GREAT SCIENCE FICTION of the 20TH CENTURY

Compiled by ROBERT SILVERBERG
and MARTIN H. GREENBERG

AVENEL BOOKS
New York

Originally published as *The Arbor House Treasury of Modern Science Fiction.*

Copyright © MCMLXXX by Robert Silverberg and Martin H. Greenberg
All rights reserved.

This 1987 edition is published by Avenel Books,
distributed by Crown Publishers, Inc., 225 Park Avenue South, New York, New York
10003, by arrangement with Arbor House Publishing Company.

Printed and Bound in the United States of America

LIBRARY OF CONGRESS CATALOGING-IN-PUBLICATION DATA

Arbor House treasury of modern science fiction.
Great science fiction of the 20th century.

Originally published: The Arbor House treasury of
modern science fiction. New York: Arbor House, c1980.
1. Science fiction, American. 2. Science fiction,
English. I. Silverberg, Robert. II. Greenberg, Martin
Harry. III. Title.
PS648.S3A7 1987   813'.0876'08   87-11523
ISBN 0-517-64124-0
h g f e d c b

The following pages constitutes an extension of the copyright page. The author gratefully acknowledges permission to include material from the following:

"Angel's Egg," by Edgar Pangborn, copyright © 1951 by World Editions, Inc. Reprinted by permission of Robert P. Mills, Ltd.

"Rescue Party," by Arthur C. Clarke, copyright © 1946, 1974, by Street & Smith Publications, Inc. Reprinted by permission of the author and the author's agents, Scott Meredith Literary Agency, Inc., 845 Third Avenue, New York, New York 10022.

"Shape," by Robert Sheckley, copyright © 1953 by Galaxy Publishing Corporation. Reprinted by permission of The Sterling Lord Agency, Inc.

"Alpha Ralpha Boulevard," by Cordwainer Smith, copyright © 1961 by Mercury Publications, Inc. Reprinted by permission of the author's agents, Scott Meredith Literary Agency, Inc. 845 Third Avenue, New York, New York 10022.

"Winter's King," by Ursula K. Le Guin, copyright © 1969, 1975 by Ursula K. Le Guin. Reprinted by permission of the author and the author's agent, Virginia Kidd.

"Or All the Seas With Oysters," by Avram Davidson, copyright © 1968 by Galaxy Publishing Corporation. Reprinted by permission of the author and his agents, Kirby McCauley, Ltd.

"Common Time," by James Blish, copyright © 1953 by Columbia Publications, Inc. Reprinted by permission of Richard Curtis Associates, Inc.

"When You Care, When You Love," by Theodore Sturgeon, copyright © 1962 by Mercury Publications, Inc. Reprinted by permission of the author and his agents, Kirby McCauley, Ltd.

"Poor Little Warrior!" by Brian W. Aldiss. Copyright © 1958 by Mercury Press, Inc. Reprinted by permission of the author.

"When It Changed," by Joanna Russ, copyright © 1972 by Harlan Ellison. Reprinted by permission of the author.

"The Bicentennial Man," by Isaac Asimov, copyright © 1976 by Random House, Inc. Reprinted by permission of the author.

"Hunting Machine," by Carol Emshwiller, copyright © 1957 by Columbia Publications, Inc. Reprinted by permission of the author and the author's agent, Virginia Kidd.

"Light of Other Days," by Bob Shaw, copyright © 1966 by The Condé Nast Publications, Inc. Reprinted by permission of the author and the author's agents, Scott Meredith Literary Agency, Inc.

"The Keys to December," by Roger Zelazny, copyright © 1966 by New Worlds SF. Reprinted by permission of the author and his agents, Kirby McCauley, Ltd.

"Of Mist, and Grass, and Sand," by Vonda N. McIntyre, copyright © 1973 by Vonda N. McIntyre. Reprinted by permission of the author.

"A Galaxy Called Rome," by Barry N. Malzberg, copyright © 1975 by Mercury Press, Inc. Originally appeared in *The Magazine of Fantasy and Science Fiction* for July, 1975 and reprinted by permission of the author.

"Stranger Station," by Damon Knight, copyright © 1956 by Fantasy House, Inc. Reprinted by permission of the author.

"The Time of His Life," by Larry Eisenberg, copyright © 1968 by Mercury Press, Inc. Reprinted by permission of the author.

"The Women Men Don't See," by James Tiptree, Jr., copyright © 1973 by Mercury Press, Inc. Reprinted by permission of the author and the author's agents, Robert P. Mills, Ltd.

"The Queen of Air and Darkness," by Poul Anderson, copyright © 1971 by Mercury Press, Inc. Reprinted by permission of the author and the author's agents, Scott Meredith Literary Agency, Inc., 845 Third Avenue, New York, New York 10022.

Contents

Introduction

The year was 1946: the early springtime of the wondrous postwar world in which we had been promised glittering new cities of sky-piercing towers, television screens for living room and telephone, and commuter helicopters in every garage. The future was about to begin after the long bleak autumn of the Depression and the grim winter of the Second World War. Europe lay in shambles, Japan still struggled in the horrifying aftermath of Hiroshima and Nagasaki but in the United States tomorrow was dawning. And in that year of 1946 two bulky books of short stories were offered to the reading public, the first two major anthologies of science fiction—Groff Conklin's *The Best of Science Fiction* and, a few months later, *Adventures in Time and Space*, edited by Raymond J. Healy and J. Francis McComas. Thus was the marvelous new era of startling technological progress provided with the first volumes of its scriptures.

Science fiction, of course, was nothing new. Scholars could trace its pedigree back to classical times; in the nineteenth century everyone had read Jules Verne, and in the early twentieth there was H.G. Wells; Aldous Huxley's *Brave New World*, a work of authentic science fiction, had been one of the most widely discussed books of the 1930s. But since 1926 another kind of science fiction had existed, almost covertly, in the United States, in magazines with names like *Amazing Stories, Wonder Stories* and *Astounding Science Fiction*. And it was from the rough, yellowing pages of those magazines that the pioneering anthologists Conklin, Healy and McComas chose the material for their two thick collections.

Much of what the early science fiction magazines published was, of course,

mere gaudy juvenile nonsense. Magazines with such flamboyant names—
Startling Stories, Marvel Stories, Super Science Stories—did not promise much
in the way of literary sophistication, and their contents pages bristled with
such titles as "Cursed Caverns of Ra," "Hell-Stuff for Planet X" and "Swords-
men of Saturn." And yet, and yet, there was so much more than simple trash
to be found in those magazines! Some were frankly aimed at boys just graduating from comic books, but a few of the magazines tried, at least some of the
time, to provide thoughtful fiction for the young men—and the occasional
woman—who would be shaping that golden world beyond time's horizon.
Behind the flashy covers, behind the foolish typography, could be found scores
of thoughtful, penetrating, fascinating glimpses of the future, particularly in
the sensational-looking but actually quite sober *Astounding Science Fiction*
edited by John Campbell.

The readers of the science fiction magazines were a tiny band numbering
in the thousands, and they thought of themselves as an elite corps of visionar-
ies. Others, seeing them carry their preposterous magazines away from the
newsstands, thought of them as crackpots. No matter: persecuted minorities
develop extraordinary internal cohesion, and those who somehow were drawn
to science fiction read it with passionate loyalty, proselytized where they dared,
published execrably mimeographed little magazines dealing with it and, naturally, tried their own hand at writing it. It was not at all unusual to see an
adolescent contributor to the cranky, quirky correspondence columns of the
magazine move on, in a year or two, to the rank of professional author. Among
those who did, in those early days, were Isaac Asimov, Ray Bradbury, Arthur
C. Clarke, Lester del Rey and Frederik Pohl. Others who had no aptitude for
writing, but who burned with the fire of centuries yet to come, entered the
sciences and helped to design the television sets, jet planes and atomic bombs
of the years just ahead.

In those ghastly but beloved science fiction magazines of the 1930s and
1940s, then, the blueprints of the future were being designed—hammered out
in a welter of split infinitives and bug-eyed monsters. And in 1946, when *The
Best of Science Fiction* and *Adventures in Time and Space* appeared, with
their contents culled almost exclusively from the magazines with the embarrassing names, science fiction suddenly emerged from the pulp-magazine underground into the brilliant light of publishing respectability.

There had been a few earlier science fiction anthologies, notably Donald A.
Wollheim's *The Pocket Book of Science Fiction* in 1943 and Phil Stong's *The
Other Worlds* in 1941. But the two 1946 volumes made a far greater impact.
For one thing, they were hardcover volumes of imposing size, *The Best* with
785 pages of small type, *Adventures* offering 997 pages even more closely set.

For another, they appeared under the auspices of large, well-established publishing houses, Random House and Crown. And—most significant of all—they were being offered not to harried and war-weary readers but to the inhabitants of that shining new postwar world. "We know that atomic power, supersonic speed, strange and marvelous new materials, devices and inventions are coming," declared the jacket copy of *The Best of Science Fiction*. "These stories give us an idea of how it will be and what it will mean to our lives and fortunes. They are a fascinating pre-view of tomorrow."

Their effect was extraordinary. The two jumbo volumes sold quite well—*Adventures in Time and Space*, in fact, is still in print more than thirty-five years later—and were followed swiftly by other compilations that skimmed the treasure trove of magazine science fiction until by 1952 a shelf of such anthologies ran to dozens of hefty books and virtually everything worthwhile from science fiction's early era had been put between hard covers. New readers, encountering the books in libraries or bookstores, were instantly converted to the futuristic literature, including many who would hardly have dreamed of investigating magazines called *Astounding Science Fiction* or *Startling Stories*. And—this is particularly true in the case of *Adventures in Time and Space*—readers of these anthologies often reported themselves changed forever by their experiences with those stories, their minds indelibly imprinted with visions of times to come.

A generation has gone by since those big books appeared. Science fiction is no longer the province of a subterranean elite. Long lines form to see the hit SF movie of the season, hundreds of paperback SF novels are published every year, libraries maintain thriving SF departments and—truly astonishing to the early faithful—high schools and colleges actually offer *courses* in the once-despised tales of robots and starships. Those of us who were lucky enough to pick up *Adventures in Time and Space* at the age of twelve or fourteen or eighteen were overwhelmed by the novelty of the ideas and images its stories offered, but no one now, not even a five-year-old, can approach science fiction with that kind of innocent receptivity to wonder, not in a world where moon walks are already dusty history, supersonic jet transport is a routine matter and telephone calls ricochet off orbiting satellites on their way from Philadelphia to Salt Lake City.

Nevertheless, the present anthology is an attempt to provide, for the readers of the 1980s and beyond, the same kind of powerful impact that *Adventures in Time and Space* and *The Best of Science Fiction* delivered thirty years back. It is the largest possible book that modern publishing economics could support, and if it is not the 997 pages at $2.95 that the original *Adventures in Time and Space* was, the fault is not ours but time's, for we live in the future, and the future is an expensive place. Still, what we offer here is a book of robust size, full of robust stories of the centuries to come—a book of dreams, visions and carefully imagined fantasies, chosen for their ability to delight, amaze, startle and entertain. Arbitrarily we have chosen to use no stories written before 1946 on the grounds that they fall into the province of our distinguished predecessors. Indeed, only a handful of the stories here date from the 1940s. Most first appeared in the 1950s and 1960s, and there are some here from the 1970s, so that we provide an extensive panorama of the evolution of science fiction since those wonderful old days. *Adventures in Time and Space* and *The Best of Science Fiction* are classic volumes, unforgettable and forever cherishable. But dozens of brilliant new writers have appeared since those books were published—and we offer here a fine fat volume of their work, which we confidently believe will be a fitting companion to the huge and wonderful collections of science fiction stories that enlivened our days and irradiated our imaginations when we were young.

—Robert Silverberg
—Martin Harry Greenberg

EDGAR PANGBORN
Angel's Egg

The two film versions of Invasion of the Body Snatchers *provide one view of an Earth invaded by aliens, but there are many other ways to handle the theme. In some stories the emphasis is on motive, in others, on how the invasion was accomplished. And in a few, we turn out to be the invaders. Edgar Pangborn's "Angel's Egg" shows us some of the most interesting alien invaders in SF in a story that opened a remarkable literary career.*

LETTER OF RECORD, BLAINE TO MC CARRAN, DATED AUGUST 10, 1951.

Mr. Cleveland McCarran
Federal Bureau of Investigation
Washington, D.C.

Dear Sir:

In compliance with your request I enclose herewith a transcript of the pertinent sections of the journal of Dr. David Bannerman, deceased. The original document is being held at this office until proper disposition can be determined.

Our investigation has shown no connection between Dr. Bannerman and any organization, subversive or otherwise. So far as we can learn, he was exactly what he seemed, an inoffensive summer resident, retired, with a small independent income—a recluse to some extent, but well spoken of by local tradesmen and other neighbors. A connection between Dr. Bannerman and the type of activity that concerns your department would seem most unlikely.

The following information is summarized from the earlier parts of Dr. Bannerman's journal, and tallies with the results of our own limited inquiry. He was born in 1898 at Springfield, Massachusetts, attended public school there, and was graduated from Harvard College in 1922, his

1

studies having been interrupted by two years' military service. He was wounded in action in Argonne, receiving a spinal injury. He earned a doctorate in biology in 1926. Delayed aftereffects of his war injury necessitated hospitalization, 1927–28. From 1929 to 1948 he taught elementary sciences in a private school in Boston. He published two textbooks in introductory biology, 1929 and 1937. In 1948 he retired from teaching: a pension and a modest income from textbook royalties evidently made this possible. Aside from the spinal deformity, which caused him to walk with a stoop, his health is said to have been fair. Autopsy findings suggested that the spinal condition must have given him considerable pain; he is not known to have mentioned this to anyone, not even to his physician, Dr. Lester Morse. There is no evidence whatever of drug addiction or alcoholism.

At one point early in his journal Dr. Bannerman describes himself as "a naturalist of the puttering type—I would rather sit on a log than write monographs: it pays off better." Dr. Morse, and others who knew Dr. Bannerman personally, tell me that this conveys a hint of his personality.

I am not qualified to comment on the material of this journal, except to say I have no evidence to support (or to contradict) Dr. Bannerman's statements. The journal has been studied only by my immediate superiors, by Dr. Morse, and by myself. I take it for granted you will hold the matter in strictest confidence.

With the journal I am also enclosing a statement by Dr. Morse, written at my request for our records and for your information. You will note that he says, with some qualifications, that "death was not inconsistent with an embolism." He has signed a death certificate on that basis. You will recall from my letter of August 5 that it was Dr. Morse who discovered Dr. Bannerman's body. Because he was a close personal friend of the deceased, Dr. Morse did not feel able to perform the autopsy himself. It was done by a Dr. Stephen Clyde of this city, and was virtually negative as regards cause of death, neither confirming nor contradicting Dr. Morse's original tentative diagnosis. If you wish to read the autopsy report in full I shall be glad to forward a copy.

Dr. Morse tells me that so far as he knows Dr. Bannerman had no near relatives. He never married. For the last twelve summers he occupied a small cottage on a back road about twenty-five miles from this city, and had few visitors. The neighbor, Steele, mentioned in the journal is a farmer, age sixty-eight, of good character, who tells me he "never got really acquainted with Dr. Bannerman."

At this office we feel that unless new information comes to light, further active investigation is hardly justified.

Respectfully yours,
Garrison Blaine
Capt., State Police
Augusta, Me.

Encl: Extract from Journal of David Bannerman, dec'd. Statement by Lester Morse, M.D.

LIBRARIAN'S NOTE: The following document, originally attached as an unofficial "rider" to the foregoing letter, was donated to this institution in 1994 through the courtesy of Mrs. Helen McCarran, widow of the martyred first president of the World Federation. Other personal and state papers of President McCarran, many of them dating from the early period when he was employed by the FBI, are accessible to public view at the Institute of World History, Copenhagen.

PERSONAL NOTE, BLAINE TO MC CARRAN, DATED AUGUST 10, 1951

Dear Cleve:

Guess I didn't make it clear in my other letter that that bastard Clyde was responsible for my having to drag you into this. He is something to handle with tongs. Happened thusly— When he came in to heave the autopsy report at me, he was already having pups just because it was so completely negative (he does have certain types of honesty), and he caught sight of a page or two of the journal on my desk. Doc Morse was with me at the time. I fear we both got upstage with him (Clyde has that effect, and we were both in a State of Mind anyway), so right away the old drip thinks he smells something subversive. Belongs to the atomize-'em-NOW-WOW-WOW school of thought—nuf sed? He went into a grand whuff-whuff about referring to Higher Authority, and I knew that meant your hive, so I wanted to get ahead of the letter I knew he'd write. I suppose his literary effort couldn't be just sort of quietly transferred to File 13, otherwise known as the Appropriate Receptacle?

He can say what he likes about my character, if any, but even I never supposed he'd take a sideswipe at his professional colleague. Doc Morse is the best of the best and would not dream of suppressing any evidence important to us, as you say Clyde's letter hints. What Doc did do was to tell Clyde, pleasantly, in the privacy of my office, to go take a flying this-and-that at the moon. I only wish I'd thought of the expression myself. So Clyde rushes off to tell teacher. See what I mean about the tongs? However (knock on wood) I don't think Clyde saw enough of the journal to get any notion of what it's all about.

As for that journal, damn it, Cleve, I don't know. If you have any ideas I want them, of course. I'm afraid I believe in angels, myself. But when I think of the effect on local opinion if the story ever gets out—brother! Here was this old Bannerman living alone with a female angel and they wuzn't even common-law married. Aw, gee. . . . And the flood of phone calls from other crackpots anxious to explain it all to me. Experts in the care and feeding of angels. Methods of angel-proofing. Angels right out-

side the window a minute ago. Make Angels a Profitable Enterprise in
Your Spare Time!!!

When do I see you? You said you might have a week clear in October.
If we could get together maybe we could make sense where there is none.
I hear the cider promises to be good this year. Try and make it. My best
to Ginny and the other young fry, and Helen of course.

                                        Respeckfully yourn,
                                        Garry

P.S. If you do see any angels down your way, and they aren't willing to
wait for a Republican Administration, by all means have them investigated by the Senate—then we'll *know* we're all nuts.

                                        G.

EXTRACT FROM JOURNAL OF DAVID BANNERMAN, JUNE 1–JULY 29, 1951

                                        June 1

It must have been at least three weeks ago when we had that flying saucer
flurry. Observers the other side of Katahdin saw it come down this side;
observers this side saw it come down the other. Size anywhere from six inches
to sixty feet in diameter (or was it cigar-shaped?) and speed whatever you
please. Seem to recall that witnesses agreed on a rosy-pink light. There was
the inevitable gobbledegookery of official explanation designed to leave everyone impressed, soothed, and disappointed. I paid scant attention to the excitement and less to the explanation—naturally, I thought it was just a flying
saucer. But now Camilla has hatched out an angel.

It would have to be Camilla. Perhaps I haven't mentioned my hens enough.
In the last day or two it has dawned on me that this journal may be of
importance to other eyes than mine, not merely a lonely man's plaything to
blunt the edge of mortality: an angel in the house makes a difference. I had
better show consideration for possible readers.

I have eight hens, all yearlings except Camilla: this is her third spring. I
boarded her two winters at my neighbor Steele's farm when I closed this shack
and shuffled my chilly bones off to Florida, because even as a pullet she had
a manner which overbore me. I could never have eaten Camilla: if she had
looked at the ax with that same expression of rancid disapproval (and she
would), I should have felt I was beheading a favorite aunt. Her only concession
to sentiment is the annual rush of maternity to the brain—normal, for a
case-hardened White Plymouth Rock.

This year she stole a nest successfully in a tangle of blackberry. By the time

I located it, I estimated I was about two weeks too late. I had to outwit her by watching from a window—she is far too acute to be openly trailed from feeding ground to nest. When I had bled and pruned my way to her hideout she was sitting on nine eggs and hating my guts. They could not be fertile, since I keep no rooster, and I was about to rob her when I saw the ninth egg was nothing of hers. It was a deep blue and transparent, with flecks of inner light that made me think of the first stars in a clear evening. It was the same size as Camilla's own. There was an embryo, but I could make nothing of it. I returned the egg to Camilla's bare and fevered breastbone and went back to the house for a long, cool drink.

That was ten days ago. I know I ought to have kept a record; I examined the blue egg every day, watching how some nameless life grew within it. The angel has been out of the shell three days now. This is the first time I have felt equal to facing pen and ink.

I have been experiencing a sort of mental lassitude unfamiliar to me. Wrong word: not so much lassitude as a preoccupation, with no sure clue to what it is that preoccupies me. By reputation I am a scientist of sorts. Right now I have no impulse to look for data; I want to sit quiet and let truth come to a relaxed mind if it will. Could be merely a part of growing older, but I doubt that. The broken pieces of the wonderful blue shell are on my desk. I have been peering at them—into them—for the last ten minutes or more. Can't call it study: my thought wanders into their blue, learning nothing I can retain in words. It does not convey much to say I have gone into a vision of open sky—and of peace, if such a thing there be.

The angel chipped the shell deftly in two parts. This was evidently done with the aid of small horny outgrowths on her elbows; these growths were sloughed off on the second day. I wish I had seen her break the shell, but when I visited the blackberry tangle three days ago she was already out. She poked her exquisite head through Camilla's neck feathers, smiled sleepily, and snuggled back into darkness to finish drying off. So what could I do, more than save the broken shell and wriggle my clumsy self out of there? I had removed Camilla's own eggs the day before—Camilla was only moderately annoyed. I was nervous about disposing of them, even though they were obviously Camilla's, but no harm was done. I cracked each one to be sure. Very frankly rotten eggs and nothing more.

In the evening of that day I thought of rats and weasels, as I should have done earlier. I prepared a box in the kitchen and brought the two in, the angel quiet in my closed hand. They are there now. I think they are comfortable.

Three days after hatching, the angel is the length of my forefinger, say three inches tall, with about the relative proportions of a six-year-old girl. Except for head, hands, and probably the soles of her feet, she is clothed in down the color of ivory; what can be seen of her skin is a glowing pink—I do mean glowing, like the inside of certain sea shells. Just above the small of her back are two stubs which I take to be infantile wings. They do not suggest an extra pair of specialized forelimbs. I think they are wholly differentiated organs; perhaps they will be like the wings on an insect. Somehow, I never thought of angels buzzing. Maybe she won't. I know very little about angels. At present the stubs are covered with some dull tissue, no doubt a protective sheath to be discarded when the membranes (if they are membranes) are ready to grow. Between the stubs is a not very prominent ridge—special musculature, I suppose. Otherwise her shape is quite human, even to a pair of minuscule mammalian buttons just visible under the down; how that can make sense in an egg-laying organism is beyond my comprehension. (Just for the record, so is a Corot landscape; so is Schubert's *Unfinished*; so is the flight of a hummingbird, or the other-world of frost on a window pane.) The down on her head has grown visibly in three days and is of different quality from the body down—later it may resemble human hair, as a diamond resembles a chunk of granite. . . .

A curious thing has happened. I went to Camilla's box after writing that. Judy*was already lying in front of it, unexcited. The angel's head was out from under the feathers, and I thought—with more verbal distinctness than such thoughts commonly take, "So here I am, a naturalist of middle years and cold sober, observing a three-inch oviparous mammal with down and wings." The thing is—she giggled. Now, it might have been only amusement at my appearance, which to her must be enormously gross and comic. But another thought formed unspoken: "I am no longer lonely." And her face (hardly bigger than a dime) immediately changed from laughter to a brooding and friendly thoughtfulness.

Judy and Camilla are old friends. Judy seems untroubled by the angel. I have no worries about leaving them alone together. I must sleep.

June 3

I made no entry last night. The angel was talking to me, and when that was finished I drowsed off immediately on a cot that I have moved into the kitchen so as to be near them.

I had never been strongly impressed by the evidence for extrasensory perception. It is fortunate my mind was able to accept the novelty, since to the

*Dr. Bannerman's dog, mentioned often earlier in the journal. A nine-year-old English setter. According to an entry of May 15, 1951, she was then beginning to go blind.
—BLAINE.

angel it is clearly a matter of course. Her tiny mouth is most expressive but moves only for that reason and for eating—not for speech. Probably she could speak to her own kind if she wished, but I dare say the sound would be outside the range of my hearing as well as my understanding.

Last night after I brought the cot in and was about to finish my puttering bachelor supper, she climbed to the edge of the box and pointed, first at herself and then at the top of the kitchen table. Afraid to let my vast hand take hold of her, I held it out flat and she sat in my palm. Camilla was inclined to fuss, but the angel looked over her shoulder and Camilla subsided, watchful but no longer alarmed.

The table top is porcelain, and the angel shivered. I folded a towel and spread a silk handkerchief on top of that; the angel sat on this arrangement with apparent comfort, near my face. I was not even bewildered. Possibly she had already instructed me to blank out my mind. At any rate, I did so, without conscious effort to that end.

She reached me first with visual imagery. How can I make it plain that this had nothing in common with my sleeping dreams? There was no weight of symbolism from my littered past; no discoverable connection with any of yesterday's commonplace; indeed, no actual involvement of my personality at all. I saw. I was moving vision, though without eyes or other flesh. And while my mind saw, it also knew where my flesh was, slumped at the kitchen table. If anyone had entered the kitchen, if there had been a noise of alarm out in the henhouse, I should have known it.

There was a valley such as I have not seen (and never will) on Earth. I have seen many beautiful places on this planet—some of them were even tranquil. Once I took a slow steamer to New Zealand and had the Pacific as a plaything for many days. I can hardly say how I knew this was not Earth. The grass of the valley was an earthly green; a river below me was a blue-and-silver thread under familiar-seeming sunlight; there were trees much like pine and maple, and maybe that is what they were. But it was not Earth. I was aware of mountains heaped to strange heights on either side of the valley—snow, rose, amber, gold. Perhaps the amber tint was unlike any mountain color I have noticed in this world at midday.

Or I may have known it was not Earth simply because her mind—dwelling within some unimaginable brain smaller than the tip of my little finger—told me so.

I watched two inhabitants of that world come flying, to rest in the field of sunny grass where my bodiless vision had brought me. Adult forms, such as my angel would surely be when she had her growth, except that both of these were male and one of them was dark-skinned. The latter was also old, with a thousand-wrinkled face, knowing and full of tranquility; the other was flushed and lively with youth; both were beautiful. The down of the brown-skinned old one was reddish tawny; the other's was ivory with hints of orange. Their wings were true membranes, with more variety of subtle iridescence than I have seen even in the wings of a dragonfly; I could not say that any color was dominant, for each motion brought a ripple of change. These two sat at their ease on the grass. I realized that they were talking to each other, though their lips did not move in speech more than once or twice. They would nod, smile, now and then illustrate something with twinkling hands.

A huge rabbit lolloped past them. I knew (thanks to my own angel's efforts, I suppose) that this animal was of the same size of our common wild ones. Later, a blue-green snake three times the size of the angels came flowing through the grass; the old one reached out to stroke its head carelessly, and I think he did it without interrupting whatever he was saying.

Another creature came, in leisured leaps. He was monstrous, yet I felt no alarm in the angels or in myself. Imagine a being built somewhat like a kangaroo up to the head, about eight feet tall, and katydid-green. Really, the thick balancing tail and enormous legs were the only kangaroolike features about him: the body above the massive thighs was not dwarfed but thick and square; the arms and hands were quite humanoid: the head was round, manlike except for its face—there was only a single nostril and his mouth was set in the vertical; the eyes were large and mild. I received an impression of high intelligence and natural gentleness. In one of his manlike hands two tools so familiar and ordinary that I knew my body by the kitchen table had laughed in startled recognition. But, after all, a garden spade and rake are basic. Once invented—I expect we did it ourselves in the Neolithic Age—there is little reason why they should change much down the millennia.

This farmer halted by the angels, and the three conversed awhile. The big head nodded agreeably. I believe the young angel made a joke; certainly the convulsions in the huge green face made me think of laughter. Then this amiable monster turned up the grass in a patch a few yards square, broke the sod and raked the surface smooth, just as any competent gardener might do —except that he moved with the relaxed smoothness of a being whose strength far exceeds the requirements of his task. . . .

I was back in my kitchen with everyday eyes. My angel was exploring the table. I had a loaf of bread there and a dish of strawberries and cream. She was trying a bread crumb; seemed to like it fairly well. I offered the strawberries; she broke off one of the seeds and nibbled it but didn't care so much for the pulp. I held up the great spoon with sugary cream; she steadied it with both hands to try some. I think she liked it. It had been most stupid of me not to realize that she would be hungry. I brought wine from the cupboard; she watched inquiringly, so I put a couple of drops on the handle of a spoon. This really pleased her: she chuckled and patted her tiny stomach, though I'm afraid it wasn't awfully good sherry. I brought some crumbs of cake, but she indicated that she was full, came close to my face, and motioned me to lower my head.

She reached toward me until she could press both hands against my forehead—I felt it only enough to know her hands were there—and she stood so a long time, trying to tell me something.

It was difficult. Pictures come through with relative ease, but now she was transmitting an abstraction of a complex kind: my clumsy brain really suffered in the effort to receive. Something did come across. I have only the crudest way of passing it on. Imagine an equilateral triangle; place the following words one at each corner—"recruiting," "collecting," "saving." The meaning she wanted to convey ought to be near the center of the triangle.

I had also the sense that her message provided a partial explanation of her errand in this lovable and damnable world.

She looked weary when she stood away from me. I put out my palm and she climbed into it, to be carried back to the nest.

She did not talk to me tonight, nor eat, but she gave a reason, coming out from Camilla's feathers long enough to turn her back and show me the wing stubs. The protective sheaths have dropped off; the wings are rapidly growing. They are probably damp and weak. She was quite tired and went back into the warm darkness almost at once.

Camilla must be exhausted, too. I don't think she has been off the nest more than twice since I brought them into the house.

June 4

Today she can fly.

I learned it in the afternoon when I was fiddling about in the garden and Judy was loafing in the sunshine she loves. Something apart from sight and sound called me to hurry back to the house. I saw my angel through the screen door before I opened it. One of her feet had caught in a hideous loop of loose wire at a break in the mesh. Her first tug of alarm must have tightened the loop so that her hands were not strong enough to force it open.

Fortunately I was able to cut the wire with a pair of shears before I lost my head; then she could free her foot without injury. Camilla had been frantic, rushing around fluffed up, but—here's an odd thing—perfectly silent. None of the recognized chicken noises of dismay: if an ordinary chick had been in trouble she would have raised the roof.

The angel flew to me and hovered, pressing her hands on my forehead. The message was clear at once: "No harm done." She flew down to tell Camilla the same thing.

Yes, in the same way. I saw Camilla standing near my feet with her neck out and head low, and the angel put a hand on either side of her scraggy comb. Camilla relaxed, clucked in the normal way, and spread her wings for a shelter. The angel went under it, but only to oblige Camilla, I think—at least, she stuck her head through the wing feathers and winked.

She must have seen something else, then, for she came out and flew back to me and touched a finger to my cheek, looked at the finger, saw it was wet, put it in her mouth, made a face and laughed at me.

We went outdoors into the sun (Camilla, too), and the angel gave me an exhibition of what flying ought to be. Not even Schubert can speak of joy as her first free flying did. At one moment she would be hanging in front of my eyes, radiant and delighted; the next instant she would be a dot of color against a cloud. Try to imagine something that would make a hummingbird seem a bit dull and sluggish.

They do hum. Softer than a hummingbird, louder than a dragonfly.

Something like the sound of hawk-moths—*Heinmaris thisbe,* for instance: the one I used to call Hummingbird Moth when I was a child.

I was frightened, naturally. Frightened first at what might happen to her, but that was unnecessary; I don't think she would be in danger from any savage animal except possibly man. I saw a Cooper's hawk slant down the visible ray toward the swirl of color where she was dancing by herself; presently she was drawing iridescent rings around him; then, while he soared in smaller circles, I could not see her, but (maybe she felt my fright) she was again in front of me, pressing my forehead in the now familiar way. I knew she was amused and caught the idea that the hawk was a "lazy character." Not quite the way I'd describe *Accipiter Cooperi,* but it's all in the point of view. I believe she had been riding his back, no doubt with her speaking hands on his terrible head.

And later I was frightened by the thought that she might not want to return to me. Can I compete with sunlight and open sky? The passage of that terror through me brought her back swiftly, and her hands said with great clarity: "Don't ever be afraid of anything—it isn't necessary for you."

Once this afternoon I was saddened by the realization that old Judy can take little part in what goes on now. I can well remember Judy running like the wind. The angel must have heard this thought in me, for she stood a long time beside Judy's drowsy head, while Judy's tail thumped cheerfully on the warm grass. . . .

In the evening the angel made a heavy meal on two or three cake crumbs and another drop of sherry, and we had what was almost a sustained conversation. I will write it in that form this time, rather than grope for anything more exact. I asked her, "How far away is your home?"

"My home is here."

"Thank God!—but I meant, the place your people came from."

"Ten light-years."

"The images you showed me—that quiet valley—that is ten light-years away?"

"Yes. But that was my father talking to you, through me. He was grown when the journey began. He is two hundred and forty years old—our years, thirty-two days longer than yours."

Mainly I was conscious of a flood of relief: I had feared, on the basis of terrestrial biology, that her explosively rapid growth after hatching must foretell a brief life. But it's all right—she can outlive me, and by a few hundred years, at that. "Your father is here now, on this planet—shall I see him?"

She took her hands away—listening, I believe. The answer was: "No. He is sorry. He is ill and cannot live long. I am to see him in a few days, when I fly a little better. He taught me for twenty years after I was born."

"I don't understand. I thought . . ."

"Later, friend. My father is grateful for your kindness to me."

I don't know what I thought about that. I felt no faintest trace of condescension in the message. "And he was showing me things he had seen with his own eyes, ten light-years away?"

"Yes." Then she wanted me to rest awhile; I am sure she knows what a huge effort it is for my primitive brain to function in this way. But before she ended the conversation by humming down to her nest she gave me this, and I received it with such clarity that I cannot be mistaken: "He says that only fifty million years ago it was a jungle there, just as Terra is now."

June 8

When I woke four days ago the angel was having breakfast, and little Camilla was dead. The angel watched me rub sleep out of my eyes, watched me discover Camilla, and then flew to me. I received this: "Does it make you unhappy?"

"I don't know exactly." You can get fond of a hen, especially a cantankerous and homely old one whose personality has a lot in common with your own.

"She was old. She wanted a flock of chicks, and I couldn't stay with her. So I . . ." Something obscure here: probably my mind was trying too hard to grasp it—". . . so I saved her life." I could make nothing else out of it. She said "saved."

Camilla's death looked natural, except that I should have expected the death contractions to muss the straw, and that hadn't happened. Maybe the angel had arranged the old lady's body for decorum, though I don't see how her muscular strength would have been equal to it—Camilla weighed at least seven pounds.

As I was burying her at the edge of the garden and the angel was humming over my head, I recalled a thing which, when it happened, I had dismissed as a dream. Merely a moonlight image of the angel standing in the nest box with her hands on Camilla's head, then pressing her mouth gently on Camilla's throat, just before the hen's head sank down out of my line of vision. Probably I actually waked and saw it happen. I am somehow unconcerned— even, as I think more about it, pleased. . . .

After the burial the angel's hands said, "Sit on the grass and we'll talk. . . . Question me. I'll tell you what I can. My father asks you to write it down."

So that is what we have been doing for the last four days, I have been going to school, a slow but willing pupil. Rather than enter anything in this journal (for in the evenings I was exhausted), I made notes as best I could. The angel has gone now to see her father and will not return until morning. I shall try to make a readable version of my notes.

Since she had invited questions, I began with something which had been bothering me, as a would-be naturalist, exceedingly. I couldn't see how creatures no larger than the adults I had observed could lay eggs as large as Camilla's. Nor could I understand why, if they were hatched in an almost adult condition and able to eat a varied diet, she had any use for that ridiculous, lovely, and apparently functional pair of breasts. When the angel grasped my difficulty she exploded with laughter—her kind, which buzzed her all over the garden and caused her to fluff my hair on the wing and pinch my earlobe. She lit on a rhubarb leaf and gave a delectably naughty representation of herself as a hen laying an egg, including the cackle. She got me to bumbling helplessly —my kind of laughter—and it was some time before we could quiet down. Then she did her best to explain.

They are true mammals, and the young—not more than two or at most three in a lifetime averaging two hundred and fifty years—are delivered in very much the human way. The baby is nursed—human fashion—until his brain begins to respond a little to their unspoken language; that takes three to four weeks. Then he is placed in an altogether different medium. She could not describe that clearly, because there was very little in my educational storehouse to help me grasp it. It is some gaseous medium that arrests bodily growth for an almost indefinite period, while mental growth continues. It took them, she says, about seven thousand years to perfect this technique after they first hit on the idea: they are never in a hurry. The infant remains under this delicate and precise control for anywhere from fifteen to thirty years, the period depending not only on his mental vigor but also on the type of lifework he tentatively elects as soon as his brain is knowing enough to make a choice. During this period his mind is guided with unwavering patience by teachers who . . ."

It seems those teachers know their business. This was peculiarly difficult for me to assimilate, although the fact came through clearly enough. In their world, the profession of teacher is more highly honored than any other—can such a thing be possible?—and so difficult to enter that only the strongest minds dare attempt it. (I had to rest a while after absorbing that.) An aspirant must spend fifty years (not including the period of infantile education) in merely getting ready to begin, and the acquisition of factual knowledge, while not understressed, takes only a small portion of those fifty years. Then—if he's good enough—he can take a small part in the elementary instruction of a few babies, and if he does well on that basis for another thirty or forty years, he is considered a fair beginner. . . . Once upon a time I lurched around stuffy classrooms trying to insert a few predigested facts (I wonder how many of them *were* facts?) into the minds of bored and preoccupied adolescents, some of whom may have liked me moderately well. I was even able to shake hands and be nice while their terribly well-meaning parents explained to me how they ought to be educated. So much of our human effort goes down the drain of futility, I sometimes wonder how we ever got as far as the Bronze Age. Somehow we did, though, and a short way beyond.

After that preliminary stage of an angel's education is finished, the baby is transferred to more ordinary surroundings, and his bodily growth completes itself in a very short time. Wings grow abruptly (as I have seen), and he reaches a maximum height of six inches (our measure). Only then does he enter on that lifetime of two hundred and fifty years, for not until then does his body begin to age. My angel has been a living personality for many years but will not celebrate her first birthday for almost a year. I like to think of that.

At about the same time that they learned the principles of interplanetary travel (approximately twelve million years ago) these people also learned how, by use of a slightly different method, growth could be arrested at any point short of full maturity. At first the knowledge served no purpose except in the control of illnesses which still occasionally struck them at that time. But when the long periods of time required for space travel were considered, the advantages became obvious.

So it happens that my angel was born ten light-years away. She was trained by her father and many others in the wisdom of seventy million years (that, she tells me, is the approximate sum of their *recorded* history), and then she was safely sealed and cherished in what my superamoebic brain regarded as a blue egg. Education did not proceed at that time; her mind went to sleep with the rest of her. When Camilla's temperature made her wake and grow again, she remembered what to do with the little horny bumps provided for her elbows. And came out—into this planet, God help her.

I wondered why her father should have chosen any combination so unreliable as an old hen and a human being. Surely he must have had plenty of excellent ways to bring the shell to the right temperature. Her answer should have satisfied me immensely, but I am still compelled to wonder about it. "Camilla was a nice hen, and my father studied your mind while you were asleep. It was a bad landing, and much was broken—no such landing was ever made before after so long a journey: forty years. Only four other grown-ups could come with my father. Three of them died en route and he is very ill. And there were nine other children to care for."

Yes, I knew she'd said that an angel thought I was good enough to be trusted with his daughter. If it upsets me, all I need do is look at her and then in the mirror. As for the explanation, I can only conclude there must be more that I am not ready to understand. I was worried about those nine others, but she assured me they were all well, and I sensed that I ought not to ask more about them at present. . . .

Their planet, she says, is closely similar to this. A trifle larger, moving in a somewhat longer orbit around a sun like ours. Two gleaming moons, smaller than ours—their orbits are such that two-moon nights come rarely. They are magic, and she will ask her father to show me one, if he can. Their year is thirty-two days longer than ours; because of a slower rotation, their day has twenty-six of our hours. Their atmosphere is mainly nitrogen and oxygen in the proportions familiar to us; slightly richer in some of the rare gases. The climate is now what we should call tropical and subtropical, but they have known glacial rigors like those in our world's past. There are only two great continental land masses, and many thousands of large islands.

Their total population is only five billion. . . .

Most of the forms of life we know have parallels there—some quite exact parallels: rabbits, deer, mice, cats. The cats have been bred to an even higher intelligence than they possess on our Earth; it is possible, she says, to have a good deal of intellectual intercourse with their cats, who learned several million years ago that when they kill, it must be done with lightning precision and without torture. The cats had some difficulty grasping the possibility of pain in other organisms, but once that educational hurdle was passed, development was easy. Nowadays many of the cats are popular storytellers; about forty million years ago they were still occasionally needed as a special police force, and served the angels with real heroism.

It seems my angel wants to become a student of animal life here on Earth. I, a teacher!—but bless her heart for the notion, anyhow. We sat and traded animals for a couple of hours last night. I found it restful, after the mental struggle to grasp more difficult matters. Judy was something new to her. They have several luscious monsters on that planet but, in her view, so have we. She told me of a blue sea snake fifty feet long (relatively harmless) that bellows cowlike and comes into the tidal marshes to lay black eggs; so I gave her a whale. She offered a bat-winged, day-flying ball of mammalian fluff as big as my head and weighing under an ounce; I matched her with a marmoset. She tried me with a small-sized pink brontosaur (very rare), but I was ready with the duck-billed platypus, and that caused us to exchange some pretty smart remarks about mammalian eggs; she bounced. All trivial in a way; also, the happiest evening in my fifty-three tangled years of life.

She was a trifle hesitant to explain these kangaroolike people, until she was sure I really wanted to know. It seems they are about the nearest parallel to human life on that planet; not a near parallel, of course, as she was careful to explain. Agreeable and always friendly souls (though they weren't always so, I'm sure) and of a somewhat more alert intelligence than we possess. Manual workers, mainly, because they prefer it nowadays, but some of them are excellent mathematicians. The first practical spaceship was invented by a group of them, with some assistance. . . .

Names offer difficulties. Because of the nature of the angelic language, they have scant use for them except for the purpose of written record, and writing naturally plays little part in their daily lives—no occasion to write a letter when a thousand miles is no obstacle to the speech of your mind. An angel's formal name is about as important to him as, say, my social security number is to me. She has not told me hers, because the phonetics on which their written language is based have no parallel in my mind. As we would speak a friend's name, an angel will project the friend's image to his friend's receiving mind. More pleasant and more intimate, I think—although it was a shock to me at first to glimpse my own ugly mug in my mind's eye. Stories are occasionally written, if there is something in them that should be preserved precisely as it was in the first telling; but in their world the true storyteller has a more important place than the printer—he offers one of the best of their quieter pleasures: a good one can hold his audience for a week and never tire them.

"What is this 'angel' in your mind when you think of me?"

"A being men have imagined for centuries, when they thought of themselves as they might like to be and not as they are."

I did not try too painfully hard to learn much about the principles of space travel. The most my brain could take in of her explanation was something like: "Rocket—then phototropism." Now, that makes scant sense. So far as I know, phototropism—movement toward light—is an organic phenomenon. One thinks of it as a response of protoplasm, in some plants and animal organisms (most of them simple), to the stimulus of light; certainly not as a force capable of moving inorganic matter. I think that whatever may be the principle she was describing, this word "phototropism" was merely the nearest thing to it in my reservoir of language. Not even the angels can create understanding out of blank ignorance. At least I have learned not to set neat limits to the possible.

(There was a time when I did, though. I can see myself, not so many years back, like a homunculus squatting at the foot of Mt. McKinley, throwing together two handfuls of mud and shouting, "Look at the big mountain *I* made!")

And if I did know the physical principles which brought them here, and could write them in terms accessible to technicians resembling myself, I would not do it.

Here is a thing I am afraid no reader of this journal will believe: these people, as I have written, learned their method of space travel some twelve million years ago. But this is the first time they have ever used it to convey them to another planet. The heavens are rich in worlds, she tells me; on many of them there is life, often on very primitive levels. No external force prevented her people from going forth, colonizing, conquering, as far as they pleased. They could have populated a galaxy. They did not, and for this reason: they believed they were not ready. More precisely: *Not good enough.*

Only some fifty million years ago, by her account, did they learn (as we may learn eventually) that intelligence without goodness is worse than high explosive in the hands of a baboon. For beings advanced beyond the level of Pithecanthropus, intelligence is a cheap commodity—not too hard to develop, hellishly easy to use for unconsidered ends. Whereas goodness is not to be achieved without unending effort of the hardest kind, within the self, whether the self be man or angel.

It is clear even to me that the conquest of evil is only one step, not the most important. For goodness, so she tried to tell me, is an altogether positive quality; the part of living nature that swarms with such monstrosities as cruelty, meanness, bitterness, greed, is not to be filled by a vacuum when these horrors are eliminated. When you clear away a poisonous gas, you try to fill the whole room with clean air. Kindness, for only one example: one who can define kindness only as the absence of cruelty has surely not begun to understand the nature of either.

They do not aim at perfection, these angels: only at the attainable. . . . That time fifty million years ago was evidently one of great suffering and confusion. War and all its attendant plagues. They passed through many centuries while advances in technology merely worsened their condition and increased the peril of self-annihilation. They came through that, in time. War was at length so far outgrown that its recurrence was impossible, and the development of wholly rational beings could begin. Then they were ready to start growing up, through millennia of self-searching, self-discipline, seeking to derive the simple from the complex, discovering how to use knowledge and not be used by it. Even then, of course, they slipped back often enough. There were what she refers to as "eras of fatigue." In their dimmer past, they had had many dark ages, lost civilizations, hopeful beginnings ending in dust. Earlier still, they had come out of the slime, as we did.

But their period of deepest uncertainty and sternest self-appraisal did not come until twelve million years ago, when they knew a universe could be theirs for the taking and knew they were not yet good enough.

They are in no more hurry than the stars. She tried to convey something tentatively, at this point, which was really beyond both of us. It had to do with time (not as I understand time) being perhaps the most essential attribute of God (not as I was ever able to understand that word). Seeing my mental exhaustion, she gave up the effort and later told me that the conception was extremely difficult for her, too—not only, I gathered, because of her youth and relative ignorance. There was also a hint that her father might not have wished her to bring my brain up to a hurdle like that one. . . .

Of course, they explored. Their little spaceships were roaming the ether before there was anything like Man on this earth—roaming and listening, observing, recording; never entering or taking part in the life of any home but their own. For five million years they even forbade themselves to go beyond their own Solar System, though it would have been easy to do so. And in the following seven million years, although they traveled to incredible distances, the same stern restraint was in force. It was altogether unrelated to what we should call fear—that, I think, is as extinct in them as hate. There was so much to do at home!—I wish I could imagine it. They mapped the heavens and played in their own sunlight.

Naturally, I cannot tell you what goodness is. I know only, moderately well, what it seems to mean to us human beings. It appears that the best of us can, with enormous difficulty, achieve a manner of life in which goodness is reasonably dominant, by a not too precarious balance, for the greater part of the time.

Often, wise men have indicated they hope for nothing better than that in our present condition. We are, in other words, a fraction alive; the rest is in the dark. Dante was a bitter masochist, Beethoven a frantic and miserable snob, Shakespeare wrote potboilers. And Christ said, "My Father, if it be possible, let this cup pass from me."

But give us fifty million years—I am no pessimist. After all, I've watched one-celled organisms on the slide and listened to Brahms' Fourth. Night before last I said to the angel, "In spite of everything, you and I are kindred."

She granted me agreement.

June 9

She was lying on my pillow this morning so that I could see her when I waked.

Her father has died, and she was with him when it happened. There was again that thought-impression that I could interpret only to mean that his life had been "saved." I was still sleep-bound when my mind asked, "What will you do?"

"Stay with you, if you wish it, for the rest of your life." Now, the last part of the message was clouded, but I am familiar with that—it seems to mean there is some further element that eludes me. I could not be mistaken about the part I did receive. It gives me amazing speculations. After all, I am only fifty-three; I might live for another thirty or forty years. . . .

She was preoccupied this morning, but whatever she felt about her father's death that might be paralleled by sadness in a human being was hidden from me. She did say her father was sorry he had not been able to show me a two-moon night.

One adult, then, remains in this world. Except to say that he is two hundred years old and full of knowledge, and that he endured the long journey without serious ill effects, she has told me little about him. And there are ten children, including herself.

Something was sparkling at her throat. When she was aware of my interest in it she took it off, and I fetched a magnifying glass. A necklace; under the glass, much like our finest human workmanship, if your imagination can reduce it to the proper scale. The stones appeared similar to the jewels we know: diamonds, sapphires, rubies, emeralds, the diamonds snapping out every color under heaven; but there were two or three very dark-purple stones unlike anything I know—not amethysts, I am sure. The necklace was strung on something more slender than cobweb, and the design of the joining clasp was too delicate for my glass to help me. The necklace had been her mother's, she told me; as she put it back around her throat I thought I saw the same shy pride that any human girl might feel in displaying a new pretty.

She wanted to show me other things she had brought, and flew to the table where she had left a sort of satchel an inch and a half long—quite a load for her to fly with, but the translucent substance is so light that when she rested the satchel on my finger I scarcely felt it. She arranged a few articles happily for my inspection, and I put the glass to work again. One was a jeweled comb; she ran it through the down on her chest and legs to show me its use. There was a set of tools too small for the glass to interpret; I learned later they were a sewing kit. A book, and some writing instrument much like a metal pencil: imagine a book and pencil that could be used comfortably by hands hardly bigger than the paws of a mouse—that is the best I can do. The book, I understand, is a blank record for her use as needed.

And finally, when I was fully awake and dressed and we had finished breakfast, she reached in the bottom of the satchel for a parcel (heavy for her) and made me understand it was a gift for me. "My father made it for you, but I put in the stone myself, last night." She unwrapped it. A ring, precisely the size for my little finger.

I broke down, rather. She understood that, and sat on my shoulder petting my earlobe till I had command of myself.

I have no idea what the jewel is. It shifts with the light from purple to jade green to amber. The metal resembles platinum in appearance except for a tinge of rose at certain angles of light. . . . When I stare into the stone, I think I see—never mind that now. I am not ready to write it down, and perhaps never will be; anyway, I must be sure.

We improved our housekeeping later in the morning. I showed her over the house. It isn't much—Cape Codder, two rooms up and two down. Every corner interested her, and when she found a shoe box in the bedroom closet, she asked for it. At her direction, I have arranged it on a chest near my bed and near the window, which will be always open; she says the mosquitoes will not bother me, and I don't doubt her. I unearthed a white silk scarf for the bottom of the box; after asking my permission (as if I could want to refuse her anything!) she got her sewing kit and snipped off a piece of the scarf several inches square, folded it on itself several times, and sewed it into a narrow pillow an inch long. So now she had a proper bed and a room of her own. I wish I had something less coarse than silk, but she insists it's nice.

We have not talked very much today. In the afternoon she flew out for an hour's play in the cloud country; when she returned she let me know that she needed a long sleep. She is still sleeping, I think; I am writing this downstairs, fearing the light might disturb her.

Is it possible I can have thirty or forty years in her company? I wonder how teachable my mind still is. I seem to be able to assimilate new facts as well as I ever could; this ungainly carcass should be durable, with reasonable care. Of course, facts without a synthetic imagination are no better than scattered bricks; but perhaps my imagination . . .

I don't know.

Judy wants out. I shall turn in when she comes back. I wonder if poor Judy's life could be—the word is certainly "saved." I must ask.

June 10

Last night when I stopped writing I did go to bed but I was restless, refusing sleep. At some time in the small hours—there was light from a single room —she flew over to me. The tensions dissolved like an illness, and my mind was able to respond with a certain calm.

I made plain (what I am sure she already knew) that I would never willingly part company with her, and then she gave me to understand that there are two alternatives for the remainder of my life. The choice, she says, is altogether mine, and I must take time to be sure of my decision.

I can live out my natural span, whatever it proves to be, and she will not leave me for long at any time. She will be there to counsel, teach, help me in anything good I care to undertake. She says she would enjoy this; for some reason she is, as we'd say in our language, fond of me. We'd have fun.

Lord, the books I could write! I fumble for words now, in the usual human way: whatever I put on paper is a miserable fraction of the potential; the words themselves are rarely the right ones. But under her guidance . . .

I could take a fair part in shaking the world. With words alone. I could preach to my own people. Before long, I would be heard.

I could study and explore. What small nibblings we have made at the sum of available knowledge! Suppose I brought in one leaf from outdoors, or one common little bug—in a few hours of studying it with her I'd know more of my own specialty than a flood of the best textbooks could tell me.

She has also let me know that when she and those who came with her have learned a little more about the human picture, it should be possible to improve my health greatly, and probably my life expectancy. I don't imagine my back could ever straighten, but she thinks the pain might be cleared away, possibly without drugs. I could have a clearer mind, in a body that would neither fail nor torment me.

Then there is the other alternative.

It seems they have developed a technique by means of which any unresisting living subject whose brain is capable of memory at all can experience a total recall. It is a byproduct, I understand, of their silent speech, and a very recent one. They have practiced it for only a few thousand years, and since their own understanding of the phenomenon is very incomplete, they classify it among their experimental techniques. In a general way, it may somewhat resemble that reliving of the past that psychoanalysis can sometimes bring about in a limited way for therapeutic purposes; but you must imagine that sort of thing tremendously magnified and clarified, capable of including every detail that has ever registered on the subject's brain; and the end result is very different. The purpose is not therapeutic, as we would understand it: quite the opposite. The end result is death. Whatever is recalled by this process is transmitted to the receiving mind, which can retain it and record any or all of it if such a record is desired; but to the subject who recalls it, it is a flowing away, without return. Thus it is not a true "remembering" but a giving. The mind is swept clear, naked of all its past, and along with memory, life withdraws also. Very quietly. At the end, I suppose it must be like standing without resistance in the engulfment of a flood time, until finally the waters close over.

That, it seems, is how Camilla's life was "saved." Now, when I finally grasped that, I laughed, and the angel of course caught my joke. I was thinking about my neighbor Steele, who boarded the old lady for me in his henhouse for a couple of winters. Somewhere safe in the angelic records there must be a hen's-eye image of the patch in the seat of Steele's pants. Well—good. And, naturally, Camilla's view of me, too: not too unkind, I hope—she couldn't help the expression on her rigid little face, and I don't believe it ever meant anything.

At the other end of the scale is the saved life of my angel's father. Recall can be a long process, she says, depending on the intricacy and richness of the mind recalling; and in all but the last stages it can be halted at will. Her father's recall was begun when they were still far out in space and he knew that he could not long survive the journey. When that journey ended, the recall had progressed so far that very little actual memory remained to him of his life on that other planet. He had what must be called a "deductive memory"; from the material of the years not yet given away, he could reconstruct what must have been; and I assume the other adult who survived the passage must have been able to shelter him from errors that loss of memory might involve. This, I infer, is why he could not show me a two-moon night. I forgot to ask her whether the images he did send me were from actual or deductive memory. Deductive, I think, for there was a certain dimness about them not present when my angel gives me a picture of something seen with her own eyes.

Jade green eyes, by the way—were you wondering?

In the same fashion, my own life could be saved. Every aspect of existence that I ever touched, that ever touched me, could be transmitted to some perfect record. The nature of the written record is beyond me, but I have no doubt of its relative perfection. Nothing important, good or bad, would be lost. And they need a knowledge of humanity, if they are to carry out whatever it is they have in mind.

It would be difficult, she tells me, and sometimes painful. Most of the effort would be hers, but some of it would have to be mine. In her period of infantile education, she elected what we should call zoology as her lifework; for that reason she was given intensive theoretical training in this technique. Right now, I guess she knows more than anyone else on this planet not only about what makes a hen tick but about how it feels to be a hen. Though a beginner, she is in all essentials already an expert. She can help me, she thinks (if I choose this alternative)—at any rate, ease me over the toughest spots, soothe away resistance, keep my courage from too much flagging.

For it seems that this process of recall is painful to an advanced intellect (she, without condescension, calls us very advanced) because, while all pretense and self-delusion are stripped away, there remains conscience, still functioning by whatever standards of good and bad the individual has developed in his lifetime. Our present knowledge of our own motives is such a pathetically small beginning!—hardly stronger than an infant's first effort to focus his eyes. I am merely wondering how much of my life (if I choose this way) will seem to me altogether hideous. Certainly plenty of the "good deeds" that I still cherish in memory like so many well-behaved cherubs will turn up with the leering aspect of greed or petty vanity or worse.

Not that I am a bad man, in any reasonable sense of the term; not a bit of it. I respect myself; no occasion to grovel and beat my chest; I'm not ashamed to stand comparison with any other fair sample of the species. But there you are: I *am* human, and under the aspect of eternity so far, plus this afternoon's newspaper, that is a rather serious thing.

Without real knowledge, I think of this total recall as something like a passage down a corridor of myriad images—now dark, now brilliant; now pleasant, now horrible—guided by no certainty except an awareness of the open blind door at the end of it. It could have its pleasing moments and its consolations. I don't see how it could ever approximate the delight and satisfaction of living a few more years in this world with the angel lighting on my shoulder when she wishes, and talking to me.

I had to ask her of how great value such a record would be to them. Very great. Obvious enough—they can be of little use to us, by their standards, until they understand us; and they came here to be of use to us as well as to themselves. And understanding us, to them, means knowing us inside out with a completeness such as our most dedicated and laborious scholars could never imagine. I remember those twelve million years: they will not touch us until they are certain no harm will come of it. On our tortured planet, however, there is a time factor. They know that well enough, of course. . . . Recall cannot begin unless the subject is willing or unresisting; to them, that has to mean willing, for any being with intellect enough to make a considered choice. Now, I wonder how many they could find who would be honestly willing to make that uneasy journey into death, for no reward except an assurance that they were serving their own kind and the angels?

More to the point, I wonder if I would be able to achieve such willingness myself, even with her help?

When this had been explained to me, she urged me again to make no hasty decision. And she pointed out to me what my thoughts were already groping at—why not both alternatives, within a reasonable limit of time? Why couldn't I have ten or fifteen years or more with her and then undertake the total recall—perhaps not until my physical powers had started toward senility? I thought that over.

This morning I had almost decided to choose that most welcome and comforting solution. Then the mailman brought my daily paper. Not that I needed any such reminder.

In the afternoon I asked her if she knew whether, in the present state of human technology, it would be possible for our folly to actually destroy this planet. She did not know, for certain. Three of the other children have gone away to different parts of the world, to learn what they can about that. But she had to tell me that such a thing has happened before, elsewhere in the heavens. I guess I won't write a letter to the papers advancing an explanation for the occasional appearance of a nova among the stars. Doubtless others have hit on the same hypothesis without the aid of angels.

And that is not all I must consider. I could die by accident or sudden disease before I had begun to give my life.

Only now, at this very late moment, rubbing my sweaty forehead and gazing into the lights of that wonderful ring, have I been able to put together some obvious facts in the required synthesis.

I don't know, of course, what forms their assistance to us will take. I suspect human beings won't see or hear much of the angels for a long time to come. Now and then disastrous decisions may be altered, and those who believe themselves wholly responsible won't quite know why their minds worked that way. Here and there, maybe an influential mind will be rather strangely nudged into a better course. Something like that. There may be sudden new discoveries and inventions of kinds that will tend to neutralize the menace of our nastiest playthings. But whatever the angels decide to do, the record and analysis of my not too atypical life will be an aid: it could even be the small weight deciding the balance between triumph and failure. That is fact one.

Two: my angel and her brothers and sisters, for all their amazing level of advancement, are of perishable protoplasm, even as I am. Therefore, if this ball of earth becomes a ball of flame, they also will be destroyed. Even if they have the means to use their spaceship again or to build another, it might easily happen that they would not learn their danger in time to escape. And for all I know, this could be tomorrow. Or tonight.

So there can no longer be any doubt as to my choice, and I will tell her when she wakes.

Tonight* there is no recall—I am to rest awhile. I see it is almost a month since I last wrote in this journal. My total recall began three weeks ago, and I have already been able to give away the first twenty-eight years of my life.

Since I no longer require normal sleep, the recall begins at night, as soon as the lights begin to go out over there in the village and there is little danger of interruption. Daytimes, I putter about in my usual fashion. I have sold Steele my hens, and Judy's life was saved a week ago; that practically winds up my affairs, except that I want to write a codicil to my will. I might as well do that now, right here in this journal, instead of bothering my lawyer. It should be legal.

> TO WHOM IT MAY CONCERN: I hereby bequeath to my friend Lester Morse, M.D., of Augusta, Maine, the ring which will be found at my death on the fifth finger of my left hand; and I would urge Dr. Morse to retain this ring in his private possession at all times, and to make provision for its disposal, in the event of his own death, to some person in whose character he places the utmost faith.
>
> (Signed) David Bannerman†

Tonight she has gone away for a while, and I am to rest and do as I please until she returns. I shall spend the time filling in some blanks in this record, but I am afraid it will be a spotty job, unsatisfactory to any readers who are subject to the blessed old itch for facts. Mainly because there is so much I no longer care about. It is troublesome to try to decide what things would

*At this point Dr. Bannerman's handwriting alters curiously. From here on he used a soft pencil instead of a pen, and the script shows signs of haste. In spite of this, however, it is actually much clearer, steadier, and easier to read than the earlier entries in his normal hand.—BLAINE.

†In spite of superficial changes in the handwriting, this signature has been certified genuine by an expert graphologist.   —BLAINE.

be considered important by interested strangers.

Except for the lack of any desire for sleep, and a bodily weariness that is not at all unpleasant, I notice no physical effects thus far. I have no faintest recollection of anything that happened earlier than my twenty-eighth birthday. My deductive memory seems rather efficient, and I am sure I could reconstruct most of the story if it were worth the bother: this afternoon I grubbed around among some old letters of that period, but they weren't very interesting. My knowledge of English is unaffected; I can still read scientific German and some French, because I had occasion to use those languages fairly often after I was twenty-eight. The scraps of Latin dating from high school are quite gone. So are algebra and all but the simplest propositions of high-school geometry: I never needed 'em. I can remember thinking of my mother after twenty-eight, but do not know whether the image this provides really resembles her; my father died when I was thirty-one, so I remember him as a sick old man. I believe I had a younger brother, but he must have died in childhood.*

Judy's passing was tranquil—pleasant for her, I think. It took the better part of a day. We went out to an abandoned field I know, and she lay in the sunshine with the angel sitting by her, while I dug a grave and then rambled off after wild raspberries. Toward evening the angel came and told me it was finished. And most interesting, she said. I don't see how there can have been anything distressing about it for Judy; after all, what hurts us worst is to have our favorite self-deceptions stripped away.

As the angel has explained it to me, her people, their cats, those kangaroo-folk, Man, and just possibly the cats on our planet (she hasn't met them yet) are the only animals she knows who are introspective enough to develop self-delusion and related pretenses. I suggested she might find something of the sort, at least in rudimentary form, among some of the other primates. She was immensely interested and wanted to learn everything I could tell her about monkeys and apes. It seems that long ago on the other planet there used to be clumsy, winged creatures resembling the angels to about the degree that the large anthropoids resemble us. They became extinct some forty million years ago, in spite of enlightened efforts to keep their kind alive. Their birth rate became insufficient for replacement, as if some necessary spark had simply flickered out; almost as if nature, or whatever name you prefer for the unknown, had with gentle finality written them off. . . .

*Dr. Bannerman's mother died in 1918 of influenza. His brother (three years older, not younger) died of pneumonia, 1906.   —BLAINE.

I have not found the recall painful, at least not in retrospect. There must have been sharp moments, mercifully forgotten, along with their causes, as if the process had gone on under anesthesia. Certainly there were plenty of incidents in my first twenty-eight years that I should not care to offer to the understanding of any but the angels. Quite often I must have been mean, selfish, base in any number of ways, if only to judge by the record since twenty-eight. Those old letters touch on a few of these things. To me, they now matter only as material for a record which is safely out of my hands.

However, to any persons I may have harmed, I wish to say this: you were hurt by aspects of my humanity which may not, in a few million years, be quite so common among us all. Against these darker elements I struggled, in my human fashion, as you do yourselves. The effort is not wasted.

It was a week after I told the angel my decision before she was prepared to start the recall. During that week she searched my present mind more closely than I should have imagined was possible: she had to be sure. During that week of hard questions I dare say she learned more about my kind than has ever gone on record even in a physician's office; I hope she did. To any psychiatrist who might question that, I offer a naturalist's suggestion: it is easy to imagine, after some laborious time, that we have noticed everything a given patch of ground can show us; but alter the viewpoint only a little—dig down a foot with a spade, say, or climb a tree branch and look downward—it's a whole new world.

When the angel was not exploring me in this fashion, she took pains to make me glimpse the satisfactions and million rewarding experiences I might have if I chose the other way. I see how necessary that was; at the time it seemed almost cruel. She had to do it, for my own sake, and I am glad that I was somehow able to stand fast to my original choice. So was she, in the end; she has even said she loves me for it. What that troubling word means to her is not within my mind: I am satisfied to take it in the human sense.

Some evening during that week—I think it was June 12—Lester dropped around for sherry and chess. Hadn't seen him in quite a while, and haven't since. There is a moderate polio scare this summer, and it keeps him on the jump. The angel retired behind some books on an upper shelf—I'm afraid it was dusty—and had fun with our chess. She had a fair view of your bald spot, Lester; later she remarked that she liked your looks, and can't you do something about that weight? She suggested an odd expedient, which I believe has occurred to your medical self from time to time—eating less.

Maybe she shouldn't have done what she did with those chess games. Nothing more than my usual blundering happened until after my first ten moves; by that time I suppose she had absorbed the principles and she took over, slightly. I was not fully aware of it until I saw Lester looking like a boiled duck: I had imagined my astonishing moves were the result of my own damn cleverness.

Seriously, Lester, think back to that evening. You've played in stiff amateur tournaments; you know your own abilities and you know mine. Ask yourself whether I could have done anything like that without help. I tell you again, I didn't study the game in the interval when you weren't there. I've never had a chess book in the library, and if I had, no amount of study would take me into your class. Haven't that sort of mentality—just your humble sparring partner, and I've enjoyed it on that basis, as you might enjoy watching a prima-donna surgeon pull off some miracle you wouldn't dream of attempting yourself. Even if your game had been way below par that evening (I don't think it was), I could never have pinned your ears back three times running, without help. That evening you were a long way out of *your* class, that's all.

I couldn't tell you anything about it at the time—she was clear on that point —so I could only bumble and preen myself and leave you mystified. But she wants me to write anything I choose in this journal, and somehow, Lester, I think you may find the next few decades pretty interesting. You're still young —some ten years younger than I. I think you'll see many things that I do wish I myself might see come to pass—or I would so wish if I were not convinced that my choice was the right one.

Most of those new events will not be spectacular, I'd guess. Many of the turns to a better way will hardly be recognized at the time for what they are, by you or anyone else. Obviously, our nature being what it is, we shall not jump into heaven overnight. To hope for that would be as absurd as it is to imagine that any formula, ideology, theory of social pattern, can bring us into Utopia. As I see it, Lester—and I think your consulting room would have told you the same even if your own intuition were not enough—there is only one battle of importance: Armageddon. And Armageddon field is within each self, world without end.

At the moment I believe I am the happiest man who ever lived.

July 20

All but the last ten years now given away. The physical fatigue (still pleasant) is quite overwhelming. I am not troubled by the weeds in my garden patch —merely a different sort of flowers where I had planned something else. An hour ago she brought me the seed of a blown dandelion, to show me how lovely it was—I don't suppose I had ever noticed. I hope whoever takes over this place will bring it back to farming: they say the ten acres below the house used to be good potato land—nice early ground.

It is delightful to sit in the sun, as if I were old.

After thumbing over earlier entries in this journal, I see I have often felt quite bitter toward my own kind. I deduce that I must have been a lonely man —much of the loneliness self-imposed. A great part of my bitterness must have been no more than one ugly byproduct of a life spent too much apart. Some of it doubtless came from objective causes, yet I don't believe I ever had more cause than any moderately intelligent man who would like to see his world a pleasanter place than it ever has been. My angel tells me that the pain in my back is due to an injury received in some early stage of the world war that still goes on. That could have soured me, perhaps. It's all right—it's all in the record.

She is racing with a hummingbird—holding back, I think, to give the ball of green fluff a break.

Another note for you, Lester. I have already indicated that my ring is to be yours. I don't want to tell you what I have discovered of its properties, for fear it might not give you the same pleasure and interest that it has given me. Of course, like any spot of shifting light and color, it is an aid to self-hypnosis. It is much, much more than that, but—find out for yourself, at some time when you are a little protected from everyday distractions. I know it can't harm you, because I know its source.

By the way, I wish you would convey to my publishers my request that they either discontinue manufacture of my *Introductory Biology* or else bring out a new edition revised in accordance with some notes you will find in the top left drawer of my library desk. I glanced through that book after my angel assured me that I wrote it, and I was amazed. However, I'm afraid my notes are messy (I call them mine by a poetic license), and they may be too advanced for the present day—though the revision is mainly a matter of leaving out certain generalities that ain't so. Use your best judgment: it's a very minor textbook, and the thing isn't too important. A last wriggle of my personal vanity.

July 27

I have seen a two-moon night.

It was given to me by that other grown-up, at the end of a wonderful visit, when he and six of those nine other children came to see me. It was last night, I think—yes, must have been. First there was a murmur of wings above the house; my angel flew in, laughing; then they were here, all about me. Full of gaiety and colored fire, showing off in every way they knew would please me. Each one had something graceful and friendly to say to me. One brought me a moving image of the St. Lawrence seen at morning from half a mile up—

clouds—eagles; now, how could he know that would delight me so much? And each one thanked me for what I had done.

But it's been so easy!

And at the end the old one—his skin is quite brown, and his down is white and gray—gave the remembered image of a two-moon night. He saw it some sixty years ago.

I have not even considered making an effort to describe it—my fingers will not hold this pencil much longer tonight. Oh—soaring buildings of white and amber, untroubled countryside, silver on curling rivers, a glimpse of open sea; a moon rising in clarity, another setting in a wreath of cloud, between them a wide wandering of unfamiliar stars; and here and there the angels, worthy after fifty million years to live in such a night. No, I cannot describe anything like that. But, you human kindred of mine, I can do something better. I can tell you that this two-moon night, glorious as it was, was no more beautiful than a night under a single moon on this ancient and familiar Earth might be—if you will imagine that the rubbish of human evil has been cleared away and that our own people have started at last on the greatest of all explorations.

July 29

Nothing now remains to give away but the memory of the time that has passed since the angel came. I am to rest as long as I wish, write whatever I want to. Then I shall get myself over to the bed and lie down as if for sleep. She tells me that I can keep my eyes open: she will close them for me when I no longer see her.

I remain convinced that our human case is hopeful. I feel sure that in only a few thousand years we may be able to perform some of the simpler preparatory tasks, such as casting out evil and loving our neighbors. And if that should prove to be so, who can doubt that in another fifty million years we might well be only a little lower than the angels?

LIBRARIAN'S NOTE: As is generally known, the original of the Bannerman Journal is said to have been in the possession of Dr. Lester Morse at the time of the latter's disappearance in 1964, and that disappearance has remained an unsolved mystery to the present day. McCarran is known to have visited Captain Garrison Blaine in October, 1951, but no record remains of that visit. Captain Blaine appears to have been a bachelor who lived alone. He was killed in line of duty, December, 1951. McCarran is believed not to have written about or discussed the Bannerman affair with anyone else. It is almost certain that he himself removed the extract and related papers from the files (unofficially, it would seem!) when he severed his connection with the FBI in 1957;

at any rate, they were found among his effects after his assassination and were released to the public, considerably later, by Mrs. McCarran.

The following memorandum was originally attached to the extract from the Bannerman Journal; it carries the McCarran initialing.

Aug. 11, 1951

The original letter of complaint written by Stephen Clyde, M.D., and mentioned in the accompanying letter of Captain Blaine, has unfortunately been lost, owing perhaps to an error in filing.

Personnel presumed responsible have been instructed not to allow such error to be repeated except if, as, and/or when necessary.

C. McC.

On the margin of this memorandum there was a penciled notation, later erased. The imprint is sufficient to show the unmistakable McCarran script. The notation read in part as follows: *Far be it from a McC. to lose his job except if, as, and/or*—the rest is undecipherable, except for a terminal word which is regrettably unparliamentary.

STATEMENT BY LESTER MORSE, M.D., DATED AUGUST 9, 1951

On the afternoon of July 30, 1951, acting on what I am obliged to describe as an unexpected impulse, I drove out to the country for the purpose of calling on my friend Dr. David Bannerman. I had not seen him nor had word from him since the evening of June 12 of this year.

I entered, as was my custom, without knocking. After calling to him and hearing no response, I went upstairs to his bedroom and found him dead. From superficial indications I judged that death must have taken place during the previous night. He was lying on his bed on his left side, comfortably disposed as if for sleep but fully dressed, with a fresh shirt and clean summer slacks. His eyes and mouth were closed, and there was no trace of the disorder to be expected at even the easiest natural death. Because of these signs I assumed, as soon as I had determined the absence of breath and heartbeat and noted the chill of the body, that some neighbor must have found him already, performed these simple rites out of respect for him, and probably notified a local physician or other responsible person. I therefore waited (Dr. Bannerman had no telephone), expecting that someone would soon call.

Dr. Bannerman's journal was on a table near his bed, open to that page on which he had written a codicil to his will. I read that part. Later, while I was waiting for others to come, I read the remainder of the journal, as I believe he wished me to do. The ring he mentions was on the fifth finger of his left hand, and it is now in my possession. When writing that codicil Dr. Bannerman must have overlooked or forgotten the fact that in his formal will, written some months earlier, he had appointed me executor. If there are legal technicalities involved, I shall be pleased to cooperate fully with the proper authorities.

The ring, however, will remain in my keeping, since that was Dr. Bannerman's expressed wish, and I am not prepared to offer it for examination or discussion under any circumstances.

The notes for a revision of one of his textbooks were in his desk, as noted in the journal. They are by no means "messy"; nor are they particularly revolutionary except insofar as he wished to rephrase, as theory or hypothesis, certain statements that I would have supposed could be regarded as axiomatic. This is not my field, and I am not competent to judge. I shall take up the matter with his publishers at the earliest opportunity.*

So far as I can determine, and bearing in mind the results of the autopsy performed by Stephen Clyde, M.D., the death of Dr. David Bannerman was not inconsistent with the presence of an embolism of some type not distinguishable by post mortem. I have so stated on the certificate of death. It would seem to be not in the public interest to leave such questions in doubt. I am compelled to add one other item of medical opinion for what it may be worth:

I am not a psychiatrist, but, owing to the demands of general practice, I have found it advisable to keep as up to date as possible with current findings and opinion in this branch of medicine. Dr. Bannerman possessed, in my opinion, emotional and intellectual stability to a better degree than anyone else of comparable intelligence in the entire field of my acquaintance, personal and professional. If it is suggested that he was suffering from a hallucinatory psychosis, I can only say that it must have been of a type quite outside my experience and not described, so far as I know, anywhere in the literature of psychopathology.

Dr. Bannerman's house, on the afternoon of July 30, was in good order. Near the open, unscreened window of his bedroom there was a coverless shoe box with a folded silk scarf in the bottom. I found no pillow such as Dr. Bannerman describes in the journal, but observed that a small section had been cut from the scarf. In this box, and near it, there was a peculiar fragrance, faint, aromatic, and very sweet, such as I have never encountered before and therefore cannot describe.

It may or may not have any bearing on the case that, while I remained in

*LIBRARIAN'S NOTE: But it seems he never did. No new edition of *Introductory Biology* was ever brought out, and the textbook has been out of print since 1952.

this house that afternoon, I felt no sense of grief or personal loss, although Dr. Bannerman had been a loved and honored friend for a number of years. I merely had, and have, a conviction that after the completion of some very great undertaking, he had found peace.

ARTHUR C. CLARKE

Rescue Party

Much of science fiction is ego-enhancing. It depicts the human species as the toughest, strongest and fittest in the universe, ready and able to take on all comers and survive. But an important part of science fiction is ego-deflating, presenting us as relatively helpless creatures, desperately in need of guidance and assistance by superior beings. Often we are just depicted as a young life form with considerable growth ahead of us. Arthur C. Clarke has been placing humanity in his version of its place throughout a good portion of his writing—as in the present selection.

Who was to blame? For three days Alveron's thoughts had come back to that question, and still he had found no answer. A creature of a less civilized or a less sensitive race would never have let it torture his mind and would have satisfied himself with the assurance that no one could be responsible for the working of fate. But Alveron and his kind had been lords of the universe since the dawn of history, since that far distant age when the time barrier had been folded around the cosmos by the unknown powers that lay beyond the beginning. To them had been given all knowledge—and with infinite knowledge went infinite responsibility. If there were mistakes and errors in the administration of the galaxy, the fault lay on the heads of Alveron and his people. And this was no mere mistake: it was one of the greatest tragedies in history.

The crew still knew nothing. Even Rugon, his closest friend and the ship's deputy captain, had been told only part of the truth. But now the doomed worlds lay less than a billion miles ahead. In a few hours, they would be landing on the third planet.

Once again Alveron read the message from base; then, with a flick of a tentacle that no human eye could have followed, he pressed the "general attention" button. Throughout the mile-long cylinder that was the galactic survey ship S9000, creatures of many races laid down their work to listen to the words of their captain.

"I know you have all been wondering," began Alveron, "why we were ordered to abandon our survey and to proceed at such an acceleration to this region of space. Some of you may realize what this acceleration means. Our ship is on its last voyage: the generators have already been running for sixty hours at ultimate overload. We will be very lucky if we return to base under our own power.

"We are approaching a sun which is about to become a nova. Detonation will occur in seven hours, with an uncertainty of one hour, leaving us a maximum of only four hours for exploration. There are ten planets in the system about to be destroyed—and there is a civilization on the third. That fact was discovered only a few days ago. It is our tragic mission to contact that doomed race and if possible to save some of its members. I know that there is little we can do in so short a time with this single ship. No other machine can possibly reach the system before detonation occurs."

There was a long pause during which there could have been no sound or movement in the whole of the mighty ship as it sped silently toward the worlds ahead. Alveron knew what his companions were thinking and he tried to answer their unspoken question.

"You will wonder how such a disaster, the greatest of which we have any record, has been allowed to occur. On one point I can reassure you. The fault does not lie with the survey.

"As you know, with our present fleet of under twelve thousand ships, it is possible to reexamine each of the eight thousand million solar systems in the galaxy at intervals of about a million years. Most worlds change very little in so short a time as that.

"Less than four hundred thousand years ago, the survey ship S5060 examined the planets of the system we are approaching. It found intelligence on none of them, though the third planet was teeming with animal life and two other worlds had once been inhabited. The usual report was submitted and the system is due for its next examination in six hundred thousand years.

"It now appears that in the incredibly short period since the last survey, intelligent life has appeared in the system. The first intimation of this occurred when unknown radio signals were detected on the planet Kulath in the system X29.35, Y34.76, Z27.93. Bearings were taken on them; they were coming from the system ahead.

"Kulath is two hundred light-years from here, so those radio waves had been on their way for two centuries. Thus for at least that period of time a civilization has existed on one of these worlds—a civilization that can generate electromagnetic waves and all that that implies.

"An immediate telescopic examination of the system was made and it was then found that the sun was in the unstable pre-nova stage. Detonation might occur at any moment, and indeed might have done so while the light waves were on their way to Kulath.

"There was a slight delay while the supervelocity scanners on Kulath II were focused on the system. They showed that the explosion had not yet occurred but was only a few hours away. If Kulath had been a fraction of a light-year farther from this sun, we should never have known of its civilization until it had ceased to exist.

"The administrator of Kulath contacted sector base immediately, and I was ordered to proceed to the system at once. Our object is to save what members we can of the doomed race, if indeed there are any left. But we have assumed that a civilization possessing radio could have protected itself against any rise of temperature that may have already occurred.

"This ship and the two tenders will each explore a section of the planet. Commander Torkalee will take Number One, Commander Orostron Number Two. They will have just under four hours in which to explore this world. At the end of that time, they must be back in the ship. It will be leaving then, with or without them. I will give the two commanders detailed instructions in the control room immediately.

"That is all. We enter atmosphere in two hours."

On the world once known as Earth the fires were dying out: there was nothing left to burn. The great forests that had swept across the planet like a tidal wave with the passing of the cities were now no more than glowing charcoal and the smoke of their funeral pyres still stained the sky. But the last hours were still to come, for the surface rocks had not yet begun to flow. The continents were dimly visible through the haze, but their outlines meant nothing to the watchers in the approaching ship. The charts they possessed were out of date by a dozen Ice Ages and more deluges than one.

The S9000 had driven past Jupiter and seen at once that no life could exist in those half-gaseous oceans of compressed hydrocarbons, now erupting furiously under the sun's abnormal heat. Mars and the outer planets they had missed, and Alveron realized that the worlds nearer the sun than Earth would be already melting. It was more than likely, he thought sadly, that the tragedy of this unknown race was already finished. Deep in his heart, he thought it might be better so. The ship could only have carried a few hundred survivors, and the problem of selection had been haunting his mind.

Rugon, chief of communications and deputy captain, came into the control room. For the last hour he had been striving to detect radiation from Earth, but in vain.

"We're too late," he announced gloomily. "I've monitored the whole spectrum and the ether's dead except for our own stations and some two-hundred-year-old programs from Kulath. Nothing in this system is radiating any more."

He moved toward the giant vision screen with a graceful flowing motion that no mere biped could ever hope to imitate. Alveron said nothing; he had been expecting this news.

One entire wall of the control room was taken up by the screen, a great black rectangle that gave an impression of almost infinite depth. Three of Rugon's slender control tentacles, useless for heavy work but incredibly swift at all manipulation, flickered over the selector dials and the screen lit up with a thousand points of light. The star field flowed swiftly past as Rugon adjusted the controls, bringing the projector to bear upon the sun itself.

No man of Earth would have recognized the monstrous shape that filled the screen. The sun's light was white no longer: great violet blue clouds covered half its surface and from them long streamers of flame were erupting into space. At one point an enormous prominence had reared itself out of the photosphere, far out even into the flickering veils of the corona. It was as though a tree of fire had taken root in the surface of the sun—a tree that stood half a million miles high and whose branches were rivers of flame sweeping through space at hundreds of miles a second.

"I suppose," said Rugon presently, "that you are quite satisfied about the astronomers' calculations. After all . . ."

"Oh, we're perfectly safe," said Alveron confidently. "I've spoken to Kulath Observatory and they have been making some additional checks through our own instruments. That uncertainty of an hour includes a private safety margin which they won't tell me in case I feel tempted to stay any longer."

He glanced at the instrument board.

"The pilot should have brought us to the atmosphere now. Switch the screen back to the planet, please. Ah, there they go!"

There was a sudden tremor underfoot and a raucous clanging of alarms, instantly stilled. Across the vision screen two slim projectiles dived toward the looming mass of Earth. For a few miles they traveled together, then they separated, one vanishing abruptly as it entered the shadow of the planet.

Slowly the huge mother ship, with its thousand times greater mass, descended after them into the raging storms that already were tearing down the deserted cities of man.

It was night in the hemisphere over which Orostron drove his tiny command. Like Torkalee, his mission was to photograph and record and to report progress to the mother ship. The little scout had no room for speci-mens or passengers. If contact was made with the inhabitants of this world, the S9000 would come at once. There would be no time for parley-ing. If there was any trouble the rescue would be by force and the expla-nations could come later.

The ruined land beneath was bathed with an eerie, flickering light, for a great auroral display was raging over half the world. But the image on the vision screen was independent of external light, and it showed clearly a waste of barren rock that seemed never to have known any form of life. Presumably this desert land must come to an end somewhere. Orostron increased his speed to the highest value he dared risk in so dense an atmosphere.

The machine fled on through the storm, and presently the desert of rock began to climb toward the sky. A great mountain range lay ahead, its peaks lost in the smoke-laden clouds. Orostron directed the scanners toward the horizon, and on the vision screen the line of mountains seemed suddenly very close and menacing. He started to climb rapidly. It was difficult to imagine a more unpromising land in which to find civilization and he wondered if it would be wise to change course. He decided against it. Five minutes later, he had his reward.

Miles below lay a decapitated mountain, the whole of its summit sheared away by some tremendous feat of engineering. Rising out of the rock and straddling the artificial plateau was an intricate structure of metal girders, supporting masses of machinery. Orostron brought his ship to a halt and spiraled down toward the mountain.

The slight Doppler blur had now vanished, and the picture on the screen was clear-cut. The latticework was supporting some scores of great metal mirrors, pointing skyward at an angle of forty-five degrees to the horizontal. They were slightly concave, and each had some complicated mechanism at its focus. There seemed something impressive and purposeful about the great array; every mirror was aimed at precisely the same spot in the sky—or beyond.

Orostron turned to his colleagues.

"It looks like some kind of observatory to me," he said. "Have you ever seen anything like it before?"

Klarten, a multitentacled, tripedal creature from a globular cluster at the edge of the Milky Way, had a different theory.

"That's communication equipment. Those reflectors are for focusing elec-tromagnetic beams. I've seen the same kind of installation on a hundred worlds before. It may even be the station that Kulath picked up—though that's rather unlikely, for the beams would be very narrow from mirrors that size."

"That would explain why Rugon could detect no radiation before we landed," added Hansur II, one of the twin beings from the planet Thargon.

Orostron did not agree at all.

"If that is a radio station, it must be built for interplanetary communication. Look at the way the mirrors are pointed. I don't believe that a race which has only had radio for two centuries can have crossed space. It took my people six thousand years to do it."

"We managed it in three," said Hansur II mildly, speaking a few seconds ahead of his twin. Before the inevitable argument could develop, Klarten began to wave his tentacles with excitement. While the others had been talking, he had started the automatic monitor.

"Here it is! Listen!"

He threw a switch, and the little room was filled with a raucous whining sound, continually changing in pitch but nevertheless retaining certain characteristics that were difficult to define.

The four explorers listened intently for a minute; then Orostron said, "Surely that can't be any form of speech! No creature could produce sounds as quickly as that!"

Hansur I had come to the same conclusion. "That's a television program. Don't you think so, Klarten?"

The other agreed.

"Yes, and each of those mirrors seems to be radiating a different program. I wonder where they're going? If I'm correct, one of the other planets in the system must lie along those beams. We can soon check that."

Orostron called the S9000 and reported the discovery. Both Rugon and Alveron were greatly excited and made a quick check of the astronomical records.

The result was surprising—and disappointing. None of the other nine planets lay anywhere near the line of transmission. The great mirrors appeared to be pointing blindly into space.

There seemed only one conclusion to be drawn, and Klarten was the first to voice it.

"They had interplanetary communication," he said. "But the station must be deserted now and the transmitters no longer controlled. They haven't been switched off and are just pointing where they were left."

"Well, we'll soon find out," said Orostron. "I'm going to land."

He brought the machine slowly down to the level of the great metal mirrors and past them until it came to rest on the mountain rock. A hundred yards away, a white stone building crouched beneath the maze of steel girders. It was windowless, but there were several doors in the wall facing them.

Orostron watched his companions climb into their protective suits and wished he could follow. But someone had to stay in the machine to keep in touch with the mother ship. Those were Alveron's instructions, and they were very wise. One never knew what would happen on a world that was being explored for the first time, especially under conditions such as these.

Very cautiously, the three explorers stepped out of the airlock and adjusted the antigravity field of their suits. Then, each with the mode of locomotion peculiar to his race, the little party went toward the building, the Hansur twins leading and Klarten following close behind. His gravity control was apparently giving trouble, for he suddenly fell to the ground, rather to the amusement of his colleagues. Orostron saw them pause for a moment at the nearest door —then it opened slowly and they disappeared from sight.

So Orostron waited with what patience he could while the storm rose around him and the light of the aurora grew even brighter in the sky. At the agreed times he called the mother ship and received brief acknowledgments from Rugon. He wondered how Torkalee was faring, halfway round the planet, but he could not contact him through the crash and thunder of solar interference.

It did not take Klarten and the Hansurs long to discover that their theories were largely correct. The building was a radio station, and it was utterly deserted. It consisted of one tremendous room with a few small offices leading from it. In the main chamber, row after row of electrical equipment stretched into the distance; lights flickered and winked on hundreds of control panels, and a dull glow came from the elements in a great avenue of vacuum tubes.

But Klarten was not impressed. The first radio sets his race had built were now fossilized in strata a thousand million years old. Man, who had possessed electrical machines for only a few centuries, could not compete with those who had known them for half the lifetime of the Earth.

Nevertheless, the party kept their recorders running as they explored the building. There was still one problem to be solved. The deserted station was broadcasting programs, but where were they coming from? The central switchboard had been quickly located. It was designed to handle scores of programs simultaneously, but the source of those programs was lost in a maze of cables that vanished underground. Back in the S9000, Rugon was trying to analyze the broadcasts and perhaps his researches would reveal their origin. It was impossible to trace cables that might lead across continents.

The party wasted little time at the deserted station. There was nothing they could learn from it, and they were seeking life rather than scientific information. A few minutes later the little ship rose swiftly from the plateau and headed toward the plains that must lie beyond the mountains. Less than three hours were still left to them.

As the array of enigmatic mirrors dropped out of sight, Orostron was struck by a sudden thought. Was it imagination, or had they all moved through a small angle while he had been waiting, as if they were still compensating for the rotation of the Earth? He could not be sure, and he dismissed the matter as unimportant. It would only mean that the directing mechanism was still working, after a fashion.

They discovered the city fifteen minutes later. It was a great, sprawling metropolis, built around a river that had disappeared, leaving an ugly scar winding its way among the great buildings and beneath bridges that looked very incongruous now.

Even from the air, the city looked deserted. But only two and a half hours were left—there was no time for further exploration. Orostron made his decision and landed near the largest structure he could see. It seemed reasonable to suppose that some creatures would have sought shelter in the strongest buildings, where they would be safe until the very end.

The deepest caves—the heart of the planet itself—would give no protection when the final cataclysm came. Even if this race had reached the outer planets, its doom would only be delayed by the few hours it would take for the ravening wavefronts to cross the solar system.

Orostron could not know that the city had been deserted not for a few days or weeks, but for over a century. For the culture of cities, which had outlasted so many civilizations had been doomed at last when the helicopter brought universal transportation. Within a few generations the great masses of mankind, knowing that they could reach any part of the globe in a matter of hours, had gone back to the fields and forests for which they had always longed. The new civilization had machines and resources of which earlier ages had never dreamed, but it was essentially rural and no longer bound to the steel and concrete warrens that had dominated the centuries before. Such cities as still remained were specialized centers of research, administration or entertainment; the others had been allowed to decay, where it was too much trouble to destroy them. The dozen or so greatest of all cities, and the ancient university towns, had scarcely changed and would have lasted for many generations to come. But the cities that had been founded on steam and iron and surface transportation had passed with the industries that had nourished them.

And so while Orostron waited in the tender, his colleagues raced through endless empty corridors and deserted halls, taking innumerable photographs but learning nothing of the creatures who had used these buildings. There were libraries, meeting places, council rooms, thousands of offices—all were empty and deep with dust. If they had not seen the radio station on its mountain aerie, the explorers could well have believed that this world had known no life for centuries.

Through the long minutes of waiting, Orostron tried to imagine where this race could have vanished. Perhaps they had killed themselves knowing that escape was impossible; perhaps they had built great shelters in the bowels of the planet and even now were cowering in their millions beneath his feet, waiting for the end. He began to fear that he would never know.

It was almost a relief when at last he had to give the order for the return. Soon he would know if Torkalee's party had been more fortunate. And he was anxious to get back to the mother ship, for as the minutes passed the suspense had become more and more acute. There had always been the thought in his mind: what if the astronomers of Kulath have made a mistake? He would begin to feel happy when the walls of the S9000 were around him. He would be happier still when they were out in space and this ominous sun was shrinking far astern.

As soon as his colleagues had entered the airlock, Orostron hurled his tiny machine into the sky and set the controls to home on the S9000. Then he turned to his friends.

"Well, what have you found?" he asked.

Klarten produced a large roll of canvas and spread it out on the floor.

"This is what they were like," he said quietly. "Bipeds, with only two arms. They seem to have managed well, in spite of that handicap. Only two eyes as well, unless there are others in the back. We were lucky to find this; it's about the only thing they left behind."

The ancient oil paintings stared stonily back at the three creatures regarding it so intently. By the irony of fate, its complete worthlessness had saved it from oblivion. When the city had been evacuated, no one had bothered to move Alderman John Richards, 1909–1974. For a century and a half he had been gathering dust while far away from the old cities the new civilization had been rising to heights no earlier culture had ever known.

"That was almost all we found," said Klarten. "The city must have been deserted for years. I'm afraid our expedition has been a failure. If there are any living beings on this world, they've hidden themselves too well for us to find them."

His commander was forced to agree.

"It was an almost impossible task," he said. "If we'd had weeks instead of hours we might have succeeded. For all we know, they may even have built shelters under the sea. No one seems to have thought of that."

He glanced quickly at the indicators and corrected the course.

"We'll be there in five minutes. Alveron seems to be moving rather quickly.

I wonder if Torkalee has found anything."

The S9000 was hanging a few miles above the seaboard of a glazing continent when Orostron homed upon it. The danger line was thirty minutes away and there was no time to lose. Skillfully, he maneuvered the little ship into its launching tube and the party stepped out of the airlock.

There was a small crowd waiting for them. That was to be expected, but Orostron could see at once that something more than curiosity had brought his friends here. Even before a word was spoken, he knew that something was wrong.

"Torkalee hasn't returned. He's lost his party and we're going to the rescue. Come along to the control room at once."

From the beginning, Torkalee had been luckier than Orostron. He had followed the zone of twilight, keeping away from the intolerable glare of the sun, until he came to the shores of an inland sea. It was a very recent sea, one of the latest of man's works, for the land it covered had been desert less than a century before. In a few hours it would be desert again, for the water was boiling and clouds of steam were rising to the skies. But they could not veil the loveliness of the great white city that overlooked the tideless sea.

Flying machines were still parked neatly round the square in which Torkalee landed. They were disappointingly primitive, though beautifully finished, and depended on rotating airfoils for support. Nowhere was there any sign of life, but the place gave the impression that its inhabitants were not very far away. Lights were still shining from some of the windows.

Torkalee's three companions lost no time in leaving the machine. Leader of the party, by seniority of rank and race was T'sinadree, who like Alveron himself had been born on one of the ancient planets of the Central Suns. Next came Alarkane, from a race which was one of the youngest in the universe and took a perverse pride in the fact. Last came one of the strange beings from the system of Palador. It was nameless, like all its kind, for it possessed no identity of its own, being merely a mobile but still dependent cell in the consciousness of its race. Though it and its fellows had long been scattered over the galaxy in the exploration of countless worlds, some unknown link still bound them together as inexorably as the living cells in a human body.

When a creature of Palador spoke, the pronoun it used was always "we." There was not, nor could there ever be, any first person singular in the language of Palador.

The great doors of the splendid building baffled the explorers, though any human child would have known their secret. T'sinadree wasted no time on them but called Torkalee on his personal transmitter. Then the three hurried aside while their commander maneuvered his machine into the best position. There was a brief burst of intolerable flame; the massive steelwork flickered once at the edge of the visible spectrum and was gone. The stones were still glowing when the eager party hurried into the building, the beams of their light projectors fanning before them.

The torches were not needed. Before them lay a great hall, flowing with light from lines of tubes along the ceiling. On either side, the hall opened out into long corridors, while straight ahead a massive stairway swept majestically toward the upper floors.

For a moment T'sinadree hesitated. Then, since one way was as good as another, he led his companions down the first corridor.

The feeling that life was near had now become very strong. At any moment, it seemed, they might be confronted by the creatures of this world. If they showed hostility—and they could scarcely be blamed if they did—the paralyzers would be used at once.

The tension was very great as the party entered the first room and only relaxed when they saw that it held nothing but machines—row after row of them, now stilled and silent. Lining the enormous room were thousands of metal filing cabinets, forming a continuous wall as far as the eye could reach. And that was all; there was no furniture, nothing but the cabinets and the mysterious machines.

Alarkane, always the quickest of the three, was already examining the cabinets. Each held many thousand sheets of tough, thin material, perforated with innumerable holes and slots. The Paladorian appropriated one of the cards and Alarkane recorded the scene together with some close-ups of the machines. Then they left. The great room, which had been one of the marvels of the world, meant nothing to them. No living eye would ever again see that wonderful battery of almost human Hollerith analyzers and the five thousand million punched cards holding all that could be recorded of each man, woman and child on the planet.

It was clear that this building had been used very recently. With growing excitement, the explorers hurried on to the next room. This they found to be an enormous library, for millions of books lay all around them on miles and miles of shelving. Here, though the explorers could not know it, were the records of all the laws that man had ever passed and all the speeches that had ever been made in his council chambers.

T'sinadree was deciding his plan of action, when Alarkane drew his attention to one of the racks a hundred yards away. It was half empty, unlike all the others. Around it books lay in a tumbled heap on the floor, as if knocked down by someone in frantic haste. The signs were unmistakable. Not long ago, other creatures had been this way. Faint wheel marks were clearly visible on the floor to the acute sense of Alarkane, though the others could see nothing. Alarkane could even detect footprints, but knowing nothing of the creatures that had formed them he could not say which way they led.

The sense of nearness was stronger than ever now, but it was nearness in time, not in space. Alarkane voiced the thoughts of the party.

"Those books must have been valuable, and someone has come to rescue them—rather as an afterthought, I should say. That means there must be a place of refuge, possibly not very far away. Perhaps we may be able to find some other clues that will lead us to it."

T'sinadree agreed; the Paladorian wasn't enthusiastic.

"That may be so," it said, "but the refuge may be anywhere on the planet, and we have just two hours left. Let us waste no more time if we hope to rescue these people."

The party hurried forward once more, pausing only to collect a few books that might be useful to the scientists at base—though it was doubtful if they could ever be translated. They soon found that the great building was composed largely of small rooms, all showing signs of recent occupation. Most of them were in a neat and tidy condition, but one or two were very much the reverse. The explorers were particularly puzzled by one room—clearly an office of some kind—that appeared to have been completely wrecked. The floor was littered with papers, the furniture had been smashed and smoke was pouring through the broken windows from the fires outside.

T'sinadree was rather alarmed.

"Surely no dangerous animal could have got into a place like this!" he exclaimed, fingering his paralyzer nervously.

Alarkane did not answer. He began to make that annoying sound which his race called "laughter." It was several minutes before he would explain what had amused him.

"I don't think any animal has done it," he said. "In fact, the explanation is very simple. Suppose *you* had been working all your life in this room, dealing with endless papers, year after year. And suddenly, you are told that you will never see it again, that your work is finished and that you can leave it forever. More than that—no one will come after you. Everything is finished. How would you make your exit, T'sinadree?"

The other thought for a moment.

"Well, I suppose I'd just tidy things up and leave. That's what seems to have happened in all the other rooms."

Alarkane laughed again.

"I'm quite sure you would. But some individuals have a different psychology. I think I should have liked the creature that used this room."

He did not explain himself further, and his two colleagues puzzled over his words for quite a while before they gave it up.

It came as something of a shock when Torkalee gave the order to return. They had gathered a great deal of information, but had found no clue that might lead them to the missing inhabitants of this world. That problem was as baffling as ever, and now it seemed that it would never be solved. There were only forty minutes left before the S9000 would be departing.

They were halfway back to the tender when they saw the semi-circular passage leading down into the depths of the building. Its architectural style was quite different from that used elsewhere, and the gently sloping floor was an irresistible attraction to creatures whose many legs had grown weary of the marble staircases which only bipeds could have built in such profusion. T'sinadree had been the worst sufferer, for he normally employed twelve legs and could use twenty when he was in a hurry, though no one had ever seen him perform this feat.

The party stopped dead and looked down the passageway with a single thought. A tunnel, leading down into the depths of Earth! At its end, they might yet find the people of this world and rescue some of them from their fate. For there was still time to call the mother ship if the need arose.

T'sinadree signaled to his commander and Torkalee brought the little machine immediately overhead. There might not be time for the party to retrace its footsteps through the maze of passages, so meticulously recorded in the Paladorian mind that there was no possibility of going astray. If speed was necessary, Torkalee could blast his way through the dozen floors above their head. In any case, it should not take long to find what lay at the end of the passage.

It took only thirty seconds. The tunnel ended quite abruptly in a very curious cylindrical room with magnificently padded seats along the walls. There was no way out save that by which they had come and it was several seconds before the purpose of the chamber dawned on Alarkane's mind. It was a pity, he thought, that they would never have time to use this. The thought was suddenly interrupted by a cry from T'sinadree. Alarkane wheeled around and saw that the entrance had closed silently behind them.

Even in that first moment of panic, Alarkane found himself thinking with some admiration: whoever they were, they knew how to build automatic machinery!

The Paladorian was the first to speak. It waved one of its tentacles toward the seats.

"We think it would be best to be seated," it said. The multiplex mind of

Palador had already analyzed the situation and knew what was coming.

They did not have long to wait before a low-pitched hum came from a grill overhead, and for the very last time in history a human, even if lifeless, voice was heard on Earth. The words were meaningless, though the trapped explorers could guess their message clearly enough.

"Choose your stations, please, and be seated."

Simultaneously, a wall panel at one end of the compartment glowed with light. On it was a simple map, consisting of a series of a dozen circles connected by a line. Each of the circles had writing alongside it, and beside the writing were two buttons of different colors.

Alarkane looked questioningly at his leader.

"Don't touch them," said T'sinadree. "If we leave the controls alone, the doors may open again."

He was wrong. The engineers who had designed the automatic subway had assumed that anyone who entered it would naturally wish to go somewhere. If they selected no intermediate station, their destination could only be the end of the line.

There was another pause while the relays and thyratrons waited for their orders. In those thirty seconds, if they had known what to do, the party could have opened the doors and left the subway. But they did not know, and the machines geared to a human psychology acted for them.

The surge of acceleration was not very great; the lavish upholstery was a luxury, not a necessity. Only an almost imperceptible vibration told of the speed at which they were traveling through the bowels of the earth, on a journey the duration of which they could not even guess. And in thirty minutes, the S9000 would be leaving the solar system.

There was a long silence in the speeding machine. T'sinadree and Alarkane were thinking rapidly. So was the Paladorian, though in a different fashion. The conception of personal death was meaningless to it, for the destruction of a single unit meant no more to the group mind than the loss of a nail-paring to a man. But it could, though with great difficulty, appreciate the plight of individual intelligences such as Alarkane and T'sinadree, and it was anxious to help them if it could.

Alarkane had managed to contact Torkalee with his personal transmitter, though the signal was very weak and seemed to be fading quickly. Rapidly he explained the situation, and almost at once the signals became clearer. Torkalee was following the path of the machine, flying above the ground under which they were speeding to their unknown destination. That was the first indication they had of the fact that they were traveling at nearly a thousand miles an hour, and very soon after that Torkalee was able to give the still more disturbing news that they were rapidly approaching the sea. While they were beneath the land, there was a hope, though a slender one, that they might stop the machine and escape. But under the ocean—not all the brains and the machinery in the great mother ship could save them. No one could have devised a more perfect trap.

T'sinadree had been examining the wall map with great attention. Its meaning was obvious, and along the line connecting the circles a tiny spot of light was crawling. It was already halfway to the first of the stations marked.

"I'm going to press one of those buttons," said T'sinadree at last. "It won't do any harm, and we may learn something."

"I agree. Which will you try first?"

"There are only two kinds, and it won't matter if we try the wrong one first. I suppose one is to start the machine and the other is to stop it."

Alarkane was not very hopeful.

"It started without any button pressing," he said. "I think it's completely automatic and we can't control it from here at all."

T'sinadree could not agree.

"These buttons are clearly associated with the stations, and there's no point in having them unless you can use them to stop yourself. The only question is, which is the right one?"

His analysis was perfectly correct. The machine could be stopped at any intermediate station. They had only been on their way ten minutes, and if they could leave now, no harm would have been done. It was just bad luck that T'sinadree's first choice was the wrong button.

The little light on the map crawled slowly through the illuminated circle without checking its speed. And at the same time Torkalee called from the ship overhead.

"You have just passed underneath a city and are heading out to sea. There cannot be another stop for nearly a thousand miles."

Alveron had given up all hope of finding life on this world. The S9000 had roamed over half the planet, never staying long in one place, descending ever and again in an effort to attract attention. There had been no response; Earth seemed utterly dead. If any of its inhabitants were still alive, thought Alveron, they must have hidden themselves in its depths where no help could reach them, though their doom would be nonetheless certain.

Rugon brought news of the disaster. The great ship ceased its fruitless searching and fled back through the storm to the ocean above which Torkalee's little tender was still following the track of the buried machine.

The scene was truly terrifying. Not since the days when Earth was born had there been such seas as this. Mountains of water were racing before the storm which had now reached velocities of many hundred miles an hour. Even at this distance from the mainland the air was full of flying debris—trees, fragments of houses, sheets of metal, anything that had not been anchored to the ground. No airborne machine could have lived for a moment in such a gale. And ever and again even the roar of the wind was drowned as the vast water-mountains met head-on with a crash that seemed to shake the sky.

Fortunately, there had been no serious earthquakes yet. Far beneath the bed of the ocean, the wonderful piece of engineering which had been the World President's private vacuum-subway was still working perfectly, unaffected by the tumult and destruction above. It would continue to work until the last minute of the Earth's existence, which, if the astronomers were right, was not much more than fifteen minutes away—though precisely how much more Alveron would have given a great deal to know. It would be nearly an hour before the trapped party could reach land and even the slightest hope of rescue.

Alveron's instructions had been precise, though even without them he would never have dreamed of taking any risks with the great machine that had been entrusted to his care. Had he been human, the decision to abandon the trapped members of his crew would have been desperately hard to make. But he came of a race far more sensitive than man, a race that so loved the things of the spirit that long ago, and with infinite reluctance, it had taken over control of the universe since only thus could it be sure that justice was being done. Alveron would need all his superhuman gifts to carry him through the next few hours.

Meanwhile, a mile below the bed of the ocean Alarkane and T'sinadree were very busy indeed with their private communicators. Fifteen minutes is not a long time in which to wind up the affairs of a lifetime. It is indeed, scarcely long enough to dictate more than a few of those farewell messages which at such moments are so much more important than all other matters.

All the while the Paladorian had remained silent and motionless, saying not a word. The other two, resigned to their fate and engrossed in their personal affairs, had given it no thought. They were startled when suddenly it began to address them in its peculiarly passionless voice.

"We perceive that you are making certain arrangements concerning your anticipated destruction. That will probably be unnecessary. Captain Alveron hopes to rescue us if we can stop this machine when we reach land again."

Both T'sinadree and Alarkane were too surprised to say anything for a moment. Then the latter gasped, "How do you know?"

It was a foolish question, for he remembered at once that there were several

Paladorians—if one could use the phrase—in the S9000, and consequently their companion knew everything that was happening in the mother ship. So he did not wait for an answer but continued. "Alveron can't do that! He daren't take such a risk!"

"There will be no risk," said the Paladorian. "We have told him what to do. It is really very simple."

Alarkane and T'sinadree looked at their companion with something approaching awe, realizing now what must have happened. In moments of crisis, the single units comprising the Paladorian mind could link together in an organization no less close than that of any physical brain. At such moments they formed an intellect more powerful than any other in the universe. All ordinary problems could be solved by a few hundred or thousand units. Very rarely, millions would be needed, and on two historic occasions the billions of cells of the entire Paladorian consciousness had been welded together to deal with emergencies that threatened the race. The mind of Palador was one of the greatest mental resources of the universe; its full force was seldom required, but the knowledge that it was available was supremely comforting to other races. Alarkane wondered how many cells had coordinated to deal with this particular emergency. He also wondered how so trivial an incident had ever come to its attention.

To that question he was never to know the answer, though he might have guessed it had he known that the chillingly remote Paladorian mind possessed an almost human streak of vanity. Long ago, Alarkane had written a book trying to prove that eventually all intelligent races would sacrifice individual consciousness and that one day only group-minds would remain in the universe. Palador, he had said, was the first of those ultimate intellects, and the vast, dispersed mind had not been displeased.

They had no time to ask any further questions before Alveron himself began to speak through their communicators.

"Alveron calling! We're staying on this planet until the detonation waves reach it, so we may be able to rescue you. You're heading toward a city on the coast which you'll reach in forty minutes at your present speed. If you cannot stop yourselves then, we're going to blast the tunnel behind and ahead of you to cut off your power. Then we'll sink a shaft to get you out—the chief engineer says he can do it in five minutes with the main projectors. So you should be safe within an hour, unless the sun blows up before."

"And if that happens, you'll be destroyed as well! You mustn't take such a risk!"

"Don't let that worry you; we're perfectly safe. When the sun detonates, the explosion wave will take several minutes to rise to its maximum. But apart from that, we're on the night side of the planet, behind an eight-thousand-mile screen of rock. When the first warning of the explosion comes, we will accelerate out of the solar system, keeping in the shadow of the planet. Under our maximum drive, we will reach the velocity of light before leaving the cone of shadow, and the sun cannot harm us then."

T'sinadree was still afraid to hope. Another objection came at once into his mind.

"Yes, but how will you get any warning, here on the night side of the planet?"

"Very easily," replied Alveron. "This world has a moon which is now visible from this hemisphere. We have telescopes trained on it. If it shows any sudden increase in brilliance, our main drive goes on automatically and we'll be thrown out of the system."

The logic was flawless. Alveron, cautious as ever, was taking no chances. It would be many minutes before the eight-thousand-mile shield of rock and metal could be destroyed by the fires of the exploding sun. In that time, the S9000 could have reached the safety of the velocity of light.

Alarkane pressed the second button when they were still several miles from the coast. He did not expect anything to happen then, assuming that the machine could not stop between stations. It seemed too good to be true when, a few minutes later, the machine's slight vibration died away and they came to a halt.

The doors slid silently apart. Even before they were fully open, the three had left the compartment. They were taking no more chances. Before them a long tunnel stretched into the distance, rising slowly out of sight. They were starting along it when suddenly Alveron's voice called from the communicators.

"Stay where you are! We're going to blast!"

The ground shuddered once, and far ahead there came the rumble of falling rock. Again the earth shook—and a hundred yards ahead the passageway vanished abruptly. A tremendous vertical shaft had been cut clean through it.

The party hurried forward again until they came to the end of the corridor and stood waiting on its lip. The shaft in which it ended was a full thousand feet across and descended into the earth as far as the torches could throw their beams. Overhead, the storm clouds fled beneath a moon that no man would have recognized, so luridly brilliant was its disk. And, most glorious of all sights, the S9000 floated high above, the great projectors that had drilled this enormous pit still glowing cherry red.

A dark shape detached itself from the mother ship and dropped swiftly toward the ground. Torkalee was returning to collect his friends. A little later,

Alveron greeted them in the control room. He waved to the great vision screen and said quietly, "See, we were barely in time."

The continent below them was slowly settling beneath the mile-high waves that were attacking its coasts. The last that anyone was ever to see of Earth was a great plain, bathed with the silver light of the abnormally brilliant moon. Across its face the waters were pouring in a glittering flood toward a distant range of mountains. The sea had won its final victory, but its triumph would be short-lived for soon sea and land would be no more. Even as the silent party in the control room watched the destruction below, the infinitely greater catastrophe to which this was only the prelude came swiftly upon them.

It was as though dawn had broken suddenly over this moonlit landscape. But it was not dawn: it was only the moon, shining with the brilliance of a second sun. For perhaps thirty seconds that awesome, unnatural light burned fiercely on the doomed land beneath. Then there came a sudden flashing of indicator lights across the control board. The main drive was on. For a second Alveron glanced at the indicators and checked their information. When he looked again at the screen, Earth was gone.

The magnificent, desperately overstrained generators quietly died when the S9000 was passing the orbit of Persephone. It did not matter; the sun could never harm them now, and although the ship was speeding helplessly out into the lonely night of interstellar space, it would only be a matter of days before rescue came.

There was irony in that. A day ago, they had been the rescuers going to the aid of a race that now no longer existed. Not for the first time Alveron wondered about the world that had just perished. He tried in vain to picture it as it had been in its glory, the streets of its cities thronged with life. Primitive though its people had been, they might have offered much to the universe. If only they could have made contact! Regret was useless; long before their coming, the people of this world must have buried themselves in its iron heart. And now they and their civilization would remain a mystery for the rest of time.

Alveron was glad when his thoughts were interrupted by Rugon's entrance. The chief of communications had been very busy ever since the takeoff, trying to analyze the programs radiated by the transmitter Orostron had discovered. The problem was not a difficult one, but it demanded the construction of special equipment, and that had taken time.

"Well, what have you found?" asked Alveron.

"Quite a lot," replied his friend. "There's something mysterious here, and I don't understand it.

"It didn't take long to find how the vision transmissions were built up, and we've been able to convert them to suit our own equipment. It seems that there were cameras all over the planet, surveying points of interest. Some of them were apparently in cities, on the tops of very high buildings. The cameras were rotating continuously to give panoramic views. In the programs we've recorded there are about twenty different scenes.

"In addition, there are a number of transmissions of a different kind, neither sound nor vision. They seem to be purely scientific—possibly instrument readings or something of that sort. All these programs were going out simultaneously on different frequency bands.

"Now there must be a reason for all this. Orostron still thinks that the station simply wasn't switched off when it was deserted. But these aren't the sort of programs such a station would normally radiate at all. It was certainly used for interplanetary relaying—Klarten was quite right there. So these people must have crossed space, since none of the other planets had any life at the time of the last survey. Don't you agree?"

Alveron was following intently.

"Yes, that seems reasonable enough. But it's also certain that the beam was pointing to none of the other planets. I checked that myself."

"I know," said Rugon. "What I want to discover is why a giant interplanetary relay station is busily transmitting pictures of a world about to be destroyed—pictures that would be of immense interest to scientists and astronomers. Someone had gone to a lot of trouble to arrange all those panoramic cameras. I am convinced that those beams were going somewhere."

Alveron started up.

"Do you imagine that there might be an outer planet that hasn't been reported?" he asked. "If so, your theory's certainly wrong. The beam wasn't even pointing in the plane of the solar system. And even if it were—just look at this."

He switched on the vision screen and adjusted the controls. Against the velvet curtain of space was hanging a blue-white sphere, apparently composed of many concentric shells of incandescent gas. Even though its immense distance made all movement invisible, it was clearly expanding at an enormous rate. At its center was a blinding point of light—the white dwarf star that the sun had now become.

"You probably don't realize just how big that sphere is," said Alveron. "Look at this."

He increased the magnification until only the center portion of the nova was visible. Close to its heart were two minute condensations, one on either side of the nucleus.

"Those are the two giant planets of the system. They have still managed to retain their existence—after a fashion. And they were several hundred million miles from the sun. The nova is still expanding—but it's already twice the size of the solar system."

Rugon was silent for a moment.

"Perhaps you're right," he said, rather grudgingly. "You've disposed of my first theory. But you still haven't satisfied me."

He made several swift circuits of the room before speaking again. Alveron waited patiently. He knew the almost intuitive powers of his friend, who could often solve a problem when mere logic seemed insufficient.

Then rather slowly, Rugon began to speak again.

"What do you think of this?" he said. "Suppose we've completely underestimated this people? Orostron did it once—he thought they could never have crossed space, since they'd only known radio for two centuries. Hansur II told me that. Well, Orostron was quite wrong. Perhaps we're all wrong. I've had a look at the material that Klarten brought back from the transmitter. He wasn't impressed by what he found, but it's a marvelous achievement for so short a time. There were devices in that station that belonged to civilizations thousands of years older. Alveron, can we follow that beam to see where it leads?"

Alveron said nothing for a full minute. He had been more than half expecting the question, but it was not an easy one to answer. The main generators had gone completely. There was no point in trying to repair them. But there was still power available, and while there was power, anything could be done in time. It would mean a lot of improvisation, and some difficult maneuvers, for the ship still had its enormous initial velocity. Yes, it could be done, and the activity would keep the crew from becoming further depressed, now that the reaction caused by the mission's failure had started to set in. The news that the nearest heavy repair ship could not reach them for three weeks had also caused a slump in morale.

The engineers, as usual, made a tremendous fuss. Again as usual, they did the job in half the time they had dismissed as being absolutely impossible. Very slowly, over many hours, the great ship began to discard the speed its main drive had given it in as many minutes. In a tremendous curve, millions of miles in radius, the S9000 changed its course and the star fields shifted around it.

The maneuver took three days, but at the end of that time the ship was limping along a course parallel to the beam that had once come from Earth. They were heading out into emptiness, the blazing sphere that had been the sun dwindling slowly behind them. By the standards of interstellar flight, they were almost stationary.

For hours Rugon strained over his instruments, driving his detector beams far ahead into space. There were certainly no planets within many light-years; there was no doubt of that. From time to time Alveron came to see him and always he had to give the same reply: "Nothing to report." About a fifth of the time Rugon's intuition let him down badly; he began to wonder if this was such an occasion.

Not until a week later did the needles of the mass-detectors quiver feebly at the ends of their scales. But Rugon said nothing, not even to his captain. He waited until he was sure, and he went on waiting until even the short-range scanners began to react and to build up the first faint pictures on the vision screen. Still he waited patiently until he could interpret the images. Then, when he knew that his wildest fancy was even less than the truth, he called his colleagues into the control room.

The picture on the vision screen was the familiar one of endless star fields, sun beyond sun to the very limits of the universe. Near the center of the screen a distant nebula made a patch of haze that was difficult for the eye to grasp.

Rugon increased the magnification. The stars flowed out of the field; the little nebula expanded until it filled the screen and then—it was a nebula no longer. A simultaneous gasp of amazement came from all the company at the sight that lay before them.

Lying across league after league of space, ranged in a vast three-dimensional array of rows and columns with the precision of a marching army, were thousands of tiny pencils of light. They were moving swiftly; the whole immense lattice holding its shape as a single unit. Even as Alveron and his comrades watched, the formation began to drift off the screen and Rugon had to recenter the controls.

After a long pause, Rugon started to speak.

"This is the race," he said softly, "that has known radio for only two centuries—the race that we believed had crept to die in the heart of its planet. I have examined those images under the highest possible magnification.

"That is the greatest fleet of which there has ever been a record. Each of those points of light represents a ship larger than our own. Of course, they are very primitive—what you see on the screen are the jets of their rockets. Yes, they dared to use rockets to bridge interstellar space! You realize what that means. It would take them centuries to reach the nearest star. The whole race must have embarked on this journey in the hope that its descendants would complete it, generations later.

"To measure the extent of their accomplishment, think of the ages it took us to conquer space and the longer ages still before we attempted to reach the stars. Even if we were threatened with annihilation, could we have done so much in so short a time? Remember, this is the youngest civilization in the universe. Four hundred thousand years ago it did not even exist. What will it be a million years from now?"

An hour later, Orostron left the crippled mother ship to make contact with the great fleet ahead. As the little torpedo disappeared among the stars, Alveron turned to his friend and made a remark that Rugon was often to remember in the years ahead.

"I wonder what they'll be like?" he mused. "Will they be nothing but wonderful engineers, with no art or philosophy? They're going to have such a surprise when Orostron reaches them—I expect it will be rather a blow to their pride. It's funny how all isolated races think they're the only people in the universe. But they should be grateful to us; we're going to save them a good many hundred years of travel."

Alveron glanced at the Milky Way, lying like a veil of silver mist across the vision screen. He waved toward it with a sweep of a tentacle that embraced the whole circle of the galaxy, from the Central Planets to the lonely suns of the Rim.

"You know," he said to Rugon, "I feel rather afraid of these people. Suppose they don't like our little federation?" He waved once more toward the star-clouds that lay massed across the screen, glowing with the light of their countless suns.

"Something tells me they'll be very determined people," he added. "We had better be polite to them. After all, we only outnumber them about a thousand million to one."

Rugon laughed at his captain's little joke.

Twenty years afterward, the remark didn't seem funny.

ROBERT SHECKLEY

Shape

"Shape" is an alien-invasion story with a unique twist. Here Mr.
Sheckley creates a situation in which the invaders can assume any
shape they want—which should make them irresistible. But don't
despair. Some parts of our planet still have a few things going for
them.

Pid the pilot slowed the ship almost to a standstill. He peered anxiously at the green planet below.

Even without instruments, there was no mistaking it. Third from its sun, it was the only planet in this system capable of sustaining life. Peacefully it swam through its gauze of clouds.

It looked very innocent. And yet, something on this planet had claimed the lives of every expedition the Glom had sent.

Pid hesitated a moment, before starting irrevocably down. He and his two crewmen were as ready now as they would ever be. Their compact displacers were stored in body pouches, inactive but ready.

Pid wanted to say something to his crew but wasn't sure how to put it.

The crew waited. Ilg the radioman had sent the final message to the Glom planet. Ger the detector read sixteen dials at once and reported, "No sign of alien activity." His body surfaces flowed carelessly.

Pid noticed the flow and knew what he had to say. Ever since they had left Glom, shape-discipline had been disgustingly lax. The invasion chief had warned him; but still he had to do something about it. It was his duty, since lower castes such as radiomen and detectors were notoriously prone to shapelessness.

"A lot of hopes are resting on this expedition," he began slowly. "We're a long way from home now."

Ger the detector nodded. Ilg the radioman flowed out of his prescribed shape and molded himself comfortably to a wall.

"However," Pid said sternly, "distance is no excuse for promiscuous shape-lessness."

Ilg flowed hastily back into proper radioman's shape.

"Exotic shapes will undoubtedly be called for," Pid went on. "And for that we have a special dispensation. But remember—any shape not assumed strictly in the line of duty is a device of The Shapeless One!"

Ger's body surfaces abruptly stopped flowing.

"That's all," Pid said and flowed into his controls. The ship started down, so smoothly coordinated that Pid felt a glow of pride.

They were good workers, he decided. He just couldn't expect them to be as shape-conscious as a high-caste pilot. Even the invasion chief had told him that.

"Pid," the invasion chief had said at their last interview, "we need this planet desperately."

"Yes, sir," Pid had said, standing at full attention, never quivering from optimum pilot's shape.

"One of you," the chief said heavily, "must get through and set up a displacer near an atomic power source. The army will be standing by at this end, ready to step through."

"We'll do it, sir," Pid said.

"This expedition has to succeed," the chief said, and his features blurred momentarily from sheer fatigue. "In strictest confidence, there's considerable unrest on Glom. The miner caste is on strike, for instance. They want a new digging shape. Say the old one is inefficient."

Pid looked properly indignant. The mining shape had been set down by the ancients fifty thousand years ago, together with the rest of the basic shapes. And now these upstarts wanted to change it!

"That's not all," the chief told him. "We've uncovered a new cult of shapelessness. Picked up almost eight thousand Glom, and I don't know how many more we missed."

Pid knew that shapelessness was a lure of The Shapeless One, the greatest evil that the Glom mind conceived of. But how, he wondered, did Glom fall for His lures?

The chief guessed his question. "Pid," he said, "I suppose it's difficult for you to understand. Do you enjoy piloting?"

"Yes, sir," Pid said simply. *Enjoy* piloting! It was his entire life! Without a ship, he was nothing.

"Not all Glom feel that way," the chief said. "I don't understand it either. All my ancestors have been invasion chiefs, back to the beginning of time. So of course *I* want to be an invasion chief. It's only natural, as well as lawful. But the lower castes don't feel that way." He shook his body sadly.

"I've told you this for a reason," the chief went on. "We Glom need more room. This unrest is caused purely by crowding. All our psychologists say so. Another planet to expand into will cure everything. So we're counting on you, Pid."

"Yes, sir," Pid said, with a glow of pride.

The chief rose to end the interview. Then he changed his mind and sat down again.

"You'll have to watch your crew," he said. "They're loyal, no doubt, but low caste. And you know the lower castes."

Pid did indeed.

"Ger, your detector, is suspected of harboring alterationist tendencies. He was once fined for assuming a quasi-hunter shape. Ilg has never had any definite charge brought against him. But I hear that he remains immobile for suspiciously long periods of time. Possibly, he fancies himself a thinker."

"But sir," Pid protested, "if they are even slightly tainted with alterationism or shapelessness, why send them on this expedition?"

The chief hesitated before answering. "There are plenty of Glom I could trust," he said slowly. "But those two have certain qualities of resourcefulness and imagination that will be needed on this expedition." He sighed. "I really don't understand why those qualities are usually linked with shapelessness."

"Yes, sir," Pid said.

"Just watch them."

"Yes, sir," Pid said again, and saluted, realizing that the interview was at an end. In his body pouch he felt the dormant displacer, ready to transform the enemy's power source into a bridge across space for the Glom hordes.

"Good luck," the chief said. "I'm sure you'll need it."

The ship dropped silently toward the surface of the enemy planet. Ger the detector analyzed the clouds below and fed data into the camouflage unit. The unit went to work. Soon the ship looked, to all outward appearances, like a cirrus formation.

Pid allowed the ship to drift slowly toward the surface of the mystery planet. He was in optimum pilot's shape now, the most efficient of the four shapes alloted to the pilot caste. Blind, deaf and dumb, an extension of his controls, all his attention was directed toward matching the velocities of the high-flying clouds, staying among them, becoming a part of them.

Ger remained rigidly in one of the two shapes allotted to detectors. He fed data into the camouflage unit, and the descending ship slowly altered into an altocumulus.

There was no sign of activity from the enemy planet.

Ilg located an atomic power source and fed the data to Pid. The pilot altered course. He had reached the lowest level of clouds, barely a mile above the surface of the planet. Now his ship looked like a fat, fleecy cumulus.

And still there was no sign of alarm. The unknown fate that had overtaken twenty previous expeditions still had not shown itself.

Dusk crept across the face of the planet as Pid maneuvered near the atomic power installation. He avoided the surrounding homes and hovered over a clump of woods.

Darkness fell, and the green planet's lone moon was veiled in clouds.

One cloud floated lower.

And landed.

"Quick, everyone out!" Pid shouted, detaching himself from the ship's controls. He assumed the pilot's shape best suited for running and raced out of the hatch. Ger and Ilg hurried after him. They stopped fifty yards from the ship and waited.

Inside the ship a circuit closed. There was a silent shudder and the ship began to melt. Plastic dissolved, metal crumpled. Soon the ship was a great pile of junk, and still the process went on. Big fragments broke into smaller fragments and split and split again.

Pid felt suddenly helpless, watching his ship scuttle itself. He was a pilot, of the pilot caste. His father had been a pilot, and his father before him stretching back to the hazy past when the Glom had first constructed ships. He had spent his entire childhood around ships, his entire manhood flying them.

Now, shipless, he was naked in an alien world.

In a few minutes there was only a mound of dust to show where the ship had been. The night wind scattered it through the forest. And then there was nothing at all.

They waited. Nothing happened. The wind sighed and the trees creaked. Squirrels chirped, and birds stirred in their nests.

An acorn fell to the ground.

Pid heaved a sigh of relief and sat down. The twenty-first Glom expedition had landed safely.

There was nothing to be done until morning, so Pid began to make plans. They had landed as close to the atomic power installation as they dared. Now they would have to get closer. Somehow, one of them had to get very near the reactor room, in order to activate the displacer.

Difficult. But Pid felt certain of success. After all, the Glom were strong on ingenuity.

Strong on ingenuity, he thought bitterly, but terribly short of radioactives. That was another reason why this expedition was so important. There was little radioactive fuel left on any of the Glom worlds.

Ages ago, the Glom had spent their store of radioactives spreading throughout their neighbor worlds, occupying the ones that they could live on. Colonization barely kept up with the mounting birthrate. New worlds were constantly needed.

This particular world, discovered in a scouting expedition, was needed. It suited the Glom perfectly. But it was too far away. They didn't have enough fuel to mount a conquering space fleet.

Luckily, there was another way. A better way.

Over the centuries, the Glom scientists had developed the displacer. A triumph of identity engineering, the displacer allowed mass to be moved instantaneously between any two linked points.

One end was set up at Glom's sole atomic energy plant. The other end had to be placed in proximity to another atomic power source and activated. Diverted power then flowed through both ends, was modified and modified again.

Then, through the miracle of identity engineering, the Glom could *step* through from planet to planet, or pour through in a great, overwhelming wave.

It was quite simple. But twenty expeditions had failed to set up the Earth-end displacer.

What had happened to them was not known.

For no Glom ship had ever returned to tell.

Before dawn they crept through the woods, taking on the coloration of the plants around them. Their displacers pulsed feebly, sensing the nearness of atomic energy.

A tiny, four-legged creature darted in front of them. Instantly, Ger grew four legs and a long, streamlined body and gave chase.

"Ger! Come back here!" Pid howled at the detector, throwing caution to the winds.

Ger overtook the animal and knocked it down. He tried to bite it, but he had neglected to grow teeth. The animal jumped free and vanished into the underbrush. Ger thrust out a set of teeth and bunched his muscles for a leap.

"Ger!"

Reluctantly, the detector turned away. He loped silently back to Pid.

"I was hungry," he said.

"You were not," Pid said sternly.

"Was," Ger mumbled, writhing with embarrassment.

Pid remembered what the chief had told him. Ger certainly did have hunter tendencies. He would have to watch him more closely.

"We'll have no more of that," Pid said. "Remember—the lure of exotic shapes is not sanctioned. Be content with the shape you were born to."

Ger nodded and melted back into the underbrush. They moved on.

At the extreme edge of the woods they could observe the atomic energy installation. Pid disguised himself as a clump of shrubbery and Ger formed himself into an old log. Ilg, after a moment's thought, became a young oak.

The installation was in the form of a long, low building, surrounded by a metal fence. There was a gate and guards in front of it.

The first job, Pid thought, was to get past that gate. He began to consider ways and means.

From the fragmentary reports of the survey parties, Pid knew that, in some ways, this race of men were like the Glom. They had pets, as the Glom did, and homes and children and a culture. The inhabitants were skilled mechanically, as were the Glom.

But there were terrific differences. The men were of fixed and immutable forms, like stones or trees. And to compensate, their planet boasted a fantastic array of species, types and kinds. This was completely unlike Glom, which had only eight distinct forms of animal life.

And evidently the men were skilled at detecting invaders, Pid thought. He wished he knew how the other expeditions had failed. It would make his job much easier.

A man lurched past them on two incredibly stiff legs. Rigidity was evident in his every move. Without looking, he hurried past.

"I know," Ger said, after the creature had moved away. "I'll disguise myself as a man, walk through the gate to the reactor room and activate my displacer."

"You can't speak their language," Pid pointed out.

"I won't speak at all. I'll ignore them. Look." Quickly Ger shaped himself into a man.

"That's not bad," Pid said.

Ger tried a few practice steps, copying the bumpy walk of the man.

"But I'm afraid it won't work," Pid said.

"It's perfectly logical," Ger pointed out.

"I know. Therefore the other expeditions must have tried it. And none of them came back."

There was no arguing that. Ger flowed back into the shape of a log. "What, then?" he asked.

"Let me think," Pid said.

Another creature lurched past on four legs instead of two. Pid recognized it as a dog, a pet of man. He watched it carefully.

The dog ambled to the gate, head down, in no particular hurry. It walked through, unchallenged, and lay down in the grass.

"Hmm," Pid said.

They watched. One of the men walked past and touched the dog on the head. The dog stuck out its tongue and rolled over on its side.

"I can do that," Ger said excitedly. He started to flow into the shape of a dog.

"No, wait," Pid said. "We'll spend the rest of the day thinking it over. This is too important to rush into."

Ger subsided sulkily.

"Come on, let's move back," Pid said. He and Ger started into the woods. Then he remembered Ilg.

"Ilg?" he called softly.

There was no answer.

"Ilg!"

"What? Oh, yes," an oak tree said and melted into a bush. "Sorry. What were you saying?"

"We're moving back," Pid said. "Were you, by any chance, thinking?"

"Oh, no," Ilg assured him. "Just resting."

Pid let it go at that. There was too much else to worry about.

They discussed it for the rest of the day, hidden in the deepest part of the woods. The only alternatives seemed to be man or dog. A tree couldn't walk past the gates, since that was not in the nature of trees. Nor could anything else, and escape notice.

Going as a man seemed too risky. They decided that Ger would sally out in the morning as a dog.

"Now get some sleep," Pid said.

Obediently his two crewmen flattened out, going immediately shapeless. But Pid had a more difficult time.

Everything looked too easy. Why wasn't the atomic installation better guarded? Certainly the men must have learned something from the expeditions they had captured in the past. Or had they killed them without asking any questions?

You couldn't tell what an alien would do.

Was that open gate a trap?

Wearily he flowed into a comfortable position on the lumpy ground. Then he pulled himself together hastily.

He had gone shapeless!

Comfort had nothing to do with duty, he reminded himself, and firmly took a pilot's shape.

But pilot's shape wasn't constructed for sleeping on damp, bumpy ground. Pid spent a restless night, thinking of ships and wishing he were flying one.

Pid awoke in the morning tired and ill-tempered. He nudged Ger.

"Let's get this over with," he said.

Ger flowed gaily to his feet.

"Come on, Ilg," Pid said angrily, looking around. "Wake up."

There was no reply.

"Ilg!" he called.

Still there was no reply.

"Help me look for him," Pid said to Ger. "He must be around here somewhere."

Together they tested every bush, tree, log and shrub in the vicinity. But none of them was Ilg.

Pid began to feel a cold panic run through him. What could have happened to the radioman?

"Perhaps he decided to go through the gate on his own," Ger suggested.

Pid considered the possibility. It seemed unlikely. Ilg had never shown much initiative. He had always been content to follow orders.

They waited. But midday came and there was still no sign of Ilg.

"We can't wait any longer," Pid said and they started through the woods. Pid wondered if Ilg *had* tried to get through the gates on his own. Those quiet types often concealed a foolhardy streak.

But there was nothing to show that Ilg had been successful. He would have to assume that the radioman was dead or captured by the men.

That left two of them to activate a displacer.

And still he didn't know what had happened to the other expeditions.

At the edge of the woods, Ger turned himself into a facsimile of a dog. Pid inspected him carefully.

"A little less tail," he said.

Ger shortened his tail.

"More ears."

Ger lengthened his ears.

"Now even them up." He inspected the finished product. As far as he could tell, Ger was perfect, from the tip of his tail to his wet, black nose.

"Good luck," Pid said.

"Thanks." Cautiously Ger moved out of the woods, walking in the lurching style of dogs and men. At the gate the guard called to him. Pid held his breath.

Ger walked past the man, ignoring him. The man started to walk over and Ger broke into a run.

Pid shaped a pair of strong legs for himself, ready to dash if Ger was caught.

But the guard turned back to his gate. Ger stopped running immediately and strolled quietly toward the main gate.

Pid dissolved his legs with a sigh of relief.

But the main door was closed! Pid hoped the detector wouldn't try to open it. That was *not* in the nature of dogs.

Another dog came running toward Ger. Ger backed away from him. The dog approached and sniffed. Ger sniffed back.

Then both of them ran around the building.

That was clever, Pid thought. There was bound to be a door in the rear.

He glanced up at the afternoon sun. As soon as the displacer was activated, the Glom armies would begin to pour through. By the time the men recovered from the shock, a million or more Glom troops would be here. With more following.

The day passed slowly, and nothing happened.

Nervously Pid watched the front of the plant. It shouldn't be taking so long if Ger was successful.

Late into the night he waited. Men walked in and out of the installation, and dogs barked around the gates. But Ger did not appear.

Ger had failed. Ilg was gone. Only he was left.

And *still* he didn't know what had happened.

By morning, Pid was in complete despair. He knew that the twenty-first Glom expedition to this planet was near the point of complete failure. Now it was all up to him.

He decided to sally out boldly in the shape of a man. It was the only possibility left.

He saw that workers were arriving in great numbers, rushing through the gates. Pid wondered if he should try to mingle with them or wait until there was less commotion. He decided to take advantage of the apparent confusion, and started to shape himself into a man.

A dog walked past the woods where he was hiding.

"Hello," the dog said.

It was Ger!

"What happened?" Pid asked with a sigh of relief. "Why were you so long? Couldn't you get in?"

"I don't know," Ger said, wagging his tail. "I didn't try."

Pid was speechless.

"I went hunting," Ger said complacently. "This form is ideal for hunting, you know. I went out the rear gate with another dog."

"But the expedition—your duty . . ."

"I changed my mind," Ger told him. "You know, pilot, I never wanted to be a detector."

"But you were *born* a detector!"

"That's true," Ger said. "But it doesn't help. I always wanted to be a hunter."

Pid shook his entire body in annoyance. "You can't," he said, very slowly, as one would explain to a Glomling. "The hunter shape is forbidden to you."

"Not here it isn't," Ger said, still wagging his tail.

"Let's have no more of this." Pid said angrily. "Get into that installation and set up your displacer. I'll try to overlook this heresy."

"I won't," Ger said. "I don't want the Glom here. They'd ruin it for the rest of us."

"He's right," an oak tree said.

"Ilg!" Pid gasped. "Where are you?"

Branches stirred. "I'm right here," Ilg said. "I've been thinking."

"But—your caste . . ."

"Pilot," Ger said sadly, "why don't you wake up? Most of the people on Glom are miserable. Only custom makes us take the caste shape of our ancestors."

"Pilot," Ilg said, "all Glom are born shapeless!"

"And being born shapeless, all Glom should have freedom of shape," Ger said.

"Exactly," Ilg said. "But he'll never understand. Now excuse me. I want to think." And the oak tree was silent.

Pid laughed humorlessly. "The men will kill you off," he said. "Just as they killed off the rest of the expeditions."

"No one from Glom has been killed," Ger told him. "The other expeditions are right here."

"Alive?"

"Certainly. The men don't even know we exist. That dog I was hunting with is a Glom from the nineteenth expedition. There are hundreds of us here, pilot. We like it."

Pid tried to absorb it all. He had always known that the lower castes were lax in caste-consciousness. But this—this was preposterous!

This planet's secret menace was—freedom!

"Join us, pilot," Ger said. "We've got a paradise here. Do you know how many species there are on this planet? An uncountable number! There's a shape to suit every need!"

Pid shook his head. There was no shape to suit *his* need. He was a pilot.

But men were unaware of the presence of the Glom. Getting near the reactor would be simple!

"The Glom Supreme Council will take care of all of you," he snarled and shaped himself into a dog. "I'm going to set up the displacer myself."

He studied himself for a moment, bared his teeth at Ger, and loped toward the gate.

The men at the gate didn't even look at him. He slipped through the main door of the building behind a man and loped down a corridor.

The displacer in his body pouch pulsed and tugged, leading him toward the reactor room.

He sprinted up a flight of stairs and down another corridor. There were footsteps around the bend, and Pid knew instinctively that dogs were not allowed inside the building.

He looked around desperately for a hiding place, but the corridor was bare. However, there were several overhead lights in the ceiling.

Pid leaped and glued himself to the ceiling. He shaped himself into a lighting fixture and hoped that the men wouldn't try to find out why he wasn't shining.

Men passed, running.

Pid changed himself into a facsimile of a man and hurried on.

He had to get closer.

Another man came down the corridor. He looked sharply at Pid, started to speak and then sprinted away.

Pid didn't know what was wrong, but he broke into a full sprint. The displacer in his body pouch throbbed and pulsed, telling him he had almost reached the critical distance.

Suddenly a terrible doubt assailed his mind. *All the expeditions had deserted! Every single Glom!*

He slowed slightly.

Freedom of shape . . . that was a strange notion. A disturbing notion.

And obviously a device of The Shapeless One, he told himself and rushed on.

At the end of the corridor was a gigantic bolted door. Pid stared at it.

Footsteps hammered down the corridor, and men were shouting.

What was wrong? How had they detected him? Quickly he examined himself and ran his fingers across his face.

He had forgotten to mold any features.

In despair he pulled at the door. He took the tiny displacer out of his pouch, but the pulse beat wasn't quite strong enough. He had to get closer to the reactor.

He studied the door. There was a tiny crack running under it. Pid went quickly shapeless and flowed under, barely squeezing the displacer through.

Inside the room he found another bolt on the inside of the door. He jammed it into place and looked around for something to prop against the door.

It was a tiny room. On one side was a lead door, leading to the reactor. There was a small window on another side, and that was all.

Pid looked at the displacer. The pulse beat was right. At last he was close enough. Here the displacer could work, drawing and altering the energy from the reactor. All he had to do was activate it.

But they had all deserted, every one of them.

Pid hesitated. *All Glom are born shapeless.* That was true. Glom children were amorphous until old enough to be instructed in the caste shape of their ancestors. But freedom of shape?

Pid considered the possibilities. To be able to take on any shape he wanted without interference! On this paradise planet he could fulfill any ambition, become anything, do anything.

Nor would he be lonely. There were other Glom here as well, enjoying the benefits of freedom of shape.

The men were beginning to break down the door. Pid was still uncertain. What should he do? Freedom . . .

But not for him, he thought bitterly. It was easy enough to be a hunter or a thinker. But he was a pilot. Piloting was his life and love. How could he do that here?

Of course, the men had ships. He could turn into a man, find a ship . . .

Never. Easy enough to become a tree or a dog. He could never pass successfully as a man.

The door was beginning to splinter from repeated blows.

Pid walked to the window to take a last look at the planet before activating the displacer.

He looked—and almost collapsed from shock.

It was really true! He hadn't fully understood what Ger had meant when he said that there were species on this planet to satisfy every need. *Every* need! Even his!

Here he could satisfy a longing of the pilot caste that went even deeper than piloting.

He looked again, then smashed the displacer to the floor. The door burst open, and in the same instant he flung himself through the window.

The men raced to the window and stared out. But they were unable to understand what they saw.

There was only a great white bird out there, flapping awkwardly but with increasing strength, trying to overtake a flight of birds in the distance.

CORDWAINER SMITH

Alpha Ralpha Boulevard

The dreamlike worlds created by the gifted "Cordwainer Smith"
(Paul M. A. Linebarger) were exceptional. He produced a "future
history" featuring such elements as the Instrumentality of Mankind,
the planet known as Old North Australia, and the underpeople.
These elements constitute one of the most memorable visions in the
history of science fiction. "Alpha Ralpha Boulevard" is a brilliant
and typical part of Professor Linebarger's vision.

We were drunk with happiness in those early years. Everybody was, especially the young people. These were the first years of the Rediscovery of Man, when the Instrumentality dug deep in the treasury, reconstructing the old cultures, the old languages and even the old troubles. The nightmare of perfection had taken our forefathers to the edge of suicide. Now under the leadership of the Lord Jestocost and the Lady Alice More, the ancient civilizations were rising like great land masses out of the sea of the past.

I myself was the first man to put a postage stamp on a letter, after sixteen thousand years. I took Virginia to hear the first piano recital. We watched at the eye-machine when cholera was released in Tasmania, and we saw the Tasmanians dancing in the streets, now that they did not have to be protected any more. Everywhere, things became exciting. Everywhere, men and women worked with a wild will to build a more imperfect world.

I myself went into a hospital and came out French. Of course I remembered my early life; I remembered it, but it did not matter. Virginia was French, too, and we had the years of our future lying ahead of us like ripe fruit hanging in an orchard of perpetual summers. We had no idea when we would die. Formerly, I would be able to go to bed and think, "The government has given me four hundred years. Three hundred and seventy-four years from now, they will stop the stroon injections and I will then die." Now I knew anything could happen. The safety devices had been turned off. The diseases ran free. With luck and hope and love, I might live a thousand years. Or I might die tomorrow. I was free.

We reveled in every moment of the day.

Virginia and I bought the first French newspaper to appear since the Most Ancient World fell. We found delight in the news, even in the advertisements. Some parts of the culture were hard to reconstruct. It was difficult to talk about foods of which only the names survived, but the homunculi and the machines, working tirelessly in Downdeep-downdeep, kept the surface of the world filled with enough novelties to fill anyone's heart with hope. We knew that all of this was make-believe, and yet it was not. We knew that when the diseases had killed the statistically correct number of people, they would be turned off; when the accident rate rose too high, it would stop without our knowing why. We knew that over us all, the Instrumentality watched. We had confidence that the Lord Jestocost and the Lady Alice More would play with us as friends and not use us as victims of a game.

Take, for example, Virginia. She had been called Menerima, which represented the coded sounds of her birth number. She was small, verging on chubby; she was compact; her head was covered with tight brown curls; her eyes were a brown so deep and so rich that it took sunlight, with her squinting against it, to bring forth the treasures of her irises. I had known her well, but never known her. I had seen her often, but never seen her with my heart, until we met just outside the hospital after becoming French.

I was pleased to see an old friend and started to speak in the Old Common Tongue, but the words jammed, and as I tried to speak it was not Menerima any longer, but someone of ancient beauty, rare and strange—someone who had wandered into these latter days from the treasure worlds of time past. All I could do was to stammer:

"What do you call yourself now?" And I said it in ancient French.

She answered in the same language, "Je m'appelle Virginia."

Looking at her and falling in love was a single process. There was something strong, something wild in her, wrapped and hidden by the tenderness and youth of her girlish body. It was as though destiny spoke to me out of the certain brown eyes, eyes which questioned me surely and wonderingly, just as we both questioned the fresh new world which lay about us.

"May I?" said I, offering her my arm, as I had learned in the hours of hypnopedia. She took my arm and we walked away from the hospital.

I hummed a tune which had come into my mind, along with the ancient French language.

She tugged gently on my arm and smiled up at me.

"What is it," she asked, "or don't you know?"

The words came soft and unbidden to my lips and I sang it very quietly, muting my voice in her curly hair, half-singing, half-whispering the popular song which had poured into my mind with all the other things which the Rediscovery of Man had given me:

> *She wasn't the woman I went to seek.*
> *I met her by the merest chance.*
> *She did not speak the French of France,*
> *But the surded French of Martinique.*
>
> *She wasn't rich. She wasn't chic.*
> *She had a most entrancing glance,*
> *And that was all. . . .*

Suddenly I ran out of words. "I seem to have forgotten the rest of it. It's called 'Macouba' and it has something to do with a wonderful island which the ancient French called Martinique."

"I know where that is," she cried. She had been given the same memories that I had. "You can see it from Earthport!"

This was a sudden return to the world we had known. Earthport stood on its single pedestal, twelve miles high, at the eastern edge of the small continent. At the top of it, the lords worked amid machines which had no meaning any more. There the ships whispered their way in from the stars. I had seen pictures of it, but I had never been there. As a matter of fact, I had never known anyone who had actually been up Earthport. Why should we have gone? We might not have been welcome, and we could always see it just as well through the pictures on the eye-machine. For Menerima—familiar, dully pleasant, dear little Menerima—to have gone there was uncanny. It made me think that in the Old Perfect World things had not been as plain or forthright as they seemed.

Virginia, the new Menerima, tried to speak in the Old Common Tongue, but she gave up and used French instead:

"My aunt," she said, meaning a kindred lady, since no one had had aunts for thousands of years, "was a Believer. She took me to the Abba-dingo. To get holiness and luck."

The old me was a little shocked; the French me was disquieted by the fact that this girl had done something unusual even before mankind itself turned to the unusual. The Abba-dingo was a long obsolete computer set partway up the column of Earthport. The homunculi treated it as a god, and occasionally people went to it. To do so was tedious and vulgar.

Or had been. Till all things became new again.

Keeping the annoyance out of my voice, I asked her, "What was it like?"

She laughed lightly, yet there was a trill to her laughter which gave me a shiver. If the old Menerima had had secrets, what might the new Virginia do? I almost hated the fate which made me love her, which made me feel that the touch of her hand on my arm was a link between me and time-forever.

She smiled at me instead of answering my question. The surfaceway was under repair; we followed a ramp down to the level of the top underground, where it was legal for true persons and hominids and homunculi to walk.

I did not like the feeling; I had never gone more than twenty minutes' trip from my birthplace. This ramp looked safe enough. There were few hominids around these days, men from the stars who (though of true human stock) had been changed to fit the conditions of a thousand worlds. The homunculi were morally repulsive, though many of them look like very handsome people; bred from animals into the shape of men, they took over the tedious chores of working with machines where no real man would wish to go. It was whispered that some of them had even bred with actual people, and I would not want my Virginia to be exposed to the presence of such a creature.

She had been holding my arm. When we walked down the ramp to the busy passage, I slipped my arm free and put it over her shoulders, drawing her closer to me. It was light enough, bright enough to be clearer than the daylight which we had left behind, but it was strange and full of danger. In the old days, I would have turned around and gone home rather than to expose myself to the presence of such dreadful beings. At this time, in this moment, I could not bear to part from my newfound love, and I was afraid that if I went back to my own apartment in the tower, she might go to hers. Anyhow, being French gave a spice to danger.

Actually, the people in the traffic looked commonplace enough. There were many busy machines, some in human forms and some not. I did not see a single hominid. Other people, whom I knew to be homunculi because they yielded the right of way to us, looked no different from the real human beings on the surface. A brilliantly beautiful girl gave me a look which I did not like —saucy, intelligent, provocative beyond all limits of flirtation. I suspected her of being a dog by origin. Among the hominids, d'persons are the ones most apt to take liberties. They even have a dogman philosopher who once produced a tape arguing that since dogs are the most ancient of men's allies, they have the right to be closer to man than any other form of life. When I saw the tape, I thought it amusing that a dog should be bred into the form of a Socrates; here, in the top underground, I was not so sure at all. What would

I do if one of them became insolent? Kill him? That meant a brush with the law and a talk with the subcommissioners of the Instrumentality.

Virginia noticed none of this.

She had not answered my question, but was asking me questions about the top underground instead. I had been there only once before, when I was small, but it was flattering to have her wondering, husky voice murmuring in my ear.

Then it happened.

At first I thought he was a man, foreshortened by some trick of the underground light. When he came closer, I saw that it was not. He must have been five feet across the shoulders. Ugly red scars on his forehead showed where the horns had been dug out of his skull. He was a homunculus, obviously derived from cattle stock. Frankly, I had never known that they left them that ill-formed.

And he was drunk.

As he came closer I could pick up the buzz of his mind. ". . . they're not people, they're not hominids, and they're not us—what are they doing here? The words they think confuse me." He had never telepathed French before.

This was bad. For him to talk was common enough, but only a few of the homunculi were telepathic—those with special jobs, such as in the Downdeep-downdeep, where only telepathy could relay instructions.

Virginia clung to me.

Thought I, in clear Common Tongue: "True men are we. You must let us pass."

There was no answer, but a roar. I do not know where he got drunk, or on what, but he did not get my message.

I could see his thoughts forming up into panic, helplessness, hate. Then he charged, almost dancing toward us, as though he could crush our bodies.

My mind focused and I threw the stop order at him.

It did not work.

Horror-stricken, I realized that I had thought French at him.

Virginia screamed.

The bull-man was upon us.

At the last moment he swerved, passed us blindly, and let out a roar which filled the enormous passage. He had raced beyond us.

Still holding Virginia, I turned around to see what had made him pass us. What I beheld was odd in the extreme.

Our figures ran down the corridor away from us—my black purple cloak flying in the still air as my image ran, Virginia's golden dress swimming out behind her as she ran with me. The images were perfect and the bull-man pursued them.

I stared around in bewilderment. We had been told that the safeguards no longer protected us.

A girl stood quietly next to the wall. I had almost mistaken her for a statue. Then she spoke.

"Come no closer. I am a cat. It was easy enough to fool him. You had better get back to the surface."

"Thank you," I said, "thank you. What is your name?"

"Does it matter?" said the girl. "I'm not a person."

A little offended, I insisted, "I just wanted to thank you." As I spoke to her I saw that she was as beautiful and as bright as a flame. Her skin was clear, the color of cream, and her hair—finer than any human hair could possibly be—was the wild golden orange of a Persian cat.

"I'm C'mell," said the girl, "And I work at Earthport."

That stopped both Virginia and me. Cat-people were below us and should be shunned, but Earthport was above us and had to be respected. Which was C'mell?

She smiled, and her smile was better suited for my eyes than for Virginia's. It spoke a whole world of voluptuous knowledge. I knew she wasn't trying to do anything to me; the rest of her manner showed that. Perhaps it was the only smile she knew.

"Don't worry," she said, "about the formalities. You'd better take these steps here. I hear him coming back."

I spun around, looking for the drunken bull-man. He was not to be seen.

"Go up here," urged C'mell. "They are emergency steps and you will be back on the surface. I can keep him from following. Was that French you were speaking?"

"Yes," said I. "How did you . . . ?"

"Get along," she said. "Sorry I asked. Hurry!"

I entered the small door. A spiral staircase went to the surface. It was below our dignity as true people to use steps, but with C'mell urging me, there was nothing else I could do. I nodded goodbye to C'mell and drew Virginia after me up the stairs.

At the surface we stopped.

Virginia gasped, "Wasn't it horrible?"

"We're safe now," said I.

"It's not safety," she said. "It's the dirtiness of it. Imagine having to talk to her!"

Virginia meant that C'mell was worse than the drunken bull-man. She sensed my reserve because she said, "The sad thing is, you'll see her again . . ."

"What! How do you know that?"

"I don't know it," said Virginia. "I guess it. But I guess good, very good. After all, I went to the Abba-dingo."

"I asked you, darling, to tell me what happened there."

She shook her head mutely and began walking down the streetway. I had no choice but to follow her. It made me a little irritable.

I asked again, more crossly, "What was it like?"

With hurt, girlish dignity she said, "Nothing, nothing. It was a long climb. The old woman made me go with her. It turned out that the machine was not talking that day, anyhow, so we got permission to drop down a shaft and to come back on the rolling road. It was just a wasted day."

She had been talking straight ahead, not to me, as though the memory were a little ugly.

Then she turned her face to me. The brown eyes looked into my eyes as though she were searching for my soul. (*Soul.* There's a word we have in French, and there is nothing quite like it in the Old Common Tongue.) She brightened and pleaded with me:

"Let's not be dull on the new day. Let's be good to the new us, Paul. Let's do something really French, if that's what we are to be."

"A café," I cried. "We need a café. And I know where one is."

"Where?"

"Two undergrounds over. Where the machines come out and where you can see the homunculi peering over the edge." The thought of homunculi peering out struck the new-me as funny, though the old-me had taken them as much for granted as clouds or windows or tables. Of course homunculi had feelings; they weren't exactly people, since they were bred from animals, but they looked just about like people, and they could talk. It took a Frenchman like the new-me to realize that those things were picturesque. More than picturesque: romantic.

Evidently Virginia thought the same, for she said, "But they're *nette,* just adorable. And what is the café called?"

"The Greasy Cat," said I.

The Greasy Cat. How was I to know that this led to a nightmare between high waters and to the winds which cried? How was I to suppose that this had anything to do with Alpha Ralpha Boulevard?

No force in the world could have taken me there if I had known.

Other new-French people had gotten to the café before us.

A waiter with a big brown moustache took our order. I looked closely at him to see if he might be a licensed homunculus, allowed to work among people because his services were indispensable; but he was not. He was pure machine, though his voice rang out with old-Parisian heartiness, and the designers had even built into him the nervous old habit of mopping the back of his hand against his big moustache, and had fixed him so that little beads of sweat showed high up on his brow, just below the hairline.

"Mademoiselle? M'sieur? Beer? Coffee? Red wine next month. The sun will shine in the quarter after the hour and after the half hour. At twenty minutes to the hour it will rain for five minutes so that you can enjoy these umbrellas. I am a native of Alsace. You may speak French or German to me."

"Anything," said Virginia. "You decide, Paul."

"Beer, please," said I. "Blond beer for both of us."

"But certainly, m'sieur," said the waiter.

He left, waving his cloth wildly over his arm.

Virginia puckered up her eyes against the sun and said, "I wish it would rain now. I've never seen real rain."

"Be patient, honey."

She turned earnestly to me. "What is 'German,' Paul?"

"Another language, another culture. I read they will bring it to life next year. But don't you like being French?"

"I like it fine," she said. "Much better than being a number. But Paul . . ." And then she stopped, her eyes blurred with perplexity.

"Yes, darling?"

"Paul," she said, and the statement of my name was a cry of hope from some depth of her mind beyond new-me, beyond old-me, beyond even the contrivances of the lords who molded us. I reached for her hand.

Said I, "You can tell me, darling."

"Paul," she said, and it was almost weeping, "Paul, why does it all happen so fast? This is our first day, and we both feel that we may spend the rest of our lives together. There's something about marriage, whatever that is, and we're supposed to find a priest, and I don't understand that, either. Paul, Paul, Paul, why does it happen so fast? I want to love you. I do love you. But I don't want to be *made* to love you. I want it to be to the real me," and as she spoke, tears poured from her eyes though her voice remained steady enough.

Then it was that I said the wrong thing.

"You don't have to worry, honey. I'm sure that the lords of the Instrumentality have programmed everything well."

At that, she burst into tears, loudly and uncontrollably. I had never seen an adult weep before. It was strange and frightening.

A man from the next table came over and stood beside me, but I did not so much as glance at him.

"Darling," said I, reasonably, "darling, we can work it out. . . ."

"Paul, let me leave you, so that I may be yours. Let me go away for a few days or a few weeks or a few years. Then, if—if—if I *do* come back, you'll know it's me and not some program ordered by a machine. For God's sake, Paul—for God's sake!" In a different voice she said, "What is God, Paul? They gave us the words to speak, but I do not know what they mean."

The man beside me spoke. "I can take you to God," he said.

"Who are you?" said I. "And who asked you to interfere?" This was not the kind of language that we had ever used when speaking the Old Common Tongue—when they had given us a new language they had built in temperament as well.

The stranger kept his politeness—he was as French as we but he kept his temper well.

"My name," he said, "is Maximilien Macht, and I used to be a Believer."

Virginia's eyes lit up. She wiped her face absentmindedly while staring at the man. He was tall, lean, sunburned. (How could he have gotten sunburned so soon?) He had reddish hair and a moustache almost like that of the robot waiter.

"You asked about God, mademoiselle," said the stranger. "God is where he has always been—around us, near us, in us."

This was strange talk from a man who looked worldly. I rose to my feet to bid him good-by. Virginia guessed what I was doing and she said, "that's nice of you, Paul. Give him a chair."

There was warmth in her voice.

The machine waiter came back with two conical beakers made of glass. They had a golden fluid in them with a cap of foam on top. I had never seen or heard of beer before, but I knew exactly how it would taste. I put imaginary money on the tray, received imaginary change, paid the waiter an imaginary tip. The Instrumentality had not yet figured out how to have separate kinds of money for all the new cultures, and of course you could not use real money to pay for food or drink. Food and drink are free.

The machine wiped his moustache, used his serviette (checked red and white) to dab the sweat off his brow and then looked inquiringly at Monsieur Macht.

"M'sieur, you will sit here?"

"Indeed," said Macht.

"Shall I serve you here?"

"But why not?" said Macht. "If these good people permit."

"Very well," said the machine, wiping his moustache with the back of his hand. He fled to the dark recesses of the bar.

All this time Virginia had not taken her eyes off Macht.

"You are a Believer?" she asked. "You are still a Believer, when you have been made French like us? How do you know you're you? Why do I love Paul? Are the lords and their machines controlling everything in us? I want to be *me*. Do you know how to be *me*?"

"Not you, mademoiselle," said Macht, "that would be too great an honor. But I am learning how to be myself. You see," he added, turning to me, "I have been French for two weeks now, and I know how much of me is myself, and how much has been added by this new process of giving us language and danger again."

The waiter came back with a small beaker. It stood on a stem, so that it looked like an evil little miniature of Earthport. The fluid it contained was milky white.

Macht lifted his glass to us. "Your health!"

Virginia stared at him as if she were going to cry again. When he and I sipped, she blew her nose and put her handkerchief away. It was the first time I had ever seen a person perform that act of blowing the nose, but it seemed to go well with our new culture.

Macht smiled at both of us, as if he were going to begin a speech. The sun came out, right on time. It gave him a halo and made him look like a devil or a saint.

But it was Virginia who spoke first.

"You have been there?"

Macht raised his eyebrows a little, frowned and said, "Yes," very quietly.

"Did you get a word?" she persisted.

"Yes." He looked glum and a little troubled.

"What did it say?"

For answer, he shook his head at her, as if there were things which should never be mentioned in public.

I wanted to break in, to find out what this was all about.

Virginia went on, heeding me not at all: "But it did say something!"

"Yes," said Macht.

"Was it important?"

"Mademoiselle, let us not talk about it."

"We must," she cried. "It's life or death." Her hands were clenched so tightly together that her knuckles showed white. Her beer stood in front of her, untouched, growing warm in the sunlight.

"Very well," said Macht, "you may ask. . . . I cannot guarantee to answer."

I controlled myself no longer. "What's all this about?"

Virginia looked at me with scorn, but even her scorn was the scorn of a lover, not the cold remoteness of the past. "Please, Paul, you wouldn't know. Wait a while. What did it say to you, M'sieur Macht?"

"That I, Maximilien Macht, would live or die with a brown-haired girl who was already betrothed." He smiled wryly. "And I do not even quite know what 'betrothed' means."

"We'll find out," said Virginia. "When did it say this?"

"Who is 'it'?" I shouted at them. "For God's sake, what is this all about?"

Macht looked at me and dropped his voice when he spoke: "The Abba-dingo." To her he said, "Last week."

Virginia turned white. "So it does work, it does, it does. Paul, darling, it said nothing to me. But it said to my aunt something which I can't ever forget!"

I held her arm firmly and tenderly and tried to look into her eyes, but she looked away. Said I, "What did it say?"

"Paul and Virginia."

"So what?" said I.

I scarcely knew her. Her lips were tense and compressed. She was not angry. It was something different, worse. She was in the grip of tension. I suppose we had not seen that for thousands of years, either. "Paul, seize this simple fact, if you can grasp it. The machine gave that woman our names—but it gave them to her twelve years ago."

Macht stood up so suddenly that his chair fell over, and the waiter began running toward us.

"That settles it," he said. "We're all going back."

"Going where?" I said.

"To the Abba-dingo."

"But why now?" said I; and, "Will it work?" said Virginia, both at the same time.

"It always works," said Macht, "if you go on the northern side."

"How do you get there?" said Virginia.

Macht frowned sadly. "There's only one way. By Alpha Ralpha Boulevard." Virginia stood up. And so did I.

Then, as I rose, I remembered. Alpha Ralpha Boulevard. It was a ruined street hanging in the sky, faint as a vapor trail. It had been a processional highway once, where conquerors came down and tribute went up. But it was ruined, lost in the clouds, closed to mankind for a hundred centuries.

"I know it," said I. "It's ruined."

Macht said nothing, but he stared at me as if I were an outsider. . . .

Virginia, very quiet and white of countenance, said, "come along."

"But why?" said I. "Why?"

"You fool," she said. "If we don't have a god, at least we have a machine. This is the only thing left on or off the world which the Instrumentality doesn't understand. Maybe it tells the future. Maybe it's an un-machine. It certainly comes from a different time. Can't you see it, darling? If it says we're us, we're *us.*"

"And if it doesn't?"

"Then we're not." Her face was sullen with grief.

"What do you mean?"

"If we're not us," she said, "we're just toys, dolls, puppets that the lords have written on. You're not you and I'm not me. But if the Abba-dingo, which knew the names Paul and Virginia twelve years before it happened—if the Abba-dingo says that we are us, I don't care if it's a predicting machine or a god or a devil or a what. I don't care, but I'll have the truth."

What could I have answered to that? Macht led, she followed and I walked third in single file. We left the sunlight of The Greasy Cat; just as we left, a light rain began to fall. The waiter, looking momentarily like the machine that he was, stared straight ahead. We crossed the lip of the underground and went down to the fast expressway.

When we came out, we were in a region of fine homes. All were in ruins. The trees had thrust their way into the buildings. Flowers rioted across the lawn, through the open doors, and blazed in the roofless rooms. Who needed a house in the open, when the population of Earth had dropped so that the cities were commodious and empty?

Once I thought I saw a family of homunculi, including little ones, peering at me as we trudged along the soft gravel road. Maybe the faces I had seen at the edge of the house were fantasies.

Macht said nothing.

Virginia and I held hands as we walked beside him. I could have been happy at this odd excursion, but her hand was tightly clenched in mine. She bit her lower lip from time to time. I knew it mattered to her—she was on a pilgrimage. (A pilgrimage was an ancient walk to some powerful place, very good for body and soul.) I didn't mind going along. In fact, they could not have kept me from coming, once she and Macht decided to leave the café. But I didn't have to take it seriously. Did I?

What did Macht want?

Who was Macht? What thoughts had that mind learned in two short weeks? How had he preceded us into a new world of danger and adventure? I did not trust him. For the first time in my life I felt alone. Always, always, up to now, I had only to think about the Instrumentality and some protector leaped fully armed into my mind. Telepathy guarded against all dangers, healed all hurts, carried each of us forward to the one hundred and forty-six thousand and ninety-seven days which had been allotted us. Now it was different. I did not know this man, and it was on him that I relied, not on the powers which had shielded and protected us.

We turned from the ruined road into an immense boulevard. The pavement was so smooth and unbroken that nothing grew on it, save where the wind and dust had deposited random little pockets of earth.

Macht stopped.

"This is it," he said. "Alpha Ralpha Boulevard."

We fell silent and looked at the causeway of forgotten empires.

To our left the boulevard disappeared in a gentle curve. It led far north of the city in which I had been reared. I knew that there was another city to the north, but I had forgotten its name. Why should I have remembered it? It was sure to be just like my own.

But to the right . . .

To the right the boulevard rose sharply, like a ramp. It disappeared into the clouds. Just at the edge of the cloud line there was a hint of disaster. I could not see for sure, but it looked to me as though the whole boulevard had been sheared off by unimaginable forces. Somewhere beyond the clouds there stood the Abba-dingo, the place where all questions were answered. . . .

Or so they thought.

Virginia cuddled close to me.

"Let's turn back," said I. "We are city people. We don't know anything about ruins."

"You can if you want to," said Macht. "I was just trying to do you a favor."

We both looked at Virginia.

She looked up at me with those brown eyes. From the eyes there came a plea older than woman or man, older than the human race. I knew what she was going to say before she said it. She was going to say that she *had* to know.

Macht was idly crushing some soft rocks near his foot.

At last Virginia spoke up: "Paul, I don't want danger for its own sake. But I meant what I said back there. Isn't there a chance that we were *told* to love each other? What sort of a life would it be if our happiness, our own selves, depended on a thread in a machine or on a mechanical voice which spoke to us when we were asleep and learning French? It may be fun to go back to the old world. I guess it is. I know that you give me a kind of happiness which I never even suspected before this day. If it's really us, we have something wonderful, and we ought to know it. But if it isn't . . ." She burst into sobs.

I wanted to say, "If it isn't, it will seem just the same," but the ominous sulky face of Macht looked at me over Virginia's shoulder as I drew her to me. There was nothing to say.

I held her close.

From beneath Macht's foot there flowed a trickle of blood. The dust drank it up.

"Macht," said I, "are you hurt?"

Virginia turned around, too.

Macht raised his eyebrows at me and said with unconcern, "No. Why?"

"The blood. At your feet."

He glanced down. "Oh, those," he said, "they're nothing. Just the eggs of some kind of an un-bird which does not even fly."

"Stop it!" I shouted telepathically, using the Old Common Tongue. I did not even try to think in our new-learned French.

He stepped back a pace in surprise.

Out of nothing there came to me a message: thankyou thankyou goodgreat gohomeplease thankyou goodgreat goaway manbad manbad manbad. . . . Somewhere an animal or bird was warning me against Macht. I thought a casual *thanks* to it and turned my attention to Macht.

He and I stared at each other. Was this what *culture* was? Were we now men? Did freedom always include the freedom to mistrust, to fear, to hate?

I liked him not at all. The words of forgotten crimes came into my mind: assassination, murder, abduction, insanity, rape, robbery. . . .

We had known none of these things and yet I felt them all.

He spoke evenly to me. We had both been careful to guard our minds against being read telepathically, so that our only means of communication were empathy and French. "It's your idea," he said, most untruthfully, "or at least your lady's. . . ."

"Has lying already come into the world," said I, "so that we walk into the clouds for no reason at all?"

"There is a reason," said Macht.

I pushed Virginia gently aside and capped my mind so tightly that the antitelepathy felt like a headache.

"Macht," said I, and I myself could hear the snarl of an animal in my own voice, "tell me why you have brought us here or I will kill you."

He did not retreat. He faced me, ready for a fight. He said, "Kill? You mean, to make me dead?" but his words did not carry conviction. Neither one of us knew how to fight, but he readied for defense and I for attack.

Underneath my thought shield an animal thought crept in: goodman goodman take him by the neck no-air he-aah no-air he-aaah like broken egg. . . .

I took the advice without worrying where it came from. It was simple. I walked over to Macht, reached my hands around his throat and squeezed. He tried to push my hands away. Then he tried to kick me. All I did was hang onto his throat. If I had been a lord or a go-captain, I might have known about fighting. But I did not, and neither did he.

It ended when a sudden weight dragged at my hands.

Out of surprise, I let go.

Macht had become unconscious. Was that *dead*?

It could not have been, because he sat up. Virginia ran to him. He rubbed his throat and said with a rough voice:

"You should not have done that."

This gave me courage. "Tell me," I spat at him, "tell me why you wanted us to come, or I will do it again."

Macht grinned weakly. He leaned his head against Virginia's arm. "It's fear," he said. "Fear."

"Fear?" I knew the word—*peur*—but not the meaning. Was it some kind of disquiet or animal alarm?

I had been thinking with my mind open; he thought back *yes*.

"But why do you like it?" I asked.

It is delicious, he thought. *It makes me sick and thrilly and alive. It is like strong medicine, almost as good as stroon. I went there before. High up, I had much fear. It was wonderful and bad and good, all at the same time. I lived a thousand years in a single hour. I wanted more of it, but I thought it would be even more exciting with other people.*

"Now I will kill you," said I in French. "You are very—very. . . ." I had to look for the word. "You are very evil."

"No," said Virginia, "let him talk."

He thought at me, not bothering with words. *This is what the lords of the Instrumentality never let us have. Fear. Reality. We were born in a stupor and we died in a dream. Even the underpeople, the animals, had more life than we did. The machines did not have fear. That's what we were. Machines who thought they were men. And now we are free.*

He saw the edge of raw red anger in my mind, and he changed the subject. *I did not lie to you. This is the way to the Abba-dingo. I have been there. It works. On this side, it always works.*

"It works," cried Virginia. "You see he says so. It works! He is telling the truth. Oh, Paul, do let's go on!"

"All right," said I, "we'll go."

I helped him rise. He looked embarrassed, like a man who has shown something of which he is ashamed.

We walked onto the surface of the indestructible boulevard. It was comfortable to the feet.

At the bottom of my mind the little unseen bird or animal babbled its thoughts at me: goodman goodman make him dead take water take water. . . .

I paid no attention as I walked forward with her and him, Virginia between us. I paid no attention.

I wish I had.

We walked for a long time.

The process was new to us. There was something exhilarating in knowing that no one guarded us, that the air was free air, moving without benefit of weather machines. We saw many birds, and when I thought at them I found their minds startled and opaque; they were natural birds, the like of which I had never seen before. Virginia asked me their names, and I outrageously applied all the bird names which we had learned in French without knowing whether they were historically right or not.

Maximilien Macht cheered up, too, and he even sang us a song, rather off key, to the effect that we would take the high road and he the low one, but that he would be in Scotland before us. It did not make sense, but the lilt was pleasant. Whenever he got a certain distance ahead of Virginia and me, I made up variations on "Macouba" and sang-whispered the phrases into her pretty ear:

> She wasn't the woman I went to seek.
> I met her by the merest chance.
> She did not speak the French of France,
> But the surded French of Martinique.

We were happy in adventure and freedom until we became hungry. Then our troubles began.

Virginia stepped up to a lamp post, struck it lightly with her fist and said, "Feed me." The post should either have opened, serving us a dinner, or else told us where, within the next few hundred yards, food was to be had. It did neither. It did nothing. It must have been broken.

With that, we began to make a game of hitting every single post.

Alpha Ralpha Boulevard had risen about half a kilometer above the surrounding countryside. The wild birds wheeled below us. There was less dust on the pavement, and fewer patches of weeds. The immense road, with no pylons below it, curved like an unsupported ribbon into the clouds.

We wearied of beating posts and there was neither food nor water.

Virginia became fretful: "It won't do any good to go back now. Food is even farther the other way. I do wish you'd brought something."

How should I have thought to carry food? Who ever carries food? Why would they carry it, when it is everywhere? My darling was unreasonable, but she was my darling and I loved her all the more for the sweet imperfections of her temper.

Macht kept tapping pillars, partly to keep out of our fight, and obtained an unexpected result.

At one moment I saw him leaning over to give the pillar of a large lamp the usual hearty but guarded *whop*—in the next instant he yelped like a dog and was sliding uphill at a high rate of speed. I heard him shout something, but could not make out the words, before he disappeared into the clouds ahead.

Virginia looked at me. "Do you want to go back now? Macht is gone. We can say that I got tired."

"Are you serious?"

"Of course, darling."

I laughed, a little angrily. She had insisted that we come, and now she was ready to turn around and give it up, just to please me.

"Never mind," said I. "It can't be far now. Let's go on."

"Paul . . ." She stood close to me. Her brown eyes were troubled, as though she were trying to see all the way into my mind through my eyes. I thought to her. *Do you want to take this way?*

"No," she said in French. "I want to say things one at a time. Paul, I do want to go to the Abba-dingo. I need to go. It's the biggest need in my life. But at the same time I don't want to go. There is something wrong up there. I would rather have you on the wrong terms than not have you at all. Something could happen."

Edgily, I demanded, "Are you getting this 'fear' that Macht was talking about?"

"Oh, no, Paul, not at all. This feeling isn't exciting. It feels like something broken in a machine. . . ."

"Listen!" I interrupted her.

From far ahead, from within the clouds, there came a sound like an animal wailing. There were words in it. It must have been Macht. I thought I heard "Take care." When I sought him with my mind, the distance made circles and I got dizzy.

"Let's follow, darling," said I.

"Yes, Paul," said she, and in her voice there was an unfathomable mixture of happiness, resignation and despair. . . .

Before we moved on, I looked carefully at her. She *was* my girl. The sky had turned yellow and the lights were not yet on. In the yellow rich sky her brown curls were tinted with gold, her brown eyes approached the black in their irises, her young and fate-haunted face seemed more meaningful than any other human face I had ever seen.

"You *are* mine," I said.

"Yes, Paul," she answered me and then smiled brightly. "*You* said it! That is doubly nice."

A bird on the railing looked sharply at us and then left. Perhaps he did not approve of human nonsense, so flung himself downward into dark air. I saw him catch himself, far below, and ride lazily on his wings.

"We're not as free as birds, darling," I told Virginia, "but we are freer than people have been for a hundred centuries."

For answer she hugged my arm and smiled at me.

"And now," I added, "to follow Macht. Put your arms around me and hold me tight. I'll try hitting that post. If we don't get dinner we may get a ride."

I felt her take hold tightly and then I struck the post.

Which post? An instant later the posts were sailing by us in a blur. The ground beneath our feet seemed steady, but we were moving at a fast rate. Even in the service underground I had never seen a roadway as fast as this. Virginia's dress was blowing so hard that it made snapping sounds like the snap of fingers. In no time at all we were in the cloud and out of it again.

A new world surrounded us. The clouds lay below and above. Here and there blue sky shone through. We were steady. The ancient engineers must have devised the walkway cleverly. We rode up, up, up without getting dizzy.

Another cloud.

Then things happened so fast that the telling of them takes longer than the event.

Something dark rushed at me from up ahead. A violent blow hit me in the chest. Only much later did I realize that this was Macht's arm trying to grab me before we went over the edge. Then we went into another cloud. Before I could even speak to Virginia a second blow struck me. The pain was terrible. I had never felt anything like that in all my life. For some reason, Virginia had fallen over me and beyond me. She was pulling at my hands.

I tried to tell her to stop pulling me because it hurt, but I had no breath. Rather than argue, I tried to do what she wanted. I struggled toward her. Only then did I realize that there was nothing below my feet—no bridge, no jetway, nothing.

I was on the edge of the boulevard, the broken edge of the upper side. There was nothing below me except for some looped cables and, far underneath them, a tiny ribbon which was either a river or a road.

We had jumped blindly across the great gap and I had fallen just far enough to catch the upper edge of the roadway on my chest.

It did not matter, the pain.

In a moment the doctor-robot would be there to repair me.

A look at Virginia's face reminded me there was no doctor-robot, no world, no Instrumentality, nothing but wind and pain. She was crying. It took a moment for me to hear what she was saying.

"I did it, I did it, darling, are you dead?"

Neither one of us was sure what "dead" meant, because people always went away at their appointed time, but we knew that it meant a cessation of life. I tried to tell her that I was living, but she fluttered over me and kept dragging me farther from the edge of the drop.

I used my hands to push myself into a sitting position.

She knelt beside me and covered my face with kisses.

At last I was able to gasp, "Where's Macht?"

She looked back. "I don't see him."

I tried to look too. Rather than have me struggle, she said, "You stay quiet. I'll look again."

Bravely she walked to the edge of the sheared-off boulevard. She looked over toward the lower side of the gap, peering through the clouds which drifted past us as rapidly as smoke sucked by a ventilator. Then she cried out:

"I see him. He looks so funny. Like an insect in the museum. He is crawling across on the cables."

Struggling to my hands and knees, I neared her and looked too. There he was, a dot moving along a thread with the birds soaring by beneath him. It looked very unsafe. Perhaps he was getting all the "fear" that he needed to keep himself happy. I did not want that "fear," whatever it was. I wanted food, water and a doctor-robot.

None of these was here.

I struggled to my feet. Virginia tried to help me but I was standing before she could do more than touch my sleeve.

"Let's go on."

"On?" she said.

"On to the Abba-dingo. There may be friendly machines up there. Here there is nothing but cold and wind, and the lights have not yet gone on."

She frowned. "But Macht . . . ?"

"It will be hours before he gets here. We can come back."

She obeyed.

Once again we went to the left of the boulevard. I told her to squeeze my waist while I struck the pillars, one by one. Surely there must have been a reactivating device for the passengers on the road.

The fourth time, it worked.

Once again the wind whipped our clothing as we raced upward on Alpha Ralpha Boulevard.

We almost fell as the road veered to the left. I caught my balance, only to have it veer the other way.

And then we stopped.

This was the Abba-dingo.

A walkway littered with white objects—knobs and rods and imperfectly formed balls about the size of my head.

Virginia stood beside me, silent.

About the size of my head? I kicked one of the objects aside and then knew, knew for sure, what it was. It was people. The inside parts. I had never seen such things before. And that, that on the ground, must once have been a hand. There were hundreds of such things along the wall.

"Come, Virginia," said I, keeping my voice even, and my thoughts hidden.

She followed without saying a word. She was curious about the things on the ground, but she did not seem to recognize them.

For my part, I was watching the wall.

At last I found them—the little doors of Abba-dingo.

One said, METEOROLOGICAL. It was not Old Common Tongue, nor was it French, but it was so close that I knew it had something to do with the behavior of air. I put my hand against the panel of the door. The panel became translucent and ancient writing showed through. There were numbers which meant nothing, words which meant nothing, and then: "Typhoon coming."

My French had not taught me what a "coming" was, but "typhoon" was plainly *typhon,* a major air disturbance. Thought I, let the weather machines take care of the matter. It had nothing to do with us.

"That's no help," said I.

"What does it mean?" she said.

"The air will be disturbed."

"Oh," said she. "That couldn't matter to us, could it?"

"Of course not."

I tried the next panel, which said FOOD. When my hand touched the little door, there was an aching creak inside the wall, as though the whole tower retched. The door opened a little bit and a horrible odor came out of it. Then the door closed again.

The third door said HELP and when I touched it nothing happened. Perhaps it was some kind of tax-collecting device from the ancient days. It yielded nothing to my touch. The fourth door was larger and already partly open at the bottom. At the top, the name of the door was PREDICTIONS. Plain enough, that one was, to anyone who knew Old French. The name at the bottom was more mysterious: PUT PAPER HERE it said, and I could not guess what it meant.

I tried telepathy. Nothing happened. The wind whistled past us. Some of the calcium balls and knobs rolled on the pavement. I tried again, trying my utmost for the imprint of long-departed thoughts. A scream entered my mind, a thin long scream which did not sound much like people. That was all.

Perhaps it did upset me. I did not feel "fear," but I was worried about Virginia.

She was staring at the ground.

"Paul," she said, "isn't that a man's coat on the ground among those funny things?"

Once I had seen an ancient X-ray in the museum, so I knew that the coat still surrounded the material which had provided the inner structure of the man. There was no ball there, so that I was quite sure he was *dead.* How could that have happened in the old days? Why did the Instrumentality let it happen? But then, the Instrumentality had always forbidden this side of the tower. Perhaps the violators had met their own punishment in some way I could not fathom.

"Look, Paul," said Virginia. "I can put my hand in."

Before I could stop her, she had thrust her hand into the flat open slot which said PUT PAPER HERE.

She screamed.

Her hand was caught.

I tried to pull at her arm, but it did not move. She began gasping with pain. Suddenly her hand came free.

Clear words were cut into the living skin. I tore my cloak off and wrapped her hand.

As she sobbed beside me I unbandaged her hand. As I did so she saw the words on her skin.

The words said, in clear French, "You will love Paul all your life."

Virginia let me bandage her hand with my cloak and then she lifted her face to be kissed. "It was worth it," she said, "it was worth all the trouble, Paul. Let's see if we can get down. Now I know."

I kissed her again and said, reassuringly, "You do know, don't you?"

"Of course," she smiled through her tears. "The Instrumentality could not have contrived this. What a clever old machine! Is it a god or a devil, Paul?"

I had not studied those words at that time, so I patted her instead of answering. We turned to leave.

At the last minute I realized that I had not tried PREDICTIONS myself.

"Just a moment, darling. Let me tear a little piece off the bandage."

She waited patiently. I tore a piece the size of my hand, and then I picked up one of the ex-person units on the ground. It may have been the front of an arm. I returned to push the cloth into the slot, but when I turned to the door, an enormous bird was sitting there.

I used my hand to push the bird aside, and he cawed at me. He even seemed to threaten me with his cries and his sharp beak. I could not dislodge him.

Then I tried telepathy. *I am a true man. Go away!*

The bird's dim mind flashed back at me nothing but *no-no-no-no-no!*

With that I struck him so hard with my fist that he fluttered to the ground. He righted himself amid the white litter on the pavement and then, opening his wings, he let the wind carry him away.

I pushed in the scrap of cloth, counted to twenty in my mind and pulled the scrap out.

The words were plain but they meant nothing: "You will love Virginia twenty-one more minutes."

Her happy voice, reassured by the prediction but still unsteady from the pain in her written-on hand, came to me as though it were far away. "What does it say, darling?"

Accidentally on purpose, I let the wind take the scrap. It fluttered away like a bird. Virginia saw it go.

"Oh," she cried disappointedly, "we've lost it! What did it say?"

"Just what yours did."

"But what words, Paul? How did it say it?"

With love and heartbreak and perhaps a little "fear," I lied to her and whispered gently,

"It said, 'Paul will always love Virginia.' "

She smiled at me radiantly. Her stocky, full figure stood firmly and happily against the wind. Once again she was the chubby, pretty Menerima whom I had noticed in our block when we both were children. And she was more than that. She was my newfound love in our newfound world. She was my mademoiselle from Martinique. The message was foolish. We had seen from the food slot that the machine was broken.

"There's no food or water here," said I. Actually, there was a puddle of water near the railing, but it had been blown over the human structural elements on the ground, and I had no heart to drink it.

Virginia was so happy that, despite her wounded hand, her lack of water and her lack of food, she walked vigorously and cheerfully.

Thought I to myself, "Twenty-one minutes. About six hours have passed. If we stay here we face unknown dangers."

Vigorously we walked downward, down Alpha Ralpha Boulevard. We had met the Abba-dingo and were still "alive." I did not think that I was "dead," but the words had been meaningless so long that it was hard to think them.

The ramp was so steep going down that we pranced like horses. The wind blew into our faces with incredible force. That's what it was, *wind,* but I looked up the word *vent* only after it was all over.

We never did see the whole tower—just the wall at which the ancient jetway had deposited us. The rest of the tower was hidden by clouds which fluttered like torn rags as they raced past the heavy material.

The sky was red on one side and a dirty yellow on the other.

Big drops of water began to strike at us.

"The weather machines are broken," I shouted to Virginia.

She tried to shout back at me but the wind carried her words away. I repeated what I had said about the weather machines. She nodded happily and warmly, though the wind was by now whipping her hair past her face and the pieces of water which fell from up above were spotting her flame golden gown. It did not matter. She clung to my arm. Her happy face smiled at me as we stamped downward, bracing ourselves against the decline in the ramp. Her brown eyes were full of confidence and life. She saw me looking at her and she kissed me on the upper arm without losing step. She was my own girl, forever, and she knew it.

The water-from-above, which I later knew was actual "rain," came in increasing volume. Suddenly it included birds. A large bird flapped his way vigorously against the whistling air and managed to stand still in front of my face, though his airspeed was many leagues per hour. He cawed in my face and then was carried away by the wind. No sooner had that one gone than another bird struck me in the body. I looked down at it but it too was carried away by the racing current of air. All I got was a telepathic echo from its bright blank mind: *no-no-no-no!*

No what? thought I. A bird's advice is not much to go upon.

Virginia grabbed my arm and stopped.

I too stopped.

The broken edge of Alpha Ralpha Boulevard was just ahead. Ugly yellow clouds swam through the break like poisonous fish hastening on an inexplicable errand.

Virginia was shouting.

I could not hear her, so I leaned down. That way her mouth could almost touch my ear.

"Where's Macht?" she shouted.

Carefully I took her to the left side of the road, where the railing gave us some protection against the heavy racing air and against the water commingled with it. By now neither of us could see very far. I made her drop to her knees. I got down beside her. The falling water pelted our backs. The light around us had turned to a dark dirty yellow.

We could still see, but we could not see much.

I was willing to sit in the shelter of the railing, but she nudged me. She wanted us to do something about Macht. What anyone could do, that was beyond me. If he had found shelter, he was safe, but if he was out on those cables, the wild pushing air would soon carry him off and then there would be no more Maximilien Macht. He would be "dead" and his interior parts would bleach somewhere on the open ground.

Virginia insisted.

We crept to the edge.

A bird swept in, true as a bullet, aiming for my face. I flinched. A wing touched me. It stung against my cheek like fire. I did not know that feathers were so tough. The birds must all have damaged mental mechanisms, thought I, if they hit people on Alpha Ralpha. That is not the right way to behave toward true people.

At last we reached the edge, crawling on our bellies. I tried to dig the fingernails of my left hand into the stonelike material of the railing, but it was flat, and there was nothing much to hold to, save for the ornamental fluting. My right arm was around Virginia. It hurt me badly to crawl forward that way because my body was still damaged from the blow against the edge of the road, on the way coming up. When I hesitated, Virginia thrust herself forward.

We saw nothing.

The gloom was around us.

The wind and the water beat at us like fists.

Her gown pulled at her like a dog worrying its master. I wanted to get her back into the shelter of the railing where we could wait for the air disturbance to end.

Abruptly, light shone all around us. It was wild electricity, which the ancients called *lightning*. Later I found that it occurs quite frequently in the areas beyond the reach of the weather machines.

The bright quick light showed us a white face staring at us. He hung on the cables below us. His mouth was open, so he must have been shouting. I shall never know whether the expression on his face showed "fear" or great happiness. It was full of excitement. The bright light went out and I thought that I heard the echo of a call. I reached for his mind telepathically and there was nothing there. Just some dim, obstinate bird thinking at me, *no-no-no-no-no!*

Virginia tightened in my arms. She squirmed around. I shouted at her in French. She could not hear.

Then I called with my mind.

Someone else was there.

Virginia's mind blazed at me, full of revulsion. "The cat girl. She is going to *touch* me!"

She twisted. My right arm was suddenly empty. I saw the gleam of a golden gown flash over the edge, even in the dim light. I reached with my mind, and I caught her cry: "Paul, Paul, I love you. Paul . . . help me!"

The thoughts faded as her body dropped.

The someone else was C'mell, whom we had first met in the corridor.

"I came to get you both," she thought at me; "not that the birds cared about her."

"What have the birds got to do with it?"

"You saved them. You saved their young, when the red-topped man was killing them all. All of us have been worried about what you true people would do to us when you were free. We found out. Some of you are bad and kill other kinds of life. Others of you are good and protect life."

Thought I, is that all there is to *good* and *bad*?

Perhaps I should not have left myself off guard. People did not have to understand fighting, but the homunculi did. They were bred amid battle and they served through troubles. C'mell, cat-girl that she was, caught me on the chin with a pistonlike fist. She had no anesthesia, and the only way—cat or no cat—that she could carry me across the cables in the "typhoon" was to have me unconscious and relaxed.

I awakened in my own room. I felt very well indeed. The doctor-robot was there. Said he: "You've had a shock. I've already reached a subcommissioner of the Instrumentality, and I can erase the memories of the last full day if you want me to."

His expression was pleasant.

Where was the racing wind? The air falling like stone around us? The water driving where no weather machines controlled it? Where was the golden gown and the wild fear-hungry face of Maximilien Macht?

I thought these things, but the doctor-robot, not being telepathic, caught none of it. I stared hard at him.

"Where," I cried, "is my own true love?"

Robots cannot sneer, but this one attempted to do so. "The naked cat-girl with the blazing hair? She left to get some clothing."

I stared at him.

His fuddy-duddy little machine mind cooked up its own nasty little thoughts: "I must say, sir, you 'free people' change very fast indeed. . . ."

Who argues with a machine? It wasn't worth answering him.

But that other machine? Twenty-one minutes. How could that work out? How could it have known? I did not want to argue with that other machine either. It must have been a very powerful leftover machine—perhaps something once used in ancient wars. I had no intention of finding out. Some people might call it a god. I call it nothing. I do not need "fear" and I do not propose to go back to Alpha Ralpha Boulevard again.

But hear, O heart of mine!—how can you ever visit the café again?

C'mell came in and the doctor-robot left.

URSULA K. LE GUIN

Winter's King

Science fiction spins its wonder around relationships—humans and aliens, men and women, humans and machines, humans and themselves—and it also frequently focuses on parents and children, as in this marvelous story by the illustrious Ursula K. Le Guin, set on the wondrous world she calls "Winter"—a setting she would also use in her magnificent novel The Left Hand of Darkness. *It concerns change and growth and important and timeless values.*

When whirlpools appear in the onward run of time and history seems to swirl around a snag, as in the curious matter of the succession of Karhide, then pictures come in handy: snapshots, which may be taken up and matched to compare the parent to the child, the young king to the old, and which may also be rearranged and shuffled till the years run straight. For despite the tricks played by instantaneous interstellar communication and just-sublightspeed interstellar travel, time (as the Plenipotentiary Axt remarked) does not reverse itself; nor is death mocked.

Thus, although the best-known picture is that dark image of a young king standing above an old king who lies dead in a corridor lit only by mirror-reflections of a burning city, set it aside awhile. Look first at the young king, a nation's pride, as bright and fortunate a soul as ever lived to the age of twenty-two; but when this picture was taken the young king had her back against a wall. She was filthy, she was trembling, and her face was blank and mad, for she had lost that minimal confidence in the world which is called sanity. Inside her head she repeated, as she had been repeating for hours or years, over and over, "I will abdicate. I will abdicate. I will abdicate." Inside her eyes she saw the red-walled rooms of the palace, the towers and streets of Erhenrang in falling snow, the lovely plains of the West Fall, the white summits of the Kargav, and she renounced them all, her kingdom. "I will

97

abdicate," she said not aloud and then, aloud, screamed as once again the person dressed in red and white approached her saying, "Majesty! A plot against your life has been discovered in the artisan school," and the humming noise began, softly. She hid her head in her arms and whispered, "Stop it, please stop it," but the humming whine grew higher and louder and nearer, relentless, until it was so high and loud that it entered her flesh, tore the nerves from their channels and made her bones dance and jangle, hopping to its tune. She hopped and twitched, bare bones strung on thin white threads, and wept dry tears and shouted, "Have them—Have them—They must—Executed—Stopped—Stop!"

It stopped.

She fell in a clattering, chattering heap to the floor. What floor? Not red tiles, not parquetry, not urine-stained cement, but the wood floor of the room in the tower, the little tower bedroom where she was safe, safe from her ogre parent, the cold, mad, uncaring king, safe to play cat's cradle with Piry and to sit by the fireside on Borhub's warm lap, as warm and deep as sleep. But there was no hiding, no safety, no sleep. The person dressed in black had come even here and had hold of her head, lifted it up, lifted on thin white strings the eyelids she tried to close.

"Who am I?"

The blank, black mask stared down. The young king struggled, sobbing because now the suffocation would begin: she would not be able to breathe until she said the name, the right name—"Gerer!"—She could breathe. She was allowed to breathe. She had recognized the black one in time.

"Who am I?" said a different voice, gently, and the young king groped for that strong presence that always brought her sleep, truce, solace. "Rebade," she whispered, "tell me what to do. . . ."

"Sleep."

She obeyed. A deep sleep and dreamless, for it was real. Dreams came at waking, now. Unreal, the horrible dry red light of sunset burned her eyes open and she stood, once more, on the palace balcony looking down at fifty thousand black pits opening and shutting. From the pits came a paroxysmic gush of sound, a shrill, rhythmic eructation: her name. Her name was roared in her ears as a taunt, a jeer. She beat her hands on the narrow brass railing and shouted at them, "I will silence you!" She could not hear her voice, only their voice, the pestilent mouths of the mob that hated her, screaming her name. "Come away, my king," said the one gentle voice, and Rebade drew her away from the balcony into the vast, red-walled quiet of the Hall of Audience. The screaming ceased with a click. Rebade's expression was as always composed, compassionate. "What will you do now?" she said in her gentle voice.

"I will—I will abdicate . . ."

"No," Rebade said calmly. "That is not right. What will you do now?"

The young king stood silent, shaking. Rebade helped her sit down on the iron cot, for the walls had darkened as they often did and drawn in all about her to a little cell. "You will call . . ."

"Call up the Erhenrang Guard. Have them shoot into the crowd. Shoot to kill. They must be taught a lesson." The young king spoke rapidly and distinctly in a loud, high voice. Rebade said, "Very good, my lord, a wise decision! Right. We shall come out all right. You are doing right. Trust me."

"I do. I trust you. Get me out of here," the young king whispered, seizing Rebade's arm, but her friend frowned. That was not right. She had driven Rebade and hope away again. Rebade was leaving now, calm and regretful, though the young king begged her to stop, to come back, for the noise was softly beginning again, the whining hum that tore the mind to pieces, and already the person in red and white was approaching across a red, interminable floor. "Majesty! A plot against your life has been discovered in the artisan school. . . ."

Down Old Harbor Street to the water's edge the street lamps burned cavernously bright. Guard Pepenerer on her rounds glanced down that slanting vault of light expecting nothing, and saw something staggering up it toward her. Pepenerer did not believe in porngropes, but she saw a porngrope, sea-beslimed, staggering on thin webbed feet, gasping dry air, whimpering. . . . Old sailors' tales slid out of Pepenerer's mind and she saw a drunk or a maniac or a victim staggering between the dank gray warehouse walls. "Now then! Hold on there!" she bellowed, on the run. The drunk, half-naked and wild-eyed, let out a yell of terror and tried to dodge away, slipped on the frost-slick stones of the street and pitched down sprawling. Pepenerer got out her gun and delivered a half-second of stun, just to keep the drunk quiet; then squatted down by her, wound up her radio and called the West Ward for a car.

Both the arms, sprawled out limp and meek on the cold cobbles, were blotched with injection marks. Not drunk; drugged. Pepenerer sniffed, but got no resinous scent of orgrevy. She had been drugged, then; thieves, or a ritual clan-revenge. Thieves would not have left the gold ring on the forefinger, a massive thing, carved, almost as wide as the finger joint. Pepenerer crouched forward to look at it. Then she turned her head and looked at the beaten, blank face in profile against the paving stones, hard lit by the glare of the street lamps. She took a new quarter-crown piece out of her pouch and looked at the left profile stamped on the bright tin, then back at the right profile stamped in light and shadow and cold stone. Then, hearing the purr of the electric car turning down from the Longway into Old Harbor Street, she stuck the coin back in her pouch, muttering to herself, "Damn fool."

King Argaven was off hunting in the mountains anyhow and had been for a couple of weeks; it had been in all the bulletins.

"You see," said Hoge the physician, "we can assume that she was mindformed; but that gives us almost nothing to go on. There are too many expert mindformers in Karhide, and in Orgoreyn for that matter. Not criminals whom the police might have a lead on, but respectable mentalists or physicians to whom the drugs are legally available. As for getting anything from her, if they had any skill at all they will have blocked everything they did to rational access. All clues will be buried, the trigger-suggestions hidden, and we simply cannot guess what questions to ask. There is no way, short of brain destruction, of going through everything in her mind; and even under hypnosis and deep drugging there would be no way now to distinguish implanted ideas or emotions from her own autonomous ones. Perhaps the aliens could do something, though I doubt their mindscience is all they boast of; at any rate it's out of reach. We have only one real hope."

"Which is?" Lord Gerer asked, stolidly.

"The king is quick and resolute. At the beginning, before they broke her, she may have known what they were doing to her and so set up some block or resistance, left herself some escape route. . . ."

Hoge's low voice lost confidence as she spoke, and trailed off in the silence of the high, red, dusky room. She drew no response from old Gerer who stood, black-clad, before the fire.

The temperature of that room in the king's palace of Erhenrang was twelve degrees Celsius where Lord Gerer stood and five degrees midway between the two big fireplaces; outside it was snowing lightly, a mild day only a few degrees below freezing. Spring had come to Winter. The fires at either end of the room roared red and gold, devouring thigh-thick logs. Magnificence, a harsh luxury, a quick splendor; fireplaces, fireworks, lightning, meteors, volcanoes; such things satisfied the people of Karhide on the world called Winter. But, except in Arctic colonies above the thirty-fifth parallel, they had never installed central heating in any building in the many centuries of their Age of Technology. Comfort was allowed to come to them rare, welcome, unsought: a gift, like joy.

The king's personal servant, sitting by the bed, turned toward the physician and the lord councillor, though she did not speak. Both at once crossed the room. The broad, hard bed, high on gilt pillars, heavy with a finery of red cloaks and coverlets, bore up the king's body almost level with their eyes. To

Gerer it appeared a ship breasting, motionless, a swift vast flood of darkness, carrying the young king into shadows, terrors, years. Then with a terror of her own the old councillor saw that Argaven's eyes were open, staring out a half-curtained window at the stars.

Gerer feared lunacy; idiocy; she did not know what she feared. Hoge had warned her: "The king will not behave 'normally,' Lord Gerer. She has suffered thirteen days of torment, intimidation, exhaustion and mindhandling. There may be brain damage, there will certainly be side- and aftereffects of drugs." Neither fear nor warning parried the shock. Argaven's bright, weary eyes turned to Gerer and paused on her blankly a moment, then saw her. And Gerer, though she could not see the black mask reflected, saw the hate, the horror, saw her young king, infinitely beloved, gasping in imbecile terror and struggling with the servant, with Hoge, with her own weakness in the effort to get away, to get away from Gerer.

Standing in the cold midst of the room where the prowlike head of the bedstead hid her from the king, Gerer heard them pacify Argaven and settle her down again. Argaven's voice sounded reedy, childishly plaintive. So the old king, Emran, had spoken in her last madness with a child's voice. Then silence, and the burning of the two great fires.

Korgry, the king's bodyservant, yawned and rubbed her eyes. Hoge measured something from a vial into a hypodermic. Gerer stood in despair. My child, my king, what have they done to you? So great a trust, so fair a promise, lost, lost. . . . So the one who looked like a lump of half-carved black rock, a heavy, prudent, rude old courtier, grieved and was passion-racked, her love and service of the young king being the world's one worth to her.

Argaven spoke aloud: "My child . . ."

Gerer winced, feeling the words torn out of her own mind; but Hoge, untroubled by love, comprehended and said softly to Argaven, "Prince Emran is well, my liege. She is with her attendants at Warrever Castle. We are in constant communication. All is well there."

Gerer heard the king's harsh breathing and came somewhat closer to the bed, though out of sight still behind the high headboard.

"Have I been sick?"

"You are not well yet," the physician said, bland.

"Where . . . ?"

"Your own room in the palace in Erhenrang."

But Gerer, coming a step closer, though not in view of the king, said, "We do not know where you have been."

Hoge's smooth face creased with a frown, though, physician as she was and so in her way ruler of them all, she dared not direct the frown at the lord councillor. Gerer's voice did not seem to trouble the king, who asked another question or two, sane and brief, and then lay quiet. Presently the servant Korgry, who had sat with her ever since she had been brought into the palace (last night, in secret, by side doors, like a shameful suicide of the last reign, but all in reverse), Korgry committed lèse-majesté: huddled forward on her high stool, she let her head droop on the side of the bed and slept. The guard at the door yielded place to a new guard, in whispers. Officials came and received a fresh bulletin for public release on the state of the king's health, in whispers. Stricken by symptoms of fever while vacationing in the High Kargav, the king had been rushed to Erhenrang and was now responding satisfactorily to treatment, etc. Physician Hoge rem ir Hogeremme at the palace has released the following statement, etc., etc. "May the wheel turn for our king," people in village houses said solemnly as they lit the fire on the altarhearth, to which elders sitting near the fire remarked, "It comes of her roving around the city at night and climbing mountains, fool tricks like that," but they kept the radio on to catch the next bulletin. A very great number of people had come and gone and loitered and chatted this day in the square before the palace, watching those who went in and out, watching the vacant balcony; there were still several hundred down there, standing around patiently in the snow. Argaven XVII was loved in her domain. After the dull brutality of King Emran's reign that had ended in the shadow of madness and the country's bankruptcy, she had come: sudden, gallant, young, changing everything; sane and shrewd, yet magnanimous. She had the fire, the splendor that suited her people. She was the force and center of a new age: one born, for once, king of the right kingdom.

"Gerer."

It was the king's voice, and Gerer hastened stiffly through the hot and cold of the great room, the firelight and dark.

Argaven was sitting up. Her arms shook and the breath caught in her throat; her eyes burned across the dark air at Gerer. By her left hand, which bore the sign ring of the Harge dynasty, lay the sleeping face of the servant, derelict, serene. "Gerer," the king said with effort and clarity, "summon the council. Tell them I will abdicate."

So crude, so simple? All the drugs, the terrorizing, the hypnosis, parahypnosis, neurone-stimulation, synapse-pairing, spotshock that Hoge had described, for this blunt result? But reasoning must wait. They must temporize. "My liege, when your strength returns . . ."

"Now. Call the council, Gerer!"

Then she broke, like a bowstring breaking, and stammered in a fury of fear that found no sense or strength to flesh itself in, and still her faithful servant slept beside her, deaf.

In the next picture things are going better, it appears. Here is King Argaven XVII in good health and good clothes, finishing a large breakfast. She talks with the nearer dozen of the forty or fifty people sharing or serving the meal (singularity is a king's prerogative, but seldom privacy), and includes the rest in the largesse of her courtesy. She looks, as everyone has said, quite herself again. Perhaps she is not quite herself again, however; something is missing, a youthful serenity, a confidence, replaced by a similar but less reassuring quality, a kind of heedlessness. Out of it she rises in wit and warmth, but always subsides to it again, that darkness which absorbs her and makes her heedless: fear, pain, resolution?

Mr. Mobile Axt, ambassador plenipotentiary to Winter from the Ekumen of the Known Worlds, who had spent the last six days on the road trying to drive an electric car faster than fifty kilometers an hour from Mishnory in Orgoreyn to Erhenrang in Karhide, overslept breakfast, and so arrived in the Hall of Audience prompt, but hungry. The old chief of the council, the king's cousin Gerer rem ir Verhen, met the alien at the door of the great hall and greeted him with the polysyllabic politeness of Karhide. The plenipotentiary responded as best he could, discerning beneath the eloquence Gerer's desire to tell him something.

"I am told the king is perfectly recovered," he said, "and I heartily hope this is true."

"It is not," the old councillor said, her voice suddenly blunt and toneless. "Mr. Axt, I tell you this trusting your confidence; there are not ten others in Karhide who know the truth. She is not recovered. She was not sick."

Axt nodded. There had of course been rumors.

"She will go alone in the city sometimes, at night, in common clothes, walking, talking with strangers. The pressures of kingship . . . She is very young." Gerer paused a moment, struggling with some suppressed emotion. "One night six weeks ago, she did not come back. A message was delivered to me and the second lord, at dawn. If we announced her disappearance, she would be killed; if we waited a half-month in silence she would be restored unhurt. We kept silent, lied to the council, sent out false news. On the thirteenth night she was found wandering in the city. She had been drugged and mindformed. By which enemy or faction we do not yet know. We must work in utter secrecy; we cannot wreck the people's confidence in her, her own confidence in herself. It is hard: she remembers nothing. But what they did is plain. They broke her will and bent her mind all to one thing. She believes she must abdicate the throne."

The voice remained low and flat; the eyes betrayed anguish. And the plenipotentiary turning suddenly saw the reflection of that anguish in the eyes of the young king.

"Holding my audience, cousin?"

Argaven smiled but there was a knife in it. The old councillor excused herself stolidly, bowed, left, a patient ungainly figure diminishing down a long corridor.

Argaven stretched out both hands to the plenipotentiary in the greeting of equals, for in Karhide the Ekumen was recognized as a sister kingdom, though not a living soul had seen it. But her words were not the polite discourse that Axt expected. All she said, and fiercely, was, "At last!"

"I left as soon as I received your message. The roads are still icy in East Orgoreyn and the West Fall; I couldn't make very good time. But I was very glad to come. Glad to leave, too." Axt smiled saying this, for he and the young king enjoyed each other's candor. What Argaven's welcome implied, he waited to see, watching, with some exhilaration, the mobile, beautiful, adrogynous face.

"Orgoreyn breeds bigots as a corpse breeds worms, as one of my ancestors remarked. I'm glad you find the air fresher here in Karhide. Come this way. Gerer told you that I was kidnapped, and so forth? Yes. It was all according to the old rules. Kidnapping is a quite formal art. If it had been one of the anti-alien groups who think your Ekumen intends to enslave the earth, they might have ignored the rules; I think it was one of the old clan factions hoping to regain power through me, the power they had in the last reign. But we don't know, yet. It's strange to know that one has seen them face to face and yet can't recognize them; who knows but that I see those faces daily? Well, no profit in such notions. They wiped out all their tracks. I am sure only of one thing. *They* did not tell me that I must abdicate."

She and the plenipotentiary were walking side by side up the long, immensely high room toward the dais and chairs at the far end. The windows were little more than slits, as usual on this cold world; fulvous strips of sunlight fell from them diagonally to the red-paved floor, dusk and dazzle in Axt's eyes. He looked up at the young king's face in that somber, shifting radiance. "Who then?"

"I did."

"When, my lord, and why?"

"When they had me, when they were remaking me to fit their mold and play their game. Why? So that I can't fit their mold and play their game!

Listen, Lord Axt, if they wanted me dead they'd have killed me. They want me alive, to govern, to be king. As such I am to follow the orders imprinted in my brain, gain their ends for them. I am their tool, their machine, waiting for the switch to be thrown. The only way to prevent that is to . . . discard the machine."

Axt was quick of understanding, that being a minimal qualification of a mobile of the Ekumen; besides, the manners and affairs of Karhide, the stresses and seditions of that lively kingdom, were well known to him. Remote though Winter was, both in space and in the physiology of its inhabitants, from the rest of the human race, yet its dominant nation, Karhide, had proved a loyal member of the Ekumen. Axt's reports were discussed in the central councils of the Ekumen eighty light-years away; the equilibrium of the whole rests in all its parts. Axt said, as they sat down in the great stiff chairs on the dais before the fire, "But they need not even throw switches, if you abdicate."

"Leaving my child as heir, and a regent of my own choice?"

"Perhaps," Axt said with caution, "they chose your regent for you."

The king frowned. "I think not," she said.

"Whom had you thought of naming?"

There was a long pause. Axt saw the muscles of Argaven's throat working as she struggled to get a word, a name, up past a block, a harsh constriction; at last she said, in a forced, strangled whisper, "Gerer."

Axt nodded, startled. Gerer had served as regent for a year after Emran's death and before Argaven's accession; he knew her honesty and her utter devotion to the young king. "Gerer serves no faction!" he said.

Argaven shook her head. She looked exhausted. After a while she said, "Could the science of your people undo what was done to me, Lord Axt?"

"Possibly. In the institute on Ollul. But if I sent for a specialist tonight, he'd get here twenty-four years from now. . . . You're sure, then, that your decision to abdicate was . . ." But a servant, coming in a side door behind them, set a small table by the plenipotentiary's chair and loaded it with fruit, sliced bread-apple, a silver tankard of ale. Argaven had noticed that her guest had missed his breakfast. Though the fare on Winter, mostly vegetable and that mostly uncooked, was dull stuff to Axt's taste, he set to gratefully; and as serious talk was unseemly over food, Argaven shifted to generalities. "Once you said, Lord Axt, that different as I am from you, and different as my people are from yours, yet we are blood kin. Was that a moral fact or a material one?"

Axt smiled at the very Karhidish distinction. "Both, my lord. As far as we know, which is a tiny corner of dusty space under the rafters of the universe, all the people we've run into are in fact human. But the kinship goes back a million years and more to the fore-eras of Hain. The ancient Hainish settled a hundred worlds."

"We call the time before my dynasty ruled Karhide 'ancient.' Seven hundred years ago!"

"So we call the Age of the Enemy 'ancient,' and that was less than six hundred years ago. Time stretches and shrinks; changes with the eye, with the age, with the star; does all except reverse itself—or repeat."

"The dream of the Ekumen, then, is to restore that truly ancient commonalty; to regather all the peoples of all the worlds at one hearth?"

Axt nodded, chewing bread-apple. "To weave some harmony among them, at least. Life loves to know itself, out to its furthest limits; to embrace complexity is its delight. Our difference is our beauty. All these worlds and the various forms and ways of the minds and lives and bodies on them—together they would make a splendid harmony."

"No harmony endures," said the young king.

"None has ever been achieved," said the plenipotentiary. "The pleasure is in trying." He drained his tankard, wiped his fingers on the woven-grass napkin.

"That was my pleasure as king," said Argaven. "It is over."

"Should . . . ?"

"It is finished. Believe me. I will keep you here, Lord Axt, until you believe me. I need your help. You are the piece the game players forgot about! You must help me. I cannot abdicate against the will of the council. They will refuse my abdication, force me to rule, and if I rule, I serve my enemies! If you will not help me, I will have to kill myself." She spoke quite evenly and reasonably, but Axt knew what even the mention of suicide, the ultimately contemptible act, cost a Karhider.

"One way or the other," said the young king.

The plenipotentiary pulled his heavy cloak closer round him; he was cold. He had been cold for seven years, here. "My lord," he said, "I am an alien on your world, with a handful of aides and a little device with which I can converse with other aliens on distant worlds. I represent power, of course, but I have none. How can I help you?"

"You have a ship on Horden Island."

"Ah. I was afraid of that," said the plenipotentiary, sighing. "Lord Argaven, that ship is set for Ollul, twenty-four light-years away. Do you know what that means?"

"My escape from my time, in which I have become an instrument of evil."

"There is no escape," said Axt with sudden intensity. "No, my lord. Forgive me. It is impossible. I could not consent. . . ."

Icy rain of spring rattled on the stones of the tower; wind whined at the angles and finials of the roof. The room was quiet, shadowy. One small shielded light burned by the door. The nurse lay snoring mildly in the bed; the baby was head down, rump up in the crib. Argaven stood beside the crib. She looked around the room, or rather saw it, knew it wholly, without looking. She too had slept here as a little child. It had been her first kingdom. It was here that she had come to suckle her child, her firstborn, had sat by the fireplace while the little mouth tugged at her breast, had hummed to the baby the songs Borhub had hummed to her. This was the center, the center of everything.

Very cautiously and gently she slipped her hand under the baby's warm, damp, downy head and put over it a chain on which hung a massive ring carved with the token of the lords of Harge. The chain was far too long, and Argaven knotted it shorter, thinking that it might twist and choke the child. So allaying that small anxiety, she tried to allay the great fear and wretchedness that filled her. She stooped down till her cheek touched the baby's cheek, whispering inaudibly, "Emran, Emran, I have to leave you, I can't take you, you have to rule for me. Be good, Emran, live long, rule well, be good, Emran. . . ."

She straightened up, turned, ran from the tower room, the lost kingdom.

She knew several ways of getting out of the palace unperceived. She took the surest and then made for the New Harbor through the bright-lit, sleet-lashed streets of Erhenrang, alone.

Now there is no picture: no seeing her. With what eye will you watch a process that is one hundred millionth percent slower than the speed of light? She is not now a king, nor a human being; she is translated. You can scarcely call fellow mortal one whose time passes seventy thousand times slower than yours. She is more than alone. It seems that she is not, any more than an uncommunicated thought is; that she goes nowhere, any more than a thought goes. And yet, at very nearly but never quite the speed of light, she voyages. She is the voyage. Quick as thought. She has doubled her age when she arrives, less than a day older, in the portion of space curved about a dust mote named Ollul, the fourth planet of a yellowish sun. And all this has passed in utter silence.

With noise now and fire and meteoric dazzle enough to satisfy a Karhider's lust for splendor, the clever ship makes earthfall, settling down in flame in the precise spot it left from some fifty-five years ago. Presently, visible, unmassive, uncertain, the young king emerges from it and stands a moment in the exitway, shielding her eyes from the light of a strange, hot sun.

Axt had of course sent notice of her coming, by instantaneous transmitter, twenty-four years ago, or seventeen hours ago, depending on how you look at it; and aides and agents of the Ekumen were on hand to greet her. Even pawns did not go unnoticed by those players of the great game, and this Gethenian was, after all, a king. One of the agents had spent a year of the twenty-four in learning Karhidish, so that Argaven could speak to someone. She spoke at once: "What news from my country?"

"Mr. Mobile Axt and his successor have sent regular summaries of events and various private messages for you; you'll find all the material in your quarters, Mr. Harge. Very briefly, the regency of Lord Gerer was uneventful and benign; there was a depression in the first two years, during which your Arctic settlements were abandoned, but at present the economy is quite stable. Your heir was enthroned at eighteen and has ruled now for seven years."

"Yes. I see," said the person who had kissed that year-old heir last night.

"Whenever you see fit, Mr. Harge, the specialists at our institute over in Belxit . . ."

"As you wish," said Mr. Harge.

They went into her mind very gently, very subtly, opening doors. For locked doors they had delicate instruments that always found the combination; and then they stood aside and let her enter. They found the person in black, who was not Gerer, and compassionate Rebade, who was not compassionate; they stood with her on the palace balcony and climbed the crevasses of nightmare with her up to the room in the tower; and at last the one who was to have been first, the person in red and white, approached her saying, "Majesty! A plot against your life . . ." And Mr. Harge screamed in abject terror, and woke up.

"Well! That was the trigger. The signal to begin tripping off the other instructions and determine the course of your phobia. An induced paranoia. Really beautifully induced, I must say. Here, drink this, Mr. Harge. No, it's just water! You might well have become a remarkably vicious ruler, increasingly obsessed by fear of plots and subversions, increasingly disaffected from your people. Not overnight, of course. That's the beauty of it. It would have taken several years for you to become a real tyrant; though they no doubt planned some boosts along the way, once Rebade wormed his way—her way —a way into your confidence. . . . Well, well, I see why Karhide is well spoken of, over at the clearinghouse. If you'll pardon my objectivity, this kind of skill and patience is quite rare. . . ." So the doctor, the mindmender, the hairy, grayish, one-sexed person from somewhere called the Cetians, went rambling on while the patient recovered herself.

"Then I did right," said Mr. Harge at last.

"You did. Abdication, suicide or escape was the only act of consequence which you could have committed of your own volition, freely. They counted on your moral veto of suicide and your council's vote on abdication. But being possessed by ambition themselves, they forgot the possibility of abnegation and left one door open for you. A door which only a strong-minded person, if you'll pardon my literalness, could choose to go through. I really must read up on this other mindscience of yours, what do you call it, foretelling? Thought it was some occultist trash, but quite evidently . . . Well, well, I expect they'll be wanting you to look in at the clearinghouse soon, to discuss your future, now that we've put your past where it belongs, eh?"

"As you wish," said Mr. Harge.

She talked with various people there in the clearinghouse of the Ekumen for the West Worlds, and when they suggested that she go to school, she assented readily. For among those mild persons, whose chief quality seemed a cool, profound sadness indistinguishable from a warm, profound hilarity— among them, the ex-king of Karhide knew herself a barbarian, unlearned and unwise.

She attended Ekumenical School. She lived in barracks near the clearing-house in Vaxtsit City with a couple of hundred other aliens, none of whom was either androgynous or an ex-king. Never having owned much that was hers alone, and never having had much privacy, she did not mind barracks life; nor was it so bad as she had expected to live among single-sexed people, although she found their condition of perpetual kemmer tiresome. She did not mind anything much, getting through the works and days with vigor and compe-tence but always a certain heedlessness, as of one whose center is somewhere else. The only discomfort was the heat, the awful heat of Ollul that rose sometimes to thirty-five degrees Celsius in the blazing interminable season when no snow fell for two hundred days on end. Even when winter came at last she sweated, for it seldom got more than ten degrees below freezing outside, and the barracks were kept sweltering—she thought—though the other aliens wore heavy sweaters all the time. She slept on top of her bed, naked and thrashing, and dreamed of the snows of the Kargav, the ice in Old Harbor, the ice scumming one's ale on cool mornings in the palace, the cold, the dear and bitter cold of Winter.

She learned a good deal. She had already learned that the Earth was, here, called Winter, and that Ollul was, here, called the Earth: one of those facts which turn the universe inside out like a sock. She learned that a meat diet causes diarrhea in the unaccustomed gut. She learned that single-sexed people, whom she tried hard not to think of as perverts, tried hard not to think of her as a pervert. She learned that when she pronounced *Ollul* as *Orrur* some people laughed. She attempted also to unlearn that she was a king. Once the school took her in hand she learned and unlearned much more. She was led, by all the machines and devices and experiences and (simplest and most demanding) words that the Ekumen had at its disposal, into an intimation of what it might be to understand the nature and history of a kingdom that was over a million years old and trillions of miles wide. When she had begun to guess the immensity of this kingdom of humanity and the durable pain and monotonous waste of its history, she began also to see what lay beyond its borders in space and time, and among naked rocks and furnace-suns and the shining desolation that goes on and on she glimpsed the sources of hilarity and serenity, the inexhaustible springs. She learned a great many facts, numbers, myths, epics, proportions, relationships, and so forth, and saw, beyond the borders of what she had learned, the unknown again, a splendid immensity. In this augmentation of her mind and being there was great satisfaction; yet she was unsatisfied. They did not always let her go on as far as she wanted into certain fields, mathematics, Cetian physics. "You started late, Mr. Harge," they said, "we have to build on the existing foundations. Besides, we want you in subjects which you can put to use."

"What use?"

They—the ethnographer Mr. Mobile Gist represented Them at the moment, across a library table—looked at her sardonically. "Do you consider yourself to be of no further use, Mr. Harge?"

Mr. Harge, who was generally reserved, spoke with sudden fury: "I do."

"A king without a country," said Gist in his flat Terran accent, "self-exiled, believed to be dead, might feel a trifle superfluous. But then, why do you think we're bothering with you?"

"Out of kindness."

"Oh, kindness . . . However kind we are, we can give you nothing that would make you happy, you know. Except . . . well. Waste is a pity. You were indubitably the right king for Winter, for Karhide, for the purposes of the Ekumen. You have a sense of balance. You might even have unified the planet. You certainly wouldn't have terrorized and fragmented the country, as the present king seems to be doing. What a waste! Only consider our hopes and needs, Mr. Harge, and your own qualifications, before you despair of being useful in your life. Forty or fifty more years of it you have to live, after all. . . ."

The last snapshot taken by alien sunlight: erect, in a Hainish-style cloak of gray, a handsome person of indeterminate sex stands, sweating profusely, on a green lawn beside the chief agent of the Ekumen in the West Worlds, the stabile, Mr. Hoalans of Alb, who can meddle (if he likes) with the destinies of forty worlds.

"I can't order you to go there, Argaven," says the stabile. "Your own conscience . . ."

"I gave up my kingdom to my conscience twelve years ago. It's had its due. Enough's enough," says Argaven Harge. Then she laughs suddenly, so that the stabile also laughs; and they part in such harmony as the powers of the Ekumen desire between human souls.

Horden Island, off the south coast of Karhide, was given as a freehold to the Ekumen by the kingdom of Karhide during the reign of Argaven XV. No one lived there. Yearly generations of seawalkies crawled up on the barren rocks and laid and hatched their eggs and raised their young and finally led them back in long single file to the sea. But once every ten or twenty years fire ran over the rocks and the sea boiled on the shores, and if any seawalkies were on the island then they died.

When the sea had ceased to boil, the plenipotentiary's little electric launch approached. The starship ran out a gossamer steel gangplank to the deck of the launch, and one person started to walk up it as another one started to walk down it, so that they met in the middle, in midair, between sea and land, an ambiguous meeting.

"Ambassador Horrsed? I'm Harge," said the one from the starship, but the one from the launch was already kneeling, saying aloud, in Karhidish, "Welcome, Argaven of Karhide!"

As he straightened up the ambassador added in a quick whisper, "You come as yourself . . . Explain when I can . . ." Behind and below him on the deck of the launch stood a sizable group of people, staring up intently at the newcomer. All were Karhiders by their looks; several were very old.

Argaven Harge stood for a minute, two minutes, three minutes, erect and perfectly motionless, though her gray cloak tugged and riffled in the cold sea wind. She looked then once at the dull sun in the west, once at the gray land north across the water, back again at the silent people grouped below her on the deck. She strode forward so suddenly that Ambassador Horrsed had to squeeze out of the way in a hurry. She went straight to one of the old people on the deck of the launch. "Are you Ker rem ir Kerheder?"

"I am."

"I knew you by the lame arm, Ker." She spoke clearly; there was no guessing what emotions she felt. "I could not know your face. After sixty years. Are there others of you I knew? I am Argaven."

They were all silent. They gazed at her.

All at once one of them, one scored and scarred with age like wood that has been through fire, stepped forward one step. "My liege, I am Bannith of the palace guard. You served with me when I was drillmaster and you a child, a young child." And the gray head bowed down suddenly, in homage, or to hide tears. Then another stepped forward, and another. The heads that bowed were gray, white, bald; the voices that hailed the king quavered. One, Ker of the crippled arm, whom Argaven had known as a shy page of thirteen, spoke fiercely to those who still stood unmoving: "This is the king. I have eyes that have seen and that see now. This is the king!"

Argaven looked at them, face after face, the bowed heads and the unbowed. "I am Argaven," she said. "I was king. Who reigns now in Karhide?"

"Emran," one answered.

"My child Emran?"

"Yes, my liege," old Bannith said; most of the faces were blank; but Ker said in her fierce shaking voice, "Argaven, Argaven reigns in Karhide! I have lived to see the bright days return. Long live the king!"

One of the younger ones looked at the others and said resolutely, "So be it. Long live the king!" And all the heads bowed low.

Argaven took their homage unperturbed, but as soon as a moment came when she could address Horrsed the plenipotentiary alone she demanded, "What is this? What has happened? Why was I misled? I was told I was to come here to assist you, as an aide, from the Ekumen. . . ."

"That was twenty-four years ago," said the ambassador, apologetically. "I've only lived here five years, my lord. Things are going very ill in Karhide. King Emran broke off relations with the Ekumen last year. I don't really know what the stabile's purpose in sending you here was at the time he sent you; but at present, we're losing Winter. So the agents on Hain suggested to me that we might move out our king."

"But I am *dead*," Argaven said wrathfully. "I have been dead for sixty years!"

"The king is dead," said Horrsed. "Long live the king."

As some of the Karhiders approached, Argaven turned from the ambassador and went over to the rail. Gray water bubbled and slid by the ship's side. The shore of the continent lay now to their left, gray patched with white. It was cold: a day of early winter in the Ice Age. The ship's engine purred softly. Argaven had not heard that purr of an electric engine for a dozen years now, the only kind of engine Karhide's slow and stable Age of Technology had chosen to employ. The sound of it was very pleasant to her.

She spoke abruptly without turning, as one who has known since infancy that there is always someone there to answer: "Why are we going east?"

"We're making for Kerm Land."

"Why Kerm Land?"

It was one of the younger ones who had come forward to answer. "Because that part of the country is in rebellion against the—against King Emran. I am a Kermlander: Perreth ner Sode."

"Is Emran in Erhenrang?"

"Erhenrang was taken by Orgoreyn six years ago. The king is in the new capital, east of the mountains—the old capital, actually, Rer."

"Emran lost the West Fall?" Argaven said and then turning full on the stout young noble, "Lost the West Fall? Lost Erhenrang?"

Perreth drew back a step, but answered promptly, "We've been in hiding behind the mountains for six years."

"The Orgota are in Erhenrang?"

"King Emran signed a treaty with Orgoreyn five years ago, ceding them the western provinces."

"A shameful treaty, your majesty," old Ker broke in, fiercer and shakier than ever. "A fool's treaty! Emran dances to the drums of Orgoreyn. All of us here are rebels, exiles. The ambassador there is an exile, in hiding!"

"The West Fall," Argaven said. "Argaven I took the West Fall for Karhide seven hundred years ago . . ." She looked round on the others again with her strange, keen, unheeding gaze. "Emran . . ." she began, but halted. "How strong are you in Kerm Land? Is the coast with you?"

"Most hearths of the South and East are with us."

Argaven was silent awhile. "Did Emran ever bear an heir?"

"No heir of the flesh, my liege," Bannith said. "She sired six."

"She has named Girvry Harge rem ir Orek as her heir," said Perreth.

"Girvry? What kind of name is that? The kings of Karhide are named Emran," Argaven said, "and Argaven."

Now at last comes the dark picture, the snapshot taken by firelight— firelight, because the power plants of Rer are wrecked, the trunk lines cut, and half the city is on fire. Snow flurries heavily down above the flames and gleams red for a moment before it melts in midair, hissing faintly.

Snow and ice and guerrilla troops keep Orgoreyn at bay on the west side of the Kargav Mountains. No help came to the old king, Emran, when her country rose against her. Her guards fled, her city burns, and now at the end she is face to face with the usurper. But she has, at the end, something of her family's heedless pride. She pays no attention to the rebels. She stares at them and does not see them, lying in the dark hallway, lit only by mirrors that reflect distant fires, the gun with which she killed herself near her hand.

Stooping over the body Argaven lifts up that cold hand and starts to take from the age-knotted forefinger the massive, carved, gold ring. But she does not do it. "Keep it," she whispers, "keep it." For a moment she bends yet lower, as if she whispered in the dead ear, or laid her cheek against that cold and wrinkled face. Then she straightens up and stands awhile and presently goes out through dark corridors, by windows bright with distant ruin, to set her house in order: Argaven, Winter's king.

AVRAM DAVIDSON

Or All the Seas
With Oysters

*Mary Shelley is widely recognized as the mother of modern science
fiction. In* Frankenstein *she asked a basic question that is at the
heart of SF: Who will prevail, humanity or humanity's creations?
The response has been countless stories of the struggles between
humans and machines, some optimistic, many increasingly pessimistic. "Or All the Seas with Oysters" is the story of such a struggle,
of the intentions and "true" (and very funny) nature of our creations.*

When the man came in to the F & O Bike Shop, Oscar greeted him with
a hearty "Hi, there!" Then, as he looked closer at the middle-aged visitor with
the eyeglasses and business suit, his forehead creased and he began to snap his
thick fingers.

"Oh, say, I know you," he muttered. "Mr.—um—name's on the tip of my
tongue, doggone it . . ." Oscar was a barrel-chested fellow. He had orange hair.

"Why, sure you do," the man said. There was a Lion's emblem in his
lapel. "Remember, you sold me a girl's bicycle with gears, for my daughter? We got to talking about that red French racing bike your partner was
working on . . ."

Oscar slapped his big hand down on the cash register. He raised his head
and rolled his eyes up. "Mr. Whatney!" Mr. Whatney beamed. "Oh, *sure*.
Gee, how could I forget? And we went across the street afterward and had
a couple a beers. Well, how you *been,* Mr. Whatney? I guess the bike—it was
an English model, wasn't it? Yeah. It must of given satisfaction or you would
of been back, huh?"

Mr. Whatney said the bicycle was fine, just fine. Then he said, "I understand there's been a change, though. You're all by yourself now. Your partner . . ."

Oscar looked down, pushed his lower lip out, nodded. "You heard, huh? Ee-up. I'm all by myself now. Over three months now."

The partnership had come to an end three months ago, but it had been faltering long before then. Ferd liked books, long-playing records and high-level conversation, Oscar liked beer, bowling and women. Any women. Any time.

The shop was located near the park; it did a big trade in renting bicycles to picnickers. If a woman was barely old enough to be *called* a woman and not quite old enough to be called an *old* woman, or if she was anywhere in between, and if she was alone, Oscar would ask, "How does that machine feel to you? All right?"

"Why . . . I guess so."

Taking another bicycle, Oscar would say, "Well, I'll just ride along a little bit with you, to make sure. Be right back, Ferd." Ferd always nodded gloomily. He knew that Oscar would not be right back. Later, Oscar would say, "Hope you made out in the shop as good as I did in the park."

"Leaving me all alone here all that time," Ferd grumbled.

And Oscar usually flared up. "Okay, then, next time *you* go and leave *me* stay here. See if I begrudge you a little fun." But he knew, of course, that Ferd —tall, thin, pop-eyed Ferd—would never go. "Do you good," Oscar said, slapping his sternum. "Put hair on your chest."

Ferd muttered that he had all the hair on his chest that he needed. He would glance down covertly at his lower arms; they were thick with long black hair, though his upper arms were slick and white. It was already like that when he was in high school, and some of the others would laugh at him—call him "Ferdie the Birdie." They knew it bothered him, but they did it anyway. How was it possible—he wondered then; he still did now— for people deliberately to hurt someone else who hadn't hurt them? How was it possible?

He worried over other things. All the time.

"The communists . . ." He shook his head over the newspaper. Oscar offered an advice about the communists in two short words. Or it might be capital punishment. "Oh, what a terrible thing if an innocent man was to be executed," Ferd moaned. Oscar said that was the guy's tough luck.

"Hand me that tire iron," Oscar said.

And Ferd worried even about other people's minor concerns. Like the time the couple came in with the tandem and the baby basket on it. Free air was all they took; then the woman decided to change the diaper and one of the safety pins broke.

"Why are there never any safety pins?" the woman fretted, rummaging here and rummaging there. "There are *never* any safety pins."

Ferd made sympathetic noises, went to see if he had any; but, though he was sure there'd been some in the office, he couldn't find them. So they drove off with one side of the diaper tied in a clumsy knot.

At lunch, Ferd said it was too bad about the safety pins. Oscar dug his teeth into a sandwich, tugged, tore, chewed, swallowed. Ferd liked to experiment with sandwich spreads—the one he liked most was cream cheese, olives, anchovy and avocado, mashed up with a little mayonnaise—but Oscar always had the same pink luncheon meat.

"It must be difficult with a baby." Ferd nibbled. "Not just traveling, but raising it."

Oscar said, "Jeez, there's drugstores in every block, and if you can't read, you can at least reckernize them."

"Drugstores? Oh, to buy safety pins, you mean."

"Yeah. Safety pins."

"But . . . you know . . . it's true . . . there's never any safety pins when you look."

Oscar uncapped his beer, rinsed the first mouthful around. "Aha! Always plenny of clothes hangers, though. Throw 'em out every month, next month same closet's full of 'm again. Now whatcha wanna do in your spare time, you invent a device which it'll make safety pins outa clothes hangers."

Ferd nodded abstractedly. "But in my spare time I'm working on the French racer. . . ." It was a beautiful machine, light, low-slung, swift, red and shining. You felt like a bird when you rode it. But, good as it was, Ferd knew he could make it better. He showed it to everybody who came into the place until his interest slackened.

Nature was his latest hobby, or, rather, reading about nature. Some kids had wandered by from the park one day with tin cans in which they had put salamanders and toads, and they proudly showed them to Ferd. After that, the work on the red racer slowed down and he spent his spare time on natural history books.

"Mimicry!" he cried to Oscar. "A wonderful thing!"

Oscar looked up interestedly from the bowling scores in the paper. "I seen Edie Adams on TV the other night, doing her imitation of Marilyn Monroe. Boy, oh, boy."

Ferd was irritated, shook his head. "Not that kind of mimicry. I mean how insects and arachnids will mimic the shapes of leaves and twigs and so on, to escape being eaten by birds or other insects and arachnids."

A scowl of disbelief passed over Oscar's heavy face. "You mean they change their *shapes*? What you giving me?"

"Oh, it's true. Sometimes the mimicry is for aggressive purposes, though —like a South African turtle that looks like a rock and so the fish swim up to it and then it catches them. Or that spider in Sumatra. When it lies on its back, it looks like a bird dropping. Catches butterflies that way."

Oscar laughed, a disgusted and incredulous noise. It died away as he turned back to the bowling scores. One hand groped at his pocket, came away, scratched absently at the orange thicket under the shirt, then went patting his hip pocket.

"Where's that pencil?" he muttered, got up, stomped into the office, pulled open drawers. His loud cry of "Hey!" brought Ferd into the tiny room.

"What's the matter?" Ferd asked.

Oscar pointed to a drawer. "Remember that time you claimed there were no safety pins here? Look—whole gahdamn drawer is full of 'em."

Ferd stared, scratched his head, said feebly that he was certain he'd looked there before. . . .

A contralto voice from outside asked, "Anybody here?"

Oscar at once forgot the desk and its contents, called, "Be right with you," and was gone. Ferd followed him slowly.

There was a young woman in the shop, a rather massively built young woman with muscular calves and a deep chest. She was pointing out the seat of her bicycle to Oscar, who was saying "Uh-huh" and looking more at her than at anything else. "It's just a little too far forward ('Uh-huh'), as you can see. A wrench is all I need ('Uh-huh'). It was silly of me to forget my tools."

Oscar repeated, "Uh-huh" automatically, then snapped to. "Fix it in a jiffy," he said, and—despite her insistence that she could do it herself—he did fix it. Though not quite in a jiffy. He refused money. He prolonged the conversation as long as he could.

"Well, thank *you*," the young woman said. "And now I've got to go."

"That machine feel all right to you now?"

"Perfectly. Thanks. . . ."

"Tell you what, I'll just ride along with you a little bit, just . . ."

Pear-shaped notes of laughter lifted the young woman's bosom. "Oh, you couldn't keep up with me! My machine is a *racer*!"

The moment he saw Oscar's eye flit to the corner, Ferd knew what he had in mind. He stepped forward. His cry of "No" was drowned out by his partner's loud, "Well, I guess this racer here can keep up with yours!"

The young woman giggled richly, said, well, they would see about that and was off. Oscar, ignoring Ferd's outstretched hand, jumped on the French bike and was gone. Ferd stood in the doorway, watching the two figures, hunched over their handlebars, vanish down the road into the park. He went slowly back inside.

It was almost evening before Oscar returned, sweaty but smiling. Smiling broadly. "Hey, what a babe!" he cried. He wagged his head, he whistled, he made gestures, noises like escaping steam. "Boy, oh, boy, what an afternoon!"

"Give me the bike," Ferd demanded.

Oscar said, yeah, sure; turned it over to him and went to wash. Ferd looked at the machine. The red enamel was covered with dust; there was mud spattered and dirt and bits of dried grass. It seemed soiled—degraded. He had felt like a swift bird when he rode it. . . .

Oscar came out wet and beaming. He gave a cry of dismay, ran over.

"Stand away," said Ferd, gesturing with the knife. He slashed the tires, the seat and seat cover, again and again.

"You crazy?" Oscar yelled. "You outa your mind? Ferd, no, don't, Ferd. . . ."

Ferd cut the spokes, bent them, twisted them. He took the heaviest hammer and pounded the frame into shapelessness, and then he kept on pounding till his breath was gasping.

"You're not only crazy," Oscar said bitterly, "you're rotten jealous. You can go to hell." He stomped away.

Ferd, feeling sick and stiff, locked up, went slowly home. He had no taste for reading, turned out the light and fell into bed, where he lay awake for hours, listening to the rustling noises of the night and thinking hot, twisted thoughts.

They didn't speak to each other for days after that, except for the necessities of the work. The wreckage of the French racer lay behind the shop. For about two weeks, neither wanted to go out back where he'd have to see it.

One morning Ferd arrived to be greeted by his partner, who began to shake his head in astonishment even before he started speaking. "How did you *do* it, how did you *do* it, Ferd? Jeez, what a beautiful job—I gotta hand it to you —no more hard feelings, huh, Ferd?"

Ferd took his hand. "Sure, sure. But what are you talking about?"

Oscar led him out back. There was the red racer, all in one piece, not a mark or scratch on it, its enamel bright as ever. Ferd gaped. He squatted down and examined it. It *was* his machine. Every change, every improvement he had made was there.

He straightened up slowly. "Regeneration . . ."

"Huh? What say?" Oscar asked. Then, "Hey, kiddo, you're all white. Whad you do, stay up all night and didn't get no sleep? Come on in and siddown. But I still don't see how you done it."

Inside, Ferd sat down. He wet his lips. He said, "Oscar—listen . . ."

"Yeah?"

"Oscar. You know what regeneration is? No? Listen. Some kinds of lizards, you grab them by the tail, the tail breaks off and they grow a new one. If a lobster loses a claw, it regenerates another one. Some kinds of worms—and hydras and starfish—you cut them into pieces, each piece will grow back the missing parts. Salamanders can regenerate lost hands, and frogs can grow legs back."

"No kidding, Ferd. But, uh, I mean: nature. Very interesting. But to get back to the bike now—how'd you manage to fix it so good?"

"I never touched it. It regenerated. Like a newt. Or a lobster."

Oscar considered this. He lowered his head, looked up at Ferd from under his eyebrows. "Well, now, Ferd . . . Look . . . How come all broke bikes don't do that?"

"This isn't an ordinary bike. I mean it isn't a real bike." Catching Oscar's look, he shouted, "Well, it's *true*!"

The shout changed Oscar's attitude from bafflement to incredulity. He got up. "So for the sake of argument, let's say all that stuff about the bugs and the eels or whatever the hell you were talking about is true. But they're alive. A bike ain't." He looked down triumphantly.

Ferd shook his leg from side to side, looked at it. "A crystal isn't, either, but a broken crystal can regenerate itself if the conditions are right. Oscar, go see if the safety pins are still in the desk. Please, Oscar?"

He listened as Oscar, muttering, pulled the desk drawers out, rummaged in them, slammed them shut, tramped back.

"Naa," he said. "All gone. Like that lady said that time, and you said, there never are any safety pins when you want 'em. They disap—Ferd? What're . . . ?"

Ferd jerked open the closet door, jumped back as a shoal of clothes hangers clattered out.

"And like *you* say," Ferd said with a twist of his mouth, "on the other hand, there are always plenty of clothes hangers. There weren't any here before."

Oscar shrugged. "I don't see what you're getting at. But anybody could of got in here and took the pins and left the hangers. *I* could of—but I didn't. Or *you* could of. Maybe . . ." He narrowed his eyes. "Maybe you walked in your sleep and done it. You better see a doctor. Jeez, you look rotten."

Ferd went back and sat down, put his head in his hands. "I feel rotten. I'm scared, Oscar. Scared of what?" He breathed noisily. "I'll tell you. Like I explained before, about how things that live in the wild places, they mimic other things there. Twigs, leaves . . . toads that look like rocks. Well, suppose there are . . . things . . . that live in people places. Cities. Houses. These things could imitate—well, other kinds of things you find in people places. . . ."

"*People* places, for crise sake!"

"Maybe they're a different kind of life form. Maybe they get their nourishment out of the elements in the air. You know what safety pins *are*—these other kinds of them? Oscar, the safety pins are the pupa forms and then they, like, *hatch*. Into the larval forms. Which look just like coat hangers. They feel like them, even, but they're not. Oscar, they're not, not really, not really, not . . ."

He began to cry into his hands. Oscar looked at him. He shook his head.

After a minute, Ferd controlled himself somewhat. He snuffled. "All these bicycles the cops find, and they hold them waiting for owners to show up, and then we buy them at the sale because no owners show up because there aren't any, and the same with the ones the kids are always trying to sell us, and they say they just found them, and they really did because they were never made in a factory. They grew. They grow. You smash them and throw them away. They regenerate."

Oscar turned to someone who wasn't there and waggled his head. "Hoo, boy," he said. Then, to Ferd: "You mean one day there's a safety pin and the next day instead there's a coat hanger?"

Ferd said, "One day there's a cocoon; the next day there's a moth. One day there's an egg; the next day there's a chicken. But with . . . these it doesn't happen in the open daytime where you can see it. But at night, Oscar—at night you can *hear* it happening. All the little noises in the nighttime, Oscar . . ."

Oscar said, "Then how come we ain't up to our belly button in bikes? If I had a bike for every coat hanger . . ."

But Ferd had considered that, too. If every codfish egg, he explained, or every oyster spawn grew to maturity, a man could walk across the ocean on the backs of all the codfish or oysters there'd be. So many died, so many were eaten by predatory creatures, that nature had to produce a maximum in order to allow a minimum to arrive at maturity. And Oscar's question was: then who, uh, eats the, uh, coat hangers?

Ferd's eyes focused through wall, buildings, park, more buildings, to the horizon. "You got to get the picture. I'm not talking about real pins or hangers. I got a name for the others—'false friends,' I call them. In high school French, we had to watch out for French words that looked like English words, but really were different. *'Faux amis,'* they call them. False friends. Pseudo-pins. Pseudo-hangers . . . Who eats them? I don't know for sure. Pseudo-vacuum cleaners, maybe?"

His partner, with a loud groan, slapped his hands against his thighs. He said, "Ferd, Ferd, for crise sake. You know what's the trouble with you? You talk about oysters, but you forgot what they're good for. You forgot there's two kinds of people in the world. Close up them books, them bug books and French books. Get out, mingle, meet people. Soak up some brew. You know what? The next time Norma—that's this broad's name with the racing bike —the next time she comes here, *you* take the red racer and *you* go out in the woods with her. I won't mind. And I don't think she will, either. Not *too* much."

But Ferd said no. "I never want to touch the red racer again. I'm afraid of it."

At this, Oscar pulled him to his feet, dragged him protestingly out to the back and forced him to get on the French machine. "Only way to conquer your fear of it!"

Ferd started off, white-faced, wobbling. And in a moment was on the ground, rolling and thrashing, screaming.

Oscar pulled him away from the machine.

"It threw me!" Ferd yelled. "It tried to kill me! Look—blood!"

His partner said it was a bump that threw him—it was his own fear. The blood? A broken spoke. Grazed his cheek. And he insisted Ferd get on the bicycle again to conquer his fear.

But Ferd had grown hysterical. He shouted that no man was safe—that mankind had to be warned. It took Oscar a long time to pacify him and to get him to go home and into bed.

He didn't tell all this to Mr. Whatney, of course. He merely said that his partner had gotten fed up with the bicycle business.

"It don't pay to worry and try to change the world," he pointed out. "I always say take things the way they are. If you can't lick 'em, join 'em."

Mr. Whatney said that was his philosophy, exactly. He asked how things were, since.

"Well . . . not *too* bad. I'm engaged, you know. Name's Norma. Crazy about bicycles. Everything considered, things aren't bad at all. More work, yes, but I can do things all my own way, so . . ."

Mr. Whatney nodded. He glanced around the shop. "I see they're still making drop-frame bikes," he said, "though, with so many women wearing slacks, I wonder they bother."

Oscar said, "Well, I dunno. I kinda like it that way. Ever stop to think that bicycles are like people? I mean, of all the machines in the world, only bikes come male and female."

Mr. Whatney gave a little giggle, said that was *right,* he had never thought of it like that before. Then Oscar asked if Mr. Whatney had anything in particular in mind—not that he wasn't always welcome.

"Well, I wanted to look over what you've got. My boy's birthday is coming up . . ."

Oscar nodded sagely. "Now here's a job," he said, "which you can't get it in any other place but here. Specialty of the house. Combines the best features of the French racer and the American standard, but it's made right here, and it comes in three models—junior, intermediate and regular. Beautiful, ain't it?"

Mr. Whatney observed that, say, that might be just the ticket. "By the way," he asked, "what's become of the French racer, the red one, used to be here?"

Oscar's face twitched. Then it grew bland and innocent and he leaned over and nudged his customer. "Oh, *that* one. Old Frenchy? Why, I put *him* out to stud!"

And they laughed and they laughed, and after they told a few more stories they concluded the sale, and they had a few beers and they laughed some more. And then they said what a shame it was about poor Ferd, poor old Ferd, who had been found in his own closet with an unraveled coat hanger coiled tightly around his neck.

JAMES BLISH

Common Time

Although not as common as tales of space travel, stories of time travel have a long and distinguished history in modern science fiction. They include attempts to alter history by influencing historical events, adventures that take place in a future reached by a time machine, encounters with one's own ancestors and many other variations. But few have ever equalled this brilliant and mystical treatment of time inverted.

> *. . . the days went slowly round and round,*
> *endless and uneventful as cycles in space.*
> *Time, and time-pieces! How many centuries did*
> *my hammock tell, as pendulum-like it swung*
> *to the ship's dull roll, and ticked the hours*
> *and ages.*—HERMAN MELVILLE, in *Mardi*

Don't move.

It was the first thought that came into Garrard's mind when he awoke, and perhaps it saved his life. He lay where he was, strapped against the padding, listening to the round hum of the engines. That in itself was wrong; he should be unable to hear the overdrive at all.

He thought to himself: *Has it begun already?*

Otherwise everything seemed normal. The DFC-3 had crossed over into interstellar velocity, and he was still alive, and the ship was still functioning. The ship should at this moment be traveling at 22.4 times the speed of light —a neat 4,157,000 miles per second.

Somehow Garrard did not doubt that it was. On both previous tries, the ships had whiffed away toward Alpha Centauri at the proper moment when the overdrive should have cut in; and the split second of residual image after they had vanished, subjected to spectroscopy, showed a Doppler shift which tallied with the acceleration predicted for that moment by Haertel.

The trouble was not that Brown and Cellini hadn't gotten away in good order. It was simply that neither of them had ever been heard from again.

Very slowly, he opened his eyes. His eyelids felt terrifically heavy. As far as he could judge from the pressure of the couch against his skin, the gravity was normal; nevertheless, moving his eyelids seemed almost an impossible job.

After long concentration, he got them fully open. The instrument chassis was directly before him, extended over his diaphragm on its elbow joint. Still without moving anything but his eyes—and those only with the utmost patience—he checked each of the meters. Velocity: 22.4 c. Operating temperature: normal. Ship temperature: 37°C. Air pressure: 778 mm. Fuel: No. 1 tank full, No. 2 tank full, No. 3 tank full, No. 4 tank nine-tenths full. Gravity: 1 g. Calendar: stopped.

He looked at it closely, though his eyes seemed to focus very slowly, too. It was, of course, something more than a calendar—it was an all-purpose clock, designed to show him the passage of seconds, as well as of the ten months his trip was supposed to take to the double star. But there was no doubt about it: the second hand was motionless.

That was the second abnormality. Garrard felt an impulse to get up and see if he could start the clock again. Perhaps the trouble had been temporary and safely in the past. Immediately there sounded in his head the injunction he had drilled into himself for a full month before the trip had begun:

Don't move!

Don't move until you know the situation as far as it can be known without moving. Whatever it was that had snatched Brown and Cellini irretrievably beyond human ken was potent and totally beyond anticipation. They had both been excellent men, intelligent, resourceful, trained to the point of diminishing returns and not a micron beyond that point—the best men in the project. Preparations for every knowable kind of trouble had been built into their ships, as they had been built into the DFC-3. Therefore, if there was something wrong nevertheless, it would be something that might strike from some commonplace quarter—and strike only once.

He listened to the humming. It was even and placid and not very loud, but it disturbed him deeply. The overdrive was supposed to be inaudible, and the tapes from the first unmanned test vehicles had recorded no such hum. The noise did not appear to interfere with the overdrive's operation or to indicate any failure in it. It was just an irrelevancy for which he could find no reason.

But the reason existed. Garrard did not intend to do so much as draw another breath until he found out what it was.

Incredibly, he realized for the first time that he had not in fact drawn one single breath since he had first come to. Though he felt not the slightest discomfort, the discovery called up so overwhelming a flash of panic that he very nearly sat bolt upright on the couch. Luckily—or so it seemed, after the panic had begun to ebb—the curious lethargy which had affected his eyelids appeared to involve his whole body, for the impulse was gone before he could summon the energy to answer it. And the panic, poignant though it had been for an instant, turned out to be wholly intellectual. In a moment, he was observing that his failure to breathe in no way discommoded him as far as he could tell—it was just there, waiting to be explained. . . .

Or to kill him. But it hadn't, yet.

Engines humming; eyelids heavy; breathing absent; calendar stopped. The four facts added up to nothing. The temptation to move something—even if it were only a big toe—was strong, but Garrard fought it back. He had been awake only a short while—half an hour at most—and already had noticed four abnormalities. There were bound to be more, anomalies more subtle than these four; but available to close examination before he had to move. Nor was there anything in particular that he had to do, aside from caring for his own wants; the project, on the chance that Brown's and Cellini's failure to return had resulted from some tampering with the overdrive, had made everything in the DFC-3 subject only to the computer. In a very real sense, Garrard was just along for the ride. Only when the overdrive was off could he adjust. . . .

Pock.

It was a soft, low-pitched noise, rather like a cork coming out of a wine bottle. It seemed to have come just from the right of the control chassis. He halted a sudden jerk of his head on the cushions toward it with a flat fiat of will. Slowly, he moved his eyes in that direction.

He could see nothing that might have caused the sound. The ship's temperature dial showed no change, which ruled out a heat noise from differential contraction or expansion—the only possible explanation he could bring to mind.

He closed his eyes—a process which turned out to be just as difficult as opening them had been—and tried to visualize what the calendar had looked like when he had first come out of anesthesia. After he got a clear and—he was almost sure—accurate picture, Garrard opened his eyes again.

The sound had been the calendar, advancing one second. It was now motionless again, apparently stopped.

He did not know how long it took the second hand to make that jump, normally; the question had never come up. Certainly the jump, when it came at the end of each second, had been too fast for the eye to follow.

Belatedly, he realized what all this cogitation was costing him in terms of essential information. The calendar had moved. Above all and before anything else, he *must* know exactly how long it took it to move again. . . .

He began to count, allowing an arbitrary five seconds lost. *One-and-a-six, one-and-a-seven, one-and-an-eight* . . .

Garrard had gotten only that far when he found himself plunged into hell.

First, and utterly without reason, a sickening fear flooded swiftly through his veins, becoming more and more intense. His bowels began to knot with infinite slowness. His whole body became a field of small, slow pulses—not so much shaking him as putting his limbs into contrary joggling motions and making his skin ripple gently under his clothing. Against the hum another sound became audible, a nearly subsonic thunder which seemed to be inside his head. Still the fear mounted, and with it came the pain, and the tenesmus —a boardlike stiffening of his muscles, particularly across his abdomen and his shoulders, but affecting his forearms almost as grievously. He felt himself beginning, very gradually, to double at the middle, a motion about which he could do precisely nothing—a terrifying kind of dynamic paralysis. . . .

It lasted for hours. At the height of it, Garrard's mind, even his very personality, was washed out utterly; he was only a vessel of horror. When some few trickles of reason began to return over that burning desert of reasonless emotion, he found that he was sitting up on the cushions, and that with one arm he had thrust the control chassis back on its elbow so that it no longer jutted over his body. His clothing was wet with perspiration, which stubbornly refused to evaporate or to cool him. And his lungs ached a little, although he could still detect no breathing.

What under God had happened? Was it this that had killed Brown and Cellini? For it would kill Garrard, too—of that he was sure—if it happened often. It would kill him even if it happened only twice more, if the next two such things followed the first one closely. At the very best it would make a slobbering idiot of him; and though the computer might bring Garrard and the ship back to Earth, it would not be able to tell the project about his tornado of senseless fear.

The calendar said that the eternity in hell had taken three seconds. As he looked at it in academic indignation, it said *pock* and condescended to make the total seizure four seconds long. With grim determination, Garrard began to count again.

He took care to establish the counting as an absolutely even, automatic process which would not stop at the back of his mind no matter what other problem he tackled along with it, or what emotional typhoons should interrupt him. Really compulsive counting cannot be stopped by anything—not the transports of love nor the agonies of empires. Garrard knew the dangers in deliberately setting up such a mechanism in his mind, but he also knew how desperately he needed to time that clock tick. He was beginning to understand what had happened to him—but he needed exact measurement before he could put that understanding to use.

Of course there had been plenty of speculation on the possible effect of the overdrive on the subjective time of the pilot, but none of it had come to much. At any speed below the velocity of light, subjective and objective time were exactly the same as far as the pilot was concerned. For an observer on Earth, time aboard the ship would appear to be vastly slowed at near-light speeds; but for the pilot himself there would be no apparent change.

Since flight beyond the speed of light was impossible—although for slightly differing reasons—by both the current theories of relativity, neither theory had offered any clue as to what would happen on board a translight ship. They would not allow that any such ship could even exist. The Haertel transformation, on which, in effect, the DFC-3 flew, was nonrelativistic: it showed that the apparent elapsed time of a translight journey should be identical in ship time and in the time of observers at both ends of the trip.

But since ship and pilot were part of the same system, both covered by the same expression in Haertel's equation, it had never occurred to anyone that the pilot and the ship might keep different times. The notion was ridiculous.

One-and-a-seven-hundred one, one-and-a-seven-hundred two, one-and-a-seven-hundred three, one-and-a-seven-hundred four . . .

The ship was keeping ship time, which was identical with observer time. It would arrive at the Alpha Centauri system in ten months. But the pilot was keeping Garrard time, and it was beginning to look as though he wasn't going to arrive at all.

It was impossible, but there it was. Something—almost certainly an unsuspected physiological side effect of the overdrive field on human metabolism, an effect which naturally could not have been detected in the preliminary, robot-piloted tests of the overdrive—had speeded up Garrard's subjective apprehension of time and had done a thorough job of it.

The second hand began a slow, preliminary quivering as the calendar's innards began to apply power to it. *Seventy-hundred-forty-one, seventy-hundred-forty-two, seventy-hundred-forty-three . . .*

At the count of 7,058 the second hand began the jump to the next graduation. It took it several apparent minutes to get across the tiny distance and several more to come completely to rest. Later still, the sound came to him:

Pock.

In a fever of thought, but without any real physical agitation, his mind began to manipulate the figures. Since it took him longer to count an individual number as the number became larger, the interval between the two calendar ticks probably was closer to 7,200 seconds than to 7,058. Figuring backward brought him quickly to the equivalence he wanted: one second in ship time was two hours in Garrard time.

Had he really been counting for what was, for him, two whole hours? There seemed to be no doubt about it. It looked like a long trip ahead.

Just how long it was going to be struck him with stunning force. Time had been slowed for him by a factor of 7,200. He would get to Alpha Centauri in just 72,000 months.

Which was . . .

Six thousand years!

II

Garrard sat motionless for a long time after that, the Nessus shirt of warm sweat swathing him persistently, refusing even to cool. There was, after all, no hurry.

Six thousand years. There would be food and water and air for all that time, or for sixty or six hundred thousand years; the ship would synthesize his needs, as a matter of course, for as long as the fuel lasted, and the fuel bred itself. Even if Garrard ate a meal every three seconds of objective, or ship, time (which, he realized suddenly, he wouldn't be able to do, for it took the ship several seconds of objective time to prepare and serve up a meal once it was ordered; he'd be lucky if he ate once a day, Garrard time), there would be no reason to fear any shortage of supplies. That had been one of the earliest of the possibilities for disaster that the project engineers had ruled out in the design of the DFC-3.

But nobody had thought to provide a mechanism which would indefinitely refurbish Garrard. After six thousand years, there would be nothing left of him but a faint film of dust on the DFC-3's dully gleaming horizontal surfaces. His corpse might outlast him awhile, since the ship itself was sterile —but eventually he would be consumed by the bacteria which he carried in his own digestive tract. He needed those bacteria to synthesize part of his B-vitamin needs while he lived, but they would consume him without compunction once he had ceased to be as complicated and delicately balanced a thing as a pilot—or as any other kind of life.

Garrard was, in short, to die before the DFC-3 had gotten fairly away from Sol; and when, after 12,000 apparent years, the DFC-3 returned to Earth, not even his mummy would be still aboard.

The chill that went through him at that seemed almost unrelated to the way he thought he felt about the discovery; it lasted an enormously long time, and insofar as he could characterize it at all, it seemed to be a chill of urgency and excitement—not at all the kind of chill he should be feeling at a virtual death sentence. Luckily it was not as intolerably violent as the last such emotional convulsion; and when it was over, two clock ticks later, it left behind a residuum of doubt.

Suppose that this effect of time-stretching was only mental? The rest of his bodily processes might still be keeping ship time; Garrard had no immediate reason to believe otherwise. If so, he would be able to move about only on ship time, too; it would take many apparent months to complete the simplest task.

But he would live, if that were the case. His mind would arrive at Alpha Centauri six thousand years older, and perhaps madder, than his body, but he would live.

If, on the other hand, his bodily movements were going to be as fast as his mental processes, he would have to be enormously careful. He would have to move slowly and exert as little force as possible. The normal human hand movement, in such a task as lifting a pencil, took the pencil from a state of rest to another state of rest by imparting to it an acceleration of about two feet per second—and, of course, decelerated it by the same amount. If Garrard were to attempt to impart to a two-pound weight, which was keeping ship time, an acceleration of 14,440 ft/sec^2 in his time, he'd have to exert a force of 900 pounds on it.

The point was not that it couldn't be done—but that it would take as much effort as pushing a stalled jeep. He'd never be able to lift that pencil with his forearm muscles alone; he'd have to put his back into the task.

And the human body wasn't engineered to maintain stresses of that magnitude indefinitely. Not even the most powerful professional weight lifter is forced to show his prowess throughout every minute of every day.

Pock.

That was the calendar again; another second had gone by. Or another two hours. It had certainly seemed longer than a second, but less than two hours, too. Evidently subjective time was an intensively recomplicated measure. Even in this world of microtime—in which Garrard's mind, at least, seemed to be operating—he could make the lapses between calendar ticks seem a little shorter by becoming actively interested in some problem or other. That would help during the waking hours, but it would help only if the rest of his body was *not* keeping the same time as his mind. If it was not, then he would lead an incredibly active, but perhaps not intolerable, mental life during the many centuries of his awake time and would be mercifully asleep for nearly as long.

Both problems—that of how much force he could exert with his body and how long he could hope to be asleep in his mind—emerged simultaneously into the forefront of his consciousness while he still sat inertly on the hammock, their terms still much muddled together. After the single tick of the calendar, the ship—or the part of it that Garrard could see from here—settled back into complete rigidity. The sound of the engines, too, did not seem to vary in frequency or amplitude, at least as far as his ears could tell. He was still not breathing. Nothing moved, nothing changed.

It was the fact that he could still detect no motion of his diaphragm or his rib cage that decided him at last. His body had to be keeping ship time, otherwise he would have blacked out from oxygen starvation long before now. That assumption explained, too, those two incredibly prolonged, seemingly sourceless saturnalias of emotion through which he had suffered: they had been nothing more or less than the response of his endocrine glands to the purely intellectual reactions he had experienced earlier. He had discovered that he was not breathing, had felt a flash of panic and had tried to sit up. Long after his mind had forgotten those two impulses, they had inched their way from his brain down his nerves to the glands and muscles involved, and actual, *physical* panic had supervened. When that was over, he actually *was* sitting up, though the flood of adrenalin had prevented his noticing the motion as he had made it. The later chill—less violent and apparently associated with the discovery that he might die long before the trip was completed—actually had been his body's response to a much earlier mental command; the abstract fever of interest he had felt while computing the time differential had been responsible for it.

Obviously, he was going to have to be very careful with apparently cold and intellectual impulses of any kind—or he would pay for them later with a prolonged and agonizing glandular reaction. Nevertheless, the discovery gave him considerable satisfaction, and Garrard allowed it free play; it certainly could not hurt him to feel pleased for a few hours, and the glandular pleasure might even prove helpful if it caught him at a moment of mental depression. Six thousand years, after all, provided a considerable number of opportunities for feeling down in the mouth; so it would be best to encourage all pleasure moments, and let the after-reaction last as long as it might. It would be the instants of panic, of fear, of gloom, which he would have to regulate sternly the moment they came into his mind; it would be those which would otherwise plunge him into four, five, six, perhaps even ten Garrard hours of emotional inferno.

Pock.

There now, that was very good: there had been two Garrard hours which he had passed with virtually no difficulty of any kind and without being especially conscious of their passage. If he could really settle down and become used to this kind of scheduling, the trip might not be as bad as he had at first feared. Sleep would take immense bites out of it; and during the waking periods he could put in one hell of a lot of creative thinking. During a single day of ship time, Garrard could get in more thinking than any philosopher of Earth could have managed during an entire lifetime. Garrard could, if he disciplined himself sufficiently, devote his mind for a century to running down the consequences of a single thought, down to the last detail and still have millennia left to go on to the next thought. What panoplies of pure reason could he not have assembled by the time 6,000 years had gone by? With sufficient concentration, he might come up with the solution to the problem of evil between breakfast and dinner of a single ship's day, and in a ship's month might put his finger on the first cause!

Pock.

Not that Garrard was sanguine enough to expect that he would remain logical or even sane throughout the trip. The vista was still grim in much of its detail. But the opportunities, too, were there. He felt a momentary regret that it hadn't been Haertel, rather than himself, who had been given such an opportunity . . .

Pock.

. . . for the old man could certainly have made better use of it than Garrard could. The situation demanded someone trained in the highest rigors of mathematics to be put to the best conceivable use. Still and all Garrard began to feel . . .

Pock.

. . . that he would give a good account of himself, and it tickled him to realize that (as long as he held on to his essential sanity) he would return . . .

Pock.

. . . to Earth after ten Earth months with knowledge centuries advanced beyond anything . . .

Pock.

. . . that Haertel knew or that anyone could know . . .

Pock.

. . . who had to work within a normal lifetime. *Pck.* The whole prospect tickled him. *Pck.* Even the clock tick seemed more cheerful. *Pck.* He felt fairly safe now *Pck* in disregarding his drilled-in command *Pck* against moving *Pck,* since in any *Pck* event the *Pck* had already *Pck* moved *Pck* without *Pck* being *Pck* harmed *Pck Pck Pck Pck Pck pckpckpckpckpckpckpck.* . . .

He yawned, stretched, and got up. It wouldn't do to be too pleased, after all. There were certainly many problems that still needed coping with, such as how to keep the impulse toward getting a ship-time task performed going, while his higher centers were following the ramifications of some purely philosophical point. And besides . . .

And besides, he had just moved.

More than that, he had just performed a complicated maneuver with his body *in normal time!*

Before Garrard looked at the calendar itself, the message it had been ticking away at him had penetrated. While he had been enjoying the protracted, glandular backwash of his earlier feeling of satisfaction, he had failed to notice, at least consciously, that the calendar was accelerating.

Good-by, vast ethical systems which would dwarf the Greeks. Good-by, calculuses aeons advanced beyond the spinor calculus of Dirac. Good-by, cosmologies by Garrard which would allot the Almighty a job as third-assistant waterboy in an n-dimensional backfield.

Good-by, also, to a project he had once tried to undertake in college—to describe and count the positions of love, of which, according to under-the-counter myth, there were supposed to be at least forty-eight. Garrard had never been able to carry his tally beyond twenty, and he had just lost what was probably his last opportunity to try again.

The microtime in which he had been living had worn off, only a few objective minutes after the ship had gone into overdrive and he had come out of the anesthetic. The long intellectual agony, with its glandular counterpoint, had come to nothing. Garrard was now keeping ship time.

Garrard sat back down on the hammock, uncertain whether to be bitter or relieved. Neither emotion satisfied him in the end; he simply felt unsatisfied. Microtime had been bad enough while it lasted; but now it was gone, and everything seemed normal. How could so transient a thing have killed Brown and Cellini? They were stable men, more stable, by his own private estimation, than Garrard himself. Yet he had come through it. Was there more to it than this?

And if there was—what, conceivably, could it be?

There was no answer. At his elbow, on the control chassis which he had thrust aside during that first moment of infinitely protracted panic, the calendar continued to tick. The engine noise was gone. His breath came and went in natural rhythm. He felt light and strong. The ship was quiet, calm, unchanging.

The calendar ticked, faster and faster. It reached and passed the first hour, ship time, of flight in overdrive.

Pock.

Garrard looked up in surprise. The familiar noise, this time, had been the hour hand jumping one unit. The minute hand was already sweeping past the past half-hour. The second hand was whirling like a propeller—and while he watched it, it speeded up to complete invisibility. . . .

Pock.

Another hour. The half-hour already passed. *Pock.* Another hour. *Pock.* Another, *Pock. Pock. Pock, Pock, Pock, Pock, pck-pck-pck-pck-pckpckpckpck.* . . .

The hands of the calendar swirled toward invisibility as time ran away with Garrard. Yet the ship did not change. It stayed there, rigid, inviolate, invulnerable. When the date tumblers reached a speed at which Garrard could no longer read them, he discovered that once more he could not move—and that, although his whole body seemed to be aflutter like that of a hummingbird, nothing coherent was coming to him through his senses. The room was dimming, becoming redder; or no, it was . . .

But he never saw the end of the process, never was allowed to look from the pinnacle of macrotime toward which the Haertel overdrive was taking him.

Pseudo-death took him first.

III

That Garrard did not die completely, and within a comparatively short time after the DFC-3 had gone into overdrive, was due to the purest of accidents; but Garrard did not know that. In fact, he knew nothing at all for an indefinite period, sitting rigid and staring, his metabolism slowed down to next to nothing, his mind almost utterly inactive. From time to time, a single wave of low-level metabolic activity passed through him—what an electrician might have termed a "maintenance turnover"—in response to the urgings of some occult survival urge; but these were of so basic a nature as to reach his consciousness not at all. This was the pseudo-death.

When the observer actually arrived, however, Garrard woke. He could make very little sense out of what he saw or felt even now; but one fact was clear: the overdrive was off—and with it the crazy alterations in time rates—and there was strong light coming through one of the ports. The first leg of the trip was over. It had been these two changes in his environment which had restored him to life.

The thing (or things) which had restored him to consciousness, however, was—it was what? It made no sense. It was a construction, a rather fragile one, which completely surrounded his hammock. No, it wasn't a construction, but evidently something alive—a living being, organized horizontally, that had arranged itself in a circle about him. No, it was a number of beings. Or a combination of all of these things.

How it had gotten into the ship was a mystery, but there it was. Or there they were.

"How do you hear?" the creature said abruptly. Its voice, or their voices, came at equal volume from every point in the circle, but not from any particular point in it. Garrard could think of no reason why that should be unusual.

"I . . ." he said. "Or we—we hear with our ears. Here."

His answer, with its unintentionally long chain of open vowel sounds, rang ridiculously. He wondered why he was speaking such an odd language.

"We-they wooed to pitch you-yours thiswise," the creature said. With a thump, a book from the DFC-3's ample library fell to the deck beside the hammock. "We wooed there and there and there for a many. You are the being-Garrard. We-they are the clinesterton beademung, with all of love."

"With all of love," Garrard echoed. The beademung's use of the language they both were speaking was odd; but again Garrard could find no logical reason why the beademung's usage should be considered wrong.

"Are—are you-they from Alpha Centauri?" he said hesitantly.

"Yes, we hear the twin radioceles, that show there beyond the gift-orifices. We-they pitched that the being-Garrard with most adoration these twins and had mind to them, soft and loud alike. How do you hear?"

This time the being-Garrard understood the question. "I hear Earth," he said. "But that is very soft, and does not show."

"Yes," said the beademung. "It is a harmony, not a first, as ours. The All-Devouring listens to lovers there, not on the radioceles. Let me-mine pitch you-yours so to have mind of the rodalent beademung and other brothers and lovers, along the channel which is fragrant to the being-Garrard."

Garrard found that he understood the speech without difficulty. The thought occurred to him that to understand a language on its own terms—

without having to put it back into English in one's own mind—is an ability that is won only with difficulty and long practice. Yet, instantly his mind said, "But it *is* English," which of course it was. The offer the clinesterton beademung had just made was enormously hearted, and he in turn was much minded and of love, to his own delighting as well as to the beademungen; that almost went without saying.

There were many matings of ships after that, and the being-Garrard pitched the harmonies of the beademungen, leaving his ship with the many gift-orifices in harmonic for the All-Devouring to love, while the beademungen made show of they-theirs.

He tried, also, to tell how he was out of love with the overdrive, which wooed only spaces and times, and made featurelings. The rodalent beademung wooed the overdrive, but it did not pitch he-them.

Then the being-Garrard knew that all the time was devoured and he must hear Earth again.

"I pitch you-them to fullest love," he told the beademungen, "I shall adore the radioceles of Alpha and Proxima Centauri, 'on Earth as it is in heaven.' Now the overdrive my-other must woo and win me and make me adore a featureling much like silence."

"But you will be pitched again," the clinesterton beademung said. "After you have adored Earth. You are much loved by Time, the All-Devouring. We-they shall wait for this othering."

Privately Garrard did not faith as much, but he said, "Yes, we-they will make a new wooing of the beademungen at some other radiant. With all of love."

On this the beademungen made and pitched adorations, and in the midst the overdrive cut in. The ship with the many gift-orifices and the being-Garrard him-other saw the twin radioceles sundered away.

Then, once more, came the pseudo-death.

IV

When the small candle lit in the endless cavern of Garrard's pseudo-dead mind, the DFC-3 was well inside the orbit of Uranus. Since the sun was still very small and distant, it made no spectacular display through the nearby port, and nothing called him from the postdeath sleep for nearly two days.

The computers waited patiently for him. They were no longer immune to his control; he could now tool the ship back to Earth himself if he so desired. But the computers were also designed to take into account the fact that he might be truly dead by the time the DFC-3 got back. After giving him a solid week, during which time he did nothing but sleep, they took over again. Radio signals began to go out, tuned to a special channel.

An hour later, a very weak signal came back. It was only a directional signal, and it made no sound inside the DFC-3—but it was sufficient to put the big ship in motion again.

It was that which woke Garrard. His conscious mind was still glazed over with the icy spume of the pseudo-death; and as far as he could see the interior of the cabin had not changed one whit, except for the book on the deck . . .

The book. The clinesterton beademung had dropped it there. But what under God was a clinesterton beademung? And what was he, Garrard, crying about? It didn't make sense. He remembered dimly some kind of experience out there by the Centauri twins . . .

. . . *the twin radioceles* . . .

There was another one of those words. It seemed to have Greek roots, but he knew no Greek—and besides, why would Centaurians speak Greek?

He leaned forward and actuated the switch which would roll the shutter off the front port, actually a telescope with a translucent viewing screen. It showed a few stars, and a faint nimbus off on one edge which might be the sun. At about one o'clock on the screen was a planet about the size of a pea which had tiny projections, like teacup handles, on each side. The DFC-3 hadn't passed Saturn on its way out; at that time it had been on the other side of the sun from the route the starship had had to follow. But the planet was certainly difficult to mistake.

Garrard was on his way home—and he was still alive and sane. Or was he still sane? These fantasies about Centaurians—which still seemed to have such a profound emotional effect upon him—did not argue very well for the stability of his mind.

But they were fading rapidly. When he discovered, clutching at the handiest fragments of the "memories," that the plural of *beademung* was *beademungen,* he stopped taking the problem seriously. Obviously a race of Centaurians who spoke Greek wouldn't also be forming weak German plurals. The whole business had obviously been thrown up by his unconscious.

But what *had* he found by the Centaurus stars?

There was no answer to that question but that incomprehensible garble about love, the All-Devouring and beademungen. Possibly, he had never seen the Centaurus stars at all, but had been lying here, cold as a mackerel, for the entire twenty months.

Or had it been 12,000 years? After the tricks the overdrive had played with time, there was no way to tell what the objective date actually was. Frantically Garrard put the telescope into action. Where was the Earth? After 12,000 years . . .

The Earth was there. Which, he realized swiftly, proved nothing. The Earth had lasted for many millions of years; 12,000 years was nothing to a planet. The moon was there, too; both were plainly visible, on the far side of the sun—but not too far to pick them out clearly, with the telescope at highest power. Garrard could even see a clear sun highlight on the Atlantic Ocean, not far east of Greenland; evidently the computers were bringing the DFC-3 in on the Earth from about twenty-three degrees north of the plane of the ecliptic.

The moon, too, had not changed. He could even see on its face the huge splash of white, mimicking the sun highlight on Earth's ocean, which was the magnesium hydroxide landing beacon, which had been dusted over the Mare Vaporum in the earliest days of space flight, with a dark spot on its southern edge which could only be the crater Monilius.

But that again proved nothing. The moon never changed. A film of dust laid down by modern man on its face would last for millennia—what, after all, existed on the moon to blow it away? The Mare Vaporum beacon covered more than 4,000 square miles; age would not dim it, nor could man himself undo it—either accidentally or on purpose—in anything under a century. When you dust an area that large on a world without atmosphere, it stays dusted.

He checked the stars against his charts. They hadn't moved; why should they have, in only 12,000 years? The pointer stars in the Dipper still pointed to Polaris. Draco, like a fantastic bit of tape, wound between the two Bears, and Cepheus and Cassiopeia, as it always had done. These constellations told him only that it was spring in the northern hemisphere of Earth.

But spring of what year?

Then, suddenly, it occurred to Garrard that he had a method of finding the answer. The moon causes tides in the Earth, and action and reaction are always equal and opposite. The moon cannot move things on Earth without itself being affected—and that effect shows up in the moon's angular momentum. The moon's distance from the Earth increases steadily by 0.6 inch every year. At the end of 12,000 years, it should be 600 feet farther away from the Earth.

Was it possible to measure? Garrard doubted it, but he got out his ephemeris and his dividers anyhow and took pictures. While he worked, the Earth grew nearer. By the time he had finished his first calculation—which was indecisive because it allowed a margin of error greater than the distances he was trying to check—Earth and moon were close enough in the telescope to permit much more accurate measurements.

Which were, he realized wryly, quite unnecessary. The computer had brought the DFC-3 back, not to an observed sun or planet, but simply to a calculated point. That Earth and moon would not be near that point when the DFC-3 returned was not an assumption that the computer could make. That the Earth was visible from here was already good and sufficient proof that no more time had elapsed than had been calculated for from the beginning.

This was hardly new to Garrard; it had simply been retired to the back of his mind. Actually he had been doing all this figuring for one reason and one reason only: because deep in his brain, set to work by himself, there was a mechanism that demanded counting. Long ago, while he was still trying to time the ship's calendar, he had initiated compulsive counting—and it appeared that he had been counting ever since. That had been one of the known dangers of deliberately starting such a mental mechanism; and now it was bearing fruit in these perfectly useless astronomical exercises.

The insight was healing. He finished the figures roughly, and that unheard moron deep inside his brain stopped counting at last. It had been pawing its abacus for twenty months now, and Garrard imagined that it was as glad to be retired as he was to feel it go.

His radio squawked and said anxiously, "DFC-3, DFC-3. Garrard, do you hear me? Are you still alive? Everybody's going wild down here. Garrard, if you hear me, call us!"

It was Haertel's voice. Garrard closed the dividers so convulsively that one of the points nipped into the heel of his hand. "Haertel, I'm here. DFC-3 to the project. This is Garrard." And then, without knowing quite why, he added: "With all of love."

Haertel, after all the hoopla was over, was more than interested in the time effects. "It certainly enlarges the manifold in which I was working," he said. "But I think we can account for it in the transformation. Perhaps even factor it out, which would eliminate it as far as the pilot is concerned. We'll see, anyhow."

Garrard swirled his highball reflectively. In Haertel's cramped old office in the project's administration shack, he felt both strange and as old, as compressed, constricted. He said, "I don't think I'd do that, Adolph. I think it saved my life."

"How?"

"I told you that I seemed to die after a while. Since I got home, I've been reading; and I've discovered that the psychologists take far less stock in the individuality of the human psyche than you and I do. You and I are physical scientists, so we think about the world as being all outside our skins—something which is to be observed, but which doesn't alter the essential *1*. But evidently, that old solipsistic position isn't quite true. Our very personalities, really, depend in large part upon *all* the things in our environment, large and small, that exist outside our skins. If by some means you could cut a human being off from every sense impression that comes to him from outside, he would cease to exist as a personality within two or three minutes. Probably he would die."

"Unquote: Harry Stack Sullivan," Haertel said, dryly. "So?"

"So," Garrard said, "think of what a monotonous environment the inside of a spaceship is. It's perfectly rigid, still, unchanging, lifeless. In ordinary interplanetary flight, in such an environment, even the most hardened spaceman may go off his rocker now and then. You know the typical spaceman's psychosis as well as I do, I suppose. The man's personality goes rigid, just like his surroundings. Usually he recovers as soon as he makes port and makes contact with a more or less normal world again.

"But in the DFC-3, I was cut off from the world around me much more severely. I couldn't look outside the ports—I was in overdrive, and there was nothing to see. I couldn't communicate with home because I was going faster than light. And then I found I couldn't move either, for an enormous long while; and that even the instruments that are in constant change for the usual spaceman wouldn't be in motion for me. Even those were fixed.

"After the time rate began to pick up, I found myself in an even more impossible box. The instruments moved, all right, but then they moved too *fast* for me to read them. The whole situation was now utterly rigid—and, in effect, I died. I froze as solid as the ship around me and stayed that way as long as the overdrive was on."

"By that showing," Haertel said dryly, "the time effects were hardly your friends."

"But they were, Adolph. Look. Your engines act on subjective time; they keep it varying along continuous curves—from far-too-slow to far-too-fast—and, I suppose, back down again. Now, this is a *situation of continuous change*. It wasn't marked enough, in the long run, to keep me out of pseudo-death; but it was sufficient to protect me from being obliterated altogether, which I think is what happened to Brown and Cellini. Those men knew that they could shut down the overdrive if they could just get to it, and they killed themselves trying. But I knew that I just had to sit and take it—and, by my great good luck, your sine-curve time variation made it possible for me to survive."

"Ah, ah," Haertel said. "A point worth considering—though I doubt that it will make interstellar travel very popular!"

He dropped back into silence, his thin mouth pursed. Garrard took a grateful pull at his drink.

At last Haertel said, "Why are you in trouble over these Centaurians? It seems to me that you have done a good job. It was nothing that you were a hero—any fool can be brave—but I see also that you *thought,* where Brown and Cellini evidently only reacted. Is there some secret about what you found when you reached those two stars?"

Garrard said, "Yes, there is. But I've already told you what it is. When I came out of the pseudo-death, I was just a sort of plastic palimpsest upon which anybody could have made a mark. My own environment, my ordinary Earth environment, was a hell of a long way off. My present surroundings were nearly as rigid as they had ever been. When I met the Centaurians—if I did, and I'm not at all sure of that—*they* became the most important thing in my world, and my personality changed to accommodate and understand them. That was a change about which I couldn't do a thing.

"Possibly I did understand them. But the man who understood them wasn't the same man you're talking to now, Adolph. Now that I'm back on Earth, I don't understand that man. He even spoke English in a way that's gibberish to me. If I can't understand myself during that period—and I can't; I don't even believe that that man was the Garrard I know—what hope have I of telling you or the project about the Centaurians? They found me in a controlled environment, and they altered me by entering it. Now that they're gone, nothing comes through; I don't even understand why I think they spoke English!"

"Did they have a name for themselves?"

"Sure," Garrard said. "They were the beademungen."

"What did they look like?"

"I never saw them."

Haertel leaned forward. "Then . . ."

"I heard them. I think." Garrard shrugged and tasted his Scotch again. He was home, and on the whole he was pleased.

But in his malleable mind he heard someone say, *On Earth, as it is in heaven;* and then, in another voice, which might also have been his own (why had he thought "him-other"?), *It is later than you think.*

"Adolph," he said, "is this all there is to it? Or are we going to go on with it from here? How long will it take to make a better starship, a DFC-4?"

"Many years," Haertel said, smiling kindly. "Don't be anxious, Garrard. You've come back, which is more than the others managed to do, and nobody will ask you to go out again. I really think that it's hardly likely that we'll get another ship built during your lifetime; and even if we do, we'll be slow to launch it. We really have very little information about what kind of playground you found out there."

"I'll go," Garrard said. "I'm not afraid to go back—I'd like to go. Now that I know how the DFC-3 behaves, I could take it out again, bring you back proper maps, tapes, photos."

"Do you really think," Haertel said, his face suddenly serious, "that we could let the DFC-3 go out again? Garrard, we're going to take that ship apart practically molecule by molecule; that's preliminary to the building of any DFC-4. And no more can we let you go. I don't mean to be cruel, but has it occurred to you that this desire to go back may be the result of some kind of posthypnotic suggestion? If so, the more badly you want to go back, the more dangerous to us all you may be. We are going to have to examine you just as thoroughly as we do the ship. If these beademungen wanted you to come back, they must have had a reason—and we have to know that reason."

Garrard nodded, but he knew that Haertel could see the slight movement of his eyebrows and the wrinkles forming in his forehead, the contractions of the small muscles which stop the flow of tears only to make grief patent on the rest of the face.

"In short," he said, *"don't move."*

Haertel looked politely puzzled. Garrard, however, could say nothing more. He had returned to humanity's common time and would never leave it again.

Not even, for all his dimly remembered promise, with all there was left in him of love.

THEODORE STURGEON

When You Care, When You Love

One dictionary defines love variously as "an intense affectionate concern," as "a passionate attraction" and as "a zero score in tennis." It is all of these and much more. It is tenderness, lust, concern. It is something people feel for other people, for all people, for all living things, for certain inanimate things, even for some abstract concepts. Within the science fiction universe Theodore Sturgeon has been the leading expert on this important subject, examining love in almost all of its dimensions.

He was beautiful in her bed.

When you care, when you love, when you treasure someone, you can watch the beloved in sleep as you watch everything, anything else—laughter, lips to a cup, a look even away from you; a stride, sun a-struggle lost in a hair-lock, a jest or a gesture—even stillness, even sleep.

She leaned close, all but breathless, and watched his lashes. Now, lashes are thick sometimes, curled, russet; these were all these and glossy besides. Look closely—there where they curve lives light in tiny serried scimitars.

All so good, so very good, she let herself deliciously doubt its reality. She would let herself believe, in a moment, that this was real, was true, was here, had at last happened. All the things her life before had ever given her, all she had ever wanted, each by each had come to her purely for wanting. Delight there might be, pride, pleasure, even glory in the new possession of gift, privilege, object, experience: her ring, hat, toy, trip to Trinidad; yet, with possession there had always been (until now) the platter called *well, of course* on which these things were served her. For had she not wanted it? But this, now—*him,* now . . . greatest of all her wants, ever; first thing in all her life to transcend want itself and knowingly become need: this she had at last, at long (how long, now) long last, this she had now for good and all, for always, forever and never a touch of *well, of course.* He was her personal miracle, he in this bed now, warm and loving her. He was the reason and the reward of it all—her family and forebears, known by so few and felt by so many, and indeed, the whole history of mankind leading up to it, and all she herself had been and done and felt; and loving him, and losing him, and seeing him dead and bringing him back—it was all for this moment and because the moment had to be, he and this peak, this warmth in these sheets, this *now* of hers. He was all life and all life's beauty, beautiful in her bed; and now she could be sure, could believe it, believe . . .

"I do," she breathed. "I do."

"What do you do?" he asked her. He had not moved, and did not now.

"Devil, I thought you were asleep."

"Well, I was. But I had the feeling someone was looking."

"Not looking," she said softly. "Watching." She was watching the lashes still and did not see them stir, but between them now lay a shining sliver of the gray cool aluminum of his surprising eyes. In a moment he would look at her—just that—in a moment their eyes would meet and it would be as if nothing new had happened (for it would be the same metal missile which had first impaled her) and also as if everything, everything were happening again. Within her, passion boiled up like a fusion fireball, so beautiful, so huge . . .

. . . and like the most dreaded thing on earth, without pause the radiance changed, shifting from the hues of all the kinds of love to all the tones of terror and the colors of a cataclysm.

She cried his name. . . .

And the gray eyes opened wide in fear for her fears and in astonishment, and he bounded up laughing, and the curl of his laughing lips turned without pause to the pale writhing of agony, and they shrank apart, too far apart while the white teeth met and while between them he shouted his hurt. He fell on his side and doubled up, grunting, gasping in pain . . . grunting, gasping, wrapped away from her, even her, unreachable even by her.

She screamed. She screamed. She . . .

A Wyke biography is hard to come by. This has been true for four generations, and more true with each, for the more the Wyke holdings grew, the less visible have been the Wyke family, for so Cap'n Gamaliel Wyke willed it after his conscience conquered him. This (for he was a prudent man) did not happen until after his retirement from what was euphemistically called the molasses trade. His ship—later, his fleet—had carried fine New England rum, made from the molasses, to Europe, having brought molasses from the West Indies to New England. Of course a paying cargo was needed for the westward crossing, to close with a third leg this profitable triangle; and what better cargo than Africans for the West Indies, to harvest the cane and work in the mills which made the molasses?

Ultimately affluent and retired, he seemed content for a time to live among his peers, carrying his broadcloth coat and snowy linen as to the manor born, limiting his personal adornment to a massive golden ring and small square gold buckles at his knee. Soberly shoptalking molasses often, rum seldom, slaves never, he dwelt with a frightened wife and a silent son, until she died and something—perhaps loneliness—coupled his brain again to his sharp old eyes and made him look about him. He began to dislike the hypocrisy of man and was honest enough to dislike himself as well, and this was a new thing for the Cap'n; he could not deny it and he could not contain it, so he left the boy with the household staff and, taking only a manservant, went into the wilderness to search his soul.

The wilderness was Martha's Vineyard, and right through a bitter winter the old man crouched by the fire when the weather closed in and, muffled in four great gray shawls, paced the beaches when it was bright, his brass telescope under his arm and his grim canny thoughts doing mighty battle with his convictions. In the late spring he returned to Wiscassett, his blunt certainty regained, his laconic curtness increased almost to the point of speechlessness. He sold out (as a startled contemporary described it) "everything that showed" and took his son, an awed obedient eleven, back to the Vineyard where to the accompaniment of tolling breakers and creaking gulls, he gave the boy an education to which all the schooling of all the Wykes for all of four generations would be mere addenda.

For in his retreat to the storms and loneliness of the inner self and the Vineyard, Gamaliel Wyke had come to terms with nothing less than the Decalogue.

He had never questioned the Ten Commandments, nor had he knowingly disobeyed them. Like many another before him, he attributed the sad state of the world and the sin of its inhabitants to their refusal to heed those rules. But in his ponderings, God himself, he at last devoutly concluded, had underestimated the stupidity of mankind. So he undertook to amend the Decalogue himself by adding ". . . or cause . . ." to each commandment, just to make it easier for a man to work with:

". . . or cause the name of the Lord to be taken in vain.

". . . or cause stealing to be done.

". . . or cause dishonor to thy father and thy mother.

". . . or cause the commission of adultery.

". . . or cause a killing to be done."

But his revelation came to him when he came to the last one. It was suddenly clear to him that all mankind's folly—all greed, lust, war, all dishonor —sprang from humanity's almost total disregard for this edict and its amendment: "Thou shalt not covet . . . *nor cause covetousness!*"

It came to him then that to arouse covetousness in another is just as deadly a sin as to kill him or to cause his murder. Yet all around the world empires rose, great yachts and castles and hanging gardens came into being, tombs and trusts and college grants, all for the purpose of arousing the envy or covetousness of the less endowed—or having that effect no matter what the motive.

Now, one way for a man as rich as Gamaliel Wyke to have resolved the matter for himself would be St. Francis's way; but (though he could not admit this or even recognize it) he would have discarded the Decalogue and his amendments, all surrounding scripture and his gnarled right arm rather than run so counter to his inborn, ingrained Yankee acquisitiveness. And another way might have been to take his riches and bury them in the sand of Martha's Vineyard, to keep them from causing covetousness; the very thought clogged his nostrils with the feel of dune sand and he felt suffocation; to him money was a living thing and should not be interred.

And so he came to his ultimate answer: make your money, enjoy it, but *never let anyone know.* Desire, he concluded, for a neighbor's wife or a neighbor's ass or for anything, presupposed knowing about these possessions. No neighbor could desire anything of his if he couldn't lay a name to it.

So Gamaliel brought weight like granite and force like gravity to bear upon the mind and soul of his son Walter, and Walter begat Jedediah, and Jedediah begat Caiaphas (who died) and Samuel, and Samuel begat Zebulon (who died) and Sylva; so perhaps the true beginning of the story of the boy who became his own mother lies with Cap'n Gamaliel Wyke and his sand-scoured, sea-deep, rock-hard revelation.

. . . fell on his side on the bed and doubled up, grunting, gasping in pain, grunting, gasping, wrapped away from her, even her, unreachable even by her.

She screamed. She screamed. She pressed herself up and away from him and ran naked into the sitting room, pawed up the ivory telephone: "Keogh" she cried; "for the love of God, *Keogh!*"

. . . and back into the bedroom where he lay openmouthing a grating horrible *uh uh!* while she wrung her hands, tried to take one of his, found it agony-tense and unaware of her. She called him, called him and once, screamed again.

The buzzer sounded with inexcusable discretion.

"Keogh!" she shouted, and the polite buzzer *shhh'd* her again—the lock, oh, the damned lock . . . she picked up her negligee and ran with it in her hand through the dressing room and the sitting room and the hall and the living room and the foyer and flung open the door. She pulled Keogh through it before he could turn away from her; she thrust one arm in a sleeve of the garment and shouted at him, "Keogh, please, please, Keogh, what's wrong with him?" and she fled to the bedroom, Keogh sprinting to keep up with her.

Then Keogh, chairman of the board of seven great corporations, board member of a dozen more, general manager of a quiet family holding company which had, for most of a century, specialized in the ownership of corporate owners, went to the bed and fixed his cool blue gaze on the agonized figure there.

He shook his head slightly.

"You called the wrong man," he snapped, and ran back to the sitting room, knocking the girl aside as if he had been a machine on tracks. He picked up the phone and said, "Get Rathburn up here. *Now.* Where's Weber? You don't? well, find him and get him here. . . . I don't care. Hire an airplane. *Buy* an airplane."

He slammed down the phone and ran back into the bedroom. He came up behind her and gently lifted the negligee onto her other shoulder, and speaking gently to her all the while, reached around her and tied the ribbon belt. "What happened?"

"N-nothing, he just . . ."

"Come on, girl—clear out of here. Rathburn's practically outside the door, and I've sent for Weber. If there's a better doctor than Rathburn, it could only be Weber, so you've got to leave it to them. Come!"

"I won't leave him."

"Come!" Keogh rapped, then murmured, looking over her shoulder at the bed, "he wants you to, can't you see? He doesn't want you to see him like this. *Right?*" he demanded, and the face, turned away and half-buried in the pillow shone sweatily; cramp mounded the muscles on the side of the mouth they could just see. Stiffly the head nodded; it was like a shudder. "And . . . shut . . . door . . . tight. . . ." he said in a clanging half-whisper.

"Come," said Keogh. And again, "Come." He propelled her away; she stumbled. Her face turned yearningly until Keogh, both hands on her, kicked at the door and it swung and the sight of the bed was gone. Keogh leaned back against the door as if the latch were not enough to hold it closed.

"What is it? Oh, what is it?"

"I don't know," he said.

"You do, you do. . . . You always know everything. . . . Why won't you let me stay with him?"

"He doesn't want that."

Overcome, inarticulate, she cried out.

"Maybe," he said into her hair, "he wants to scream too."

She struggled—oh, strong, lithe and strong she was. She tried to press past him. He would not budge, so at last, at last she wept.

He held her in his arms again, as he had not done since she used to sit on his lap as a little girl. He held her in his arms and looked blindly toward the unconcerned bright morning, seen soft-focused through the cloud of her hair. And he tried to make it stop, the morning, the sun, and time, but . . .

. . . but there is one certain thing only about a human mind, and that is that it acts, moves, works ceaselessly while it lives. The action, motion, labor differ from that of a heart, say, or an epithelial cell, in that the latter have functions and in any circumstance perform their functions. Instead of a function, mind has a duty, that of making of a hairless ape a human being. . . . Yet as if to prove how trivial a difference there is between mind and muscle, mind must move, to some degree, always change, to some degree, always while it lives, like a stinking sweat gland. . . . Holding her, Keogh thought about Keogh.

The biography of Keogh is somewhat harder to come by than that of a Wyke. This is not in spite of having spent merely half a lifetime in this moneyed shadow; it is because of it. Keogh was a Wyke in all but blood and breeding: Wyke owned him and all he owned, which was a great deal.

He must have been a child once, a youth; he could remember if he wished but did not care to. Life began for him with the *summa cum laude,* the degrees in both business and law and (so young) the year and a half with Hinnegan and Bache and then the incredible opening at the International Bank; the impossible asked of him in the Zurich-Plenum affair and his performance of it and the shadows which grew between him and his associates over the years, while for him the light grew and grew as to the architecture of his work until at last he was admitted to Wyke and was permitted to realize that Wyke *was* Zurich and Plenum and the International Bank and Hinnegan and Bache; was indeed his law school and his college and much, so very much more. And finally sixteen—good heavens, it was eighteen—years ago, when he became general manager and the shadows dark to totally black between him and any other world, while the light, his own huge personal illumination, exposed almost to him alone an industrial-financial complex unprecedented in his country and virtually unmatched in the world.

But then, the beginning, the *other* beginning, was when old Sam Wyke called him in so abruptly that morning, when (though general manager with many a board chairman, all unbeknownst, under him in rank) he was still the youngest man in that secluded office.

"Keogh," said old Sam, "this is my kid. Take 'er out. Give 'er anything she wants. Be back here at six." He had then kissed the girl on the crown of her dark straw hat, gone to the door, turned and barked, "You see her show off or brag, Keogh, you fetch her a good one, then and there, hear? I don't care what else she does, but don't you let her wave something she's got at someone that hasn't got it. That's rule one." He had then breezed out, leaving a silent, startled young mover of mountains locking gazes with an unmoving mouse of an eleven-year-old girl. She had luminous pale skin, blue-black, silky-shining hair and thick level black brows.

The *summa cum laude,* the acceptance at Hinnegan and Bache—all such things, they were beginnings that he knew were beginnings. This he would not know for some time that it was a beginning, any more than he could realize that he had just heard the contemporary version of Cap'n Gamaliel's "Thou shalt not . . . cause covetousness." At the moment, he could only stand nonplused for a moment, then excuse himself and go to the treasurer's office, where he scribbled a receipt and relieved the petty cash box of its by no means petty contents. He got his hat and coat and returned to the president's office. Without a word the child rose and moved with him to the door.

They lunched and spent the afternoon together and were back at six. He bought her whatever she wanted at one of the most expensive shops in New York. He took her to just the places of amusement she asked him to.

When it was all over he returned the stack of bills to the petty cash box, less the one dollar and twenty cents he had paid out. For at the shop—the largest toy store in the world—she had carefully selected a sponge rubber ball, which they packed for her in a cubical box. This she carried carefully by its string for the rest of the afternoon.

They lunched from a pushcart. He had one hot dog with kraut; she had two with relish.

They rode uptown on the top of a Fifth Avenue double-decker open-top bus.

They went to the zoo in Central Park and bought one bag of peanuts for the girl and the pigeons and one bag of buns for the girl and the bears.

Then they took another double-decker back downtown, and that was it; that was the afternoon.

He remembered clearly what she looked like then: like a straw-hatted wren, for all it was a well-brushed wren. He could not remember what they had talked about, if indeed they had talked much at all. He was prepared to forget the episode, or at least to put it neatly in the *Trivia: Misc.: Closed* file in his compartmented mind when, a week later, old Sam tossed him a stack of papers and told him to read them through and come and ask questions if he thought he had to. The only question which came to mind when he had read them was "Are you sure you want to go through with this?" and that was not the kind of question one asked old Sam. So he thought it over very carefully and came up with "Why me?" and old Sam looked him up and down and growled, "she likes you, that's why."

And so it was that Keogh and the girl lived together in a cotton mill town in the South for a year. Keogh worked in the company store. The girl worked in the mill; twelve-year-old girls worked in cotton mills in the South in those days. She worked the morning shift and half the evening shift and had three hours' school in the afternoons. Up until ten o'clock on Saturday nights they watched the dancing from the sidelines. On Sundays they went to the Baptist church. Their name while they were there was Harris. Keogh used to worry frantically when she was out of his sight, but one day when she was crossing the catwalk over the water-circulating sump, a sort of oversized well beside the mill, the catwalk broke and pitched her into the water. Before she could so much as draw a breath a Negro stoker appeared out of nowhere—actually, out of the top of the coal chute—and leaped in and had her and handed her up to the sudden crowd. Keogh came galloping up from the company store as they were pulling the stoker out, and after seeing that the girl was all right, knelt beside the man, whose leg was broken.

"I'm Mr. Harris, her father. You'll get a reward for this. What's your name?"

The man beckoned him close, and as he bent down, the stoker, in spite of his pain, grinned and winked. "You don' owe me a thang, Mr. Keogh," he murmured. In later times, Keogh would be filled with rage at such a confidence, would fire the man out of hand: this first time he was filled with wonder and relief. After that, things were easier on him, as he realized that the child was surrounded by Wyke's special employees, working on Wyke land in a Wyke mill and paying rent in a Wyke row house.

In due time the year was up. Someone else took over, and the girl, now named Kevin and with a complete new background in case anyone should ask, went off for two years to a very exclusive Swiss finishing school, where she dutifully wrote letters to a Mr. and Mrs. Kevin who held large acreage in the Pennsylvania mountains, and who just as dutifully answered her.

Keogh returned to his own work, which he found in apple-pie order, with every one of the year's transactions beautifully abstracted for him and an extra amount, over and above his astronomical salary, tucked away in one of his accounts—an amount that startled even Keogh. He missed her at first, which he expected. But he missed her every single day for two solid years, a disturbance he could not explain, did not examine and discussed with no one.

All the Wykes, old Sam once grunted to him, did something of the sort. He, Sam, had been a logger in Oregon and a year and a half as utility man, then ordinary seaman on a coastwise tanker.

Perhaps some deep buried part of Keogh's mind thought that when she returned from Switzerland they would go for catfish in an old flat-bottomed boat again or that she would sit on his lap while he suffered on the hard benches of the once-a-month picture show. The instant he saw her on her return from Switzerland he knew that would never be. He knew he was entering some new phase; it troubled and distressed him and he put it away in the dark inside himself; he could do that; he was strong enough. And she —well, she flung her arms around him and kissed him; but when she talked with this new vocabulary, this deft school finish, she was strange and awesome to him, like an angel. Even a loving angel is strange and awesome. . . .

They were together again then for a long while, but there were no more hugs. He became a Mr. Stark in the Cleveland office of a brokerage house and she boarded with an elderly couple, went to the local high school and had a part-time job filing in his office. This was when she learned the ins and outs of the business, the size of it. It would be hers. It became hers while they were in Cleveland: old Sam died very suddenly. They slipped away to the funeral but were back at work on Monday. They stayed there for another eight months; she had a great deal to learn. In the fall she entered a small private college and Keogh saw nothing of her for a year.

"Shhh," he breathed to her, crying, and *shhh!* said the buzzer.

"The doctor . . ."

"Go take a bath," he said. He pushed her.

She half-turned under his hand, faced him again blazing. "No!"

"You can't go in there, you know," he said, going for the door. She glared at him, but her lower lip trembled.

Keogh opened the door. "In the bedroom."

"Who . . .?" Then the doctor saw the girl, her hands knotted together, her face twisted, and had his answer. He was a tall man, gray, with quick hands, a quick step, swift words. He went straight through foyer, hall and rooms and into the bedroom. He closed the door behind him. There had been no discussion, no request and refusal; Dr. Rathburn had simply, quickly, quietly shut them out.

"Go take a bath."

"No."

"Come on." He took her wrist and led her to the bathroom. He reached into the shower stall and turned on the side jets. There were four at each corner; the second from the top was scented. Apple blossom. "Go on."

He moved toward the door. She stood where he had let go of her wrist, pulling at her hands. "Go on," he said again. "Just a quick one. Do you good." He waited. "Or do you want me to douse you myself? I bet I still can."

She flashed him a look; indignation passed instantly as she understood what he was trying to do. The rare spark of mischief appeared in her eyes and, in perfect imitation of a mill row red-neck, she said, "Y'all try it an ah'll tall th' shurff ah ain't rightly you' chile." But the effort cost her too much and she cried again. He stepped out and softly closed the door.

He was waiting by the bedroom when Rathburn slid out and quickly shut the door on the grunt, the gasp.

"What is it?" asked Keogh.

"Wait a minute." Rathburn strode to the phone. Keogh said, "I sent for Weber."

Rathburn came almost ludicrously to a halt. "Wow," he said. "Not bad diagnosing, for a layman. Is there anything you can't do?"

"I can't understand what you're talking about," said Keogh testily.

"Oh, I thought you knew. Yes, I'm afraid it's in Weber's field. What made you guess?"

Keogh shuddered. "I saw a mill hand take a low blow once. I know *he* wasn't hit. What exactly is it?"

Rathburn darted a look around. "Where is she?" Keogh indicated the bathroom. "I told her to take a shower."

"Good," said the doctor. He lowered his voice. "Naturally I can't tell without further examination and lab . . ."

"*What is it?*" Keogh demanded, not loud, but with such violence that Rathburn stepped back a pace.

"It could be choriocarcinoma."

Tiredly, Keogh wagged his head. "Me diagnose that? I can't even spell it. What is it?" He caught himself up, as if he had retrieved the word from thin air and run it past him again. "I know what the last part of it means."

"One of the . . ." Rathburn swallowed, and tried again. "One of the more vicious forms of cancer. And it . . ." He lowered his voice again. "It doesn't always hit this hard."

"Just how serious is it?"

Rathburn raised his hands and let them fall.

"Bad, eh? Doc—*how bad . . . ?*"

"Maybe some day we can . . ." Rathburn's lowered voice at last disappeared. They hung there, each on the other's pained gaze.

"How much time?"

"Maybe six weeks."

"*Six weeks!*"

"Shh," said Rathburn nervously.

"Weber . . ."

"Weber knows more about internal physiology than anybody. But I don't know if that will help. It's a little like . . . your, uh, house is struck by lightning, flattened, burned to the ground. You can examine it and the weather reports and, uh, know exactly what happened. Maybe some day we can . . ." he said again, but he said it so hopelessly that Keogh, through the roiling mists of his own terror, pitied him and half-instinctively put out a hand. He touched the doctor's sleeve and stood awkwardly.

"What are you going to do?"

Rathburn looked at the closed bedroom door. "What I did." He made a gesture with a thumb and two fingers. "Morphine."

"And that's all?"

"Look, I'm a GP. Ask Weber, will you?"

Keogh realized that he had pushed the man as far as he could in his search for a crumb of hope; if there was none, there was no point in trying to squeeze it out. He asked, "Is there anyone working on it? Anything new? Can you find out?"

"Oh, I will, I will. But Weber can tell you off the top of his head more than I could find out in six mon . . . in a long time."

A door opened. She came out, hollow-eyed, but pink and glowing in a long white terry-cloth robe. "Dr. Rathburn . . ."

"He's asleep."

"Thank God. Does it . . . ?"

"There's no pain."

"What is it? What happened to him?"

"Well, I wouldn't like to say for sure. . . . We're waiting for Dr. Weber. He'll know."

"But—but is he . . . ?"

"He'll sleep the clock around."

"Can I . . . ?" The timidity, the caution, Keogh realized, was so unlike her. "Can I see him?"

"He's fast asleep!"

"I don't care. I'll be quiet. I won't—touch him or anything."

"Go ahead," said Rathburn. She opened the bedroom door and eagerly, silently slipped inside.

"You'd think she was trying to make sure he was there."

Keogh, who knew her so very well, said, "she is."

But a biography of Guy Gibbon is *really* hard to come by. For he was no exceptional executive, who for all his guarded anonymity wielded so much power that he must be traceable by those who knew where to look and what to look for and cared enough to process detail like a mass spectroscope. Neither was Guy Gibbon born heir to countless millions, the direct successor to a procession of giants.

He came from wherever it is most of us come from, the middle or the upper-middle or the upper-lower middle or the lower-upper middle or some other indefinable speck in the midrange of the interflowing striations of society (the more they are studied, the less they mean). He belonged to the Wykes entity for only eight and a half weeks, after all. Oh, the bare details might not be too hard to come by (birth date, school record) and certain main facts (father's occupation, mother's maiden name) as well, perhaps, as a highlight or two (divorce, perhaps, or a death in the family), but a biography, a real biography, which does more than describe, which *explains* the man—and few do—now, *this* is an undertaking.

Science, it is fair to assume, can do what all the king's horses and all the king's men could not do, and totally restore a smashed egg. Given equipment enough, and time enough . . . but isn't this a way of saying, "Given money enough"? For money can be not only means, but motive. So if enough money went into the project, perhaps the last unknown, the last vestige of anonymity could be removed from a man's life story, even a young man from (as the snobs say) nowhere, no matter how briefly—though intimately—known.

The most important thing, obviously, that ever happened to Guy Gibbon in his life was his first encounter with the Wyke entity, and like many a person before and since, he had not the faintest idea he had done so. It was when he was in his late teens, and he and Sammy Stein went trespassing.

Sammy was a school sidekick, and this particular day he had a secret; he had been very insistent on the day's outing, but refused to say why. He was a burly-shouldered, good-natured, reasonably chinless boy whose close friendship with Guy was based almost exclusively on the attraction of opposite poles. And since, of the many kinds of fun they had had, the most fun was going trespassing; he wanted it that way on this particular occasion.

"Going trespassing," as an amusement, had more or less invented itself when they were in their early teens. They lived in a large city surrounded (unlike many today) by old suburbs, not new ones. These included large— some, more than large—estates and mansions, and it was their greatest delight to slip through a fence or over a wall and, profoundly impressed by their own bravery, slip through field and forest, lawn and drive, like Indian scouts in settler country. Twice they had been caught, once to have dogs set on them —three boxers and two mastiffs, which certainly would have torn them to very small pieces if the boys had not been more lucky than swift—and once by a dear little old lady who swamped them sickeningly with jelly sandwiches and lonely affection. But over the saga of their adventures, their two captures served to spice the adventure; two failures out of a hundred successes (for many of these places were visited frequently) was a proud record.

So they took a trolley to the end of the line and walked a mile and went straight ahead where the road turned at a discreet *No Admittance* sign of expensive manufacture and a high degree of weathering. They proceeded through a small wild wood and came at last to an apparently unscalable granite wall.

Sammy had discovered this wall the week before, roaming alone; he had waited for Guy to accompany him before challenging it, and Guy was touched. He was also profoundly excited by the wall itself. Anything this size should have been found, conjectured about, campaigned against, battled and conquered long since. But as well as being a high wall, a long wall and mysterious, it was a distant wall, a discreet wall. No road touched it but its own driveway, which was primitive, meandering and led to ironbound, solid oak gates without a chink or crack to peek through.

They could not climb it nor breach it—but they crossed it. An ancient maple on this side held hands with a chestnut over the crown of the wall, and they went over like a couple of squirrels.

They had, in their ghostlike way, haunted many an elaborate property, but never had they seen such maintenance, such manicure, such polish of a piece of land and, as Sammy said, awed out of his usual brashness, as they stood in a solid marble pergola overlooking green plush acres of rolling lawn, copses of carven boxwood, parklike woods and streams with little Japanese bridges and, in their bends, humorful little rock gardens: "And there's goddamn *miles* of it."

They had wandered a bit, that first time, and had learned that there were after all some people there. They saw a tractor far away, pulling a slanted gang of mowers across one of the green plush fields. (The owners doubtless called it a lawn; it was a field.) The machines, rare in that time, cut a swath all of thirty feet wide. "And that," Sammy said, convulsing them, "ain't hay." And then they had seen the house. . . .

Well, a glimpse. Breaking out of the woods, Guy had felt himself snatched back. "House up there," said Sammy. "Someone'll see us." There was a confused impression of a white hill that was itself the house, or part of it; towers, turrets, castellations, crenellations; a fairy-tale palace set in this legendary landscape. They had not been able to see it again; it was so placed that it could be approached nowhere secretly nor even spied upon. They were struck literally speechless by the sight and for most of an hour had nothing to say, and that expressible only by wags of the head. Ultimately they referred to it as "the shack," and it was in this vein that they later called their final discovery "the ol' swimmin' hole."

It was across a creek and over a wooded hill. Two more hills rose to meet the wood, and cupped between the three was a pond, perhaps a lake. It was roughly L-shaped, and all around it were shadowed inlets, grottoes, inconspicuous stone steps leading here to a rustic pavilion set about with flowers, there to a concealed forest glade harboring a tiny formal garden.

But the lake, the ol' swimmin' hole . . .

They went swimming, splashing as little as possible and sticking to the shore. They explored two inlets to the right (a miniature waterfall and a tiny beach of obviously imported golden sand) and three to the left (a square-cut one, lined with tile the color of patina, with a black glass diving tower overhanging water that must have been dredged to twenty feet; a little beach of snow-white sand; and one they dared not enter for fear of harming the fleet of perfect sailing ships, none more than a foot long, which lay at anchor; but they trod water until they were bone cold, gawking at the miniature model waterfront with little pushcarts in the street, and lamp posts, and old-fashioned houses) and then, weary, hungry and awestruck, they had gone home.

And Sammy cracked the secret he had been keeping—the thing which he felt made this day an occasion: he was to go wild-hairing off the next day in an effort to join Chennault in China.

Guy Gibbon, overwhelmed, made the only gesture he could think of: he devotedly swore he would not go trespassing again until Sammy got back.

"Death from choriocarcinoma," Dr. Weber began, "is the result of . . ."

"But he won't die," she said. "I won't let him."

"My dear," Dr. Weber was a small man with round shoulders and a hawk's face. "I don't mean to be unkind, but I can use all the euphemisms and kindle all the false hope, or I can do as you have asked me to do—explain the condition and make a prognosis. I can't do both."

Dr. Rathburn said gently, "Why don't you go and lie down? I'll come when we've finished here and tell you all about it."

"I don't want to lie down," she said fiercely. "And I wasn't asking you to spare me anything, Dr. Weber. I simply said I would not let him die. There's nothing in that statement which keeps you from telling me the truth."

Keogh smiled. Weber caught him at it and was startled; Keogh saw his surprise. "I know her better than you do," he said, with a touch of pride. "You don't have to pull any punches."

"Thanks, Keogh," she said. She leaned forward. "Go ahead, Dr. Weber."

Weber looked at her. Snatched from his work two thousand miles away, brought to a place he had never known existed, of a magnificence which attacked his confidence in his own eyes, meeting a woman of power—every sort of power—quite beyond his experience . . . Weber had thought himself beyond astonishment. Shock, grief, fear, deprivation like hers he had seen before, of course; what doctor has not? but when Keogh had told her baldly that this disease killed in six weeks, *always,* she had flinched, closed her eyes for an interminable moment and had then said softly, "Tell us everything you can about this—this disease, doctor." And she had added, for the first time, "He isn't going to die. I won't let him;" and the way she held her head, the way her full voice handled the words, he almost believed her. Heaven knows, he wished he could. And so he found he could be astonished yet again.

He made an effort to detach himself and became not a man, not this particular patient's doctor, but a sort of source book. He began again:

"Death from choriocarcinoma is a little unlike other deaths from malignancies. Ordinarily a cancer begins locally and sends its chains and masses of wild cells growing through the organ on which it began. Death can result from the failure of that organ; liver, kidney, brain, what have you. Or the cancer suddenly breaks up and spreads through the body, starting colonies throughout the system. This is called metastasis. Death results then from the loss of efficiency of many organs instead of just one. Of course, both these things can happen—the almost complete impairment of the originally cancerous organ and metastatic effects at the same time.

"Chorio, on the other hand, doesn't originally involve a vital organ. Vital to the species, perhaps, but not to the individual." He permitted himself a dry smile. "This is probably a startling concept to most people in this day and age, but it's nonetheless true. However, sex cells, at their most basic and primitive, have peculiarities not shared by other body cells.

"Have you ever heard of the condition known as ectopic pregnancy?" He directed his question at Keogh, who nodded. "A fertilized ovum fails to descend to the uterus; instead it attaches itself to the side of the very fine tube between the ovaries and the womb. And at first everything proceeds well with it—and this is the point I want you to grasp—because in spite of the fact that only the uterus is truly specialized for this work, the tube wall not only supports the growing ovum but also feeds it. It actually forms what we call a counterplacenta; it enfolds the early fetus and nurtures it. The fetus, of course, has a high survival value and is able to get along quite well on the plasma which the counterplacenta supplies it with. And it grows—it grows fantastically. Since the tube is very fine—you'd have difficulty getting the smallest sewing needle up through it—it can no longer contain the growing fetus, and ruptures. Unless it is removed at that time, the tissues outside will quite as readily take on the work of a real placenta and uterus, and in six or seven months, if the mother survives that long, will create havoc in the abdomen.

"All right then: back to chorio. Since the cells involved are sex cells and cancerous to boot, they divide and redivide wildly, without pattern or special form. They develop in an infinite variety of shapes and sizes and forms. The law of averages dictates that a certain number of these—and the number of distorted cells is astronomical—resemble fertilized ova. Some of them resemble them so closely that I personally would not enjoy the task of distinguishing between them and the real thing. However, the body as a whole is not that particular; anything which even roughly resembles a fertilized egg cell is capable of commanding that counterplacenta.

"Now consider the source of these cells—physiologically speaking, gland tissue—a mass of capillary tubes and blood vessels. Each and every one of these does its best to accept and nurture these fetal imitations, down to the tiniest of them. The thin walls of the capillaries, however, break down easily under such an effort, and the imitations—selectively, the best of them, too, because the tissues yield most readily to them—they pass into the capillaries and then into the bloodstream.

"There is one place and only one place where they can be combed out; and it's a place rich in oxygen, lymph, blood and plasma: the lungs. The lungs enthusiastically take on the job of forming placentae for these cells and nurturing them. But for every segment of lung given over to gestating an imitation fetus, there is one less segment occupied with the job of oxygenating blood. Ultimately the lungs fail, and death results from oxygen starvation."

Rathburn spoke up. "For years chorio was regarded as a lung disease, and the cancerous gonads as a sort of side effect."

"But lung cancer . . ." Keogh began to object.

"It isn't lung cancer, don't you see? Given enough time, it might be, through metastasis. But there is never enough time. Chorio doesn't have to wait for that, to kill. That's why it's so swift." He tried not to look at the girl and failed; he said it anyway: "And certain."

"Just exactly how do you treat it?"

Weber raised his hands and let them fall. It was precisely the gesture Rathburn had made earlier, and Keogh wondered distantly whether they taught it in medical schools. "Something to kill the pain. Orchidectomy might make the patient last a little longer, by removing the supply of wild cells to the bloodstream. But it wouldn't save him. Metastasis has already taken place by the time the first symptom appears. The cancer becomes generalized . . . perhaps the lung condition is only God's mercy."

"What's 'orchidectomy'?" asked Keogh.

"Amputation of the—uh—source," said Rathburn uncomfortably.

"No!" cried the girl.

Keogh sent her a pitying look. There was that about him which was cynical, sophisticated and perhaps coldly angry at anyone who lived as he could never live, had what he could never have. It was a stirring of the grave ancient sin which old Cap'n Gamaliel had isolated in his perspicacious thoughts. Sure, amputate, if it'll help, he thought. What do you think you're preserving—his virility? What good's it to you now?'. . . But sending her the look, he encountered something different from the romantically based horror and shock he expected. Her thick level brows were drawn together, her whole face intense with taut concentration. "Let me think," she said, oddly.

"You really should . . ." Rathburn began, but she shushed him with an impatient gesture. The three men exchanged a glance and settled back; it was as if someone, something, had told them clearly and specifically to wait. What they were waiting for, they could not imagine.

The girl sat with her eyes closed. A minute crawled by. "Daddy used to say," she said, so quietly that she must surely be talking to herself, "that there's always a way. All you have to do is think of it."

There was another long silence, and she opened her eyes. There was a burning down in them somewhere; it made Keogh uneasy. She said, "And once he told me that I could have anything I wanted; all it had to be was . . . possible. And . . . the only way you can find out if a thing is impossible is to try it."

"That wasn't Sam Wyke," said Keogh. "That was Keogh."

She wet her lips and looked at them each in turn. She seemed not to see them at all. "I'm not going to let him die," she said. "You'll see."

Sammy Stein came back two years later on leave, and full of plans to join the Army Air Force. He'd had, as he himself said, the hell kicked out of him in China and a lot of the hellishness as well. But there was enough of the old

Sammy left to make wild wonderful plans about going trespassing; and they knew just where they were going. The new Sammy, however, demanded a binge and a broad first.

Guy, two years out of high school, working for a living and by nature neither binger nor wencher, went along only too gladly. Sam seemed to have forgotten about the "ol' swimmin' hole" at first, and halfway through the evening, in a local bar-and-dance emporium, Guy was about to despair of his ever remembering it when Sam himself brought it up, recalling to Guy that he had once written Sam a letter asking Sam if it had really happened. Guy had, in his turn, forgotten the letter, and after that they had a good time with "remember when"—and they made plans to go trespassing the very next day and bring a lunch. And start early.

Then there was a noisy involvement with some girls and a lot more drinks, and out of the haze and movement somewhere after midnight, Guy emerged on a sidewalk looking at Sammy shoveling a girl into a taxicab. "Hey!" he called out, "what about the you know, ol' swimmin' hole?"

"Call me Abacus, you can count on me," Sammy said and laughed immoderately. The girl with him pulled at his arm; he shook her off and weaved over to Guy. "Listen," he said and gave a distorted wink, "if this makes—and it will—I'm starting no early starts. Tell you what, you go on out there and meet me by that sign says keep out or we'll castigate you. Say eleven o'clock. If I can't make it by then I'm dead or something." He bellowed at the cab, "You gon' kill me, honey?" and the girl called back, "I will if you don't get into this taxi." "See what I mean?" said Sammy in a grand drunken non sequitor, "I got to go get killed." He zigged away, needing no zag because even walking sidewise he reached the cab in a straight line, and Guy saw no more of him that leave.

That was hard to take, mostly because there was no special moment at which he knew Sammy wasn't coming. He arrived ten minutes late, after making a superhuman effort to get there. His stomach was sour from the unaccustomed drinking and he was sandy-eyed and ache-jointed from lack of sleep. He knew that the greater probability was that Sammy had not arrived yet or would not at all; yet the nagging possibility existed that he had come early and gone straight in. Guy waited around for a full hour, and some more minutes until the little road was clear of traffic and sounds of traffic, and then plunged alone into the woods, past the no trespassing sign, and in to the wall. He had trouble finding the two trees, and once over the wall, he could not get his bearings for a while; he was pleased, of course, to find the unbelievably perfect lawns still there by the flawless acre, the rigidly controlled museums of carven box, the edge-trimmed, rolled-gravel walks meandering prettily through the woods. The pleasure, however, was no more than confirmation of his memory and went no further; the day was spoiled.

Guy reached the lake at nearly one o'clock, hot, tired, ravenously hungry and unpleasantly nervous. The combination hit him in the stomach and made it echo; he sat down on the bank and ate. He wolfed down the food he had brought for himself and Sammy's as well—odds and ends carelessly tossed into a paper sack in the bleary early hours. The cake was moldy but he ate it anyway. The orange juice was warm and had begun to ferment. And stubbornly, he determined to swim because that was what he had come for.

He chose the beach with the golden sand. Under a thick cover of junipers he found a stone bench and table. He undressed here and scuttled across the beach and into the water.

He had meant it to be a mere dip, so he could say he'd done it. But around the little headland to the left was the rectangular cove with the diving platform; and he remembered the harbor of model ships; and then movement diagonally across the foot of the lake's *L* caught his eye, and he saw models —not the anchored ships this time, but racing sloops, which put out from an inlet and crossed its mouth and sailed in again; they must be mounted on some sort of underwater wheel or endless chain, and they moved as the breeze took them. He all but boiled straight across to them, then decided to be wise and go round.

He swam to the left and the rocky shore and worked his way along it. Clinging close (the water seemed bottomless here) he rounded the point and came face to face (literally; they touched) with a girl.

She was young—near his age—and his first impression was of eyes of too complex an architecture, blue white teeth with pointed canines quite unlike the piano-key regularity considered beautiful in these times and a wide cape of rich brown hair afloat around her shoulders. By then his gasp was completed, and in view of the fact that in gasping he had neglected to remove his mouth from the water, he was shut off from outside impressions for a strangling time until he felt a firm grasp on his left biceps and found himself returned to the side of the rock.

"Th-thanks," he said hoarsely as she swam back a yard and trod water. "I'm not supposed to be here," he added inanely.

"I guess I'm not either. But I thought you lived here. I thought you were a faun."

"Boy, am I glad to hear that. I mean about you. All I am is a trespasser. Boy."

"I'm not a boy."

"It was just a finger of speech," he said, using one of the silly expressions which come to a person as he grows, and blessedly pass. She seemed not to react to it at all, for she said gravely, "You have the most beautiful eyes I have ever seen. They are made of aluminum. And your hair is all wiggly."

He could think of nothing to say to that, but tried; all that emerged was, "Well, it's early yet," and suddenly they were laughing together. She was so strange, so different. She spoke in a grave, unaccented and utterly incautious idiom as if she thought strange thoughts and spoke them right out. "Also," she said, "you have lovely lips. They're pale blue. You ought to get out of the water."

"I can't!"

She considered that for a moment, treading away from him and then back to the yard's distance. "Where are your things?"

He pointed across the narrow neck of the lake which he had circumnavigated.

"Wait for me over there," she said and suddenly swam close, so close she could dip her chin and look straight into his eyes. "You got to," she said fiercely.

"Oh, I will," he promised and struck out for the opposite shore. She hung to the rock, watching him.

Swimming, reaching hard, stretching for distance warmed him, and the chill and its accompanying vague ache diminished. Then he had a twinge of stomachache, and he drew up his knees to ease it. When he tried to extend himself again, he could, but it hurt too much. He drew up his knees again, and the pain followed inward so that to flex again was out of the question. He drew his knees up still tighter, and tighter still followed the pain. He needed air badly by then, threw up his head, tried to roll over on his back; but with his knees drawn up, everything came out all wrong. He inhaled at last because he had to, but the air was gone away somewhere; he floundered upward for it until the pressure in his ears told him he was swimming downward. Blackness came upon him and receded and came again; he let it come for a tired instant and was surrounded by light and drew one lungful of air and one of water and got the blackness again; this time it stayed with him. . . .

Still beautiful in her bed, but morphine-clouded, flypapered and unstruggling in viscous sleep, he lay with monsters swarming in his veins. . . .

Quietly, in a corner of the room, she spoke with Keogh:

"You don't understand me. You didn't understand me yesterday when I cried out at the idea of that—that operation. Keogh, I love him, but I'm *me*. Loving him doesn't mean I've stopped thinking. Loving him means I'm more me than ever, not less. It means I can do anything I did before, only more, only better. That's why I fell in love with him. That's why I am in love with him. Weren't you ever in love, Keogh?"

He looked at the way her hair fell and the earnest placement of her thick soft brows, and he said, "I haven't thought much about it."

" 'There's always a way. All you have to do is think of it,' " she quoted. "Keogh, I've accepted what Dr. Rathburn said. After I left you yesterday I went to the library and tore the heart out of some books. . . . They're right, Rathburn and Weber. And I've thought and I've thought . . . trying the way daddy would, to turn everything upside down and backward, to look for a new way of thinking. He won't die, Keogh; I'm not going to let him die."

"You said you accepted . . ."

"Oh, part of him. Most of him, if you like. We all die, bit by bit, all the time, and it doesn't bother us because most of the dead parts are replaced. He'll . . . he'll lose more parts sooner, but—after it's over, he'll be himself again." She said it with superb confidence—perhaps it was childlike. If so, it was definitely not childish.

"You have an idea," said Keogh positively. As he had pointed out to the doctors, he knew her.

"All those—those things in his blood," she said quietly. "The struggle they go through . . . they're trying to survive; did you ever think of it that way, Keogh? They want to live. They want most terribly to go on living."

"I hadn't thought about it."

"His body wants them to live too. It welcomes them wherever they lodge. Dr. Weber said so."

"You've got hold of something," said Keogh flatly, "and whatever it is I don't think I like it."

"I don't want you to like it," she said in the same strange quiet voice. He looked swiftly at her and saw again the burning deep in her eyes. He had to look away. She said, "I want you to hate it. I want you to fight it. You have one of the most wonderful minds I have ever known, Keogh, and I want you to think up every argument you can think of against it. For every argument I'll find an answer, and then we'll know what to do."

"You'd better go ahead," he said reluctantly.

"I had a pretty bad quarrel with Dr. Weber this morning," she said suddenly.

"This m . . . when?" He looked at his watch; it was still early.

"About three, maybe four. In his room. I went there and woke him up."

"Look, you don't do things like that to Weber!"

"I do. Anyway, he's gone."

He rose to his feet, the rare bright patches of anger showing in his cheeks.

He took a breath, let it out, and sat down again. "You'd better tell me about it."

"In the library," she said, "there's a book on genetics, and it mentions some experiments on Belgian hares. The does were impregnated without sperm, with some sort of saline or alkaline solution."

"I remember something about it." He was well used to her circuitous way of approaching something important. She built conversational points, not like a hired contractor, but like an architect. Sometimes she brought in portions of her lumber and stacked them beside the structure. If she ever did that, it was material she needed and would use. He waited.

"The does gave birth to baby rabbits, all female. The interesting thing was that they were identical to each other and to the mother. Even the blood-vessel patterns in the eyeball were so similar that an expert might be fooled by photographs of them. 'Impossibly similar' is what one of the experimenters called it. They had to be identical because everything they inherited was from the mother. I woke Dr. Weber up to tell him about that."

"And he told you he'd read the book."

"He wrote it," she said gently. "And then I told him that if he could do that with a Belgian hare, he could do it with"—she nodded toward her big bed—"him."

Then she was quiet while Keogh rejected the idea, found it stuck to his mind's hand, not to be shaken off; brought it to his mind's eye and shuddered away from it, shook again and failed, slowly brought it close and turned it over and turned it again.

"Take one of those—those things like fertilized ova—make it grow . . ."

"You don't *make* it grow. It wants desperately to grow. And not one of them, Keogh. You have thousands. You have hundreds more every hour."

"Oh my God."

"It came to me when Dr. Rathburn suggested the operation. It came to me all at once, a miracle. If you love someone that much," she said, looking at the sleeper, "miracles happen. But you have to be willing to help them happen." She looked at him directly with an intensity that made him move back in his chair. "I can have anything I want—all it has to be is possible. We just have to make it possible. That's why I went to Dr. Weber this morning. To ask him."

"He said it wasn't possible."

"He said that at first. After a half-hour or so he said the odds against it were in the billions or trillions . . . but you see, as soon as he said that, he was saying it was possible."

"What did you do then?"

"I dared him to try."

"And that's why he left?"

"Yes."

"You're mad," he said before he could stop himself. She seemed not to resent it. She sat calmly, waiting.

"Look," said Keogh at last, "Weber said those distorted—uh—*things* were *like* fertilized ova. He never said they were. He could have said—well, I'll say it for him—they're *not* fertilized ova."

"But he did say they were—some of them, anyway, and especially those that reached the lungs—were very much like ova. How close do you have to get before there's no real difference at all?"

"It can't be. It just can't."

"Weber said that. And I asked him if he had ever tried."

"All right, all right! It can't happen, but just to keep this silly argument going, suppose you got something that would grow. You won't, of course. But if you did, how would you keep it growing. It has to be fed, it has to be kept at a certain critical temperature, a certain amount of acid or alkali will kill it. . . . You don't just plant something like that in the yard."

"Already they've taken ova from one cow, planted them in another and gotten calves. There's a man in Australia who plans to raise blooded cattle from scrub cows that way."

"You *have* done your homework."

"Oh, that isn't all. There's a Dr. Carrel in New Jersey who has been able to keep chicken tissue alive for months—he says indefinitely—in a nutrient solution, in a temperature-controlled jar in his lab. It grows, Keogh! It grows so much he has to cut it away every once in a while."

"This is crazy. This is—it's insane," he growled. "And what do you think you'll get if you bring one of these monsters to term?"

"We'll bring thousands of them to term," she said composedly. "And one of them will be—*him.*" She leaned forward abruptly, and her even tone of voice broke; a wildness grew through her face and voice, and though it was quiet, it shattered him: "It will be his flesh, the pattern of him, his own substance grown again. His hair, Keogh. His fingerprints. His—eyes. His—his *self.*"

"I can't . . ." Keogh shook himself like a wet spaniel, but it changed nothing; he was still here, she, the bed, the sleeper and this dreadful, this inconceivably horrible, wrong idea.

She smiled then, put out her hand and touched him; incredibly, it was a mother's smile, warm and comforting, a mother's loving, protective touch; her voice was full of affection. "Keogh, if it won't work, it won't work, no matter what we do. Then you'll be right. I think it will work. It's what I want. Don't you want me to have what I want?"

He had to smile, and she smiled back. "You're a young devil," he said ardently. "Got me coming and going, haven't you? Why did you want me to fight it?"

"I didn't," she said, "but if you fight me you'll come up with problems nobody else could possibly think of, and once we've thought of them, we'll be ready, don't you see? I'll fight with you, Keogh," she said, shifting her strange bright spectrum from tenderness to a quiet, convinced, invincible certainty, "I'll fight with you, I'll lift and carry, I'll buy and sell and kill if I have to, but I am going to bring him back. You know something, Keogh?"

"What?"

She waved her hand in a gesture that included him, the room, the castle and grounds and all the other castles and grounds; the pseudonyms, the ships and trains, the factories and exchanges, the mountains and acres and mines and banks and the thousands upon thousands of people which, taken together, were Wyke: "I always knew that all this *was,*" she said, "and I've come to understand that this is mine. But I used to wonder, sometimes, what it was all *for.* Now I know. Now I know."

A mouth on his mouth, a weight on his stomach. He felt boneless and nauseated, limp as grease drooling. The light around him was green, and all shapes blurred.

The mouth on his mouth, the weight on his stomach, a breath of air, welcome but too warm, too moist. He needed it desperately but did not like it and found a power plant full of energy to gather it up in his lungs and fling it away; but his weakness so filtered all that effort that it emerged in a faint bubbling sigh.

The mouth on his mouth again and the weight on his stomach and another breath. He tried to turn his head but someone held him by the nose. He blew out the needed, unsatisfactory air and replaced it by a little gust of his own inhalation. On this he coughed; it was too rich, pure, too good. He coughed as one does over a pickle barrel; good air hurt his lungs.

He felt his head and shoulders lifted, shifted, by which he learned that he had been flat on his back on stone, or something flat and quite that hard, and was now on smooth firm softness. The good sharp air came and went, his weak coughs fewer, until he fell into a dazed peace. The face that bent over his was too close to focus, or he had lost the power to focus; either way, he didn't care. Drowsily he stared up into the blurred brightness of that face and listened uncritically to the voice. . . .

. . . The voice crooning wordlessly and comfortingly, and somehow, in its wordlessness, creating new expressions for joy and delight for which words would not do. Then after all there were words, half-sung, half-whispered; and he couldn't catch them, and he couldn't catch them and then . . . and then he was sure he heard: "How could it be, such a magic as that: all this and the eyes as well . . ." Then, demanding, "You are the shape of the not-you: tell me, are *you* in there?"

He opened his eyes wide and saw her face clearly at last and the dark hair, and the eyes were green—true deep sea green. Her tangled hair, drying, crowned her like vines, and the leafy roof close above seemed part of her and the green eyes, and threw green light on the unaccountably blonde transparency of her cheeks. He genuinely did not know, at the moment, what she was. She had said to him (was it years ago?) "I thought you were a faun. . . ." He had not, at the moment, much consciousness, not to say whimsy, at his command; she was simply something unrelated to anything in his experience.

He was aware of griping, twisting pain rising, filling, about to explode in his upper abdomen. Some thick wire within him had kinked, and knowing well that it should be unbent, he made a furious, rebellious effort and pulled it through. The explosion came, but in nausea, not in agony. Convulsively he turned his head, surged upward and let it go.

He saw with too much misery to be horrified the bright vomit surging on and around her knee and running into the crevice between thigh and calf where she had her leg bent and tucked under her, and the clots left there as the fluid ran away. And she . . .

She sat where she was, held his head, cradled him in her arms, soothed him and crooned to him and said that was good, good; he'd feel better now. The weakness floored him and receded; then shakily he pressed away from her, sat up, bowed his head and gasped for breath. "Whooo," he said.

"Boy," she said; and she said it in exact concert with him. He clung to his shins and wiped the nausea tears from his left eye, then his right, on his kneecap. "Boy, oh, boy," he said, and she said it with him in concert.

So at last he looked at her.

He looked at her and would never forget what he saw and exactly the way it was. Late sunlight made into lace by the bower above clothed her; she leaned toward him, one small hand flat on the ground, one slim supporting arm straight and straight down; her weight turned up that shoulder and her head tilted toward it as if drawn down by the heavy darkness of her hair. It gave a sense of yielding, as if she were fragile, which he knew she was not. Her other hand lay open across one knee, the palm up and the fingers not quite relaxed, as if they held something; and indeed they did, for a spot of light, gold turned coral by her flesh, lay in her palm. She held it just so, just right, unconsciously, and her hand held that rare knowledge that closed, a hand may not give nor receive. For his lifetime he had it all, each tiniest part, even to the gleaming big toenail at the underside of her other calf. And she was smiling, and her complex eyes adored.

Guy Gibbon knew his life's biggest moment during the moment itself, a rarity in itself, and of all times of life, it was time to say the unforgettable, for anything he said now would be.

He shuddered, and then smiled back at her. "Oh . . . *boy*," he breathed.

And again they were laughing together until, puzzled, he stopped and asked, "Where am I?"

She would not answer, so he closed his eyes and puzzled it out. Pine bower . . . undress somewhere . . . swimming. Oh, swimming. And then across the lake, and he had met . . . He opened his eyes and looked at her and said, "You." Then swimming back, cold, his gut full of too much food and warm juice and moldy cake to boot, and, ". . . You must have saved my life."

"Well, somebody had to. You were dead."

"I should've been."

"No!" she cried. "Don't you ever say that again!" And he could see she was absolutely serious.

"I only meant, for stupidity. I ate a lot of junk and some cake I think was moldy. Too much, when I was hot and tired, and then like a bonehead I went right into the water, so anybody who does that deserves to . . ."

"I meant it," she said levelly, "never again. Didn't you ever hear of the old tradition of the field of battle, when one man saved another's life, that life became his to do what he wanted with?"

"What do you want to do with mine?"

"That depends," she said thoughtfully. "You have to give it. I can't just take it." She knelt then and sat back on her heels, her hands trailing pine needles across the bower's paved stone floor. She bowed her head and her hair swung forward. He thought she was watching him through it; he could not be sure.

He said, and the thought grew so large that it quelled his voice and made him whisper, "Do you want it?"

"Oh, yes," she said, whispering too. When he moved to her and put her hair back to see if she was watching him, he found her eyes closed, and tears pressed through. He reached for her gently, but before he could touch her she sprang up and straight at the leafy wall. Her long golden body passed through it without a sound and seemed to hang suspended outside; then it was gone. He put his head through and saw her flashing along under green water. He hesitated, then got an acrid whiff of his own vomit. The water looked clean and the golden sand just what he ached to scrub himself with. He climbed out of the bower and floundered clumsily down the bank and into the water.

After his first plunge he came up and spun about, looking for her, but she was gone.

Numbly he swam to the tiny beach and, kneeling, scoured himself with the fine sand. He dived and rinsed, and then (hoping) scrubbed himself all over again. And rinsed. But he did not see her.

He stood in the late rays of the sun to dry and looked off across the lake. His heart leaped when he saw white movement and sank again as he saw it was just the wheel of boats bobbing and sliding there.

He plodded up to the bower—now at last he saw it was the one behind which he had undressed—and he sank down on the bench.

This was a place where tropical fish swam in ocean water where there was no ocean and where fleets of tiny perfect boats sailed with no one sailing them and no one watching and where priceless statues stood hidden in clipped and barbered glades deep in the woods and—and he hadn't seen it all; what other impossibilities were possible in this impossible place?

And besides, he'd been sick. (He wrinkled his nostrils.) Damn near . . . drowned. Out of his head for sure, for a while anyway. She couldn't be real. Hadn't he noticed a greenish cast to her flesh, or was that just the light? . . . Anybody who could make a place like this, run a place like this, could jimmy up some kind of machine to hypnotize you like in the science fiction stories.

He stirred uneasily. Maybe someone was watching him even now.

Hurriedly, he began to dress.

So she wasn't real. Or maybe all of it wasn't real. He'd bumped into that other trespasser across the lake there, and that was real, but then when he'd almost drowned, he'd dreamed up the rest.

Only—he touched his mouth. He'd dreamed up someone blowing the breath back into him. He'd heard about that somewhere, but it sure wasn't what they were teaching this year at the Y.

You are the shape of the not-you. Are you in there?

What did that mean?

He finished dressing dazedly. He muttered, "What'd I hafta go an' eat that goddamn cake for?" He wondered what he would tell Sammy. If she wasn't real, Sammy wouldn't know what he was talking about. If she was real there's only one thing he would talk about, yes, and from then on. You mean you had her in that place and all you did was throw up on her? No—he wouldn't tell Sammy. Or anybody.

And he'd be a bachelor all his life.

Boy, oh, boy. What an introduction. First she has to save your life and then you don't know what to say and then, oh, look what you had to go and do. But anyway—she wasn't real.

He wondered what her name was. Even if she wasn't real. Lots of people don't use their real names.

He climbed out of the bower and crossed the silent pine carpet behind it, and he shouted. It was not a word at all, and had nothing about it that tried to make it one.

She was standing there waiting for him. She wore a quiet brown dress and low heels and carried a brown leather pocketbook, and her hair was braided and tied neatly and sedately in a coronet. She looked, too, as if she had turned down some inward tone control so that her skin did not radiate. She looked ready to disappear, not into thin air, but into a crowd—any crowd, as soon as she could get close to one. In a crowd he would have walked right past her, certainly, but for the shape of her eyes. She stepped up to him quickly and laid her hand on his cheek and laughed up at him. Again he saw the whiteness of those unusual eyeteeth, so sharp . . . "You're blushing!" she said.

No blusher in history was ever stopped by that observation. He asked, "Which way do you go?"

She looked at his eyes, one, the other, both, quickly; then folded her long hands together around the strap of her pocketbook and looked down at them.

"With you," she said softly.

This was only one of the many things she said to him, moment by moment, which gained meaning for him as time went on. He took her back to town and to dinner and then to the West Side address she gave him and they stood outside it all night talking. In six weeks they were married.

"How could I argue?" said Weber to Dr. Rathburn.

They stood together watching a small army of workmen swarming over the gigantic stone barn a quarter-mile from the castle, which, incidentally, was invisible from this point and unknown to the men. Work had begun at three the previous afternoon, continued all night. There was nothing, nothing at all that Dr. Weber had specified which was not only given him, but on the site or already installed.

"I know," said Rathburn, who did.

"Not only, how could I argue," said Weber, "why should I? A man has plans, ambitions. That Keogh, what an approach! That's the first thing he went after—my plans for myself. That's where he starts. And suddenly everything you ever wanted to do or be or have is handed to you or promised to you, and no fooling about the promise either."

"*Oh,* no. They don't need to fool anybody. . . . You want to pass a prognosis?"

"You mean on the youngster there?" He looked at Rathburn. "Oh—that's not what you mean. . . . You're asking me if I can bring one of those surrogate fetuses to term. An opinion like that would make a damn fool out of a man, and this is no job for a damn fool. All I can tell you is, I tried it—and that is something I wouldn't've dreamed of doing if it hadn't been for her and her crazy idea. I left here at four in the morning with some throat smears, and by nine I had a half-dozen of them isolated and in nutrient solution. Beef blood plasma—the quickest thing I could get ready. And I got mitosis. They divided, and in a few hours I could see two of 'em dimpling to form the gastrosphore. That was evidence enough to get going; that's all I think and that's all I told them on the phone. And by the time I got here," he added, waving toward the big barn, "there's a research lab four-fifths built, big enough for a city medical center. Argue?" he demanded, returning to Dr. Rathburn's original question. "How could I argue? Why should I? . . . And that *girl.* She's a force, like gravity. She can turn on so much pressure, and I mean by herself and personally, that she could probably get anything in the world she wanted even if she didn't own it, the world I mean. Put that in the northeast entrance!" he bellowed at a foreman. "I'll be down to show you just where it goes." He turned to Rathburn; he was a man on fire. "I got to go."

"Anything I can do," said Dr. Rathburn, "just say it."

"That's the wonderful part of it," said Weber. "That's what everybody around here keeps saying, and they mean it!" He trotted down toward the barn, and Rathburn turned toward the castle.

About a month after his last venture at trespassing, Guy Gibbon was coming home from work when a man at the corner put away a newspaper and, still folding it, said, "Gibbon?"

"That's right," said Guy, a little sharply.

The man looked him up and down, quickly, but giving an impression of such thoroughness, efficiency and experience that Guy would not have been surprised to learn that the man had not only catalogued his clothes and their source, their state of maintenance and a computation therefrom of his personal habits, but also his state of health and even his blood type. "My name's Keogh," said the man. "Does that mean anything to you?"

"No."

"Sylva never mentioned the name?"

"Sylva! N-no, she didn't."

"Let's go somewhere and have a drink. I'd like to talk to you." Something had pleased this man; Guy wondered what. "Well, okay," he said. "Only I don't drink much, but well, okay."

They found a bar in the neighborhood with booths in the back. Keogh had a Scotch and soda, and Guy, after some hesitation, ordered beer. Guy said, "You know her?"

"Most of her life. Do you?"

"What? Well, sure. We're going to get married." He looked studiously into his beer and said uncomfortably, "Who are you anyway, Mr. Keogh?"

"You might say," said Keogh, "I'm *in loco parentis.*" He waited for a response, then added, "Sort of a guardian."

"She never said anything about a guardian."

"I can understand that. What has she told you about herself?"

Guy's discomfort descended to a level of shyness, diffidence, even a touch of fear—which did not alter the firmness of his words, however they were spoken. "I don't know you, Mr. Keogh. I don't think I ought to answer any questions about Sylva. Or me. Or anything." He looked up at the man. Keogh searched deeply, then smiled. It was an unpracticed and apparently slightly painful process with him, but it was genuine for all that. "Good!" he barked, and rose. "Come on." He left the booth and Guy, more than a little startled, followed. They went to the phone booth in the corner. Keogh dropped in a nickel, dialed and waited, his eyes fixed on Guy. Then Guy had to listen to one side of the conversation:

"I'm here with Guy Gibbon." (Guy had to notice that Keogh identified himself only with his voice.)

. . . "Of course I knew about it. That's a silly question, girl."

. . . "Because it *is* my business. *You* are my business."

. . . "Stop it? I'm not trying to stop anything. I just have to know, that's all."

. . . "All right. All right. . . . He's here. He won't talk about you or anything, which is good. Yes, very good. Will you please tell him to open up?"

And he handed the receiver to a startled Guy, who said tremulously, "Uh, hello," to it while watching Keogh's impassive face.

Her voice suffused and flooded him, changed this whole unsettling experience to something different and good. "Guy, darling."

"Sylva . . ."

"It's all right. I should have told you sooner, I guess. It had to come some time. Guy, you can tell Keogh anything you like. Anything he asks."

"Why, honey? Who is he, anyway?"

There was a pause, then a strange little laugh. "He can explain that better than I can. You want us to be married, Guy?"

"Oh, yes!"

"Well, all right then. Nobody can change that, nobody but you. And listen, Guy, I'll live anywhere, any way you want to live. That's the real truth and all of it, do you believe me?"

"I always believe you."

"All right then. So that's what we'll do. Now you go and talk to Keogh. Tell him anything he wants to know. He has to do the same. I love you, Guy."

"Me too," said Guy, watching Keogh's face. "Well, okay then," he added when she said nothing further. "'Bye." He hung up.

He and Keogh had a long talk.

"It hurts him," she whispered to Dr. Rathburn.

"I know." He shook his head sympathetically. "There's just so much morphine you can ram into a man, though."

"Just a little more?"

"Maybe a little," he said sadly. He went to his bag and got the needle. Sylva kissed the sleeping man tenderly and left the room. Keogh was waiting for her.

He said, "This has got to stop, girl."

"Why?" she responded ominously.

"Let's get out of here."

She had known Keogh so long and so well that she was sure he had no surprises for her. But this voice, this look, these were something new in Keogh. He held the door for her, so she preceded him through it and then went where he silently led.

They left the castle and took the path through a heavy copse and over the brow of the hill which overlooked the barn. The parking lot, which had once been a barnyard, was full of automobiles. A white ambulance approached; another was unloading at the northeast platform. A muffled generator purred somewhere behind the building, and smoke rose from the stack of the new stone boiler room at the side. They both looked avidly at the building but did not comment. The path took them along the crest of the hill and down toward the lake. They went to a small forest clearing in which stood an eight-foot Diana, the huntress Diana, chaste and fleet-footed, so beautifully finished she seemed not like marble at all, not like anything cold or static. "I always had the idea," said Keogh, "that nobody can lie anywhere near her."

She looked up at the Diana.

"Not even to themselves," said Keogh, and plumped down on a marble bench.

"Let's have it," she said.

"You want to make Guy Gibbon happen all over again. It's a crazy idea and it's a big one too. But lots of things were crazier and some bigger, and now they're commonplace. I won't argue on how crazy it is, or how big."

"What then?"

"I've been trying, the last day or so, to back 'way out, far off, get a look at this thing with some perspective. Sylva, you've forgotten something."

"Good," she said. "Oh, good. I knew you'd think of things like this before it was too late."

"So you can find a way out?" Slowly he shook his head. "Not this time. Tighten up the Wyke guts, girl, and make up your mind to quit."

"Go ahead."

"It's just this. I don't believe you're going to get your carbon copy, mind you, but you just might. I've been talking to Weber, and by God you just about might. But if you do, all you've got is a container, and nothing to fill it with. Look, girl, a man isn't blood and bone and body cells, and that's all."

He paused, until she said, "Go on, Keogh."

He demanded, "You love this guy?"

"Keogh!" She was amused.

"Whaddaya love?" he barked. "That skrinkly hair? The muscles, skin? His nat'ral equipment? The eyes, voice?"

"All that," she said composedly.

"All that, and that's all?" he demanded relentlessly. "Because if your answer is yes, you can have what you want, and more power to you and good riddance. I don't know anything about love, but I will say this: if that's all there is to it, the hell with it."

"Well, of *course* there's more."

"Ah. And where are you going to get that, girl? Listen, a man is the skin and bone he stands in, plus what's in his head, plus what's in his heart. You mean to reproduce Guy Gibbon, but you're not going to do it by duplicating his carcass. You want to duplicate the whole man, you're going to have to make him live the same life again. And that you can't do."

She looked up at the Diana for a long time. Then, "Why not?" she breathed.

"I'll tell you why not," he said angrily. "Because first of all you have to find out *who he is.*"

"*I* know who he is!"

He spat explosively on the green moss by the bench. It was totally uncharacteristic and truly shocking. "You don't know a particle, and I know even less. I had his back against a wall one time for better than two hours, trying to find out who he is. He's just another kid, is all. Nothing much in school, nothing much at sports, same general tastes and feelings as six zillion other ones like him. Why him, Sylva? Why him? What did you ever see in a guy like that to be worth the marrying?"

"I . . . didn't know you disliked him."

"Oh, hell, girl, I don't! I never said that. I can't—I can't even find anything to dislike!"

"You don't know him the way I do."

"There, I agree. I don't and I couldn't. Because you don't know anything either—you *feel*, but you don't *know*. If you want to see Guy Gibbon again, or a reasonable facsimile, he's going to have to live by a script from the day he's born. He'll have to duplicate every experience that this kid here ever had."

"All right," she said quietly.

He looked at her, stunned. He said, "And before he can do that, we have to write the script. And before we can write it, we have to get the material somehow. What do you expect to do—set up a foundation or something dedicated to the discovery of each and every moment this—this unnoticeable young man ever lived through? And do it secretly because while he's growing up he can't ever know? Do you know how much that would cost, how many people it would involve?"

"That would be all right," she said.

"And suppose you had it, a biography written like a script, twenty years of a lifetime, every day, every hour you could account for; now you're going to have to arrange for a child, from birth, to be surrounded by people who are going to play this script out—and who will never let anything else happen to him but what's in the script, and who will never let him know."

"That's it! That's it!" she cried.

He leaped to his feet and swore at her. He said, "I'm not planning this, you love-struck lunatic, I'm objecting to it!"

"Is there any more?" she cried eagerly. "Keogh, Keogh, try—try hard. How do we start? What do we do first? Quick, Keogh."

He looked at her, thunderstruck, and at last sank down on the bench and began to laugh weakly. She sat by him, held his hand, her eyes shining. After a time he sobered and turned to her. He drank the shine of those eyes for a while; and after, his brain began to function again . . . on Wyke business . . .

"The main source of who he is and what he's done," he said at last, "won't be with us much longer. . . . We better go tell Rathburn to get him off the morphine. He has to be able to think."

"All right," she said. "All right."

When the pain got too much to permit him to remember any more, they tried a little morphine again. For a while they found a balance between recollection and agony, but the agony gained. Then they severed his spinal cord so he couldn't feel it. They brought in people—psychiatrist, stenographers, even a professional historian.

In the rebuilt barn, Weber tried animal hosts, cows even, and primates—everything he could think of. He got some results, though no good ones. He tried humans too. He couldn't cross the bridge of body tolerance; the uterus will not support an alien fetus any more than the hand will accept the graft of another's finger.

So he tried nutrient solutions. He tried a great many. Ultimately he found one that worked. It was the blood plasma of pregnant women.

He placed the best of the quasi-ova between sheets of sterilized chamois. He designed automatic machinery to drip the plasma in at arterial tempo, drain it at a veinous rate, keep it at body temperature.

One day fifty of them died because of choloform used in one of the adhesives. When light seemed to affect them adversely, Weber designed containers of bakelite. When ordinary photography proved impractical he designed a new kind of film sensitive to heat, the first infrared film.

The viable fetuses he had at sixty days showed the eye spot, the spine, the buds of arms, a beating heart. Each and every one of them consumed, or was bathed in, over a gallon of plasma a day, and at one point there were one hundred and seventy-four thousand of them. Then they began to die off—some malformed, some chemically unbalanced, many for reasons too subtle even for Weber and his staff.

When he had done all he could, when he could only wait and see, he had fetuses seven months along and growing well. There were twenty-three of them. Guy Gibbon was dead quite awhile by then, and his widow came to see Weber and tiredly put down a stack of papers and reports, urged him to read, begged him to call her as soon as he had.

He read them, he called her. He refused what she asked.

She got hold of Keogh. He refused to have anything to do with such an idea. She made him change his mind. Keogh made Weber change his mind.

The stone barn hummed with construction again and new machinery. The cold tank was four by six feet inside, surrounded by coils and sensing devices. They put her in it.

By that time the fetuses were eight and a half months along. There were four left.

One made it.

AUTHOR'S NOTE: To the reader, but especially to the reader in his early twenties, let me ask: did you ever have the feeling that you were getting pushed around? Did you ever want to do something, and have all sorts of obstacles thrown in your way until you had to give up, while on the other hand some other thing you wanted was made easy for you? Did you ever feel that certain strangers know who you are? Did you ever meet a girl who made you explode inside, who seemed to like you—and who was mysteriously plucked out of your life, as if she shouldn't be in the script?

Well, we've all had these feelings. Yet if you've read the above, you'll allow it's a little more startling than just a story. It reads like an analogy, doesn't it? I mean, it doesn't have to be a castle, or the ol' swimmin' hole, and the names have been changed to protect the innocent . . . author.

Because it could be about time for her to wake up, aged only two or three years for her twenty-year cold sleep. And when she meets you, it's going to be the biggest thing that ever happened to you since the last time.

PHILIP JOSÉ FARMER

The Shadow of Space

A great advantage of science fiction is its ability to offer a sense of perspective to intelligent readers, to remind us that there is a lot "out there" besides us. But how do you react when you are so large that you can hold entire galaxies in your hand? What are your responsibilities then?

I

The klaxon cleared its plastic throat and began to whoop. Alternate yellow and reds pulsed on the consoles wrapped like bracelets around the wrists of the captain and the navigator. The huge auxiliary screens spaced on the bulkheads of the bridge also flashed red and yellow.

Captain Grettir, catapulted from his reverie, and from his chair, stood up. The letters and numerals 20-G-DZ-R hung burning on a sector of each screen and spurted up from the wrist-console, spread out before his eyes, then disappeared, only to rise from the wrist-console again and magnify themselves and thin into nothing. Over and over again. 20-G-DZ-R. The code letters indicating that the alarm originated from the corridor leading to the engine room.

He turned his wrist and raised his arm to place the lower half of the console at the correct viewing and speaking distance.

"Twenty-G-DZ-R, report!"

The flaming, expanding, levitating letters died out, and the long high-cheekboned face of MacCool, chief engineer, appeared as a tiny image on the sector of the console. It was duplicated on the bridge bulkhead screens. It rose and grew larger, shooting towards Grettir, then winking out to be followed by a second ballooning face.

Also on the wrist-console's screen, behind MacCool, were Comas, a petty officer, and Grinker, a machinist's mate. Their faces did not float up because they were not in the central part of the screen. Behind them was a group of marines and an 88-K cannon on a floating sled.

"It's the Wellington woman," MacCool said. "She used the photer, low-power setting, to knock out the two guards stationed at the engine-room port. Then she herded us—me, Comas, Grinker—out. She said she'd shoot us if we resisted. And she welded the grille to the bulkhead so it can't be opened unless it's burned off.

"I don't know why she's doing this. But she's reconnected the drive wires to a zander bridge so she can control the acceleration herself. We can't do a thing to stop her unless we go in after her."

He paused, swallowed and said, "I could send men outside and have them try to get through the engine room airlock or else cut through the hull to get her. While she was distracted by this, we could make a frontal attack down the corridor. But she says she'll shoot anybody that gets too close. We could lose some men. She means what she says."

"If you cut a hole in the hull, she'd be out of air, dead in a minute," Grettir said.

"She's in a space suit," MacCool replied. "That's why I didn't have this area sealed off and gas flooded in."

Grettir hoped his face was not betraying his shock. Hearing an exclamation from Wang, seated near him, Grettir turned his head. He said, "How in the hell did she get out of sick bay?"

He realized at the same time that Wang could not answer that question. MacCool said, "I don't know, sir. Ask Doctor Wills."

"Never mind that now!"

Grettir stared at the sequence of values appearing on the navigator's auxiliary bulkhead-screen. The 0.5 of light speed had already climbed to 0.96. It changed every four seconds. The 0.96 became 0.97, then 0.98, 0.99 and then 1.0. And then 1.1 and 1.2.

Grettir forced himself to sit back down. If anything was going to happen, it would have done so by now; the TSN-X cruiser *Sleipnir*, 280 million tons, would have been converted to pure energy.

A nova, bright but very brief, would have gouted in the heavens. And the orbiting telescopes of Earth would see the flare in 20.8 light-years.

"What's the state of the *emc* clamp and acceleration-dissipaters?" Grettir said.

"No strain—yet," Wang said. "But the power drain . . . if it continues . . . five megakilowatts per two seconds, and we're just beginning."

"I think," Grettir said slowly, "that we're going to find out what we intended to find out. But it isn't going to be under the carefully controlled conditions we had planned."

The Terran Space Navy experimental cruiser *Sleipnir* had left its base on Asgard, eighth planet of Altair (alpha Aquilae), twenty-eight shipdays ago. It was under orders to make the first attempt of a manned ship to exceed the velocity of light. If its mission was successful, men could travel between Earth and the colonial planets in weeks instead of years. The entire galaxy might be opened to Earth.

Within the past two weeks, the *Sleipnir* had made several tests at 0.8 times the velocity of light, the tests lasting up to two hours at a time.

The *Sleipnir* was equipped with enormous motors and massive clamps, dissipaters and space-time structure expanders ("hole-openers") required for near-lightspeeds and beyond. No ship in Terrestrial history had ever had such power or the means to handle such power.

The drive itself—the cubed amplification of energy produced by the controlled mixture of matter, antimatter and half-matter—gave an energy that could eat its way through the iron core of a planet. But part of that energy had to be diverted to power the energy-mass conversion "clamp" that kept the ship from being transformed into energy itself. The "hole-opener" also required vast power. This device—officially the space-time structure expander, or neutralizer—"unbent" the local curvature of the universe and so furnished a "hole" through which the *Sleipnir* traveled. This hole nullified 99.3 percent of the resistance the *Sleipnir* would normally have encountered.

Thus the effects of speeds approaching and even exceeding lightspeed, would be modified, even if not entirely avoided. The *Sleipnir* should not contract along its length to zero nor attain infinite mass when it reached the speed of light. It contracted, and it swelled, yes, by only $1/777{,}777$ what it should have. The ship would assume the shape of a disk—but much more slowly than it would without its openers, clamps and dissipaters.

Beyond the speed of light, who knew what would happen? It was the business of the *Sleipnir* to find out. But, Grettir thought, not under these conditions. Not willy-nilly.

"Sir!" MacCool said, "Wellington threatens to shoot anybody who comes near the engine room."

He hesitated, then said, "Except you. She wants to speak to you. But she doesn't want to do it over the intercom. She insists that you come down and talk to her face to face." Grettir bit his lower lip and made a sucking sound.

"Why me?" he said, but he knew why, and MacCool's expression showed that he also knew.

"I'll be down in a minute. Now, isn't there any way we can connect a bypass, route a circuit around her or beyond her and get control of the drive again?"

"No, sir!"

"Then she's cut through the engine-room deck and gotten to the redundant circuits also?"

MacCool said, "She's crazy, but she's clear-headed enough to take all precautions. She hasn't overlooked a thing."

Grettir said, "Wang! What's the velocity now?"

"Two point three sl/pm, sir!"

Grettir looked at the huge starscreen on the "forward" bulkhead of the bridge. Black except for a few glitters of white, blue, red, green, and the galaxy called XD-Two that lay dead ahead. The galaxy had been the size of an orange, and it still was. He stared at the screen for perhaps a minute, then said, "Wang, am I seeing right? The red light from XD-Two is shifting toward the blue, right?"

"Right, sir!"

"Then . . . why isn't XD-Two getting bigger? We're overhauling it like a fox after a rabbit."

Wang said, "I think it's getting closer, sir. But we're getting bigger."

II

Grettir rose from the chair. "Take over while I'm gone. Turn off the alarm; tell the crew to continue their normal duties. If anything comes up while I'm in the engine area, notify me at once."

The exec saluted. "Yes, sir!" she said huskily.

Grettir strode off the bridge. He was aware that the officers and crewmen seated in the ring of chairs in the bridge were looking covertly at him. He stopped for a minute to light up a cigar. He was glad that his hands were not shaking, and he hoped that his expression was confident. Slowly, repressing the impulse to run, he continued across the bridge and into the jump-shaft. He stepped off backward into the shaft and nonchalantly blew out smoke while he sank out of sight of the men in the bridge. He braced himself against the quick drop and then the thrusting deceleration. He had set the controls for Dock 14; the doors slid open; he walked into a corridor where a g-car and operator waited for him. Grettir climbed in, sat down and told the crewman where to drive.

Two minutes later, he was with MacCool. The chief engineer pointed down the corridor. Near its end on the floor were two still unconscious marines. The door to the engine room was open. The secondary door, the grille, was shut. The lights within the engine room had been turned off. Something white on the other side of the grille moved. It was Donna Wellington's face, visible through the helmet.

"We can't keep this acceleration up," Grettir said. "We're already going far faster than even unmanned experimental ships have been allowed to go. There are all sorts of theories about what might happen to a ship at these speeds, all bad."

"We've disproved several by now," MacCool said. He spoke evenly, but his forehead was sweaty and shadows hung under his eyes.

MacCool continued, "I'm glad you got here, sir. She just threatened to cut the *emc* clamp wires if you didn't show within the next two minutes."

He gestured with both hands to indicate a huge expanding ball of light.

"I'll talk to her," Grettir said. "Although I can't imagine what she wants."

MacCool looked dubious. Grettir wanted to ask him what the hell he was thinking but thought better of it. He said, "Keep your men at this post. Don't even look as if you're coming after me."

"And what do we do, sir, if she shoots you?"

Grettir winced. "Use the cannon. And never mind hesitating if I happen to be in the way. Blast her! But make sure you use a beam short enough to get her but not long enough to touch the engines."

"May I ask why we don't do that before you put your life in danger?" MacCool said.

Grettir hesitated, then said, "My main responsibility is to the ship and its crew. But this woman is very sick; she doesn't realize the implications of her actions. Not fully anyway. I want to talk her out of this, if I can."

He unhooked the communicator from his belt and walked down the corridor toward the grille and the darkness behind it and the whiteness that moved. His back prickled. The men were watching him intently. God knew what they were saying, or at least thinking, about him. The whole crew had been amused for some time by Donna Wellington's passion for him and his inability to cope with her. They had said she was mad about him, not realizing that she really was mad. They had laughed. But they were not laughing now.

Even so, knowing that she was truly insane, some of them must be blaming him for this danger. Undoubtedly, they were thinking that if he had handled her differently, they would not now be so close to death.

He stopped just one step short of the grille. Now he could see Wellington's face, a checkerboard of blacks and whites. He waited for her to speak first. A full minute passed, then she said, "Robert!"

The voice, normally low-pitched and pleasant, was now thin and strained.

"Not Robert. Eric," he said into the communicator. "Captain Eric Grettir, Mrs. Wellington."

There was a silence. She moved closer to the grille. Light struck one eye, which gleamed bluely.

"Why do you hate me so, Robert?" she said plaintively. "You used to love me. What did I do to make you turn against me?"

"I am *not* your husband," Grettir said. "Look at me. Can't you see that I am not Robert Wellington? I am Captain Grettir of the *Sleipnir*. You *must* see who I *really* am, Mrs. Wellington. It is very important."

"You don't love me!" she screamed. "You are trying to get rid of me by pretending you're another man! But it won't work! I'd know you anywhere, you beast! You beast! I hate you, Robert!"

Involuntarily, Grettir stepped back under the intensity of her anger. He saw her hand come up from the shadows and the flash of light on a handgun. It was too late then; she fired; a beam of whiteness dazzled him.

Light was followed by darkness.

Ahead, or above, there was a disk of grayness in the black. Grettir traveled slowly and spasmodically toward it, as if he had been swallowed by a whale but was being ejected toward the open mouth, the muscles of the leviathan's throat working him outward.

Far behind him, deep in the bowels of the whale, Donna Wellington spoke. "Robert?"

"Eric!" he shouted. "I'm *Eric!*"

The *Sleipnir*, barely on its way out from Asgard, dawdling at 6,200 kilometers per second, had picked up the Mayday call. It came from a spaceship midway between the twelfth and thirteenth planet of Altair. Although Grettir could have ignored the call without reprimand from his superiors, he altered course, and he found a ship wrecked by a meteorite. Inside the hull was half the body of a man. And a woman in deep shock.

Robert and Donna Wellington were second-generation Asgardians, Ph.D.'s in biotatology, holding master's papers in astrogation. They had been searching for specimens of "space plankton" and "space hydras," forms of life born in the regions between Altair's outer planets.

The crash, the death of her husband and the shattering sense of isolation, dissociation and hopelessness during the eighty-four hours before rescue had twisted Mrs. Wellington. Perhaps twisted was the wrong word. Fragmented was a better description.

From the beginning of what at first seemed recovery, she had taken a superficial resemblance of Grettir to her husband for an identity. Grettir had been gentle and kind with her at the beginning and had made frequent visits to sick bay. Later, advised by Doctor Wills, he had been severe with her.

. And so the unforseen result.

Donna Wellington screamed behind him and, suddenly, the twilight circle ahead became bright, and he was free. He opened his eyes to see faces over him. Doctor Wills and MacCool. He was in sick bay.

MacCool smiled and said, "For a moment, we thought . . ."

"What happened?" Grettir said. Then, "I know what she did. I mean . . ."

"She fired full power at you," MacCool said. "But the bars of the grille absorbed most of the energy. You got just enough to crisp the skin off your face and to knock you out. Good thing you closed your eyes in time."

Grettir sat up. He felt his face; it was covered with a greasy ointment, pain-deadening and skin-growing *resec*.

"I got a hell of a headache."

Doctor Wills said, "It'll be gone in a minute."

"What's the situation?" Grettir said. "How'd you get me away from her?"

MacCool said, "I had to do it, Captain. Otherwise, she'd have taken another shot at you. The cannon blasted what was left of the grille. Mrs. Wellington . . ."

"She's dead?"

"Yes. But the cannon didn't get her. Strange. She took her suit off, stripped to the skin. Then she went out through the airlock in the engine room. Naked, as if she meant to be the bride of Death. We almost got caught in the outrush of air, since she fixed the controls so that the inner port remained open. It was close, but we got the port shut in time."

Grettir said, "I . . . never mind. Any damage to the engine room?"

"No. And the wires are reconnected for normal operation. Only . . ."

"Only what?"

MacCool's face was so long he looked like a frightened bloodhound.

"Just before I reconnected the wires, a funny . . . peculiar . . . thing happened. The whole ship, and everything inside the ship, went through a sort of distortion. Wavy, as if we'd all become wax and were dripping. Or flags flapping in a wind. The bridge reports that the fore of the ship seemed to expand like a balloon, then became ripply, and the entire effect passed through the ship. We all got nauseated while the waviness lasted."

There was silence, but their expressions indicated that there was more to be said.

"Well?"

MacCool and Wills looked at each other. MacCool swallowed and said, "Captain, we don't know where in hell we are!"

III

On the bridge, Grettir examined the forward EXT. screen. There were no stars. Space everywhere was filled with a light as gray and as dull as that of a false dawn on Earth. In the gray glow, at a distance as yet undetermined, were a number of spheres. They looked small, but if they were as large as the one immediately aft of the *Sleipnir*, they were huge.

The sphere behind them, estimated to be at a distance of fifty kilometers, was about the size of Earth's moon, relative to the ship. Its surface was as smooth and as gray as a ball of lead.

Darl spoke a binary code into her wrist-console, and the sphere on the starscreen seemed to shoot toward them. It filled the screen until Darl changed the line-of-sight. They were looking at about 20 degrees of arc of the limb of the sphere.

"There it is!" Darl said. A small object floated around the edge of the sphere and seemed to shoot toward them. She magnified it, and it became a small gray sphere.

"It orbits round the big one," she said.

Darl paused, then said, "We—the ship—came *out* of that small sphere. *Out* of it. *Through* its skin."

"You mean we had been inside it?" Grettir said. "And now we're outside it?"

"Yes, sir! Exactly!"

She gasped and said, "Oh, oh—sir!"

Around the large sphere, slightly above the plane of the orbit of the small sphere but within its sweep in an inner orbit, sped another object. At least fifty times as large as the small globe, it caught up with the globe, and the two disappeared together around the curve of the primary.

"Wellington's body!" Grettir said.

He turned away from the screen, took one step, and turned around again. "It's not right! She should be trailing along behind us or at least parallel with us, maybe shooting off at an angle but still moving in our direction.

"But she's been grabbed by the big sphere! She's in orbit! And her size; gargantuan! It doesn't make sense! It shouldn't be!"

"Nothing should," Wang said.

"Take us back," Grettir said. "Establish an orbit around the primary, on the same plane as the secondary but farther out, approximately a kilometer and a half from it."

Darl's expression said, "Then what?"

Grettir wondered if she had the same thought as he. The faces of the others on the bridge were doubtful. The fear was covered but leaking out. He could smell the rotten bubbles. Had they guessed, too?

"What attraction does the primary have on the ship?" he said to Wang.

"No detectable influence whatsoever, sir. The *Sleipnir* seems to have a neutral charge, neither positive nor negative in relation to any of the spheres. Or to Wellington's . . . body."

Grettir was slightly relieved. His thoughts had been so wild that he had not been able to consider them as anything but hysterical fantasies. But Wang's answer showed that Grettir's idea was also his. Instead of replying in terms of gravitational force, he had talked as if the ship were a subatomic particle.

But if the ship was not affected by the primary, why had Wellington's corpse been attracted by the primary?

"Our velocity in relation to the primary?" Grettir said.

"We cut off the acceleration as soon as the wires were reconnected," Wang said.

"This was immediately after we came out into this . . . this space. We didn't apply any retrodrive. Our velocity, as indicated by power consumption, is ten megaparsecs per minute. That is," he added after a pause, "what the instruments show. But our radar, which should be totally ineffective at this velocity, indicates fifty kilometers per minute, relative to the big sphere."

Wang leaned back in his chair as if he expected Grettir to explode into incredulity. Grettir lit up another cigar. This time, his hands shook. He blew out a big puff of smoke and said, "Obviously, we're operating under different quote laws unquote *out here.*"

Wang sighed softly. "So you think so, too, captain? Yes, different *laws.* Which means that every time we make a move through this space, we can't know what the result will be. May I ask what you plan to do, sir?"

By this question, which Wang would never have dared to voice before, though he had doubtless often thought it, Grettir knew that the navigator shared his anxiety. The umbilical had been ripped out; Wang was hurting and bleeding inside. Was he, too, beginning to float away in a gray void? Bereft as no man had even been bereft?

It takes a special type of man or woman to lose himself from Earth or his native planet, to go out among the stars so far that the natal sun is not even a faint glimmer. It also takes special conditioning for the special type of man.

He has to believe, in the deepest part of his unconscious, that his ship is a piece of Mother Earth. He has to believe; otherwise, he goes to pieces.

It can be done. Hundreds do it. But nothing had prepared even these farfarers for absolute divorce from the universe itself.

Grettir ached with the dread of the void. The void was coiling up inside him, a gray serpent, a slither of nothingness. Coiling. And what would happen when it uncoiled?

And what would happen to the crew when they were informed—as they must be—of the utter dissociation?

There was only one way to keep their minds from slipping their moorings. They must believe that they could get back into the world. Just as he must believe it.

"I'll play it by ear," Grettir said.

"What? Sir?"

"Play it by ear!" Grettir said more harshly than he had intended. "I was merely answering your question. Have you forgotten you asked me what I meant to do?"

"Oh, no, sir," Wang said. "I was just thinking . . ."

"Keep your mind on the job," Grettir said. He told Darl he would take over. He spoke the code to activate the ALL-STATIONS; a low rising-falling sound went into every room of the *Sleipnir*, and all screens flashed a black-and-green checked pattern. Then the warnings, visual and audible, died out, and the captain spoke.

He talked for two minutes. The bridgemen looked as if the lights had been turned off in their brains. It was almost impossible to grasp the concept of their being outside their universe. As difficult was thinking of their unimaginably vast native cosmos as only an "electron" orbiting around the nucleus of an "atom." If what the captain said was true (how could it be?), the ship was in the space between the superatoms of a supermolecule of a superuniverse.

Even though they knew that the *Sleipnir* had ballooned under the effect of nearly 300,000 times the speed of light, they could not wrap the fingers of their minds around the concept. It turned to smoke and drifted away.

It took ten minutes, ship's time, to turn and to complete the maneuvers which placed the *Sleipnir* in an orbit parallel to but outside the secondary, or, as Grettir thought of it, "our universe." He gave his chair back to Darl and paced back and forth across the bridge while he watched the starscreen.

If they were experiencing the sundering, the cutting-off, they were keeping it under control. They had been told by their captain that they *were* going back in, not that they would make a *try* at reentry. They had been through much with him, and he had never failed them. With this trust, they could endure the agony of dissolution.

As the *Sleipnir* established itself parallel to the secondary, Wellington's body curved around the primary again and began to pass the small sphere and ship. The arms of the mountainous body were extended stiffly to both sides, and her legs spread out. In the gray light, her skin was bluish black from the ruptured veins and arteries below the skin. Her red hair, coiled in a Psyche knot, looked black. Her eyes, each of which was larger than the bridge of the *Sleipnir*, were open, bulging clots of black blood. Her lips were pulled back in a grimace, the teeth like a soot-streaked portcullis.

Cartwheeling, she passed the sphere and the ship.

Wang reported that there were three "shadows" on the surface of the primary. Those were keeping pace with the secondary, the corpse and the ship. Magnified on the bridge bulkhead-screen, each "shadow" was the silhouette of one of the three orbiting bodies. The shadows were only about one shade darker than the surface and were caused by a shifting pucker in the primary skin. The surface protruded along the edges of the shadows and formed a shallow depression within the edges.

If the shadow of the *Sleipnir* was a true indication of the shape of the vessel, the *Sleipnir* had lost its needle shape and was a spindle, fat at both ends and narrow-waisted.

When Wellington's corpse passed by the small sphere and the ship, her shadow or "print" reversed itself in shape. Where the head of the shadow should have been, the feet now were and vice versa.

She disappeared around the curve of the primary and, on returning on the other side, her shadow had again become a "true" reflection. It remained so until she passed the secondary, after which the shadow once more reversed itself.

Grettir had been informed that there seemed to be absolutely no matter in the space outside the spheres. There was not one detectable atom or particle. Moreover, despite the lack of any radiation, the temperature of the hull, and ten meters beyond the hull, was a fluctuating seventy degrees plus-or-minus twenty degrees Fahrenheit.

IV

Three orbits later, Grettir knew that the ship had diminished greatly in size. Or else the small sphere had expanded. Or both changes occurred. Moreover, on the visual screen, the secondary had lost its spherical shape and become a fat disk during the first circling of the ship to establish its orbit.

Grettir was puzzling over this and thinking of calling Van Voorden, the physicist chief, when Wellington's corpse came around the primary again. The body caught up with the other satellites, and for a moment the primary, secondary, and the *Sleipnir* were in a line, strung on an invisible cord.

Suddenly, the secondary and the corpse jumped toward each other. They ceased their motion when within a quarter kilometer of each other. The secondary regained its globular form as soon as it had attained its new orbit. Wellington's arms and legs, during this change in position, moved in as if she had come to life. Her arms folded themselves across her breasts, and her legs drew up so that her thighs were against her stomach.

Grettir called Van Voorden. The physicist said, "Out here, the cabin boy —if we had one—knows as much as I do about what's going on or what to expect. The data, such as they are, are too inadequate, too confusing. I can only suggest that there was an interchange of energy between Wellington and the secondary."

"A quantum jump?" Grettir said. "If that's so, why didn't the ship experience a loss or gain?"

Darl said, "Pardon, sir. But it did. There was a loss of fifty megakilowatts in zero point eight second."

Van Voorden said, "The *Sleipnir* may have decreased in relative size because of decrease in velocity. Or maybe velocity had nothing to do with it or only partially, anyway. Maybe the change in spatial interrelationships among bodies causes other changes. In shape, size, energy transfer and so forth. I don't know. Tell me, how big is the woman—corpse—relative to the ship now?"

"The radar measurements say she's eighty-three times as large. She increased. Or we've decreased."

Van Voorden's eyes grew even larger. Grettir thanked him and cut him off. He ordered the *Sleipnir* to be put in exactly the same orbit as the secondary but ten dekameters ahead of it.

Van Voorden called back. "The jump happened when we were in line with the other three bodies. Maybe the *Sleipnir* is some sort of *geometrical catalyst* under certain conditions. That's only an analogy, of course."

Wang verbally fed the order into the computer-interface, part of his wrist-console. The *Sleipnir* was soon racing ahead of the sphere. Radar reported that the ship and secondary were now approximately equal in size. The corpse, coming around the primary again, was still the same relative size as before.

Grettir ordered the vessel turned around so that the nose would be facing the sphere. This accomplished, he had the velocity reduced. The retrodrive braked them while the lateral thrusts readjusted forces to keep the ship in the same orbit. Since the primary had no attraction for the *Sleipnir,* the ship had to remain in orbit with a constant rebalancing of thrusts. The sphere, now ballooning, inched toward the ship.

"Radar indicates we're doing twenty-six point six dekameters per second relative to the primary," Wang said. "Power drain indicates we're making twenty-five thousand times the speed of light. That, by the way, is not proportionate to what we were making when we left our world."

"More braking," Grettir said. "Cut it down to fifteen dekameters."

The sphere swelled, filled the screen, and Grettir involuntarily braced himself for the impact, even though he was so far from expecting one that he had not strapped himself into a chair. There had been none when the ship had broken through the "skin" of the universe.

Grettir had been told of the distorting in the ship when it had left the universe and so was not entirely surprised. Nevertheless, he could not help being both frightened and bewildered when the front part of the bridge abruptly swelled and then rippled. Screen, bulkheads, deck and crew waved as if they were cloth in a strong wind. Grettir felt as if he were being folded into a thousand different angles at the same time.

Then Wang cried out, and the others repeated his cry. Wang rose from his seat and put his hands out before him. Grettir, standing behind and to one side of him, was frozen as he saw dozens of little objects, firefly-size, burning brightly, slip *through* the starscreen and bulkhead and drift toward him. He came out of his paralysis in time to dodge one tiny whitely glowing ball. But another struck his forehead, causing him to yelp.

A score of the bodies passed by him. Some were white; some blue; some green; one was topaz. They were at all levels, above his head, even with his waist, one almost touching the deck. He crouched down to let two pass over him, and as he did so, he saw Nagy, the communications officer, bent over and vomiting. The stuff sprayed out of his mouth and caught a little glow in it and snuffed it out in a burst of smoke.

Then the forepart of the bridge had reasserted its solidity and constancy of shape. There were no more burning objects coming through.

Grettir turned to see the aft bulkheads of the bridge quivering in the wake of the wave. And they, too, became normal. Grettir shouted the "override" code so that he could take control from Wang, who was screaming with pain. He directed the ship to change its course to an "upward vertical" direction. There was no "upward" sensation, because the artificial g-field within the ship readjusted. Suddenly, the forward part of the bridge became distorted again, and the waves reached through the fabric of the ship and the crew.

The starscreen, which had been showing nothing but the blackness of space, speckled by a few stars, now displayed the great gray sphere in one corner and the crepuscular light. Grettir, fighting the pain in his forehead and the nausea, gave another command. There was a delay of possibly thirty seconds, and then the *Sleipnir* began the turn that would take it back into a parallel orbit with the secondary.

Grettir, realizing what was happening shortly after being burned, had taken the *Sleipnir* back out of the universe. He put in a call for corpsmen and Doctor Wills and then helped Wang from his chair. There was an odor of burned flesh and hair in the bridge which the air-conditioning system had not as yet removed. Wang's face and hands were burned in five or six places, and part of the long coarse black hair on the right side of his head was burned.

Three corpsmen and Wills ran into the bridge. Wills started to apply a pseudoprotein jelly on Grettir's forehead, but Grettir told him to take care of Wang first. Wills worked swiftly and then, after spreading the jelly over Wang's burns and placing a false-skin bandage over the burns, treated the captain. As soon as the jelly was placed on his forehead, Grettir felt the pain dissolve.

"Third degree," Wills said. "It's lucky those things—whatever they are—weren't larger."

Grettir picked up his cigar, which he had dropped on the deck when he had first seen the objects racing toward him. The cigar was still burning. Near it lay a coal, swiftly blackening. He picked it up gingerly. It felt warm but could be held without too much discomfort.

Grettir extended his hand, palm up, so that the doctor could see the speck of black matter in it. It was even smaller than when it had floated into the bridge through the momentarily "opened" interstices of the molecules composing the hull and bulkheads.

"This is *a galaxy*," he whispered.

Doc Wills did not understand. "A galaxy of our universe," Grettir added.

Doc Wills paled, and he gulped loudly.

"You mean . . . ?"

Grettir nodded.

Wills said, "I hope . . . not our . . . Earth's . . . galaxy!"

"I doubt it," Grettir said. "We were on the edge of the star fields farthest out, that is, the closest to the—skin?—of our universe. But if we had kept on going . . ."

Wills shook his head. Billions of stars, possibly millions of inhabitable, hence inhabited, planets, were in that little ball of fire, now cool and collapsed.

Trillions of sentient beings and an unimaginable number of animals had died when their world collided with Grettir's forehead.

Wang, informed of the true cause of his burns, became ill again. Grettir ordered him to sick bay and replaced him with Gomez. Van Voorden entered the bridge. He said, "I suppose our main objective has to be our reentry. But why couldn't we make an attempt to penetrate the primary, the nucleus? Do you realize what an astounding . . . ?"

Grettir interrupted. "I realize. But our fuel supply is low, very low. If—I mean, *when* we get back through the 'skin,' we'll have a long way to go before we can return to base. Maybe too long. I don't dare exceed a certain speed during reentry because of our size. It would be too dangerous. . . . I don't want to wipe out any more galaxies. God knows the psychological problems we are going to have when the guilt really hits. Right now, we're numbed. *No!* We're not going to do any exploring!"

"But there may be no future investigations permitted!" Van Voorden said. "There's too much danger to the universe itself to allow any more research by ships like ours!"

"Exactly," Grettir said. "I sympathize with your desire to do scientific research. But the safety of the ship and crew comes first. Besides, I think that if I were to order an exploration, I'd have mutiny on my hands. And I couldn't blame my men. Tell me, Van Voorden, don't you feel a sense of . . . dissociation?"

Van Voorden nodded and said, "But I'm willing to fight it. There is so much . . ."

"So much to find out," Grettir said. "Agreed. But the authorities will have to determine if that is to be done."

Grettir dismissed him. Van Voorden marched off. But he did not give the impression of a powerful anger. He was, Grettir thought, secretly relieved at the captain's decision. Van Voorden had made his protest for Science's sake. But as a human being, Van Voorden must want very much to get "home."

V

At the end of the ordered maneuver, the *Sleipnir* was in the same orbit as the universe but twenty kilometers ahead and again pointed toward it. Since there was no attraction between ship and primary, the *Sleipnir* had to use power to maintain the orbit; a delicate readjustment of lateral thrust was constantly required.

Grettir ordered braking applied. The sphere expanded on the starscreen, and then there was only a gray surface displayed. To the viewers the surface did not seem to spin, but radar had determined that the globe completed a revolution on its polar axis once every thirty-three seconds.

Grettir did not like to think of the implications of this. Van Voorden undoubtedly had received the report, but he had made no move to notify the captain. Perhaps, like Grettir, he believed that the fewer who thought about it, the better.

The mock-up screen showed, in silhouette form, the relative sizes of the approaching spheres and the ship. The basketball was the universe; the toothpick, the *Sleipnir*. Grettir hoped that this reduction would be enough to avoid running into any more galaxies. Immediately after the vessel penetrated the "skin," the *Sleipnir* would be again braked, thus further diminishing it. There should be plenty of distance between the skin and the edge of the closest star fields.

"Here we go," Grettir said, watching the screen which indicated in meters the gap between ship and sphere. Again he involuntarily braced himself.

There was a rumble, a groan. The deck slanted upward, then rolled to port. Grettir was hurled to the deck, spun over and over and brought up with stunning impact against a bulkhead. He was in a daze for a moment and by the time he had recovered, the ship had reasserted its proper attitude. Gomez had placed the ship into "level" again. He had a habit of strapping himself into the navigator's chair although regulations did not require it unless the captain ordered it.

Grettir asked for a report on any damage and, while waiting for it, called Van Voorden. The physicist was bleeding from a cut on his forehead.

"Obviously," he said, "it requires a certain force to penetrate the outer covering or energy shield or whatever it is that encloses the universe. We didn't have it. So . . ."

"Presents quite a problem," Grettir said. "If we go fast enough to rip through, we're too large and may destroy entire galaxies. If we go too slow, we can't get through."

He paused, then said, "I can think of only one method. But I'm ignorant of the consequences, which might be disastrous. Not for us but for the universe. I'm not sure I should even take such a chance."

He was silent so long that Van Voorden could not restrain himself. "Well?"

"Do you think that if we could make a hole in the skin, the rupture might result in some sort of collapse or cosmic disturbance?"

"You want to beam a hole in the skin?" Van Voorden said slowly. His skin was pale, but it had been that color before Grettir asked him the question.

Grettir wondered if Van Voorden was beginning to crumble under the "dissociation."

"Never mind," Grettir said. "I shouldn't have asked you. You can't know what the effects would be any more than anyone else. I apologize. I must have been trying to make you share some of the blame if anything went wrong. Forget it."

Van Voorden stared, and he was still looking blank when Grettir cut off his image. He paced back and forth, once stepping over a tiny black object on the deck and then grimacing when he realized that it was too late for care. Millions of stars, billions of planets, trillions of creatures. All cold and dead. And if he experimented further in trying to get back into the native cosmos, then what? A collapsing universe?

Grettir stopped pacing and said aloud, "We came through the skin twice without harm to it. So we're going to try the beam!"

Nobody answered him, but the look on their faces was evidence of their relief. Fifteen minutes later, the *Sleipnir* was just ahead of the sphere and facing it. After an unvarying speed and distance from the sphere had been maintained for several minutes, laser beams measured the exact length between the tip of the cannon and the surface of the globe.

The chief gunnery officer, Abdul White Eagle, set one of the fore cannons. Grettir delayed only a few seconds in giving the next order. He clenched his teeth so hard he almost bit the cigar in two, groaned slightly then said, "Fire!"

Darl transmitted the command. The beam shot out, touched the skin and vanished.

The starscreen showed a black hole in the gray surface at the equator of the sphere. The hole moved away and then was gone around the curve of the sphere. Exactly thirty-three seconds later, the hole was in its original position. It was shrinking. By the time four rotations were completed, the hole had closed in on itself.

Grettir sighed and wiped the sweat off his forehead. Darl reported that the hole would be big enough for the ship to get through by the second time it came around. After that, it would be too small.

"We'll go through during the second rotation," Grettir said. "Set up the compigator for an automatic entry; tie the cannon in with the compigator. There shouldn't be any problem. If the hole shrinks too fast, we'll enlarge it with the cannon."

He heard Darl say, "Operation begun, sir!" as Gomez spoke into his console. The white beam spurted out in a cone, flicked against the "shell" or "skin" and disappeared. A circle of blackness three times the diameter of the ship came into being and then moved to one side of the screen. Immediately, under the control of the compigator, the retrodrive of the *Sleipnir* went into action. The sphere loomed; a gray wall filled the starscreen. Then the edge of the hole came into view, and a blackness spread over the screen.

"We're going to make it," Grettir thought. "The compigator can't make a mistake."

He looked around him. The bridgemen were strapped to their chairs now. Most of the faces were set, they were well disciplined and brave. But if they felt as he did—they must—they were shoving back a scream far down in them. They could not endure this "homesickness" much longer. And after they got through, were back in the womb, he would have to permit them a most unmilitary behavior. They would laugh, weep, shout. And so would he.

The nose of the *Sleipnir* passed through the hole. Now; if anything went wrong, the fore cannon could not be used. But it was impossible that . . .

The klaxon whooped. Darl screamed, "Oh my God! Something's wrong! The hole's shrinking too fast!"

Grettir roared, "Double the speed! No! Halve it!"

Increasing the forward speed meant a swelling in size of the *Sleipnir* but a contraction of the longitudinal axis and a lengthening of the lateral. The *Sleipnir* would get through the hole faster, but it would also narrow the gap between its hull and the edges of the hole.

Halving the speed, on the other hand, though it would make the ship smaller in relation to the hole, would also make the distance to be traversed greater. This might mean that the edges would still hit the ship.

Actually, Grettir did not know what order should be given or if any order would have an effect upon their chance to escape. He could only do what seemed best.

The grayness spread out from the perimeter of the starscreen. There was a screech of severed plastic running through the ship, quivering the bulkheads and decks, a sudden push forward of the crew as they felt the inertia, then a release as the almost instantaneous readjustment of the internal g-field canceled the external effects.

Everybody in the bridge yelled. Grettir forced himself to cut off his shout. He watched the starscreen. They were out in the gray again. The huge sphere shot across the screen. In the corner was the secondary and then a glimpse of a giant blue-black foot. More grayness. A whirl of other great spheres in the distance. The primary again. The secondary. Wellington's hand, like a malformed squid of the void.

When Grettir saw the corpse again, he knew that the ship had been deflected away from the sphere and was heading toward the corpse. He did not, however, expect a collision. The orbital velocity of the dead woman was greater than that of the secondary or of the *Sleipnir*.

Grettir, calling for a damage report, heard what he had expected. The nose of the ship had been sheared off. Bearing forty-five crewmen with it, it was now inside the "universe," heading toward a home it would never reach. The passageways leading to the cut-off part had been automatically sealed, of course, so that there was no danger of losing air.

But the retrodrives had also been sliced off. The *Sleipnir* could drive forward but could not brake itself unless it was first turned around to present its aft to the direction of motion.

VI

Grettir gave the command to stabilize the ship first, then to reverse it. MacCool replied from the engine room that neither maneuver was, at the moment, possible. The collision and the shearing had caused malfunctions in the control circuits. He did not know what the trouble was, but the electronic trouble-scanner was searching through the circuits. A moment later, he called back to say that the device was itself not operating properly and that the troubleshooting would have to be done by his men until the device had been repaired.

MacCool was disturbed. He could not account for the breakdown because, theoretically, there should have been none. Even the impact and loss of the fore part should not have resulted in loss of circuit operation.

Grettir told him to do what he could. Meanwhile, the ship was tumbling and was obviously catching up with the vast corpse. There had been another inexplainable interchange of energy, position and momentum, and the *Sleipnir* and Mrs. Wellington were going to collide.

Grettir unstrapped himself and began walking back and forth across the bridge. Even though the ship was cartwheeling, the internal g-field neutralized the effect for the crew. The vessel seemed level and stable unless the starscreen was looked at.

Grettir asked for a computation of when the collision would take place and of what part of the body the *Sleipnir* would strike. It might make a difference whether it struck a soft or hard part. The difference would not result in damage to the ship, but it would affect the angle and velocity of the rebound path. If the circuits were repaired before the convergence, or just after, Grettir would have to know what action to take.

Wang replied that he had already asked the compigator for an estimate of the area of collision if conditions remained as they were. Even as he spoke, a coded card issued from a slot in the bulkhead. Wang read it, handed it to Grettir.

Grettir said, "At any other time, I'd laugh. So we will return—literally—to the womb."

The card had also indicated that, the nearer the ship got to Wellington, the slower was its velocity. Moreover, the relative size of the ship, as reported by radar, was decreasing in direct proportion to its proximity to the body.

Gomez said, "I think we've come under the influence of that . . . woman, as if she's become a planet and had captured a satellite. Us. She doesn't have any gravitational attraction or any charge in relation to us. But . . ."

"But there are other factors," Grettir said to her. "Maybe they are spatial relations, which, in this 'space,' may be the equivalent of gravity."

The *Sleipnir* was now so close that the body entirely filled the starscreen when the ship was pointed toward it. First, the enormous head came into view. The blood-clotted and bulging eyes stared at them. The nose slid by like a Brobdingnagian guillotine; the mouth grinned at them as if it were to enjoy gulping them down. Then the neck, a diorite column left exposed by the erosion of softer rock; the cleavage of the blackened Himalayan breasts; the naval, the eye of a hurricane.

Then she went out of sight, and the secondary and primary and the gray-shrouded giants far off wheeled across the screen.

Grettir used the ALL-STATIONS to tell the nonbridge personnel what was happening. "As soon as MacCool locates the trouble, we will be on our way out. We have plenty of power left, enough to blast our way out of a hundred corpses. Sit tight. Don't worry. It's just a matter of time."

He spoke with a cheerfulness he did not feel, although he had not lied to them. Nor did he expect any reaction, positive or negative. They must be as numb as he. Their minds, their entire nervous systems, were boggling.

Another card shot out from the bulkhead-slot, a corrected impact prediction. Because of the continuing decrease in size of the vessel, it would strike the corpse almost dead center in the naval. A minute later, another card predicted impact near the coccyx. A third card revised that to collision with the top of the head. A fourth changed that to a strike on the lower part on the front of the right leg.

Grettir called Van Voorden again. The physicist's face shot up from the surface of Grettir's wrist-console but was stationary on the auxiliary bulkhead-screen. This gave a larger view and showed Van Voorden looking over his wrist-console at a screen on his cabin-bulkhead. It offered the latest impact report in large burning letters.

"Like the handwriting on the wall in the days of King Belshazzar," Van Voorden said. "And I am a Daniel come to judgment. So we're going to hit her leg, heh. *Many, many tickle up her shin.* Hee, hee!"

Grettir stared uncomprehendingly at him, then cut him off. A few seconds later, he understood Van Voorden's pun. He did not wonder at the man's levity at a moment so grave. It was a means of relieving his deep anxiety and bewilderment. It might also mean that he was already cracking up, since it was out of character with him. But Grettir could do nothing for him at that moment.

As the *Sleipnir* neared the corpse, it continued to shrink. However, the dwindling was not at a steady rate nor could the times of shrinkage be predicted. It operated in spurts of from two to thirty seconds' duration at irregular intervals. And then, as the three-hundredth card issued from the slot, it became evident that, unless some new factor entered, the *Sleipnir* would spin into the gaping mouth. While the head rotated "downward," the ship would pass through the great space between the lips.

And so it was. On the starscreen, the lower lip, a massive ridge, wrinkled with mountains and pitted with valleys, appeared. Flecks of lipstick floated by, black-red Hawaiis. A tooth like a jagged skyscraper dropped out of sight.

The *Sleipnir* settled slowly into the darkness. The walls shot away and upward. The blackness outside knotted. Only a part of the gray "sky" was visible during that point of the cartwheel when the forepart of the starscreen was directed upward. Then the opening became a thread of gray, a strand, and was gone.

Strangely—or was it so odd?—the officers and crew lost their feeling of dissociation. Grettir's stomach expanded with relief; the dreadful fragmenting was gone. He now felt as if something had been attached, or reattached, to his naval. Rubb, the psychology officer, reported that he had taken a survey of one out of fifty of the crew, and each described similar sensations.

Despite this, the personnel were free of only one anxiety and were far from being out of danger. The temperature had been slowly mounting ever since the ship had been spun off the secondary and had headed toward the corpse. The power system and air-conditioning had stabilized at eighty degrees Fahrenheit for a while. But the temperature of the hull had gone upwards at a geometric progression, and the outer hull was now 2500 K. There was no danger of it melting as yet; it could resist up to 56,000 K. The air-conditioning demanded more and more power, and after thirty minutes ship's time, Grettir had had to let the internal temperature rise to ninety-eight point two degrees Fahrenheit to ease the load.

Grettir ordered everybody into space suits, which could keep the wearers at a comfortable temperature. Just as the order was carried out, MacCool reported that he had located the source of malfunction.

"The Wellington woman did it!" he shouted. "She sure took care of us! She inserted a monolith subparticle switch in the circuits; the switch had a timer which operated the switch after a certain time had elapsed. It was only coincidence that the circuits went blank right after we failed to get back into our world!"

VII

"So she wanted to be certain that we'd be wrecked if she was frustrated in her attempts in the engine room," Grettir said. "You'd better continue the search for other microswitches or sabotage devices."

MacCool's face was long.

"We're ready to operate now only . . . hell! We can't spare any power now because we need all we can get to keep the temperature down. I can spare enough to cancel the tumble. But that's all."

"Forget it for now," Grettir said. He had contacted Van Voorden, who seemed to have recovered. He confirmed the captain's theory about the rise in temperature. It was the rapid contraction of the ship that was causing the emission of heat.

"How is this contraction possible?" Grettir said. "Are the atoms of the ship, and of our bodies, coming closer together? If so, what happens when they come into contact with each other?"

"We've already passed that point of diminishment," Van Voorden said. "I'd say that our own atoms are shrinking also."

"But that's not possible," Grettir replied. Then, "Forget about that remark. What is possible? Whatever happens is possible."

Grettir cut him off and strode back and forth and wished that he could smoke a cigar. He had intended to talk about what the *Sleipnir* would find if it had managed to break back into its native universe. It seemed to Grettir that the universe would have changed so much that no one aboard the ship would recognize it. Every time the secondary—the universe—completed a revolution on its axis, trillions of Earth years, maybe quadrillions, may have passed. The Earth's sun may have become a lightless clot in space or even have disappeared altogether. Man, who might have survived on other planets, would no longer be homo sapiens.

Moreover, when the *Sleipnir* attained a supercosmic mass on its way out of the universe, it may have disastrously affected the other masses in the universe.

Yet none of these events may have occurred. It was possible that time inside that sphere was absolutely independent of time outside it. The notion was not so fantastic. God almighty! Less than seventy minutes ago, Donna Wellington had been inside the ship. Now the ship was inside her.

And when the electrons and the nuclei of the atoms composing the ship and the crew came into contact, what then? Explosion?

Or were the elements made up of divisible subelements, and collapse would go on toward the inner infinity? He thought of the twentieth-century stories of a man shrinking until the molecules became clusters of suns and the nuclei were the suns and the electrons were the planets. Eventually, the hero found himself on an electron-planet with atmosphere, seas, rivers, plains, mountains, trees, animals and aboriginal sentients.

These stories were only fantasies. Atomic matter was composed of wavicles, stuff describable in terms of both waves and particles. The parahomunculus hero would be in a cosmos as bewildering as that encountered by the crew of the *Sleipnir* on breaking into the extrauniverse space.

That fantasy galloping across the sky of his mind, swift as the original *Sleipnir*, eight-legged horse of All-Father Odin of his ancestors' religion, would have to be dismissed. Donna Wellington was not a female Ymir, the primeval giant out of whose slain corpse was formed the world, the skull the sky, the blood the sea, the flesh the Earth, the bones the mountains.

No, the heat of contraction would increase until the men cooked in their suits. What happened after that would no longer be known to the crew and hence of no consequence.

"Captain!"

MacCool's face was on the auxiliary screen, kept open to the engine room. "We'll be ready to go in a minute."

Sweat mingled with tears to blur the image of the engineer's face. "We'll make it then," Grettir said.

Four minutes later, the tumble was stopped, the ship was pointed upward and was on its way out. The temperature began dropping inside the ship at one degree Fahrenheit per thirty seconds. The blackness was relieved by a gray thread. The thread broadened into ribbon, and then the ribbon became the edges of two mountain ridges, one below and the one above hanging upside down.

"This time," Grettir said, "we'll make a hole more than large enough."

Van Voorden entered the bridge as the *Sleipnir* passed through the break.

Grettir said, "The hole repairs itself even more quickly than it did the last time. That's why the nose was cut off. We didn't know that the bigger the hole, the swifter the rate of reclosure."

Van Voorden said, "Thirty-six hundred billion years old or even more! Why bother to go home when home no longer exists?"

"Maybe there won't be that much time gone," Grettir said. "Do you remember Minkowski's classical phrase? *From henceforth space in itself and time in itself sink to mere shadows, and only a kind of union of the two preserves an independent existence.*

"That phrase applied to the world inside the sphere, our world. Perhaps *out here* the union is somehow dissolved, the marriage of space and time is broken. Perhaps no time, or very little, has elapsed in our world."

"It's possible," Van Voorden said. "But you've overlooked one thing, captain. If our world has not been marked by time while we've been gone, *we* have been marked. Scarred by unspace and untime. I'll never believe in cause and effect and order throughout the cosmos again. I'll always be suspicious and anxious. I'm a ruined man."

Grettir started to answer but could not make himself heard. The men and women on the bridge were weeping, sobbing or laughing shrilly. Later, they would think of that *out there* as a nightmare and would try not to think of it at all. And if other nightmares faced them here, at least they would be nightmares they knew.

ROBERT A. HEINLEIN
"All You Zombies—"

Solipsism is the theory that nothing really exists outside the self. It is a philosophical position that has some profound political and social implications, and it can be a terrifying concept in the hands of a skilled writer like Robert A. Heinlein.

2217 Time Zone V (EST) 7 November 1970—NYC-Pop's Place: I was polishing a brandy snifter when the unmarried mother came in. I noted the time—10:17 P.M. zone five, or eastern time, November 7, 1970. Temporal agents always notice time and date; we must.

The unmarried mother was a man twenty-five years old, no taller than I am, childish features and a touchy temper. I didn't like his looks—I never had— but he was a lad I was here to recruit, he was my boy. I gave him my best barkeep's smile.

Maybe I'm too critical. He wasn't swish; his nickname came from what he always said when some nosy type asked him his line: "I'm an unmarried mother." If he felt less than murderous he would add: "At four cents a word. I write confession stories."

If he felt nasty, he would wait for somebody to make something of it. He had a lethal style of infighting, like a female cop—one reason I wanted him. Not the only one.

He had a load on and his face showed that he despised people more than usual. Silently I poured a double shot of Old Underwear and left the bottle. He drank it, poured another.

I wiped the bar top. "How's the unmarried mother racket?"

His fingers tightened on the glass and he seemed about to throw it at me; I felt for the sap under the bar. In temporal manipulation you try to figure everything, but there are so many factors that you never take needless risks.

I saw him relax that tiny amount they teach you to watch for in the bureau's training school. "Sorry," I said. "Just asking, 'How's business?' Make it 'How's the weather?' "

He looked sour. "Business is okay. I write 'em, they print 'em, I eat."

I poured myself one, leaned toward him. "Matter of fact," I said, "you write a nice stick—I've sampled a few. You have an amazingly sure touch with the woman's angle."

It was a slip I had to risk; he never admitted what pen names he used. But he was boiled enough to pick up only the last. " 'Woman's angle!' " he repeated with a snort. "Yeah, I know the woman's angle. I should."

"So?" I said doubtfully. "Sisters?"

"No. You wouldn't believe me if I told you."

"Now, now," I answered mildly, "bartenders and psychiatrists learn that nothing is stronger than truth. Why, son, if you heard the stories I do—well, you'd make yourself rich. Incredible."

"You don't know what 'incredible' means!"

"So? Nothing astonishes me. I've always heard worse."

He snorted again. "Want to bet the rest of the bottle?"

"I'll bet a full bottle." I placed one on the bar.

"Well . . ." I signaled my other bartender to handle the trade. We were at the far end, a single-stool space that I kept private by loading the bar top by it with jars of pickled eggs and other clutter. A few were at the other end watching the fights and somebody was playing the juke box—private as a bed where we were.

"Okay," he began, "to start with, I'm a bastard."

"No distinction around here," I said.

"I mean it," he snapped. "My parents weren't married."

"Still no distinction," I insisted. "Neither were mine."

"When . . ." He stopped, gave me the first warm look I ever saw on him. "You mean that?"

"I do. A one-hundred-percent bastard. In fact," I added, "no one in my family ever marries. All bastards."

"Oh, that." I showed it to him. "It just looks like a wedding ring; I wear it to keep women off." It is an antique I bought in 1985 from a fellow operative —he had fetched it from pre-Christian Crete. "The Worm Ouroboros . . . the World Snake that eats its own tail, forever without end. A symbol of the great paradox."

He barely glanced at it. "If you're really a bastard, you know how it feels. When I was a little girl . . ."

"Wups!" I said. "Did I hear you correctly?"

"Who's telling this story? When I was a little girl . . . Look, ever hear of Christine Jorgenson? Or Roberta Cowell?"

"Uh, sex-change cases? You're trying to tell me . . ."

"Don't interrupt or swelp me, I won't talk. I was a foundling, left at an orphanage in Cleveland in 1945 when I was a month old. When I was a little girl, I envied kids with parents. Then, when I leaned about sex—and, believe me, Pop, you learn fast in an orphanage . . ."

"I know."

". . . I made a solemn vow that any kid of mine would have both a pop and a mom. It kept me 'pure,' quite a feat in that vicinity—I had to learn to fight to manage it. Then I got older and realized I stood darn little chance of getting married—for the same reason I hadn't been adopted." He scowled. "I was horse-faced and bucktoothed, flat-chested and straight-haired."

"You don't look any worse than I do."

"Who cares how a barkeep looks? Or a writer? But people wanting to adopt pick little blue-eyed golden-haired morons. Later on, the boys want bulging breasts, a cute face, and an oh-you-wonderful-male manner." He shrugged. "I couldn't compete. So I decided to join the WENCHES."

"Eh?"

"Women's Emergency National Corps, Hospitality and Entertainment Section, what they now call Space Angels—Auxiliary Nursing Group, Extraterrestrial Legions."

I knew both terms, once I had them chronized. We use still a third name. It's that elite military service corps: Women's Hospitality Order Refortifying and Encouraging Spacemen. Vocabulary shift is the worst hurdle in time jumps—did you know that "service station" once meant a dispensary for petroleum fractions? Once on an assignment in the Churchill Era, a woman said to me, "Meet me at the service station next door"—which is not what it sounds; a "service station" (then) wouldn't have a bed in it.

He went on: "It was when they first admitted you can't send men into space for months and years and not relieve the tension. You remember how the wowsers screamed?—that improved my chance, since volunteers were scarce. A gal had to be respectable, preferably virgin (they liked to train them from scratch), above average mentally, and stable emotionally. But most volunteers were old hookers, or neurotics who would crack up ten days off Earth. So I didn't need looks; if they accepted me, they would fix my buck teeth, put a wave in my hair, teach me to walk and dance and how to listen to a man pleasingly, and everything else—plus training for the prime duties. They would even use plastic surgery if it would help—nothing too good for our boys.

"Best yet, they made sure you didn't get pregnant during your enlistment

—and you were almost certain to marry at the end of your hitch. Same way today, ANGELS marry spacers—they talk the language.

"When I was eighteen I was placed as a 'mother's helper.' This family simply wanted a cheap servant but I didn't mind as I couldn't enlist till I was twenty-one. I did housework and went to night school—pretending to continue my high school typing and shorthand but going to a charm class instead, to better my chances for enlistment.

"Then I met this city slicker with his hundred-dollar bills." He scowled. "The no-good actually did have a wad of hundred-dollar bills. He showed me one night, told me to help myself.

"But I didn't. I liked him. He was the first man I ever met who was nice to me without trying games with me. I quit night school to see him oftener. It was the happiest time of my life.

"Then one night in the park the games began."

He stopped. I said, "And then?"

"And then *nothing!* I never saw him again. He walked me home and told me he loved me—and kissed me good night and never came back." He looked grim. "If I could find him, I'd kill him!"

"Well," I sympathized, "I know how you feel. But killing him—just for doing what comes naturally—hmm . . . Did you struggle?"

"Huh? What's that got to do with it?"

"Quite a bit. Maybe he deserves a couple of broken arms for running out on you, but . . ."

"He deserves worse than that! Wait till you hear. Somehow I kept anyone from suspecting and decided it was all for the best. I hadn't really loved him and probably would never love anybody—and I was more eager to join the WENCHES than ever. I wasn't disqualified, they didn't insist on virgins. I cheered up.

"It wasn't until my skirts got tight that I realized."

"Pregnant?"

"He had me higher 'n a kite! Those skinflints I lived with ignored it as long as I could work—then kicked me out and the orphanage wouldn't take me back. I landed in a charity ward surrounded by other big bellies and trotted bedpans until my time came.

"One night I found myself on an operating table, with a nurse saying, 'Relax. Now breathe deeply.'

"I woke up in bed, numb from the chest down. My surgeon came in. 'How do you feel?' he says cheerfully.

" 'Like a mummy.'

" 'Naturally. You're wrapped like one and full of dope to keep you numb.

You'll get well—but a Caesarian isn't a hangnail.'

" 'Caesarian' I said. 'Doc—*did I lose the baby?*'

" 'Oh, no. Your baby's fine.'

" 'Oh. Boy or girl?'

" 'A healthy little girl. Five pounds, three ounces.'

"I relaxed. It's something, to have made a baby. I told myself I would go somewhere and tack 'Mrs.' on my name and let the kid think her papa was dead—no orphanage for *my* kid!

"But the surgeon was talking. 'Tell me, uh . . .' He avoided my name. 'Did you ever think your glandular setup was odd?'

"I said, 'Huh? Of course not. What are you driving at?'

"He hesitated. 'I'll give you this in one dose, then a hypo to let you sleep off your jitters. You'll have 'em.'

" 'Why?' I demanded.

" 'Ever hear of that Scottish physician who was female until she was thirty-five, then had surgery and became legally and medically a man? Got married. All okay.'

" 'What's that got to do with me?'

" 'That's what I'm saying. You're a man.'

"I tried to sit up. *'What?'*

" 'Take it easy. When I opened you, I found a mess. I sent for the chief of surgery while I got the baby out, then we held a consultation with you on the table—and worked for hours to salvage what we could. You had two full sets of organs, both immature, but with the female set well enough developed for you to have a baby. They could never be any use to you again, so we took them out and rearranged things so that you can develop properly as a man.' He put a hand on me. 'Don't worry. You're young, your bones will readjust, we'll watch your glandular balance—and make a fine young man out of you.'

"I started to cry. 'What about my *baby?*'

" 'Well, you can't nurse her, you haven't milk enough for a kitten. If I were you, I wouldn't see her—put her up for adoption.'

" *'No!'*

"He shrugged. 'The choice is yours; you're her mother—well, her parent. But don't worry now; we'll get you well first.'

"Next day they let me see the kid and I saw her daily—trying to get used to her. I had never seen a brand-new baby and had no idea how awful they look—my daughter looked like an orange .monkey. My feelings changed to cold determination to do right by her. But four weeks later that didn't mean anything."

"Eh?"

"She was snatched."

" 'Snatched?' "

The unmarried mother almost knocked over the bottle we had bet. "Kidnapped—stolen from the hospital nursery!" He breathed hard. "How's that for taking the last a man's got to live for?"

"A bad deal," I agreed. "Let's pour you another. No clues?"

"Nothing the police could trace. Somebody came to see her, claimed to be her uncle. While the nurse had her back turned, he walked out with her."

"Description?"

"Just a man, with a face-shaped face, like yours or mine." He frowned. "I think it was the baby's father. The nurse swore it was an older man but he probably used makeup. Who else would swipe my baby? Childless women pull such stunts—but whoever heard of a man doing it?"

"What happened to you then?"

"Eleven more months of that grim place and three operations. In four months I started to grow a beard; before I was out I was shaving regularly . . . and no longer doubted that I was male." He grinned wryly. "I was staring down nurses' necklines."

"Well," I said, "seems to me you came through okay. Here you are, a normal man, making good money, no real troubles. And the life of a female is not an easy one."

He glared at me. "A lot you know about it!"

"So?"

"Ever hear the expression 'a ruined woman'?"

"Mmm, years ago. Doesn't mean much today."

"I was as ruined as a woman can be; that bum *really* ruined me—I was no longer a woman . . . and I didn't know *how* to be a man."

"Takes getting used to, I suppose."

"You have no idea. I don't mean learning how to dress, or not walking into the wrong rest room; I learned those in the hospital. But how could I *live?* What job could I get? Hell, I couldn't even drive a car. I didn't know a trade; I couldn't do manual labor—too much scar tissue, too tender.

"I hated him for having ruined me for the WENCHES, too, but I didn't know how much until I tried to join the Space Corps instead. One look at my belly and I was marked unfit for military service. The medical officer spent time on me just from curiosity; he had read about my case.

"So I changed my name and came to New York. I got by as a fry cook, then rented a typewriter and set myself up as a public stenographer—what a laugh! In four months I typed four letters and one manuscript. The manuscript was for *Real Life Tales* and a waste of paper, but the goof who wrote it sold it.

Which gave me an idea; I bought a stack of confession magazines and studied them." He looked cynical. "Now you know how I get the authentic woman's angle on an unmarried-mother story . . . through the only version I haven't sold—the true one. Do I win the bottle?"

I pushed it toward him. I was upset myself, but there was work to do. I said, "Son, you still want to lay hands on that so-and-so?"

His eyes lighted up—a feral gleam.

"Hold it!" I said. "You wouldn't kill him?"

He chuckled nastily. "Try me."

"Take it easy. I know more about it than you think I do. I can help you. I know where he is."

He reached across the bar. *"Where is he?"*

I said softly, "Let go my shirt, sonny—or you'll land in the alley and we'll tell the cops you fainted." I showed him the sap.

He let go. "Sorry. But where is he?" He looked at me. "And how do you know so much?"

"All in good time. There are records—hospital records, orphanage records, medical records. The matron of your orphanage was Mrs. Fetherage—right? She was followed by Mrs. Gruenstein—right? Your name, as a girl, was Jane —right? And you didn't tell me any of this—right?"

I had him baffled and a bit scared. "What's this? You trying to make trouble for me?"

"No indeed. I've your welfare at heart. I can put this character in your lap. You do to him as you see fit—and I guarantee that you'll get away with it. But I don't think you'll kill him. You'd be nuts to—and you aren't nuts. Not quite."

He brushed it aside. "Cut the noise. *Where is he?"*

I poured him a short one; he was drunk but anger was offsetting it. "Not so fast. I do something for you—you do something for me."

"Uh . . . what?"

"You don't like your work. What would you say to high pay, steady work, unlimited expense account, your own boss on the job and lots of variety and adventure?"

He stared. "I'd say, 'Get those goddamn reindeer off my roof!' Shove it, pop —there's no such job."

"Okay, put it this way: I hand him to you, you settle with him, then try my job. If it's not all I claim—well, I can't hold you."

He was wavering; the last drink did it. "When d'yuh d'liver 'im?" he said thickly.

He shoved out his hand. "It's a deal!"

"If it's a deal—*right now!*"

I nodded to my assistant to watch both ends, noted the time—2300—started to duck through the gate under the bar—when the juke box blared out: "I'm My Own Grandpaw!" The service man had orders to load it with Americana and classics because I couldn't stomach the "music" of 1970, but I hadn't known that tape was in it. I called out, "Shut that off! Give the customer his money back." I added, "Storeroom, back in a moment," and headed there with my unmarried mother following.

It was down the passage across from the johns, a steel door to which no one but my day manager and I had a key; inside was a door to an inner room to which only I had a key. We went there.

He looked blearily around at windowless walls. "Where is 'e?"

"Right away." I opened a case, the only thing in the room; it was a USFF Coordinates Transformer Field Kit, series 1992, mod. II—a beauty, no moving parts, weight twenty-three kilos fully charged and shaped to pass as a suitcase. I had adjusted it precisely earlier that day; all I had to do was to shake out the metal net which limits the transformation field.

Which I did. "What's that?" he demanded.

"Time machine," I said and tossed the net over us.

"Hey!" he yelled and stepped back. There is a technique to this; the net has to be thrown so that the subject will instinctively step back *onto* the metal mesh, then you close the net with both of you inside completely—else you might leave shoe soles behind or a piece of foot, or scoop up a slice of floor. But that's all the skill it takes. Some agents con a subject into the net; I tell the truth and use that instant of utter astonishment to flip the switch. Which I did.

1030-VI-3 April 1963—Cleveland, Ohio-Apex Bldg.: "Hey!" he repeated. "Take this damn thing off!"

"Sorry," I apologized and did so, stuffed the net into the case, closed it. "You said you wanted to find him."

"But—you said that was a time machine!"

I pointed out a window. "Does that look like November? Or New York?" While he was gawking at new buds and spring weather, I reopened the case, took out a packet of hundred-dollar bills, checked that the numbers and signatures were compatible with 1963. The Temporal Bureau doesn't care how much you spend (it costs nothing) but they don't like unnecessary anachronisms. Too many mistakes, and a general court-martial will exile you for a year in a nasty period, say 1974 with its strict rationing and forced labor. I never make such mistakes; the money was okay.

He turned around and said, "What happened?"

"He's here. Go outside and take him. Here's expense money." I shoved it at him and added, "Settle him, then I'll pick you up."

Hundred-dollar bills have a hypnotic effect on a person not used to them. He was thumbing them unbelievingly as I eased him into the hall, locked him out. The next jump was easy, a small shift in era.

7100-VI-10 March 1964—Cleveland, Ohio-Apex Bldg.: There was a notice under the door saying that my lease expired next week; otherwise the room looked as it had a moment before. Outside, trees were bare and snow threatened; I hurried, stopping only for contemporary money and a coat, hat and topcoat I had left there when I leased the room. I hired a car, went to the hospital. It took twenty minutes to bore the nursery attendant to the point where I could swipe the baby without being noticed. We went back to the Apex Building. This dial setting was more involved, as the building did not yet exist in 1945. But I had precalculated it.

0100-VI-20 September 1945—Cleveland, Ohio-Skyview Motel: Field kit, baby and I arrived in a motel outside town. Earlier I had registered as "Gregory Johnson, Warren, Ohio," so we arrived in a room with curtains closed, windows locked and doors bolted, and the floor cleared to allow for waver as the machine hunts. You can get a nasty bruise from a chair where it shouldn't be —not the chair, of course, but backlash from the field.

No trouble. Jane was sleeping soundly; I carried her out, put her in a grocery box on the seat of a car I had provided earlier, drove to the orphanage, put her on the steps, drove two blocks to a "service station" (the petroleum-products sort) and phoned the orphanage, drove back in time to see them taking the box inside, kept going and abandoned the car near the motel—walked to it and jumped forward to the Apex Building in 1963.

2200-VI-24 April 1963—Cleveland, Ohio-Apex Bldg.: I had cut the time rather fine—temporal accuracy depends on span, except on return to zero. If I had it right, Jane was discovering, out in the park this balmy spring night, that she wasn't quite as "nice" a girl as she had thought. I grabbed a taxi to the home of those skinflints, had the hackie wait around a corner while I lurked in shadows.

Presently I spotted them down the street, arms around each other. He took her up on the porch and made a long job of kissing her good night—longer than I thought. Then she went in and he came down the walk, turned away.

I slid into step and hooked an arm in his. "That's all, son," I announced quietly. "I'm back to pick you up."

"*You!*" He gasped and caught his breath.

"Me. Now you know who *he* is—and after you think it over you'll know who you are . . . and if you think hard enough, you'll figure out who the baby is . . . and who *I* am."

He didn't answer, he was badly shaken. It's a shock to have it proved to you that you can't resist seducing yourself. I took him to the Apex Building and we jumped again.

2300-VIII-12 August 1985—Sub Rockies Base: I woke the duty sergeant, showed my ID, told the sergeant to bed my companion down with a happy pill and recruit him in the morning. The sergeant looked sour, but rank is rank, regardless of era; he did what I said—thinking, no doubt, that the next time we met he might be the colonel and I the sergeant. Which can happen in our corps. "What name?" he asked.

I wrote it out. He raised his eyebrows. "Like so, eh? *Hmm . . .*"

"You just do your job, sergeant." I turned to my companion.

"Son, your troubles are over. You're about to start the best job a man ever held—and you'll do well. *I know.*"

"That you will!" agreed the sergeant. "Look at me—born in 1917—still around, still young, still enjoying life." I went back to the jump room, set everything on preselected zero.

2301-V-7 November 1970—NYC-Pop's Place: I came out of the storeroom carrying a fifth of Drambuie to account for the minute I had been gone. My assistant was arguing with the customer who had been playing "I'm My Own Grandpaw!" I said, "Oh, let him play it, then unplug it." I was very tired.

It's rough, but somebody must do it and it's very hard to recruit anyone in the later years, since the Mistake of 1972. Can you think of a better source than to pick people all fouled up where they are and give them well-paid, interesting (even though dangerous) work in a necessary cause? Everybody knows now why the Fizzle War of 1963 fizzled. The bomb with New York's number on it didn't go off, a hundred other things didn't go as planned—all arranged by the likes of me.

But not the Mistake of 1972; that one is not our fault—and can't be undone; there's no paradox to resolve. A thing either is, or it isn't, now and forever amen. But there won't be another like it; an order dated 1992 takes precedence any year.

I closed five minutes early, leaving a letter in the cash register telling my day manager that I was accepting his offer to buy me out, so see my lawyer as I was leaving on a long vacation. The bureau might or might not pick up his payments, but they want things left tidy. I went to the room back of the storeroom and forward to 1993.

2200-VII-12 January 1993—Sub Rockies Annex-HQ Temporal DOL: I checked in with the duty officer and went to my quarters, intending to sleep for a week. I had fetched the bottle we bet (after all, I won it) and took a drink before I wrote my report. It tasted foul and I wondered why I had ever liked Old Underwear. But it was better than nothing; I don't like to be cold sober, I think too much. But I don't really hit the bottle either; other people have snakes—I have people.

I dictated my report; forty recruitments all okayed by the Psych Bureau—counting my own, which I knew would be okayed. I was here, wasn't I? Then I taped a request for assignment to operations; I was sick of recruiting. I dropped both in the slot and headed for bed.

My eye fell on "The By-Laws of Time," over my bed:

> *Never Do Yesterday What Should Be Done Tomorrow.*
> *If at Last You Do Succeed, Never Try Again.*
> *A Stitch in Time Saves Nine Billion.*
> *A Paradox May Be Paradoctored.*
> *It Is Earlier When You Think.*
> *Ancestors Are Just People.*
> *Even Jove Nods.*

They didn't inspire me the way they had when I was a recruit; thirty subjective-years of time jumping wears you down. I undressed and when I got down to the hide I looked at my belly. A Caesarian leaves a big scar but I'm so hairy now that I don't notice it unless I look for it.

Then I glanced at the ring on my finger.

The snake that eats its own tail, forever and ever . . . I *know* where *I* came from—but *where did all you zombies come from?*

I felt a headache coming on, but a headache powder is one thing I do not take. I did once—and you all went away.

So I crawled into bed and whistled out the light.

You aren't really there at all. There isn't anybody but me—Jane—here alone in the dark.

I miss you dreadfully!

JACK FINNEY

I'm Scared

A major complaint frequently leveled at science fiction is that it is escapist literature, fluff for people who do not want to be bothered with "serious" fiction. Some of it is, of course—and some is more serious and mature in concept and execution. This is nowhere more apparent than in this remarkable story of the need to escape and the dangers this need represents. Although it first appeared in 1951, it is very much a story for the 1980s.

I'm very badly scared, not so much for myself—I'm a gray-haired man of sixty-six, after all—but for you and everyone else who has not yet lived out his life. For I believe that certain dangerous things have recently begun to happen in the world. They are noticed here and there, idly discussed, then dismissed and forgotten. Yet I am convinced that unless these occurrences are recognized for what they are, the world will be plunged into a nightmare. Judge for yourself.

One evening last winter I came home from a chess club to which I belong. I'm a widower; I live alone in a small but comfortable three-room apartment overlooking Fifth Avenue. It was still fairly early, and I switched on a lamp beside my leather easy chair, picked up a murder mystery I'd been reading and turned on the radio; I did not, I'm sorry to say, notice which station it was tuned to.

The tubes warmed, and the music of an accordion—faint at first, then louder—came from the loudspeaker. Since it was good music for reading, I adjusted the volume control and began to read.

Now I want to be absolutely factual and accurate about this, and I do not claim that I paid close attention to the radio. But I do know that presently the music stopped and an audience applauded. Then a man's voice, chuckling and pleased with the applause, said, "All right, all right," but the applause continued for several more seconds. During that time the voice once more chuckled appreciatively, then firmly repeated, "All right," and the applause died down. "That was Alec Somebody-or-other," the radio voice said, and I went back to my book.

But I soon became aware of this middle-aged voice again; perhaps a change of tone as he turned to a new subject caught my attention. "And now, Miss Ruth Greeley," he was saying, "of Trenton, New Jersey. Miss Greeley is a pianist; that right?" A girl's voice, timid and barely audible, said, "that's right, Major Bowes." The man's voice—and now I recognized his familiar singsong delivery—and, "And what are you going to play?"

The girl replied, " 'La Paloma.' " The man repeated it after her, as an announcement: " 'La Paloma.' " There was a pause, then an introductory chord sounded from a piano, and I resumed my reading.

As the girl played, I was half aware that her style was mechanical, her rhythm defective; perhaps she was nervous. Then my attention was fully aroused once more by a gong which sounded suddenly. For a few notes more the girl continued to play falteringly, not sure what to do. The gong sounded jarringly again, the playing abruptly stopped and there was a restless murmur from the audience. "All right, all right," said the familiar voice, and I realized I'd been expecting this, knowing it would say just that. The audience quieted, and the voice began, "Now . . ."

The radio went dead. For the smallest fraction of a second no sound issued from it but its own mechanical hum. Then a completely different program came from the loudspeaker; the recorded voices of Bing Crosby and his son were singing the concluding bars of "Sam's Song," a favorite of mine. So I returned once more to my reading, wondering vaguely what had happened to the other program, but not actually thinking about it until I finished my book and began to get ready for bed.

Then, undressing in my bedroom, I remembered that Major Bowes was dead. Years had passed, half a decade, since that dry chuckle and familiar, "All right, all right," had been heard in the nation's living rooms.

Well, what does one do when the apparently impossible occurs? It simply made a good story to tell friends, and more than once I was asked if I'd recently heard Moran and Mack, a pair of radio comedians popular some twenty-five years ago, or Floyd Gibbons, an old-time news broadcaster. And there were other joking references to my crystal radio set.

But one man—this was at a lodge meeting the following Thursday—listened to my story with utter seriousness, and when I had finished he told me a queer little story of his own. He is a thoughtful, intelligent man, and as I listened I was not frightened, but puzzled at what seemed to be a connecting link, a common denominator, between this story and the odd behavior of my radio. Since I am retired and have plenty of time, I took the trouble, the following day, of making a two-hour train trip to Connecticut in order to verify the story firsthand. I took detailed notes, and the story appears in my files now as follows:

Case 2. Louis Trachnor, coal and wood dealer, R.F.D. 1, Danbury, Connecticut, age fifty-four.

On July 20, 1950, Mr. Trachnor told me, he walked out on the front porch of his house about six o'clock in the morning. Running from the eaves of his house to the floor of the porch was a streak of gray paint, still damp. "It was about the width of an eight-inch brush," Mr. Trachnor told me, "and it looked like hell because the house was white. I figured some kids did it in the night for a joke, but if they did, they had to get a ladder up to the eaves and you wouldn't figure they'd go to that much trouble. It wasn't smeared, either; it was a careful job, a nice even stripe straight down the front of the house."

Mr. Trachnor got a ladder and cleaned off the gray paint with turpentine.

In October of that same year Mr. Trachnor painted his house. "The white hadn't held up so good, so I painted it gray. I got to the front last and finished about five one Saturday afternoon. Next morning when I came out I saw a streak of white right down the front of the house. I figured it was the damn kids again because it was the same place as before. But when I looked close, I saw it wasn't new paint; it was the old white I'd painted over. Somebody had done a nice careful job of cleaning off the new paint in a long stripe about eight inches wide right down from the eaves! Now who the hell would go to that trouble? I just can't figure it out."

Do you see the link between this story and mine? Suppose for a moment that something had happened, on each occasion, to disturb briefly the orderly progress of time. That seemed to have happened in my case; for a matter of some seconds I apparently heard a radio broadcast that had been made years before. Suppose, then, that no one had touched Mr. Trachnor's house but himself; that he had painted his house in October, but that through some fantastic mix-up in time, a portion of that paint appeared on his house the previous summer. Since he had cleaned the paint off at that time, a broad stripe of new gray paint was missing *after* he painted his house in the fall.

I would be lying, however, if I said I really believed this. It was merely an intriguing speculation, and I told both these little stories to friends, simply as curious anecdotes. I am a sociable person, see a good many people, and occasionally I heard other odd stories in response to mine.

Someone would nod and say, "Reminds me of something I heard recently . . ." and I would have one more to add to my collection. A man on Long Island received a telephone call from his sister in New York one Friday evening. She insists that she did not make this call until the following Monday, three days later. At the Forty-fifth Street branch of the Chase National Bank, I was shown a check deposited the day before it was written. A letter was delivered on East Sixty-eighth Street in New York City, just seventeen minutes after it was dropped into a mailbox on the main street of Green River, Wyoming.

And so on, and so on; my stories were now in demand at parties, and I told myself that collecting and verifying them was a hobby. But the day I heard Julia Eisenberg's story, I knew it was no longer that.

Case 17. Julia Eisenberg, office worker, New York City, age thirty-one.
Miss Eisenberg lives in a small walk-up apartment in Greenwich Village. I talked to her there after a chess-club friend who lives in her neighborhood had repeated to me a somewhat garbled version of her story, which was told to him by the doorman of the building he lives in.

In October 1947, about eleven at night, Miss Eisenberg left her apartment to walk to the drugstore for toothpaste. On her way back, not far from her apartment, a large black and white dog ran up to her and put his front paws on her chest.

"I made the mistake of petting, him," Miss Eisenberg told me, "and from then on he simply wouldn't leave. When I went into the lobby of my building, I actually had to push him away to get the door closed. I felt sorry for him, poor hound, and a little guilty because he was still sitting at the door an hour later when I looked out my front window."

This dog remained in the neighborhood for three days, discovering and greeting Miss Eisenberg with wild affection each time she appeared on the street. "When I'd get on the bus in the morning to go to work, he'd sit on the curb looking after me in the most mournful way, poor thing. I wanted to take him in, but I knew he'd never go home then, and I was afraid whoever owned him would be sorry to lose him. No one in the neighborhood knew whom he belonged to, and finally he disappeared."

Two years later a friend gave Miss Eisenberg a three-week-old puppy. "My apartment is really too small for a dog, but he was such a darling I couldn't resist. Well, he grew up into a nice big dog who ate more than I did."

Since the neighborhood was quiet and the dog well behaved, Miss Eisenberg usually unleashed him when she walked him at night, for he never strayed far. "One night—I'd last seen him sniffing around in the dark a few doors down—I called to him and he didn't come back. And he never did; I never saw him again.

"Now our street is a solid wall of brownstone buildings on both sides with locked doors and no areaways. He *couldn't* have disappeared like that, he just *couldn't.* But he did."

Miss Eisenberg hunted for her dog for many days afterward, inquired of neighbors, put ads in the papers, but she never found him. "Then one night I was getting ready for bed; I happened to glance out the front window down at the street, and suddenly I remembered something I'd forgotten all about. I remembered the dog I'd chased away over two years before." Miss Eisenberg looked at me for a moment, then she said flatly, "It was the same dog. If you own a dog you know him, you can't be mistaken, and I tell you it was the same dog. Whether it makes sense or not, my dog was lost—I chased him away—two years before he was born."

She began to cry silently, the tears running down her face. "Maybe you think I'm crazy, or a little lonely and overly sentimental about a dog. But you're wrong." She brushed at her tears with a handkerchief. "I'm a well-balanced person, as much as anyone is these days, at least, and I tell you I *know* what happened."

It was at that moment, sitting in Miss Eisenberg's neat, shabby living room, that I realized fully that the consequences of these odd little incidents could be something more than merely intriguing; that they might, quite possibly, be tragic. It was in that moment that I began to be afraid.

I have spent the last eleven months discovering and tracking down these strange occurrences, and I am astonished and frightened at how many there are. I am astonished and frightened at how much more frequently they are happening now, and—I hardly know how to express this—at their increasing power to tear human lives tragically apart. This is an example, selected almost at random, of the increasing strength of—whatever it is that is happening in the world.

Case 34. Paul V. Kerch, accountant, the Bronx, age thirty-one.

On a bright clear Sunday afternoon, I met an unsmiling family of three at their Bronx apartment: Mr. Kerch, a chunky, darkly good-looking young man; his wife, a pleasant-faced dark-haired woman in her late twenties, whose attractiveness was marred by circles under her eyes; and their son, a nice-looking boy of six or seven. After introductions, the boy was sent to his room at the back of the house to play.

"All right," Mr. Kerch said wearily then and walked toward a bookcase, "let's get at it. You said on the phone that you know the story in general." It was half a question, half a statement.

"Yes," I said.

He took a book from the top shelf and removed some photographs from it. "There are the pictures." He sat down on the davenport beside me with the photographs in his hand. "I own a pretty good camera. I'm a fair amateur photographer, and I have a darkroom setup in the kitchen; do my own developing. Two weeks ago we went down to Central Park." His voice was a tired monotone, as though this was a story he'd repeated many times, aloud and in his own mind. "It was nice, like today, and the kid's grandmothers have been pestering us for pictures, so I took a whole roll of films, pictures of all of us. My camera can be set up and focused and it will snap the picture automatically a few seconds later, giving me time to get around in front of it and get in the picture myself."

There was a tired, hopeless look in his eyes as he handed me all but one of the photographs. "These are the first ones I took," he said. The photographs were all fairly large, perhaps seven by three and a half inches, and I examined them closely.

They were ordinary enough, very sharp and detailed, and each showed the family of three in various smiling poses. Mr. Kerch wore a light business suit, his wife had on a dark dress and a cloth coat and the boy wore a dark suit with knee-length pants. In the background stood a tree with bare branches. I glanced up at Mr. Kerch, signifying that I had finished my study of the photographs.

"The last picture," he said, holding it in his hand ready to give to me, "I took exactly like the others. We agreed on the pose, I set the camera, walked around in front, and joined my family. Monday night I developed the whole roll. This is what came out on the last negative." He handed me the photograph.

For an instant it seemed to me like merely one more photograph in the group; then I saw the difference. Mr. Kerch looked much the same, bareheaded and grinning broadly, but he wore an entirely different suit. The boy, standing beside him, wore long pants, was a good three inches taller, obviously older, but equally obviously the same boy. The woman was an entirely different person. Dressed smartly, her light hair catching the sun, she was very pretty and attractive. She was smiling into the camera and holding Mr. Kerch's hand.

I looked up at him. "Who is this?"

Wearily, Mr. Kerch shook his head. "I don't know," he said suddenly, then exploded: "I don't *know!* I've never seen her in my life!" He turned to look at his wife, but she would not return his glance, and he turned back to me, shrugging. "Well, there you have it," he said. "The whole story." And he stood up, thrusting both hands into his trouser pockets and began to pace about the room, glancing often at his wife, talking to *her* actually, though he addressed his words to me. "So who is she? How could the camera have snapped that picture? I've never seen that woman in my life!"

I glanced at the photograph again, then bent closer. "The trees here are in full bloom," I said. Behind the solemn-faced boy, the grinning man and smiling woman, the trees of Central Park were in full summer leaf.

Mr. Kerch nodded. "I know," he said bitterly. "And you know what *she* says?" he burst out, glaring at his wife. "She says that *is* my wife in the photograph, my *new* wife a couple of years from now! God!" He snapped both hands down on his head. "The ideas a woman can get!"

"What do you mean?" I glanced at Mrs. Kerch, but she ignored me, remaining silent, her lips tight.

Kerch shrugged hopelessly. "She says that photograph shows how things will be a couple of years from now. She'll be dead or"—he hesitated, then said the word bitterly—"divorced, and I'll have our son and be married to the woman in the picture."

We both looked at Mrs. Kerch, waiting until she was obliged to speak.

"Well, if it isn't so," she said, shrugging a shoulder, "then tell me what that picture does mean."

Neither of us could answer that, and a few minutes later I left. There was nothing much I could say to the Kerches; certainly I couldn't mention my conviction that, whatever the explanation of the last photograph, their married life was over? . . .

Case 72. Lieutenant Alfred Eichler, New York Police Department, age thirty-three.

In the late evening of January 9, 1951, two policemen found a revolver lying just off a gravel path near an East Side entrance to Central Park. The gun was examined for fingerprints at the police laboratory and several were found. One bullet had been fired from the revolver and the police fired another which was studied and classified by a ballistics expert. The fingerprints were checked and found in police files; they were those of a minor hoodlum with a record of assault.

A routine order to pick him up was sent out. A detective called at the rooming house where he was known to live, but he was out, and since no unsolved shootings had occurred recently, no intensive search for him was made that night.

The following evening a man was shot and killed in Central Park with the same gun. This was proved ballistically past all question of error. It was soon learned that the murdered man had been quarreling with a friend in a nearby tavern. The two men, both drunk, had left the tavern together. And the second man was the hoodlum whose gun had been found the previous night and which was still locked in a police safe.

As Lieutenant Eichler said to me, "it's impossible that the dead man was killed with that same gun, but he was. Don't ask me how, though, and if anybody thinks we'd go into court with a case like that, they're crazy."

Case 111. Captain Hubert V. Rihm, New York Police Department, retired, aged sixty-six.

I met Captain Rihm by appointment one morning in Stuyvesant Park, a patch of greenery, wood benches and asphalt surrounded by the city on lower Second Avenue. "You want to hear about the Fentz case, do you?" he said, after we had introduced ourselves and found an empty bench. "All right, I'll tell you. I don't like to talk about it—it bothers me—but I'd like to see what you think." He was a big, rather heavy man with a red, tough face, and he wore an old police jacket and uniform cap with the insignia removed.

"I was up at City Mortuary," he began as I took out my notebook and pencil, "at Bellevue about twelve one night, drinking coffee with one of the interns. This was in June of 1950, just before I retired, and I was in Missing Persons. They brought this guy in and he was a funny-looking character. Had a beard. A young guy, maybe thirty, but he wore regular muttonchop whiskers, and his clothes were funny-looking. Now I was thirty years on the force and I've seen a lot of queer guys killed on the streets. We found an Arab once in full regalia, and it took us a week to find out who he was. So it wasn't just the way the guy looked that bothered me; it was the stuff we found in his pockets."

Captain Rihm turned on the bench to see if he'd caught my interest, then continued. "There was about a dollar in change in the dead guy's pocket, and one of the boys picked up a nickel and showed it to me. Now you've seen plenty of nickels, the new ones with Jefferson's picture, the buffalo nickels they made before that, and once in a while you still even see the old Liberty-head nickels; they quit making them before the first world war. But this one was even older than that. It had a shield on the front, a United States shield, and a big five on the back; I used to see that kind when I was a boy. And the funny thing was, that old nickel looked new; what coin dealers call 'mint condition,' like it was made the day before yesterday. The date on that nickel was 1876, and there wasn't a coin in his pocket dated any later."

Captain Rihm looked at me questioningly. "Well," I said, glancing up from my notebook, "that could happen."

"Sure it could," he answered in a satisfied tone, "but all the pennies he had were Indian-head pennies. Now when did you see one of them last? There was even a silver three-cent piece; looked like an old-style dime, only smaller. And the bills in his wallet, every one of them, were old-time bills, the big kind."

Captain Rihm leaned forward and spat on the patch, a needle jet of tobacco juice and an expression of a policeman's annoyed contempt for anything deviating from an orderly norm.

"Over seventy bucks in cash, and not a federal reserve note in the lot. There were two yellow-back tens. Remember them? They were payable in gold. The rest were old national-bank notes; you remember them too. Issued direct by local banks, personally signed by the bank president; that kind used to be counterfeited a lot.

"Well," Captain Rihm continued, leaning back on the bench and crossing his knees, "there was a bill in his pocket from a livery stable on Lexington Avenue; three dollars for feeding and stabling his horse and washing a carriage. There was a brass slug in his pocket good for a five-cent beer at some saloon. There was a letter postmarked Philadelphia, June 1876, with an old-style two-cent stamp and a bunch of cards in his wallet. The cards had his name and address on them, and so did the letter."

"Oh," I said, a little surprised, "you identified him right away, then?"

"Sure. Rudolph Fentz, some address on Fifth Avenue—I forget the exact number—in New York City. No problem at all." Captain Rihm leaned forward and spat again. "Only that address wasn't a residence. It's a store, and it has been for years, and nobody there ever heard of any Rudolph Fentz, and there's no such name in the phone book either. Nobody ever called or made any inquiries about the guy, and Washington didn't have his prints. There was a tailor's name in his coat, a lower Broadway address, but nobody there ever heard of this tailor."

"What was so strange about his clothes?"

The captain said, "Well, did you ever know anyone who wore a pair of pants with big black-and-white checks, cut very narrow, no cuffs, and pressed without a crease?"

I had to think for a moment. "Yes," I said then, "my father, when he was a very young man, before he was married; I've seen old photographs."

"Sure," said Captain Rihm, "and he probably wore a short sort of cutaway coat with two cloth-covered buttons at the back, a vest with lapels, a tall silk hat, a big, black oversized bow tie on a turned-up stiff collar and button shoes."

"That's how this man was dressed?"

"Like seventy-five years ago! And him no more than thirty years old. There was a label in his hat, a Twenty-third Street hat store that went out of business around the turn of the century. Now what do you make out of a thing like that?"

"Well," I said carefully, "there's nothing much you can make of it. Apparently someone went to a lot of trouble to dress up in an antique style—the coins and bills I assume he could buy at a coin dealer's—and then he got himself killed in a traffic accident."

"Got himself killed is right. Eleven-fifteen at night in Times Square—the theaters letting out, busiest time and place in the world—and this guy shows up in the middle of the street, gawking and looking around at the cars and up at the signs like he'd never seen them before. The cop on duty noticed him, so you can see how he must have been acting. The lights change, the traffic starts up, with him in the middle of the street, and instead of waiting, the damn fool, he turns and tries to make it back to the sidewalk. A cab got him and he was dead when he hit."

For a moment Captain Rihm sat chewing his tobacco and staring angrily at a young woman pushing a baby carriage, though I'm sure he didn't see her. The young mother looked at him in surprise as she passed, and the captain continued:

"Nothing you can make out of a thing like that. We found out nothing. I started checking through our file of old phone books, just as routine, but without much hope because they only go back so far. But in the 1939 summer edition I found a Rudolph Fentz, Jr., somewhere on East Fifty-second Street. He'd moved away in 'forty-two, though, the building super told me, and was a man in his sixties besides, retired from business; used to work in a bank a few blocks away, the super thought. I found the bank where he'd worked, and they told me he'd retired in 'forty, and had been dead for five years; his widow was living in Florida with a sister.

"I wrote to the widow, but there was only one thing she could tell us, and that was no good. I never even reported it, not officially, anyway. Her husband's father had disappeared when her husband was a boy maybe two years old. He went out for a walk around ten one night—his wife thought cigar smoke smelled up the curtains, so he used to take a little stroll before he went to bed and smoke a cigar—and he didn't come back and was never seen or heard of again. The family spent a good deal of money trying to locate him, but they never did. This was in the middle 1870s some time; the old lady wasn't sure of the exact date. Her husband hadn't ever said too much about it.

"And that's all," said Captain Rihm. "Once I put in one of my afternoons of hunting through a bunch of old police records. And I finally found the missing persons file for 1876, and Rudolph Fentz was listed, all right. There wasn't much of a description, and no fingerprints, of course. I'd give a year of my life, even now, and maybe sleep better nights, if they'd had his fingerprints. He was listed as twenty-nine years old, wearing full muttonchop whiskers, a tall silk hat, dark coat and checked pants. That's about all it said. Didn't say what kind of tie or vest or if his shoes were the button kind. His name was Rudolph Fentz and he lived at this address on Fifth Avenue; it must have been a residence then. Final disposition of case: not located.

"Now, I hate that case," Captain Rihm said quietly. "I hate it and I wish I'd never heard of it. What do you think?" he demanded suddenly, angrily. "You think this guy walked off into thin air in 1876 and showed up again in 1950?"

I shrugged noncommittally, and the captain took it to mean no.

"No, of course not," he said. "Of *course* not—but give me some other explanation."

I could go on. I could give you several hundred such cases. A sixteen-year-old girl walked out of her bedroom one morning, carrying her clothes in her hand because they were too big for her and she was quite obviously eleven years old again. And there are other occurrences too horrible for print. All of them have happened in the New York City area alone, all within the last few years; and I suspect thousands more have occurred and are occurring, all over the world. I could go on, but the point is this: What is happening, and *why?* I believe that I know.

Haven't you noticed, too, on the part of nearly everyone you know, a growing rebellion against the *present?* And an increasing longing for the past? I have. Never before in all my long life have I heard so many people wish that they lived "at the turn of the century" or "when life was simpler" or "worth living" or "when you could bring children into the world and count on the future" or simply "in the good old days." People didn't talk that way when I was young! The present was a glorious time! But they talk that way now.

For the first time in man's history, man is desperate to escape the present. Our newsstands are jammed with escape literature, the very name of which is significant. Entire magazines are devoted to fantastic stories of escape—to other times, past and future, to other worlds and planets—escape to anywhere but here and now. Even our larger magazines, book publishers and Hollywood are beginning to meet the rising demand for this kind of escape. Yes, there is a craving in the world like a thirst, a terrible mass pressure that you can almost feel, of millions of minds struggling against the barriers of time. I am utterly convinced that this terrible mass pressure of millions of minds is already, slightly but definitely, affecting time itself. In the moments when this happens—when the almost universal longing to escape is greatest—my incidents occur. Man is disturbing the clock of time, and I am afraid it will break. When it does, I leave to your imagination the last few hours of madness that will be left to us; all the countless moments that now make up our lives suddenly ripped apart and chaotically tangled in time.

Well, I have lived most of my life; I can be robbed of only a few more years.

But it seems too bad—this universal craving to escape what could be a rich, productive, happy world. We live on a planet well able to provide a decent life for every soul on it, which is all ninety-nine of a hundred human beings ask. Why in the world can't we have it?

WILLIAM TENN

Child's Play

One of the favorite topics of science fiction is time travel, the paradoxes of which have provided some of SF's finest moments. The challenge to the writer is to maintain perfect logic while producing an entertaining and significant story. Another theme is the artifact from the future and its effect on an individual of the present, equally difficult to portray convincingly. The author has succeeded brilliantly, we think, in this lighthearted yet sinister story.

After the man from the express company had given the door an untipped slam, Sam Weber decided to move the huge crate under the one light bulb in his room. It was all very well for the messenger to drawl, "I dunno. We don't send 'em; we just deliver 'em, mister"—but there must be some sensible explanation.

With a grunt that began as an anticipatory reflex and ended on a note of surprised annoyance, Sam shoved the box forward the few feet necessary. It was heavy enough; he wondered how the messenger had carried it up the three flights of stairs.

He straightened and frowned down at the garish card which contained his name and address as well as the legend—"Merry Christmas, 2353."

A joke? He didn't know anyone who'd think it funny to send a card dated over four hundred years in the future. Unless one of the comedians in his law school graduating class meant to record his opinion as to when Weber would be trying his first case. Even so . . .

The letters were shaped strangely, come to think of it, sort of green streaks instead of lines. And the card was a sheet of gold!

Sam decided he was really interested. He ripped the card aside, tore off the flimsy wrapping material—and stopped.

There was no top to the box, no slit in its side, no handle anywhere in sight.

It seemed to be a solid, cubical mass of brown stuff. Yet he was positive something had rattled inside when it was moved.

He seized the corners and strained and grunted till it lifted. The underside was as smooth and innocent of openings as the rest. He let it thump back to the floor.

"Ah, well," he said, philosophically, "it's not the gift; it's the principle involved."

Many of his gifts still required appreciative notes. He'd have to work up something special for Aunt Maggie. Her neckties were things of cubistic horror, but he hadn't even sent her a lone handkerchief this Christmas. Every cent had gone into buying that brooch for Tina. Not quite a ring, but maybe she'd consider that under the circumstances . . .

He turned to walk to his bed which he had drafted into the additional service of desk and chair. He kicked at the great box disconsolately. "Well, if you won't open, you won't open."

As if smarting under the kick, the box opened. A cut appeared on the upper surface, widened rapidly and folded the top back and down on either side like a valise. Sam clapped his forehead and addressed a rapid prayer to every god from Set to Father Divine. Then he remembered what he'd said.

"Close," he suggested.

The box closed, once more as smooth as a baby's bottom.

"Open."

The box opened.

So much for the sideshow, Sam decided. He bent down and peered into the container.

The interior was a crazy mass of shelving on which rested vials filled with blue liquids, jars filled with red solids, transparent tubes showing yellow and green and orange and mauve and other colors which Sam's eyes didn't quite remember. There were seven pieces of intricate apparatus on the bottom which looked as if tube-happy radio hams had assembled them. There was also a book.

Sam picked the book off the bottom and noted numbly that while all its pages were metallic, it was lighter than any paper book he'd ever held.

He carried the book over to the bed and sat down. Then he took a long, deep breath and turned to the first page. *"Gug,"* he said, exhaling his long, deep breath.

In mad, green streaks of letters:

> Bild-a-Man Set 3. This set is intended solely for the use of children between the ages of eleven and thirteen. The equipment, much more

advanced than Bild-a-Man Sets 1 and 2, will enable the child of this age group to build and assemble complete adult humans in perfect working order. The retarded child may also construct the babies and mannikins of the earlier kits. Two disassembleators are provided so that the set can be used again and again with profit. As with Sets 1 and 2, the aid of a census keeper in all disassembling is advised. Refills and additional parts may be acquired from The Bild-a-Man Company, 928 Diagonal Level, Glunt City, Ohio. Remember—only with a Bild-a-Man can you build a man!

Weber squeezed his eyes shut. What was that gag in the movie he'd seen last night? Terrific gag. Terrific picture, too. Nice Technicolor. Wonder how much the director made a week? The cameraman? Five hundred? A thousand?

He opened his eyes warily. The box was still a squat cube in the center of his room. The book was still in his shaking hand. And the page read the same.

"Only with a Bild-a-Man can you build a man!" Heaven help a neurotic young lawyer at a time like this!

There was a price list on the next page for "refills and additional parts." Things like one liter of hemoglobin and three grams of assorted enzymes were offered for sale in terms of one slunk fifty and three slunks forty-five. A note on the bottom advertised Set 4: "The thrill of building your first live Martian!"

Fine print announced *pat. pending 2348.*

The third page was a table of contents. Sam gripped the edge of the mattress with one sweating hand and read:

CHAPTER I— A Child's Garden of Biochemistry
CHAPTER II— Making Simple Living Things Indoors and Out
CHAPTER III— Mannikins and What Makes Them Do the World's Work
CHAPTER IV— Babies and Other Small Humans
CHAPTER V— Twins for Every Purpose, Twinning Yourself and Your Friends
CHAPTER VI— What You Need to Build a Man
CHAPTER VII— Completing the Man
CHAPTER VIII— Disassembling the Man
CHAPTER IX— New Kinds of Life for Your Leisure Moments

Sam dropped the book back into the box and ran for the mirror. His face was still the same, somewhat like bleached chalk, but fundamentally the same. He hadn't twinned or grown himself a mannikin or devised a new kind of life for his leisure moments. Everything was snug as a bug in a bughouse.

Very carefully he pushed his eyes back into the proper position in their sockets.

"Dear Aunt Maggie," he began writing feverishly. "Your ties made the most beautiful gift of my Christmas. My only regret is . . .

My only regret is that I have but one life to give for my Christmas present. Who could have gone to such fantastic lengths for a practical joke? Lew Knight? Even Lew must have some reverence in his insensitive body for the institution of Christmas. And Lew didn't have the brains or the patience for a job so involved.

Tina? Tina had the fine talent for complication, all right. But Tina, while possessing a delightful abundance of all other physical attributes, was badly lacking in funnybone.

Sam drew the leather envelope forth and caressed it. Tina's perfume seemed to cling to the surface and move the world back into focus.

The metallic greeting card glinted at him from the floor. Maybe the reverse side contained the sender's name. He picked it up, turned it over.

Nothing but blank gold surface. He was sure of the gold; his father had been a jeweler. The very value of the sheet was rebuttal to the possibility of a practical joke. Besides, again, what was the point?

"Merry Christmas, 2353." Where would humanity be in four hundred years? Traveling to the stars, or beyond—to unimaginable destinations? Using little mannikins to perform the work of machines and robots? Providing children with . . .

There might be another card or note inside the box. Weber bent down to remove its contents. His eye noted a large grayish jar and the label etched into its surface: *Dehydrated Neurone Preparation, for human construction only.*

He backed away and glared. "Close!"

The thing melted shut. Weber sighed his relief at it and decided to go to bed.

He regretted while undressing that he hadn't thought to ask the messenger the name of his firm. Knowing the delivery service involved would be useful in tracing the origin of this gruesome gift.

"But then," he repeated as he fell asleep, "it's not the gift—it's the principle! Merry Christmas, me."

The next morning when Lew Knight breezed in with his "Good morning, counselor," Sam waited for the first sly ribbing to start. Lew wasn't the man to hide his humor behind a bushel. But Lew buried his nose in *The New York State Supplement* and kept it there all morning. The other five young lawyers in the communal office appeared either too bored or too busy to have Bild-a-Man sets on their conscience. There were no sly grins, no covert glances, no leading questions.

Tina walked in at ten o'clock, looking like a pinup girl caught with her clothes on.

"Good morning, counselors," she said.

Each in his own way, according to the peculiar gland secretions he was enjoying at the moment, beamed, drooled or nodded a reply. Lew Knight drooled. Sam Weber beamed.

Tina took it all in and analyzed the situation while she fluffed her hair about. Her conclusions evidently involved leaning markedly against Lew Knight's desk and asking what he had for her to do this morning.

Sam bit savagely into Hackleworth *On Torts.* Theoretically, Tina was employed by all seven of them as secretary, switchboard operator and receptionist. Actually, the most faithful performance of her duties entailed nothing more daily than the typing and addressing of two envelopes with an occasional letter to be sealed inside. Once a week there might be a wistful little brief which was never to attain judicial scrutiny. Tina therefore had a fair library of fashion magazines in the first drawer of her desk and a complete cosmetics laboratory in the other two; she spent one-third of her working day in the ladies' room swapping stocking prices and sources with other secretaries; she devoted the other two-thirds religiously to that one of her employers who as of her arrival seemed to be in the most masculine mood. Her pay was small but her life was full.

Just before lunch, she approached casually with the morning's mail. "Didn't think we'd be too busy this morning, counselor . . ." she began.

"You thought incorrectly, Miss Hill," he informed her with a brisk irritation that he hoped became him well; "I've been waiting for you to terminate your social engagements so that we could get down to what occasionally passes for business."

She was as startled as an uncushioned kitten. "But—but this isn't Monday. Somerset & Ojack only send you stuff on Mondays."

Sam winced at the reminder that if it weren't for the legal drudgework he received once a week from Somerset & Ojack he would be a lawyer in name only, if not in spirit only. "I have a letter, Miss Hill," he replied steadily. "Whenever you assemble the necessary materials, we can get on with it."

Tina returned in a head-shaking moment with stenographic pad and pencils.

"Regular heading, today's date," Sam began. "Address it to Chamber of Commerce, Glunt City, Ohio. Gentlemen: Would you inform me if you have registered currently with you a firm bearing the name of the Bild-a-Man Company or a firm with any name at all similar? I am also interested in whether a firm bearing the above or related name has recently made known its intention of joining your community. This inquiry is being made informally on behalf of a client who is interested in a product of this organization whose address he has mislaid. Signature and then this P.S.—My client is also curious as to the business possibilities of a street known as Diagonal Avenue or Diagonal Level. Any data on this address and the organizations presently located there will be greatly appreciated."

Tina batted wide blue eyes at him. "Oh, Sam," she breathed, ignoring the formality he had introduced, "oh, Sam, you have another client. I'm so glad. He looked a little sinister, but in *such* a distinguished manner that I was certain . . ."

"Who? Who looked a little sinister?"

"Why, your new cli-ent." Sam had the uncomfortable feeling that she had almost added, "stu-pid." "When I came in this morning, there was this terribly tall old man in a long black overcoat talking to the elevator operator. He turned to me—the elevator operator, I mean—and said, 'This is Mr. Weber's secretary. She'll be able to tell you anything you want to know.' Then he sort of winked which I thought was sort of impolite, you know, considering. Then this old man looked at me hard and I felt distinctly uncomfortable and he walked away muttering, 'Either disjointed or predatory personalities. Never normal. Never balanced.' Which I didn't think was very polite, either, I'll have you know, if he *is* your new client!" She sat back and began breathing again.

Tall, sinister old men in long black overcoats pumping the elevator operator about him. Hardly a matter of business. He had no skeletons in his personal closet. Could it be connected with his unusual Christmas present? Sam hummed mentally.

" . . . but she is my favorite aunt, you know," Tina was saying. "And she came in so unexpectedly."

The girl was explaining about their Christmas date. Sam felt a rush of affection for her as she leaned forward.

"Don't bother," he told her. "I know you couldn't help breaking the date. I was a little sore when you called me, but I got over it; never-hold-a-grudge-against-a-pretty-girl-Sam, I'm known as. How about lunch?"

"Lunch?" She gestured distractedly. "I promised Lew—Mr. Knight, that is—but he wouldn't mind if you came along."

"Fine. Let's go." This would be helping Lew to a spoonful of his own medicine.

Lew Knight took the business of having acrowd instead of a party for lunch as badly as Sam hoped he would. Unfortunately, Lew was able to describe details of his forthcoming case, the probable fees and possible distinction to be reaped thereof. After one or two attempts to bring an interesting will he was rephrasing for Somerset & Ojack into the conversation, Sam subsided into daydreams. Lew immediately dropped *Rosenthal* vs. *Rosenthal* and leered at Tina conversationally.

Outside the restaurant, snow discolored into slush. Most of the stores were removing Christmas displays. Sam noticed construction sets for children, haloed by tinsel and glittering with artificial snow. Build a radio, a skyscraper, an airplane. But "Only with a Bild-a-Man can you . . ."

"I'm going home," he announced suddenly. "Something important I just remembered. If anything comes up, call me there."

He was leaving Lew a clear field, he told himself, as he found a seat on the subway. But the bitter truth was that the field was almost as clear when he was around as when he wasn't. Lupine Lew Knight, he had been called in law school; since the day when he had noticed that Tina had the correct proportions of dress-filling substance, Sam's chances had been worth a crowbar at Fort Knox.

Tina hadn't been wearing his brooch today. Her little finger, right hand, however, had sported an unfamiliar and garish little ring. "Some got it," Sam philosophized. "Some don't got it. I don't got it."

But it would have been nice, with Tina, to have got it.

As he unlocked the door of his room he was surprised by an unmade bed telling with rumpled stoicism of a chambermaid who'd never come. This hadn't happened before—of course! He'd never locked his room before.

The girl must have thought he wanted privacy.

Maybe he had.

Aunt Maggie's ties glittered obscenely at the foot of the bed. He chucked them into the closet as he removed his hat and coat. Then he went over to the washstand and washed his hands, slowly. He turned around.

This was it. At last the great cubical bulk that had been lurking quietly in the corner of his vision was squarely before him. It was there and it undoubtedly contained all the outlandish collection he remembered.

"Open," he said, and the box opened.

The book, still open to the metallic table of contents, was lying at the bottom of the box. Part of it had slipped into the chamber of a strange piece of apparatus. Sam picked both out gingerly.

He slipped the book out and noticed the apparatus consisted mostly of some sort of binoculars, supported by a coil and tube arrangement and bearing on a flat green plate. He turned it over. The underside was lettered in the same streaky way as the book. *Combination Electron Microscope and Workbench.*

Very carefully he placed it on the floor. One by one, he removed the others, from the *Junior Biocalibrator* to the *Jiffy Vitalizer*. Very respectfully he ranged against the box in five multicolored rows the phials of lymph and the jars of basic cartilage. The walls of the chest were lined with indescribably thin and wrinkled sheets; a slight pressure along their edges expanded them into three-dimensional outlines of human organs whose shape and size could be varied with pinching any part of their surface—most indubitably molds.

Quite an assortment. If there was anything solidly scientific to it, that box might mean unimaginable wealth. Or some very useful publicity. Or—well, it should mean something!

If there was anything solidly scientific to it.

Sam flopped down onto the bed and opened to *A Child's Garden of Biochemistry.*

At nine that night he squatted next to the combination electron microscope and workbench and began opening certain small bottles. At nine forty-seven Sam Weber made his first simple living thing.

It wasn't much, if you used the first chapter of Genesis as your standard. Just a primitive brown mold that, in the field of the microscope, fed diffidently on a piece of pretzel, put forth a few spores and died in about twenty minutes. But *he* had made it. He had constructed a specific life form to feed on the constituents of a specific pretzel; it could survive nowhere else.

He went out to supper with every intention of getting drunk. After just a little alcohol, however, the *deiish* feeling returned and he scurried back to his room.

Never again that evening did he recapture the exultation of the brown mold, though he constructed a giant protein molecule and a whole slew of filterable viruses.

He called the office in the little corner drugstore which was his breakfast nook. "I'll be home all day," he told Tina.

She was a little puzzled. So was Lew Knight, who grabbed the phone. "Hey, counselor, you building up a neighborhood practice? Kid Blackstone is missing out on a lot of cases. Two ambulances have already clanged past the building."

"Yeah," said Sam. "I'll tell him when he comes in."

The weekend was almost upon him, so he decided to take the next day off as well. He wouldn't have any real work till Monday when the Somerset & Ojack basket would produce his lone egg.

Before he returned to his room, he purchased a copy of an advanced bacteriology. It was amusing to construct—with improvements!—unicellular creatures whose very place in the scheme of classification was a matter for argument among scientists of his own day. The Bild-a-Man manual, of course, merely gave a few examples and general rules; but with the descriptions in the bacteriology, the world was his oyster.

Which was an idea: he made a few oysters. The shells weren't hard enough, and he couldn't quite screw his courage up to the eating point, but they were most undeniably bivalves. If he cared to perfect his technique, his food problem would be solved.

The manual was fairly easy to follow and profusely illustrated with pictures that expanded into solidity as the page was opened. Very little was taken for granted; involved explanations followed simpler ones. Only the allusions were occasionally obscure: "This is the principle used in the phanphophlink toys." "When your teeth are next yokekkled or demortoned, think of the *Bacterium cyanogenum* and the humble part it plays." "If you have a rubicular mannikin around the house, you needn't bother with the chapter on mannikins."

After a brief search had convinced Sam that whatever else he now had in his apartment he didn't have a rubicular mannikin, he felt justified in turning to the chapter on mannikins. He had conquered completely this feeling of being Pop playing with Junior's toy train: already he had done more than the world's top biologists ever dreamed of for the next generation and what might not lie ahead—what problems might he not yet solve?

"Never forget that mannikins are constructed for one purpose and one purpose only." I won't, Sam promised. "Whether they are sanitary mannikins, tailoring mannikins, printing mannikins or even sunevviarry mannikins, they are each constructed with one operation of a given process in view. When you make a mannikin that is capable of more than one function, you are committing a crime so serious as to be punishable by public admonition."

"To construct an elementary mannikin . . ."

It was very difficult. Three times he tore down developing monstrosities and began anew. It wasn't till Sunday afternoon that the mannikin was complete —or rather, incomplete.

Long arms it had—although by an error, one was slightly longer than the other—a faceless head and a trunk. No legs. No eyes or ears, no organs of reproduction. It lay on his bed and gurgled out of the red rim of a mouth that was supposed to serve both for ingress and excretion of food. It waved the long arms, designed for some one simple operation not yet invented, in slow circles.

Sam, watching it, decided that life could be as ugly as an open field latrine in midsummer.

He had to disassemble it. Its length—three feet from almost boneless fingers to tapering, sealed-off trunk—precluded the use of the tiny disassembleator with which he had taken apart the oysters and miscellaneous small creations. There was a bright yellow notice on the large diassembleator, however: "To be used only under the direct supervision of a census keeper. Call formula A76 or unstable your id."

"Formula A76" meant about as much as "sunevviarry," and Sam decided his id was already sufficiently unstabled, thank you. He'd have to make out without a census keeper. The big disassembleator probably used the same general principles as the small one.

He clamped it to a bedpost and adjusted the focus. He snapped the switch set in the smooth underside.

Five minutes later the mannikin was a bright, gooey mess on his bed.

The large disassembleator, Sam was convinced as he tidied his room, did require the supervision of a census keeper. Some sort of keeper anyway. He rescued as many of the legless creature's constituents as he could, although he doubted he'd be using the set for the next fifty years or so. He certainly wouldn't ever use the disassembleator again; much less spectacular and disagreeable to shove the whole thing into a meat grinder and crank the handle as it squashed inside.

As he locked the door behind him on his way to a gentle binge, he made a mental note to purchase some fresh sheets the next morning. He'd have to sleep on the floor tonight.

Wrist-deep in Somerset & Ojack minutiae, Sam was conscious of Lew Knight's stares and Tina's puzzled glances. If they only knew, he exulted! But Tina would probably just think it "marr-vell-ouss!" and Lew Knight might make some crack like "Hey! Kid Frankenstein himself!" Come to think of it, though, Lew would probably have worked out some method of duplicating, to a limited extent, the contents of the Bild-a-Man set and marketing it commercially. Whereas he—well, there were other things you could do with the gadget. Plenty of other things.

"Hey, counselor," Lew Knight was perched on the corner of his desk, "what are these long weekends we're taking? You might not make as much money in the law, but does it look right for an associate of mine to sell magazine subscriptions on the side?"

Sam stuffed his ears mentally against the emery-wheel voice. "I've been writing a book."

"A law book? *Weber on Bankruptcy?*"

"No, a juvenile. *Lew Knight, The Neanderthal Nitwit.*"

"Won't sell. The title lacks punch. Something like *Knights, Knaves and Knobheads* is what the public goes for these days. By the way, Tina tells me you two had some sort of understanding about New Year's Eve and she doesn't think you'd mind if I took her out instead. I don't think you'd mind either, but I may be prejudiced. Especially since I have a table reservation at Cigale's where there's usually less of a crowd of a New Year's Eve than at the Automat."

"I don't mind."

"Good," said Knight approvingly as he moved away. "By the way, I won that case. Nice juicy fee, too. Thanks for asking."

Tina also wanted to know if he objected to the new arrangements when she brought the mail. Again, he didn't. Where had he been for over two days? He had been busy, very busy. Something entirely new. Something important.

She stared down at him as he separated offers of used cars guaranteed not to have been driven over a quarter of a million miles from caressing reminders that he still owed half the tuition for the last year of law school and when was he going to pay it?

Came a letter that was neither bill nor ad. Sam's heart momentarily lost interest in the monotonous round of pumping that was its lot as he stared at a strange postmark: Glunt City, Ohio.

> Dear Sir:
>   There is no firm in Glunt City at the present time bearing any name similar to "Bild-a-Man Company" nor do we know of any such organization planning to join our little community. We also have no thoroughfare called "Diagonal"; our north-south streets are named after Indian tribes while our east-west avenues are listed numerically in multiples of five.
>   Glunt City is a restricted residential township; we intend to keep it that. Only small retailing and service establishments are permitted here. If you are interested in building a home in Glunt City and can furnish proof of white, Christian, Anglo-Saxon ancestry on both sides of your family for fifteen generations, we would be glad to furnish further information.
>
> THOMAS H. PLANTAGENET, *Mayor.*
>
> P.S. An airfield for privately owned jet and propeller-driven aircraft is being built outside the city limits.

That was sort of that. He would get no refills on any of the phials and bottles even if he had a loose slunk or two with which to pay for the stuff. Better go easy on the material and conserve it as much as possible. But no disassembling!

Would the Bild-a-Man Company begin manufacturing at Glunt City some time in the future when it had developed into an industrial metropolis against the constricted wills of its restricted citizenry? Or had his package slid from some different track in the human time stream, some era to be born on an other-dimensional earth? There would have to be a common origin to both, else why the English wordage? And could there be a purpose in his having received it, beneficial—or otherwise?

Tina had been asking a question. Sam detached his mind from shapeless speculation and considered her quite-the-opposite features.

"So if you'd still like me to go out with you New Year's Eve, all I have to do is tell Lew that my mother expects to suffer from her gallstones and I have to stay home. Then I think you could buy the Cigale reservations from him cheap."

"Thanks a lot, Tina, but very honestly I don't have the loose cash right now. You and Lew make a much more logical couple anyhow."

Lew Knight wouldn't have done that. Lew cut throats with carefree zest. But Tina did seem to go with Lew as a type.

Why? Until Lew had developed a raised eyebrow where Tina was concerned, it had been Sam all the way. The rest of the office had accepted the fact and moved out of their path. It wasn't only a question of Lew's greater success and financial well-being: just that Lew had decided he wanted Tina and had got her.

It hurt. Tina wasn't special; she was no cultural companion, no intellectual equal; but he wanted her. He liked being with her. She was the woman he desired, rightly or wrongly, whether or not there was a sound basis to their relationship. He remembered his parents before a railway accident had orphaned him: they were theoretically incompatible, but they had been terribly happy together.

He was still wondering about it the next night as he flipped the pages of "Twinning yourself and your friends." It would be interesting to twin Tina.

"One for me, one for Lew."

Only the horrible possibility of an error was there. His mannikin had not been perfect; its arms had been of unequal length. Think of a physically lopsided Tina, something he could never bring himself to disassemble, limping extraneously through life.

And then the book warned: "Your constructed twin, though resembling you in every obvious detail, has not had the slow and guarded maturity you have enjoyed. He or she will not be as stable mentally, much less able to cope with unusual situations, much more prone to neurosis. Only a professional carnuplicator, using the finest equipment, can make an exact copy of a human personality. Yours will be able to live and even reproduce, but cannot ever be accepted as a valid and responsible member of society."

Well, he could chance that. A little less stability in Tina would hardly be noticeable; it might be more desirable.

There was a knock. He opened the door, guarding the box from view with his body. His landlady.

"Your door has been locked for the past week, Mr. Weber. That's why the chambermaid hasn't cleaned the room. We thought you didn't want anyone inside."

"Yes." He stepped into the hall and closed the door behind him. "I've been doing some highly important legal work at home."

"Oh." He sensed a murderous curiosity and changed the subject.

"Why all the fine feathers, Mrs. Lipanti—New Year's Eve party?"

She smoothed her frilled black dress self-consciously. "Y-yes. My sister and her husband came in from Springfield today and we were going to make a night of it. Only . . . only the girl who was supposed to come over and mind their baby just phoned and said she isn't feeling well. So I guess we won't go unless somebody else, I mean unless we can get someone else to take care . . . I mean, somebody who doesn't have a previous engagement and who wouldn't . . ." Her voice trailed away in assumed embarrassment as she realized the favor was already asked.

Well, after all, he wasn't doing anything tonight. And she had been remarkably pleasant those times when he had to operate on the basis of "Of course I'll have the rest of the rent in a day or so." But why did any one of the earth's two billion humans, when in the possession of an unpleasant buck, pass it automatically to Sam Weber?

Then he remembered Chapter IV on babies and other small humans. Since the night when he had separated the mannikin from its constituent parts, he'd been running through the manual as an intellectual exercise. He didn't feel quite up to making some weird error on a small human. But twinning wasn't supposed to be as difficult.

Only by Gog and by Magog, by Aesculapius the physician and Kildare the doctor, he would not disassemble this time. There must be other methods of disposal possible in a large city on a dark night. He'd think of something.

"I'd be glad to watch the baby for a few hours." He started down the hall to anticipate her polite protest. "Don't have a date tonight myself. No, don't mention it, Mrs. Lipanti. Glad to do it."

In the landlady's apartment, her nervous sister briefed him doubtfully. "And that's the only time she cries in a low, steady way so if you move fast there won't be much damage done. Not much, anyway."

He saw them to the door. "I'll be fast enough," he assured the mother. "Just so I get a hint."

Mrs. Lipanti paused at the door. "Did I tell you about the man who was asking after you this afternoon?"

Again? "A sort of tall old man in a long black overcoat?"

"With the most frightening way of staring into your face and talking under his breath. Do you know him?"

"Not exactly. What did he want?"

"Well, he asked if there was a Sam Weaver living here who was a lawyer and had been spending most of his time in his room for the past week. I told him we had a Sam Weber—your first name *is* Sam?—who answered to that description, but that the last Weaver had moved out over a year ago. He just looked at me for a while and said, 'Weaver, Weber—they might have made an error,' and walked out without so much as a good-by or excuse me. Not what I call a polite gentleman."

Thoughtfully Sam walked back to the child. Strange how sharp a mental picture he had formed of this man! Possibly because the two women who had met him thus far had been very impressionable, although to hear their stories the impression was there to be received.

He doubted there was any mistake: the man had been looking for him on both occasions; his knowledge of Sam's vacation from foolscap this past week proved that. It did seem as if he weren't interested in meeting him until some moot point of identity should be established beyond the least shadow of a doubt. Something of a legal mind, that.

The whole affair centered around the Bild-a-Man set, he was positive. This skulking investigation hadn't started until after the gift from 2353 had been delivered—and Sam had started using it.

But till the character in the long black overcoat paddled up to Sam Weber personally and stated his business, there wasn't very much he could do about it.

Sam went upstairs for his junior biocalibrator.

He propped the manual open against the side of the bed and switched the instrument on to full scanning power. The infant gurgled thickly as the calibrator was rolled slowly over its fat body and a section of metal tape unwound from the slot with, according to the manual, a completely detailed physiological description.

It was detailed. Sam gasped as the tape, running through the enlarging viewer, gave information on the child for which a pediatrician would have taken out at least three mortgages on his immortal soul. Thyroid capacity, chromosome quality, cerebral content. All broken down into neat subheads of data for construction purposes. Rate of skull expansion in minutes for the next ten hours; rate of cartilage transformation; changes in hormone secretions while active and at rest.

This was a blueprint; it was like taking canons from a baby.

Sam left the child to a puzzled contemplation of its navel and sped upstairs. With the tape as a guide, he clipped sections of the molds into the required smaller sizes. Then, almost before he knew it consciously, he was constructing a small human.

He was amazed at the ease with which he worked. Skill was evidently acquired in this game; the mannikin had been much harder to put together. The matter of duplication and working from an informational tape simplified his problems, though.

The child took form under his eyes.

He was finished just an hour and a half after he had taken his first measurements. All except the vitalizing.

A moment's pause, here. The ugly prospect of disassembling stopped him for a moment, but he shook it off. He had to see how well he had done the job. If this child could breathe, what was not possible to him! Besides he couldn't keep it suspended in an inanimate condition very long without running the risk of ruining his work and the materials.

He started the vitalizer.

The child shivered and began a low, steady cry. Sam tore down to the landlady's apartment again and scooped up a square of white linen left on the bed for emergencies. Oh well, some more clean sheets.

After he had made the necessary repairs, he stood back and took a good look at it. He was in a sense a papa. He felt as proud.

It was a perfect little creature, glowing and round with health.

"I have twinned," he said happily.

Every detail correct. The two sides of the face correctly inexact, the duplication of the original child's lunch at the very same point of digestion. Same hair, same eyes—or was it? Sam bent over the infant. He could have sworn the other was a blonde. This child had dark hair which seemed to grow darker as he looked.

He grabbed it with one hand and picked up the Junior Biocalibrator with the other.

Downstairs, he placed the two babies side by side on the big bed. No doubt about it. One was blonde; the other, his plagiarism, was now a definite brunette.

The biocalibrator showed other differences: Slightly faster pulse for his model. Lower blood count. Minutely higher cerebral capacity, although the content was the same. Adrenalin and bile secretions entirely unalike.

It added up to error. His child might be the superior specimen, or the inferior one, but he had not made a true copy. He had no way of knowing at the moment whether or not the infant he had built could grow into a human maturity. The other could.

Why? He had followed directions faithfully, had consulted the calibrator tape at every step. And this had resulted. Had he waited too long before starting the vitalizer? Or was it just a matter of insufficient skill?

Close to midnight, his watch delicately pointed out. It would be necessary to remove evidences of baby-making before the Sisters Lipanti came home. Sam considered possibilities swiftly.

He came down in a few moments with an old tablecloth and a cardboard carton. He wrapped the child in the tablecloth, vaguely happy that the temperature had risen that night, then placed it in the carton.

The child gurgled at the adventure. Its original on the bed *goo*ed in return. Sam slipped quietly out into the street.

Male and female drunks stumbled along tootling on tiny trumpets. People wished each other a *hic* Happy New Year as he strode down the necessary three blocks.

As he turned left, he saw the sign: "Urban Foundling Home." There was a light burning over a side door. Convenient, but that was a big city for you.

Sam shrank into the shadow of an alley for a moment as a new idea occurred to him. This had to look genuine. He pulled a pencil out of his breast pocket and scrawled on the side of the carton in as small handwriting as he could manage:

Please take good care of my darling little girl. I am not married.

Then he deposited the carton on the doorstep and held his finger on the bell until he heard movement inside. He was across the street and in the alley again by the time a nurse had opened the door.

It wasn't until he walked into the boardinghouse that he remembered about the navel. He stopped and tried to recall. No, he had built his little girl without a navel! Her belly had been perfectly smooth. That's what came of hurrying! Shoddy workmanship.

There might be a bit of to-do in the foundling home when they unwrapped the kid. How would they explain it?

Sam slapped his forehead. "Me and Michelangelo. He adds a navel, I forget one!"

Except for an occasional groan, the office was fairly quiet the second day of the New Year.

He was going through the last intriguing pages of the book when he was aware of two people teetering awkwardly near his desk. His eyes left the manual reluctantly: "New kinds of life for your leisure moments" was really fascinating!

Tina and Lew Knight.

Sam digested the fact that neither of them was perched on his desk.

Tina wore the little ring she'd received for Christmas on the third finger of her left hand; Lew was experimenting with a sheepish look and finding it difficult.

"Oh, Sam. Last night, Lew . . . Sam, we wanted you to be the first . . . Such a surprise, like that, I mean! Why I almost . . . Naturally we thought this would be a little difficult . . . Sam, we're going, I mean we expect . . ."

" . . . to be married," Lew Knight finished in what was almost an undertone. For the first time since Sam had known him he looked uncertain and suspicious of life, like a man who finds a newly hatched octopus in his breakfast orange juice.

"You'd adore the way Lew proposed," Tina was gushing. "So roundabout. And so shy. I told him afterward that I thought for a moment he was talking of something else entirely. I did have trouble understanding you, didn't I, dear?"

"Huh? Oh, yeah, you had trouble understanding me." Lew stared at his former rival. "Much of a surprise?"

"Oh, no. No surprise at all. You two fit together so perfectly that I knew it right from the first." Sam mumbled his felicitations, conscious of Tina's searching glances. "And now, if you'll excuse me, there's something I have to take care of immediately. A special sort of wedding present."

Lew was disconcerted. "A wedding present. This early?"

"Why, certainly," Tina told him. "It isn't very easy to get just the right thing. And a special friend like Sam naturally wants to get a very special gift."

Sam decided he had taken enough. He grabbed the manual and his coat and dodged through the door.

By the time he came to the red stone steps of the boardinghouse, he had reached the conclusion that the wound, while painful, had definitely missed his heart. He was in fact chuckling at the memory of Lew Knight's face when his landlady plucked at his sleeve.

"That man was here again today, Mr. Weber. He said he wanted to see you."

"Which man? The tall, old fellow?"

Mrs. Lipanti nodded, her arms folded complacently across her chest. "Such an unpleasant person! When I told him you weren't in, he insisted I take him up to your room. I said I couldn't do that without your permission and he looked at me fit to kill. I've never believed in the evil eye myself—although I always say where there is smoke there must be fire—but if there is such a thing as an evil eye, he has it."

"Will he be back?"

"Yes. He asked me when you usually return and I said about eight o'clock, figuring that if you didn't want to meet him it would give you time to change your clothes and wash up and leave before he gets here. And, Mr. Weber, if you'll excuse me for saying this, I don't think you want to meet him."

"Thanks. But when he comes in at eight, show him up. If he's the right person, I'm in illegal possession of his property. I want to know where this property originates."

In his room, he put the manual away carefully and told the box to open. The junior biocalibrator was not too bulky and newspaper would suffice to cover it. He was on his way uptown in a few minutes with the strangely shaped parcel under his arm.

Did he still want to duplicate Tina, he pondered? Yes, in spite of everything. She was still the woman he desired more than any he had ever known; and with the original married to Lew, the replica would have no choice but himself. Only—the replica would have Tina's characteristics up to the moment the measurements were taken; she might insist on marrying Lew as well.

That would make for a bit of a mad situation. But he was still miles from that bridge. It might even be amusing. . . .

The possibility of error was more annoying. The Tina he would make might be off-center in a number of ways: reds might overlap pinks; like an imperfectly reproduced color photograph she might, in time, come to digest her own stomach; there could very easily be a streak of strange and incurable insanity implicit in his model which would not assert itself until a deep mutual affection had flowered and borne fruit. As yet, he was no great shakes as a twinner and human mimeographer; the errors he had made on Mrs. Lipanti's niece demonstrated his amateur standing.

Sam knew he would never be able to dismantle Tina if she proved defective. Outside of the chivalrous concepts and almost superstitious reverence for womankind pressed into him by a small-town boyhood, there was the unmitigated horror he felt at the idea of such a beloved object going through the same disintegrating process as—well, the mannikin. But if he overlooked an essential in his construction, what other recourse would there be?

Solution: nothing must be overlooked. Sam grinned bitterly as the ancient elevator swayed up to his office. If he only had time for a little more practice with a person whose reactions he knew so exactly that any deviation from the norm would be instantly obvious! But the strange old man would be calling tonight, and, if his business concerned "Bild-a-Man" sets, Sam's experiments might be abruptly curtailed. And where would he find such a person? He had few real friends and no intimate ones. And, to be at all valuable, it would have to be someone he knew as well as himself.

Himself!

"Floor, sir." The elevator operator was looking at him reproachfully. Sam's exultant shout had caused him to bring the carrier to a spasmodic stop six inches under the floor level, something he had not done since that bygone day when he had first nervously reached for the controls. He felt his craftmanship was under a shadow as he morosely closed the door behind the lawyer.

And why not himself? He knew his own physical attributes better than he knew Tina's; any mental instability on the part of his reproduced self would be readily discernible long before it reached the point of psychosis or worse. And the beauty of it was that he would have no compunction in disassembling a superfluous Sam Weber. Quite the contrary: the horror in that situation would be the continued existence of a duplicate personality; its removal would be a relief.

Twinning himself would provide the necessary practice in a familiar medium. Ideal. He'd have to take careful notes so that if anything went wrong he'd know just where to avoid going off the track in making his own personal Tina.

And maybe the old geezer wasn't interested in the set at all. Even if he was, Sam could take his landlady's advice and not be at home when he called. Silver linings wherever he looked.

Lew Knight stared at the instrument in Sam's hands. "What in the sacred name of Blackstone and all his commentaries is that? Looks like a lawn mower for a window box!"

"It's, uh, sort of a measuring gadget. Gives the right size for one thing and another and this and that. Won't be able to get you the wedding present I have in mind unless I know the right size. Or sizes. Tina, would you mind stepping out into the hall?"

"Nooo." She looked dubiously at the gadget. "It won't hurt?"

It wouldn't hurt a bit, Sam assured her. "I just want to keep this a secret from Lew till after the ceremony."

She brightened at that and preceded Sam through the door. "Hey, counselor," one of the other young lawyers called at Lew as they left. "Hey, counselor, don't let him do that. Possession is nine points, Sam always says. He'll never bring her back."

Lew chuckled weakly and bent over his work.

"Now I want you to go into the ladies' room," Sam explained to a bewildered Tina. "I'll stand guard outside and tell the other customers that the place is out of order. If another woman is inside wait until she leaves. Then strip."

"Strip?" Tina squealed.

He nodded. Then very carefully, emphasizing every significant detail of operation, he told her how to use the junior biocalibrator. How she must be careful to kick the switch and set the tape running. How she must cover every external square inch of her body. "This little arm will enable you to lower it down your back. No questions now. Git."

She was back in fifteen minutes, fluffing her dress into place and studying the tape with a rapt frown. "This is the *strangest* thing. According to the spool, my iodine content . . ."

Sam snaffled the biocalibrator hurriedly. "Don't give it another thought. It's a code, kind of. Tells me just what size and how many of what kind. You'll be crazy about the gift when you see it."

"I know I will." She bent over him as he knelt and examined the tape to make certain she had applied the instrument correctly. "You know, Sam, I always felt your taste was perfect. I want you to come and visit us often after we're married. You can have such beautiful ideas! Lew is a bit too . . . too businesslike, isn't he? I mean it's necessary for success and all that, but success isn't everything. I mean you have to have culture, too. You'll help me keep cultured, won't you, Sam?"

"Sure," Sam said vaguely. The tape was complete. Now to get started! "Anything I can do—glad to help."

He rang for the elevator and noticed the forlorn uncertainty with which she watched him. "Don't worry, Tina. You and Lew will be very happy together. And you'll love this wedding present." But not as much as I will, he told himself as he stepped into the elevator.

Back in his room, he emptied the machine and undressed. In a few moments he had another tape on himself. He would have liked to consider it for a while, but being this close to the goal made him impatient. He locked the door, cleaned his room hurriedly of accumulated junk—remembering to grunt in annoyance at Aunt Maggie's ties: the blue and red one almost lighted up the room—ordered the box to open—and he was ready to begin.

First the water. With the huge amount of water necessary to the human body, especially in the case of an adult, he might as well start collecting it now. He had bought several pans and it would take his lone faucet some time to fill them all.

As he placed the first pot under the tap, Sam wondered suddenly if its chemical impurities might affect the end product. Of course it might! These children of 2353 would probably take absolutely pure H_2O as a matter of daily use; the manual hadn't mentioned the subject, but how did he know what kind of water they had available? Well, he'd boil this batch over his chemical stove; when he got to making Tina he could see about getting *aqua* completely *pura*.

Score another point for making a simulacrum of Sam first.

While waiting for the water to boil, he arranged his supplies to positions of maximum availability. They were getting low. That baby had taken up quite a bit of useful ingredients; too bad he hadn't seen his way clear to disassembling it. That meant if there were any argument in favor of allowing the replica of himself to go on living, it was now invalid. He'd have to take it apart in order to have enough for Tina II. (Or Tina prime?)

He leafed through Chapters VI, VII and VIII on the ingredients, completion and disassembling of a man. He'd been through this several times before; but he'd passed more than one law exam on the strength of a last-minute review.

The constant reference to mental instability disturbed him. "The humans constructed with this set will, at the very best, show most of the superstitious tendencies and neurosis compulsions of medieval mankind. In the long run they are not normal; take great care not to consider them such." Well, it wouldn't make too much difference in Tina's case—and that was all that was important.

When he had finished adjusting the molds to the correct sizes, he fastened the vitalizer to the bed. Then—very, very slowly and with repeated glances at the manual, he began to duplicate Sam Weber. He learned more of his physical limitations and capabilities in the next two hours than any man had ever known since the day when an inconspicuous primate had investigated the possibilities of ground locomotion upon the nether extremities alone.

Strangely enough, he felt neither awe nor exultation. It was like building a radio receiver for the first time. Child's play.

Most of the phials and jars were empty when he had finished. The damp molds were stacked inside the box, still in their three-dimensional outline. The manual lay neglected on the floor.

Sam Weber stood near the bed looking down at Sam Weber on the bed.

All that remained was vitalizing. He daren't wait too long or imperfections might set in and the errors of the baby be repeated. He shook off a nauseating feeling of unreality, made certain that the big disassembleator was within reach and set the jiffy vitalizer in motion.

The man on the bed coughed. He stirred. He sat up.

"Wow!" he said. "Pretty good, if I do say so myself!" And then he had leaped off the bed and seized the disassembleator. He tore great chunks of wiring out of the center, threw it to the floor and kicked it into shapelessness.

"No Sword of Damocles going to hang over *my* head," he informed an open-mouthed Sam Weber. "Although, I could have used it on you, come to think of it."

Sam eased himself to the mattress and sat down. His mind stopped rearing and whinnied to a halt. He had been so impressed with the helplessness of the baby and the mannikin that he had never dreamed of the possibility that his duplicate would enter upon life with such enthusiasm. He should have, though; this was a full-grown man, created at a moment of complete physical and mental activity.

"This is bad," he said at last in a hoarse voice. "You're unstable. You can't be admitted into normal society."

"I'm unstable?" his image asked. "Look who's talking! The guy who's been mooning his way through his adult life, who wants to marry an overdressed, conceited collection of biological impulses that would come crawling on her knees to any man sensible enough to push the right buttons. . . ."

"You leave Tina's name out of this," Sam told him, feeling acutely uncomfortable at the theatrical phrase.

His double looked at him and grinned. "Okay, I will. But not her body! Now, look here, Sam or Weber or whatever you want me to call you, you can live your life and I'll live mine. I won't even be a lawyer if that'll make you happy. But as far as Tina is concerned, now that there are no ingredients to make a copy—that was a rotten escapist idea, by the way—I have enough of your likes and dislikes to want her badly. And I can have her, whereas you can't. You don't have the gumption."

Sam leaped to his feet and doubled his fists. Then he saw the other's entirely equal size and slightly more assured twinkle. There was no point in fighting —that would end in a draw, at best. He went back to reason.

"According to the manual," he began, "you are prone to neurosis. . . ."

"The manual! The manual was written for children of four centuries hence, with quite a bit of selective breeding and scientific education behind them. Personally, I think I'm a . . ."

There was a double knock on the door. "Mr. Weber."

"Yes," they both said simultaneously.

Outside, the landlady gasped and began speaking in an uncertain voice. "Th-that gentleman is downstairs. He'd like to see you. Shall I tell him you're in?"

"No, I'm not at home," said the double.

"Tell him I left an hour ago," said Sam at exactly the same moment.

There was another, longer gasp and the sound of footsteps receding hurriedly.

"That's one clever way to handle a situation," Sam's facsimile exploded. "Couldn't you keep your mouth shut? The poor woman's probably gone off to have a fit."

"You forget that this is my room and you are just an experiment that went wrong," Sam told him hotly. "I have just as much right, in fact more right . . . hey, what do you think you're doing?"

The other had thrown open the closet door and was stepping into a pair of pants. "Just getting dressed. You can wander around in the nude if you find it exciting, but I want to look a bit respectable."

"I undressed to take my measurements . . . or your measurements. Those are my clothes, this is my room . . ."

"Look, take it easy. You could never prove it in a court of law. Don't make me go into that cliché about what's yours is mine and so forth."

Heavy feet resounded through the hall. They stopped outside the room. Cymbals seemed to clash all around them and there was a panic-stricken sense of unendurable heat. Then shrill echoes fled into the distance. The walls stopped shuddering.

Silence and a smell of burning wood.

They whirled in time to see a terribly tall, terribly old man in a long black overcoat walking through the smoldering remains of the door. Much too tall for the entrance, he did not stoop as he came in; rather, he drew his head down into his garment and shot it up again. Instinctively, they moved close together.

His eyes, all shiny black iris without any whites, were set back deep in the shadow of his head. They reminded Sam Weber of the scanners on the biocalibrator: they tabulated, deduced, rather than saw.

"I was afraid I would be too late," he rumbled at last in weird, clipped tones. "You have already duplicated yourself, Mr. Weber, making necessary unpleasant rearrangements. And the duplicate has destroyed the disassembleator. Too bad. I shall have to do it manually. An ugly job."

He came farther into the room until they could almost breathe their fright upon him. "This affair has already dislocated four major programs, but we had to move in accepted cultural grooves and be absolutely certain of the recipient's identity before we could act to withdraw the set. Mrs. Lipanti's collapse naturally stimulated emergency measures."

The duplicate cleared his throat. "You are . . ."

"Not exactly human. A humble civil servant of precision manufacture. I am census keeper for the entire twenty-ninth oblong. You see, your set was intended for the Thregander children, who are on a field trip in this oblong.

One of the Threganders who has a Weber chart requested the set through the chrondromos which, in an attempt at the supernormal, unstabled without carnuplicating. You therefore received the package instead. Unfortunately, the unstabling was so complete that we were forced to locate you by indirect methods."

The census keeper paused and Sam's double hitched his pants nervously. Sam wished he had anything—even a fig leaf—to cover his nakedness. He felt like a character in the Garden of Eden trying to build up a logical case for apple-eating. He appreciated glumly how much more than Bild-a-Man sets clothes had to do with the making of a man.

"We will have to recover the set, of course," the staccato thunder continued, "and readjust any discrepancies it has caused. Once the matter has been cleared up, however, your life will be allowed to resume its normal progression. Meanwhile, the problem is which of you is the original Sam Weber?"

"I am," they both quavered—and turned to glare at each other.

"Difficulties," the old man rumbled. He sighed like an arctic wind. "I always have difficulties! Why can't I ever have a simple case like a carnuplicator?"

"Look here," the duplicate began. "The original will be . . ."

"Less unstable and of better emotional balance than the replica," Sam interrupted. "Now, it seems . . ."

"That you should be able to tell the difference," the other concluded breathlessly. "From what you see and have seen of us, can't you decide which is the more valid member of society?"

What a pathetic confidence, Sam thought, the fellow was trying to display! Didn't he know he was up against someone who could really discern mental differences? This was no fumbling psychiatrist of the present; here was a creature who could see through externals to the most coherent personality beneath.

"I can, naturally. Now, just a moment." He studied them carefully, his eyes traveling with judicious leisure up and down their bodies. They waited, fidgeting, in a silence that pounded.

"Yes," the old man said at last. "Yes. Quite."

He walked forward.

A long, thin arm shot out.

He started to disassemble Sam Weber.

"But listennnnn . . ." began Weber in a yell that turned into a high scream and died in a liquid mumble.

"It would be better for your sanity if you didn't watch," the census keeper suggested.

The duplicate exhaled slowly, turned away and began to button a shirt. Behind him the mumbling continued, rising and falling in pitch.

"You see," came the clipped, rumbling accents, "it's not the gift we're afraid of letting you have—it's the principle involved. Your civilization isn't ready for it. You understand."

"Perfectly," replied the counterfeit Weber, knotting Aunt Maggie's blue and red tie.

JAMES H. SCHMITZ

Grandpa

Science fiction is partly an exercise in extrapolation—the author takes known facts, patterns or tendencies and projects these into the future. But there are some areas about which we know very little. One of these is exobiology, the science devoted to the study of life beyond the planet Earth. Yet aliens are one of the core elements of modern science fiction, and they have been depicted in a bewildering array of shapes, sizes, colors, substances and degrees of plausibility —but rarely better than in this fine story of an encounter between humans and an alien.

A green-winged, downy thing as big as a hen fluttered along the hillside to a point directly above Cord's head and hovered there, twenty feet above him. Cord, a fifteen-year-old human being, leaned back against a skipboat parked on the equator of a world that had known human beings for only the past four Earth years, and eyed the thing speculatively. The thing was, in the free and easy terminology of the Sutang Colonial Team, a swamp bug. Concealed in the downy fur back of the bug's head was a second, smaller, semi-parasitical thing, classed as a bug rider.

The bug itself looked like a new species to Cord. Its parasite might or might not turn out to be another unknown. Cord was a natural research man; his first glimpse of the odd flying team had sent endless curiosities thrilling through him. How did that particular phenomenon tick, and why? What fascinating things, once you'd learned about it, could you get it to *do?*

Normally, he was hampered by circumstances in carrying out any such investigation. The colonial team was a practical, hardworking outfit—two thousand people who'd been given twenty years to size up and tame down the brand-new world of Sutang to the point where a hundred thousand colonists could be settled on it in reasonable safety and comfort. Even junior colonial students like Cord were expcted to confine their curiosity to the pattern of research set up by the station to which they were attached. Cord's inclination toward independent experiments had got him into disfavor with his immediate superiors before this.

He sent a casual glance in the direction of the Yoger Bay Colonial Station behind him. No signs of human activity about that low, fortresslike bulk in the hill. Its central lock was still closed. In fifteen minutes, it was scheduled to be opened to let out the planetary regent, who was inspecting the Yoger Bay Station and its principal activities today.

Fifteen minutes was time enough to find out something about the new bug, Cord decided.

But he'd have to collect it first.

He slid out one of the two handguns holstered at his side. This one was his own property: a Vanadian projectile weapon. Cord thumbed it to position for anesthetic small-game missiles and brought the hovering swamp bug down, drilled neatly and microscopically through the head.

As the bug hit the ground, the rider left its back. A tiny scarlet demon, round and bouncy as a rubber ball, it shot toward Cord in three long hops, mouth wide to sink home inch-long, venom-dripping fangs. Rather breathlessly, Cord triggered the gun again and knocked it out in midleap. A new species, all right! Most bug riders were harmless plant-eaters, mere suckers of vegetable juice. . . .

"Cord!" A feminine voice.

Cord swore softly. He hadn't heard the central lock click open. She must have come around from the other side of the station.

"Hi, Grayan!" he shouted innocently without looking around. "Come see what I got! New species!"

Grayan Mahoney, a slender, black-haired girl two years older than himself, came trotting down the hillside toward him. She was Sutang's star colonial student and the station manager, Nirmond, indicated from time to time that she was a fine example for Cord to pattern his own behavior on. In spite of that, she and Cord were good friends, but she bossed him around considerably.

"Cord, you dope!" she scowled as she came up. "Quit acting like a collector! If the regent came out now, you'd be sunk. Nirmond's been telling her about you!"

"Telling her what?" Cord asked, startled.

"For one," Grayan reported, "that you don't keep up on your assigned work. Two, that you sneak off on one-man expeditions of your own at least once a month and have to be rescued . . ."

"Nobody," Cord interrupted hotly, "has had to rescue me yet!"

"How's Nirmond to know you're alive and healthy when you just drop out of sight for a week?" Grayan countered. "Three," she resumed checking the items off on slim fingertips, "he complained that you keep private zoological gardens of unidentified and possibly deadly vermin in the woods back of the station. And four . . . well, Nirmond simply doesn't want the responsibility for you any more!" She held up the four fingers significantly.

"Golly!" gulped Cord, dismayed. Summed up tersely like that, his record *didn't* look too good.

"Golly is right! I keep warning you! Now Nirmond wants the regent to send you back to Vanadia—and there's a starship coming into New Venus forty-eight hours from now!" New Venus was the colonial team's main settlement on the opposite side of Sutang.

"What'll I do?"

"Start acting like you had good sense mainly." Grayan grinned suddenly. "I talked to the regent, too—Nirmond isn't rid of you yet! But if you louse up on our tour of the Bay Farms today, you'll be off the team for good!"

She turned to go. "You might as well put the skipboat back; we're not using it. Nirmond's driving us down to the edge of the bay in a treadcar, and we'll take a raft from there. Don't let them know I warned you!"

Cord looked after her, slightly stunned. He hadn't realized his reputation had become as bad as all that! To Grayan, whose family had served on colonial teams for the past four generations, nothing worse was imaginable than to be dismissed and sent back ignominiously to one's own homeworld. Much to his surprise, Cord was discovering now that he felt exactly the same way about it!

Leaving his newly bagged specimens to revive by themselves and flutter off again, he hurriedly flew the skipboat around the station and rolled it back into its stall.

Three rafts lay moored just offshore in the marshy cove, at the edge of which Nirmond had stopped the treadcar. They looked somewhat like exceptionally broad-brimmed, well-worn sugarloaf hats floating out there, green and leathery. Or like lily pads twenty-five feet across, with the upper section of a big, gray green pineapple growing from the center of each. Plant animals of some sort. Sutang was too new to have had its phyla sorted out into anything remotely like an orderly classification. The rafts were a local oddity which had been investigated and could be regarded as harmless and moderately useful. Their usefulness lay in the fact that they were employed as a rather slow means of transportation about the shallow, swampy waters of the Yoger Bay. That was as far as the team's interest in them went at present.

The regent had stood up from the back seat of the car where she was sitting next to Cord. There were only four in the party; Grayan was up front with Nirmond.

"Are those our vehicles?" The regent sounded amused.

Nirmond grinned, a little sourly. "Don't underestimate them, Dane! They could become an important economic factor in this region in time. But, as a matter of fact, these three are smaller than I like to use." He was peering about the reedy edges of the cove. "There's a regular monster parked here usually. . . ."

Grayan turned to Cord. "Maybe Cord knows where Grandpa is hiding."

It was well meant, but Cord had been hoping nobody would ask him about Grandpa. Now they all looked at him.

"Oh, you want Grandpa?" he said, somewhat flustered. "Well, I left him . . . I mean I saw him a couple of weeks ago about a mile south from here. . . ."

Grayan sighed. Nirmond grunted and told the regent, "The rafts tend to stay wherever they're left, providing it's shallow and muddy. They use a hair-root system to draw chemicals and microscopic nourishment directly from the bottom of the bay. Well—Grayan, would you like to drive us there?"

Cord settled back unhappily as the treadcar lurched into motion. Nirmond suspected he'd used Grandpa for one of his unauthorized tours of the area, and Nirmond was quite right.

"I understand you're an expert with these rafts, Cord," Dane said from beside him. "Grayan told me we couldn't find a better steersman, or pilot, or whatever you call it, for our trip today."

"I can handle them," Cord said, perspiring. "They don't give you any trouble!" He didn't feel he'd made a good impression on the regent so far. Dane was a young, handsome-looking woman with an easy way of talking and laughing, but she wasn't the head of the Sutang Colonial Team for nothing. She looked quite capable of shipping out anybody whose record wasn't up to par.

"There's one big advantage our beasties have over a skipboat, too," Nirmond remarked from the front seat. "You don't have to worry about a snapper trying to climb on board with you!" He went on to describe the stinging ribbon-tentacles the rafts spread around them under water to discourage creatures that might make a meal off their tender underparts. The snappers and two or three other active and aggressive species of the bay hadn't yet learned it was foolish to attack armed human beings in a boat, but they would skitter hurriedly out of the path of a leisurely perambulating raft.

Cord was happy to be ignored for the moment. The regent, Nirmond and

Grayan were all Earth people, which was true of most of the members of the team; and Earth people made him uncomfortable, particularly in groups. Vanadia, his own homeworld, had barely graduated from the status of Earth colony itself, which might explain the difference. All the Earth people he'd met so far seemed dedicated to what Grayan Mahoney called the Big Picture, while Nirmond usually spoke of it as "Our Purpose Here." They acted strictly in accordance with their team regulations—sometimes, in Cord's opinion, quite insanely. Because now and then the regulations didn't quite cover a new situation and then somebody was likely to get killed. In which case, the regulations would be modified promptly, but Earth people didn't seem otherwise disturbed by such events.

Grayan had tried to explain it to Cord:

"We can't really ever *know* in advance what a new world is going to be like! And once we're there, there's too much to do, in the time we've got, to study it inch by inch. You get your job done, and you take a chance. But if you stick by the regulations you've got the best chances of surviving anybody's been able to figure out for you . . ."

Cord felt he preferred to just use good sense and not let regulations or the job get him into a situation he couldn't figure out for himself.

To which Grayan replied impatiently that he hadn't yet got the Big Picture. . . .

The treadcar swung around and stopped, and Grayan stood up in the front seat, pointing. "That's Grandpa, over there!"

Dane also stood up and whistled softly, apparently impressed by Grandpa's fifty-foot spread. Cord looked around in surprise. He was pretty sure this was several hundred yards from the spot where he'd left the big raft two weeks ago; and as Nirmond said, they didn't usually move about by themselves.

Puzzled, he followed the others down a narrow path to the water, hemmed in by tree-sized reeds. Now and then he got a glimpse of Grandpa's swimming platform, the rim of which just touched the shore. Then the path opened out, and he saw the whole raft lying in sunlit, shallow water; and he stopped short, startled.

Nirmond was about to step up on the platform, ahead of Dane.

"Wait!" Cord shouted. His voice sounded squeaky with alarm. "Stop!"

He came running forward.

They had frozen where they stood, looked around swiftly. Then glanced back at Cord coming up. They were well trained.

"What's the matter, Cord?" Nirmond's voice was quiet and urgent.

"Don't get on that raft—it's changed!" Cord's voice sounded wobbly, even to himself. "Maybe it's not even Grandpa. . . ."

He saw he was wrong on the last point before he'd finished the sentence. Scattered along the rim of the raft were discolored spots left by a variety of heat-guns, one of which had been his own. It was the way you goaded the sluggish and mindless things into motion. Cord pointed at the cone-shaped central projection. "There—his head! He's sprouting!"

"Sprouting?" the station manager repeated uncomprehendingly. Grandpa's head, as befitted his girth, was almost twelve feet high and equally wide. It was armor-plated like the back of a saurian to keep off plant-suckers, but two weeks ago it had been an otherwise featureless knob, like those on all other rafts. Now scores of long, kinky, leafless vines had grown out from all surfaces of the cone, like green wires. Some were drawn up like tightly coiled springs, others trailed limply to the platform and over it. The top of the cone was dotted with angry red buds, rather like pimples, which hadn't been there before either. Grandpa looked unhealthy.

"Well," Nirmond said, "so it is. Sprouting!" Grayan made a choked sound. Nirmond glanced at Cord as if puzzled. "Is that all that was bothering you, Cord?"

"Well, sure!" Cord began excitedly. He hadn't caught the significance of the word "all"; his hackles were still up, and he was shaking. "None of them ever . . ."

Then he stopped. He could tell by their faces that they hadn't got it. Or rather, that they'd got it all right but simply weren't going to let it change their plans. The rafts were classified as harmless, according to the regulations. Until proved otherwise, they would continue to be regarded as harmless. You didn't waste time quibbling with the regulations—apparently even if you were the planetary regent. You didn't feel you had the time to waste.

He tried again. "Look . . ." he began. What he wanted to tell them was that Grandpa with one unknown factor added wasn't Grandpa any more. He was an unpredictable, oversized life form, to be investigated with cautious thoroughness till you knew what the unknown factor meant.

But it was no use. They knew all that. He stared at them helplessly. "I . . ."

Dane turned to Nirmond. "Perhaps you'd better check," she said. She didn't add, "to reassure the boy!" but that was what she meant.

Cord felt himself flushing terribly. They thought he was scared—which he was—and they were feeling sorry for him, which they had no right to do. But there was nothing he could say or do now except watch Nirmond walk steadily across the platform. Grandpa shivered slightly a few times, but the rafts always did that when someone first stepped on them. The station manager stopped before one of the kinky sprouts, touched it and then gave it a tug. He reached up and poked at the lowest of the budlike growths. "Odd-looking things!" he called back. He gave Cord another glance. "Well, everything seems harmless enough, Cord. Coming aboard, everyone?"

It was like dreaming a dream in which you yelled and yelled at people and couldn't make them hear you! Cord stepped up stiff-legged on the platform behind Dane and Grayan. He knew exactly what would have happened if he'd hesitated even a moment. One of them would have said in a friendly voice, careful not to let it sound too contemptuous: "You don't have to come along if you don't want to, Cord!"

Grayan had unholstered her heat-gun and was ready to start Grandpa moving out into the channels of the Yoger Bay.

Cord hauled out his own heat-gun and said roughly, "I was to do that!"

"All right, Cord." She gave him a brief, impersonal smile, as if he were someone she'd met for the first time that day, and stood aside.

They were so infuriatingly polite! He was, Cord decided, as good as on his way back to Vanadia right now.

For a while, Cord almost hoped that something awesome and catastrophic would happen promptly to teach the team people a lesson. But nothing did. As always, Grandpa shook himself vaguely and experimentally when he felt the heat on one edge of the platform and then decided to withdraw from it, all of which was standard procedure. Under the water, out of sight, were the raft's working sections: short, thick leaf-structures shaped like paddles and designed to work as such, along with the slimy nettle-streamers which kept the vegetarians of the Yoger Bay away, and a jungle of hair roots through which Grandpa sucked nourishments from the mud and the sluggish waters of the bay, and with which he also anchored himself.

The paddles started churning, the platform quivered, the hair roots were hauled out of the mud; and Grandpa was on his ponderous way.

Cord switched off the heat, reholstered his gun, and stood up. Once in motion, the rafts tended to keep traveling unhurriedly for quite a while. To stop them, you gave them a touch of heat along their leading edge; and they could be turned in any direction by using the gun lightly on the opposite side of the platform.

It was simple enough. Cord didn't look at the others. He was still burning inside. He watched the reed beds move past and open out, giving him glimpses of the misty, yellow and green and blue expanse of the brackish bay ahead. Behind the mist, to the west, were the Yoger Straits, tricky and ugly water when the tides were running; and beyond the straits lay the open sea, the great Zlanti Deep, which was another world entirely and one of which he hadn't seen much as yet.

Suddenly he was sick with the full realization that he wasn't likely to see any more of it now! Vanadia was a pleasant enough planet; but the wildness and strangeness were long gone from it. It wasn't Sutang.

Grayan called from beside Dane, "What's the best route from here into the farms, Cord?"

"The big channel to the right," he answered. He added somewhat sullenly, "We're headed for it!"

Grayan came over to him. "The regent doesn't want to see all of it," she said, lowering her voice. "The algae and plankton beds first. Then as much of the mutated grains as we can show her in about three hours. Steer for the ones that have been doing best, and you'll keep Nirmond happy!"

She gave him a conspiratorial wink. Cord looked after her uncertainly. You couldn't tell from her behavior that anything was wrong. Maybe . . .

He had a flare of hope. It was hard not to like the team people, even when they were being rock-headed about their regulations. Perhaps it was that purpose that gave them their vitality and drive, even though it made them remorseless about themselves and everyone else. Anyway, the day wasn't over yet. He might still redeem himself in the regent's opinion. Something might happen . . .

Cord had a sudden cheerful, if improbable, vision of some bay monster plunging up on the raft with snapping jaws, and of himself alertly blowing out what passed for the monster's brains before anyone else—Nirmond, in particular—was even aware of the threat. The bay monsters shunned Grandpa, of course, but there might be ways of tempting one of them.

So far, Cord realized, he'd been letting his feelings control him. It was time to start thinking!

Grandpa first. So he'd sprouted—green vines and red buds, purpose unknown, but with no change observable in his behavior patterns otherwise. He was the biggest raft in this end of the bay, though all of them had been growing steadily in the two years since Cord had first seen one. Sutang's seasons changed slowly; its year was somewhat more than five Earth years long. The first team members to land here hadn't yet seen a full year pass.

Grandpa then was showing a seasonal change. The other rafts, not quite so far developed, would be reacting similarly a little later. Plant animals—they might be blossoming, preparing to propagate.

"Grayan," he called, "how do the rafts get started? When they're small, I mean."

Grayan looked pleased; and Cord's hopes went up a little more. Grayan was on his side again anyway!

"Nobody knows yet," she said. "We were just talking about it. About half of the coastal marsh fauna of the continent seems to go through a preliminary larval stage in the sea." She nodded at the red buds on the raft's cone. "It *looks* as if Grandpa is going to produce flowers and let the wind or tide take the seeds out through the straits."

It made sense. It also knocked out Cord's still half-held hope that the change in Grandpa might turn out to be drastic enough, in some way, to justify his reluctance to get on board. Cord studied Grandpa's armored head carefully once more—unwilling to give up that hope entirely. There was a series of vertical gummy black slits between the armor plates, which hadn't been in evidence two weeks ago either. It looked as if Grandpa was beginning to come apart at the seams. Which might indicate that the rafts, big as they grew to be, didn't outlive a full seasonal cycle, but came to flower at about this time of Sutang's year and died. However, it was a safe bet that Grandpa wasn't going to collapse into senile decay before they completed their trip today.

Cord gave up on Grandpa. The other notion returned to him—perhaps he could coax an obliging bay monster into action that would show the regent he was no sissy!

Because the monsters were there, all right.

Kneeling at the edge of the platform and peering down into the wine-colored, clear water of the deep channel they were moving through, Cord could see a fair selection of them at almost any moment.

Some five or six snappers, for one thing. Like big, flattened crayfish, chocolate brown mostly, with green and red spots on their carapaced backs. In some areas they were so thick you'd wonder what they found to live on, except that they ate almost anything, down to chewing up the mud in which they squatted. However, they preferred their food in large chunks and alive, which was one reason you didn't go swimming in the bay. They would attack a boat on occasion; but the excited manner in which the ones he saw were scuttling off toward the edges of the channel showed they wanted to have nothing to do with a big moving raft.

Dotted across the bottom were two-foot round holes which looked vacant at the moment. Normally, Cord knew, there would be a head filling each of those holes. The heads consisted mainly of triple sets of jaws, held open patiently like so many traps to grab at anything that came within range of the long, wormlike bodies behind the heads. But Grandpa's passage, waving his stingers like transparent pennants through the water, had scared the worms out of sight, too.

Otherwise, mostly schools of small stuff—and then a flash of wicked scarlet, off to the left behind the raft, darting out from the reeds, turning its needle-nose into their wake.

Cord watched it without moving. He knew that creature, though it was rare in the bay and hadn't been classified. Swift, vicious—alert enough to snap swamp bugs out of the air as they fluttered across the surface. And he'd tantalized one with fishing tackle once into leaping up on a moored raft, where it had flung itself about furiously until he was able to shoot it.

No fishing tackle. A handkerchief might just do it, if he cared to risk an arm. . . .

"What fantastic creatures!" Dane's voice just behind him.

"Yellowheads," said Nirmond. "They've got a high utility rating. Keep down the bugs."

Cord stood up casually. It was no time for tricks! The reed bed to their right was thick with yellowheads, a colony of them. Vaguely froggy things, man-sized and better. Of all the creatures he'd discovered in the bay, Cord liked them least. The flabby, sacklike bodies clung with four thin limbs to the upper sections of the twenty-foot reeds that lined the channel. They hardly ever moved, but their huge, bulging eyes seemed to take in everything that went on about them. Every so often, a downy swamp bug came close enough; and a yellowhead would open its vertical, enormous, tooth-lined slash of a mouth, extend the whole front of its face like a bellows in a flashing strike; and the bug would be gone. They might be useful, but Cord hated them.

"Ten years from now we should know what the cycle of coastal life is like," Nirmond said. "When we set up the Yoger Bay Station there were no yellowheads here. They came the following year. Still with traces of the oceanic larval form; but the metamorphosis was almost complete. About twelve inches long. . . ."

Dane remarked that the same pattern was duplicated endlessly elsewhere. The regent was inspecting the yellowhead colony with field glasses; she put them down now, looked at Cord and smiled. "How far to the farms?"

"About twenty minutes."

"The key," Nirmond said, "seems to be the Zlanti Basin. It must be almost a soup of life in spring."

"It is," nodded Dane, who had been here in Sutang's spring, four Earth years ago. "It's beginning to look as if the basin alone might justify colonization. The question is still"—she gestured toward the yellowheads—"how do creatures like that get there?"

They walked off toward the other side of the raft, arguing about ocean currents. Cord might have followed. But something splashed back of them, off to the left and not too far back. He stayed, watching.

After a moment, he saw the big yellowhead. It had slipped down from its reedy perch, which was what had caused the splash. Almost submerged at the water line, it stared after the raft with huge pale green eyes. To Cord, it seemed to look directly at him. In that moment, he knew for the first time why he didn't like yellowheads. There was something very like intelligence in that look, an alien calculation. In creatures like that, intelligence seemed out of place. What use could they have for it?

A little shiver went over him when it sank completely under the water and he realized it intended to swim after the raft. But it was mostly excitement. He had never seen a yellowhead come down out of the reeds before. The obliging monster he'd been looking for might be presenting itself in an unexpected way.

Half a minute later, he watched it again, swimming awkwardly far down. It had no immediate intention of boarding at any rate. Cord saw it come into the area of the raft's trailing stingers. It maneuvered its way between them with curiously human swimming motions and went out of sight under the platform.

He stood up, wondering what it meant. The yellowhead had appeared to know about the stingers; there had been an air of purpose in every move of its approach. He was tempted to tell the others about it, but there was the moment of triumph he could have if it suddenly came slobbering up over the edge of the platform and he nailed it before their eyes.

It was almost time anyway to turn the raft in toward the farms. If nothing happened before then. . . .

He watched. Almost five minutes, but no sign of the yellowhead. Still wondering, a little uneasy, he gave Grandpa a calculated needling of heat.

After a moment, he repeated it. Then he drew a deep breath and forgot all about the yellowhead.

"Nirmond!" he called sharply.

The three of them were standing near the center of the platform, next to the big armored cone, looking ahead at the farms. They glanced around.

"What's the matter now, Cord?"

Cord couldn't say it for a moment. He was suddenly, terribly scared again. Something had gone wrong!

"The raft won't turn!" he told them.

"Give it a real burn this time!" Nirmond said.

Cord glanced up at him. Nirmond, standing a few steps in front of Dane and Grayan as if he wanted to protect them, had begun to look a little strained, and no wonder. Cord already had pressed the gun to three different points on the platform; but Grandpa appeared to have developed a sudden anesthesia for heat. They kept moving out steadily toward the center of the bay.

Now Cord held his breath, switched the heat on full and let Grandpa have it. A six-inch patch on the platform blistered up instantly, turned brown, then black . . .

Grandpa stopped dead. Just like that.

"That's right! Keep burn . . ." Nirmond didn't finish his order.

A giant shudder. Cord staggered back toward the water. Then the whole edge of the raft came curling up behind him and went down again, smacking the bay with a sound like a cannon shot. He flew forward off his feet, hit the platform face down and flattened himself against it. It swelled up beneath him. Two more enormous slaps and joltings. Then quiet. He looked round for the others.

He lay within twelve feet of the central cone. Some twenty or thirty of the mysterious new vines the cone had spouted were stretched out stiffly toward him now, like so many thin green fingers. They couldn't quite reach him. The nearest tip was still ten inches from his shoes.

But Grandpa had caught the others, all three of them. They were tumbled together at the foot of the cone, wrapped in a stiff network of green vegetable ropes, and they didn't move.

Cord drew his feet up cautiously, prepared for another earthquake reaction. But nothing happened. Then he discovered that Grandpa was back in motion on his previous course. The heat-gun had vanished. Gently, he took out the Vanadian gun.

"Cord? It didn't get you?" It was the regent.

"No," he said, keeping his voice low. He realized suddenly he'd simply assumed they were all dead. Now he felt sick and shaky.

"What are you doing?"

Cord looked at Grandpa's big armor-plated head with a certain hunger. The cones were hollowed out inside; the station's lab had decided their chief function was to keep enough air trapped under the rafts to float them. But in that central section was also the organ that controlled Grandpa's overall reactions.

He said softly, "I got a gun and twelve heavy-duty explosive bullets. Two of them will blow that cone apart."

"No good, Cord!" the pain-racked voice told him. "If the thing sinks, we'll die anyway. You have anesthetic charges for that gun of yours?"

He stared at her back. "Yes."

"Give Nirmond and the girl a shot each, before you do anything else. Directly into the spine, if you can. But don't come any closer. . . ."

Somehow, Cord couldn't argue with that voice. He stood up carefully. The gun made two soft spitting sounds.

"All right," he said hoarsely. "What do I do now?"

Dane was silent a moment. "I'm sorry, Cord. I can't tell you that. I'll tell you what I can . . ."

She paused for some seconds again. "This thing didn't try to kill us, Cord. It could have easily. It's incredibly strong. I saw it break Nirmond's legs. But as soon as we stopped moving, it just held us. They were both unconscious then.

"You've got that to go on. It was trying to pitch you within reach of its vines or tendrils, or whatever they are, wasn't it?"

"I think so," Cord said shakily. That was what had happened, of course; and at any moment Grandpa might try again.

"Now it's feeding us some sort of anesthetic of its own through those vines. Tiny thorns. A sort of numbness . . ." Dane's voice trailed off a moment. Then she said clearly, "Look, Cord, it seems we're food it's storing up! You get that?"

"Yes," he said.

"Seeding time for the rafts. There are analogues. Live food for its seed probably; not for the raft. One couldn't have counted on that. Cord?"

"Yes. I'm here."

"I want," said Dane, "to stay awake as long as I can. But there's really just one other thing—this raft's going somewhere. To some particularly favorable location. And that might be very near shore. You might make it in then; otherwise it's up to you. But keep your head and wait for a chance. No heroics, understand?"

"Sure, I understand," Cord told her. He realized then that he was talking reassuringly, as if it weren't the planetary regent but someone like Grayan.

"Nirmond's the worst," Dane said. "The girl was knocked unconscious at once. If it weren't for my arm . . . But, if we can get help in five hours or so, everything should be all right. Let me know if anything happens, Cord."

"I will," Cord said gently again. Then he sighted his gun carefully at a point between Dane's shoulder blades, and the anesthetic chamber made its soft, spitting sound once more. Dane's taut body relaxed slowly, and that was all.

There was no point Cord could see in letting her stay awake; because they weren't going anywhere near shore.

The reed beds and the channels were already behind them, and Grandpa hadn't changed direction by the fraction of a degree. He was moving out into the open bay—and he was picking up company!

So far, Cord could count seven big rafts within two miles of them; and on the three that were closest he could make out a sprouting of new green vines. All of them were traveling in a straight direction; and the common point they were all headed for appeared to be the roaring center of the Yoger Straits, now some three miles away!

Behind the straits, the cold Zlanti Deep—the rolling fogs, and the open sea!

It might be seeding time for the rafts, but it looked as if they weren't going to distribute their seeds in the bay. . . .

For a human being, Cord was a fine swimmer. He had a gun and he had a knife, in spite of what Dane had said; he might have stood a chance among the killers of the bay. But it would be a very small chance, at best. And it wasn't, he thought, as if there weren't still other possibilities. He was going to keep his head.

Except by accident, of course, nobody was going to come looking for them in time to do any good. If anyone did look, it would be around the Bay Farms. There were a number of rafts moored there; and it would be assumed they'd used one of them. Now and then something unexpected happened and some-body simply vanished—by the time it was figured out just what had happened on this occasion, it would be much too late.

Neither was anybody likely to notice within the next few hours that the rafts had started migrating out of the swamps through the Yoger Straits. There was a small weather station a little inland on the north side of the straits, which used a helicopter occasionally. It was about as improbable, Cord decided dismally, that they'd use it in the right spot just now as it would be for a jet transport to happen to come in low enough to spot them.

The fact that it was up to him, as the regent had said, sank in a little more after that! Cord had never felt so lonely.

Simply because he was going to try it sooner or later, he carried out an experiment next that he knew couldn't work. He opened the gun's anesthetic chamber and counted out fifty pellets—rather hurriedly because he didn't particularly want to think of what he might be using them for eventually. There were around three hundred charges left in the chamber then; and in the next few minutes Cord carefully planted a third of them in Grandpa's head.

He stopped after that. A whale might have shown signs of somnolence under a lesser load. Grandpa paddled on undisturbed. Perhaps he had become a little numb in spots, but his cells weren't equipped to distribute the soporific effect of that type of drug.

There wasn't anything else Cord could think of doing before they reached the straits. At the rate they were moving, he calculated that would happen in something less than an hour; and if they did pass through the straits, he was going to risk a swim. He didn't think Dane would have disapproved, under the circumstances. If the raft simply carried them all out into the foggy vastness of the Zlanti Deep, there would be no practical chance of survival left at all.

Meanwhile, Grandpa was definitely picking up speed. And there were other changes going on—minor ones, but still a little awe-inspiring to Cord. The pimply-looking red buds that dotted the upper part of the cone were opening out gradually. From the center of most of them protruded now something like a thin, wet, scarlet worm: a worm that twisted weakly, extended itself by an inch or so, rested and twisted again and stretched up a little farther, groping into the air. The vertical black slits between the armor plates looked somehow deeper and wider than they had been even some minutes ago; a dark, thick liquid dripped slowly from several of them.

Under other circumstances Cord knew he would have been fascinated by these developments in Grandpa. As it was, they drew his suspicious attention only because he didn't know what they meant.

Then something quite horrible happened suddenly. Grayan started moaning loudly and terribly and twisted almost completely around. Afterward, Cord knew it hadn't been a second before he stopped her struggles and the sounds together with another anesthetic pellet; but the vines had tightened their grip on her first, not flexibly but like the digging, bony green talons of some monstrous bird of prey. If Dane hadn't warned him. . . .

White and sweating, Cord put his gun down slowly while the vines relaxed again. Grayan didn't seem to have suffered any additional harm; and she would certainly have been the first to point out that his murderous rage might have been as intelligently directed against a machine. But for some moments Cord continued to luxuriate furiously in the thought that, at any instant he chose, he could still turn the raft very quickly into a ripped and exploded mess of sinking vegetation.

Instead, and more sensibly, he gave both Dane and Nirmond another shot, to prevent a similar occurrence with them. The contents of two such pellets, he knew, would keep any human being torpid for at least four hours. Five shots . . .

Cord withdrew his mind hastily from the direction it was turning into; but it wouldn't stay withdrawn. The thought kept coming up again; until at last he had to recognize it:

Five shots would leave the three of them completely unconscious, whatever else might happen to them, until they either died from other causes or were given a counteracting agent.

Shocked, he told himself he couldn't do it. It was exactly like killing them.

But then, quite steadily, he found himself raising the gun once more, to bring the total charge for each of the three team people up to five. And if it was the first time in the last four years Cord had felt like crying, it also seemed to him that he had begun to understand what was meant by using your head —along with other things.

Barely thirty minutes later, he watched a raft as big as the one he rode go sliding into the foaming white waters of the straits a few hundred yards ahead, and dart off abruptly at an angle, caught by one of the swirling currents. It pitched and spun, made some headway and was swept aside again. And then it righted itself once more. Not like some blindly animated vegetable, Cord thought, but like a creature that struggled with intelligent purpose to maintain its chosen direction.

At least, they seemed practically unsinkable. . . .

Knife in hand, he flattened himself against the platform as the straits roared just ahead. When the platform jolted and tilted up beneath him, he rammed the knife all the way into it and hung on. Cold water rushed suddenly over him, and Grandpa shuddered like a laboring engine. In the middle of it all, Cord had the horrified notion that the raft might release its unconscious human prisoners in its struggle with the straits. But he underestimated Grandpa in that. Grandpa also hung on.

Abruptly, it was over. They were riding a long swell, and there were three other rafts not far away. The straits had swept them together, but they seemed to have no interest in one another's company. As Cord stood up shakily and began to strip off his clothes, they were visibly drawing apart again. The platform of one of them was half-submerged; it must have lost too much of the air that held it afloat and, like a small ship, it was foundering.

From this point, it was only a two-mile swim to the shore north of the straits and another mile inland from there to the Straits Head Station. He didn't know about the current but the distance didn't seem too much, and he couldn't bring himself to leave knife and gun behind. The bay creatures loved warmth and mud; they didn't venture beyond the straits. But Zlanti Deep bred its own killers, though they weren't often observed so close to shore.

Things were beginning to look rather hopeful.

Thin, crying voices drifted overhead, like the voices of curious cats as Cord knotted his clothes into a tight bundle, shoes inside. He looked up. There were four of them circling there; magnified seagoing swamp bugs, each carrying an unseen rider. Probably harmless scavengers—but the ten-foot wingspread was impressive. Uneasily, Cord remembered the venomously carnivorous rider he'd left lying beside the station.

One of them dipped lazily and came sliding down toward him. It soared overhead and came back, to hover about the raft's cone.

The bug rider that directed the mindless flier hadn't been interested in him at all! Grandpa was baiting it!

Cord stared in fascination. The top of the cone was alive now with a softly wriggling mass of the scarlet, wormlike extrusions that had started sprouting before the raft left the bay. Presumably, they looked enticingly edible to the bug rider.

The flier settled with an airy fluttering and touched the cone. Like a trap springing shut, the green vines flashed up and around it, crumpling the brittle wings, almost vanishing into the long soft body. . . .

Barely a second later, Grandpa made another catch, this one from the sea itself. Cord had a fleeting glimpse of something like a small, rubbery seal that flung itself out of the water upon the edge of the raft, with a suggestion of desperate haste—and was flipped on instantly against the cone where the vines clamped it down beside the flier's body.

It wasn't the enormous ease with which the unexpected kill was accomplished that left Cord standing there, completely shocked. It was the shattering of his hopes to swim to shore from here. Fifty yards away, the creature from which the rubbery thing had been fleeing showed briefly on the surface, as it turned away from the raft; and the glance was all he needed. The ivory white body and gaping jaws were similar enough to those of the sharks of Earth to indicate the pursuer's nature. The important difference was that, wherever the white hunters of the Zlanti Deep went, they went by the thousands.

Stunned by that incredible piece of bad luck, still clutching his bundled clothes, Cord stared toward shore. Knowing what to look for, he could spot the telltale roilings of the surface now—the long, ivory gleams that flashed through the swells and vanished again. Shoals of smaller things burst into the air in sprays of glittering desperation and fell back.

He would have been snapped up like a drowning fly before he'd covered a twentieth of that distance!

But almost another full minute passed before the realization of the finality of his defeat really sank in.

Grandpa was beginning to eat!

Each of the dark slits down the sides of the cone was a mouth. So far only one of them was in operating condition, and the raft wasn't able to open that one very wide as yet. The first morsel had been fed in, however: the bug rider the vines had plucked out of the flier's downy neck fur. It took Grandpa several minutes to work it out of sight, small as it was. But it was a start.

Cord didn't feel quite sane any more. He sat there, clutching his bundle of clothes and only vaguely aware of the fact that he was shivering steadily under the cold spray that touched him now and then, while he followed Grandpa's activities attentively. He decided it would be at least some hours before one of that black set of mouths grew flexible and vigorous enough to dispose of a human being. Under the circumstances, it couldn't make much difference to the other human beings here; but the moment Grandpa reached for the first of them would also be the moment he finally blew the raft to pieces. The white hunters were cleaner eaters, at any rate; and that was about the extent to which he could still control what was going to happen.

Meanwhile, there was the very faint chance that the weather station's helicopter might spot them. . . .

Meanwhile also, in a weary and horrified fascination, he kept debating the mystery of what could have produced such a nightmarish change in the rafts. He could guess where they were going by now; there were scattered strings of them stretching back to the straits or roughly parallel to their own course, and the direction was that of the plankton-swarming pool of the Zlanti Basin, a thousand miles to the north. Given time, even mobile lily pads like the rafts had been could make that trip for the benefit of their seedlings. But nothing in their structure explained the sudden change into alert and capable carnivores.

He watched the rubbery little seal-thing being hauled up to a mouth next. The vines broke its neck; and the mouth took it in up to the shoulders and then went on working patiently at what was still a trifle too large a bite. Meanwhile, there were more thin cat cries overhead; and a few minutes later, two more sea bugs were trapped almost simultaneously and added to the larder. Grandpa dropped the dead seal-thing and fed himself another bug rider. The second rider left its mount with a sudden hop, sank its teeth viciously into one of the vines that caught it again and was promptly battered to death against the platform.

Cord felt a resurge of unreasoning hatred against Grandpa. Killing a bug was about equal to cutting a branch from a tree; they had almost no life-awareness. But the rider had aroused his partisanship because of its appearance of intelligent action—and it was in fact closer to the human scale in that feature than to the monstrous life form that had, mechanically, but quite successfully, trapped both it and the human beings. Then his thoughts had drifted again; and he found himself speculating vaguely on the curious symbiosis in which the nerve systems of two creatures as dissimilar as the bugs and their riders could be linked so closely that they functioned as one organism.

Suddenly an expression of vast and stunned surprise appeared on his face. Why—now he knew!

Cord stood up hurriedly, shaking with excitement, the whole plan complete in his mind. And a dozen long vines snaked instantly in the direction of his sudden motion, and groped for him, taut and stretching. They couldn't reach him, but their savagely alert reaction froze Cord briefly where he was. The platform was shuddering under his feet, as if in irritation at his inaccessibility; but it couldn't be tilted up suddenly here to throw him within the grasp of the vines, as it could around the edges.

Still, it was a warning! Cord sidled gingerly around the cone till he had gained the position he wanted, which was on the forward half of the raft. And then he waited. Waited long minutes, quite motionless, until his heart stopped pounding and the irregular angry shivering of the surface of the raft-thing died away and the last vine tendril had stopped its blind groping. It might help a lot if, for a second or two after he next started moving, Grandpa wasn't too aware of his exact whereabouts

He looked back once to check how far they had gone by now beyond the Straits Head Station. It couldn't he decided, be even an hour behind them. Which was close enough, by the most pessimistic count—if everything else worked out all right! He didn't try to think out in detail what that "everything else" could include because there were factors that simply couldn't be calculated in advance. And he had an uneasy feeling that speculating too vividly about them might make him almost incapable of carrying out his plan.

At last, moving carefully, Cord took the knife in his left hand but left the gun holstered. He raised the tightly knotted bundle of clothes slowly over his head, balanced in his right hand. With a long, smooth motion he tossed the bundle back across the cone, almost to the opposite edge of the platform.

It hit with a soggy thump. Almost immediately, the whole far edge of the raft buckled and flapped up to toss the strange object to the reaching vines.

Simultaneously, Cord was racing forward. For a moment, his attempt to divert Grandpa's attention seemed completely successful—then he was pitched to his knees as the platform came up.

He was within eight feet of the edge. As it slapped down again, he threw himself desperately forward.

An instant later, he was knifing down through cold, clear water, just ahead of the raft, then twisting and coming up again.

The raft was passing over him. Clouds of tiny sea creatures scattered through its dark jungle of feeding roots. Cord jerked back from a broad, wavering streak of glassy greenness, which was a stinger, and felt a burning jolt on his side, which meant he'd been touched lightly by another. He bumped on blindly through the slimy black tangles of hair roots that covered the bottom of the raft; then green half-light passed over him, and he burst up into the central bubble under the cone.

Half-light and foul, hot air. Water slapped around him, dragging him away again—nothing to hang onto here! Then above him, to his right, molded against the interior curve of the cone as if it had grown there from the start, the froglike, man-sized shape of the yellowhead.

The raft rider. . . .

Cord reached up and caught Grandpa's symbiotic partner and guide by a flabby hind leg, pulled himself half out of the water and struck twice with the knife, fast while the pale green eyes were still opening.

He'd thought the yellowhead might need a second or so to detach itself from its host, as the bug riders usually did, before it tried to defend itself. This one merely turned its head; the mouth slashed down and clamped on Cord's left arm above the elbow. His right hand sank the knife through one staring eye and the yellowhead jerked away, pulling the knife from his grasp.

Sliding down, he wrapped both hands around the slimy leg and hauled with all his weight. For a moment more, the yellowhead hung on. Then the countless neural extensions that connected it now with the raft came free in a succession of sucking, tearing sounds; and Cord and the yellowhead splashed into the water together.

Black tangle of roots again—and two more electric burns suddenly across his back and legs! Strangling, Cord let go. Below him, for a moment, a body was turning over and over with oddly human motions; then a solid wall of water thrust him up and aside, as something big and white struck the turning body and went on.

Cord broke the surface twelve feet behind the raft. And that would have been that, if Grandpa hadn't already been slowing down.

After two tries, he floundered back up on the platform and lay there gasping and coughing awhile. There were no indications that his presence was resented now. A few vine tips twitched uneasily, as if trying to remember previous functions, when he came limping up presently to make sure his three companions were still breathing, but Cord never noticed that.

They were still breathing, and he knew better than to waste time trying to help them himself. He took Grayan's heat-gun from its holster. Grandpa had come to a full stop.

Cord hadn't had time to become completely sane again, or he might have worried now whether Grandpa, violently sundered from his controlling partner, was still capable of motion on his own. Instead, he determined the approximate direction of the Straits Head Station, selected a corresponding spot on the platform and gave Grandpa a light tap of heat.

Nothing happened immediately. Cord sighed patiently and stepped up the heat a little.

Grandpa shuddered gently. Cord stood up.

Slowly and hesitatingly at first, then with steadfast—though now again brainless—purpose, Grandpa began paddling back toward the Straits Head Station.

HENRY KUTTNER
Private Eye

*Numerous writers have attempted to combine the mystery story with
science fiction, and although there have been some successes, there
are also problems. The kind of future scientific breakthroughs commonplace in SF should make the apprehension of criminals much
easier than it is today. It is not surprising, then, that some of the
finest fusions of science fiction and the mystery focus not on the
capture of the offender, but rather on the way in which the criminal
committed the crime under conditions in which escape from detec-
tion is almost impossible. "Private Eye" is a superb example.*

The forensic sociologist looked closely at the image on the wall screen. Two
figures were frozen there, one in the act of stabbing the other through the
heart with an antique letter cutter once used at Johns Hopkins for surgery.
That was before the ultramicrotome, of course.

"As tricky a case as I've ever seen," the sociologist remarked. "If we can
make a homicide charge stick on Sam Clay, I'll be a little surprised."

The tracer engineer twirled a dial and watched the figures on the screen
repeat their actions. One—Sam Clay—snatched the letter cutter from a desk
and plunged it into the other man's heart. The victim fell down dead. Clay
started back in apparent horror. Then he dropped to his knees beside the
twitching body and said wildly that he didn't mean it. The body drummed
its heels upon the rug and was still.

"That last touch was nice," the engineer said.

"Well, I've got to make the preliminary survey," the sociologist sighed,
settling in his dictachair and placing his fingers on the keyboard. "I doubt if
I'll find any evidence. However, the analysis can come later. Where's Clay
now?"

"His mouthpiece put in a *habeas mens.*"

"I didn't think we'd be able to hold him. But it was worth trying. Imagine, just one shot of scop and he'd have told the truth. Ah, well. We'll do it the hard way, as usual. Start the tracer, will you? It won't make sense till we run it chronologically, but one must start somewhere. Good old Blackstone," the sociologist said, as on the screen, Clay stood up, watching the corpse revive and arise, and then pulled the miraculously clean paper cutter out of its heart, all in reverse.

"Good old Blackstone," he repeated. "On the other hand, sometimes I wish I'd lived in Jeffreys's time. In those days, homicide was homicide."

Telepathy never came to much. Perhaps the developing faculty went underground in response to a familiar natural law after the new science appeared —omniscience. It wasn't really that, of course. It was a device for looking into the past. And it was limited to a fifty-year span; no chance of seeing the arrows at Agincourt or the homunculi of Bacon. It was sensitive enough to pick up the "fingerprints" of light and sound waves imprinted on matter, descramble and screen them and reproduce the image of what had happened. After all, a man's shadow can be photographed on concrete if he's unlucky enough to be caught in an atomic blast. Which is something. The shadow's about all there is left.

However, opening the past like a book didn't solve all problems. It took generations for the maze of complexities to iron itself out, though finally a tentative check and balance was reached. The right to kill has been sturdily defended by mankind since Cain rose up against Abel. A good many idealists quoted, "The voice of thy brother's blood crieth unto me from the ground." But that didn't stop the lobbyists and the pressure groups. Magna Carta was quoted in reply. The right to privacy was defended desperately.

And the curious upshot of this imbalance came when the act of homicide was declared nonpunishable unless intent and forethought could be proved. Of course, it was considered at least naughty to fly into a rage and murder someone on impulse, and there was a nominal punishment—imprisonment, for example—but in practice this never worked because so many defenses were possible. Temporary insanity. Undue provocation. Self-defense. Manslaughter, second-degree homicide, third degree, fourth degree—it went on like that. It was up to the state to prove that the killer had planned his killing in advance; only then would a jury convict. And the jury, of course, had to waive immunity and take a scop test, to prove the box hadn't been packed. But no defendant ever waived immunity.

A man's home wasn't his castle—not with the Eye able to enter it at will and scan his past. The device couldn't interpret, and it couldn't read his mind;

it could only see and listen. Consequently the sole remaining fortress of privacy was the human mind. And that was defended to the last ditch. No truth serum, no hypnoanalysis, no third degree, no leading questions.

If, by viewing the prisoner's past actions, the prosecution could prove forethought and intent, okay.

Otherwise, Sam Clay would go scot-free. Superficially, it appeared as though Andrew Vanderman had, during a quarrel, struck Clay across the face with a stingaree whip. Anyone who has been stung by a Portuguese man-of-war can understand that, at this point, Clay could plead temporary insanity and self-defense, as well as undue provocation and possible justification. Only the curious cult of the Alaskan Flagellantes, who make the stingaree whips for their ceremonials, know how to endure the pain. The Flagellantes even like it; the pre-ritual drug they swallow transmutes pain into pleasure. Not having swallowed this drug, Sam Clay very naturally took steps to protect himself—irrational steps, perhaps, but quite logical and defensible ones.

Nobody but Clay knew that he had intended to kill Vanderman all along. That was the trouble. Clay couldn't understand why he felt so let down.

The screen flickered. It went dark. The engineer chuckled.

"My, my. Locked up in a dark closet at the age of four. What one of those old-time psychiatrists would have made of that. Or do I mean obimen? Shamans? I forget. They interpreted dreams, anyway."

"You're confused. It . . . "

"Astrologers! No, it wasn't either. The ones I mean went in for symbolism. They used to spin prayer wheels and say 'A rose is a rose is a rose,' didn't they? To free the unconscious mind?"

"You've got the typical layman's attitude toward antique psychiatric treatments."

"Well, maybe they had something, at that. Look at quinine and digitalis. The United Amazon natives used those long before science discovered them. But why use eye of newt and toe of frog? To impress the patient?"

"No, to convince themselves," the sociologist said. "In those days the study of mental aberrations drew potential psychotics, so naturally there was unnecessary mumbo jumbo. Those medicos were trying to fix their own mental imbalance while they treated their patients. But it's a science today, not a religion. We've found out how to allow for individual psychotic deviation in the psychiatrist himself, so we've got a better chance of finding true north. However, let's get on with this. Try ultraviolet. Oh, never mind. Somebody's letting him out of that closet. The devil with it. I think we've cut back far enough. Even if he was frightened by a thunderstorm at the age of three months, that can be filed under Gestalt and ignored. Let's run through this chronologically. Give it the screening for . . . let's see. Incidents involving these persons: Vanderman, Mrs. Vanderman, Josephine Wells—and these places: the office, Vanderman's apartment, Clay's place . . ."

"Got it."

"Later we can recheck for complicating factors. Right now we'll run the superficial survey. Verdict first, evidence later," he added, with a grin. "All we need is a motive. . . ."

"What about this?"

A girl was talking to Sam Clay. The background was an apartment, grade B-2.

"I'm sorry, Sam. It's just that . . . well, these things happen."

"Yeah. Vanderman's got something I haven't got, apparently."

"I'm in love with him."

"Funny. I thought all along you were in love with me."

"So did I . . . for a while."

"Well, forget it. No, I'm not angry, Bea. I'll even wish you luck. But you must have been pretty certain how I'd react to this."

"I'm sorry. . . ."

"Come to think of it, I've always let you call the shots. Always."

Secretly—and this the screen could not show—he thought: Let her? I wanted it that way. It was so much easier to leave the decisions up to her. Sure, she's dominant, but I guess I'm just the opposite. And now it's happened again.

It always happens. I was loaded with weight-cloths from the start. And I always felt I had to toe the line, or else. Vanderman—that cocky, arrogant air of his. Reminds me of somebody. I was locked up in a dark place; I couldn't breathe. I forget. What . . . who . . . my father. No, I don't remember. But my life's been like that. He always watched me, and I always thought some day I'd do what *I* wanted—but I never did. Too late now. He's been dead quite a while.

He was always so sure I'd knuckle under. If I'd only defied him once. . . ."

Somebody's always pushing me in and closing the door. So I can't use my abilities. I can't prove I'm competent. Prove it to myself, to my father, to Bea, to the whole world. If only I could—I'd like to push Vanderman into a dark place and lock the door. A dark place, like a coffin. It would be satisfying to surprise him that way. It would be fine if I killed Andrew Vanderman.

"Well, that's the beginning of a motive," the sociologist said. "Still, lots of people get jilted and don't turn homicidal. Carry on."

"In my opinion, Bea attracted him because he wanted to be bossed," the engineer remarked. "He'd given up."

"Protective passivity."

The wire tapes spun through the screening apparatus, A new scene showed on the oblong panel. It was the Paradise Bar.

Anywhere you sat in the Paradise Bar, a competent robot analyzer instantly studied your complexion and facial angles, and switched on lights, in varying tints and intensities that showed you off to best advantage. The joint was popular for business deals. A swindler could look like an honest man there. It was also popular with women and slightly passé teleo talent. Sam Clay looked rather like an ascetic young saint. Andrew Vanderman looked noble, in a grim way, like Richard Coeur-de-Lion offering Saladin his freedom, though he knew it wasn't really a bright thing to do. *Noblesse oblige,* his firm jaw seemed to say, as he picked up the silver decanter and poured. In ordinary light, Vanderman looked slightly more like a handsome bulldog. Also, away from the Paradise Bar, he was redder around the chops, a choleric man.

"As to that deal we were discussing," Clay said, "you can go to . . ."

The censoring juke box blared out a covering bar or two.

Vanderman's reply was unheard as the music got briefly louder, and the lights shifted rapidly to keep pace with his sudden flush.

"It's perfectly easy to outwit these censors," Clay said. "They're keyed to familiar terms of profane abuse, not to circumlocutions. If I said that the arrangement of your chromosomes would have surprised your father . . . you see?" He was right. The music stayed soft.

Vanderman swallowed nothing. "Take it easy," he said. "I can see why you're upset. Let me say first of all . . ."

"*Hijo* . . ."

But the censor was proficient in Spanish dialects. Vanderman was spared hearing another insult.

". . . that I offered you a job because I think you're a very capable man. You have potentialities. It's not a bribe. Our personal affairs should be kept out of this."

"All the same, Bea was engaged to me."

"Clay, are you drunk?"

"Yes," Clay said, and threw his drink into Vanderman's face. The music began to play Wagner very, very loudly. A few minutes later, when the waiters interfered, Clay was supine and bloody, with a mashed nose and a bruised cheek. Vanderman had skinned his knuckles.

"That's a motive," the engineer said.

"Yes, it is, isn't it? But why did Clay wait a year and a half? And remember what happened later. I wonder if the murder itself was just a symbol? If Vanderman represented, say, what Clay considered the tyrannical and oppressive force of society in general—synthesized in the representative image . . . oh, nonsense. Obviously Clay was trying to prove something to himself, though. Suppose you cut forward now. I want to see this in normal chronology, not backward. What's the next selection?"

"Very suspicious. Clay got his nose fixed up and then went to a murder trial."

He thought: I can't breathe. Too crowded in here. Shut up in a box, a closet, a coffin, ignored by the spectators and the vested authority on the bench. What would I do if I were in the dock, like that chap? Suppose they convicted? That would spoil it all. Another dark place—if I'd inherited the right genes, I'd have been strong enough to beat up Vanderman. But I've been pushed around too long.

I keep remembering that song.

> Stray in the herd and the boss said kill it,
> So I shot him in the rump with the handle of a skillet.

A deadly weapon that's in normal usage wouldn't appear dangerous. But if it could be used homicidally—no, the Eye could check on that. All you can conceal these days is motive. But couldn't the trick be reversed? Suppose I got Vanderman to attack me with what he thought was the handle of a skillet, but which I knew was a deadly weapon. . . ."

The trial Sam Clay was watching was fairly routine. One man had killed another. Counsel for the defense contended that the homicide had been a matter of impulse and that, as a matter of fact, only assault and battery plus culpable negligence, at worst, could be proved, and the latter was canceled by an act of God. The fact that the defendant inherited the decedent's fortune, in Martial oil, made no difference. Temporary insanity was the plea.

The prosecuting attorney showed films of what had happened before the fact. True, the victim hadn't been killed by the blow, merely stunned. But the affair had occurred on an isolated beach, and when the tide came in . . .

Act of God, the defense repeated hastily.

The screen showed the defendant some days before his crime, looking up the tide table in a news tape. He also, it appeared, visited the site and asked a passing stranger if the beach was often crowded. "Nope," the stranger said, "it ain't crowded after sundown. Gits too cold. Won't do you no good, though. Too cold to swim then."

One side matched *Actus non facit reum, nisi mens sit rea*—"The act does not make a man guilty, unless the mind be also guilty"—against *Acta exteriora indicant interiora secreta*—"By the outward acts we are to judge of the inward thoughts." Latin legal basics were still valid, up to a point. A man's past remained sacrosanct, provided—and here was the joker—that he possessed the right of citizenship. And anyone accused of a capital crime was automatically suspended from citizenship until his innocence had been established.

Also, no past-tracing evidence could be introduced into a trial unless it could be proved that it had direct connection with the crime. The average citizen did have a right of privacy against tracing. Only if accused of a serious crime was that forfeit, and even then evidence uncovered could be used only in correlation with the immediate charge. There were various loopholes, of course, but theoretically a man was safe from espionage as long as he stayed within the law.

Now a defendant stood in the dock, his past opened. The prosecution showed recordings of a ginger blonde blackmailing him, and that clinched the motive and the verdict—guilty. The condemned man was led off in tears. Clay got up and walked out of the court. From his appearance, he seemed to be thinking.

He was. He had decided that there was only one possible way in which he could kill Vanderman and get away with it. He couldn't conceal the deed itself or the actions leading up to it, or any written or spoken word. All he could hide were his own thoughts. And, without otherwise betraying himself, he'd have to kill Vanderman so that his act would appear justified, which meant covering his tracks for yesterday as well as for tomorrow and tomorrow.

Now, thought Clay, this much can be assumed: if I stand to lose by Vanderman's death instead of gaining, that will help considerably. I must juggle that somehow. But I mustn't forget that at present I have an obvious motive. First, he stole Bea. Second, he beat me up.

So I must make it seem as though he's done me a favor—somehow.

I must have an opportunity to study Vanderman carefully, and it must be a normal, logical, waterproof opportunity. Private secretary. Something like that. The Eye's in the future now, after the fact, but it's watching me . . .

I must remember that. *It's watching me now!*

All right. Normally, I'd have thought of murder at this point. That can't and shouldn't be disguised. I must work out of the mood gradually, but meanwhile . . .

He smiled.

Going off to buy a gun, he felt uncomfortable, as though that prescient Eye, years in the future, could with a wink summon the police. But it was separated from him by a barrier of time that only the natural processes could shorten. And, in fact, it had been watching him since his birth. You could look at it that way. . . .

He could defy it. The Eye couldn't read thoughts.

He bought the gun and lay in wait for Vanderman in a dark alley. But first he got thoroughly drunk. Drunk enough to satisfy the Eye.

After that . . .

"Feel better now?" Vanderman asked, pouring another coffee.

Clay buried his face in his hands.

"I was crazy," he said, his voice muffled. "I must have been. You'd better t-turn me over to the police."

"We can forget about that end of it, Clay. You were drunk, that's all. And I . . . well, I . . ."

"I pull a gun on you . . . try to kill you . . . and you bring me up to your place and . . ."

"You didn't use that gun, Clay. Remember that. You're no killer. All this has been my fault. I needn't have been so blasted tough with you," Vanderman said, looking like Coeur-de-Lion in spite of uncalculated amber fluorescence.

"I'm no good. I'm a failure. Every time I try to do something, a man like you comes along and does it better. I'm a second-rater."

"Clay, stop talking like that. You're just upset, that's all. Listen to me. You're going to straighten up. I'm going to see that you do. Starting tomorrow, we'll work something out. Now drink your coffee."

"You know," Clay said, "you're quite a guy."

So the magnanimous idiot's fallen for it, Clay thought, as he was drifting happily off to sleep. Fine. That begins to take care of the Eye. Moreover, it starts the ball rolling with Vanderman. Let a man do you a favor and he's your pal. Well, Vanderman's going to do me a lot more favors. In fact, before I'm through, I'll have every motive for wanting to keep him alive.

Every motive visible to the naked Eye.

Probably Clay had not heretofore applied his talents in the right direction, for there was nothing second-rate about the way he executed his homicide plan. In that, he proved very capable. He needed a suitable channel for his ability, and perhaps he needed a patron. Vanderman fulfilled that function; probably it salved his conscience for stealing Bea. Being the man he was, Vanderman needed to avoid even the appearance of ignobility. Naturally strong and ruthless, he told himself he was sentimental. His sentimentality never reached the point of actually inconveniencing him, and Clay knew enough to stay within the limits.

Nevertheless it is nerve-racking to know you're living under the scrutiny of an extratemporal Eye. As he walked into the lobby of the V Building a month later, Clay realized that light vibrations reflected from his own body were driving irretrievably into the polished onyx walls and floor, photographing themselves there, waiting for a machine to unlock them, someday, sometime, for some man perhaps in this very city, who as yet didn't know even the name of Sam Clay. Then, sitting in his relaxer in the spiral lift moving swiftly up inside the walls, he knew that those walls were capturing his image, stealing it, like some superstition he remembered . . . ah?

Vanderman's private secretary greeted him. Clay let his gaze wander freely across that young person's neatly dressed figure and mildly attractive face. She said that Mr. Vanderman was out, and the appointment was for three, not two, wasn't it? Clay referred to a notebook. He snapped his fingers.

"Three—you're right, Miss Wells. I was so sure it was two I didn't even bother to check up. Do you think he might be back sooner? I mean, is he out or in conference?"

"He's out, all right, Mr. Clay," Miss Wells said. "I don't think he'll be back much sooner than three. I'm sorry."

"Well, may I wait in here?"

She smiled at him efficiently. "Of course. There's stereo and the magazine spools are in that case."

She went back to her work, and Clay skimmed through an article about the care and handling of lunar filchards. It gave him an opportunity to start a conversation by asking Miss Wells if she liked filchards. It turned out that she had no opinion whatsoever of filchards, but the ice had been broken.

This is the cocktail acquaintance, Clay thought. I may have a broken heart, but, naturally, I'm lonesome.

The trick wasn't to get engaged to Miss Wells so much as to fall in love with her convincingly. The Eye never slept. Clay was beginning to wake at night with a nervous start and lie there looking up at the ceiling. But darkness was no shield.

"The question is," said the sociologist at this point, "whether or not Clay was acting for an audience."

"You mean us?"

"Exactly. It just occurred to me. Do you think he's been behaving perfectly naturally?"

The engineer pondered.

"I'd say yes. A man doesn't marry a girl only to carry out some other plan, does he? After all, he'd get himself involved in a whole new batch of responsibilities."

"Clay hasn't married Josephine Wells yet, however," the sociologist countered. "Besides, that responsibility angle might have applied a few hundred years ago, but not now." He went off at random. "Imagine a society where, after divorce, a man was forced to support a perfectly healthy, competent woman! It was vestigial, I know—a throwback to the days when only males could earn a living—but imagine the sort of women who were willing to accept such support. That was reversion to infancy if I ever . . ."

The engineer coughed.

"Oh," the sociologist said. "Oh, . . . yes. The question is, would Clay have got himself engaged to a woman unless he really . . ."

"Engagements can be broken."

"This one hasn't been broken yet, as far as we know. And *we know.*"

"A normal man wouldn't plan on marrying a girl he didn't care anything about, unless he had some stronger motive—I'll go along that far."

"But how normal is Clay?" the sociologist wondered. "Did he know in advance we'd check back on his past? Did you notice that he cheated at solitaire?"

"Proving?"

"There are all kinds of trivial things you don't do if you think people are looking. Picking up a penny in the street, drinking soup out of the bowl, posing before a mirror—the sort of foolish or petty things everyone does when alone. Either Clay's innocent, or he's a very clever man. . . ."

He was a very clever man. He never intended the engagement to get as far as marriage, though he knew that in one respect marriage would be a precaution. If a man talks in his sleep, his wife will certainly mention the fact. Clay considered gagging himself at night if the necessity should arise. Then he realized that if he talked in his sleep at all, there was no insurance against talking too much the very first time he had an auditor. He couldn't risk such a break. But there was no necessity, after all. Clay's problem, when he thought it over, was simply: how can I be sure I don't talk in my sleep?

He solved that easily enough by renting a narcohypnotic supplementary course in common trade dialects. This involved studying while awake and getting the information repeated in his ear during slumber. As a necessary preparation for the course, he was instructed to set up a recorder and chart the depth of his sleep, so the narcohypnosis could be keyed to his individual rhythms. He did this several times, rechecked once a month thereafter and was satisfied. There was no need to gag himself at night.

He was glad to sleep provided he didn't dream. He had to take sedatives after a while. At night, there was relief from the knowledge that an Eye watched him always, an Eye that could bring him to justice, an Eye whose omnipotence he could not challenge in the open. But he dreamed about the Eye.

Vanderman had given him a job in the organization, which was enormous. Clay was merely a cog, which suited him well enough, for the moment. He didn't want any more favors yet. Not till he had found out the extent of Miss Wells's duties—Josephine, her Christian name was. That took several months, but by that time friendship was ripening into affection. So Clay asked Vanderman for another job. He specified. It wasn't obvious, but he was asking for work that would, presently, fit him for Miss Wells's duties.

Vanderman probably still felt guilty about Bea; he'd married her and she was in Antarctica now, at the casino. Vanderman was due to join her, so he scribbled a memorandum, wished Clay good luck and went to Antarctica, bothered by no stray pangs of conscience. Clay improved the hour by courting Josephine ardently.

From what he had heard about the new Mrs. Vanderman, he felt secretly relieved. Not long ago, when he had been content to remain passive, the increasing dominance of Bea would have satisfied him, but no more. He was learning self-reliance and liked it. These days, Bea was behaving rather badly. Given all the money and freedom she could use, she had too much time on her hands. Once in a while Clay heard rumors that made him smile secretly. Vanderman wasn't having an easy time of it. A dominant character, Bea— but Vanderman was no weakling himself.

After a while Clay told his employer he wanted to marry Josephine Wells. "I guess that makes us square," he said. "You took Bea away from me and I'm taking Josie away from you."

"Now wait a minute," Vanderman said. "I hope you don't . . ."

"My fiancée, your secretary. That's all. The thing is, Josie and I are in love." He poured it on, but carefully. It was easier to deceive Vanderman than the Eye, with its trained technicians and forensic sociologists looking through it. He thought, sometimes, of those medieval pictures of an immense eye, and that reminded him of something vague and distressing, though he couldn't isolate the memory.

After all, what could Vanderman do? He arranged to have Clay given a raise. Josephine, always conscientious, offered to keep on working for a while, till office routine was straightened out, but it never did get straightened out, somehow. Clay deftly saw to that by keeping Josephine busy. She didn't have to bring work home to her apartment, but she brought it, and Clay gradually began to help her when he dropped by. His job, plus the narcohypnotic courses, had already trained him for this sort of tricky organizational work. Vanderman's business was highly specialized—planetwide exports and imports, and what with keeping track of specific groups, seasonal trends, sectarian holidays and so forth, Josephine, as a sort of animated memorandum book for Vanderman, had a more than full-time job.

She and Clay postponed marriage for a time. Clay—naturally enough—began to appear mildly jealous of Josephine's work, and she said she'd quit soon. But one night she stayed on at the office, and he went out in a pet and got drunk. It just happened to be raining that night. Clay got tight enough to walk unprotected through the drizzle and to fall asleep at home in his wet clothes. He came down with influenza. As he was recovering, Josephine got it.

Under the circumstances, Clay stepped in—purely a temporary job—and took over his fiancée's duties. Office routine was extremely complicated that week, and only Clay knew the ins and outs of it. The arrangement saved Vanderman a certain amount of inconvenience, and, when the situation resolved itself, Josephine had a subsidiary job and Clay was Vanderman's private secretary.

"I'd better know more about him," Clay said to Josephine. "After all, there must be a lot of habits and foibles he's got that need to be catered to. If he wants lunch ordered up, I don't want to get smoked tongue and find out he's allergic to it. What about his hobbies?"

But he was careful not to pump Josephine too hard, because of the Eye. He still needed sedatives to sleep.

The sociologist rubbed his forehead.

"Let's take a break," he suggested. "Why does a guy want to commit murder anyway?"

"For profit, one sort or another."

"Only partly, I'd say. The other part is an unconscious desire to be punished —usually for something else. That's why you get accident prones. Ever think about what happens to murderers who feel guilty and yet who aren't punished by the law? They must live a rotten sort of life—always accidentally stepping in front of speedsters; cutting themselves with an ax—accidentally; accidentally touching wires full of juice. . . ."

"Conscience, eh?"

"A long time ago, people thought God sat in the sky with a telescope and watched everything they did. They really lived pretty carefully in the Middle Ages—the first Middle Ages, I mean. Then there was the era of disbelief, where people had nothing to believe in very strongly—and finally we get this." He nodded toward the screen. "A universal memory. By extension, it's a universal social conscience, an externalized one. It's exactly the same as the medieval concept of God—omniscience."

"But not omnipotence."

"Mm."

All in all, Clay kept the Eye in mind for a year and a half. Before he said or did anything whatsoever, he reminded himself of the Eye and made certain that he wasn't revealing his motive to the judging future. Of course, there was —would be—an Ear, too, but that was a little too absurd. One couldn't visualize a large, disembodied Ear decorating the wall like a plate in a plate holder. All the same, whatever he said would be as important evidence— sometime—as what he did. So Sam Clay was very careful indeed and behaved like Caesar's wife. He wasn't exactly defying authority, but he was certainly circumventing it.

Superficially Vanderman was more like Caesar, and his wife was not above reproach, these days. She had too much money to play with. And she was finding her husband too strong-willed a person to be completely satisfactory. There was enough of the matriarch in Bea to make her feel rebellion against Andrew Vanderman, and there was a certain lack of romance. Vanderman had little time for her. He was busy these days, involved with a whole string of deals which demanded much of his time. Clay, of course, had something to do with that. His interest in his new work was most laudable. He stayed up nights plotting and planning as though expecting Vanderman to make him a full partner. In fact, he even suggested this possibility to Josephine. He wanted it on the record. The marriage date had been set, and Clay wanted to move before then; he had no intention of being drawn into a marriage of convenience after the necessity had been removed.

One thing he did, which had to be handled carefully, was to get the whip. Now, Vanderman was a fingerer. He liked to have something in his hands while he talked. Usually it was a crystalline paperweight with a miniature thunderstorm in it, complete with lightning, when it was shaken. Clay put this where Vanderman would be sure to knock it off and break it. Meanwhile, he had plugged one deal with Callisto Ranches for the sole purpose of getting a whip for Vanderman's desk. The natives were proud of their leatherwork and their silversmithing, and a nominal make-weight always went with every deal they closed. Thus, presently, a handsome miniature whip, with Vanderman's initials on it, lay on the desk, coiled into a loop, acting as a paperweight except when he picked it up and played with it while he talked.

The other weapon Clay wanted was already there—an antique paper knife, once called a surgical scalpel. He never let his gaze rest on it too long, because of the Eye.

The other whip came. He absentmindedly put it in his desk and pretended to forget it. It was a sample of the whips made by the Alaskan Flagellantes for use in their ceremonies and was wanted because of some research being done into the pain-neutralizing drugs the Flagellantes used. Clay, of course, had engineered this deal, too. There was nothing suspicious about that; the firm stood to make a sound profit. In fact, Vanderman had promised him a percentage bonus at the end of the year on every deal he triggered. It would be quite a lot. It was December; a year and a half had passed since Clay first recognized that the Eye would seek him out.

He felt fine. He was careful about the sedatives, and his nerves, though jangled, were nowhere near the snapping point. It had been a strain, but he had trained himself so that he would make no slips. He visualized the Eye in the walls, in the ceiling, in the sky, everywhere he went. It was the only way to play completely safe. And very soon now it would pay off. But he would have to do it soon; such a nervous strain could not be continued indefinitely.

A few details remained. He carefully arranged matters—under the Eye's very nose, so to speak—so that he was offered a well-paying position with another firm. He turned it down.

And, one night, an emergency happened to arise so that Clay, very logically, had to go to Vanderman's apartment.

Vanderman wasn't there. Bea was. She had quarreled violently with her husband. Moreover, she had been drinking. (This, too, he had expected.) If the situation had not worked out exactly as he wanted, he would have tried again—and again—but there was no need.

Clay was a little politer than necessary. Perhaps too polite; certainly Bea, that incipient matriarch, was led down the garden path, a direction she was not unwilling to take. After all, she had married Vanderman for his money, found him as dominant as herself and now saw Clay as an exaggerated symbol of both romance and masculine submissiveness.

The camera eye hidden in the wall in a decorative bas-relief, was grinding away busily, spooling up its wire tape in a way that indicated Vanderman was a suspicious as well as a jealous husband. But Clay knew about this gadget, too. At the suitable moment he stumbled against the wall in such a fashion that the device broke. Then, with only that other Eye spying on him, he suddenly became so virtuous that it was a pity Vanderman couldn't witness his *volte-face*.

"Listen, Bea," he said, "I'm sorry, but I didn't understand. It's no good. I'm not in love with you any more. I was once, sure, but that was quite awhile ago. There's somebody else, and you ought to know it by now."

"You still love me," Bea said with intoxicated firmness. "We belong together."

"Bea. Please. I hate to have to say this, but I'm grateful to Andrew Vanderman for marrying you. I . . . well, you got what you wanted, and I'm getting what I want. Let's leave it at that."

"I'm used to getting what *I* want, Sam. Opposition is something I don't like. Especially when I know you really . . ."

She said a good deal more, and so did Clay—he was perhaps unnecessarily harsh. But he had to make the point, for the Eye, that he was no longer jealous of Vanderman.

He made the point.

The next morning he got to the office before Vanderman, cleaned up his desk and discovered the stingaree whip still in its box. "Oops," he said, snapping his fingers—the Eye watched, and this was the crucial period. Perhaps it would all be over within the hour. Every move from now on would have to be specially calculated in advance, and there could be no slightest deviation. The Eye was everywhere—literally everywhere.

He opened the box, took out the whip and went into the inner sanctum. He tossed the whip on Vanderman's desk, so carelessly that a stylus rack toppled. Clay rearranged everything, leaving the stingaree whip near the edge of the desk and placing the Callistan silver-leather whip at the back, half-concealed behind the inter-office visor-box. He didn't allow himself more than a casual sweeping glance to make sure the paper knife was still there.

Then he went out for coffee.

Half an hour later he got back, picked up a few letters for signature from the rack and walked into Vanderman's office. Vanderman looked up from behind his desk. He had changed a little in a year and a half; he was looking older, less noble, more like an aging bulldog. Once, Clay thought coldly, this man stole my fiancée and beat me up.

Careful. Remember the Eye.

There was no need to do anything but follow the plan and let events take their course. Vanderman had seen the spy films, all right, up to the point where they had gone blank, when Clay fell against the wall. Obviously he hadn't really expected Clay to show up this morning. But to see the louse grinning hello, walking across the room, putting some letters down on his desk . . . !

Clay was counting on Vanderman's short temper, which had not improved over the months. Obviously the man had been simply sitting there, thinking unpleasant thoughts, and just as Clay had known would happen, he picked up the whip and began to finger it. But it was the stingaree whip this time.

"Morning," Clay said cheerfully to his stunned employer. His smile became one-sided. "I've been waiting for you to check this letter to the Kirghiz kovar breeders. Can we find a market for two thousand of those ornamental horns?"

It was at this point that Vanderman, bellowing, jumped to his feet, swung the whip and sloshed Clay across the face. There is probably nothing more painful than the bite of a stingaree whip.

Clay staggered back. He had not known it would hurt so much. For an instant the shock of the blow knocked every other consideration out of his head, and blind anger was all that remained.

Remember the Eye!

He remembered it. There were dozens of trained men watching everything he did just now. Literally he stood on an open stage surrounded by intent observers who made notes on every expression of his face, every muscular flection, every breath he drew.

In a moment Vanderman would be dead—but Sam Clay would not be alone. An invisible audience from the future was fixing him with cold, calculating eyes. He had one more thing to do and the job would be over. Do it— carefully, carefully!—while they watched.

Time stopped for him. *The job would be over.*

It was very curious. He had rehearsed this series of actions so often in the privacy of his mind that his body was going through with it now without further instructions. His body staggered back from the blow, recovered balance, glared at Vanderman in shocked fury, poised for a dive at that paper knife in plain sight on the desk.

That was what the outward and visible Sam Clay was doing. But the inward and spiritual Sam Clay went through quite a different series of actions.

The job would be over.

And what was he going to do after that?

The inward and spiritual murderer stood fixed with dismay and surprise, staring at a perfectly empty future. He had never looked beyond this moment. He had made no plans for his life beyond the death of Vanderman. But now —he had no enemy but Vanderman. When Vanderman was dead, what would he fix upon to orient his life? What would he work at then? His job would be gone, too. And he liked his job.

Suddenly he knew how much he liked it. He was good at it. For the first time in his life, he had found a job he could do really well.

You can't live a year and a half in a new environment without acquiring new goals. The change had come imperceptibly. He was a good operator; he'd discovered that he could be successful. He didn't have to kill Vanderman to prove that to himself. He'd proved it already without committing murder.

In that time stasis which had brought everything to a full stop he looked at Vanderman's red face and he thought of Bea, and of Vanderman as he had come to know him—and he didn't want to be a murderer.

He didn't want Vanderman dead. He didn't want Bea. The thought of her made him feel a little sick. Perhaps that was because he himself had changed from passive to active. He no longer wanted or needed a dominant woman. He could make his own decisions. If he were choosing now, it would be someone more like Josephine. . . .

Josephine. That image before his mind's stilled eye was suddenly very pleasant. Josephine with her mild, calm prettiness, her admiration for Sam Clay, the successful businessman, the rising young importer in Vanderman, Inc. Josephine whom he was going to marry—of course he was going to marry her. He loved Josephine. He loved his job. All he wanted was the status quo, exactly as he had achieved it. Everything was perfect right now—as of maybe thirty seconds ago.

But that was a long time ago—thirty seconds. A lot can happen in half a minute. A lot had happened. Vanderman was coming at him again, the whip raised. Clay's nerves crawled at the anticipation of its burning impact across his face a second time. If he could get hold of Vanderman's wrist before he struck again—if he could talk fast enough . . .

The crooked smile was still on his face. It was part of the pattern, in some dim way he did not quite understand. He was acting in response to conditioned reflexes set up over a period of many months of rigid self-training. His body was already in action. All that had taken place in his mind had happened so fast there was no physical hiatus at all. His body knew its job and it was doing the job. It was lunging forward toward the desk and the knife, and he could not stop it.

All this had happened before. It had happened in his mind, the only place where Sam Clay had known real freedom in the past year and a half. In all that time he had forced himself to realize that the Eye was watching every outward move he made. He had planned each action in advance and schooled himself to carry it through. Scarcely once had he let himself act purely on impulse. Only in following the plan exactly was there safety. He had indoctrinated himself too successfully.

Something was wrong. This wasn't what he'd wanted. He was still afraid, weak, failing. . . .

He lurched against the desk, clawed at the paper knife, and, knowing failure, drove it into Vanderman's heart.

"It's a tricky case," the forensic sociologist said to the engineer. "Very tricky."

"Want me to run it again?"

"No, not right now. I'd like to think it over. Clay . . . that firm that offered him another job. The offer's withdrawn now, isn't it? Yes, I remember—they're fussy about the morals of their employees. It's insurance or something, I don't know. Motive. Motive, now."

The sociologist looked at the engineer.

The engineer said, "A year and a half ago he had a motive. But a week ago he had everything to lose and nothing to gain. He's lost his job and that bonus, he doesn't want Mrs. Vanderman any more, and as for that beating Vanderman once gave him . . . ah?"

"Well, he did try to shoot Vanderman once, and he couldn't, remember? Even though he was full of Dutch courage. But—something's wrong. Clay's been avoiding even the appearance of evil a little too carefully. Only I can't put my finger on anything, blast it."

"What about tracing back his life farther? We only got to his fourth year."

"There couldn't be anything useful that long ago. It's obvious he was afraid of his father and hated him, too. Typical stuff, basic psych. The father symbolizes judgment to him. I'm very much afraid Sam Clay is going to get off scot-free."

"But if you think there's something haywire . . ."

"The burden of proof is up to us," the sociologist said.

The visor sang. A voice spoke softly.

"No, I haven't got the answer yet. Now? All right. I'll drop over."

He stood up.

"The DA wants a consultation. I'm not hopeful, though. I'm afraid the state's going to lose this case. That's the trouble with the externalized conscience. . . ."

He didn't amplify. He went out, shaking his head, leaving the engineer staring speculatively at the screen. But within five minutes he was assigned to another job—the bureau was understaffed—and he didn't have a chance to investigate on his own until a week later. Then it didn't matter any more.

For, a week later, Sam Clay was walking out of the court an acquitted man. Bea Vanderman was waiting for him at the foot of the ramp. She wore black, but obviously her heart wasn't in it.

"Sam," she said.

He looked at her.

He felt a little dazed. It was all over. Everything had worked out exactly according to plan. And nobody was watching him now. The Eye had closed. The invisible audience had put on its hats and coats and left the theater of Sam Clay's private life. From now on he could do and say precisely what he liked with no censoring watcher's omnipresence to check him. He could act on impulse again.

He had outwitted society. He had outwitted the Eye and all its minions in all their technological glory. He, Sam Clay, private citizen. It was a wonderful thing, and he could not understand why it left him feeling so flat.

That had been a nonsensical moment, just before the murder. The moment of relenting. They say you get the same instant's frantic rejection on the verge of a good many important decisions—just before you marry, for instance. Or —what was it? Some other common instance he'd often heard of. For a second it eluded him. Then he had it. The hour before marriage—and the instant after suicide. After you've pulled the trigger or jumped off the bridge. The instant of wild revulsion when you'd give anything to undo the irrevocable. Only, you can't. It's too late. The thing is done.

Well, he'd been a fool. Luckily, it *had* been too late. His body took over and forced him to success he'd trained it for. About the job—it didn't matter. He'd get another. He'd proved himself capable. If he could outwit the Eye itself, what job existed he couldn't lick if he tried? Except—nobody knew exactly how good he was. How could he prove his capabilities? It was infuriating to achieve such phenomenal success after a lifetime of failures and never to get the credit for it. How many men must have tried and failed where he had tried and succeeded? Rich men, successful men, brilliant men who had yet failed in the final test of all—the contest with the Eye, their own lives at stake. Only Sam Clay had passed that most important test in the world—and he could never claim credit for it.

". . . knew they wouldn't convict," Bea's complacent voice was saying.

Clay blinked at her. "What?"

"I said I'm so glad you're free, darling. I knew they wouldn't convict you.

I knew that from the very beginning." She smiled at him, and for the first time it occurred to him that Bea looked a little like a bulldog. It was something about her lower jaw. He thought that when her teeth were closed together the lower set probably rested just outside the upper. He had an instant's impulse to ask her about it. Then he decided he had better not.

"You knew, did you?" he said.

She squeezed his arm. What an ugly lower jaw that was. How odd he'd never noticed it before. And behind the heavy lashes, how small her eyes were. How mean.

"Let's go where we can be alone," Bea said, clinging to him. "There's such a lot to talk about."

"We *are* alone," Clay said, diverted for an instant to his original thoughts. "Nobody's watching." He glanced up at the sky and down at the mosaic pavement. He drew a long breath and let it out slowly. "Nobody," he said.

"My speeder's parked right over here. We can . . ."

"Sorry, Bea."

"What do you mean?"

"I've got business to attend to."

"Forget business. Don't you understand that we're free now, both of us?"

He had a horrible feeling he knew what she meant.

"Wait a minute," he said, because this seemed the quickest way to end it. "I killed your husband, Bea. Don't forget that."

"You were acquitted. It was self-defense. The court said so."

"It . . ." He paused, glanced up quickly at the high wall of the Justice Building and began a one-sided, mirthless smile. It was all right; there was no Eye now. There never would be again. He was unwatched.

"You mustn't feel guilty, even within yourself," Bea said firmly. "It wasn't your fault. It simply wasn't. You've got to remember that. You *couldn't* have killed Andrew except by accident, Sam, so . . ."

"What? What do you mean by that?"

"Well, after all. I know the prosecution kept trying to prove you'd planned to kill Andrew all along, but you mustn't let what they said put any ideas in your head. I know you, Sam. I knew Andrew. You couldn't have planned a thing like that, and even if you had, it wouldn't have worked."

The half-smile died.

"It wouldn't?"

She looked at him steadily.

"Why, you couldn't have managed it," she said. "Andrew was the better man, and we both know it. He'd have been too clever to fall for anything . . ."

"Anything a second-rater like me could dream up?" Clay swallowed. His lips tightened. "Even you—what's the idea? What's your angle now—that we second-raters ought to get together?"

"Come on," she said and slipped her arm through his. Clay hung back for a second. Then he scowled, looked back at the Justice Building and followed Bea toward her speeder.

The engineer had a free period. He was finally able to investigate Sam Clay's early childhood. It was purely academic now, but he liked to indulge his curiosity. He traced Clay back to the dark closet when the boy was four, and used ultraviolet. Sam was huddled in a corner, crying silently, staring up with frightened eyes at a top shelf.

What was on that shelf the engineer could not see.

He kept the beam focused on the closet and cast back rapidly through time. The closet often opened and closed, and sometimes Sam Clay was locked in it as punishment, but the upper shelf held its mystery until . . .

It was in reverse. A woman reached to that shelf, took down an object, walked backward out of the closet to Sam Clay's bedroom and went to the wall by the door. This was unusual, for generally it was Sam's father who was warden of the closet.

She hung up a framed picture of a single huge staring eye floating in space. There was a legend under it. The letters spelled out: THOU GOD SEEST ME.

The engineer kept on tracing. After a while it was night. The child was in bed, sitting up wide-eyed, afraid. A man's footsteps sounded on the stair. The scanner told all secrets but those of the inner mind. The man was Sam's father, coming up to punish him for some childish crime committed earlier. Moonlight fell upon the wall beyond which the footsteps approached, showing how the wall quivered a little to the vibrations of the feet, and the Eye in its frame quivered, too. The boy seemed to brace himself. A defiant half-smile showed on his mouth, crooked, unsteady.

This time he'd keep that smile, no matter what happened. When it was over he'd still have it, so his father could see it, and the Eye could see it and they'd know he hadn't given in. He hadn't . . . he . . .

The door opened.

He couldn't help it. The smile faded and was gone.

"Well, what was eating him?" the engineer demanded.

The sociologist shrugged. "You could say he never did really grow up. It's axiomatic that boys go through a phase of rivalry with their fathers. Usually that's sublimated; the child grows up and wins, in one way or another. But

Sam Clay didn't. I suspect he developed an externalized conscience very early. Symbolizing partly his father, partly God, an Eye and society—which fulfills the role of protective, punishing parent, you know."

"It still isn't evidence."

"We aren't going to get any evidence on Sam Clay. But that doesn't mean he's got away with anything, you know. He's always been afraid to assume the responsibilities of maturity. He never took on an optimum challenge. He was afraid to succeed at anything because that symbolic Eye of his might smack him down. When he was a kid, he might have solved his entire problem by kicking his old man in the shins. Sure, he'd have got a harder whaling, but he'd have made some move to assert his individuality. As it is, he waited too long. And then he defied the wrong thing, and it wasn't really defiance, basically. Too late now. His formative years are past. The thing that might really solve Clay's problem would be his conviction for murder—but he's been acquitted. If he'd been convicted, then he could prove to the world that he'd hit back. He'd kicked his father in the shins, kept that defiant smile on his face, killed Andrew Vanderman. I think that's what he actually has wanted all along—recognition. Proof of his own ability to assert himself. He had to work hard to cover his tracks—if he made any—but that was part of the game. By winning it he's lost. The normal ways of escape are closed to him. He always had an Eye looking down at him."

"Then the acquittal stands?"

"There's still no evidence. The state's lost its case. But I . . . I don't think Sam Clay has won his. Something will happen." He sighed. "It's inevitable, I'm afraid. Sentence first, you see. Verdict afterward. The sentence was passed on Clay a long time ago."

Sitting across from him in the Paradise Bar behind a silver decanter of brandy in the center of the table, Bea looked lovely and hateful. It was the lights that made her lovely. They even managed to cast their shadows over that bulldog chin and under her thick lashes the small, mean eyes acquired an illusion of beauty. But she still looked hateful. The lights could do nothing about that. They couldn't cast shadows into Sam Clay's private mind or distort the images there.

He thought of Josephine. He hadn't made up his mind fully yet about that. But if he didn't quite know what he wanted, there was no shadow of doubt about what he *didn't* want—no possible doubt whatever.

"You need me, Sam," Bea told him over her brimming glass.

"I can stand on my own feet. I don't need anybody."

It was the indulgent way she looked at him. It was the smile that showed her teeth. He could see as clearly as if he had X-ray vision how the upper teeth would close down inside the lower when she shut her mouth. There would be a lot of strength in a jaw like that. He looked at her neck and saw the thickness of it and thought how firmly she was getting her grip upon him, how she maneuvered for position and waited to lock her bulldog clamp deep into the fabric of his life again.

"I'm going to marry Josephine, you know," he said.

"No, you're not. You aren't the man for Josephine. I know that girl, Sam. For a while you may have had her convinced you were a go-getter. But she's bound to find out the truth. You'd be miserable together. You need me, Sam darling. You don't know what you want. Look at the mess you got into when you tried to act on your own. Oh, Sam, why don't you stop pretending? You know you never were a planner. You . . . what's the matter, Sam?"

His sudden burst of laughter had startled both of them. He tried to answer her, but the laughter wouldn't let him. He lay back in his chair and shook with it until he almost strangled. He had come so close, so desperately close to bursting out with a boast that would have been confession. Just to convince the woman. Just to shut her up. He must care more about her good opinion than he had realized until now. But that last absurdity was too much. It was only ridiculous now. Sam Clay not a planner!

How good it was to let himself laugh, now. To let himself go without having to think ahead. Acting on impulse again, after those long months of rigid repression. No audience from the future was clustering around this table, analyzing the quality of his laughter, observing that it verged on hysteria, measuring it against all possible occasions in the past that could not explain its exact depth and duration.

All right, so it was hysteria. Who cared? He deserved a little blow-off like this after all he'd been through. He'd risked so much, and achieved so much —and in the end gained nothing, not even glory except in his own mind. He'd gained nothing, really, except the freedom to be hysterical if he felt like it. He laughed and laughed and laughed, hearing the shrill note of lost control in his own voice and not caring.

People were turning to stare. The bartender looked over at him uneasily, getting ready to move if this went on. Bea stood up, leaned across the table, shook him by the shoulder.

"Sam, what's the matter! Sam, do get hold of yourself! You're making a spectacle of me, Sam! What *are* you laughing at?"

With a tremendous effort he forced the laughter back in his throat. His breath still came heavily and little bursts of merriment kept bubbling up so that he could hardly speak, but he got the words out somehow. They were probably the first words he had spoken without rigid censorship since he first put his plan into operation. And the words were these.

"I'm laughing at the way I fooled you. I fooled everybody! You think I didn't know what I was doing every minute of the time? You think I wasn't planning, every step of the way? It took me eighteen months to do it, but I killed Andrew Vanderman with malice aforethought, and nobody can ever prove I did it." He giggled foolishly. "I just wanted you to know," he added in a mild voice.

And it wasn't until he got his breath back and began to experience that feeling of incredible, delightful, incomparable relief that he knew what he had done.

She was looking at him without a flicker of expression on her face. Total blank was all that showed. There was a dead silence for a quarter of a minute. Clay had the feeling that his words must have rung from the roof, that in a moment the police would come in to hale him away. But the words had been quietly spoken. No one had heard but Bea.

And now, at last, Bea moved. She answered him, but not in words. The bulldog face convulsed suddenly and overflowed with laughter.

As he listened, Clay felt all that flood of glorious relief ebbing away. For he saw that she did not believe him. And there was no way he could prove the truth.

"Oh, you silly little man," Bea gasped when words came back to her. "You had me almost convinced for a minute. I almost believed you. I . . ." Laughter silenced her again; consciously silvery laughter made heads turn. That conscious note in it warned him that she was up to something. Bea had had an idea. His own thoughts outran hers and he knew in an instant before she spoke exactly what the idea was and how she would apply it. He said: "I *am* going to marry Josephine," in the very instant that Bea spoke.

"You're going to marry me," she said flatly. "You've got to. You don't know your own mind, Sam. I know what's best for you and I'll see you do it. Do you understand me, Sam?

"The police won't realize that was only a silly boast," she told him. "They'll believe you. You wouldn't want me to tell them what you just said, would you, Sam?"

He looked at her in silence, seeing no way out. This dilemma had sharper horns than anything he could have imagined. For Bea did not and would not believe him, no matter how he yearned to convince her, while the police undoubtedly would believe him, to the undoing of his whole investment in time, effort and murder. He had said it. It was engraved upon the walls and in the echoing air, waiting for that invisible audience in the future to observe.

No one was listening now, but a word from Bea could make them reopen the case.

A word from Bea.

He looked at her, still in silence, but with a certain cool calculation beginning to dawn in the back of his mind.

For a moment Sam Clay felt very tired indeed. In that moment he encompassed a good deal of tentative future time. In his mind he said yes to Bea, married her, lived an indefinite period as her husband. And he saw what that life would be like. He saw the mean small eyes watching him, the relentlessly gripping jaw set, the tyranny that would emerge slowly or not slowly, depending on the degree of his subservience, until he was utterly at the mercy of the woman who had been Andrew Vanderman's widow.

Sooner or later, he thought clearly to himself, *I'd kill her.*

He'd have to kill. That sort of life, with that sort of woman, wasn't a life Sam Clay could live indefinitely. And he'd proved his ability to kill and go free.

But what about Andrew Vanderman's death?

Because they'd have another case against him then. This time it had been qualitative: the next time, the balance would shift toward quantitative. If Sam Clay's wife died, Sam Clay would be investigated no matter how she died. Once a suspect, always a suspect in the eyes of the law. The Eye of the law. They'd check back. They'd return to this moment, while he sat there revolving thoughts of death in his mind. And they'd return to five minutes ago and listen to him boast that he had killed Vanderman.

A good lawyer might get him off. He could claim it wasn't the truth. He could say he had been goaded to an idle boast by the things Bea said. He might get away with that, and he might not. Scop would be the only proof, and he couldn't be compelled to take scop.

But—no. That wasn't the answer. That wasn't the way out. He could tell by the sick, sinking feeling inside him. There had been just one glorious moment of release after he'd made his confession to Bea, and from then on everything seemed to run downhill again.

But that moment had been the goal he'd worked toward all this time. He didn't know what it was or why he wanted it. But he recognized the feeling when it came. He wanted it back.

This helpless feeling, this impotence—was this the total sum of what he had achieved? Then he'd failed, after all. Somehow, in some strange way he could only partly understand, he had failed; killing Vanderman hadn't been the answer at all. He wasn't a success. He was a second-rater, a passive, helpless worm whom Bea would manage and control and drive, eventually, to . . .

"What's the matter, Sam?" Bea asked solicitously.

"You think I'm a second-rater, don't you?" he said. "You'll never believe I'm not. You think I couldn't have killed Vanderman except by accident. You'll never believe I could possibly have defied . . ."

"What?" she asked, when he did not go on.

There was a new note of surprise in his voice.

"But it wasn't defiance," he said slowly. "I just hid and dodged. Circumvented. I hung dark glasses on an Eye because I was afraid of it. But—that wasn't defiance. So—what I really was trying to prove . . ."

She gave him a startled, incredulous stare as he stood up.

"Sam! What are you doing?" Her voice cracked a little.

"Proving something," Clay said, smiling crookedly and glancing up from Bea to the ceiling. "Take a good look," he said to the Eye as he smashed her skull with the decanter.

ROBERT SILVERBERG

Sundance

Rarely has mankind hesitated to wipe out creatures that get in its way on the path of conquest—even when the creatures happen to be fellow human beings. One hopes that the dark past will not be replayed when we move outward to colonize the worlds of other suns; if we find intelligent species out there we will, presumably, respect their rights to their own worlds. But how can we know if a species is truly intelligent? How, in fact, can we be sure of anything in a universe where reality sometimes seems like a matter of opinion?

Today you liquidated about 50,000 Eaters in Sector A, and now you are spending an uneasy night. You and Herndon flew east at dawn with the green-gold sunrise at your backs and sprayed the neural pellets over a thousand hectares along the Forked River. You flew on into the prairie beyond the river, where the Eaters have already been wiped out, and had lunch sprawled on that thick, soft carpet of grass where the first settlement is expected to rise. Herndon picked some juiceflowers, and you enjoyed half an hour of mild hallucinations. Then, as you headed toward the copter to begin an afternoon of further pellet spraying, he said suddenly, "Tom, how would you feel about this if it turned out that the Eaters weren't just animal pests? That they were *people*, say, with a language and rites and a history and all?"

You thought of how it had been for your own people.

"They aren't," you said.

"Suppose they were. Suppose the Eaters . . ."

"They aren't. Drop it."

Herndon has this streak of cruelty in him that leads him to ask such questions. He goes for the vulnerabilities; it amuses him. All night now his casual remark has echoed in your mind. Suppose the Eaters . . . Suppose the Eaters . . . Suppose . . . Suppose . . .

You sleep for a while and dream, and in your dreams you swim through rivers of blood.

Foolishness. A feverish fantasy. You know how important it is to exterminate the Eaters fast before the settlers get here. They're just animals and not even harmless animals at that; ecology-wreckers is what they are, devourers of oxygen-liberating plants, and they have to go. A few have been saved for zoological study. The rest must be destroyed. Ritual extirpation of undesirable beings, the old, old story. But let's not complicate our job with moral qualms, you tell yourself. Let's not dream of rivers of blood.

The Eaters don't even *have* blood, none that could flow in rivers, anyway. What they have is, well, a kind of lymph that permeates every tissue and transmits nourishment along the interfaces. Waste products go out the same way, osmotically. In terms of process, it's structurally analogous to your own kind of circulatory system, except there's no network of blood vessels hooked to a master pump. The life-stuff just oozes through their bodies as though they were amoebas or sponges or some other low-phylum form. Yet they're definitely high-phylum in nervous system, digestive setup, limb-and-organ template, and so forth. Odd, you think. The thing about aliens is that they're alien, you tell yourself, not for the first time.

The beauty of their biology for you and your companions is that it lets you exterminate them so neatly.

You fly over the grazing grounds and drop the neural pellets. The Eaters find and ingest them. Within an hour the poison has reached all sectors of the body. Life ceases; a rapid breakdown of cellular matter follows, the Eater literally falling apart molecule by molecule the instant that nutrition is cut off; the lymphlike stuff works like acid; a universal lysis occurs; flesh and even the bones, which are cartilaginous, dissolve. In two hours, a puddle on the ground. In four, nothing at all left. Considering how many millions of Eaters you've scheduled for extermination here, it's sweet of the bodies to be self-disposing. Otherwise what a charnel house this world would become!

Suppose the Eaters . . .

Damn Herndon. You almost feel like getting a memory-editing in the morning. Scrape his stupid speculations out of your head. If you dared. If you dared.

In the morning he does not dare. Memory-editing frightens him; he will try to shake free of his newfound guilt without it. The Eaters, he explains to himself, are mindless herbivores, the unfortunate victims of human expansionism, but not really deserving of passionate defense. Their extermination is not tragic; it's just too bad. If Earthmen are to have this world, the Eaters must relinquish it. There's a difference, he tells himself, between the elimination of the Plains Indians from the American prairie in the nineteenth century and the destruction of the bison on that same prairie. One feels a little wistful about the slaughter of the thundering herds; one regrets the butchering of millions of the noble brown woolly beasts, yes. But one feels outrage, not mere wistful regret, at what was done to the Sioux. There's a difference. Reserve your passions for the proper cause.

He walks from his bubble at the edge of the camp toward the center of things. The flagstone path is moist and glistening. The morning fog has not yet lifted, and every tree is bowed, the long, notched leaves heavy with droplets of water. He pauses, crouching, to observe a spider-analog spinning its asymmetrical web. As he watches, a small amphibian, delicately shaded turquoise, glides as inconspicuously as possible over the mossy ground. Not inconspicuously enough; he gently lifts the little creature and puts it on the back of his hand. The gills flutter in anguish, and the amphibian's sides quiver. Slowly, cunningly, its color changes until it matches the coppery tone of the hand. The camouflage is excellent. He lowers his hand and the amphibian scurries into a puddle. He walks on.

He is forty years old, shorter than most of the other members of the expedition, with wide shoulders, a heavy chest, dark glossy hair, a blunt, spreading nose. He is a biologist. This is his third career, for he has failed as an anthropologist and as a developer of real estate. His name is Tom Two Ribbons. He has been married twice but has had no children. His great-grandfather died of alcoholism; his grandfather was addicted to hallucinogens; his father had compulsively visited cheap memory-editing parlors. Tom Two Ribbons is conscious that he is failing a family tradition, but he has not yet found his own mode of self-destruction.

In the main building he discovers Herndon, Julia, Ellen, Schwartz, Chang, Michaelson and Nichols. They are eating breakfast; the others are already at work. Ellen rises and comes to him and kisses him. Her short soft yellow hair tickles his cheeks. "I love you," she whispers. She has spent the night in Michaelson's bubble. "I love you," he tells her and draws a quick vertical line of affection between her small pale breasts. He winks at Michaelson, who nods, touches the tops of two fingers to his lips and blows them a kiss. We are all good friends here, Tom Two Ribbons thinks.

"Who drops pellets today?" he asks.

"Mike and Chang," says Julia. "Sector C."

Schwartz says, "Eleven more days and we ought to have the whole peninsula clear. Then we can move inland."

"If our pellet supply holds up," Chang points out.

Herndon says, "Did you sleep well, Tom?"

"No," says Tom. He sits down and taps out his breakfast requisition. In the west, the fog is beginning to burn off the mountains. Something throbs in the back of his neck. He has been on this world nine weeks now, and in that time it has undergone its only change of season, shading from dry weather to foggy. The mists will remain for many months. Before the plains parch again, the Eaters will be gone and the settlers will begin to arrive. His food slides down the chute and he seizes it. Ellen sits beside him. She is a little more than half his age; this is her first voyage; she is their keeper of records, but she is also skilled at editing. "You look troubled," Ellen tells him. "Can I help you?"

"No. Thank you."

"I hate it when you get gloomy."

"It's a racial trait," says Tom Two Ribbons.

"I doubt that very much."

"The truth is that maybe my personality reconstruct is wearing thin. The trauma level was so close to the surface. I'm just a walking veneer, you know."

Ellen laughs prettily. She wears only a sprayon half-wrap. Her skin looks damp; she and Michaelson have had a swim at dawn. Tom Two Ribbons is thinking of asking her to marry him when this job is over. He has not been married since the collapse of the real estate business. The therapist suggested divorce as part of the reconstruct. He sometimes wonders where Terry has gone and whom she lives with now. Ellen says, "You seem pretty stable to me, Tom."

"Thank you," he says. She is young. She does not know.

"If it's just a passing gloom I can edit it out in one quick snip."

"Thank you," he says. "No."

"I forgot. You don't like editing."

"My father . . ."

"Yes?"

"In fifty years he pared himself down to a thread," Tom Two Ribbons says. "He had his ancestors edited away, his whole heritage, his religion, his wife, his sons, finally his name. Then he sat and smiled all day. Thank you, no editing."

"Where are you working today?" Ellen asks.

"In the compound, running tests."

"Want company? I'm off all morning."

"Thank you, no," he says, too quickly. She looks hurt. He tries to remedy his unintended cruelty by touching her arm lightly and saying, "maybe this afternoon, all right? I need to commune awhile. Yes?"

"Yes," she says and smiles and shapes a kiss with her lips.

After breakfast he goes to the compound. It covers a thousand hectares east of the base; they have bordered it with neural-field projectors at intervals of eighty meters, and this is a sufficient fence to keep the captive population of two hundred Eaters from straying. When all the others have been exterminated, this study group will remain. At the southwest corner of the compound stands a lab bubble from which the experiments are run: metabolic, psychological, physiological, ecological. A stream crosses the compound diagonally. There is a low ridge of grassy hills at its eastern edge. Five distinct copses of tightly clustered knifeblade trees are separated by patches of dense savanna. Sheltered beneath the grass are the oxygen-plants, almost completely hidden except for the photosynthetic spikes that jut to heights of three or four meters at regular intervals and for the lemon-colored respiratory bodies, chest high, that make the grassland sweet and dizzying with exhaled gases. Through the fields move the Eaters in a straggling herd, nibbling delicately at the respiratory bodies.

Tom Two Ribbons spies the herd beside the stream and goes toward it. He stumbles over an oxygen-plant hidden in the grass but deftly recovers his balance and, seizing the puckered orifice of the respiratory body, inhales deeply. His despair lifts. He approaches the Eaters. They are spherical, bulky, slow-moving creatures, covered by masses of coarse orange fur. Saucerlike eyes protrude above narrow rubbery lips. Their legs are thin and scaly like a chicken's, and their arms are short and held close to their bodies. They regard him with bland lack of curiosity. "Good morning, brothers!" is the way he greets them this time, and he wonders why.

I noticed something strange today. Perhaps I simply sniffed too much oxygen in the fields; maybe I was succumbing to a suggestion Herndon planted; or possibly it's the family masochism cropping out. But while I was observing the Eaters in the compound, it seemed to me, for the first time, that they were behaving intelligently, that they were functioning in a ritualized way.

I followed them around for three hours. During that time they uncovered half a dozen outcroppings of oxygen-plants. In each case they went through a stylized pattern of action before starting to munch. They:

Formed a straggly circle around the plants.

Looked toward the sun.

Looked toward their neighbors on left and right around the circle.

Made fuzzy neighing sounds *only* after having done the foregoing.

Looked toward the sun again.

Moved in and ate.

If this wasn't a prayer of thanksgiving, a saying of grace, then what was it? And if they're advanced enough spiritually to say grace, are we not therefore committing genocide here? Do chimpanzees say grace? Christ, we wouldn't even wipe out chimps the way we're cleaning out the Eaters! Of course, chimps don't interfere with human crops, and some kind of coexistence would be possible, whereas Eaters and human agriculturalists simply can't function on the same planet. Nevertheless, there's a moral issue here. The liquidation effort is predicated on the assumption that the intelligence level of the Eaters is about on a par with that of oysters, or, at best, sheep. Our consciences stay clear because our poison is quick and painless and because the Eaters thoughtfully dissolve upon dying, sparing us the mess of incinerating millions of corpses. But if they pray . . . .

I won't say anything to the others just yet. I want more evidence, hard, objective. Films, tapes, record cubes. Then we'll see. What if I can show that we're exterminating intelligent beings? My family knows a little about genocide, after all, having been on the receiving end just a few centuries back. I doubt that I could halt what's going on here. But at the very least I could withdraw from the operation. Head back to Earth and stir up public outcries.

I hope I'm imagining this.

I'm not imagining a thing. They gather in circles; they look to the sun; they neigh and pray. They're only balls of jelly on chicken legs, but they give thanks for their food. Those big round eyes now seem to stare accusingly at me. Our tame herd here knows what's going on: that we have descended from the stars to eradicate their kind and that they alone will be spared. They have no way of fighting back or even of communicating their displeasure, but they *know*. And hate us. Jesus, we have killed two million of them since we got here, and in a metaphorical way I'm stained with blood, and what will I do, what can I do?

I must move very carefully, or I'll end up drugged and edited.

I can't let myself seem like a crank, a quack, an agitator. I can't stand up and *denounce!* I have to find allies. Herndon, first. He surely is onto the truth; he's the one who nudged *me* to it, that day we dropped pellets. And I thought he was merely being vicious in his usual way!

I'll talk to him tonight.

He says, "I've been thinking about that suggestion you made. About the Eaters. Perhaps we haven't made sufficiently close psychological studies. I mean, if they really *are* intelligent . . ."

Herndon blinks. He is a tall man with glossy dark hair, a heavy beard, sharp cheekbones. "Who says they are, Tom?"

"You did. On the far side of the Forked River, you said . . ."

"It was just a speculative hypothesis. To make conversation."

"No, I think it was more than that. You really believed it."

Herndon looks troubled. "Tom, I don't know what you're trying to start, but don't start it. If I for a moment believed we were killing intelligent creatures, I'd run for an editor so fast I'd start an implosion wave."

"Why did you ask me that thing, then?" Tom Two Ribbons says.

"Idle chatter."

"Amusing yourself by kindling guilts in somebody else? You're a bastard, Herndon. I mean it."

"Well, look, Tom, if I had any idea that you'd get so worked up about a hypothetical suggestion . . ." Herndon shakes his head. "The Eaters aren't intelligent beings. Obviously. Otherwise we wouldn't be under orders to liquidate them."

"Obviously," says Tom Two Ribbons.

Ellen said, "No, I don't know what Tom's up to. But I'm pretty sure he needs a rest. It's only a year and a half since his personality reconstruct, and he had a pretty bad breakdown back then."

Michaelson consulted a chart. "He's refused three times in a row to make his pellet-dropping run. Claiming he can't take time away from his research. Hell, we can fill in for him, but it's the idea that he's ducking chores that bothers me."

"What kind of research is he doing?" Nichols wanted to know.

"Not biological," said Julia. "He's with the Eaters in the compound all the time, but I don't see him making any tests on them. He just watches them."

"And talks to them," Chang observed.

"And talks, yes," Julia said.

"About what?" Nichols asked.

"Who knows?"

Everyone looked at Ellen. "You're closest to him," Michaelson said. "Can't you bring him out of it?"

"I've got to know what he's in, first," Ellen said. "He isn't saying a thing."

You know that you must be very careful, for they outnumber you, and their concern for your mental welfare can be deadly. Already they realize you are disturbed, and Ellen has begun to probe for the source of the disturbance. Last night you lay in her arms and she questioned you, obliquely, skillfully, and you knew what she is trying to find out. When the moons appeared she suggested that you and she stroll in the compound among the sleeping Eaters. You declined, but she sees that you have become involved with the creatures.

You have done probing of your own—subtly, you hope. And you are aware that you can do nothing to save the Eaters. An irrevocable commitment has been made. It is 1876 all over again; these are the bison, these are the Sioux, and they must be destroyed, for the railroad is on its way. If you speak out here, your friends will calm you and pacify you and edit you, for they do not see what you see. If you return to Earth to agitate, you will be mocked and recommended for another reconstruct. You can do nothing. You can do nothing.

You cannot save, but perhaps you can record.

Go out into the prairie. Live with the Eaters; make yourself their friend; learn their ways. Set it down, a full account of their culture, so that at least that much will not be lost. You know the techniques of field anthropology. As was done for your people in the old days, do now for the Eaters.

He finds Michaelson. "Can you spare me for a few weeks?" he asks.

"Spare you, Tom? What do you mean?"

"I've got some field studies to do. I'd like to leave the base and work with Eaters in the wild."

"What's wrong with the ones in the compound?"

"It's the last chance with wild ones, Mike. I've got to go."

"Alone or with Ellen?"

"Alone."

Michaelson nods slowly. "All right, Tom. Whatever you want. Go. I won't hold you here."

I dance in the prairie under the green gold sun. About me the Eaters gather. I am stripped; sweat makes my skin glisten; my heart pounds. I talk to them with my feet, and they understand.

They understand.

They have a language of soft sounds. They have a god. They know love and awe and rapture. They have rites. They have names. They have a history. Of all this I am convinced.

I dance on thick grass.

How can I reach them? With my feet, with my hands, with my grunts, with my sweat. They gather by the hundreds, by the thousands, and I dance. I must not stop. They cluster about me and make their sounds. I am a conduit for strange forces. My great-grandfather should see me now! Sitting on his porch in Wyoming, the firewater in his hand, his brain rotting—see me now, old one! See the dance of Tom Two Ribbons! I talk to these strange ones with my feet under a sun that is the wrong color. I dance. I dance.

"Listen to me," I say. "I am your friend, I alone, the only one you can trust. Trust me, talk to me, teach me. Let me preserve your ways, for soon the destruction will come."

I dance, and the sun climbs, and the Eaters murmur.

There is the chief, I dance toward him, back, toward, I bow, I point to the sun, I imagine the being that lives in that ball of flame, I imitate the sounds of these people, I kneel, I rise, I dance. Tom Two Ribbons dances for you.

I summon skills my ancestors forgot. I feel the power flowing in me. As they danced in the days of the bison, I dance now, beyond the Forked River.

I dance, and now the Eaters dance too. Slowly, uncertainly, they move toward me, they shift their weight, lift leg and leg, sway about. "Yes, like that!" I cry. "Dance!"

We dance together as the sun reaches noon height.

Now their eyes are no longer accusing. I see warmth and kinship. I am their brother, their red-skinned tribesman, he who dances with them. No longer do they seem clumsy to me. There is a strange ponderous grace in their movements. They dance. They dance. They caper about me. Closer, closer, closer!

We move in holy frenzy.

They sing, now, a blurred hymn of joy. They throw forth their arms, unclench their little claws. In unison they shift weight, left foot forward, right, left, right. Dance, brothers, dance, dance, dance! They press against me. Their flesh quivers; their smell is a sweet one. They gently thrust me across the field to a part of the meadow where the grass is deep and untrampled. Still dancing, we seek the oxygen-plants and find clumps of them beneath the grass, and they make their prayer and seize them with their awkward arms, separating the respiratory bodies from the photosynthetic spikes. The plants, in anguish, release floods of oxygen. My mind reels. I laugh and sing. The Eaters are nibbling the lemon-colored perforated globes, nibbling the stalks as well. They thrust their plants at me. It is a religious ceremony, I see. Take from us, eat with us, join with us, this is the body, this is the blood, take, eat, join. I bend forward and put a lemon-colored globe to my lips. I do not bite; I nibble, as they do, my teeth slicing away the skin of the globe. Juice spurts into my mouth while oxygen drenches my nostrils. The Eaters sing hosannas. I should be in full paint for this, paint of my forefathers, feathers, too, meeting their religion in the regalia of what should have been mine. Take, eat, join. The juice of the oxygen-plant flows in my veins. I embrace my brothers. I sing, and as my voice leaves my lips it becomes an arch that glistens like new steel, and I pitch my song lower, and the arch turns to tarnished silver. The Eaters crowd close. The scent of their bodies is fiery red to me. Their soft cries are puffs of steam. The sun is very warm; its rays are tiny jagged pings of puckered sound, close to the top of my range of hearing, plink! plink! plink! The thick grass hums to me, deep and rich, and the wind hurls points of flame along the prairie. I devour another oxygen-plant and then a third. My brothers laugh and shout. They tell me of their gods, the god of warmth, the god of food, the god of pleasure, the god of death, the god of holiness, the god of wrongness, and the others. They recite for me the names of their kings, and I hear their voices as splashes of green mold on the clean sheet of the sky. They instruct me in their holy rites. I must remember this, I tell myself, for when it is gone it will never come again. I continue to dance. They continue to dance. The color of the hills becomes rough and coarse, like abrasive gas. Take, eat, join. Dance. They are so gentle!

I hear the drone of the copter, suddenly.

It hovers far overhead. I am unable to see who flies in it. "No," I scream. "Not here! Not these people! Listen to me! This is Tom Two Ribbons! Can't you hear me? I'm doing a field study here! You have no right . . . !"

My voice makes spirals of blue moss edged with red sparks. They drift upward and are scattered by the breeze.

I yell, I shout, I bellow. I dance and shake my fists. From the wings of the copter the jointed arms of the pellet-distributors unfold. The gleaming spigots extend and whirl. The neural pellets rain down into the meadow, each tracing a blazing track that lingers in the sky. The sound of the copter becomes a furry carpet stretching to the horizon, and my shrill voice is lost in it.

The Eaters drift away from me, seeking the pellets, scratching at the roots of the grass to find them. Still dancing, I leap into their midst, striking the pellets from their hands, hurling them into the stream, crushing them to powder. The Eaters growl black needles at me. They turn away and search for more pellets. The copter turns and flies off, leaving a trail of dense oily sound. My brothers are gobbling the pellets eagerly.

There is no way to prevent it.

Joy consumes them and they topple and lie still. Occasionally a limb twitches; then even this stops. They begin to dissolve. Thousands of them melt on the prairie, sinking into shapelessness, losing their spherical forms, flattening, ebbing into the ground. The bonds of the molecules will no longer hold. It is the twilight of protoplasm. They perish. They vanish. For hours I walk the prairie. Now I inhale oxygen; now I eat a lemon-colored globe. Sunset begins with the ringing of leaden chimes. Black clouds make brazen trumpet calls in the east and the deepening wind is a swirl of coaly bristles. Silence comes. Night falls. I dance. I am alone.

The copter comes again, and they find you, and you do not resist as they

gather you in. You are beyond bitterness. Quietly you explain what you have
done and what you have learned, and why it is wrong to exterminate these
people. You describe the plant you have eaten and the way it affects your
senses, and as you talk of the blessed synesthesia, the texture of the wind and
the sound of the clouds and the timbre of the sunlight, they nod and smile
and tell you not to worry, that everything will be all right soon, and they touch
something cold to your forearm, so cold that it is a whir and a buzz and the
deintoxicant sinks into your vein and soon the ecstasy drains away, leaving only
the exhaustion and the grief.

He says, "We never learn a thing, do we? We export all our horrors to the
stars. Wipe out the Armenians, wipe out the Jews, wipe out the Tasmanians,
wipe out the Indians, wipe out everyone who's in the way, and then come out
here and do the same damned murderous thing. You weren't with me out
there. You didn't dance with them. You didn't see what a rich, complex
culture the Eaters have. Let me tell you about their tribal structure. It's dense:
seven levels of matrimonial relationships, to begin with, and an exogamy factor
that requires . . ."

Softly Ellen says, "Tom, darling, nobody's going to harm the Eaters."

"And the religion," he goes on. "Nine gods, each one an aspect of *the* god.
Holiness and wrongness both worshiped. They have hymns, prayers, a theol-
ogy. And we, the emissaries of the god of wrongness . . ."

"We're not exterminating them," Michaelson says. "Won't you understand
that, Tom? This is all a fantasy of yours. You've been under the influence of
drugs, but now we're clearing you out. You'll be clean in a little while. You'll
have perspective again."

"A fantasy?" he says bitterly. "A drug dream? I stood out in the prairie and
saw you drop pellets. And I watched them die and melt away. I didn't dream
that."

"How can we convince you?" Chang asks earnestly. "What will make you
believe? Shall we fly over the Eater country with you and show you how many
millions there are?"

"But how many millions have been destroyed?" he demands.

They insist that he is wrong. Ellen tells him again that no one has ever
desired to harm the Eaters. "This is a scientific expedition, Tom. We're here
to *study* them. It's a violation of all we stand for to injure intelligent life
forms."

"You admit that they're intelligent?"

"Of course. That's never been in doubt."

"Then why drop the pellets?" he asks. "Why slaughter them?"

"None of that has happened, Tom," Ellen says. She takes his hand between her cool palms. "Believe us. Believe us."

He says bitterly, "If you want me to believe you, why don't you do the job properly? Get out the editing machine and go to work on me. You can't simply *talk* me into rejecting the evidence of my own eyes."

"You were under drugs all the time," Michaelson says.

"I've never taken drugs! Except for what I ate in the meadow, when I danced—and that came after I had watched the massacre going on for weeks and weeks. Are you saying that it's a retroactive delusion?"

"No, Tom," Schwartz says. "You've had this delusion all along. It's part of your therapy, your reconstruct. You came here programmed with it."

"Impossible," he says.

Ellen kisses his fevered forehead. "It was done to reconcile you to mankind, you see. You had this terrible resentment of the displacement of your people in the nineteenth century. You were unable to forgive the industrial society for scattering the Sioux, and you were terribly full of hate. Your therapist thought that if you could be made to participate in an imaginary modern extermination, if you could come to see it as a necessary operation, you'd be purged of your resentment and able to take your place in society as . . ."

He thrusts her away. "Don't talk idiocy! If you knew the first thing about reconstruct therapy, you'd realize that no reputable therapist could be so shallow. There are no one-to-one correlations in reconstructs. No, don't touch me. Keep away. Keep away."

He will not let them persuade him that this is merely a drug-born dream. It is no fantasy, he tells himself, and it is no therapy. He rises. He goes out. They do not follow him. He takes a copter and seeks his brothers.

Again I dance. The sun is much hotter today. The Eaters are more numerous. Today I wear paint, today I wear feathers. My body shines with my sweat. They dance with me, and they have a frenzy in them that I have never seen before. We pound the trampled meadow with our feet. We clutch for the sun with our hands. We sing, we shout, we cry. We will dance until we fall.

This is no fantasy. These people are real, and they are intelligent, and they are doomed. This I know.

We dance. Despite the doom, we dance.

My great-grandfather comes and dances with us. He too is real. His nose is like a hawk's, not blunt like mine, and he wears the big headdress, and his muscles are like cords under his brown skin. He sings, he shouts, he cries.

Others of my family join us.

We eat the oxygen-plants together. We embrace the Eaters. We know, all of us, what it is to be hunted.

The clouds make music and the wind takes on texture and the sun's warmth has color.

We dance. We dance. Our limbs know no weariness.

The sun grows and fills the whole sky, and I see no Eaters now, only my own people, my father's fathers across the centuries, thousands of gleaming skins, thousands of hawks' noses, and we eat the plants, and we find sharp sticks and thrust them into our flesh, and the sweet blood flows and dries in the blaze of the sun, and we dance, and we dance, and some of us fall from weariness, and we dance, and the prairie is a sea of bobbing headdresses, an ocean of feathers, and we dance, and my heart makes thunder, and my knees become water, and the sun's fire engulfs me, and I dance, and I fall, and I dance, and I fall, and I fall, and I fall.

Again they find you and bring you back. They give you the cool snout on your arm to take the oxygen-plant drug from your veins, and then they give you something else so you will rest. You rest and you are very calm. Ellen kisses you and you stroke her soft skin, and then the others come in and they talk to you, saying soothing things, but you do not listen, for you are searching for realities. It is not an easy search. It is like falling through many trapdoors, looking for the one room whose floor is not hinged. Everything that has happened on this planet is your therapy, you tell yourself, designed to reconcile an embittered aborigine to the white man's conquest; nothing is really being exterminated here. You reject that and fall through and realize that this must be the therapy of your friends; they carry the weight of accumulated centuries of guilt and have come here to shed that load, and you are here to ease them of their burden, to draw their sins into yourself and give them forgiveness. Again you fall through and see that the Eaters are mere animals who threaten the ecology and must be removed; the culture you imagined for them is your hallucination, kindled out of old churnings. You try to withdraw your objections to this necessary extermination, but you fall through again and discover that there is no extermination except in your mind, which is troubled and disordered by your obsession with the crime against your ancestors, and you sit up, for you wish to apologize to these friends of yours, these innocent scientists whom you have called murderers. And you fall through.

JOHN VARLEY

In the Bowl

The qualities that make a piece of fiction memorable are varied: characters who capture the reader's emotions, vivid imagery, skillful writing, careful attention to detail, imaginative plotting, making the unusual seem commonplace. "In the Bowl" has all of these qualities and more. It offers the reader beautifully worked out scientific advances, convincing alien backgrounds, considerable dramatic tension and attractive protagonists. It is also one of the most interesting and unusual love stories in all of science fiction.

Never buy anything at a secondhand organ bank. And while I'm handing out good advice, don't outfit yourself for a trip to Venus until you *get* to Venus.

I wish I had waited. But while shopping around at Coprates a few weeks before my vacation, I happened on this little shop and was talked into an infraeye at a very good price. What I should have asked myself was what was an infraeye doing on Mars in the first place?

Think about it. No one wears them on Mars. If you want to see at night, it's much cheaper to buy a snooperscope. That way you can take the damn thing off when the sun comes up. So this eye must have come back with a tourist from Venus. And there's no telling how long it sat there in the vat until this sweet-talking old guy gave me his line about how it belonged to a nice little old schoolteacher who never . . . ah, well. You've probably heard it before.

If only the damn thing had gone on the blink before I left Venusburg. You know Venusburg: town of steamy swamps and sleazy hotels where you can get mugged as you walk down the public streets, lose a fortune at the gaming tables, buy any pleasure in the known universe, hunt the prehistoric monsters that wallow in the fetid marshes that are just a swamp-buggy ride out of town. You do? Then you should know that after hours—when they turn all the holos off and the place reverts to an ordinary cluster of silvery domes sitting in darkness and eight-hundred-degree temperature and pressure enough to give you a sinus headache just *thinking* about it, when they shut off all the tourist razzle-dazzle—it's no trouble to find your way to one of the rental agencies around the spaceport and get medicanical work done. They'll accept Martian money. Your Solar Express Card is honored. Just walk right in, no waiting.

However . . .

I had caught the daily blimp out of Venusburg just hours after I touched down, happy as a clam, my infraeye working beautifully. By the time I landed in Cui-Cui Town, I was having my first inklings of trouble. Barely enough to notice; just the faintest hazing in the right-side peripheral vision. I shrugged it off. I had only three hours in Cui-Cui before the blimp left for Last Chance. I wanted to look around. I had no intention of wasting my few hours in a body shop getting my eye fixed. If it was still acting up at Last Chance, then I'd see about it.

Cui-Cui was more to my liking than Venusburg. There was not such a cast-of-thousands feeling there. On the streets of Venusburg the chances are about ten to one against meeting a real human being; everyone else is a holo put there to spice up the image and help the streets look not quite so *empty*. I quickly tired of zoot-suited pimps that I could see right through trying to sell me boys and girls of all ages. What's the *point?* Just try to touch one of those beautiful people.

In Cui-Cui the ratio was closer to fifty-fifty. And the theme was not decadent corruption, but struggling frontier. The streets were very convincing mud, and the wooden storefronts were tastefully done. I didn't care for the eight-legged dragons with eyestalks that constantly lumbered through the place, but I understand they are a memorial to the fellow who named the town. That's all right, but I doubt if he would have liked to have one of the damn things walk through him like a twelve-ton tank made of pixie dust.

I barely had time to get my feet "wet" in the "puddles" before the blimp was ready to go again. And the eye trouble had cleared up. So I was off to Last Chance.

I should have taken a cue from the name of the town. And I had every opportunity to do so. While there, I made my last purchase of supplies for the bush. I was going out where there were no air stations on every corner, and so I decided I could use a tagalong.

Maybe you've never seen one. They're modern science's answer to the backpack. Or maybe to the mule train, though in operation you're sure to be reminded of the safari bearers in old movies, trudging stolidly along behind the white hunter with bales of supplies on their heads. The thing is a pair of metal legs exactly as long as your legs, with equipment on the top and an umbilical cord attaching the contraption to your lower spine. What it does is provide you with the capability of living on the surface for four weeks instead of the five days you get from your Venus-lung.

The medico who sold me mine had me lying right there on his table with my back laid open so he could install the tubes that carry air from the tanks in the tagalong into my Venus-lung. It was a golden opportunity to ask him to check the eye. He probably would have, because while he was hooking me up he inspected and tested my lung and charged me nothing. He wanted to know where I bought it, and I told him Mars. He clucked, and said it seemed all right. He warned me not ever to let the level of oxygen in the lung get too low, to always charge it up before I left a pressure dome, even if I was only going out for a few minutes. I assured him that I knew all that and would be careful. So he connected the nerves into a metal socket in the small of my back and plugged the tagalong into it. He tested it several ways and said the job was done.

And I didn't ask him to look at the eye. I just wasn't thinking about the eye then. I'd not even gone out on the surface yet, so I'd no real occasion to see it in action. Oh, things looked a little different, even in visible light. There were different colors and very few shadows, and the image I got out of the infraeye was fuzzier than the one from the other eye. I could close one eye, then the other, and see a real difference. But I wasn't thinking about it.

So I boarded the blimp the next day for the weekly scheduled flight to Lodestone, a company mining town close to the Fahrenheit Desert. Though how they were able to distinguish a desert from anything else on Venus was still a mystery to me. I was enraged to find that, though the blimp left half-loaded, I had to pay two fares: one for me, and one for my tagalong. I thought briefly of carrying the damn thing in my lap but gave it up after a ten-minute experiment in the depot. It was full of sharp edges and poking angles, and the trip was going to be a long one. So I paid. But the extra expense had knocked a large hole in my budget.

From Cui-Cui the steps got closer together and harder to reach. Cui-Cui is two thousand kilometers from Venusburg, and it's another thousand to Lodestone. After that the passenger service is spotty. I did find out how Venusians defined a desert, though. A desert is a place not yet inhabited by human beings. So long as I was still able to board a scheduled blimp, I wasn't there yet.

The blimps played out on me in a little place called Prosperity. Population seventy-five humans and one otter. I thought the otter was a holo playing in the pool in the town square. The place didn't look prosperous enough to afford a real pool like that with real water. But it was. It was a transient town catering to prospectors. I understand that a town like that can vanish overnight if the prospectors move on. The owners of the shops just pack up and haul the whole thing away. The ratio of the things you see in a frontier town to what really is there is something like a hundred to one.

I learned with considerable relief that the only blimps I could catch out of Prosperity were headed in the direction I had come from. There was nothing at all going the other way. I was happy to hear that and felt it was only a matter of chartering a ride into the desert. Then my eye faded out entirely.

I remember feeling annoyed; no, more than annoyed. I was really angry. But I was still viewing it as a nuisance rather than a disaster. It was going to be a matter of some lost time and some wasted money.

I quickly learned otherwise. I asked the ticket seller (this was in a saloon-drugstore-arcade; there was no depot in Prosperity) where I could find some-one who'd sell and install an infraeye. He laughed at me.

"Not out here you won't brother," he said. "Never have had anything like that out here. Used to be a medico in Ellsworth, three stops back on the local blimp, but she moved back to Venusburg a year ago. Nearest thing now is in Last Chance."

I was stunned. I knew I was heading out for the deadlands, but it had never occurred to me that any place would be lacking in something so basic as a medico. Why, you might as well not sell food or air as not sell medicanical services. People might actually *die* out here. I wondered if the planetary government knew about this disgusting situation.

Whether they did or not, I realized that an incensed letter to them would do me no good. I was in a bind. Adding quickly in my head, I soon discovered that the cost of flying back to Last Chance and buying a new eye would leave me without enough money to return to Prosperity and still make it back to Venusburg. My entire vacation was about to be ruined just because I tried to cut some corners buying a used eye.

"What's the matter with the eye?" the man asked me.

"Huh? Oh, I don't know. I mean, it's just stopped working. I'm blind in it, that's what's wrong." I grasped at a straw, seeing the way he was studying my eye.

"Say, you don't know anything about it, do you?"

He shook his head and smiled ruefully at me. "Naw. Just a little here and there. I was thinking if it was the muscles that was giving you trouble, bad tracking or something like that . . ."

"No. No vision at all."

"Too bad. Sounds like a shot nerve to me. I wouldn't try to fool around with that. I'm just a tinkerer." He clucked his tongue sympathetically. "You want that ticket back to Last Chance?"

I didn't know what I wanted just then. I had planned this trip for two years. I almost bought the ticket, then thought what the hell. I was here, and I should at least look around before deciding what to do. Maybe there was someone here who could help me. I turned back to ask the clerk if he knew anyone, but he answered before I got it out.

"I don't want to raise your hopes too much," he said, rubbing his chin with a broad hand. "Like I say, it's not for sure, but . . ."

"Yes, what is it?"

"Well, there's a kid lives around here who's pretty crazy about medico stuff. Always tinkering around, doing odd jobs for people, fixing herself up; you know the type. The trouble is she's pretty loose in her ways. You might end up worse when she's through with you than when you started."

"I don't see how," I said. "It's not working at all; what could she do to make it any worse?"

He shrugged. "It's your funeral. You can probably find her hanging around the square. If she's not there, check the bars. Her name's Ember. She's got a pet otter that's always with her. But you'll know her when you see her."

Finding Ember was no problem. I simply backtracked to the square and there she was, sitting on the stone rim of the fountain. She was trailing her toes in the water. Her otter was playing on a small waterslide, looking immensely pleased to have found the only open body of water within a thousand kilometers.

"Are you Ember?" I asked, sitting down beside her.

She looked up at me with that unsettling stare a Venusian can inflict on a foreigner. It comes of having one blue or brown eye and one that is all red with no white. I looked that way myself, but I didn't have to look at it.

"What if I am?"

Her apparent age was about ten or eleven. Intuitively, I felt that it was probably very close to her actual age. Since she was supposed to be handy at medicanics, I could have been wrong. She had done some work on herself, but of course there was no way of telling how extensive it might have been. Mostly it seemed to be cosmetic. She had no hair on her head. She had replaced it with a peacock fan of feathers that kept falling into her eyes. Her scalp skin had been transplanted to her lower legs and forearms, and the hair there was long, blonde and flowing. From the contours of her face I was sure that her skull was a mass of file marks and bone putty from where she'd fixed the understructure to reflect the face she wished to wear.

"I was told that you know a little medicanics. You see, this eye has . . ."

She snorted. "I don't know who would have told you *that.* I know a hell of a lot about medicine. I'm not just a backyard tinkerer. Come on, Malibu."

She started to get up, and the otter looked back and forth between us. I don't think he was ready to leave the pool.

"Wait a minute. I'm sorry if I hurt your feelings. Without knowing anything about you I'll admit that you must know more about it than anyone else in town."

She sat back down, finally had to grin at me.

"So you're in a spot, right? It's me or no one. Let me guess: you're here on vacation, that's obvious. And either time or money is preventing you from going back to Last Chance for professional work." She looked me up and down. "I'd say it was money."

"You hit it. Will you help me?"

"That depends." She moved closer and squinted into my infraeye. She put her hands on my cheeks to hold my head steady. There was nowhere for me to look but at her face. There were no scars visible on her; at least she was that good. Her upper canines were about five millimeters longer than the rest of her teeth.

"Hold still. Where'd you get this?"

"Mars."

"Thought so. It's a Gloom Piercer, made by Northern Bio. Cheap model; they peddle 'em mostly to tourists. Maybe ten, twelve years old."

"Is it the nerve? The guy I talked to . . ."

"Nope." She leaned back and resumed splashing her feet in the water. "Retina. The right side is detached, and it's flopped down over the fovea. Probably wasn't put on very tight in the first place. They don't make those things to last more than a year."

I sighed and slapped my knees with my palms. I stood up, held out my hand to her.

"Well, I guess that's that. Thanks for your help."

She was surprised. "Where you going?"

"Back to Last Chance, then to Mars to sue a certain organ bank. There are laws for this sort of thing on Mars."

"Here, too. But why go back? I'll fix it for you."

We were in her workshop, which doubled as her bedroom and kitchen. It was just a simple dome without a single holo. It was refreshing after the ranch-style houses that seemed to be the rage in Prosperity. I don't wish to sound chauvinistic, and I realize that Venusians need some sort of visual stimulation, living as they do in a cloud-covered desert. Still, the emphasis on illusion there was never to my liking. Ember lived next door to a man who lived in a perfect replica of the Palace at Versailles. She told me that when he shut his holo generators off the residue of his *real* possessions would have fit in a knapsack. Including the holo generator.

"What brings you to Venus?"

"Tourism."

She looked at me out of the corner of her eye as she swabbed my face with nerve deadener. I was stretched out on the floor, since there was no furniture in the room except a few work tables.

"All right. But we don't get many tourists this far out. If it's none of my business, just say so."

"It's none of your business."

She sat up. "Fine. Fix your own eye." She waited with a half-smile on her face. I eventually had to smile, too. She went back to work, selecting a spoon-shaped tool from a haphazard pile at her knees.

"I'm an amateur geologist. Rock hound, actually. I work in an office, and weekends I get out in the country and hike around. The rocks are an excuse to get me out there, I guess."

She popped the eye out of its socket and reached in with one finger to deftly unhook the metal connection along the optic nerve. She held the eyeball up to the light and peered into the lens.

"You can get up now. Pour some of this stuff into the socket and squint down on it." I did as she asked and followed her to the workbench.

She sat on a stool and examined the eye more closely. Then she stuck a syringe into it and drained out the aqueous humor, leaving the orb looking like a turtle egg that's dried in the sun. She sliced it open and started probing carefully. The long hairs on her forearms kept getting in the way, so she paused and tied them back with rubber bands.

"Rock hound," she mused. "You must be here to get a look at the blast jewels."

"Right. Like I said, I'm strictly a small-time geologist. But I read about them and saw one once in a jeweler's shop in Phobos. So I saved up and came to Venus to try and find one of my own."

"That should be no problem. Easiest gems to find in the known universe. Too bad. People out here were hoping they could get rich off them." She shrugged. "Not that there's not some money to be made off them. Just not the fortune everybody was hoping for. Funny; they're as rare as diamonds used to be, and to make it even better, they don't duplicate in the lab the way diamonds do. Oh, I guess they could make 'em, but it's way too much trouble." She was using a tiny device to staple the detached retina back onto the rear surface of the eye.

"Go on."

"Huh?"

"Why can't they make them in the lab?"

She laughed. "You *are* an amateur geologist. Like I said, they could, but it'd cost too much. They're a blend of a lot of different elements. A lot of aluminum, I think. That's what makes rubies red, right?"

"Yes."

"It's the other impurities that make them so pretty. And you have to make them in high pressure and heat, and they're so unstable that they usually blow before you've got the right mix. So it's cheaper to go out and pick 'em up."

"And the only place to pick them up is in the middle of the Fahrenheit Desert."

"Right." She seemed to be finished with her stapling. She straightened up to survey her work with a critical eye. She frowned, then sealed up the incision she had made and pumped the liquid back in. She mounted it in a caliper and aimed a laser at it, then shook her head when she read some figures on a readout by the laser.

"It's working," she said. "But you really got a lemon. The iris is out of true. It's an ellipse, about .24 eccentric. It's going to get worse. See that brown discoloration on the left side? That's progressive decay in the muscle tissue, poisons accumulating in it. And you're a dead cinch for cataracts in about four months."

I couldn't see what she was talking about, but I pursed my lips as if I did.

"But will it last that long?"

She smirked at me. "Are you looking for a six-month warranty? Sorry, I'm not a member of the VMA. But if it isn't legally binding, I guess I'd feel safe in saying it ought to last that long. Maybe."

"You sure go out on a limb, don't you?"

"It's good practice. We future medicos must always be on the alert for malpractice suits. Lean over here and I'll put it in."

"What I was wondering," I said, as she hooked it up and eased it back into the socket, "is whether I'd be safe going out in the desert for four weeks with this eye."

"No," she said promptly, and I felt a great weight of disappointment. "Nor with any eye," she quickly added. "Not if you're going alone."

"I see. But you think the eye would hold up?"

"Oh, sure. But you wouldn't. That's why you're going to take me up on my astounding offer and let me be your guide through the desert."

I snorted. "You think so? Sorry, this is going to be a solo expedition. I planned it that way from the first. That's what I go out rock hunting for in the first place: to be alone." I dug my credit meter out of my pouch. "Now, how much do I owe you?"

She wasn't listening but was resting her chin on her palm and looking wistful.

"He goes out so he can be alone, did you hear that, Malibu?" The otter looked up at her from his place on the floor. "Now take me, for instance. Me, I know what being alone is all about. It's the crowds and big cities I crave. Right, old buddy?" The otter kept looking at her, obviously ready to agree to anything.

"I suppose so," I said. "Would a hundred be all right?" That was about half what a registered medico would have charged me, but like I said, I was running short.

"You're not going to let me be your guide? Final word?"

"No. Final. Listen, it's not you, it's just . . ."

"I know. You want to be alone. No charge. Come on, Malibu." She got up and headed for the door. Then she turned around.

"I'll be seeing you," she said, and winked at me.

It didn't take me too long to understand what the wink had been all about. I can see the obvious on the third or fourth go-around.

The fact was that Prosperity was considerably bemused to have a tourist in its midst. There wasn't a rental agency or hotel in the entire town. I had thought of that but hadn't figured it would be too hard to find someone willing to rent his private skycycle if the price was right. I'd been saving out a large chunk of cash for the purpose of meeting extortionate demands in that department. I felt sure the locals would be only too willing to soak a tourist.

But they weren't taking. Just about everyone had a skycycle, and absolutely everyone who had one was uninterested in renting it. They were a necessity to anyone who worked out of town, which everyone did, and they were hard to get. Freight schedules were as spotty as the passenger service. And every person who turned me down had a helpful suggestion to make. As I say, after the fourth or fifth such suggestion I found myself back in the town square. She was sitting just as she had been the first time, trailing her feet in the water. Malibu never seemed to tire of the waterslide.

"Yes," she said, without looking up. "It so happens that I *do* have a skycycle for rent."

I was exasperated, but I had to cover it up. She had me over the proverbial barrel.

"Do you always hang around here?" I asked. "People tell me to see you about a skycycle and tell me to look here, almost like you and this fountain are a hyphenated word. What else do you do?"

She fixed me with a haughty glare. "I repair eyes for dumb tourists. I also do body work for everyone in town at only twice what it would cost them in Last Chance. And I do it damn well, too, though those rubes'd be the last to admit it. No doubt Mr. Lamara at the ticket station told you scandalous lies about my skills. They resent it because I'm taking advantage of the cost and time it would take them to get to Last Chance and pay merely inflated prices, instead of the outrageous ones I charge them."

I had to smile, though I was sure I was about to become the object of some outrageous prices myself. She was a shrewd operator.

"How old are you?" I found myself asking, then almost bit my tongue. The last thing a proud and independent child likes to discuss is age. But she surprised me.

"In mere chronological time, eleven Earth years. That's just over six of your years. In real, internal time, of course, I'm ageless."

"Of course. Now about that cycle . . ."

"Of course. But I evaded your earlier question. What I do besides sit here is irrelevant, because while sitting here I am engaged in contemplating eternity. I'm diving into my naval, hoping to learn the true depth of the womb. In short, I'm doing my yoga exercises." She looked thoughtfully out over the water to her pet. "Besides, it's the only pool in a thousand kilometers." She grinned at me and dived flat over the water. She cut it like a knife blade and torpedoed out to her otter, who set up a happy racket of barks.

When she surfaced near the middle of the pool, out by the jets and falls, I called to her.

"What about the cycle?"

She cupped her ear, though she was only about fifteen meters away.

"I said what about the cycle?"

"I can't hear you," she mouthed. "You'll have to come out here."

I stepped into the pool, grumbling to myself. I could see that her price included more than just money.

"I can't swim," I warned.

"Don't worry, it won't get much deeper than that." It was up to my chest. I sloshed out until I was on tiptoe, then grabbed at a jutting curlicue on the fountain. I hauled myself up and sat on the wet Venusian marble with water trickling down my legs.

Ember was sitting at the bottom of the waterslide, thrashing her feet in the water. She was leaning flat against the smooth rock. The water that sheeted over the rock made a bow wave at the crown of her head. Beads of water ran off her head feathers. Once again she made me smile. If charm could be sold, she could have been wealthy. What am I talking about? Nobody ever sells anything *but* charm, in one way or another. I got a grip on myself before she tried to sell me the north and south poles. In no time at all I was able to see her as an avaricious, cunning little guttersnipe again.

"One billion solar marks per hour, not a penny less," she said from that sweet little mouth.

There was no point in negotiating from an offer like that. "You brought me out here to hear *that?* I'm really disappointed in you. I didn't take you for a tease, I really didn't. I thought we could do business. I . . ."

"Well, if that offer isn't satisfactory, try this one. Free of charge, except for oxygen and food and water." She waited, threshing the water with her feet.

Of course there would be some teeth in that. In an intuitive leap of truly cosmic scale, a surmise worthy of an Einstein, I saw the string. She saw me make that leap, knew I didn't like where I had landed and her teeth flashed at me. So once again, and not for the last time, I had to either strangle her or smile at her. I smiled. I don't know how, but she had this knack of making her opponents like her even as she screwed them.

"Are you a believer in love at first sight?" I asked her, hoping to throw her off guard. Not a chance.

"Maudlin wishful thinking, at best," she said. "You have *not* bowled me over, mister . . ."

"Kiku."

"Nice. Martian name?"

"I suppose so. I never really thought of it. I'm not rich, Ember."

"Certainly not. You wouldn't have put yourself in my hands if you were."

"Then why are you so attracted to me? Why are you so determined to go with me, when all I want from you is to rent your cycle? If I was that charming, I would have noticed it by now."

"Oh, I don't know," she said, with one eyebrow climbing up her forehead. "There's *something* about you that I find absolutely fascinating. Irresistible, even." She pretended to swoon.

"Want to tell me what it is?"

She shook her head. "Let that be my little secret for now."

I was beginning to suspect she was attracted to me by the shape of my neck —so she could sink her teeth into it and drain my blood. I decided to let it lie. Hopefully she'd tell me more in the days ahead. Because it looked like there would be days together, many of them.

"When can you be ready to leave?"

"I packed right after I fixed your eye. Let's get going."

Venus is spooky. I thought and thought, and that's the best way I can describe it.

It's spooky partly because of the way you see it. Your right eye—the one that sees what's called visible light—shows you only a small circle of light that's illuminated by your hand torch. Occasionally there's a glowing spot of molten metal in the distance, but it's far too dim to see by. Your infraeye pierces those shadows and gives you a blurry picture of what lies outside the torchlight, but I would have almost rather been blind.

There's no good way to describe how this dichotomy affects your mind. One eye tells you that everything beyond a certain point is shadowy, while the other shows you what's in those shadows. Ember says that after a while your brain can blend the two pictures as easily as it does for binocular vision. I never reached that point. The whole time I was there I was trying to reconcile the two pictures.

I don't like standing in the bottom of a bowl a thousand kilometers wide. That's what you see. No matter how high you climb or how far you go, you're still standing in the bottom of that bowl. It has something to do with the bending of the light rays by the thick atmosphere, if I understand Ember correctly.

Then there's the sun. When I was there it was nighttime, which means that the sun was a squashed ellipse hanging just above the horizon in the east, where it had set weeks and weeks ago. Don't ask me to explain it. All I know is that the sun never sets on Venus. Never, no matter where you are. It just gets flatter and flatter and wider and wider until it oozes around to the north or south, depending on where you are, becoming a flat, bright line of light until it begins pulling itself back together in the west, where it's going to rise in a few weeks.

Ember says that at the equator it becomes a complete circle for a split second when it's actually directly underfoot. Like the lights of a terrific stadium. All this happens up at the rim of the bowl you're standing in, about ten degrees above the theoretical horizon. It's another refraction effect.

You don't see it in your left eye. Like I said, the clouds keep out virtually all of the visible light. It's in your right eye. The color is what I got to think of as infrablue.

It's quiet. You begin to miss the sound of your own breathing, and if you think about that too much, you begin to wonder why you *aren't* breathing. You know, of course, except the hindbrain, which never likes it at all. It doesn't matter to the autonomic nervous system that your Venus-lung is dribbling oxygen directly into your bloodstream; those circuits aren't made to understand things; they are primitive and very wary of improvements. So I was plagued by a feeling of suffocation, which was my medulla getting even with me, I guess.

I was also pretty nervous about the temperature and pressure. Silly, I know. Mars would kill me just as dead without a suit, and do it more slowly and painfully into the bargain. If my suit failed here, I doubt if I'd have felt anything. It was just the thought of that incredible pressure being held one millimeter away from my fragile skin by a force field that, physically speaking, isn't even there. Or so Ember told me. She might have been trying to get my goat. I mean, lines of magnetic force have no physical reality, but they're *there*, aren't they?

I kept my mind off it. Ember was there and she knew about such things.

What she couldn't adequately explain to me was why a skycycle didn't have a motor. I thought about that a lot, sitting on the saddle and pedaling my ass off with nothing to look at but Ember's silver-plated buttocks.

She had a tandem cycle, which meant four seats; two for us and two for our tagalongs. I sat behind Ember, and the tagalongs sat in two seats off to our right. Since they aped our leg movements with exactly the same force we applied, what we had was a four-human-power cycle.

"I can't figure out for the life of me," I said on our first day out, "what would have been so hard about mounting an engine on this thing and using some of the surplus power from our packs."

"Nothing hard about it, lazy," she said, without turning around. "Take my advice as a fledgling medico; this is much better for you. If you *use* the muscles you're wearing, they'll last you a lot longer. It makes you feel healthier and keeps you out of the clutches of money-grubbing medicos. I *know*. Half my work is excising fat from flabby behinds and digging varicose veins out of legs. Even out here, people don't get more than twenty years' use of their legs before they're ready for a trade-in. That's pure waste."

"I think I should have had a trade-in before we left. I'm about done in. Can't we call it a day?"

She tut-tutted, but touched a control and began spilling hot gas from the balloon over our heads. The steering vanes sticking out at our sides tilted, and we started a slow spiral to the ground.

We landed at the bottom of the bowl—my first experience with it, since all my other views of Venus had been from the air where it isn't so noticeable. I stood looking at it and scratching my head while Ember turned on the tent and turned off the balloon.

The Venusians use null fields for just about everything. Rather than try to cope with a technology that must stand up to the temperature and pressure extremes, they coat everything in a null field and let it go at that. The balloon on the cycle was nothing but a standard globular field with a discontinuity at the bottom for the air heater. The cycle body was protected with the same kind of field that Ember and I wore, the kind that follows the surface at a set distance. The tent was a hemispherical field with a flat floor.

It simplified a lot of things. Airlocks, for instance. What we did was simply to walk into the tent. Our suit fields vanished as they were absorbed into the tent field. To leave one need merely walk through the wall again, and the suit would form around you.

I plopped myself down on the floor and tried to turn my hand torch off. To my surprise, I found that it wasn't built to turn off. Ember turned on the camp fire and noticed my puzzlement.

"Yes, it is wasteful," she conceded. "There's something in a Venusian that hates to turn out a light. You won't find a light switch on the entire planet. You may not believe this, but I was shocked silly a few years ago when I heard about light switches. The idea had never occurred to me. See what a provincial I am?"

That didn't sound like her. I searched her face for clues to what had brought on such a statement, but I could find nothing. She was sitting in front of the campfire with Malibu on her lap, preening her feathers.

I gestured at the fire, which was a beautifully executed holo of snapping, crackling logs with a heater concealed in the center of it.

"Isn't that an uncharacteristic touch? Why didn't you bring a fancy house like the ones in town?"

"I like the fire. I don't like phony houses."

"Why not?"

She shrugged. She was thinking of other things. I tried another tack.

"Does your mother mind you going into the desert with strangers?"

She shot me a look I couldn't read.

"How should I know? I don't live with her. I'm emancipated. I think she's in Venusburg." I had obviously touched a tender area, so I went cautiously.

"Personality conflicts?"

She shrugged again, not wanting to get into it.

"No. Well, yes, in a way. She wouldn't emigrate from Venus. I wanted to leave and she wanted to stay. Our interests didn't coincide. So we went our own ways. I'm working my way toward passage off-planet."

"How close are you?"

"Closer than you might think." She seemed to be weighing something in her mind, sizing me up. I could hear the gears grind and the cash register bells cling as she studied my face. Then I felt the charm start up again, like the flicking of one of those nonexistent light switches.

"See, I'm as close as I've ever been to getting off Venus. In a few weeks, I'll be there. As soon as we get back with some blast jewels. Because you're going to adopt me."

I think I was getting used to her. I wasn't rocked by that, though it was nothing like what I had expected to hear. I had been thinking vaguely along the lines of blast jewels. She picks some up along with me, sells them and buys a ticket off-planet, right?

That was silly, of course. She didn't need *me* to get blast jewels. She was the guide, not I, and it was her cycle. She could get as many jewels as she wanted, and probably already had. This scheme had to have something to do with me, personally, as I had known back in town and forgotten about. There was something she wanted from me.

"That's why you had to go with me? That's the fatal attraction? I don't understand."

"Your passport. I'm in love with your passport. On the blank labeled 'citizenship' it says 'Mars.' Under age it says, oh . . . about seventy-three." She was within a year, though I keep my appearance at about thirty.

"So?"

"So, my dear Kiku, you are visiting a planet which is groping its way into the stone age. A medieval planet, Mr. Kiku, that sets the age of majority at thirteen—a capricious and arbitrary figure, as I'm sure you'll agree. The laws of this planet state that certain rights of free citizens are withheld from minor citizens. Among these are liberty, the pursuit of happiness and the ability *to get out of the goddamn place!*" She startled me with her fury, coming so hard on the heels of her usual amusing glibness. Her fists were clenched. Malibu, sitting in her lap, looked sadly up at his friend, then over to me.

She quickly brightened and bounced up to prepare dinner. She would not respond to my questions. The subject was closed for the day.

I was ready to turn back the next day. Have you ever had stiff legs? Probably not; if you go in for that sort of thing—heavy physical labor—you are probably one of those health nuts and keep yourself in shape. I wasn't in shape, and I thought I'd die. For a panicky moment I thought I *was* dying.

Luckily, Ember had anticipated it. She knew I was a desk jockey, and she knew how pitifully underconditioned Martians tend to be. Added to the sedentary lifestyles of most modern people, we Martians come off even worse than the majority because Mars's gravity never gives us much of a challenge no matter how hard we try. My leg muscles were like soft noodles.

She gave me an old-fashioned massage and a new-fangled injection that killed off the accumulated poisons. In an hour I began to take a flickering interest in the trip. So she loaded me onto the cycle and we started off on another leg of the journey.

There's no way to measure the passage of time. The sun gets flatter and wider, but it's much too slow to see. Sometime that day we passed a tributary of the Reynolds-wrap River. It showed up as a bright line in my right eye, as a crusted, sluggish semi-glacier in my left. Molten aluminum, I was told. Malibu knew what it was and barked plaintively for us to stop so he could go for a slide. Ember wouldn't let him.

You can't get lost on Venus, not if you can still see. The river had been visible since we left Prosperity, though I hadn't known what it was. We could still see the town behind us and the mountain range in front of us and even the desert. It was a little way up the slope of the bowl. Ember said that meant it was still about three days' journey away from us. It takes practice to judge distance. Ember kept trying to point out Venusburg, which was several thousand kilometers behind us. She said it was easily visible as a tiny point on a clear day. I never spotted it.

We talked a lot as we pedaled. There was nothing else to do and, besides, she was fun to talk to. She told me more of her plan for getting off Venus and filled my head with her naive ideas of what other planets were like.

It was a subtle selling campaign. We started off with her being the advocate for her crazy plan. At some point it evolved into an assumption. She took it as settled that I would adopt her and take her to Mars with me. I half believed it myself.

On the fourth day I began to notice that the bowl was getting higher in front of us. I didn't know what was causing it until Ember called a halt and we hung there in the air. We were facing a solid line of rock that sloped gradually upward to a point about fifty meters higher than we were.

"What's the matter?" I asked, glad of the rest.

"The mountains are higher," she said matter-of-factly. "Let's turn to the right and see if we can find a pass."

"Higher? What are you talking about?"

"Higher. You know, taller, sticking up more than they did the last time I was around, of slightly greater magnitude in elevation, bigger than . . ."

"I know the definition of higher," I said. "But why? Are you sure?"

"Of course I'm sure. The air heater for the balloon is going flat-out; we're as high as we can go. The last time I came through here, it was plenty to get me across. But not today."

"Why?"

"Condensation. The topography can vary quite a bit here. Certain metals and rocks are molten on Venus. They boil off on a hot day, and they can condense on the mountaintops where it's cooler. Then they melt when it warms up and flow back to the valleys."

"You mean you brought me here in the middle of winter?"

She threw me a withering glance.

"You're the one who booked passage for winter. Besides, it's night, and it's not even midnight yet. I hadn't thought the mountains would be this high for another week."

"Can't we get around?"

She surveyed the slope critically.

"There's a permanent pass about five hundred kilometers to the east. But that would take us another week. Do you want to?"

"What's the alternative?"

"Parking the cycle here and going on foot. The desert is just over this range. With any luck we'll see our first jewels today."

I was realizing that I knew far too little about Venus to make a good decision. I had finally admitted to myself that I was lucky to have Ember along to keep me out of trouble.

"We'll do what you think best."

"All right. Turn hard left and we'll park."

We tethered the cycle by a long tungsten-alloy rope. The reason for that, I learned, was to prevent it from being buried in case there was more condensation while we were gone. It floated at the end of the cable with its heaters going full blast. And we started up the mountain.

Fifty meters doesn't sound like much. And it's not, on level ground. Try it sometime on a seventy-five-degree slope. Luckily for us, Ember had seen this possibility and come prepared with Alpine equipment. She sank pitons here and there and kept us together with ropes and pulleys. I followed her lead, staying slightly behind her tagalong. It was uncanny how that thing followed her up, placing its feet in precisely the spots she had stepped. Behind me, my tagalong was doing the same thing. Then there was Malibu, almost running along, racing back to see how we were doing, going to the top and chattering about what was on the other side.

I don't suppose it would have been much for a mountain climber. Personally I'd have preferred to slide on down the mountainside and call it quits. I would have, but Ember just kept going up. I don't think I've ever been so tired as the moment when we reached the top and stood looking over the desert.

Ember pointed ahead of us.

"There's one of the jewels going off now," she said.

"Where?" I asked, barely interested. I could see nothing.

"You missed it. It's down lower. They don't form up this high. Don't worry, you'll see more by and by."

And down we went. This wasn't too hard. Ember set the example by sitting down in a smooth place and letting go. Malibu was close behind her, squealing happily as he bounced and rolled down the slippery rock face. I saw Ember hit a bump and go flying in the air to come down on her head. Her suit was already stiffened. She continued to bounce her way down, frozen in a sitting position.

I followed them down in the same way. I didn't much care for the idea of bouncing around like that, but I cared even less for a slow, painful descent. It wasn't too bad. You don't feel much after your suit freezes in impact mode. It expands slightly away from your skin and becomes harder than metal, cushioning you from anything but the most severe blows that could bounce your brain against your skull and give you internal injuries. We never got going nearly fast enough for that.

Ember helped me up at the bottom after my suit unfroze. She looked like she had enjoyed the ride. I hadn't. One bounce seemed to have impacted my back slightly. I didn't tell her about it but just started off after her, feeling a pain with each step.

"Where on Mars do you live?" she asked brightly.

"Uh? Oh, at Coprates. That's on the northern slope of the canyon."

"Yes, I know. Tell me more about it. Where will we live? Do you have a surface apartment, or are you stuck down in the underground? I can hardly wait to see the place."

She was getting on my nerves. Maybe it was just the lower-back pain.

"What makes you think you're going with me?"

"But of course you're taking me back. You said, just . . ."

"I said nothing of the sort. If I had a recorder I could prove it to you. No, our conversations over the last days have been a series of monologues. You tell me what fun you're going to have when we get to Mars, and I just grunt something. That's because I haven't the heart, or haven't *had* the heart, to tell you what a hare-brained scheme you're talking about."

I think I had finally managed to drive a barb into her. At any rate, she didn't say anything for a while. She was realizing that she had overextended herself and was counting the spoils before the battle was won.

"What's hare-brained about it?" she said at last.

"Just everything."

"No, come on, tell me."

"What makes you think I want a daughter?"

She seemed relieved. "Oh, don't worry about that. I won't be any trouble. As soon as we land, you can file dissolution papers. I won't contest it. In fact, I can sign a binding agreement not to contest anything before you even adopt me. This is strictly a business arrangement, Kiku. You don't have to worry about being a mother to me. I don't need one. I'll . . ."

"What makes you think it's just a business arrangement to *me?*" I exploded. "Maybe I'm old-fashioned. Maybe I've got funny ideas. But I won't enter into an adoption of convenience. I've already had my one child, and I was a good parent. I won't adopt you just to get you to Mars. That's my final word."

She was studying my face. I think she decided I meant it.

"I can offer you twenty thousand marks."

I swallowed hard.

"Where did you get that kind of money?"

"I told you I've been soaking the good people of Prosperity. What the hell is there for me to spend it on out here? I've been putting it away for an emergency like this. Up against an unfeeling Neanderthal with funny ideas about right and wrong, who . . ."

"That's enough of that." I'm ashamed to say that I was tempted. It's unpleasant to find that what you had thought of as moral scruples suddenly seem not quite so important in the face of a stack of money. But I was helped along by my backache and the nasty mood it had given me.

"You think you can buy me. Well, I'm not for sale. I told you, I think it's wrong."

"Well *damn* you, Kiku, damn you to hell." She stomped her foot hard on the ground, and her tagalong redoubled the gesture. She was going to go on damning me, but we were blasted by an explosion as her foot hit the ground.

It had been quiet before, as I said. There's no wind, no animals, hardly anything to make a sound on Venus. But when a sound gets going, watch out. That thick atmosphere is murder. I thought my head was going to come off. The sound waves battered against our suits, partially stiffening them. The only thing that saved us from deafness was the millimeter of low-pressure air between the suit field and our eardrums. It cushioned the shock enough that we were left with just a ringing in our ears.

"What was that?" I asked.

Ember sat down on the ground. She hung her head, uninterested in anything but her own disappointment.

"Blast jewel," she said. "Over that way." She pointed, and I could see a dull glowing spot about a kilometer off. There were dozens of smaller points of light —infralight—scattered around the spot.

"You mean you set it off just by stomping the ground?"

She shrugged. "They're unstable. They're full of nitroglycerine, as near as anyone can figure."

"Well, let's go pick up the pieces."

"Go ahead." She was going limp on me. And she stayed that way, no matter how I cajoled her. By the time I finally got her on her feet, the glowing spots were gone, cooled off. We'd never find them now. She wouldn't talk to me as we continued down into the valley. All the rest of the day we were accompanied by distant gunshots.

We didn't talk much the next day. She tried several times to reopen the negotiations, but I made it clear that my mind was made up. I pointed out to her that I had rented her cycle and services according to the terms she had set. Absolutely free, she had said, except for consumables, which I had paid for. There had been no mention of adoption. If there had, I assured her, I would have turned her down just as I was doing now. Maybe I even believed it.

That was during the short time the morning after our argument when it seemed like she was having no more to do with the trip. She just sat there in the tent while I made breakfast. When it came time to go, she pouted and said she wasn't going looking for blast jewels, that she'd just as soon stay right there or turn around.

After I pointed out our verbal contract, she reluctantly got up. She didn't like it, but honored her word.

Hunting blast jewels proved to be a big anticlimax. I'd had visions of scouring the countryside for days. Then the exciting moment of finding one. Eureka! I'd have howled. The reality was nothing like that. Here's how you hunt blast jewels: you stomp down hard on the ground, wait a few seconds, then move on and stomp again. When you see and hear an explosion, you simply walk to where it occurred and pick them up. They're scattered all over, lit up in the infrared bands from the heat of the explosion. They might as well have had neon arrows flashing over them. Big adventure.

When we found one, we'd pick it up and pop it into a cooler mounted on our tagalongs. They are formed by the pressure of the explosion, but certain parts of them are volatile at Venus temperatures. These elements will boil out and leave you with a grayish powder in about three hours if you don't cool them down. I don't know why they lasted as long as they did. They were considerably hotter than the air when we picked them up. So I thought they should have melted right off.

Ember said it was the impaction of the crystalline lattice that gave the jewels the temporary strength to outlast the temperature. Things behave differently in the temperature and pressure extremes of Venus. As they cooled off, the lattice was weakened and a progressive decay set in. That's why it was important to get them as soon as possible after the explosion to get unflawed gems.

We spent the whole day at that. Eventually we collected about ten kilos of gems, ranging from pea size up to a few the size of an apple.

I sat beside the campfire and examined them that night. Night by my watch, anyway. Another thing I was beginning to miss was the twenty-five-hour cycle of night and day. And while I was at it, moons. It would have cheered me up considerably to spot Diemos or Phobos that night. But the sun just squatted up there in the horizon, moving slowly to the north in preparation for its transition to the morning sky.

The jewels were beautiful, I'll say that much for them. They were a wine-red color, tinged with brown. But when the light caught them right, there was no predicting what I might see. Most of the raw gems were coated with a dull substance that hid their full glory. I experimented with chipping some of them. What was left behind when I flaked off the patina was a slippery surface that sparkled even in candlelight. Ember showed me how to suspend them from a string and strike them. Then they would ring like tiny bells, and every once in a while one would shed all its imperfections and emerge as a perfect eight-sided equilateral.

I was cooking for myself that day. Ember had cooked from the first, but she no longer seemed interested in buttering me up.

"I hired on as a guide," she pointed out, with considerable venom. "Webster's defines guide as . . ."

"I know what a guide is."

"And it says nothing about cooking. Will you marry me?"

"No." I wasn't even surprised.

"Same reasons?"

"Yes. I won't enter into an agreement like that lightly. Besides, you're too young."

"Legal age is twelve. I'll be twelve in one week."

"That's too young. On Mars you must be fourteen."

"What a dogmatist. You're not kidding, are you? Is it really fourteen?"

That's typical of her lack of knowledge of the place she was trying so hard to get to. I don't know where she got her ideas about Mars. I finally concluded that she made them up whole in her daydreams.

We ate the meal I prepared in silence, toying with our collection of jewels. I estimated that I had about a thousand marks' worth of uncut stones. And I was getting tired of the Venusian bush. I figured on spending another day collecting, then heading back for the cycle. It would probably be a relief for both of us. Ember could start laying traps for the next stupid tourist to reach town, or even head for Venusburg and try in earnest.

When I thought of that, I wondered why she was still out here. If she had the money to pay the tremendous bribe she had offered me, why wasn't she in town where the tourists were as thick as flies? I was going to ask her that. But she came up to me and sat down very close.

"Would you like to make love?" she asked.

I'd had about enough inducements. I snorted, got up and walked through the wall of the tent.

Once outside, I regretted it. My back was hurting something terrible, and I belatedly realized that my inflatable mattress would not go through the wall of the tent. If I got it through somehow, it would only burn up. But I couldn't back out after walking like that. I felt committed. Maybe I couldn't think straight because of the backache; I don't know. Anyway, I picked out a soft-looking spot of ground and lay down.

I can't say it was all that soft.

I came awake in the haze of pain. I knew, without trying, that if I moved I'd get a knife in my back. Naturally I wasn't anxious to try.

My arm was lying on something soft. I moved my head—confirming my suspicions about the knife—and saw that it was Ember. She was asleep, lying on her back. Malibu was curled up in her arm.

She was a silver-plated doll, with her mouth open and a look of relaxed vulnerability on her face. I felt a smile growing on my lips, just like the ones she had coaxed out of me back in Prosperity. I wondered why I'd been treating her so badly. At least it seemed to me that morning that I'd been treating her badly. Sure, she'd used me and tricked me and seemed to want to use me again. But what had she hurt? Who was suffering for it? I couldn't think of anyone at the moment. I resolved to apologize to her when she woke up and try to start over again. Maybe we could even reach some sort of accommodation on this adoption business.

And while I was at it, maybe I could unbend enough to ask her to take a look at my back. I hadn't even mentioned it to her, probably for fear of getting deeper in her debt. I was sure she wouldn't have taken payment for it in cash. She preferred flesh.

I was about to awaken her, but I happened to glance on my other side. There was something there. I almost didn't recognize it for what it was.

It was three meters away, growing from the cleft of two rocks. It was globular, half a meter across and glowing a dull reddish color. It looked like a soft gelatin.

It was a blast jewel, before the blast.

I was afraid to talk, then remembered that talking would not affect the atmosphere around me and could not set off the explosion. I had a radio transmitter in my throat and a receiver in my ear. That's how you talk on Venus: you subvocalize and people can hear you.

Moving very carefully, I reached over and gently touched Ember on the shoulder.

She came awake quietly, stretched and started to get up.

"Don't move," I said, in what I hoped was a whisper. It's hard to do when you're subvocalizing, but I wanted to impress on her that something was wrong.

She came alert, but didn't move.

"Look over to your right. Move very slowly. Don't scrape against the ground or anything. I don't know what to do."

She looked, said nothing.

"You're not alone, Kiku," she finally whispered. "This is one I never heard of."

"How did it happen?"

"It must have formed during the night. No one knows much about how they form or how long it takes. No one's ever been closer than about five hundred meters to one. They always explode before you can get that close. Even the vibrations from the prop of a cycle will set them off before you can get close enough to see them."

"So what do we do?"

She looked at me. It's hard to read expressions on a reflective face, but I think she was scared. I know I was.

"I'd say sit tight."

"How dangerous is this?"

"Brother. I don't know. There's going to be quite a bang when that monster goes off. Our suits will protect us from most of it. But it's going to lift us and accelerate us *very* fast. That kind of sharp acceleration can mess up your insides. I'd say a concussion at the very least."

I gulped. "Then . . ."

"Just sit tight. I'm thinking."

So was I. I was frozen there with a hot knife somewhere in my back. I knew I'd have to squirm sometime.

The damn thing was moving.

I blinked, afraid to rub my eyes, and looked again. No, it wasn't. Not on the outside anyway. It was more like the movement you can see inside a living cell beneath a microscope. Internal flows, exchanges of fluids from here to there. I watched it and was hypnotized.

There were worlds in the jewel. There was ancient Barsoom of my childhood fairy tales; there was Middle Earth with brooding castles and sentient forests. The jewel was a window into something unimaginable, a place where there were no questions and no emotions but a vast awareness. It was dark and wet without menace. It was growing and yet complete as it came into being. It was bigger than this ball of hot mud called Venus and had its roots down in the core of the planet. There was no corner of the universe that it did not reach.

It was aware of me. I felt it touch me and felt no surprise. It examined me in passing but was totally uninterested. I posed no questions for it, whatever it was. It already knew me and had always known me.

I felt an overpowering attraction. The thing was exerting no influence on me; the attraction was a yearning within me. I was reaching for a completion that the jewel possessed and I knew I could never have. Life would always be a series of mysteries for me. For the jewel, there was nothing but awareness. Awareness of everything.

I wrenched my eyes away at the last possible instant. I was covered in sweat, and I knew I'd look back in a moment. It was the most beautiful thing I will ever see.

"Kiku, listen to me."

"What?" I remembered Ember as from a huge distance.

"Listen. Wake up. Don't look at that thing."

"Ember, do you see anything? Do you feel something?"

"I see something. I . . . I don't want to talk about it. I can't talk about it. Wake up, Kiku, and don't look back."

I felt as if I were already a pillar of salt; so why not look back? I knew that my life would never be quite what it had been. It was like some sort of involuntary religious conversion, as though I knew what the universe was for all of a sudden. The universe was a beautiful silk-lined box for the display of the jewel I had just beheld.

"Kiku, that thing should already have gone off. We shouldn't be here. I moved when I woke up. I tried to sneak up on one before and got five hundred meters away from it. I set my foot down soft enough to walk on water, and it blew. So this thing can't be here."

"That's nice," I said. "How do we cope with the fact that it *is* here?"

"All right, all right, it is here. But it must not be finished. It must not have enough nitro in it yet to blow up. Maybe we can get away."

I looked back at it, then away again. It was as if my eyes were welded to it with elastic bands; they'd stretch enough to let me turn away, but they kept pulling me back.

"I'm not sure I want to."

"I know," she whispered. "I . . . hold on, don't look back. We have to get away."

"Listen," I said, looking at her with an act of will. "Maybe one of us can get away. Maybe both. But it's more important that you not be injured. If I'm hurt, you can maybe fix me up. If you're hurt, you'll probably die, and if we're both hurt, we're dead."

"Yeah. So?"

"So, I'm closer to the jewel. You can start backing away from it first, and I'll follow you. I'll shield you from the worst of the blast, if it goes off. How does that sound?"

"Not too good." But she thought it over and could see no flaws in my reasoning. I think she didn't relish being the protected instead of the heroine. Childish, but natural. She proved her maturity by bowing to the inevitable.

"All right. I'll try to get ten meters from it. I'll let you know when I'm there, and you can move back. I think we can survive it at ten meters."

"Twenty."

"But . . . oh, all right. Twenty. Good luck, Kiku. I think I love you." She paused. "Uh, Kiku?"

"What is it? You should get moving. We don't know how long it'll stay stable."

"All right. But I have to say this. My offer last night, the one that got you so angry?"

"Yeah?"

"Well, it wasn't meant as a bribe. I mean, like the twenty thousand marks. I just . . . well, I don't know much about that yet. I guess it was the wrong time?"

"Yeah, but don't worry about it. Just get moving."

She did, a centimeter at a time. It was lucky that neither of us had to worry about holding our breath. I think the tension would have been unbearable.

And I looked back. I couldn't help it. I was in the sanctuary of a cosmic church when I heard her calling me. I don't know what sort of power she used to reach me where I was. She was crying.

"Kiku, please listen to me."

"Huh? Oh, what is it?"

She sobbed in relief. "Oh, Christ, I've been calling you for an hour. *Please* come on. Over here, I'm back far enough."

My head was foggy. "Oh, Ember, there's no hurry. I want to look at it just another minute. Hang on."

"No! If you don't start moving right this minute, I'm coming back and I'll drag you out."

"You can't do . . . oh, all right, I'm coming." I looked over at her sitting on her knees. Malibu was beside her. The little otter was staring in my direction. I looked at her and took a sliding step, scuttling on my back. My back was not something to think about.

I got two meters back, then three. I had to stop to rest. I looked at the jewel, then back at Ember. It was hard to tell which drew me more strongly. I must have reached a balance point. I could have gone either way.

Then a small silver streak came at me, running as fast as it could go. It reached me and dived across.

"Malibu!" Ember screamed. I turned. The otter seemed happier than I ever saw him, even in the waterslide in town. He leaped, right at the jewel . . .

Regaining consciousness was a very gradual business. There was no dividing line between different states of awareness for two reasons: I was deaf, and I was blind. So I cannot say when I went from dreams to reality; the blend was too uniform, there wasn't enough change to notice.

I don't remember learning that I was deaf and blind. I don't remember learning the hand-spelling language that Ember talked to me with. The first rational moment that I can recall as such was when Ember was telling me her plans to get back to Prosperity.

I told her to do whatever she felt best, that she was in complete control. I was desolated to realize that I was not where I had thought I was. My dreams had been of Barsoom. I thought I had become a blast jewel and had been waiting in a sort of detached ecstasy for the moment of explosion.

She operated on my left eye and managed to restore some vision. I could see things that were a meter from my face, hazily. Everything else was shadows. At least she was able to write things on sheets of paper and hold them up for me to see. It made things quicker. I learned that she was deaf, too. And Malibu was dead. Or might be. She had put him in the cooler and thought she might be able to patch him up when she got back. If not, she could always make another otter.

I told her about my back. She was shocked to hear that I had hurt it on the slide down the mountain, but she had sense enough not to scold me about it. It was short work to fix it up. Nothing but a bruised disk, she told me.

It would be tedious to describe all of our trip back. It was difficult because neither of us knew much about blindness. But I was able to adjust pretty quickly. Being led by the hand was easy enough, and I stumbled only rarely after the first day. On the second day we scaled the mountains, and my tagalong malfunctioned. Ember discarded it and we traded off with hers. We could only do it when I was sitting still, as hers was made for a much shorter person. If I tried to walk with it, it quickly fell behind and jerked me off balance.

Then it was a matter of being set on the cycle and pedaling. There was nothing to do but pedal. I missed the talking we did on the way out. I missed the blast jewel. I wondered if I'd ever adjust to life without it.

But the memory had faded when we arrived back at Prosperity. I don't think the human mind can really contain something of that magnitude. It was slipping away from me by the hour, as a dream fades away in the morning. I found it hard to remember what it was that was so great about the experience. To this day, I can't really tell about it except in riddles. I'm left with shadows. I feel like an earthworm who has been shown a sunset and has no place to store the memory.

Back in town it was a simple matter for Ember to restore our hearing. She just didn't happen to be carrying any spare eardrums in her first-aid kit.

"It was an oversight," she told me. "Looking back, it seems obvious that the most likely injury from a blast jewel would be burst eardrums. I just didn't think."

"Don't worry about it. You did beautifully."

She grinned at me. "Yes, I did, didn't I?"

The vision was a larger problem. She didn't have any spare eyes and no one in town was willing to sell one of theirs at any price. She gave me one of hers as a temporary measure. She kept her infraeye and took to wearing an eye patch over the other. It made her look bloodthirsty. She told me to buy another at Venusburg, as our blood types weren't much of a match. My body would reject it in about three weeks.

The day came for the weekly departure of the blimp to Last Chance. We were sitting in her workshop, facing each other with our legs crossed and the pile of blast jewels between us.

They looked awful. Oh, they hadn't changed. We had even polished them up until they sparkled three times as much as they had back in the firelight of our tent. But now we could see them for the rotten, yellowed, broken fragments of bone that they were. We had told no one what we had seen out in the Fahrenheit Desert. There was no way to check on it, and all our experience had been purely subjective. Nothing that would stand up in a laboratory. We were the only ones who knew their true nature. Probably we would always remain the only ones. What could we tell anyone?

"What do you think will happen?" I asked.

She looked at me keenly. "I think you already know that."

"Yeah." Whatever they were, however they survived and reproduced, the one fact we knew for sure was that they couldn't survive within a hundred kilometers of a city. Once there had been blast jewels in the very spot where we were sitting. And humans do expand. Once again, we would not know what we were destroying.

I couldn't keep the jewels. I felt like a ghoul. I tried to give them to Ember, but she wouldn't have them either.

"Shouldn't we tell someone?" Ember asked.

"Sure. Tell anyone you want. Don't expect people to start tiptoeing until you can prove something to them. Maybe not even then."

"Well, it looks like I'm going to spend a few more years tiptoeing. I find I just can't bring myself to stomp on the ground."

I was puzzled. "Why? You'll be on Mars. I don't think the vibrations will travel that far."

She stared at me. "What's this?"

There was a brief confusion; then I found myself apologizing profusely to her, and she was laughing and telling me what a dirty rat I was, then taking it back and saying I could play that kind of trick on her anytime I wanted.

It was a misunderstanding. I honestly thought I had told her about my change of heart while I was deaf and blind. It must have been a dream because she hadn't gotten it and had assumed the answer was a permanent no. She had said nothing about adoption since the explosion.

"I couldn't bring myself to pester you about it any more after what you did for me," she said, breathless with excitement. "I owe you a lot, maybe my life. And I used you badly when you first got here."

I denied it and told her I had thought she was not talking about it because she thought it was in the bag.

"When did you change your mind?" she asked.

I thought back. "At first I thought it was while you were caring for me when I was so helpless. Now I can recall when it was. It was shortly after I walked out of the tent for that last night on the ground."

She couldn't find anything to say about that. She just beamed at me. I began to wonder what sort of papers I'd be signing when we got to Venusburg: adoption, or marriage contract.

I didn't worry about it. It's uncertainties like that which make life interesting. We got up together, leaving the pile of jewels on the floor. Walking softly, we hurried out to catch the blimp.

RAY BRADBURY

Kaleidoscope

*"What's it like out there?" is a question that has occupied the minds
and dreams of human beings since time immemorial. It is also one
of the basic speculations of modern science fiction, and stories of
space travel have entranced millions of readers over the years. Here
Ray Bradbury takes us on a tragic yet beautiful journey through outer
space and reminds us that every accomplishment extracts its price.*

THE first concussion cut the ship up the side like a giant can opener. The
men were thrown into space like a dozen wriggling silverfish. They were
scattered into a dark sea; and the ship, in a million pieces, went on like a
meteor swarm seeking a lost sun.

"Barkley, Barkley, where are you?"

The sound of voices calling like lost children on a cold night.

"Woode, Woode!"

"Captain!"

"Hollis, Hollis, this is Stone."

"Stone, this is Hollis. Where are you?"

"I don't know, how can I? Which way is up? I'm falling. Good gosh, I'm
falling."

They fell. They fell as pebbles fall in the long autumns of childhood, silver
and thin. They were scattered as jackstones are scattered from a gigantic
throw. And now instead of men there were only voices—all kinds of voices.
Disembodied and impassioned, in varying degrees of terror and resignation.

"We're going away from each other."

This was true. Hollis, swinging head over heels, knew this was true. He knew
it with a vague acceptance. They were parting to go their separate ways, and
nothing could bring them back. They were wearing their sealed-tight space

suits with the glass tubes over their pale faces, but they hadn't had time to lock on their force units. With them, they could be small lifeboats in space, saving themselves, saving others, collecting together, finding each other until they were an island of men with some plan. But without the force units snapped to their shoulders they were meteors, senseless, each going to a separate and irrevocable fate.

A period of perhaps ten minutes elapsed while the first terror died and a metallic calm took its place. Space began to weave their strange voices in and out, on a great dark loom, crossing, recrossing, making a final pattern.

"Stone to Hollis. How long can we talk by phone?"

"It depends on how fast you're going your way and I'm going mine."

"An hour, I make it."

"That should do it," said Hollis, abstracted and quiet.

"What happened?" said Hollis, a minute later.

"The rocket blew up, that's all. Rockets do blow up."

"Which way are you going?"

"It looks like I'll hit the sun."

"It's Earth for me. Back to old Mother Earth at ten thousand miles per hour. I'll burn like a match." Hollis thought of it with a queer abstraction of mind. He seemed to be removed from his body, watching it fall down and down through space, as objective as he had been in regard to the first falling snowflakes of a winter season long gone.

The others were silent, thinking of the destiny that had brought them to this, falling, falling, and nothing they could do to change it. Even the captain was quiet, for there was no command or plan he knew that could put things back together again.

"Oh, it's a long way down, oh, it's a long way down, a long, long, long way down," said a voice. "I don't want to die, I don't want to die, it's a long way down."

"Who's that?"

"I don't know."

"Stimson, I think. Stimson, is that you?"

"It's a long way and I don't like it, oh God, I don't like it."

"Stimson, this is Hollis, Stimson, you hear me?"

A pause while they fell separate from one another.

"Stimson?"

"Yes," he replied at last.

"Stimson, take it easy, we're all in the same fix."

"I don't want to be here, I want to be somewhere else."

"There's a chance we'll be found."

"I must be, I must be," said Stimson. "I don't believe this, I don't believe any of this is happening."

"It's a bad dream," said someone.

"Shut up!" said Hollis.

"Come and make me," said the voice. It was Applegate. He laughed noisily, with a similar objectivity. "Come and shut me up."

Hollis for the first time felt the impossibility of his position. A great anger filled him, for he wanted more than anything in existence at this moment to be able to do something to Applegate. He had wanted for many years to do something and now it was too late. Applegate was only a telephonic voice.

Falling, falling, falling!

Now, as if they had discovered the horror, two of the men began to scream. In a nightmare, Hollis saw one of them float by, very near, screaming and screaming.

"Stop it!" The man was almost at his fingertips, screaming insanely. He would never stop. He would go on screaming for a million miles, as long as he was in radio range, disturbing all of them, making it impossible for them to talk to one another.

Hollis reached out. It was best this way. He made the extra effort and touched the man. He grasped the man's ankle and pulled himself up along the body until he reached the head. The man screamed and clawed frantically, like a drowning swimmer. The screaming filled the universe.

One way or the other, thought Hollis. The sun or Earth or meteors will kill him, so why not now?

He smashed the man's glass mask with his iron fist. The screaming stopped. He pushed off from the body and let it spin away on its own course, falling, falling.

Falling, falling down space went Hollis and the rest of them in the long, endless dropping and whirling of silent terror.

"Hollis, you still there?"

Hollis did not speak, but felt the rush of heat in his face.

"This is Applegate again."

"All right, Applegate."

"Let's talk. We haven't anything else to do."

The captain cut in. "That's enough of that. We've got to figure a way out of this."

"Captain, why don't you shut up?" said Applegate.

"What!"

"You heard me, captain. Don't pull your rank on me, you're ten thousand

miles away by now, and let's not kid ourselves. As Stimson puts it, it's a long
way down."

"See here, Applegate!"

"Can it. This is a mutiny of one. I haven't a dang thing to lose. Your ship
was a bad ship and you were a bad captain and I hope you roast when you
hit the sun."

"I'm ordering you to stop!"

"Go on, order me again!" Applegate smiled across ten thousand miles. The
captain was silent. Applegate continued, "Where were we, Hollis? Oh, yes,
I remember. I hate you, too. But you know that. You've known it for a long
time."

Hollis clenched his fists, hopelessly.

"I want to tell you something," said Applegate. "Make you happy I was the
one who blackballed you with the Rocket Company five years ago."

A meteor flashed by. Hollis looked down and his left hand was gone. Blood
spurted. Suddenly there was no air in his suit. He had enough air in his lungs
to move his right hand over and twist a knob at his left elbow, tightening the
joint and sealing the leak. It had happened so quickly that he was not surprised.
Nothing surprised him any more. The air in the suit came back to normal in
an instant now that the leak was sealed. And the blood that had flowed so
swiftly was pressured as he fastened the knob yet tighter, until it made a
tourniquet.

All of this took place in a terrible silence on his part. And the other men
chatted. That one man, Lespere, went on and on with his talk about his wife
on Mars, his wife on Venus, his wife on Jupiter, his money, his wondrous
times, his drunkenness, his gambling, his happiness. On and on, while they
all fell, fell. Lespere reminisced on the past, happy, while he fell to his death.

It was so very odd. Space, thousands of miles of space, and these voices
vibrating in the center of it. No one visible at all, and only the radio waves
quivering and trying to quicken other men into emotion.

"Are you angry, Hollis?"

"No." And he was not. The abstraction had returned and he was a thing
of dull concrete, forever falling nowhere.

"You wanted to get to the top all your life, Hollis. And I ruined it for you.
You always wondered what happened. I put the black mark on you just before
I was tossed out myself."

"That isn't important," said Hollis. And it was not. It was gone. When life
is over it is like a flicker of bright film, an instant on the screen, all of its
prejudices and passions condensed and illumined for an instant on space, and
before you could cry out. There was a happy day, there a bad one, there an

evil face, there a good one, the film burned to a cinder, the screen was dark.

From this outer edge of his life, looking back, there was only one remorse, and that was only that he wished to go on living. Did all dying people feel this way, as if they had never lived? Does life seem that short, indeed, over and down before you took a breath? Did it seem this abrupt and impossible to everyone, or only to himself, here, now with a few hours left to him for thought and deliberation?

One of the other men was talking. "Well, I had me a good life. I had a wife on Mars and one on Venus and one on Earth and one on Jupiter. Each of them had money and they treated me swell. I had a wonderful time. I got drunk and once I gambled away twenty thousand dollars."

"But you're here now," thought Hollis. "I didn't have any of those things. When I was living I was jealous of you, Lespere, when I had another day ahead of me I envied you your women and your good times. Women frightened me and I went into space, always wanting them, and jealous of you for having them, and money, and as much happiness as you could have in your own wild way. But now, falling here, with everything over, I'm not jealous of you any more, because it's over for you as it is over for me, and right now it's like it never was." Hollis craned his face forward and shouted into the telephone.

"It's all over, Lespere!"

Silence.

"It's just as if it never was, Lespere!"

"Who's that?" Lespere's faltering voice.

"This is Hollis."

He was being mean. He felt the meanness, the senseless meanness of dying. Applegate had hurt him, now he wanted to hurt another. Applegate and space had both wounded him.

"You're out here, Lespere. It's all over. It's just as if it had never happened, isn't it?"

"No."

"When anything's over, it's just like it never happened. Where's your life any better than mine, now? While it was happening, yes, but now? Now is what counts. Is it any better, is it?"

"Yes, it's better!"

"How!"

"Because I got my thoughts; I remember!" cried Lespere, far away, indignant, holding his memories to his chest with both hands.

And he was right. With a feeling of cold water gushing through his head and his body, Hollis knew he was right. There were differences between memories and dreams. He had only dreams of things he had wanted to do, while Lespere had memories of things done and accomplished. And this knowledge began to pull Hollis apart, with a slow, quivering precision.

"What good does it do you?" he cried to Lespere. "Now? When a thing's over it's not good any more. You're no better off than me."

"I'm resting easy," said Lespere. "I've had my turn. I'm not getting mean at the end, like you."

"Mean?" Hollis turned the word on his tongue. He had never been mean, as long as he could remember, in his life. He had never dared to be mean. He must have saved it all of these years for such a time as this. "Mean." He rolled the word into the back of his mind. He felt tears start in his eyes and roll down his face. Someone must have heard his gasping voice.

"Take it easy, Hollis."

It was, of course, ridiculous. Only a minute before he had been giving advice to others, to Stimson, he had felt a braveness which he had thought to be the genuine thing, and now he knew that it had been nothing but shock and the objectivity possible in shock. Now he was trying to pack a lifetime of suppressed emotion into an interval of minutes.

"I know how you feel, Hollis," said Lespere, now twenty thousand miles away, his voice fading. "I don't take it personally."

But aren't we equal, his wild mind wondered. Lespere and I? Here, now? If a good thing's over it's done, and what good is it? You die anyway. But he knew he was rationalizing, for it was like trying to tell the difference between a live man and a corpse. There was a spark in one, and not in the other, an aura, a mysterious element.

So it was with Lespere and himself; Lespere had lived a good full life, and it made him a different man now, and he, Hollis, had been as good as dead for many years. They came to death by separate paths and, in all likelihood, if there were kinds of deaths, their kinds would be as different as night from day. The quality of death, like that of life, must be of infinite variety, and if one has already died once, then what is there to look for in dying for once and all, as he was now?

It was a second later that he discovered his right foot was cut sheer away. It almost made him laugh. The air was gone from his suit again, he bent quickly, and there was blood, and the meteor had taken flesh and suit away to the ankle. Oh, death in space was most humorous, it cut you away, piece by piece, like a black and invisible butcher. He tightened the valve at the knee, his head swirling into pain, fighting to remain aware, and with the valve tightened, the blood retained, the air kept, he straightened up and went on falling, falling, for that was all there was left to do.

"Hollis?"

Hollis nodded sleepily, tired of waiting for death.

"This is Applegate again," said the voice.

"Yes."

"I've had time to think. I listened to you. This isn't good. It makes us mean. This is a bad way to die. It brings all the bile out. You listening, Hollis?"

"Yes."

"I lied. A minute ago. I lied. I didn't blackball you. I don't know why I said that. Guess I wanted to hurt you. You seemed the one to hurt. We've always fought. Guess I'm getting old fast and repenting fast. I guess listening to you be mean made me ashamed. Whatever the reason, I want you to know I was an idiot, too. There's not an ounce of truth in what I said. To heck with you."

Hollis felt his heart began to work again. It seemed as if it hadn't worked for five minutes, but now all of his limbs began to take color and warmth. The shock was over, and the successive shocks of anger and terror and loneliness were passing. He felt like a man emerging from a cold shower in the morning, ready for breakfast and a new day.

"Thanks, Applegate."

"Don't mention it. Up your nose, you slob."

"Where's Stimson, how is he?"

"Stimson?"

They listened.

No answer.

"He must be gone."

"I don't think so. Stimson!"

They listened again.

They could hear a long, slow, hard breathing in their phones.

"That's him. Listen."

"Stimson!"

No reply.

Only the slow, hard breathing.

"He won't answer."

"He's gone insane, God help him."

"That's it. Listen."

The silent breathing, the quiet.

"He's closed up like a clam. He's in himself, making a pearl. Listen to the poet, will you? He's happier than us now, anyway."

They listened to Stimson float away.

"Hey," said Stone.

"What?" Hollis called across space, for Stone, of all of them, was a good friend.

"I've got myself into a meteor swarm, some little asteroids."

"Meteors?"

"I think it's the Myrmidone cluster that goes out past Mars and in toward Earth once every five years. I'm right in the middle. It's like a big kaleidoscope. You get all kinds of colors and shapes and sizes. God, it's beautiful, all the metal."

Silence.

"I'm going with them," said Stone. "They're taking me off with them. I'll be damned." He laughed tightly.

Hollis looked to see, but saw nothing. There were only the great jewelries of space, the diamonds and sapphires and emerald mists and velvet inks of space, with God's voice mingling among the crystal fires. There was a kind of wonder and imagination in the thought of Stone going off in the meteor swarm, out past Mars for years and coming in toward Earth every five years, passing in and out of the planet's ken for the next million years, Stone and the Myrmidone cluster eternal and unending, shifting and shaping like the kaleidoscope colors when you were a child and held the long tube to the sun and gave it a twirl.

"So long, Hollis." Stone's voice, very faint now. "So long."

"Good luck," shouted Hollis across thirty thousand miles.

"Don't be funny," said Stone, and was gone.

The stars closed in.

Now all the voices were fading, each on its own trajectory, some to the sun, others into farthest space. And Hollis himself. He looked down. He, of all the others, was going back to Earth alone.

"So long."

"Take it easy."

"So long, Hollis." That was Applegate.

The many good-bys. The short farewells. And now the great loose brain was disintegrating. The components of the brain, which had worked so beautifully and efficiently in the skull case of the rocket ship racing through space, were dying off one by one, the meaning of their life together was falling apart. And as a body dies when the brain ceases functioning, so the spirit of the ship and their long time together and what they meant to one another was dying. Applegate was now no more than a finger blown from the parent body, no longer to be despised and worked against. The brain was exploded, and the senseless, useless fragments of it were far-scattered. The voices faded and now all of space was silent. Hollis was alone, falling.

They were all alone. Their voices had died like echoes of the words of God spoken and vibrating in the starred space. There went the captain to the sun;

there Stone with the meteor swarm; there Stimson, tightened and unto himself; there Applegate toward Pluto; there Smith and Turner and Underwood and all the rest, the shards of the kaleidoscope that had formed a thinking pattern for so long, now hurled apart.

And I? thought Hollis. What can I do? Is there anything I can do now to make up for a terrible and empty life? If I could do one good thing to make up for the meanness I collected all these years and didn't even know was in me? But there's no one here but myself, and how can you do good all alone? You can't. Tomorrow night I'll hit Earth's atmosphere.

I'll burn, he thought, and be scattered in ashes all over the continental lands. I'll be put to use. Just a little bit, but ashes are ashes and they'll add to the land.

He fell swiftly, like a bullet, like a pebble, like an iron weight, objective, objective all of the time now, not sad or happy or anything, but only wishing he could do a good thing now that everyone was gone, a good thing for just himself to know about.

When I hit the atmosphere, I'll burn like a meteor.

"I wonder," he said, "if anyone'll see me."

The small boy on the country road looked up and screamed. "Look, mom, look! A falling star!"

The blazing white star fell down the sky of dusk in Illinois.

"Make a wish," said his mother. "Make a wish."

KURT VONNEGUT, JR.

Unready to Wear

When first propounded in the last century, Charles Darwin's then-controversial theory of evolution by natural selection had a profound effect on society, particularly the beliefs of organized religion, for it explicitly challenged religious notions of how we got on this planet and implicitly challenged then-current assumptions about where our species was headed. The future of our kind is also the stuff of modern science fiction, as Kurt Vonnegut, Jr. shows us in this haunting story of human evolution.

I DON'T SUPPOSE the oldsters, those of us who weren't born into it, will ever feel quite at home being amphibious—amphibious in the new sense of the word. I still catch myself feeling blue about things that don't matter any more.

I can't help worrying about my business, for instance—or what used to be my business. After all, I spent thirty years building the thing up from scratch, and now the equipment is rusting and getting clogged with dirt. But even though I know it's silly of me to care what happens to the business, I borrow a body from a storage center every so often and go around the old hometown and clean and oil as much of the equipment as I can.

Of course, all in the world the equipment was good for was making money, and Lord knows there's plenty of that lying around. Not as much as there used to be, because there at first some people got frisky and threw it all around, and the wind blew it every which way. And a lot of go-getters gathered up piles of the stuff and hid it somewhere. I hate to admit it, but I gathered up close to a half million myself and stuck it away. I used to get it out and count it sometimes, but that was years ago. Right now I'd be hard put to say where it is.

But the worrying I do about my old business is bush league stuff compared to the worrying my wife, Madge, does about our old house. That thing is what

353

she herself put in thirty years on while I was building the business. Then no sooner had we gotten nerve enough to build and decorate the place than everybody we cared anything about got amphibious. Madge borrows a body once a month and dusts the place, though the only thing a house is good for now is keeping termites and mice from getting pneumonia.

Whenever it's my turn to get into a body and work as an attendant at the local storage center, I realize all over again how much tougher it is for women to get used to being amphibious.

Madge borrows bodies a lot oftener than I do, and that's true of women in general. We have to keep three times as many women's bodies in stock as men's bodies, in order to meet the demand. Every so often, it seems as though a woman just *has* to have a body and doll it up in clothes and look at herself in a mirror. And Madge, God bless her, I don't think she'll be satisfied until she's tried on every body in every storage center on Earth.

It's been a fine thing for Madge, though. I never kid her about it, because it's done so much for her personality. Her old body, to tell you the plain blunt truth, wasn't anything to get excited about, and having to haul the thing around made her gloomy a lot of the times in the old days. She couldn't help it, poor soul, any more than anybody else could help what sort of body they'd been born with, and I loved her in spite of it.

Well, after we'd learned to be amphibious, and after we'd built the storage centers and laid in body supplies and opened them to the public, Madge went hog-wild. She borrowed a platinum blonde body that had been donated by a burlesque queen, and I didn't think we'd ever get her out of it. As I say, it did wonders for her self-confidence.

I'm like most men and don't care particularly what body I get. Just the strong, good-looking, healthy bodies were put in storage, so one is as good as the next one. Sometimes, when Madge and I take bodies out together for old times' sake, I let her pick out one for me to match whatever she's got on. It's a funny thing how she always picks a blond, tall one for me.

My old body, which she claims she loved for a third of a century, had black hair, and was short and paunchy, too, there toward the last. I'm human and I couldn't help being hurt when they scrapped it after I'd left it, instead of putting it in storage. It was a good, homey, comfortable body; nothing fast and flashy, but reliable. But there isn't much call for that kind of body at the centers, I guess. I never ask for one, at any rate.

The worst experience I ever had with a body was when I was flimflammed into taking out the one that had belonged to Dr. Ellis Konigswasser. It belongs to the Amphibious Pioneers' Society and only gets taken out once a year for the big Pioneers' Day parade, on the anniversary of Konigswasser's discovery. Everybody said it was a great honor for me to be picked to get into Konigswasser's body and lead the parade.

Like a plain damn fool, I believed them.

They'll have a tough time getting me into that thing again—ever. Taking that wreck out certainly made it plain why Konigswasser discovered how people could do without their bodies. That old one of his practically *drives* you out. Ulcers, headaches, arthritis, fallen arches—a nose like a pruning hook, piggy little eyes and a complexion like a used steamer trunk. He was and still is the sweetest person you'd ever want to know, but, back when he was stuck with that body, nobody got close enough to find out.

We tried to get Konigswasser back into his old body to lead us when we first started having the Pioneers' Day parades, but he wouldn't have anything to do with it, so we always have to flatter some poor boob into taking on the job. Konigswasser marches, all right, but as a six-foot cowboy who can bend beer cans double between his thumb and middle finger.

Konigswasser is just like a kid with that body. He never gets tired of bending beer cans with it and we all have to stand around in our bodies after the parade and watch as though we were very impressed.

I don't suppose he could bend very much of anything back in the old days.

Nobody mentions it to him, since he's the grand old man of the Amphibious Age, but he plays hell with the bodies. Almost every time he takes one out, he busts it, showing off. Then somebody has to get into a surgeon's body and sew it up again.

I don't mean to be disrespectful of Konigswasser. As a matter of fact, it's a respectful thing to say that somebody is childish in certain ways because it's people like that who seem to get all the big ideas.

There is a picture of him in the old days down at the Historical Society and you can see from that that he never did grow up as far as keeping up his appearance went—doing what little he could with the rattletrap body nature had issued him.

His hair was down below his collar, he wore his pants so low that his heels wore through the legs above the cuffs and the lining of his coat hung down in festoons all around the bottom. And he'd forget meals and go out into the cold or wet without enough clothes on, and he would never notice sickness until it almost killed him. He was what we used to call absentminded. Looking back now, of course, we say he was starting to be amphibious.

Konigswasser was a mathematician, and he did all his living with his mind. The body he had to haul around with that wonderful mind was about as much use to him as a flatcar of scrap iron. Whenever he got sick and *had* to pay some attention to his body, he'd rant somewhat like this:

"The mind is the only thing about human beings that's worth anything. Why does it have to be tied to a bag of skin, blood, hair, meat, bones and tubes? No wonder people can't get anything done, stuck for life with a parasite that has to be stuffed with food and protected from weather and germs all the time. And the fool thing wears out anyway—no matter how much you stuff and protect it!

"Who," he wanted to know, "really wants one of the things? What's so wonderful about protoplasm that we've got to carry so damned many pounds of it with us wherever we go?

"Trouble with the world," said Konigswasser, "isn't too many people—it's too many bodies."

When his teeth went bad on him and he had to have them all out and he couldn't get a set of dentures that were at all comfortable, he wrote in his diary, "If living matter was able to evolve enough to get out of the ocean, which was really quite a pleasant place to live, it certainly ought to be able to take another step and get out of bodies, which are pure nuisances when you stop to think about them."

He wasn't a prude about bodies, understand, and he wasn't jealous of people who had better ones than he did. He just thought bodies were a lot more trouble than they were worth.

He didn't have great hopes that people would really evolve out of their bodies in his time. He just wished they would. Thinking hard about it, he walked through a park in his shirt-sleeves and stopped off at the zoo to watch the lions being fed. Then, when the rainstorm turned to sleet, he headed back home and was interested to see firemen on the edge of a lagoon, where they were using a pulmotor on a drowned man.

Witnesses said the old man had walked right into the water and had kept going without changing his expression until he'd disappeared. Konigswasser got a look at the victim's face and said he'd never seen a better reason for suicide. He started for home again and was almost there before he realized that that was his own body lying back there.

He went back to reoccupy the body just as the firemen got it breathing again, and he walked it home, more as a favor to the city than anything else. He walked it into his front closet, got out of it again and left it there.

He took it out only when he wanted to do some writing or turn the pages of a book, or when he had to feed it so it would have enough energy to do the few odd jobs he gave it. The rest of the time, it sat motionless in the closet, looking dazed and using almost no energy. Konigswasser told me the other day that he used to run the thing for about a dollar a week, just taking it out when he really needed it.

But the best part was that Konigswasser didn't have to sleep any more, just because *it* had to sleep; or be afraid any more, just because *it* thought it might get hurt; or go looking for things *it* seemed to think it had to have. And, when *it* didn't feel well, Konigswasser kept out of it until it felt better, and he didn't have to spend a fortune keeping the thing comfortable.

When he got his body out of the closet to write, he did a book on how to get out of one's own body, which was rejected without comment by twenty-three publishers. The twenty-fourth sold two million copies, and the book changed human life more than the invention of fire, numbers, the alphabet, agriculture, or the wheel. When somebody told Konigswasser that, he snorted that they were damning his book with faint praise. I'd say he had a point there.

By following the instructions in Konigswasser's book for about two years, almost anybody could get out of his body whenever he wanted to. The first step was to understand what a parasite and dictator the body was most of the time, then to separate what the body wanted or didn't want from what you yourself—your psyche—wanted or didn't want. Then, by concentrating on what you wanted and ignoring as much as possible what the body wanted beyond plain maintenance, you made your psyche demand its right and become self-sufficient.

That's what Konigswasser had done without realizing it, until he and his body had parted company in the park, with his psyche going to watch the lions eat and with his body wandering out of control into the lagoon.

The final trick of separation, once your psyche grew independent enough, was to start your body walking in some direction and suddenly take your psyche off in another direction. You couldn't do it standing still, for some reason—you had to walk.

At first, Madge's and my psyches were clumsy at getting along outside our bodies, like the first sea animals that got stranded on land millions of years ago and who could just waddle and squirm and gasp in the mud. But we became better at it with time because the psyche can naturally adapt so much faster than the body.

Madge and I had good reason for wanting to get out. Everybody who was crazy enough to try to get out at the first had good reasons. Madge's body was sick and wasn't going to last a lot longer. With her going in a little while, I couldn't work up enthusiasm for sticking around much longer myself. So we studied Konigswasser's book and tried to get Madge out of her body before it died. I went along with her to keep either one of us from getting lonely.

And we just barely made it—six weeks before her body went all to pieces.

That's why we get to march every year in the Pioneers' Day Parade. Not everybody does—only the first five thousand of us who turned amphibious. We were guinea pigs, without much to lose one way or another, and we were the ones who proved to the rest how pleasant and safe it was—a heck of a lot safer than taking chances in a body year in and year out.

Sooner or later, almost everybody had a good reason for giving it a try. There got to be millions and finally more than a billion of us—invisible, insubstantial, indestructible, and, by golly, true to ourselves, no trouble to anybody and not afraid of anything.

When we're not in bodies, the Amphibious Pioneers can meet on the head of a pin. When we get into bodies for the Pioneers' Day Parade, we take up over fifty thousand square feet, have to gobble more than three tons of food to get enough energy to march; and lots of us catch colds or worse and get sore because somebody's body accidentally steps on the heel of somebody else's body and get jealous because some bodies get to lead and others have to stay in ranks, and—oh, hell, I don't know what all.

I'm not crazy about the parade. With all of us there, close together in bodies —well, it brings out the worst in us, no matter how good our psyches are. Last year, for instance, Pioneers' Day was a scorcher. People couldn't help being out of sorts, stuck in sweltering, thirsty bodies for hours.

Well, one thing led to another, and the parade marshal offered to beat the daylights out of my body with his body if my body got out of step again. Naturally, being parade marshal, he had the best body that year, except for Konigswasser's cowboy, but I told him to soak his fat head, anyway. He swung, and I ditched my body right there and didn't even stick around long enough to find out if he connected. He had to haul my body back to the storage center himself.

I stopped being mad at him the minute I got out of the body. I understood, you see. Nobody but a saint could be really sympathetic or intelligent for more than a few minutes at a time in a body—or happy, either, except in short spurts. I haven't met an amphibian yet who wasn't easy to get along with and cheerful and interesting—as long as he was outside a body. And I haven't met one yet who didn't turn a little sour when he got into one.

The minute you get in, chemistry takes over—glands making you excitable or ready to fight or hungry or mad or affectionate, or—well, you never know *what's* going to happen next.

That's why I can't get sore at the enemy, the people who are against the amphibians. They never get out of their bodies and won't try to learn. They don't want anybody else to do it, either, and they'd like to make the amphibians get back into bodies and stay in them.

After the tussle I had with the parade marshal, Madge got wind of it and left *her* body right in the middle of the Ladies' Auxiliary. And the two of us, feeling full of devilment after getting shed of the bodies and the parade, went over to have a look at the enemy.

I'm never keen on going over to look at them. Madge likes to see what the women are wearing. Stuck with their bodies all the time, the enemy women change their clothes and hair and cosmetic styles a lot oftener than we do on the women's bodies in the storage centers.

I don't get much of a kick out of the fashions, and almost everything else you see and hear in enemy territory would bore a plaster statue into moving away.

Usually, the enemy is talking about old-style reproduction, which is the clumsiest, most comical, most inconvenient thing anyone could imagine, compared with what the amphibians have in that line. If they aren't talking about that, then they're talking about food, the gobs of chemicals they have to stuff into their bodies. Or they'll talk about fear, which we used to call politics—job politics, social politics, government politics.

The enemy hates that, having us able to peek in on them any time we want to, while they can't ever see us unless we get into bodies. They seem to be scared to death of us, though being scared of amphibians makes as much sense as being scared of the sunrise. They could have the whole world, except the storage centers, for all the amphibians care. But they bunch together as though we were going to come whooping out of the sky and do something terrible to them at any moment.

They've got contraptions all over the place that are supposed to detect amphibians. The gadgets aren't worth a nickel, but they seem to make the enemy feel good—like they were lined up against great forces, but keeping their nerve and doing important, clever things about it. Know-how—all the time they're patting each other about how much know-how they've got, and about how we haven't got anything by comparison. If know-how means weapons, they're dead right.

I guess there is a war on between them and us. But we never do anything about holding up our side of the war, except to keep our parade sites and our storage centers secret and to get out of bodies every time there's an air raid or the enemy fires a rocket or something.

That just makes the enemy madder because the raids and rockets and all cost plenty, and blowing up things nobody needs anyway is a poor return on the taxpayers' money. We always know what they're going to do next, and when and where, so there isn't any trick to keeping out of their way.

But they are pretty smart, considering they've got bodies to look after besides doing their thinking, so I always try to be cautious when I go over to watch them. That's why I wanted to clear out when Madge and I saw a storage center in the middle of one of their fields. We hadn't talked to anybody lately about what the enemy was up to, and the center looked awfully suspicious.

Madge was optimistic, the way she's been ever since she borrowed that burlesque queen's body, and she said the storage center was a sure sign that the enemy had seen the light, that they were getting ready to become amphibious themselves.

Well, it looked like it. There was a brand-new center, stocked with bodies and open for business, as innocent as you please. We circled it several times, and Madge's circles got smaller and smaller, as she tried to get a close look at what they had in the way of ladies' ready-to-wear.

"Let's beat it," I said.

"I'm just looking," said Madge. "No harm in looking."

Then she saw what was in the main display case, and she forgot where she was or where she'd come from.

The most striking woman's body I'd ever seen was in the case—six feet tall and built like a goddess. But that wasn't the payoff. The body had copper-colored skin, chartreuse hair and fingernails, and a gold lamé evening gown. Beside that body was the body of a blond, male giant in a pale blue field marshal's uniform, piped in scarlet and spangled with medals.

I think the enemy must have swiped the bodies in a raid on one of our outlying storage centers and padded and dyed them and dressed them up.

"Madge, come back!" I said.

The copper-colored woman with the chartreuse hair moved. A siren screamed and soldiers rushed from hiding places to grab the body Madge was in.

The center was a trap for amphibians!

The body Madge hadn't been able to resist had its ankles tied together, so Madge couldn't take the few steps she had to take if she was going to get out of it again.

The soldiers carted her off triumphantly as a prisoner of war. I got into the only body available, the fancy field marshal, to try to help her. It was a hopeless situation, because the field marshal was bait, too, with its ankles tied. The soldiers dragged me after Madge.

The cocky young major in charge of the soldiers did a jig along the shoulder of the road, he was so proud. He was the first man ever to capture an amphibian, which was really something from the enemy's point of view. They'd been at war with us for years, and spent God knows how many billions of dollars, but catching us was the first thing that made any amphibians pay much attention to them.

When we got to the town, people were leaning out of windows and waving their flags and cheering the soldiers and hissing Madge and me. Here were all the people who didn't want to be amphibious, who thought it was terrible for anybody to be amphibious—people of all colors, shapes, sizes and nationalities joined together to fight the amphibians.

It turned out that Madge and I were going to have a big trial. After being tied up every which way in jail all night, we were taken to a courtroom where television cameras stared at us.

Madge and I were worn to frazzles because neither one of us had been cooped up in a body that long since I don't know when. Just when we needed to think more than we ever had, in jail before the trial, the bodies developed hunger pains and we couldn't get them comfortable on the cots, no matter how we tried; and, of course, the bodies just had to have their eight hours sleep.

The charge against us was a capital offense on the books of the enemy—*desertion*. As far as the enemy was concerned, the amphibians had all turned yellow and run out on their bodies just when their bodies were needed to do brave and important things for humanity.

We didn't have a hope of being acquitted. The only reason there was a trial at all was that it gave them an opportunity to sound off about why they were so right and we were so wrong. The courtroom was jammed with their big brass, all looking angry and brave and noble.

"Mr. Amphibian," said the prosecutor, "you are old enough, aren't you, to remember when all men had to face up to life in their bodies, and work and fight for what they believed in?"

"I remember when the bodies were always getting into fights, and nobody seemed to know why, or how to stop it," I said politely. "The only thing everybody seemed to believe in was that they didn't like to fight."

"What would you say of a soldier who ran away in the face of fire?" he wanted to know.

"I'd say he was scared silly."

"He was helping to lose the battle, wasn't he?"

"Oh, sure." There wasn't any argument on that one.

"Isn't that what the amphibians have done—run out on the human race in the face of the battle of life?"

"Most of us are still alive, if that's what you mean," I said.

It was true. We hadn't licked death and weren't sure we wanted to, but we'd certainly lengthened life something amazing, compared to the span you could expect in a body.

"You ran out on your responsibilities!" he said.

"Like you'd run out of a burning building, sir," I said.

"Leaving everyone else to struggle on alone!"

"They can all get out the same door that we got out of. You can all get out any time you want to. All you do is figure out what you want and what your body wants, and concentrate on . . ."

The judge banged his gavel until I thought he'd split it. Here they'd burned every copy of Konigswasser's book they could find, and there I was giving a course in how to get out of a body over a whole television network.

"If you amphibians had your way," said the prosecutor, "everybody would run out on his responsibilities and let life and progress as we know them disappear completely."

"Why, sure," I agreed. "That's the point."

"Men would no longer work for what they believe in?" he challenged.

"I had a friend back in the old days who drilled holes in little square thingamajigs for seventeen years in a factory and he never did get a very clear idea of what they were for. Another one I knew grew raisins for a glassblowing company, and the raisins weren't for anybody to eat, and he never did find out why the company bought them. Things like that make me sick—now that I'm in a body, of course—and what I used to do for a living makes me even sicker."

"Then you despise human beings and everything they do," he said.

"I like them fine—better than I ever did before. I just think it's a dirty shame what they have to do to take care of their bodies. You ought to get amphibious and see how happy people can be when they don't have to worry about where their body's next meal is coming from, or how to keep it from freezing in the wintertime, or what's going to happen to them when their body wears out."

"And that, sir, means the end of ambition, the end of greatness!"

"Oh, I don't know what about that," I said. "We've got some pretty great people on our side. They'd be great in *or* out of bodies. It's the end of fear is what it is." I looked right into the lens of the nearest television camera. "And *that's* the most wonderful thing that ever happened to people."

Down came the judge's gavel again, and the brass started to shout me down. The television men turned off their cameras, and all the spectators, except for the biggest brass, were cleared out. I knew I'd really said something. All anybody would be getting on his television set now was organ music.

When the confusion died down, the judge said the trial was over and that Madge and I were guilty of desertion.

Nothing I could do could get us in any worse, so I talked back.

"Now I understand you poor fish," I said. "You couldn't get along without fear. That's the only skill you've got—how to scare yourselves and other people into doing things. That's the only fun you've got, watching people jump for fear of what you'll do to their bodies or take away from their bodies."

Madge got in her two cents' worth. "The only way you can get any response from anybody is to scare them."

"Contempt of court!" said the judge.

"The only way you can scare people is if you can keep them in their bodies," I told him.

The soldiers grabbed Madge and me and started to drag us out of the courtroom.

"This means war!" I yelled.

Everything stopped right there and the place got very quiet.

"We're already at war," said a general uneasily.

"Well, *we're* not," I answered, "but we will be, if you don't untie Madge and me this instant." I was fierce and impressive in that field marshal's body.

"You haven't any weapons," said the judge, "no know-how. Outside of bodies, amphibians are nothing."

"If you don't cut us loose by the time I count ten," I told him, "the amphibians will occupy the bodies of the whole kit and caboodle of you and march you right off the nearest cliff. The place is surrounded." That was hogwash, of course. Only one person can occupy a body at a time, but the enemy couldn't be sure of that. "One! Two! Three!"

The general swallowed, turned white, and waved his hand vaguely.

"Cut them loose," he said weakly.

The soldiers, terrified, too, were glad to do it. Madge and I were freed.

I took a couple of steps, headed my spirit in another direction, and that beautiful field marshal, medals and all, went crashing down the staircase like a grandfather clock.

I realized that Madge wasn't with me. She was still in that copper-colored body with the chartreuse hair and fingernails.

"What's more," I heard her saying, "in payment for all the trouble you've caused us, this body is to be addressed to me at New York, delivered in good condition no later than next Monday."

"Yes, ma'am," said the judge.

When we got home, the Pioneers' Day Parade was just breaking up at the local storage center, and the parade marshal got out of his body and apologized to me for acting the way he had.

"Heck, Herb," I said, "you don't need to apologize. You weren't yourself. You were parading around in a body."

That's the best part of being amphibious, next to not being afraid—people forgive you for whatever fool thing you might have done in a body.

Oh, there are drawbacks, I guess, the way there are drawbacks to everything. We still have to work off and on, maintaining the storage centers and getting food to keep the community bodies going. But that's a small drawback, and all the big drawbacks I ever heard of aren't real ones, just old-fashioned thinking by people who can't stop worrying about things they used to worry about before they turned amphibious.

As I say, the oldsters will probably never get really used to it. Every so often, I catch myself getting gloomy over what happened to the pay-toilet business it took me thirty years to build.

But the youngsters don't have any hangovers like that from the past. They don't even worry much about something happening to the storage centers, the way us oldsters do.

So I guess maybe that'll be the next step in evolution—to break clean like those first amphibians who crawled out of the mud into the sunshine, and who never did go back to the sea.

ALGIS BUDRYS

Wall of Crystal, Eye of Night

Much science fiction (like literature in general) concerns the quest, the seeking of some object or goal. But once you attain your object, you have to hold on to it. And this (in fictional form) sometimes leads to the chase, which can be even more memorable and exciting, as in this powerful and startling story.

I

Soft as the voice of a mourning dove, the telephone sounded at Rufus Sollenar's desk. Sollenar himself was standing fifty paces away, his leonine head cocked, his hands flat in his hip pockets, watching the nighted world through the crystal wall that faced out over Manhattan Island. The window was so high that some of what he saw was dimmed by low clouds hovering over the rivers. Above him were stars; below him the city was traced out in light and brimming with light. A falling star—an interplanetary rocket—streaked down toward Long Island Facility like a scratch across the soot on the doors of hell.

Sollenar's eyes took it in, but he was watching the total scene, not any particular part of it. His eyes were shining.

When he heard the telephone, he raised his left hand to his lips. "Yes?" The hand glittered with utilijem rings; the effect was that of an attempt at the sort of copper binding that was once used to reinforce the ribbing of wooden warships.

His personal receptionist's voice moved from the air near his desk to the air near his ear. Seated at the monitor board in her office, wherever in this building her office was, the receptionist told him: "Mr. Ermine says he has an appointment."

"No." Sollenar dropped his hand and returned to his panorama. When he had been twenty years younger—managing the modest optical factory that had provided the support of three generations of Sollenars—he had very much wanted to be able to stand in a place like this and feel as he imagined men felt in such circumstances. But he felt unimaginable, now.

To be here was one thing. To have almost lost the right and regained it at the last moment was another. Now he knew that not only could he be here today but that tomorrow, and tomorrow, he could still be here. He had won. His gamble had given him EmpaVid—and EmpaVid would give him all.

The city was not merely a prize set down before his eyes. It was a dynamic system he had proved he could manipulate. He and the city were one. It buoyed and sustained him; it supported him, here in the air, with stars above and light-thickened mist below.

The telephone mourned: "Mr. Ermine states he has a firm appointment."

"I've never heard of him." And the left hand's utilijems fell from Sollenar's lips again. He enjoyed such toys. He raised his right hand, sheathed in insubstantial midnight blue silk in which the silver threads of metallic wiring ran subtly toward the fingertips. He raised the hand, and touched two fingers together: music began to play behind and before him. He made contact between another combination of finger circuits, and a soft, feminine laugh came from the terrace at the other side of the room, where connecting doors had opened. He moved toward it. One layer of translucent drapery remained across the doorway, billowing lightly in the breeze from the terrace. Through it, he saw the taboret with its candle lit; the iced wine in the stand beside it; the two fragile chairs; Bess Allardyce, slender and regal, waiting in one of them —all these, through the misty curtain, like either the beginning or the end of a dream.

"Mr. Ermine reminds you the appointment was made for him at the annual business dinner of the International Association of Broadcasters in 1998."

Sollenar completed his latest step, then stopped. He frowned down at his left hand. "Is Mr. Ermine with the IAB's Special Public Relations Office?"

"Yes," the voice said after a pause.

The fingers of Sollenar's right hand shrank into a cone. The connecting door closed. The girl disappeared. The music stopped. "All right. You can tell Mr. Ermine to come up." Sollenar went to sit behind his desk.

The office door chimed. Sollenar crooked a finger of his left hand, and the door opened. With another gesture, he kindled the overhead lights near the door and sat in shadow as Mr. Ermine came in.

Ermine was dressed in rust-colored garments. His figure was spare, and his hands were empty. His face was round and soft, with long dark sideburns. His scalp was bald. He stood just inside Sollenar's office and said, "I would like some light to see you by, Mr. Sollenar."

Sollenar crooked his little finger.

The overhead lights came to soft light all over the office. The crystal wall became a mirror, with only the strongest city lights glimmering through it. "I only wanted to see you first," said Sollenar; "I thought perhaps we'd met before."

"No," Ermine said, walking across the office. "It's not likely you've ever seen me." He took a card case out of his pocket and showed Sollenar proper identification. "I'm not a very forward person."

"Please sit down," Sollenar said. "What may I do for you?"

"At the moment, Mr. Sollenar, I'm doing something for you."

Sollenar sat back in his chair. "Are you? Are you, now?" He frowned at Ermine. "When I became a party to the bylaws passed at the '98 dinner, I thought a Special Public Relations Office would make a valuable asset to the organization. Consequently, I voted for it, and for the powers it was given. But I never expected to have any personal dealings with it. I barely remembered you people had carte blanche with any IAB member."

"Well, of course, it's been awhile since '98," Ermine said. "I imagine some legends have grown up around us. Industry gossip—that sort of thing."
"Yes."

"But we don't restrict ourselves to an enforcement function, Mr. Sollenar. You haven't broken any bylaws, to our knowledge."

"Or mine. But nobody feels one hundred percent secure. Not under these circumstances." Nor did Sollenar yet relax his face into its magnificent smile. "I'm sure you've found that out."

"I have a somewhat less ambitious older brother who's with the Federal Bureau of Investigation. When I embarked on my own career, he told me I could expect everyone in the world to react like a criminal, yes," Ermine said, paying no attention to Sollenar's involuntary blink. "It's one of the complicating factors in a profession like my brother's, or mine. But I'm here to advise you, Mr. Sollenar. Only that."

"In what matter, Mr. Ermine?"

"Well, your corporation recently came into control of the patents for a new video system. I understand that this in effect makes your corporation the licensor for an extremely valuable sales and entertainment medium. Fantastically valuable."

"EmpaVid," Sollenar agreed. "Various subliminal stimuli are broadcast with and keyed to the overt subject matter. The home receiving unit contains feedback sensors which determine the viewer's reaction to these stimuli and intensify some while playing down others in order to create complete emotional rapport between the viewer and the subject matter. EmpaVid, in other words, is a system for orchestrating the viewer's emotions. The home unit is self-contained, semiportable and not significantly bulkier than the standard TV receiver. EmpaVid is compatible with standard TV receivers—except, of course, that the subject matter seems thin and vaguely unsatisfactory on a standard receiver. So the consumer shortly purchases an EV unit." It pleased Sollenar to spell out the nature of his prize.

"At a very reasonable price. Quite so, Mr. Sollenar. But you had several difficulties in finding potential licensees for this system, among the networks."

Sollenar's lips pinched out.

Mr. Ermine raised one finger. "First, there was the matter of acquiring the patents from the original inventor, who was also approached by Cortwright Burr."

"Yes, he was," Sollenar said in a completely new voice.

"Competition between Mr. Burr and yourself is long-standing and intense."

"Quite intense," Sollenar said, looking directly ahead of him at the one blank wall of the office. Burr's offices were several blocks downtown in that direction.

"Well, I have no wish to enlarge on that point, Mr. Burr being an IAB member in standing as good as yours, Mr. Sollenar. There was, in any case, a further difficulty in licensing EV, due to the very heavy cost involved in equipping broadcasting stations and network relay equipment for this sort of transmission."

"Yes, there was."

"Ultimately, however, you succeeded. You pointed out, quite rightly, that if just one station made the change, and if just a few EV receivers were put into public places within the area served by that station, normal TV outlets could not possibly compete for advertising revenue."

"Yes."

"And so your last difficulties were resolved a few days ago, when your EmpaVid Unlimited—pardon me; when EmpaVid, a subsidiary of the Sollenar Corporation—became a major stockholder in the Transworld TV Network."

"I don't understand, Mr. Ermine," Sollenar said. "Why are you recounting this? Are you trying to demonstrate the power of your knowledge? All these transactions are already matters of record in the IAB confidential files, in accordance with the bylaws."

Ermine held up another finger. "You're forgetting I'm only here to advise you. I have two things to say. They are:

"These transactions are on file with the IAB because they involve a great number of IAB members and an increasingly large amount of capital. Also, Transworld's exclusivity, under the IAB bylaws, will hold good only until thirty-three percent market saturation has been reached. If EV is as good as it looks, that will be quite soon. After that, under the bylaws, Transworld will be restrained from making effective defenses against patent infringement by competitors. Then all of the IAB's membership and much of their capital will be involved with EV. Much of that capital is already in anticipatory motion. So a highly complex structure now ultimately depends on the integrity of the Sollenar Corporation. If Sollenar stock falls in value, not just you but many IAB members will be greatly embarrassed. Which is another way of saying EV must succeed."

"I know all that! What of it? There's no risk. I've had every related patent on Earth checked. There will be no catastrophic obsolescence of the EV system."

Ermine said, "There are engineers on Mars. Martian engineers. They're a dying race, but no one knows what they can still do."

Sollenar raised his massive head.

Ermine said, "Late this evening, my office learned that Cortwright Burr has been in close consultation with the Martians for several weeks. They have made some sort of machine for him. He was on the flight that landed at the facility a few moments ago."

Sollenar's fists clenched. The lights crashed off and on, and the room wailed. From the terrace came a startled cry, and a sound of smashed glass.

Mr. Ermine nodded, excused himself, and left.

A few moments later, Mr. Ermine stepped out at the pedestrian level of the Sollenar Building. He strolled through the landscaped garden and across the frothing brook toward the central walkay down the avenue. He paused at a hedge to pluck a blossom and inhale its odor. He walked away, holding it in his naked fingers.

II

Drifting slowly on the thread of his spinneret, Rufus Sollenar came gliding down the wind above Cortwright Burr's building.

The building, like a spider, touched the ground at only the points of its legs.

It held its wide, low bulk spread like a parasol over several downtown blocks. Sollenar, manipulating the helium-filled plastic drifter far above him, steered himself with jets of compressed gas from plastic bottles in the drifter's structure.

Only Sollenar himself, in all this system, was not effectively transparent to the municipal antiplane radar. And he himself was wrapped in long, fluttering streamers of dull black, metallic sheeting. To the eye, he was amorphous and nonreflective. To electronic sensors, he was a drift of static much like a sheet of foil picked by the wind from some careless trash heap. To all of the senses of all interested parties he was hardly there at all—and, thus, in an excellent position for murder.

He fluttered against Burr's window. There was the man, crouched over his desk. What was that in his hands—a pomander?

Sollenar clipped his harness to the edges of the cornice. Swayed out against it, his sponge-soled boots pressed to the glass, he touched his left hand to the window and described a circle. He pushed; there was a thud on the carpeting in Burr's office, and now there was no barrier to Sollenar. Doubling his knees against his chest, he catapulted forward, the riot pistol in his right hand. He stumbled and fell to his knees, but the gun was up.

Burr jolted up behind his desk. The little sphere of orange-gold metal, streaked with darker bronze, its surface vermicular with encrustations, was still in his hands. "Him!" Burr cried out as Sollenar fired.

Gasping, Sollenar watched the charge strike Burr. It threw his torso backward faster than his limbs and head could follow without dangling. The choked-down pistol was nearly silent. Burr crashed backward to end, transfixed, against the wall.

Pale and sick, Sollenar moved to take the golden ball. He wondered where Shakespeare could have seen an example such as this, to know an old man could have so much blood in him.

Burr held the prize out to him. Staring with eyes distended by hydrostatic pressure, his clothing raddled and his torso grinding its broken bones, Burr stalked away from the wall and moved as if to embrace Sollenar. It was queer, but he was not dead.

Shuddering, Sollenar fired again.

Again Burr was thrown back. The ball spun from his splayed fingers as he once more marked the wall with his body.

Pomander, orange, whatever—it looked valuable.

Sollenar ran after the rolling ball. And Burr moved to intercept him, nearly faceless, hunched under a great invisible weight that slowly yielded as his back groaned.

Sollenar took a single backward step.

Burr took a step toward him. The golden ball lay in a far corner. Sollenar raised the pistol despairingly and fired again. Burr tripped backward on tiptoe, his arms like windmills, and fell atop the prize.

Tears ran down Sollenar's cheeks. He pushed one foot forward . . . and Burr, in his corner, lifted his head and began to gather his body for the effort of rising.

Sollenar retreated to the window, the pistol sledging backward against his wrist and elbow as he fired the remaining shots in the magazine.

Panting, he climbed up into the window frame and clipped the harness to his body, craning to look over his shoulder . . . as Burr—shredded, leaking blood and worse than blood—advanced across the office.

He cast off his holds on the window frame and clumsily worked the drifter controls. Far above him, volatile ballast spilled out and dispersed in the air long before it touched ground. Sollenar rose, sobbing. . . .

And Burr stood in the window, his shattered hands on the edges of the cut circle, raising his distended eyes steadily to watch Sollenar in flight across the enigmatic sky.

Where he landed, on the roof of a building in his possession, Sollenar had a disposal unit for his gun and his other trappings. He deferred for a time the question of why Burr had failed at once to die. Empty-handed, he returned uptown.

He entered his office, called and told his attorneys the exact times of departure and return and knew the question of dealing with municipal authorities was thereby resolved. That was simple enough, with no witnesses to complicate the matter. He began to wish he hadn't been so irresolute as to leave Burr without the thing he was after. Surely, if the pistol hadn't killed the man—an old man with thin limbs and spotted skin—he could have wrestled that thin-limbed, bloody old man aside—that spotted old man—and dragged himself and his prize back to the window, for all that the old man would have clung to him and clutched at his legs and fumbled for a handhold on his somber disguise of wrappings—that broken, immortal old man.

Sollenar raised his hand. The great window to the city grew opaque.

Bess Allardyce knocked softly on the door from the terrace. He would have thought she'd returned to her own apartments many hours ago. Tortuously pleased, he opened the door and smiled at her, feeling the dried tears crack on the skin of his cheeks.

He took her proffered hands. "You waited for me," he sighed. "A long time for anyone as beautiful as you to wait."

She smiled back at him. "Let's go out and look at the stars."

"Isn't it chilly?"

"I made spiced hot cider for us. We can sip it and think."

He let her draw him out onto the terrace. He leaned on the parapet, his arm around her pulsing waist, his cape drawn around both their shoulders.

"Bess, I won't ask if you'd stay with me no matter what the circumstances. But it might be a time will come when I couldn't bear to live in this city. What about that?"

"I don't know," she answered honestly.

And Cortwright Burr put his hand up over the edge of the parapet, between them.

Sollenar stared down at the straining knuckles, holding the entire weight of the man dangling against the sheer face of the building. There was a sliding, rustling noise, and the other hand came up, searched blindly for a hold and found it, hooked over the stone. The fingers tensed and rose, their tips flattening at the pressure as Burr tried to pull his head and shoulders up to the level of the parapet.

Bess breathed, "Oh, look at them! He must have torn them terribly climbing up!" Then she pulled away from Sollenar and stood staring at him, her hand to her mouth. "But he *couldn't* have climbed! We're so high!"

Sollenar beat at the hands with the heels of his palms, using the direct, trained blows he had learned at his athletic club.

Bone splintered against the stone. When the knuckles were broken the hands instantaneously disappeared, leaving only streaks behind them. Sollenar looked over the parapet. A bundle shrank from sight, silhouetted against the lights of the pedestrian level and the avenue. It contracted to a pinpoint. Then, when it reached the brook and water flew in all directions, it disappeared in a final sunburst, endowed with glory by the many lights which found momentary reflection down there.

"Bess, leave me! Leave me, please!" Rufus Sollenar cried out.

III

Rufus Sollenar paced his office, his hands held safely still in front of him, their fingers spread and rigid.

The telephone sounded, and his secretary said to him, "Mr. Solenar, you are ten minutes from being late at the TTV Executives' Ball. This is a First Class obligation."

Sollenar laughed. "I thought it was when I originally classified it."

"Are you now planning to renege, Mr. Sollenar?" the secretary inquired politely.

Certainly, Sollenar thought. He could as easily renege on the ball as a king could on his coronation.

"Burr, you scum, what have you done to me?" he asked the air, and the telephone said, "Beg pardon?"

"Tell my valet," Sollenar said. "I'm going." He dismissed the phone. His hands cupped in front of his chest. A firm grip on emptiness might be stronger than any prize in a broken hand.

Carrying in his chest something he refused to admit was terror, Sollenar made ready for the ball.

But only a few moments after the first dance set had ended, Malcolm Levier of the local TTV station executive staff looked over Sollenar's shoulder and remarked, "Oh, there's Cort Burr, dressed like a gallows bird."

Sollenar, glittering in the costume of the Medici, did not turn his head. "Is he? What would he want here?"

Levier's eyebrows arched. "He holds a little stock. He has entrée. But he's late." Levier's lips quirked. "It must have taken him some time to get that makeup on."

"Not in good taste, is it?"

"Look for yourself."

"Oh, I'll do better than that," Sollenar said. "I'll go and talk to him awhile. Excuse me, Levier." And only then did he turn around, already started on his first pace toward the man.

But Cortwright Burr was only a pasteboard imitation of himself as Sollenar had come to know him. He stood to one side of the doorway, dressed in black and crimson robes, with black leather gauntlets on his hands, carrying a staff of weathered, natural wood. His face was shadowed by a sackcloth hood, the eyes well hidden. His face was powdered gray, and some blend of livid colors hollowed his cheeks. He stood motionless as Sollenar came up to him.

As he had crossed the floor, each step regular, the eyes of bystanders had followed Sollenar, until, anticipating his course, they found Burr waiting. The noise level of the ball shrank perceptibly, for the lesser revelers who chanced to be present were sustaining it all alone. The people who really mattered here were silent and watchful.

The thought was that Burr, defeated in business, had come here in some insane reproach to his adversary, in this lugubrious, distasteful clothing. Why, he looked like a corpse. Or worse.

The question was, what would Sollenar say to him? The wish was that Burr would take himself away, back to his estates or to some other city. New York was no longer for Cortwright Burr. But what would Sollenar say to him now to drive him back to where he hadn't the grace to go willingly?

"Cortwright," Sollenar said in a voice confined to the two of them. "So your Martian immortality works."

Burr said nothing.

"You got that in addition, didn't you? You knew how I'd react. You knew you'd need protection. Paid the Martians to make you physically invulnerable? It's a good system. Very impressive. Who would have thought the Martians knew so much? But who here is going to pay attention to you now? Get out of town, Cortwright. You're past your chance. You're dead as far as these people are concerned—all you have left is your skin."

Burr reached up and surreptitiously lifted a corner of his fleshed mask. And there he was, under it. The hood retreated an inch, and the light reached his eyes; and Sollenar had been wrong, Burr had less left than he thought.

"Oh, no, no, Cortwright," Sollenar said softly. "No, you're right—I can't stand up to that."

He turned and bowed to the assembled company. "Good night!" he cried, and walked out of the ballroom.

Someone followed him down the corridor to the elevators. Sollenar did not look behind him.

"I have another appointment with you now," Ermine said at his elbow.

They reached the pedestrian level. Sollenar said: "There's a café. We can talk there."

"Too public, Mr. Sollenar. Let's simply stroll and converse." Ermine lightly took his arm and guided him along the walkway. Sollenar noticed then that Ermine was costumed so cunningly that no one could have guessed the appearance of the man.

"Very well," Sollenar said.

"Of course."

They walked together, casually. Ermine said, "Burr's driving you to your death. Is it because you tried to kill him earlier? Did you get his Martian secret?"

Sollenar shook his head.

"You didn't get it." Ermine sighed. "That's unfortunate. I'll have to take steps."

"Under the bylaws," Sollenar said, "I cry *laissez-faire.*"

Ermine looked up, his eyes twinkling. *"Laissez-faire?* Mr. Sollenar, do you have any idea how many of our members are involved in your fortunes? *They* will cry *laissez-faire*, Mr. Sollenar, but clearly you persist in dragging them down with you. No, sir, Mr. Sollenar, my office now forwards an immediate recommendation to the Technical Advisory Committee of the IAB that Mr. Burr probably has a system superior to yours and that stock in Sollenar, Incorporated, had best be disposed of."

"There's a bench," Sollenar said. "Let's sit down."

"As you wish." Ermine moved beside Sollenar to the bench, but remained standing.

"What is it, Mr. Sollenar?"

"I want your help. You advised me on what Burr had. It's still in his office building, somewhere. You have resources. We can get it."

"*Laissez-faire*, Mr. Sollenar. I visited you in an advisory capacity. I can do no more."

"For a partnership in my affairs could you do more?"

"Money?" Ermine tittered. "For me? Do you know the conditions of my employment?"

If he had thought, Sollenar would have remembered. He reached out tentatively. Ermine anticipated him.

Ermine bared his left arm and sank his teeth into it. He displayed the arm. There was no quiver of pain in voice or stance. "It's not a legend, Mr. Sollenar. It's quite true. We of our office must spend a year, after the nerve surgery, learning to walk without the feel of our feet, to handle objects without crushing them or letting them slip or damaging ourselves. Our mundane pleasures are auditory, olfactory and visual. Easily gratified at little expense. Our dreams are totally interior, Mr. Sollenar. The operation is irreversible. What would you buy for me with your money?"

"What would I buy for myself?" Sollenar's head sank down between his shoulders.

Ermine bent over him. "Your despair is your own, Mr. Sollenar. I have official business with you."

He lifted Sollenar's chin with a forefinger. "I judge physical interference to be unwarranted at this time. But matters must remain so that the IAB members involved with you can recover the value of their investments in EV. Is that perfectly clear, Mr. Sollenar? You are hereby enjoined under the bylaws, as enforced by the Special Public Relations Office." He glanced at his watch. "Notice was served at one twenty-seven, city time."

"One twenty-seven," Sollenar said. "City time." He sprang to his feet and raced down a companionway to the taxi level.

Mr. Ermine watched him quizzically.

He opened his costume, took out his omnipresent medical kit and sprayed coagulant over the wound in his forearm. Replacing the kit, he adjusted his clothing and strolled down the same companionway Sollenar had run. He raised an arm, and a taxi flittered down beside him. He showed the driver a card, and the cab lifted off with him, its lights glaring in a priority pattern, far faster than Sollenar's ordinary legal limit allowed.

IV

Long Island Facility vaulted at the stars in great kangaroo leaps of arch and cantilever span, jeweled in glass and metal as if the entire port were a mechanism for navigating interplanetary space. Rufus Sollenar paced its esplanades, measuring his steps, holding his arms still, for the short time until he could board the Mars rocket.

Erect and majestic, he took a place in the lounge and carefully sipped liqueur, once the liner had boosted away from Earth and coupled in its Faraday main drives.

Mr. Ermine settled into the place beside him.

Sollenar looked over at him calmly. "I thought so."

Ermine nodded. "Of course you did. But I didn't almost miss you. I was here ahead of you. I have no objection to your going to Mars, Mr. Sollenar. *Laissez-faire.* Provided I can go along."

"Well," Rufus Sollenar said. "Liqueur?" He gestured with his glass.

Ermine shook his head. "No, thank you," he said delicately.

Sollenar said, "Even your tongue?"

"Of course my tongue, Mr. Sollenar. I taste nothing, I touch nothing." Ermine smiled. "But I feel no pressure."

"All right, then," Rufus Sollenar said crisply. "We have several hours to landing time. You sit and dream your interior dreams, and I'll dream mine." He faced around in his chair and folded his arms across his chest.

"Mr. Sollenar," Ermine said gently.

"Yes?"

"I am once again with you by appointment as provided under the bylaws."

"State your business, Mr. Ermine."

"You are not permitted to lie in an unknown grave, Mr. Sollenar. Insurance policies on your life have been taken out at a high premium rate. The IAB members concerned cannot wait the statutory seven years to have you declared dead. Do what you will, Mr. Sollenar, but I must take care I witness your death. From now on, I am with you wherever you go."

Sollenar smiled. "I don't intend to die. Why should I die, Mr. Ermine?"

"I have no idea, Mr. Sollenar. But I know Cortwright Burr's character. And isn't that he, seated there in the corner? The light is poor, but I think he's recognizable."

Across the lounge, Burr raised his head and looked into Sollenar's eyes. He raised a hand near his face, perhaps merely to signify greeting. Rufus Sollenar faced front.

"A worthy opponent, Mr. Sollenar," Ermine said. "A persevering, unforgiving, ingenious man. And yet . . ." Ermine seemed a little touched by bafflement. "And yet it seems to me, Mr. Sollenar, that he got you running rather easily. What *did* happen between you, after my advisory call?"

Sollenar turned a terrible smile on Ermine. "I shot him to pieces. If you'd peel his face, you'd see."

Ermine sighed. "Up to this moment, I had thought perhaps you might still salvage your affairs."

"Pity, Mr. Ermine? Pity for the insane?"

"Interest. I can take no part in your world. Be grateful, Mr. Sollenar. I am not the same gullible man I was when I signed my contract with IAB so many years ago."

Sollenar laughed. Then he stole a glance at Burr's corner.

The ship came down at Abernathy Field in Aresia, the terrestrial city. Industrialized, prefabricated, jerry-built and clamorous, the storm-proofed buildings huddled, but huddled proudly, at the desert's edge.

Low on the horizon was the Martian settlement—the buildings so skillfully blended with the landscape, so eroded, so much abandoned that the uninformed eye saw nothing. Sollenar had been to Mars—on a tour. He had seen the natives in their nameless dwelling place; arrogant, venomous and weak. He had been told, by the paid guide, that they trafficked with Earthmen as much as they cared to and kept to their place on the rim of Earth's encroachment, observing.

"Tell me, Ermine," Sollenar said quietly as they walked across the terminal lobby. "You're to kill me, aren't you, if I try to go on without you?"

"A matter of procedure, Mr. Sollenar," Ermine said evenly. "We cannot risk the investment capital of so many IAB members."

Sollenar sighed. "If I were any other member, how I would commend you, Mr. Ermine! Can we hire a car for ourselves, then, somewhere nearby?"

"Going out to see the engineers?" Ermine asked. "Who would have thought they'd have something valuable for sale?"

"I want to show them something," Sollenar said.

"What thing, Mr. Sollenar?"

They turned the corner of a corridor with branching hallways here and there, not all of them busy. "Come here," Sollenar said, nodding toward one of them.

They stopped out of sight of the lobby and the main corridor. "Come on," Sollenar said. "A little farther."

"No," Ermine said. "This is farther than I really wish. It's dark here."

"Wise too late, Mr. Ermine," Sollenar said, his arms flashing out.

One palm impacted against Ermine's solar plexus and the other against the muscle at the side of his neck, but not hard enough to kill. Ermine collapsed, starved for oxygen, while Sollenar silently cursed having been cured of murder. Then Sollenar turned and ran.

Behind him Ermine's body struggled to draw breath by reflex alone.

Moving as fast as he dared, Sollenar walked back and reached the taxi lock, pulling a respirator from a wall rack as he went. He flagged a car and gave his destination, looking behind him. He had seen nothing of Cortwright Burr since setting foot on Mars. But he knew that, soon or late, Burr would find him.

A few moments later Ermine got to his feet. Sollenar's car was well away. Ermine shrugged and went to the local broadcasting station.

He commandeered a private desk, a firearm and immediate time on the IAB interoffice circuit to Earth. When his call acknowledgment had come back to him from his office there, he reported:

"Sollenar is en route to the Martian city. He wants a duplicate of Burr's device, of course, since he smashed the original when he killed Burr. I'll follow and make final disposition. The disorientation I reported previously is progressing rapidly. Almost all his responses now are inappropriate. On the flight out, he seemed to be staring at something in an empty seat. Quite often when spoken to he obviously hears something else entirely. I expect to catch one of the next few flights back."

There was no point in waiting for comment to wend its way back from Earth. Ermine left. He went to a cab rank and paid the exorbitant fee for transportation outside Aresian city limits.

Close at hand, the Martian city was like a welter of broken pots. Shards of wall and roof joined at savage angles and pointed to nothing. Underfoot, drifts of vitreous material, shaped to fit no sane configuration and broken to fit such a mosaic as no church would contain, rocked and slid under Sollenar's hurrying feet.

What from Aresia had been a solid front of dun color was here a façade of red, green and blue splashed about centuries ago and since then weathered only enough to show how bitter the colors had once been. The plum-colored sky stretched over all this like a frigid membrane, and the wind blew and blew.

Here and there, as he progressed, Sollenar saw Martian arms and heads protruding from the rubble. Sculptures.

He was moving toward the heart of the city, where some few unbroken structures persisted. At the top of a heap of shards he turned to look behind him. There was the dust plume of his cab, returning to the city. He expected to walk back—perhaps to meet someone on the road, all alone on the Martian plain if only Ermine would forebear from interfering. Searching the flat, thin-aired landscape, he tried to pick out the plodding dot of Cortwright Burr. But not yet.

He turned and ran down the untrustworthy slope.

He reached the edge of the maintained area. Here the rubble was gone, the ancient walks swept, the statues kept upright on their pediments. But only broken walls suggested the fronts of the houses that had stood here. Knifing their sides up through the wind-rippled sand that only constant care kept off the street, the shadow houses fenced his way and the sculptures were motionless as hope. Ahead of him, he saw the buildings of the engineers. There was no heap to climb and look to see if Ermine followed close behind.

Sucking his respirator, he reached the building of the Martian engineers.

A sounding strip ran down the doorjamb. He scratched his fingernails sharply along it and the magnified vibration, ducted throughout the hollow walls, rattled his plea for entrance.

V

The door opened, and Martians stood looking. They were splendidly limbed and slight, their faces framed by folds of leathery tissue. Their mouths were lipped with horn as hard as dentures and pursed, forever ready to masticate. They were pleasant neither to look at nor, Sollenar knew, to deal with. But Cortwright Burr had done it. And Sollenar needed to do it.

"Does anyone here speak English?" he asked.

"I," said the central Martian, his mouth opening to the sound, closing to end the reply.

"I would like to deal with you."

"Whenever," the Martian said, and the group at the doorway parted deliberately to let Sollenar in.

Before the door closed behind him, Sollenar looked back. But the rubble of the abandoned sectors blocked his line of sight into the desert.

"What can you offer? And what do you want?" the Martian asked. Sollenar stood half-ringed by them, in a room whose corners he could not see in the uncertain light.

"I offer you terrestrial currency."

The English-speaking Martian—the Martian who had admitted to speaking English—turned his head slightly and spoke to his fellows. There were clacking sounds as his lips met. The others reacted variously, one of them suddenly gesturing with what seemed a disgusted flip of his arm before he turned without further word and stalked away, his shoulders looking like the shawled back of a very old and very hungry woman.

"What did Burr give you?" Sollenar asked.

"Burr." The Martian cocked his head. His eyes were not multifaceted, but gave that impression.

"He was here and he dealt with you. Not long ago. On what basis?"

"Burr. Yes. Burr gave us currency. We will take currency from you. For the same thing we gave him?"

"For immortality, yes."

"Im . . . This is a new word."

"Is it? For the secret of not dying?"

"Not dying? You think we have not-dying for sale here?" The Martian spoke to the others again. Their lips clattered. Others left, like the first one had, moving with great precision and very slow step and no remaining tolerance for Sollenar.

Sollenar cried out, "What did you sell him, then?"

The principal engineer said, "We made an entertainment device for him."

"A little thing. This size." Sollenar cupped his hands.

"You have seen it, then."

"Yes. And nothing more? That was all he bought here?"

"It was all we had to sell—or give. We don't yet know whether Earthmen will give us things in exchange for currency. We'll see, when we next need something from Aresia."

Sollenar demanded, "How did it work? This thing you sold him."

"Oh, it lets people tell stories to themselves."

Sollenar looked closely at the Martian. "What kind of stories?"

"Any kind," the Martian said blandly. "Burr told us what he wanted. He had drawings with him of an Earthman device that used pictures on a screen and broadcast sounds to carry the details of the story told to the auditor."

"He stole those patents! He couldn't have used them on Earth."

"And why should he? Our device needs to convey no precise details. Any mind can make its own. It only needs to be put into a situation, and from there it can do all the work. If an auditor wishes a story of contact with other sexes, for example, the projector simply makes it seem to him, the next time he is with the object of his desire, that he is getting positive feedback—that he is arousing a similar response in that object. Once that has been established for him, the auditor may then leave the machine, move about normally, conduct his life as usual—but always in accordance with the basic situation. It is, you see, in the end a means of introducing system into his view of reality. Of course, his society must understand that he is not in accord with reality, for some of what he does cannot seem rational from an outside view of him. So some care must be taken, but not much. If many such devices were to enter his society, soon the circumstances would become commonplace, and the society would surely readjust to allow for it," said the English-speaking Martian.

"The machine creates any desired situation in the auditor's mind?"

"Certainly. There are simple predisposing tapes that can be inserted as desired. Love, adventure, cerebration—it makes no difference."

Several of the bystanders clacked sounds out to each other. Sollenar looked at them narrowly. It was obvious there had to be more than one English speaker among these people.

"And the device you gave Burr," he asked the engineer, neither calmly nor hopefully, "what sort of stories could its auditors tell themselves?"

The Martian cocked his head again. It gave him the look of an owl at a bedroom window. "Oh, there was one situation we were particularly instructed to include. Burr said he was thinking ahead to showing it to an acquaintance of his.

"It was a situation of adventure, of adventure with the fearful. And it was to end in loss and bitterness." The Martian looked even more closely at Sollenar. "Of course, the device does not specify details. No one but the auditor can know what fearful thing inhabits his story or precisely how the end of it would come. You would, I believe, be Rufus Sollenar? Burr spoke of you and made the noise of laughing."

Sollenar opened his mouth. But there was nothing to say.

"You want such a device?" the Martian asked. "We've prepared several since Burr left. He spoke of machines that would manufacture them in astronomical numbers. We, of course, have done our best with our poor hands."

Sollenar said: "I would like to look out your door."

"Pleasure."

Sollenar opened the door slightly. Mr. Ermine stood in the cleared street, motionless as the shadow buildings behind him. He raised one hand in a gesture of unfelt greeting as he saw Sollenar, then put it back on the stock of his rifle. Sollenar closed the door and turned to the Martian. "How much currency do you want?"

"Oh, all you have with you. You people always have a good deal with you when you travel."

Sollenar plunged his hands into his pockets and pulled out his billfold, his change, his keys, his jeweled radio; whatever was there, he rummaged out onto the floor, listening to the sound of rolling coins.

"I wish I had more here," he laughed. "I wish I had the amount that man out there is going to recover when he shoots me."

The Martian engineer cocked his head. "But your dream is over, Mr. Sollenar," he clacked dryly. "Isn't it?"

"Quite so. But you to your purposes and I to mine. Now give me one of those projectors. And set it to predispose a situation I am about to specify to you. Take however long it needs. The audience is a patient one." He laughed, and tears gathered in his eyes.

Mr. Ermine waited, isolated from the cold, listening to hear whether the rifle stock was slipping out of his fingers. He had no desire to go into the Martian building after Sollenar and involve third parties. All he wanted was to put Sollenar's body under a dated marker with as little trouble as possible.

Now and then he walked a few paces backward and forward, to keep from losing muscular control at his extremities because of low skin temperature. Sollenar must come out soon enough. He had no food supply with him, and though Ermine did not like the risk of engaging a man like Sollenar in a starvation contest, there was no doubt that a man with no taste for fuel could outlast one with the acquired reflexes of eating.

The door opened and Sollenar came out.

He was carrying something. Perhaps a weapon. Ermine let him come closer while he raised and carefully sighted his rifle. Sollenar might have some Martian weapon or he might not. Ermine did not particularly care. If Ermine died, he would hardly notice it—far less than he would notice a botched ending to a job of work already roiled by Sollenar's breakaway at the space field. If Ermine died, some other SPRO agent would be assigned almost immediately. No matter what happened, SPRO would stop Sollenar before he ever reached Abernathy Field.

So there was plenty of time to aim an unhurried, clean shot.

Sollenar was closer, now. He seemed to be in a very agitated frame of mind. He held out whatever he had in his hand.

It was another one of the Martian entertainment machines. Sollenar seemed to be offering it as a token to Ermine. Ermine smiled.

"What can you offer me, Mr. Sollenar?" he said, and shot.

The golden ball rolled away over the sand. "There, now," Ermine said. *"Now,* wouldn't you sooner be me than you? And where is the thing that made the difference between us?"

He shivered. He was chilly. Sand was blowing against his tender face, which had been somewhat abraded during his long wait.

He stopped, transfixed.

He lifted his head.

Then, with a great swing of his arms, he sent the rifle whirling away. "The wind!" he sighed into the thin air. "I feel the wind." He leapt into the air, and sand flew away from his feet as he landed. He whispered to himself, "I feel the ground!"

He stared in tremblant joy at Sollenar's empty body. "What have you given me?" Full of his own rebirth, he swung his head up at the sky again and cried in the direction of the sun, "Oh, you squeezing, nibbling people who made me incorruptible and thought that was the end of me!"

With love he buried Sollenar, and with reverence he put up the marker, but he had plans for what he might accomplish with the facts of this transaction and the myriad others he was privy to.

A sharp bit of pottery had penetrated the sole of his shoe and gashed his foot, but he, not having seen it, hadn't felt it. Nor would he see it or feel it even when he changed his stockings; for he had not noticed the wound when it was made. It didn't matter. In a few days it would heal, though not as rapidly as if it had been properly attended to.

Vaguely, he heard the sound of Martians clacking behind their closed door as he hurried out of the city, full of revenge and reverence for his savior.

FREDERIK POHL

Day Million

*"Day Million" is a story about love and the sexual relationships that
are a part of love between men and women. But this is also a science
fiction story, and the sex in the text is* different. *For one thing, the
lovers can live apart because they can "use" programmed memories
and stimuli to experience sexual acts. And for another thing—well,
read on. Mr. Pohl has written one of the most effective stories of
rapid social change that you will ever come across.*

On this day I want to tell you about, which will be about ten thousand years
from now, there were a boy, a girl and a love story.

Now, although I haven't said much so far, none of it is true. The boy was
not what you and I would normally think of as a boy, because he was a hundred
and eighty-seven years old. Nor was the girl a girl, for other reasons. And the
love story did not entail that sublimation of the urge to rape, and concurrent
postponement of the instinct to submit, which we at present understand in
such matters. You won't care much for this story if you don't grasp these facts
at once. If, however, you will make the effort you'll likely enough find it
jam-packed, chock-full and tiptop-crammed with laughter, tears and poignant
sentiment which may, or may not, be worthwhile. The reason the girl was not
a girl was that she was a boy.

How angrily you recoil from the page! You say, who the hell wants to read
about a pair of queers? Calm yourself. Here are no hot-breathing secrets of
perversion for the coterie trade. In fact, if you were to see this girl you would
not guess that she was in any sense a boy. Breasts, two; reproductive organs,
female. Hips, callipygean; face hairless, supraorbital lobes nonexistent. You
would term her female on sight, although it is true that you might wonder just
what species she was a female of, being confused by the tail, the silky pelt and
the gill slits behind each ear.

Now you recoil again. Cripes, man, take my word for it. This is a sweet kid, and if you, as a normal male, spent as much as an hour in a room with her you would bend heaven and Earth to get her in the sack. Dora—we will call her that; her "name" was omicron-Dibase seven-group-totter-oot S Doradus 5314, the last part of which is a color specification corresponding to a shade of green—Dora, I say, was feminine, charming and cute. I admit she doesn't sound that way. She was, as you might put it, a dancer. Her art involved qualities of intellection and expertise of a very high order, requiring both tremendous natural capacities and endless practice; it was performed in null gravity and I can best describe it by saying that it was something like the performance of a contortionist and something like classical ballet, maybe resembling Danilova's dying swan. It was also pretty damned sexy. In a symbolic way, to be sure; but face it, most of the things we call "sexy" are symbolic, you know, except perhaps an exhibitionist's open clothing. On Day Million when Dora danced, the people who saw her panted, and you would too.

About this business of her being a boy. It didn't matter to her audiences that genetically she was a male. It wouldn't matter to you, if you were among them, because you wouldn't know it—not unless you took a biopsy cutting of her flesh and put it under an electron microscope to find the XY chromosome —and it didn't matter to them because they didn't care. Through techniques which are not only complex but haven't yet been discovered, these people were able to determine a great deal about the aptitudes and easements of babies quite a long time before they were born—at about the second horizon of cell division, to be exact, when the segmenting egg is becoming a free blastocyst —and then they naturally helped those aptitudes along. Wouldn't we? If we find a child with an aptitude for music we give him a scholarship to Juilliard. If they found a child whose aptitudes were for being a woman, they made him one. As sex had long been dissociated from reproduction this was relatively easy to do and caused no trouble, and no, or at least very little, comment.

How much is "very little"? Oh, about as much as would be caused by our own tampering with divine will by filling a tooth. Less than would be caused by wearing a hearing aid. Does it still sound awful? Then look closely at the next busty babe you meet and reflect that she may be a Dora, for adults who are genetically male but somatically female are far from unknown even in our own time. An accident of environment in the womb overwhelms the blueprints of heredity. The difference is that with us it happens only by accident and we don't know about it except rarely, after close study; whereas the people of Day Million did it often, on purpose, because they wanted to.

Well, that's enough to tell you about Dora. It would only confuse you to add that she was seven feet tall and smelled of peanut butter. Let us begin our story.

On Day Million, Dora swam out of her house, entered a transportation tube, was sucked briskly to the surface in its flow of water and ejected in its plume of spray to an elastic platform in front of her—ah—call it her rehearsal hall. "Oh, hell!" she cried in pretty confusion, reaching out to catch her balance and finding herself tumbled against a total stranger, whom we will call Don.

They met cute. Don was on his way to have his legs renewed. Love was the farthest thing from his mind. But when, absentmindedly taking a shortcut across the landing platform for submarinites and finding himself drenched, he discovered his arms full of the loveliest girl he had ever seen, he knew at once they were meant for each other. "Will you marry me?" he asked. She said softly, "Wednesday," and the promise was like a caress.

Don was tall, muscular, bronze and exciting. His name was no more Don than Dora's was Dora, but the personal part of it was Adonis in tribute to his vibrant maleness, and so we will call him Don for short. His personality color code, in angstrom units, was 5290, or only a few degrees bluer than Dora's 5314—a measure of what they had intuitively discovered at first sight: that they possessed many affinities of taste and interest.

I despair of telling you exactly what it was that Don did for a living—I don't mean for the sake of making money, I mean for the sake of giving purpose and meaning to his life, to keep him from going off his nut with boredom— except to say that it involved a lot of traveling. He traveled in interstellar spaceships. In order to make a spaceship go really fast, about thirty-one male and seven genetically female human beings had to do certain things, and Don was one of the thirty-one. Actually, he contemplated options. This involved a lot of exposure to radiation flux—not so much from his own station in the propulsive system as in the spillover from the next stage, where a genetic female preferred selections, and the subnuclear particles making the selections she preferred demolished themselves in a shower of quanta. Well, you don't give a rat's ass for that, but it meant that Don had to be clad at all times in a skin of light, resilient, extremely strong copper-colored metal. I have already mentioned this, but you probably thought I meant he was sunburned.

More than that, he was a cybernetic man. Most of his ruder parts had been long since replaced with mechanisms of vastly more permanence and use. A cadmium centrifuge, not a heart, pumped his blood. His lungs moved only when he wanted to speak out loud, for a cascade of osmotic filters rebreathed oxygen out of his own wastes. In a way, he probably would have looked peculiar to a man from the twentieth century, with his glowing eyes and seven-fingered hands. But to himself, and of course to Dora, he looked mighty manly and grand. In the course of his voyages Don had circled Proxima Centauri, Procyon and the puzzling worlds of Mira Ceti; he had carried agricultural templates to the planets of Canopus and brought back warm, witty pets from the pale companion of Aldebaran. Blue-hot or red-cool, he had seen a thousand stars and their ten thousand planets. He had, in fact, been traveling the star lanes, with only brief leaves on Earth, for pushing two centuries. But you don't care about that, either. It is people who make stories, not the circumstances they find themselves in, and you want to hear about these two people. Well, they made it. The great thing they had for each other grew and flowered and burst into fruition on Wednesday, just as Dora had promised. They met at the encoding room, with a couple of well-wishing friends apiece to cheer them on, and while their identities were being taped and stored they smiled and whispered to each other and bore the jokes of their friends with blushing repartee. Then they exchanged their mathematical analogues and went away, Dora to her dwelling beneath the surface of the sea and Don to his ship.

It was an idyll, really. They lived happily ever after—or anyway, until they decided not to bother any more and died.

Of course, they never set eyes on each other again.

Oh, I can see you now, you eaters of charcoal-broiled steak, scratching an incipient bunion with one hand and holding this story with the other, while the stereo plays d'Indy or Monk. You don't believe a word of it, do you? Not for one minute. People wouldn't live like that, you say with a grunt as you get up to put fresh ice in a drink.

And yet there's Dora, hurrying back through the flushing commuter pipes toward her underwater home (she prefers it there; has had herself somatically altered to breathe the stuff). If I tell you with what sweet fulfillment she fits the recorded analogue of Don into the symbol manipulator, hooks herself in and turns herself on . . . if I try to tell you any of that you will simply stare. Or glare; and grumble, what the hell kind of love-making is this? And yet I assure you, friend, I really do assure you that Dora's ecstasies are as creamy and passionate as any of James Bond's lady spies', and one hell of a lot more so than anything you are going to find in "real life." Go ahead, glare and grumble. Dora doesn't care. If she thinks of you at all, her thirty-times-great-great-grandfather, she thinks you're a pretty primordial sort of brute. You are. Why, Dora is farther removed from you than you are from the australopithecines of five thousand centuries ago. You could not swim a second in the strong currents of her life. You don't think progress goes in a straight line, do you? Do you recognize that it is an ascending, accelerating, maybe even exponential curve? It takes hell's own time to get started, but when it goes it goes like a bomb. And you, you Scotch-drinking steak eater in your relaxacizing chair, you've just barely lighted the primacord of the fuse. What is it now, the six or seven hundred thousandth day after Christ? Dora lives in Day Million. Ten thousand years from now. Her body fats are polyunsaturated, like Crisco. Her wastes are hemodialyzed out of her bloodstream while she sleeps—that means she doesn't have to go to the bathroom. On whim to pass a slow half-hour, she can command more energy than the entire nation of Portugal can spend today, and use it to launch a weekend satellite or remold a crater on the moon. She loves Don very much. She keeps his every gesture, mannerism, nuance, touch of hand, thrill of intercourse, passion of kiss stored in symbolic-mathematical form. And when she wants him, all she has to do is turn the machine on and she has him.

And Don, of course, has Dora. Adrift on a sponson city a few hundred yards over her head, or orbiting Arcturus fifty light-years away, Don has only to command his own symbol-manipulator to rescue Dora from the ferrite files and bring her to life for him, and there she is; and rapturously, tirelessly they love all night. Not in the flesh, of course; but then his flesh has been extensively altered and it wouldn't really be much fun. He doesn't need the flesh for pleasure. Genital organs feel nothing. Neither do hands or breasts, or lips; they are only receptors, accepting and transmitting impulses. It is the brain that feels; it is the interpretation of those impulses that make agony or orgasm, and Don's symbol-manipulator gives him the analogue of cuddling, the analogue of kissing, the analogue of wild, ardent hours with the eternal, exquisite and incorruptible analogue of Dora. Or Diane. Or sweet Rose, or laughing Alicia; for to be sure, they have each of them exchanged analogues before, and will again.

Rats, you say, it looks crazy to me. And you—with your after-shave lotion and your little red car, pushing papers across a desk all day and chasing tail all night—tell me, just how the hell do you think you would look to Tiglath-Pileser, say, or Attila the Hun?

ALFRED BESTER
Hobson's Choice

Alienation is a common theme in all areas of literature, including science fiction. The treatment of this theme can take many forms, but usually ends up being rather depressing. Here Alfred Bester presents an alienated man with a very serious problem, but that does not prevent the story from being quite humorous when viewed from afar.

This is a warning to accomplices like you, me and Addyer.

Can you spare price of one cup coffee, honorable sir? I am indigent organism which are hungering.

By day, Addyer was a statistician. He concerned himself with such matters as statistical tables, averages and dispersions, groups that are not homogeneous and random sampling. At night, Addyer plunged into an elaborate escape fantasy divided into two parts. Either he imagined himself moved back in time a hundred years with a double armful of the *Encyclopaedia Britannica*, best-sellers, hit plays and gambling records; or else he imagined himself transported forward in time a thousand years to the Golden Age of perfection.

There were other fantasies which Addyer entertained on odd Thursdays, such as (by a fluke) becoming the only man left on earth with a world of passionate beauties to fecundate; such as acquiring the power of invisibility which would enable him to rob banks and right wrongs with impunity; such as possessing the mysterious power of working miracles.

Up to this point you and I and Addyer are identical. Where we part company is in the fact that Addyer was a statistician.

Can you spare cost of one cup coffee, honorable miss? For blessed charitability? I am beholden.

On Monday, Addyer rushed into his chief's office, waving a sheaf of papers. "Look here, Mr. Grande," Addyer sputtered. "I've found something fishy. Extremely fishy . . . In the statistical sense, that is."

"Oh, hell," Grande answered. "You're not supposed to be finding anything. We're in between statistics until the war's over."

"I was leafing through the Interior Department's reports. D'you know our population's up?"

"Not after the atom bomb it isn't," said Grande. "We've lost double what our birthrate can replace." He pointed out the window to the twenty-five-foot stub of the Washington Monument. "There's your documentation."

"But our population's up 3.0915 percent." Addyer displayed his figures. "What about that, Mr. Grande?"

"Must be a mistake somewhere," Grande muttered after a moment's inspection. "You'd better check."

"Yes, sir," said Addyer scurrying out of the office. "I knew you'd be interested, sir. You're the ideal statistician, sir." He was gone.

"Poop," said Grande and once again began computing the quantity of bored respirations left to him. It was his personalized anesthesia.

On Tuesday, Addyer discovered that there was no correlation between the mortality/birthrate ratio and the population increase. The war was multiplying mortality and reducing births; yet the population was minutely increasing. Addyer displayed his discovery to Grande, received a pat on the back and went home to a new fantasy in which he woke up a million years in the future, learned the answer to the enigma and decided to remain amid snow-capped mountains and snow-capped bosoms, safe under the aegis of a culture saner than Aureomycin.

On Wednesday, Addyer requisitioned the comptometer and file and ran a test check on Washington, D.C. To his dismay he discovered that the population of the former capital was down 0.0029 percent. This was distressing, and Addyer went home to escape into a dream about Queen Victoria's Golden Age where he amazed and confounded the world with his brilliant output of novels, plays and poetry, all cribbed from Shaw, Galsworthy and Wilde.

Can you spare price of one coffee, honorable sir? I am distressed individual needful of chariting.

On Thursday, Addyer tried another check, this time on the city of Philadelphia. He discovered that Philadelphia's population was up 0.0959 percent. Very encouraging. He tried a rundown on Little Rock. Population up 1.1329 percent. He tested St. Louis. Population up 2.0924 percent . . . and this despite the complete extinction of Jefferson County owing to one of those military mistakes of an excessive nature.

"My God!" Addyer exclaimed, trembling with excitement. "The closer I get to the center of the country, the greater the increase. But it was the center of the country that took the heaviest punishment in the buz-raid. What's the answer?"

That night he shuttled back and forth between the future and the past in his ferment, and he was down at the shop by 7 A.M. He put a twenty-four-hour claim on the compo and files. He followed up his hunch and he came up with a fantastic discovery which he graphed in approved form. On the map of the remains of the United States he drew concentric circles in colors illustrating the areas of population increase. The red, orange, yellow, green and blue circles formed a perfect target around Finney County, Kansas.

"Mr. Grande," Addyer shouted in a high statistical passion, "Finney County has got to explain this."

"You go out there and get that explanation," Grande replied, and Addyer departed.

"Poop," muttered Grande and began integrating his pulse rate with his eye-blink.

Can you spare price of one coffee, dearly madam? I am starveling organism requiring nutritiousment.

Now, travel in those days was hazardous. Addyer took ship to Charleston (there were no rail connections remaining in the North Atlantic states) and was wrecked off Hatteras by a rogue mine. He drifted in the icy waters for seventeen hours, muttering through his teeth: "Oh, Christ! If only I'd been born a hundred years ago."

Apparently this form of prayer was potent. He was picked up by a navy sweeper and shipped to Charleston where he arrived just in time to acquire a subcritical radiation burn from a raid which fortunately left the railroad unharmed. He was treated for the burn from Charleston to Macon (change) from Birmingham to Memphis (bubonic plague) to Little Rock (polluted water) to Tulsa (fallout quarantine) to Kansas City (the O.K. Bus Co. Accepts No Liability for Lives Lost through Acts of War) to Lyonesse, Finney County, Kansas.

And there he was in Finney County with its great magma pits and scars and radiation streaks; whole farms blackened and razed; whole highways so blasted they looked like dotted lines; whole population 4-F. Clouds of soot and fallout neutralizers hung over Finney County by day, turning it into a Pittsburgh on a still afternoon. Auras of radiation glowed at night, highlighted by the blinking red warning beacons, turning the county into one of those overexposed night photographs, all blurred and cross-hatched by deadly slashes of light.

After a restless night in the Lyonesse Hotel, Addyer went over to the county seat for a check on their birth records. He was armed with the proper credentials, but the county seat was not armed with the statistics. That excessive military mistake again. It had extinguished the seat.

A little annoyed, Addyer marched off to the County Medical Association office. His idea was to poll the local doctors on births. There was an office and one attendant who had been a practical nurse. He informed Addyer that Finney County had lost its last doctor to the army eight months previous. Midwives might be the answer to the birth enigma but there was no record of midwives. Addyer would simply have to canvass from door to door, asking if any lady within practiced that ancient profession.

Further piqued, Addyer returned to the Lyonesse Hotel and wrote on a slip of tissue paper: HAVING DATA DIFFICULTIES. WILL REPORT AS SOON AS INFORMATION AVAILABLE. He slipped the message into an aluminum capsule, attached it to his sole surviving carrier pigeon and dispatched it to Washington with a prayer. Then he sat down at his window and brooded.

He was aroused by a curious sight. In the street below, the O.K. Bus Co. had just arrived from Kansas City. The old coach wheezed to a stop, opened its door with some difficulty and permitted a one-legged farmer to emerge. His burned face was freshly bandaged. Evidently this was a well-to-do burgess who could afford to travel for medical treatment. The bus backed up for the return trip to Kansas City and honked a warning horn. That was when the curious sight began.

From nowhere . . . absolutely nowhere . . . a horde of people appeared. They skipped from back alleys, from behind rubble piles; they popped out of stores, they filled the street. They were all jolly, healthy, brisk, happy. They laughed and chatted as they climbed into the bus. They looked like hikers and tourists, carrying knapsacks, carpetbags, box lunches and even babies. In two minutes the bus was filled. It lurched off down the road, and as it disappeared Addyer heard happy singing break out and echo from the walls of rubble.

"I'll be damned," he said.

He hadn't heard spontaneous singing in over two years. He hadn't seen a carefree smile in over three years. He felt like a color-blind man who was seeing the full spectrum for the first time. It was uncanny. It was also a little blasphemous.

"Don't those people know there's a war on?" he asked himself.

And a little later: "They looked too healthy. Why aren't they in uniform?"

And last of all: "Who *were* they anyway?"

That night Addyer's fantasy was confused.

> *Can you spare price of one cup coffee, kindly sir? I am estrangered and faintly from hungering.*

The next morning Addyer arose early, hired a car at an exorbitant fee, found he could not buy any fuel at any price and ultimately settled for a lame horse. He was allergic to horse dander and suffered asthmatic tortures as he began his house-to-house canvass. He was discouraged when he returned to the Lyonesse Hotel that afternoon. He was just in time to witness the departure of the O.K. Bus Co.

Once again a horde of happy people appeared and boarded the bus. Once again the bus hirpled off down the broken road. Once again the joyous singing broke out.

"I *will* be damned," Addyer wheezed.

He dropped into the county surveyor's office for a large-scale map of Finney County. It was his intent to plot the midwife coverage in accepted statistical manner. There was a little difficulty with the surveyor who was deaf, blind in one eye and spectacleless in the other. He could not read Addyer's credentials with any faculty or facility. As Addyer finally departed with the map, he said to himself, "I think the old idiot thought I was a spy."

And later he muttered, "Spies?"

And just before bedtime: "Holy Moses! Maybe *that's* the answer to *them.* "

That night he was Lincoln's secret agent, anticipating Lee's every move, outwitting Jackson, Johnston and Beauregard, foiling John Wilkes Booth, and being elected President of the United States by 1968.

The next day the O.K. Bus Co. carried off yet another load of happy people.

And the next.

And the next.

"Four hundred tourists in five days," Addyer computed. "The country's filled with espionage."

He began loafing around the streets trying to investigate these joyous travelers. It was difficult. They were elusive before the bus arrived. They had a friendly way of refusing to pass the time. The locals of Lyonesse knew nothing about them and were not interested. Nobody was interested in much more than painful survival these days. That was what made the singing obscene.

After seven days of cloak-and-dagger and seven days of counting, Addyer suddenly did the big take. "It adds up," he said. "Eighty people a day leaving Lyonesse. Five hundred a week. Twenty-five thousand a year. Maybe that's the answer to the population increase." He spent fifty-five dollars on a telegram to Grande with no more than a hope of delivery. The telegram read: "EUREKA. I HAVE FOUND (IT)."

Can you spare price of lone cup coffee, honorable madam? I am not tramp-handler but destitute life form.

Addyer's opportunity came the next day. The O.K. Bus Co. pulled in as usual. Another crowd assembled to board the bus, but this time there were too many. Three people were refused passage. They weren't in the least annoyed. They stepped back, waved energetically as the bus started, shouted instructions for future reunions and then quietly turned and started off down the street.

Addyer was out of his hotel room like a shot. He followed the trio down the main street, turned left after them onto Fourth Avenue, passed the ruined schoolhouse, passed the demolished telephone building, passed the gutted library, railroad station, Protestant church, Catholic church . . . and finally reached the outskirts of Lyonesse and then open country.

Here he had to be more cautious. It was difficult stalking the spies with so much of the dusky road illuminated by warning lights. He wasn't suicidal enough to think of hiding in radiation pits. He hung back in an agony of indecision and was at last relieved to see them turn off the broken road and enter the old Baker farmhouse.

"Ah-ha!" said Addyer.

He sat down at the edge of the road on the remnants of a missile and asked himself: "Ah-ha what?" He could not answer, but he knew where to find the answer. He waited until dusk deepened to darkness and then slowly wormed his way forward toward the farmhouse.

It was while he was creeping between the deadly radiation glows and only occasionally butting his head against grave markers that he first became aware of two figures in the night. They were in the barnyard of the Baker place and were performing most peculiarly. One was tall and thin. A man. He stood stock-still, like a lighthouse. Upon occasion he took a slow, stately step with infinite caution and waved an arm in slow motion to the other figure. The second was also a man. He was stocky and trotted jerkily back and forth.

As Addyer approached, he heard the tall man say: "Rooo booo fooo mooo hwaaa looo fooo."

Whereupon the trotter chattered, "Wd-nk-kd-ik-md-pd-ld-nk."

Then they both laughed: the tall man like a locomotive, the trotter like a chipmunk. They turned. The trotter rocketed into the house. The tall man drifted in. And that was amazingly that.

"Oh-ho," said Addyer.

At that moment a pair of hands seized him and lifted him from the ground. Addyer's heart constricted. He had time for one convulsive spasm before something vague was pressed against his face. As he lost consciousness his last idiotic thought was of telescopes.

Can you spare price of solitary coffee for no-loafing unfortunate, honorable sir? Charity will blessings.

When Addyer awoke he was lying on a couch in a small whitewashed room. A gray-haired gentleman with heavy features was seated at a desk alongside the couch, busily ciphering on bits of paper. The desk was cluttered with what appeared to be intricate timetables. There was a small radio perched on one side.

"L-Listen . . ." Addyer began faintly.

"Just a minute, Mr. Addyer," the gentleman said pleasantly. He fiddled with the radio. A glow germinated in the middle of the room over a circular copper plate and coalesced into a girl. She was extremely nude and extremely attractive. She scurried to the desk, patted the gentleman's head with the speed of a pneumatic hammer. She laughed and chattered, "Wd-nk-tk-ik-lt-nk."

The gray-haired man smiled and pointed to the door. "Go outside and walk it off," he said. She turned and streaked through the door.

"It has something to do with temporal rates," the gentleman said to Addyer. "I don't understand it. When they come forward they've got accumulated momentum." He began ciphering again. "Why in the world did you have to come snooping, Mr. Addyer?"

"You're spies," Addyer said. "She was talking Chinese."

"Hardly. I'd say it was French. Early French. Middle fifteenth century."

"Middle fifteenth century!" Addyer exclaimed.

"That's what I'd say. You begin to acquire an ear for those stepped-up tempos. Just a minute, please."

He switched the radio on again. Another glow appeared and solidified into a nude man. He was stout, hairy and lugubrious. With exasperating slowness he said, "Mooo fooo blooo wawww hawww pooo."

The gray-haired man pointed to the door. The stout man departed in slow motion.

"The way I see it," the gray-haired man continued conversationally, "when they come back they're swimming against the time current. That slows 'em down. When they come forward, they're swimming with the current. That speeds 'em up. Of course, in any case it doesn't last longer than a few minutes. It wears off."

"What?" Addyer said. "Time travel?"

"Yes. Of course."

"That thing . . ." Addyer pointed to the radio. "A time machine?"

"That's the idea. Roughly."

"But it's too small."

The gray-haired man laughed.

"What is this place anyway? What are you up to?"

"It's a funny thing," the gray-haired man said. "Everybody used to speculate about time travel. How it would be used for exploration, archaeology, historical and social research and so on. Nobody ever guessed what the real use would be. . . . Therapy."

"Therapy? You mean medical therapy?"

"That's right. Psychological therapy for the misfits who won't respond to any other cure. We let them emigrate. Escape. We've set up stations every quarter century. Stations like this."

"I don't understand."

"This is an immigration office."

"Oh, my God!" Addyer shot up from the couch. "Then you're the answer to the population increase. Yes? That's how I happened to notice it. Mortality's up so high and birth's down so low these days that your time-addition becomes significant. Yes?"

"Yes, Mr. Addyer."

"Thousands of you coming here. From where?"

"From the future, of course. Time travel wasn't developed until C/H 127. That's . . . oh, say, A.D. 2505 your chronology. We didn't set up our chain of stations until C/H 189."

"But those fast-moving ones. You said they came forward from the past."

"Oh, yes, but they're all from the future originally. They just decided they went too far back."

"Too far?"

The gray-haired man nodded and reflected. "It's amusing, the mistakes people will make. They become unrealistic when they read history. Lose contact with facts. Chap I knew . . . wouldn't be satisfied with anything less than Elizabethan times. 'Shakespeare,' he said. 'Good Queen Bess. Spanish Armada. Drake and Hawkins and Raleigh. Most virile period in history. The Golden Age. That's for me.' I couldn't talk sense into him, so we sent him back. Too bad."

"Well?" Addyer asked.

"Oh, he died in three weeks. Drank a glass of water. Typhoid."

"You didn't inoculate him? I mean, the army when it sends men overseas always . . ."

"Of course we did. Gave him all the immunization we could. But diseases evolve and change too. New strains develop. Old strains disappear. That's what causes pandemics. Evidently our shots wouldn't take against the Elizabethan typhoid. Excuse me . . ."

Again the glow appeared. Another nude man appeared, chattered briefly and then whipped through the door. He almost collided with the nude girl who poked her head in, smiled and called in a curious accent, "Ie vous prie de me pardonner. Quy estoit cette gentilhomme?"

"I was right," the gray-haired man said. "That's Medieval French. They haven't spoken like that since Rabelais." To the girl he said, "Middle English, please. The American dialect."

"Oh, I'm sorry, Mr. Jelling. I get so damned fouled up with my linguistics. Fouled? Is that right? Or do they say . . ."

"Hey!" Addyer cried in anguish.

"They say it, but only in private these years. Not before strangers."

"Oh, yes. I remember. Who was that gentleman who just left?"

"Peters."

"From Athens?"

"That's right."

"Didn't like it, eh?"

"Not much. Seems the Peripatetics didn't have plumbing."

"Yes. You begin to hanker for a modern bathroom after a while. Where do I get some clothes . . . or don't they wear clothes this century?"

"No, that's a hundred years forward. Go see my wife. She's in the outfitting room in the barn. That's the big red building."

The tall lighthouse-man Addyer had first seen in the farmyard suddenly manifested himself behind the girl. He was now dressed and moving at normal speed. He stared at the girl; she stared at him. "Splem!" they both cried. They embraced and kissed shoulders.

"St'u my rock-ribbering rib-rockery to heart the hearts two," the man said.

"Heart's too, argal, too heart," the girl laughed.

"Eh? Then you st'u too."

They embraced again and left.

"What was that? Future talk?" Addyer asked. "Shorthand?"

"Shorthand?" Jelling exclaimed in a surprised tone. "Don't you know rhetoric when you hear it? That was thirtieth-century rhetoric, man. We don't talk anything else up there. Prosthesis, Diastole, Epergesis, Metabasis, Hendiadys . . . And we're all born scanning."

"You don't have to sound so stuck-up," Addyer muttered enviously. "I could scan too if I tried."

"You'd find it damned inconvenient trying at your time of life."

"What difference would that make?"

"It would make a big difference," Jelling said, "because you'd find that living is the sum of conveniences. You might think plumbing is pretty unimportant compared to ancient Greek philosophers. Lots of people do. But the fact is, we already know the philosophy. After a while you get tired of seeing the great men and listening to them expound the material you already know. You begin to miss the conveniences and familiar patterns you used to take for granted."

"That," said Addyer, "is a superficial attitude."

"You think so? Try living in the past by candlelight, without central heating, without refrigeration, canned foods, elementary drugs. . . . Or, futurewise, try living with Berganlicks, the Twenty-Two Commandments, duodecimal calendars and currency, or try speaking in meter, planning and scanning each sentence before you talk . . . and damned for a contemptible illiterate if you forget yourself and speak spontaneously in your own tongue."

"You're exaggerating," Addyer said. "I'll bet there are times where I could be very happy. I've thought about it for years, and I . . . ."

"Tcha!" Jelling snorted. "The great illusion. Name one."

"The American Revolution."

"Pfui! No sanitation. No medicine. Cholera in Philadelphia. Malaria in New York. No anesthesia. The death penalty for hundreds of small crimes and petty infractions. None of the books and music you like best. None of the jobs or professions for which you've been trained. Try again."

"The Victorian Age."

"How are your teeth and eyes? In good shape? They'd better be. We can't send your inlays and spectacles back with you. How are your ethics? In bad shape? They'd better be or you'd starve in that cutthroat era. How do you feel about class distinctions? They were pretty strong in those days. What's your religion? You'd better not be a Jew or Catholic or Quaker or Moravian or any minority. What's your politics? If you're a reactionary today the same opinions would make you a dangerous radical a hundred years ago. I don't think you'd be happy."

"I'd be safe."

"Not unless you were rich; and we can't send money back. Only the flesh. No, Addyer, the poor died at the average age of forty in those days . . . worked out, worn out. Only the privileged survived, and you wouldn't be one of the privileged."

"Not with my superior knowledge?"

Jelling nodded wearily. "I knew *that* would come up sooner or later. What superior knowledge? Your hazy recollection of science and invention? Don't be a damned fool, Addyer. You enjoy your technology without the faintest idea of how it works."

"It wouldn't have to be hazy recollection. I could prepare."

"What, for instance?"

"Oh . . . say, the radio. I could make a fortune inventing the radio."

Jelling smiled. "You couldn't invent radio until you'd first invented the hundred allied technical discoveries that went into it. You'd have to create an entire new industrial world. You'd have to discover the vacuum rectifier and create an industry to manufacture it; the self-heterodyne circuit, the non-radiating neutrodyne receiver and so forth. You'd have to develop electric power production and transmission and alternating current. You'd have to—but why belabor the obvious? Could you invent internal combustion before the development of fuel oils?"

"My God!" Addyer groaned.

"And another thing," Jelling went on grimly. "I've been talking about technological tools, but language is a tool too; the tool of communication. Did you ever realize that all the studying you might do could never teach you how a language was really used centuries ago? Do you know how the Romans pronounced Latin? Do you know the Greek dialects? Could you learn to speak and think in Gaelic, seventeenth-century Flemish, Old Low German? Never. You'd be a deaf-mute."

"I never thought about it that way," Addyer said slowly.

"Escapists never do. All they're looking for is a vague excuse to run away."

"What about books? I could memorize a great book and . . ."

"And what? Go back far enough into the past to anticipate the real author? You'd be anticipating the public too. A book doesn't become great until the public's ready to understand it. It doesn't become profitable until the public's ready to buy it."

"What about going forward into the future?" Addyer asked.

"I've already told you. It's the same problem only in reverse. Could a medieval man survive in the twentieth century? Could he stay alive in street traffic? Drive cars? Speak the language? Think in the language? Adapt to the tempo, ideas and coordinations you take for granted? Never. Could someone from the twenty-fifth century adapt to the thirtieth? Never."

"Well, then," Addyer said angrily, "if the past and future are so uncomfortable, what are those people traveling around for?"

"They're not traveling," Jelling said. "They're running."

"From what?"

"Their own time."

"Why?"

"They don't like it."

"Why not?"

"Do you like yours? Does any neurotic?"

"Where are they going?"

"Any place but where they belong. They keep looking for the Golden Age. Tramps! Time stiffs! Never satisfied. Always searching, shifting . . . bumming through the centuries. Pfui! Half the panhandlers you meet are probably time bums stuck in the wrong century."

"And those people coming here . . . they think *this* is a Golden Age?"

"They do."

"They're crazy," Addyer protested. "Have they seen the ruins? The radiation? The war? The anxiety? The hysteria?"

"Sure. That's what appeals to them. Don't ask me why. Think of it this way: you like the American Colonial period, yes?"

"Among others."

"Well, if you told Mr. George Washington the reasons why you liked his time, you'd probably be naming everything he hated about it."

"But that's not a fair comparison. This is the worst age in all history."

Jelling waved his hand. "That's how it looks to you. Everybody says that in every generation; but take my word for it, no matter when you live and how you live, there's always somebody else somewhere else who thinks you live in the Golden Age."

"Well, I'll be damned," Addyer said.

Jelling looked at him steadily for a moment. "You will be," he said sorrowfully. "I've got bad news for you, Addyer. We can't let you remain. You'll talk and make trouble, and our secret's got to be kept. We'll have to send you out one-way."

"I can talk wherever I go."

"But nobody'll pay attention to you outside your own time. You won't make sense. You'll be an eccentric . . . a lunatic . . . a foreigner . . . safe."

"What if I come back?"

"You won't be able to get back without a visa, and I'm not tattooing any visa on you. You won't be the first we've had to transport if that's any consolation to you. There was a Japanese, I remember . . ."

"Then you're going to send me somewhere in time? Permanently?"

"That's right. I'm really very sorry."

"To the future or the past?"

"You can take your choice. Think it over while you're getting undressed."

"You don't have to act so mournful," Addyer said. "It's a great adventure. A high adventure. It's something I've always dreamed."

"That's right. It's going to be wonderful."

"I could refuse," Addyer said nervously.

Jelling shook his head. "We'd only drug you and send you anyway. It might as well be your choice."

"It's a choice I'm delighted to make."

"Sure. That's the spirit, Addyer."

"Everybody says I was born a hundred years too soon."

"Everybody generally says that . . . unless they say you were born a hundred years too late."

"Some people say that too."

"Well, think it over. It's a permanent move. Which would you prefer . . . the phonetic future or the poetic past?"

Very slowly Addyer began to undress as he undressed each night when he began the prelude to his customary fantasy. But now his dreams were faced with fulfillment and the moment of decision terrified him. He was a little blue and rather unsteady on his legs when he stepped to the copper disk in the center of the floor. In answer to Jelling's inquiry he muttered his choice. Then he turned argent in the aura of an incandescent glow and disappeared from his time forever.

Where did he go? You know. I know. Addyer knows. Addyer traveled to the land of our pet fantasy. He escaped into the refuge that is our refuge, to the time of our dreams; and in practically no time at all he realized that he had in truth departed from the only time for himself.

Through the vistas of the years every age but our own seems glamorous and golden. We yearn for the yesterdays and tomorrows, never realizing that we are faced with Hobson's choice . . . that today, bitter or sweet, anxious or calm, is the only day for us. The dream of time is the traitor, and we are all accomplices to the betrayal of ourselves.

Can you spare price of one coffee, honorable sir? No, sir, I am not panhandling organism. I am starveling Japanese transient stranded in this somiserable year. Honorable sir! I beg in tears for holy charity. Will you donate to this destitute person one ticket to township of Lyonesse? I want to beg on knees for visa. I want to go back to year 1945 again. I want to be in Hiroshima again. I want to go home.

JACK VANCE

The Gift of Gab

"Everything is relative" is a truism that is frequently forgotten. The relativeness of things depends to a large extent on the limitations to our ability to measure, and to measure accurately. In studying human attributes, one of most the controversial is the measurement of relative intelligence. How much more difficult it will be to communicate with and appreciate the intelligence of aliens, as Jack Vance makes clear in this important and moving story.

Middle afternoon had come to the Shallows; the wind had died, the sea was listless and spread with silken gloss. In the south a black broom of rain hung under the clouds; elsewhere the air was thick with pink murk. Thick crusts of seaweed floated over the Shallows; one of these supported the Bio-Minerals raft, a metal rectangle two hundred feet long, a hundred feet wide.

At four o'clock an air horn high on the mast announced the change of shift. Sam Fletcher, assistant superintendent, came out of the mess hall, crossed the deck to the office, slid back the door, looked in. Where Carl Raight usually sat, filling out his production report, the chair was empty. Fletcher looked over his shoulder, down the deck toward the processing house, but Raight was nowhere in sight. Strange. Fletcher crossed the office, checked the day's tonnage:

Rhodium trichloride 4.01
Tantalum sulphide 0.87
Tripyridyl rhenichloride 0.43

The gross tonnage, by Fletcher's calculations, came to 5.31—an average shift. He still led Raight in the Pinch-bottle Sweepstakes. Tomorrow was the end of the month; Fletcher could hardly fail to make off with Raight's Haig

& Haig. Anticipating Raight's protests and complaints, Fletcher smiled and whistled through his teeth. He felt cheerful and confident. Another month would bring to an end his six-month contract; then it was back to Starholme with six months' pay to his credit.

Where in thunder was Raight? Fletcher looked out the window. In his range of vision was the helicopter—guyed to the deck against the Sabrian line-squalls—the mast, the black hump of the generator, the water tank and at the far end of the raft, the pulverizers, the leaching vats, the Tswett columns and the storage bins.

A dark shape filled the door. Fletcher turned, but it was Agostino, the day-shift operator, who had just now been relieved by Blue Murphy, Fletcher's operator.

"Where's Raight?" asked Fletcher.

Agostino looked around the office.

"I thought he was in here."

"I thought he was over in the works."

"No, I just came from there."

Fletcher crossed the room, looked into the washroom. "Wrong again."

Agostino turned away. "I'm going up for a shower." He looked back from the door. "We're low on barnacles."

"I'll send out the barge." Fletcher followed Agostino out on deck, headed for the processing house.

He passed the dock where the barges were tied up, entered the pulverizing room. The number one rotary was grinding barnacles for tantalum; the number two was pulverizing rhenium-rich sea slugs. The ball mill waited for a load of coral, orange-pink with nodules of rhodium salts.

Blue Murphy, who had a red face and a meager fringe of red hair, was making a routine check of bearings, shafts, chains, journals, valves and gauges. Fletcher called in his ear to be heard over the noise of the crushers, "Has Raight come through?"

Murphy shook his head.

Fletcher went on into the leaching chamber where the first separation of salts from the pulp was effected, through the forest of Tswett tubes and once more out upon the deck. No Raight. He must have gone on ahead to the office.

But the office was empty.

Fletcher continued around to the mess hall. Agostino was busy with a bowl of chili. Dave Jones, the hatchet-faced steward, stood in the doorway to the galley.

"Raight been here?" asked Fletcher.

Jones, who never used two words when one would do, gave his head a morose shake. Agostino looked around. "Did you check the barnacle barge? He might have gone out to the shelves."

Fletcher looked puzzled. "What's wrong with Mahlberg?"

"He's putting new teeth on the dragline bucket."

Fletcher tried to recall the lineup of barges along the dock. If Mahlberg, the barge tender, had been busy with repairs, Raight might well have gone out himself. Fletcher drew himself a cup of coffee. "That's where he must be." He sat down. "It's not like Raight to put in free overtime."

Mahlberg came into the mess hall. "Where's Carl? I want to order some more teeth for the bucket."

"He's gone fishing," said Agostino.

Mahlberg laughed at the joke. "Catch himself a nice wire eel maybe. Or a dekabrach."

Dave Jones grunted. "He'll cook it himself."

"Seems like a dekabrach should make good eatin'," said Mahlberg, "close as they are to a seal."

"Who likes seal?" growled Jones.

"I'd say they're more like mermaids," Agostino remarked, "with ten-armed starfish for heads."

Fletcher put down his cup. "I wonder what time Raight left?"

Mahlberg shrugged; Agostino looked blank.

"It's only an hour out to the shelves. He ought to be back by now."

"He might have had a breakdown," said Mahlberg. "Although the barge has been running good."

Fletcher rose to his feet. "I'll give him a call." He left the mess hall, returned to the office, where he dialed T_3 on the intercom screen—the signal for the barnacle barge.

The screen remained blank.

Fletcher waited. The neon bulb pulsed off and on, indicating the call of the alarm on the barge.

No reply.

Fletcher felt a vague disturbance. He left the office, went to the mast, rode up the man-lift to the cupola. From here he could overlook the half-acre of raft, the five-acre crust of seaweed and a great circle of ocean.

In the far northeast distance, up near the edge of the Shallows, the new Pelagic Recoveries raft showed as a small dark spot, almost smeared from sight by the haze. To the south, where the Equatorial Current raced through a gap in the Shallows, the barnacle shelves were strung out in a long loose line. To the north, where the Macpherson Ridge, rising from the deeps, came within thirty feet of breaking the surface, aluminium piles supported the sea slug traps. Here and there floated masses of seaweed, sometimes anchored to the bottom, sometimes maintained in place by action of the currents.

Fletcher turned binoculars along the line of barnacle shelves, spotted the barge immediately. He steadied his arms, screwed up the magnification, focused on the control cabin. He saw no one, although he could not hold the binoculars steady enough to make sure.

Fletcher scrutinized the rest of the barge.

Where was Carl Raight? Possibly in the control cabin, out of sight.

Fletcher descended to the deck, went around to the processing house, looked in. "Hey, Blue!"

Murphy appeared, wiping his big red hands on a rag.

"I'm taking the launch out to the shelves," said Fletcher. "The barge is out there, but Raight doesn't answer the screen."

Murphy shook his big bald head in puzzlement. He accompanied Fletcher to the dock, where the launch floated at moorings. Fletcher heaved at the painter, swung in the stern of the launch, jumped down on the deck.

Murphy called down to him, "Want me to come along? I'll get Hans to watch the works." Hans Heinz was the engineering mechanic.

Fletcher hesitated. "I don't think so. If anything's happened to Raight— well, I can manage. Just keep an eye on the screen. I might call back in."

He stepped into the cockpit, seated himself, closed the dome over his head, started the pump.

The launch rolled and bounced, picked up speed, shoved its blunt nose under the surface, submerged till only the dome was clear.

Fletcher disengaged the pump; water rammed in through the nose, converted to steam, spat aft.

Bio-Minerals became a gray blot in the pink haze, while the outlines of the barge and the shelves became hard and distinct and gradually grew large. Fletcher destaged the power; the launch surfaced, coasted up to the dark hull, grappled with magnetic balls that allowed barge and launch to surge independently on the slow swells.

Fletcher slid back the dome, jumped up to the deck.

"Raight! Hey, Carl!"

There was no answer.

Fletcher looked up and down the deck. Raight was a big man, strong and active—but there might have been an accident. Fletcher walked down the deck toward the control cabin. He passed the number one hold, heaped with black green barnacles. At the number two hold the boom was winged out, with the grab engaged on a shell, ready to hoist it clear of the water.

The number three hold was still unladen. The control cabin was empty.

Carl Raight was nowhere aboard the barge.

He might have been taken off by helicopter or launch, or he might have fallen over the side. Fletcher made a slow check of the dark water in all directions. He suddenly leaned over the side, trying to see through the surface reflections. But the pale shape under the water was a dekabrach, long as a man, sleek as satin, moving quietly about its business.

Fletcher looked thoughtfully to the northeast, where the Pelagic Recoveries raft floated behind a curtain of pink murk. It was a new venture, only three months old, owned and operated by Ted Chrystal, former biochemist on the Bio-Minerals raft. The Sabrian Ocean was inexhaustible; the market for metal was insatiable; the two rafts were in no sense competitors. By no stretch of imagination could Fletcher conceive Chrystal or his men attacking Carl Raight.

He must have fallen overboard.

Fletcher returned to the control cabin, climbed the ladder to the flying bridge on top. He made a last check of the water around the barge, although he knew it to be a useless gesture—the current, moving through the gap at a steady two knots, would have swept Raight's body out over the deeps. Fletcher scanned the horizon. The line of shelves dwindled away into the pink gloom. The mast on the Bio-Minerals raft marked the sky to the northwest. The Pelagic Recoveries raft could not be seen. There was no living creature in sight.

The screen signal sounded from the cabin. Fletcher went inside. Blue Murphy was calling from the raft. "What's the news?"

"None whatever," said Fletcher.

"What do you mean?"

"Raight's not out here."

The big red face creased. "Just who is out there?"

"Nobody. It looks like Raight fell over the side."

Murphy whistled. There seemed nothing to say. Finally he asked, "Any idea how it happened?"

Fletcher shook his head. "I can't figure it out."

Murphy licked his lips. "Maybe we ought to close down."

"Why?" asked Fletcher.

"Well—reverence to the dead, you might say."

Fletcher grinned crookedly. "We might as well keep running."

"Just as you like. But we're low on the barnacles."

"Carl loaded a hold and a half . . ." Fletcher hesitated, heaved a deep sigh. "I might as well shake in a few more shelves."

Murphy winced. "It's a squeamish business, Sam. You haven't a nerve in your body."

"It doesn't make any difference to Carl now," said Fletcher. "We've got to scrape barnacles sometime. There's nothing to be gained by moping."

"I suppose you're right," said Murphy dubiously.

"I'll be back in a couple hours."

"Don't go overboard like Raight now."

The screen went blank. Fletcher reflected that he was in charge, superintendent of the raft, until the arrival of the new crew, a month away. Responsibility, which he did not particularly want, was his.

He went slowly back out on deck, climbed into the winch pulpit. For an hour he pulled sections of shelves from the sea, suspended them over the hold while scraper arms wiped off the black green clusters, then slid the shelves back into the ocean. Here was where Raight had been working just before his disappearance. How could he have fallen overboard from the winch pulpit?

Uneasiness inched along Fletcher's nerves, up into his brain. He shut down the winch, climbed down the pulpit. He stopped short, staring at the rope on the deck.

It was a strange rope—glistening, translucent, an inch thick. It lay in a loose loop on the deck and one end led over the side. Fletcher started down, then hesitated. Rope? Certainly none of the barge's equipment.

Careful, thought Fletcher.

A hand scraper hung on the king post, a tool like a small adze. It was used for manual scraping of the shelves, if for some reason the automatic scrapers failed. It was two steps distant, across the rope. Fletcher stepped down to the deck. The rope quivered; the loop contracted, snapped around Fletcher's ankles.

Fletcher lunged, caught hold of the scraper. The rope gave a cruel jerk; Fletcher sprawled flat on his face and the scraper jarred out of his hands. He kicked, struggled, but the rope drew him easily toward the gunwale. Fletcher made a convulsive grab for the scraper, barely reached it. The rope was lifting his ankles to pull him over the rail. Fletcher strained forward, hacked again and again. The rope sagged, fell apart, snaked over the side.

Fletcher gained his feet, staggered to the rail. Down into the water slid the rope, out of sight among the oily reflections of the sky. Then, for half a second, a wave-front held itself perpendicular to Fletcher's line of vision. Three feet under the surface swam a dekabrach. Fletcher saw the pink golden cluster of arms, radiating like the arms of a starfish, the black patch at their core which might be an eye.

Fletcher drew back from the gunwale, puzzled, frightened, oppressed by the nearness of death. He cursed his stupidity, his reckless carelessness; how could he have been so undiscerning as to remain out here loading the barge? It was clear from the first that Raight had never died by accident. Something had killed Raight, and Fletcher had invited it to kill him too. He limped to the control cabin, started the pumps. Water sucked in through the bow orifice, thrust out through the vents. The barge moved out away from the shelves; Fletcher set the course to northwest, toward Bio-Minerals, then went out on deck.

Day was almost at an end; the sky was darkening to maroon; the gloom grew thick as bloody water. Geidion, a dull red giant, largest of Sabria's two suns, dropped out of the sky. For a few minutes only the light from blue-green Atreus played on the clouds. The gloom changed its quality to pale green, which by some illusion seemed brighter than the previous pink. Atreus sank and the sky went dark.

Ahead shone the Bio-Minerals masthead light, climbing into the sky as the barge approached. Fletcher saw the black shapes of men outlined against the glow. The entire crew was waiting for him; the two operators, Agostino and Murphy, Mahlberg the barge tender, Damon the biochemist, Dave Jones the steward, Manners the technician, Hans Heinz the engineer.

Fletcher docked the barge, climbed the soft stairs hacked from the wadded seaweed, stopped in front of the silent men. He looked from face to face. Waiting on the raft they had felt the strangeness of Raight's death more vividly than he had; so much showed in their expressions.

Fletcher, answering the unspoken question, said, "It wasn't an accident. I know what happened."

"What?" someone asked.

"There's a thing like a white rope," said Fletcher. "It slides up out of the sea. If a man comes near it, it snaps around his leg and pulls him overboard."

Murphy asked in a hushed voice, "You're sure?"

"It just about got me."

Damon the biochemist asked in a skeptical voice, "A live rope?"

"I suppose it might have been alive."

"What else could it have been?"

Fletcher hesitated. "I looked over the side. I saw dekabrachs. One for sure, maybe two or three others."

There was silence. The men looked out over the water. Murphy asked in a wondering voice, "then the dekabrachs are the ones?"

"I don't know," said Fletcher in a strained sharp voice. "A white rope, or fiber, nearly snared me. I cut it apart. When I looked over the side I saw dekabrachs."

The men made hushed noises of wonder and awe.

Fletcher turned away, started toward the mess hall. The men lingered on the deck, examining the ocean, talking in subdued voices. The lights of the raft shone past them, out into the darkness. There was nothing to be seen.

Later in the evening Fletcher climbed the stairs to the laboratory over the office, to find Eugene Damon busy at the microfilm viewer.

Damon had a thin long-jawed face, lank blond hair, a fanatic's eyes. He was industrious and thorough, but he worked in the shadow of Ted Chrystal, who had quit Bio-Minerals to bring his own raft to Sabria. Chrystal was a man of great ability. He had adapted the vanadium-sequestering sea slug of Earth to Sabrian waters; he had developed the tantalum barnacle from a rare and sickly species into the hardy high-yield producer that it was. Damon worked twice the hours that Chrystal had put in, and although he performed his routine duties efficiently, he lacked the flair and imaginative resource which Chrystal used to leap from problem to solution without apparent steps in between.

He looked up when Fletcher came into the lab, then applied himself once more to the microscreen.

Fletcher watched a moment. "What are you looking for?" he asked presently.

Damon responded in the ponderous, slightly pedantic manner that sometimes amused, sometimes irritated, Fletcher. "I've been searching the index to identify the long white 'rope' which attacked you."

Fletcher made a noncommittal sound, went to look at the settings on the microfile throw-out. Damon had coded for "long," "thin," dimension classification "E, F, G." On these instructions, the selector scanning the entire roster of Sabrian life forms, had pulled the cards of seven organisms.

"Find anything?" Fletcher asked.

"Not so far." Damon slid another card into the viewer. "Sabrian Annelid, RRS-4924," read the title, and on the screen appeared a schematic outline of a long segmented worm. The scale showed it to be about two and a half meters long.

Fletcher shook his head. "The thing that got me was four or five times that long. And I don't think it was segmented."

"That's the most likely of the lot so far," said Damon. He turned a quizzical glance up at Fletcher. "I imagine you're pretty sure about this . . . long white marine 'rope'?"

Fletcher ignored him, scooped up the seven cards, dropped them back into the file, looked in the code book, reset the selector.

Damon had the codes memorized and was able to read directly off the dials. " 'Appendages'—'long'—'dimensions D, E, F, G'."

The selector kicked three cards into the viewer.

The first was a pale saucer which swam like a skate, trailing four long whiskers. "That's not it," said Fletcher.

The second was a black bullet-shaped water beetle, with a posterior flagellum.

"Not that one."

The third was a kind of mollusk, with a plasm based in selenium, silicon, fluorine and carbon. The shell was a hemisphere of silicon carbide with a hump from which protruded a thin prehensile tendril.

The creature bore the name "Stryzkal's Monitor," after Esteban Stryzkal, the famous pioneer taxonomist of Sabria.

"That might be the guilty party," said Fletcher.

"It's not mobile," objected Damon. "Stryzkal finds it anchored to the North Shallows pegmatite dykes in conjunction with the dekabrach colonies."

Fletcher was reading the descriptive material. " 'The feeler is elastic without observable limit, and apparently functions as a food-gathering, spore-disseminating, exploratory organ. The monitor typically is found near the dekabrach colonies. Symbiosis between the two life forms is not impossible.' "

Damon looked at him questioningly. "Well?"

"I saw some dekabrachs out along the shelves."

"You can't be sure you were attacked by a monitor," Damon said dubiously. "After all, they don't swim."

"So they don't," said Fletcher, "according to Stryzkal."

Damon started to speak, then noticing Fletcher's expression, said in a subdued voice, "Of course there's room for error. Not even Stryzkal could work out much more than a summary of planetary life."

Fletcher had been reading the screen. "Here's Chrystal's analysis of the one he brought up."

They studied the elements and primary compounds of a Stryzkal monitor's constitution.

"Nothing of commercial interest," said Fletcher.

Damon was absorbed in a personal chain of thought. "Did Chrystal actually go down and trap a monitor?"

"That's right. In the water bug. He spent lots of time underwater."

"Everybody to their own methods," said Damon shortly.

Fletcher dropped the cards back into the file. "Whether you like him or not, he's a good field man. Give the devil his due."

"It seems to me that the field phase is over and done with," muttered Damon. "We've got the production line set up; it's a full-time job trying to increase the yield. Of course I may be wrong."

Fletcher laughed, slapped Damon on the skinny shoulder. "I'm not finding fault, Gene. The plain fact is that there's too many avenues for one man to explore. We could keep four men busy."

"Four men?" said Damon. "A dozen is more like it. Three different proto-plasmic phases on Sabria to the single carbon group on Earth! Even Stryzkal only scratched the surface!"

He watched Fletcher for a while, then asked curiously, "What are you after now?"

Fletcher was once more running through the index. "What I came in here to check. The dekabrachs."

Damon leaned back in his chair. "Dekabrachs? Why?"

"There's lots of things about Sabria we don't know," said Fletcher mildly. "Have you ever been down to look at a dekabrach colony?"

Damon compressed his mouth. "No, I certainly haven't."

Fletcher dialed for the dekabrach card.

It snapped out of the file into the viewer. The screen showed Stryzkal's original photo-drawing, which in many ways conveyed more information than the color stereos. The specimen depicted was something over six feet long, with a pale seal-like body terminating in three propulsive vanes. At the head radiated the ten arms from which the creature derived its name—flexible members eighteen inches long, surrounding the black disk which Stryzkal assumed to be an eye.

Fletcher skimmed through the rather sketchy account of the creature's habitat, diet, reproductive methods and protoplasmic classification. He frowned in dissatisfaction. "There's not much information here—considering that they're one of the more important species. Let's look at the anatomy."

The dekabrach's skeleton was based on an anterior dome of bone and three flexible cartilaginous vertebrae, each terminating in a propulsive vane.

The information on the card came to an end. "I thought you said Chrystal made observations on the dekabrachs," growled Damon.

"So he did."

"If he's such a howling good field man, where're his data?"

Fletcher grinned. "Don't blame me, I just work here." He put the card through the screen again.

Under General Comments, Stryzkal had noted, "Dekabrachs appear to belong in the Sabrian Class A group, the silicocarbonitride phase, although they deviate in important respects." He had added a few lines of speculation regarding dekabrach relationships to other Sabrian species.

Chrystal merely made the comment, "Checked for commercial application; no specific recommendation."

Fletcher made no comment.

"How closely did he check?" asked Damon.

"In his usual spectacular way. He went down in the water bug, harpooned one of them, dragged it to the laboratory. Spent three days dissecting it."

"Precious little he's noted here," grumbled Damon. "If I worked three days on a new species like the dekabrachs, I could write a book."

They watched the information repeat itself.

Damon stabbed out with his long bony finger. "Look! That's been blanked over. See those black triangles in the margin? Cancellation marks!"

Fletcher rubbed his chin. "Stranger and stranger."

"It's downright mischievous," Damon cried indignantly, "erasing material without indicating motive or correction."

Fletcher nodded slowly. "It looks like somebody's going to have to consult Chrystal." He considered. "Well—why not now?" He descended to the office, called the Pelagic Recoveries raft.

Chrystal himself appeared on the screen. He was a large blond man with blooming pink skin and an affable innocence that camouflaged the directness of his mind; his plumpness similarly disguised a powerful musculature. He greeted Fletcher with cautious heartiness. "How's it going on Bio-Minerals? Sometimes I wish I was back with you fellows—this working on your own isn't all it's cracked up to be."

"We've had an accident over here," said Fletcher. "I thought I'd better pass on a warning."

"Accident?" Chrystal looked anxious. "What's happened?"

"Carl Raight took the barge out—and never came back."

Chrystal was shocked. "That's terrible! How . . . why . . ."

"Apparently something pulled him in. I think it was a monitor mollusk—Stryzkal's monitor."

Chrystal's pink face wrinkled in puzzlement. "A monitor? Was the barge over shallow water? But there wouldn't be water that shallow. I don't get it."

"I don't either."

Chrystal twisted a cube of white metal between his fingers. "That's certainly strange. Raight must be—dead?"

Fletcher nodded sombrely. "That's the presumption. I've warned everybody here not to go out alone; I thought I'd better do the same for you."

"That's decent of you, Sam." Chrystal frowned, looked at the cube of metal, put it down. "There's never been trouble on Sabria before."

"I saw dekabrachs under the barge. They might be involved somehow."

Chrystal looked blank. "Dekabrachs? They're harmless enough."

Fletcher nodded noncommittally. "Incidentally, I tried to check on dekabrachs in the microlibrary. There wasn't much information. Quite a bit of material has been canceled out."

Chrystal raised his pale eyebrows. "Why tell me?"

"Because you might have done the canceling."

Chrystal looked aggrieved. "Now why should I do something like that? I worked hard for Bio-Minerals, Sam—you know that as well as I do. Now I'm trying to make money for myself. It's no bed of roses, I'll tell you." He touched the cube of white metal, then noticing Fletcher's eyes on it, pushed it to the side of his desk, against *Cosey's Universal Handbook of Constants and Physical Relationships*.

After a pause Fletcher asked, "Well, did you or didn't you blank out part of the dekabrach story?"

Chrystal frowned in deep thought. "I might have canceled one or two ideas that turned out bad—nothing very important. I have a hazy idea that I pulled them out of the bank."

"Just what were those ideas?" Fletcher asked in a sardonic voice.

"I don't remember offhand. Something about feeding habits, probably. I suspected that the deks ingested plankton, but that doesn't seem to be the case."

"No?"

"They browse on underwater fungus that grows on the coral banks. That's my best guess."

"Is that all you cut out?"

"I can't think of anything more."

Fletcher's eyes went back to the cube of metal. He noticed that it covered the handbook title from the angle of the *v* in "Universal" to the center of the *o* in "of." "What's that you've got on your desk, Chrystal? Interesting yourself in metallurgy?"

"No, no," said Chrystal. He picked up the cube, looked at it critically. "Just a bit of alloy. I'm checking it for resistance to reagents. Well, thanks for calling, Sam."

"You don't have any personal ideas on how Raight got it?"

Chrystal looked surprised. "Why on earth do you ask me?"

"You know more about the dekabrachs than anyone else on Sabria."

"I'm afraid I can't help you, Sam."

Fletcher nodded. "Good night."

"Good night, Sam."

Fletcher sat looking at the blank screen. Monitor mollusks—dekabrachs—the blanked microfilm. There was a drift here whose direction he could not identify. The dekabrachs seemed to be involved and, by association, Chrystal. Fletcher put no credence in Chrystal's protestations; he suspected that Chrystal lied as a matter of policy on almost any subject. Fletcher's mind went to the cube of metal. Chrystal had seemed rather too casual, too quick to brush the matter aside. Fletcher brought out his own handbook. He measured the distance between the fork of the *v* and the center of the *o:* 4.9 centimeters. Now, if the block represented a kilogram mass, as was likely with such sample blocks—Fletcher calculated. In a cube, 4.9 centimeters on a side was 119 cubic centimeters. Hypothesizing a mass of 1,000 grams, the density worked out to 8.4 grams per cubic centimeters.

Fletcher looked at the figure. In itself it was not particularly suggestive. It might be one of a hundred alloys. There was no point in going too far on a string of hypotheses—still, he looked in the handbook. Nickel, 8.6 grams per cubic centimeters. Cobalt, 8.7 grams per cubic centimeters. Niobium, 8.4 grams per cubic centimeters.

Fletcher sat back, considered. Niobium? An element costly and tedious to synthesize, with limited natural resources and an unsatisfied market. The idea was stimulating. Had Chrystal developed a biological source of niobium? If so, his fortune was made.

Fletcher relaxed in his chair. He felt done in—mentally and physically. His mind went to Carl Raight. He pictured the body drifting loosely and haphazardly through the night, sinking through miles of water into places where light would never reach. Why had Carl Raight been pillaged of life?

Fletcher began to ache with anger and frustration at the futility, the indignity of Raight's passing. Carl Raight was too good a man to be dragged to his death in the dark ocean of Sabria.

Fletcher jerked himself upright, marched out of the office, up the steps to the laboratory.

Damon was still busy with his routine work. He had three projects under way: two involving the sequestering of platinum by species of Sabrian algae; the third was an attempt to increase the rhenium absorption of an Alphard-alpha flat sponge. In each case his basic technique was the same: subjecting succeeding generations to an increasing concentration of metallic salt under conditions favoring mutation. Certain of the organisms would presently begin to make functional use of the metal; they would be isolated and transferred to Sabrian brine. A few might survive the shock: some might adapt to the new conditions and begin to absorb the now necessary element.

By selective breeding the desirable qualities of these latter organisms would be intensified; they would then be cultivated on a large-scale basis and the inexhaustible Sabrian waters would presently be made to yield another product.

Coming into the lab, Fletcher found Damon arranging trays of algae cultures in geometrically exact lines. He looked rather sourly over his shoulder at Fletcher.

"I talked to Chrystal," said Fletcher.

Damon became interested. "What did he say?"

"He says he might have wiped a few bad guesses off the film."

"Ridiculous," snapped Damon.

Fletcher went to the table, looked thoughtfully along the row of algae cultures. "Have you run into any niobium on Sabria, Gene?"

"Niobium? No. Not in any appreciable concentration. There are traces in the ocean, naturally. I believe one of the corals shows a set of niobium lines." He cocked his head with birdlike inquisitiveness. "Why do you ask?"

"Just an idea, wild and random."

"I don't suppose Chrystal gave you any satisfaction?"

"None at all."

"Then what's the next move?"

Fletcher hitched himself up on the table. "I'm not sure. There's not much I can do. Unless . . ." He hesitated.

"Unless what?"

"Unless I make an underwater survey myself."

Damon was appalled. "What do you hope to gain by that?"

Fletcher smiled. "If I knew, I wouldn't need to go. Remember, Chrystal went down, then came back up and stripped the microfile."

"I realize that," said Damon. "Still, I think it's rather . . . well, foolhardy, after what's happened."

"Perhaps, perhaps not." Fletcher slid off the table to the deck. "I'll let it ride till tomorrow anyway."

He left Damon making out his daily check sheet, descended to the main deck.

Blue Murphy was waiting at the foot of the stairs. Fletcher said, "Well, Murphy?"

The round red face displayed a puzzled front. "Agostino up there with you?"

Fletcher stopped short. "No."

"He should have relieved me half an hour ago. He's not in the dormitory; he's not in the mess hall."

"Good God," said Fletcher, "another one?"

Murphy looked over his shoulder at the ocean. "They saw him about an hour ago in the mess hall."

"Come on," said Fletcher. "Let's search the raft."

They looked everywhere—processing house, the cupola on the mast, all the nooks and crannies a man might take it into his head to explore. The barges were all at dock; the launch and catamaran swung at their moorings; the helicopter hulked on the deck with drooping blades.

Agostino was nowhere aboard the raft. No one knew where Agostino had gone; no one knew exactly when he had left.

The crew of the raft collected in the mess hall, making small nervous motions, looking out of the portholes over the ocean.

Fletcher could think of very little to say. "Whatever is after us—and we don't know what it is—it can surprise us and it's watching. We've got to be careful—more than careful!"

Murphy pounded his fist softly on the table. "But what can we do? We can't just stand around like silly cows!"

"Sabria is theoretically a safe planet," said Damon. "According to Stryzkal and the Galactic Index, there are no hostile life forms here."

Murphy snorted, "I wish old Stryzkal was here now to tell me."

"He might be able to theorize back Raight and Agostino." Dave Jones looked at the calendar. "A month to go."

"We'll only run one shift," said Fletcher, "until we get replacements."

"Call them reinforcements," muttered Mahlberg.

"Tomorrow," said Fletcher, "I'm going to take the water bug down, look around and get an idea what's going on. In the meantime, everybody better carry hatchets or cleavers."

There was soft sound on the windows, on the deck outside. "Rain," said Mahlberg. He looked at the clock on the wall. "Midnight."

The rain hissed through the air, drummed on the walls; the decks ran with water and the masthead lights glared through the slanting streaks.

Fletcher went to the streaming windows, looked toward the process house. "I guess we better button up for the night. There's no reason to . . ." He squinted through the window, then ran to the door and out into the rain.

Water pelted into his face, he could see very little but the glare of the lights in the rain. And a hint of white along the shining gray black of the deck like an old white plastic hose.

A snatch at his ankles: his feet were yanked from under him. He fell flat upon the streaming metal.

Behind him came the thud of feet; there were excited curses, a clang and scrape; the grip on Fletcher's ankles loosened.

Fletcher jumped up, staggered back against the mast. "Something's in the process house," he yelled.

The men pounded off through the rain; Fletcher came after.

But there was nothing in the process house. The doors were wide; the rooms were bright. The squat pulverizers stood on either hand, behind were the pressure tanks, the vats, the pipes of six different colors.

Fletcher pulled the master switch; the hum and grind of the machinery died. "Let's lock up and get back to the dormitory."

Morning was the reverse of evening; first the green gloom of Atreus, warming to pink as Geidion rose behind the clouds. It was a blustery day, with squalls trailing dark curtains all around the compass.

Fletcher ate breakfast, dressed in a skintight coverall threaded with heating filaments, then a waterproof garment with a plastic head-dome.

The water bug hung on davits at the east edge of the raft, a shell of transparent plastic with the pumps sealed in a metal cell amidships. Submerging, the hull filled with water through valves, which then closed; the bug could submerge to four hundred feet, the hull resisting about half the pressure, the enclosed water the rest. The effect on the passenger was a pressure of two hundred feet—safely short of depth delirium.

Fletcher lowered himself into the cockpit; Murphy connected the hoses from the air tanks to Fletcher's helmet, then screwed the port shut. Mahlberg and Hans Heinz winged out the davits. Murphy went to stand by the hoist control; for a moment he hesitated, looking from the dark pink-dappled water to Fletcher and back at the water.

Fletcher waved his hand. "Lower away." His voice came from the loudspeaker on the bulkhead behind them.

Murphy swung the handle. The bug eased down. Water gushed in through the valves, up around Fletcher's body, over his head. Bubbles rose from the helmet exhaust valve.

Fletcher tested the pumps, then cast off the grapples. The bug slanted down into the water.

Murphy sighed. "He's got more nerve than I'm ever likely to have."

"He can get away from whatever's after him," said Damon. "He might well be safer than we are here on the raft."

Murphy clapped him on the shoulder. "Damon, my lad—you can climb. Up on top of the mast you'll be safe; it's unlikely that they'll come there to tug you into the water." Murphy raised his eyes to the cupola a hundred feet over the deck. "And I think that's where I'd take myself—if only someone would bring me my food."

Heinz pointed to the water. "There go the bubbles. He went under the raft. Now he's headed north."

The day became stormy. Spume blew over the raft, and it meant a drenching to venture out on deck. The clouds thinned enough to show the outlines of Geidion and Atreus, a blood orange and a lime.

Suddenly the winds died; the ocean flattened into an uneasy calm. The crew sat in the mess hall drinking coffee, talking in staccato uneasy voices.

Damon became restless and went up to his laboratory. He came running back down into the mess hall.

"Dekabrachs—they're under the raft! I saw them from the observation deck!"

Murphy shrugged. "They're safe from me."

"I'd like to get hold of one," said Damon. "Alive."

"Don't we have enough trouble already?" growled Dave Jones.

Damon explained patiently. "We know nothing about dekabrachs. They're a highly developed species. Chrystal destroyed all the data we had, and I should have at least one specimen."

Murphy rose to his feet. "I suppose we can scoop one up in a net."

"Good," said Damon. "I'll set up the big tank to receive it."

The crew went out on deck where the weather had turned sultry. The ocean was flat and oily; haze blurred sea and sky together in a smooth gradation of color, from dirty scarlet near the raft to pale pink overhead.

The boom was winged out, a parachute net was attached and lowered quietly into the water. Heinz stood by the winch; Murphy leaned over the rail, staring intently down into the water.

A pale shape drifted out from under the raft. "Lift!" bawled Murphy.

The line snapped taut; the net rose out of the water in a cascade of spray. In the center a six-foot dekabrach pulsed and thrashed, gill slits gasping for water.

The boom swung inboard; the net tripped; the dekabrach slid into the plastic tank.

It darted forward and backward; the plastic dented and bulged where it struck. Then it floated quiet in the center, head-tentacles folded back against the torso.

All hands crowded around the tank. The black eye-spot looked back through the transparent walls.

Murphy asked Damon, "Now what?"

"I'd like the tank lifted to the deck outside the laboratory where I can get at it."

"No sooner said than done."

The tank was hoisted and swung to the spot Damon had indicated; Damon went excitedly off to plan his research.

The crew watched the dekabrach for ten or fifteen minutes, then drifted back to the mess hall.

Time passed. Gusts of wind raked up the ocean into a sharp steep chop. At two o'clock the loudspeaker hissed; the crew stiffened, raised their heads.

Fletcher's voice came from the diaphragm. "Hello aboard the raft. I'm about two miles northwest. Stand by to haul me aboard."

"*Hah!*" cried Murphy, grinning. "He made it."

"I gave odds against him of four to one," Mahlberg said. "I'm lucky nobody took them."

"Get a move on; he'll be alongside before we're ready."

The crew trooped out to the landing. The water bug came sliding over the ocean, its glistening back riding the dark disorder of the waters.

It slipped quietly up to the raft; grapples clamped to the plates fore and aft. The winch whined, the bug lifted from the water, draining its ballast of water.

Fletcher, in the cockpit, looked tense and tired. He climbed stiffly out of the bug, stretched, unzipped the waterproof suit, pulled off the helmet.

"Well, I'm back." He looked around the group. "Surprised?"

"I'd have lost money on you," Mahlberg told him.

"What did you find out?" asked Damon. "Anything?"

Fletcher nodded. "Plenty. Let me get into clean clothes. I'm wringing wet —sweat." He stopped short, looking up at the tank on the laboratory deck. "When did that come aboard?"

"We netted it about noon," said Murphy. "Damon wanted to look one over."

Fletcher stood looking up at the tank with his shoulders drooping.

"Something wrong?" asked Damon.

"No," said Fletcher. "We couldn't have it worse than it is already." He turned away toward the dormitory.

The crew waited for him in the mess hall; twenty minutes later he appeared. He drew himself a cup of coffee, sat down.

"Well," said Fletcher. "I can't be sure—but it looks as if we're in trouble."

"Dekabrachs?" asked Murphy.

Fletcher nodded.

"I knew it!" Murphy cried in triumph. "You can tell by looking at the blatherskites they're up to no good."

Damon frowned, disapproving of emotional judgments. "Just what is the situation?" he asked Fletcher. "At least, as it appears to you?"

Fletcher chose his words carefully. "Things are going on that we've been unaware of. In the first place, the dekabrachs are socially organized."

"You mean to say—they're intelligent?"

Fletcher shook his head. "I don't know for sure. It's possible. It's equally possible that they live by instinct, like social insects."

"How in the world . . ." began Damon; Fletcher held up a hand. "I'll tell you just what happened; you can ask all the questions you like afterward." He drank his coffee.

"When I went down under, naturally I was on the alert and kept my eyes peeled. I felt safe enough in the water bug—but funny things have been happening, and I was a little nervous.

"As soon as I was in the water I saw the dekabrachs—five or six of them." Fletcher paused, sipped his coffee.

"What were they doing?" asked Damon.

"Nothing very much. Drifting near a big monitor which had attached itself to the seaweed. The arm was hanging down like a rope—clear out of sight. I edged the bug in just to see what the deks would do; they began backing away. I didn't want to waste too much time under the raft, so I swung off north, toward the deeps. Halfway there I saw an odd thing; in fact I passed it and swung around to take another look.

"There were about a dozen deks. They had a monitor—and this one was really big. A giant. It was hanging on a set of balloons or bubbles—some kind of pods that kept it floating, and the deks were easing it along. In this direction."

"In this direction, eh?" mused Murphy.

"What did you do?" asked Manners.

"Well, perhaps it was all an innocent outing—but I didn't want to take any chances. The arm of this monitor would be like a hawser. I turned the bug at the bubbles, burst some, scattered the rest. The monitor dropped like a stone. The deks took off in different directions. I figured I'd won that round. I kept on going north, and pretty soon I came to where the slope starts down into the deeps. I'd been traveling about twenty feet under; now I lowered to two hundred. I had to turn on the lights of course—this red twilight doesn't penetrate water too well." Fletcher took another gulp of coffee. "All the way across the Shallows I'd been passing over coral banks and dodging forests of kelp. Where the shelf slopes down to the deeps the coral gets to be something fantastic—I suppose there's more water movement, more nourishment, more oxygen. It grows a hundred feet high, in spires and towers, umbrellas, platforms, arches—white, pale blue, pale green.

"I came to the edge of a cliff. It was a shock—one minute my lights were on the coral, all these white towers and pinnacles—then there was nothing. I was over the deeps. I got a little nervous." Fletcher grinned. "Irrational, of course. I checked the fathometer—bottom was twelve thousand feet down. I still didn't like it and turned around, swung back. Then I noticed lights off to my right. I turned my own off, moved in to investigate. The lights spread out as if I was flying over a city—and that's just about what it was."

"Dekabrachs?" asked Damon.

Fletcher nodded. "Dekabrachs."

"You mean—they built it themselves? Lights and all?"

Fletcher frowned. "That's what I can't be sure of. The coral has grown into shapes that give them little cubicles to swim in and out of and do whatever they'd want to do in a house. Certainly they don't need protection from the rain. They hadn't built these coral grottoes in the sense that we build a house —but it didn't look like natural coral either. It's as if they made the coral grow to suit them."

Murphy said doubtfully, "Then they're intelligent."

"No, not necessarily. After all, wasps build complicated nests with no more equipment than a set of instincts."

"What's your opinion?" asked Damon. "Just what impression does it give?"

Fletcher shook his head. "I can't be sure. I don't know what kind of standards to apply. 'Intelligence' is a word that means a lot of different things, and the way we generally use it is artificial and specialized."

"I don't get you," said Murphy. "Do you mean these deks are intelligent or don't you?"

Fletcher laughed. "Are men intelligent?"

"Sure. So they say, at least."

"Well, what I'm trying to get across is that we can't use man's intelligence as a measure of the dekabrach's mind. We've got to judge him by a different set of values—dekabrach values. Men use tools of metal, ceramic, fiber: inorganic stuff—at least, dead. I can imagine a civilization dependent upon living tools—specialized creatures the master group uses for special purposes. Suppose the dekabrachs live on this basis? They force the coral to grow in the shape they want. They use the monitors for derricks or hoists, or snares, or to grab at something in the upper air."

"Apparently, then," said Damon, "you believe that the dekabrachs are intelligent."

Fletcher shook his head. "Intelligence is just a word—a matter of definition. What the deks do may not be susceptible to human definition."

"It's beyond me," said Murphy, settling back in his chair.

Damon pressed the subject. "I am not a metaphysicist or a semanticist. But it seems that we might apply, or try to apply, a crucial test."

"What difference does it make one way or the other?" asked Murphy.

Fletcher said, "It makes a big difference where the law is concerned."

"Ah," said Murphy, "the doctrine of responsibility."

Fletcher nodded. "We could be yanked off the planet for injuring or killing intelligent autochthones. It's been done."

"That's right," said Murphy. "I was on Alkaid Two when Graviton Corporation got in that kind of trouble."

"So if the deks are intelligent, we've got to watch our step. That's why I looked twice when I saw the dek in the tank."

"Well—are they or aren't they?" asked Mahlberg.

"There's one crucial test," Damon repeated.

The crew looked at him expectantly.

"Well?" asked Murphy. "Spill it."

"Communication."

Murphy nodded thoughtfully. "That seems to make sense." He looked at Fletcher. "Did you notice them communicating?"

Fletcher shook his head. "Tomorrow I'll take a camera out and a sound recorder. Then we'll know for sure."

"Incidentally," said Damon, "why were you asking about niobium?"

Fletcher had almost forgotten. "Chrystal had a chunk on his desk. Or maybe he did—I'm not sure."

Damon nodded. "Well, it may be coincidence, but the deks are loaded with it."

Fletcher stared.

"It's in their blood, and there's a strong concentration in the interior organs."

Fletcher sat with his cup halfway to his mouth. "Enough to make a profit on?"

Damon nodded. "Probably a hundred grams or more in the organism."

"Well, well," said Fletcher. "That's very interesting indeed."

Rain roared down during the night; a great wind came up, lifting and driving the rain and spume. Most of the crew had gone to bed; all except Dave Jones the steward and Manners the radioman, who sat up over a chessboard.

A new sound rose over the wind and rain—a metallic groaning, a creaking discord that presently became too loud to ignore. Manners jumped to his feet, went to the window.

"The mast!"

Dimly it could be seen through the rain, swaying like a reed, the arc of oscillation increasing with each swing.

"What can we do?" cried Jones.

One set of guy lines snapped. "Nothing now."

"I'll call Fletcher." Jones ran for the passage to the dormitory.

The mast gave a sudden jerk, poised long seconds at an unlikely angle, then toppled across the process house.

Fletcher appeared, stared out the window. With the masthead light no longer shining down, the raft was dark and ominous. Fletcher shrugged, turned away. "There's nothing we can do tonight. It's not worth a man's life to go out on that deck."

In the morning, examination of the wreckage revealed that two of the guy lines had been sawed or clipped cleanly through. The mast, of lightweight construction, was quickly cut apart and the twisted segments dragged to a corner of the deck. The raft seemed bald and flat.

"Someone or something," said Fletcher, "is anxious to give us as much trouble as possible." He looked across the leaden-ink ocean to where the Pelagic Recoveries raft floated beyond the range of vision.

"Apparently," said Damon, "you refer to Chrystal."

"I have suspicions."

Damon glanced out across the water. "I'm practically certain."

"Suspicion isn't proof," said Fletcher. "In the first place, what would Chrystal hope to gain by attacking us?"

"What would the dekabrachs gain?"

"I don't know," said Fletcher. "I'd like to find out." He went to dress himself in the submarine suit.

The water bug was made ready. Fletcher plugged a camera into the external mounting, connected a sound recorder to a sensitive diaphragm in the skin. He seated himself, pulled the blister over his head.

The water bug was lowered into the ocean. It filled with water, and its glistening back disappeared under the surface.

The crew patched the roof of the process house, jury-rigged an antenna.

The day passed; twilight came and plum-colored evening.

The loudspeaker hissed and sputtered; Fletcher's voice, tired and tense, said, "Stand by; I'm coming in."

The crew gathered by the rail, straining their eyes through the dusk.

One of the dully glistening wave-fronts held its shape, drew closer and became the water bug.

The grapples were dropped; the water bug drained its ballast and was hoisted into the chocks.

Fletcher jumped down to the deck, leaned limply against one of the davits. "I've had enough submerging to last me awhile."

"What did you find out?" Damon asked anxiously.

"I've got it all on film. I'll run it off as soon as my head stops ringing."

Fletcher took a hot shower, then came down to the mess hall and ate the bowl of stew Jones put in front of him, while Manners transferred the film Fletcher had shot from camera to projector.

"I've made up my mind to two things," said Fletcher. "First, the deks are intelligent. Second, if they communicate with each other, it's by means imperceptible to human beings."

Damon blinked, surprised and dissatisfied. "That's almost a contradiction."

"Just watch," said Fletcher. "You can see for yourself."

Manners started the projector; the screen went bright.

"The first few feet show nothing very much," said Fletcher. "I drove directly out to the end of the shelf and cruised along the edge of the deeps. It drops away like the end of the world—straight down. I found a big colony about ten miles west of the one I found yesterday—almost a city."

" 'City' implies civilization," Damon asserted in a didactic voice.

Fletcher shrugged. "If civilization means manipulation of environment—somewhere I've heard that definition—they're civilised."

"But they don't communicate?"

"Check the film for yourself."

The screen was dark with the color of the ocean. "I made a circle out over the deeps," said Fletcher, "turned off my lights, started the camera and came in slow."

A pale constellation appeared in the center of the screen, separated into a swarm of sparks. They brightened and expanded; behind them appeared the outlines, tall and dim, of coral minarets, towers, spires and spikes. They defined themselves as Fletcher moved closer. From the screen came Fletcher's recorded voice. "These formations vary in height from fifty to two hundred feet, along a front of about half a mile."

The picture expanded. Black holes showed on the face of the spires; pale dekabrach shapes swam quietly in and out. "Notice," said the voice, "the area in front of the colony. It seems to be a shelf, or a storage yard. From up here it's hard to see; I'll drop down a hundred feet or so."

The picture changed; the screen darkened. "I'm dropping now—depthmeter reads three hundred and sixty feet . . . three eighty. . . . I can't see too well; I hope the camera is getting it all."

Fletcher commented, "You're seeing it better now than I could; the luminous areas in the coral don't shine too strongly down there."

The screen showed the base of the coral structures and a nearly level bench fifty feet wide. The camera took a quick swing, peered down over the verge into blackness.

"I was curious," said Fletcher. "The shelf didn't look natural. It isn't. Notice the outlines on down? They're just barely perceptible. The shelf is artificial—a terrace, a front porch."

The camera swung back to the bench, which now appeared to be marked off into areas vaguely differentiated in color.

Fletcher's voice said, "Those colored areas are like plots in a garden—there's a different kind of plant or weed or animal on each of them. I'll come in closer. Here are monitors." The screen showed two or three dozen heavy hemispheres, then passed on to what appeared to be eels with saw edges along their sides, attached to the bench by a sucker. Next were float bladders, then a great number of black cones with very long loose tails.

Damon said in a puzzled voice, "What keeps them there?"

"You'll have to ask the dekabrachs," said Fletcher.

"I would if I knew how."

"I still haven't seen them do anything intelligent," said Murphy.

"Watch," said Fletcher.

Into the field of vision swam a pair of dekabrachs, black eye-spots staring out of the screen at the men in the mess hall.

"Dekabrachs," came Fletcher's voice from the screen.

"Up to now, I don't think they noticed me," Fletcher himself commented. "I carried no lights and made no contrast against the background. Perhaps they felt the pump."

The dekabrachs turned together, dropped sharply for the shelf.

"Notice," said Fletcher. "They saw a problem, and the same solution occurred to both at the same time. There was no communication."

The dekabrachs had diminished to pale blurs on one of the dark areas along the shelf.

"I didn't know what was happening," said Fletcher, "but I decided to move. And then—the camera doesn't show this—I felt bumps on the hull, as if someone were throwing rocks. I couldn't see what was going on until something hit the dome right in front of my face. It was a little torpedo with a long nose like a knitting needle. I took off fast before the deks tried something else."

The screen went black. Fletcher's voice said, "I'm out over the deeps, running parallel with the edge of the shallows." Indeterminate shapes swam across the screen, pale wisps blurred by watery distance. "I came back along the edge of the shelf," said Fletcher, "and found the colony I saw yesterday."

Once more the screen showed spires, tall structures, pale blue, pale green, ivory. "I'm going in close," came Fletcher's voice. "I'm going to look in one of those holes." The towers expanded; ahead was a dark hole.

"Right here I turned on the nose light," said Fletcher. The black hole suddenly became a bright cylindrical chamber fifteen feet deep. The walls were lined with glistening colored globes, like Christmas tree ornaments. A dekabrach floated in the center of the chamber. Translucent tendrils ending in knobs extended from the chamber walls and seemed to be punching and kneading the seal-smooth hide.

"I don't know what's going on," said Fletcher, "but the dek doesn't like me looking in on him."

The dekabrach backed to the rear of the chamber; the knobbed tendrils jerked away into the walls.

"I looked into the next hole."

Another black hole became a bright chamber as the searchlight burned in. A dekabrach floated quietly, holding a sphere of pink jelly before its eye. The wall tendrils were not to be seen.

"This one didn't move," said Fletcher. "He was asleep or hypnotized or too scared. I started to take off—and there was the most awful thump. I thought I was a goner."

The screen gave a great lurch. Something dark hurtled past and into the depths.

"I looked up," said Fletcher. "I couldn't see anything but about a dozen deks. Apparently they'd floated a big rock over me and dropped it. I started the pump and headed for home."

The screen went blank.

Damon was impressed. "I agree that they show patterns of intelligent behavior. Did you detect any sounds?"

"Nothing. I had the recorder going all the time. Not a vibration other than the bumps on the hull."

Damon's face was wry with dissatisfaction. "They must communicate some-how—how could they get along otherwise?"

"Not unless they're telepathic," said Fletcher. "I watched carefully. They make no sounds or motions to each other—none at all."

Manners asked, "Could they possibly radiate radio waves? Or infrared?"

Damon said glumly, "The one in the tank doesn't."

"Oh, come now," said Murphy, "are there no intelligent races that don't communicate?"

"None," said Damon. "They use different methods—sounds, signals, radia-tion—but all communicate."

"How about telepathy?" Heinz suggested.

"We've never come up against it; I don't believe we'll find it here," said Damon.

"My personal theory," said Fletcher, "is that they think alike and don't need to communicate."

Damon shook his head dubiously.

"Assume that they work on a basis of communal empathy," Fletcher went on, "that this is the way they've evolved. Men are individualistic; they need speech. The deks are identical; they're aware of what's going on without words." He reflected a few seconds. "I suppose, in a certain sense, they do communicate. For instance, a dek wants to extend the garden in front of its tower. It possibly waits till another dek comes near, then carries out a rock—indicating what it wants to do."

"Communication by example," said Damon.

"That's right—if you can call it communication. It permits a measure of cooperation—but clearly no small talk, no planning for the future or traditions of the past."

"Perhaps not even awareness of past or future; perhaps no awareness of time!" cried Damon.

"It's hard to estimate their native intelligence. It might be remarkably high, or it might be low; the lack of communication must be a terrific handicap."

"Handicap or not," said Mahlberg, "they've certainly got us on the run."

"And why?" cried Murphy, pounding the table with his big red fist. "That's the question. We've never bothered them. And all of a sudden, Raight's gone, and Agostino. Also our mast. Who knows what they'll think of tonight? Why? That's what I want to know."

"That," said Fletcher, "is a question I'm going to put to Ted Chrystal tomorrow."

Fletcher dressed himself in clean blue twill, ate a silent breakfast and went out to the flight deck.

Murphy and Mahlberg had thrown the guy lines off the helicopter and wiped the dome clean of salt film.

Fletcher climbed into the cabin, twisted the inspection knob. Green light—everything in order.

Murphy said half-hopefully, "Maybe I'd better come with you, Sam—if there's any chance of trouble?"

"Trouble? Why should there be trouble?"

"I wouldn't put much past Chrystal."

"I wouldn't either," said Fletcher. "But—there won't be any trouble."

He started the blades. The ram tubes caught hold; the copter lifted, slanted up, away from the raft and off into the northeast. Bio-Minerals became a bright tablet on the irregular wad of seaweed.

The day was dull, brooding, windless, apparently building up for one of the tremendous electrical storms which came every few weeks. Fletcher accelerated, thinking to get his errand over with as soon as possible.

Miles of ocean slid past; Pelagic Recoveries appeared ahead.

Twenty miles southwest from the raft, Fletcher overtook a small barge laden with raw material for Chrystal's macerators and leaching columns; he noticed that there were two men aboard, both huddled inside the plastic canopy. Pelagic Recoveries perhaps had its troubles too, thought Fletcher.

Chrystal's raft was little different from Bio-Minerals, except that the mast still rose from the central deck and there was activity in the process house. They had not shut down, whatever their troubles.

Fletcher landed on the flight deck. As he stopped the blades, Chrystal came out of the office—a big blond man with a round jocular face.

Fletcher jumped down to the deck. "Hello, Ted," he said in a guarded voice.

Chrystal approached with a cheerful smile. "Hello, Sam! Long time since we've seen you." He shook hands briskly. "What's new at Bio-Minerals? Certainly too bad about Carl."

"That's what I want to talk about." Fletcher looked around the deck. Two of the crew stood watching. "Can we go to your office?"

"Sure, by all means." Chrystal led the way to the office, slid back the door. "Here we are."

Fletcher entered the office. Chrystal walked behind his desk. "Have a seat." He sat down in his own chair. "Now—what's on your mind? But first, how about a drink? You like Scotch, as I recall."

"Not today, thanks." Fletcher shifted in his chair. "Ted, we're up against a serious problem here on Sabria, and we might as well talk plainly about it."

"Certainly," said Chrystal. "Go right ahead."

"Carl Raight's dead. And Agostino."

Chrystal's eyebrows rose in shock. "Agostino too? How?"

"We don't know. He just disappeared."

Chrystal took a moment to digest the information. Then he shook his head in perplexity. "I can't understand it. We've never had trouble like this before."

"Nothing happening over here?"

Chrystal frowned. "Well—nothing to speak of. Your call put us on our guard."

"The dekabrachs seem to be responsible."

Chrystal blinked and pursed his lips, but said nothing.

"Have you been going out after dekabrachs, Ted?"

"Well now, Sam . . ." Chrystal hesitated, drumming his fingers on the desk. "That's hardly a fair question. Even if we were working with dekabrachs— or polyps or club moss or wire eels—I don't think I'd want to say, one way or the other."

"I'm not interested in your business secrets," said Fletcher. "The point is this: the deks appear to be an intelligent species. I have reason to believe that you're processing them for their niobium content. Apparently they're doing their best to retaliate and don't care who they hurt. They've killed two of our men. I've got a right to know what's going on."

Chrystal nodded. "I can understand your viewpoint—but I don't follow your chain of reasoning. For instance, you told me that a monitor had done in Raight. Now you say dekabrach. Also, what leads you to believe I'm going for niobium?"

"Let's not try to kid each other, Ted."

Chrystal looked shocked, then annoyed.

"When you were still working for Bio-Minerals," Fletcher went on, "you discovered that the deks were full of niobium. You wiped all that information out of the files, got financial backing, built this raft. Since then you've been hauling in dekabrachs."

Chrystal leaned back, surveyed Fletcher coolly. "Aren't you jumping to conclusions?"

"If I am, all you've got to do is deny it."

"Your attitude isn't very pleasant, Sam."

"I didn't come here to be pleasant. We've lost two men; also our mast. We've had to shut down."

"I'm sorry to hear that . . ." began Chrystal.

Fletcher interrupted: "So far, Chrystal, I've given you the benefit of the doubt."

Chrystal was surprised. "How so?"

"I'm assuming you didn't know the deks were intelligent, that they're protected by the Responsibility Act."

"Well?"

"Now you know. You don't have the excuse of ignorance."

Chrystal was silent for a few seconds. "Well, Sam—these are all rather astonishing statements."

"Do you deny them?"

"Of course I do!" said Chrystal with a flash of spirit.

"And you're not processing dekabrach?"

"Easy now. After all, Sam, this is my raft. You can't come aboard and chase me back and forth. It's high time you understood it."

Fletcher drew himself a little away, as if Chrystal's mere proximity were unpleasant.

"You're not giving me a plain answer."

Chrystal leaned back in his chair, put his fingers together, puffed out his cheeks. "I don't intend to."

The barge that Fletcher had passed on his way was edging close to the raft. Fletcher watched it work against the mooring stage, snap its grapples. He asked, "What's on that barge?"

"Frankly, it's none of your business."

Fletcher rose to his feet, went to the window. Chrystal made uneasy protesting noises. Fletcher ignored him. The two barge handlers had not emerged from the control cabin. They seemed to be waiting for a gangway which was being swung into position by the cargo boom.

Fletcher watched in growing curiosity and puzzlement. The gangway was built like a trough with high plywood walls.

He turned to Chrystal, "What's going on out there?"

Chrystal was chewing his lower lip, rather red in the face. "Sam, you came storming over here, making wild accusations, calling me dirty names—by implication—and I don't say a word. I try to allow for the strain you're under; I value the goodwill between our two outfits. I'll show you some documents that will prove once and for all . . ." He sorted through a sheaf of miscellaneous pamphlets.

Fletcher stood by the window with half an eye for Chrystal, half for what was occurring out on deck.

The gangway was dropped into position; the barge handlers were ready to disembark.

Fletcher decided to see what was going on. He started for the door.

Chrystal's face went stiff and cold. "Sam, I'm warning you, don't go out there!"

"Why not?"

"Because I say so."

Fletcher slid open the door; Chrystal made a motion to jump up from his chair; then he slowly sank back.

Fletcher walked out to the door, crossed the deck toward the barge.

A man in the process house saw him through the window and made urgent gestures.

Fletcher hesitated, then turned to look at the barge. A couple more steps and he could look into the hold. He stepped forward, craned his neck. From the corner of his eye, he saw the gestures becoming frantic. The man disappeared from the window.

The hold was full of limp white dekabrachs.

"Get back, you fool!" came a yell from the process house.

Perhaps a faint sound warned Fletcher; instead of backing away, he threw himself to the deck. A small object flipped over his head from the direction of the ocean with a peculiar fluttering buzz. It struck a bulkhead, dropped—

a fishlike torpedo, with a long needlelike proboscis. It came flapping toward Fletcher, who rose to his feet and ran crouching and dodging back toward the office.

Two more of the fishlike darts missed him by inches; Fletcher hurled himself through the door into the office.

Chrystal had not moved from the desk. Fletcher went panting up to him. "Pity I didn't get stuck, isn't it?"

"I warned you not to go out there."

Fletcher turned to look across the deck. The barge handlers ran down the troughlike gangway to the process house. A glittering school of dartfish flickered up out of the water, struck at the plywood.

Fletcher turned back to Chrystal. "I saw dekabrachs in that barge. Hundreds of them."

Chrystal had regained whatever composure he had lost. "Well? What if there are?"

"You know they're intelligent as well as I do."

Chrystal smilingly shook his head.

Fletcher's temper was going raw. "You're ruining Sabria for all of us!"

Chrystal held up his hand. "Easy, Sam. Fish are fish."

"Not when they're intelligent and kill men in retaliation."

Chrystal wagged his head. "*Are* they intelligent?"

Fletcher waited until he could control his voice. "Yes. They are."

Chrystal reasoned with him. "How do you know they are? Have you talked with them?"

"Naturally I haven't talked with them."

"They display a few social patterns. So do seals."

Fletcher came up closer, glared down at Chrystal. "I'm not going to argue definitions with you. I want you to stop hunting dekabrach because you're endangering lives aboard both our rafts."

Chrystal leaned back a trifle. "Now, Sam, you know you can't intimidate me."

"You've killed two men; I've escaped by inches three times now. I'm not running that kind of risk to put money in your pocket."

"You're jumping to conclusions," Chrystal protested. "In the first place you've never proved . . ."

"I've proved enough! You've got to stop. That's all there is to it!"

Chrystal slowly shook his head. "I don't see how you're going to stop me, Sam." He brought his hand up from under the desk; it held a small gun. "Nobody's going to bulldoze me, not on my own raft."

Fletcher reacted instantly, taking Chrystal by surprise. He grabbed Chrystal's wrist, banged it against the angle of the desk. The gun flashed, seared a groove in the desk, fell from Chrystal's limp fingers to the floor. Chrystal hissed and cursed, bent to recover it, but Fletcher leaped over the desk, pushed him over backward in his chair. On the way Chrystal kicked at Fletcher's face, caught him a glancing blow on the cheek that sent Fletcher to his knees.

Both men dived for the gun; Fletcher reached it first, rose to his feet, backed to the wall. "Now we know where we stand."

"Put down that gun!"

Fletcher shook his head. "I'm putting you under arrest—civilian arrest. You're coming to Bio-Minerals until the inspector arrives."

Chrystal seemed dumbfounded. "What?"

"I said I'm taking you to the Bio-Minerals raft. The inspector is due in three weeks, and I'll turn you over to him."

"You're crazy, Fletcher."

"Perhaps. But I'm taking no chances with you." Fletcher motioned with the gun. "Get going. Out to the copter."

Chrystal coolly folded his arms. "I'm not going to move. You can't scare me by waving a gun."

Fletcher raised his arm, sighted, pulled the trigger. The jet of fire grazed Crystal's rump. Chrystal jumped, clapped his hand to the scorch.

"Next shot will be somewhat closer," said Fletcher.

Chrystal glared like a boar from a thicket. "You realize I can bring kidnapping charges against you?"

"I'm not kidnapping you. I'm placing you under arrest."

"I'll sue Bio-Minerals for everything they've got."

"Unless Bio-Minerals sues you first. Get going!"

The entire crew met the helicopter: Damon, Blue Murphy, Manners, Hans Heinz, Mahlberg and Dave Jones.

Chrystal jumped haughtily to the deck, surveyed the men with whom he had once worked. "I've got something to say to you men."

The crew watched him silently.

Chrystal jerked his thumb at Fletcher. "Sam's got himself a peck of trouble. I told him I'm going to throw the book at him and that's what I'm going to do." He looked from face to face. "If you men help him, you'll be accessories. I advise you, take that gun away from him and fly me back to my raft."

He looked around the circle, but met only coolness and hostility. He shrugged angrily. "Very well, you'll be liable for the same penalties as Fletcher. Kidnapping is a serious crime, don't forget."

Murphy asked Fletcher, "what shall we do with the varmint?"

"Put him in Carl's room; that's the best place for him. Come on, Chrystal."

Back in the mess hall, after locking the door on Chrystal, Fletcher told the crew, "I don't need to tell you—be careful of Chrystal. He's tricky. Don't talk to him. Don't run any errands of any kind. Call me if he wants anything. Everybody got that straight?"

Damon asked dubiously, "Aren't we getting in rather deep water?"

"Do you have an alternative suggestion?" asked Fletcher. "I'm certainly willing to listen."

Damon thought. "Wouldn't he agree to stop hunting dekabrach?"

"No. He refused point-blank."

"Well," said Damon reluctantly, "I guess we're doing the right thing. But we've got to prove a criminal charge. The inspector won't care whether or not Chrystal's cheated Bio-Minerals."

Fletcher said, "If there's any backfire on this, I'll take full responsibility."

"Nonsense," said Murphy. "We're all in this together. I say you did just right. In fact, we ought to hand the sculpin over to the deks and see what they'd say to him."

After a few minutes Fletcher and Damon went up to the laboratory to look at the captive dekabrach. It floated quietly in the center of the tank, the ten arms at right angles to its body, the black eye area staring through the glass.

"If it's intelligent," said Fletcher, "it must be as interested in us as we are in it."

"I'm not so sure it's intelligent," said Damon stubbornly. "Why doesn't it try to communicate?"

"I hope the inspector doesn't think along the same lines," said Fletcher. "After all, we don't have an airtight case against Chrystal."

Damon looked worried. "Bevington isn't a very imaginative man. In fact, he's rather official in his outlook."

Fletcher and the dekabrach examined each other. "I know it's intelligent —but how can I prove it?"

"If it's intelligent," Damon insisted doggedly, "it can communicate."

"If it can't," said Fletcher, "then it's our move."

"What do you mean?"

"We'll have to teach it."

Damon's expression became so perplexed and worried that Fletcher broke into laughter.

"I don't see what's funny," Damon complained. "After all, what you propose is . . . well, it's unprecedented."

"I suppose it is," said Fletcher. "But it's got to be done, nevertheless. How's your linguistic background?"

"Very limited."

"Mine is even more so."

They stood looking at the dekabrach.

"Don't forget," said Damon, "we've got to keep it alive. That means, we've got to feed it." He gave Fletcher a caustic glance. "I suppose you'll admit it eats."

"I know for sure it doesn't live by photosynthesis," said Fletcher. "There's just not enough light. I believe Chrystal mentioned on the microfilm that it ate coral fungus. Just a minute." He started for the door.

"Where are you going?"

"To check with Chrystal. He's certainly noted their stomach contents."

"He won't tell you," Damon said at Fletcher's back.

Fletcher returned ten minutes later.

"Well?" asked Damon in a skeptical voice.

Fletcher looked pleased with himself. "Coral fungus mostly. Bits of tender young skelp shoots, stylax worms, sea oranges."

"Chrystal told you all this?" asked Damon incredulously.

"That's right. I explained to him that he and the dekabrach were both our guests, that we planned to treat them exactly alike. If the dekabrach ate well, so would Chrystal. That was all he needed."

Later, Fletcher and Damon stood in the laboratory watching the dekabrach ingest black green balls of fungus.

"Two days," said Damon sourly, "and what have we accomplished? Nothing."

Fletcher was less pessimistic. "We've made progress in a negative sense. We're pretty sure it has no auditory apparatus, that it doesn't react to sound and apparently lacks means for making sound. Therefore, we've got to use visual methods to make contact."

"I envy you your optimism," Damon declared. "The beast has given no grounds to suspect either the capacity or the desire for communication."

"Patience," said Fletcher. "It still probably doesn't know what we're trying to do and probably fears the worst."

"We not only have to teach it a language," grumbled Damon, "we've got to introduce it to the idea that communication is possible. And then invent a language."

Fletcher grinned. "Let's get to work."

"Certainly," said Damon. "But how?"

They inspected the dekabrach, and the black eye area stared back through the wall of the tank. "We've got to work out a set of visual conventions," said Fletcher. "The ten arms are its most sensitive organs and presumably are controlled by the most highly organized section of its brain. So—we work out a set of signals based on the dek's arm movements."

"Does that give us enough scope?"

"I should think so. The arms are flexible tubes of muscle. They can assume at least five distinct positions: straight forward, diagonal forward, perpendicular, diagonal back and straight back. Since the beast has ten arms, evidently there are ten to the fifth power combinations—a hundred thousand."

"Certainly adequate."

"It's our job to work out syntax and vocabulary—a little difficult for an engineer and a biochemist, but we'll have a go at it."

Damon was becoming interested in the project. "It's merely a matter of consistency and sound basic structure. If the dek's got any comprehension whatever, we'll put it across."

"If we don't," said Fletcher, "we're gone geese—and Chrystal winds up taking over the Bio-Minerals raft."

They seated themselves at the laboratory table.

"We have to assume that the deks have no language," said Fletcher.

Damon grumbled uncertainly and ran his fingers through his hair in annoyed confusion. "Not proven. Frankly, I don't think it's even likely. We can argue back and forth about whether they *could* get along on communal empathy and such like—but that's a couple of light-years from answering the question whether they *do*.

"They could be using telepathy as we said; they could also be emitting modulated X rays, establish long and short code signals in some unknown-to-us subspace, hyperspace or interspace—they *could* be doing almost anything we never heard of.

"As I see it, our best bet—and best hope—is that they *do* have some form of encoding system by which they communicate among themselves. Obviously, as you know, they have to have an internal coding-and-communication system; that's what a neuromuscular structure, with feedback loops, is. Any complex organism has to have communication internally. The whole point of this requirement of language as a means of classifying alien life forms is to distinguish between true communities of individual thinking entities and the communal insect type of apparent intelligence.

"Now *if* they've got an antlike or beelike city over there, we're sunk, and Chrystal wins. You can't teach an ant to talk; the nest group has intelligence, but the individual doesn't.

"So we've got to assume they do have a language—or, to be more general, a formalized encoding system for intercommunication.

"We can also assume it uses a pathway not available to our organisms. That sound sensible to you?"

Fletcher nodded. "Call it a working hypothesis, anyway. We know we haven't seen any indication the dek has tried to signal us."

"Which suggests the creature is not intelligent."

Fletcher ignored the comment. "If we knew more about their habits, emotions, attitudes, we'd have a better framework for this new language."

"It seems placid enough."

The dekabrach moved its arms back and forth idly. The visual surface studied the two men.

"Well," said Fletcher with a sign, "first a system of notation." He brought forward a model of the dekabrach's head, which Manners had constructed. The arms were of flexible conduit and could be bent into various positions. "We number the arms zero to nine around the clock, starting with this one here at the top. The five positions—forward, diagonal forward, erect, diagonal back and back—we call A, B, K, X, Y. K is normal position, and when an arm is at K it won't be noted."

Damon nodded his agreement. "That's sound enough."

"The logical first step would seem to be numbers."

Together they worked out a system of numeration, and constructed a chart:

The colon (:) indicates a composite signal: i.e., two or more separate signals.

Number	0	1	2	et cetera
Signal	OY	1Y	2Y	et cetera
	10	11	12	et cetera
	OY,1Y	OY,1Y:	OY,1Y:	et cetera
		1Y	2Y	et cetera
	20	21	22	et cetera
	OY,2Y	OY,2Y:	OY,2Y	et cetera
		1Y	2Y	et cetera
	100	101	102	et cetera
	OX,1Y	OX,1Y:	OX,1Y:	et cetera
		1Y	2Y	et cetera
	110	111	112	et cetera
	OX,1Y:	OX,1Y:	OX,1Y:	et cetera
	OY,1Y	OY,1Y:	OY,1Y	et cetera
		1Y	2Y	et cetera
	120	121	122	et cetera
	OX,1Y:	OX,1Y:	OX,1Y:	et cetera
	OY,2Y	OY,2Y:	OY,2Y:	et cetera
		1Y	2Y	et cetera
	200	201	202	et cetera
	OX,2Y			et cetera

1000	et cetera
OB,1Y	et cetera
2000	et cetera
OB,2Y	et cetera

Damon said, "It's consistent—but possibly cumbersome; for instance, to indicate five thousand seven hundred sixty-six, it's necessary to make the signal . . . let's see: OB, 5Y, then OX, 7Y, then OY, 6Y, then 6Y."

"Don't forget that these are signals, not vocalizations," said Fletcher. "Even so, it's no more cumbersome than 'five thousand seven hundred sixty-six'."

"I suppose you're right."

"Now—words."

Damon leaned back in his chair. "We can't just build a vocabulary and call it a language."

"I wish I knew more linguistic theory," said Fletcher. "Naturally, we won't go into any abstractions."

"Our basic English structure might be a good idea," Damon mused, "with English parts of speech. That is, nouns are things, adjectives are attributes of things, verbs are the displacements which things undergo or the absence of displacement."

Fletcher reflected. "We could simplify even further to nouns, verbs and verbal modifiers."

"Is that feasible? How, for instance, would you say 'the large raft'?"

"We'd use a verb meaning 'to grow big'. 'Raft expanded.' Something like that."

"Humph," grumbled Damon. "You don't envisage a very expressive language."

"I don't see why it shouldn't be. Presumably the deks will modify whatever we give them to suit their own needs. If we get across just a basic set of ideas, they'll take it from there. Or by that time someone'll be out here who knows what he's doing."

"Okay," said Damon, "get on with your Basic Dekabrach."

"First, let's list the ideas a dek would find useful and familiar."

"I'll take the nouns," said Damon. "You take the verbs; you can also have your modifiers." He wrote. "No. 1: water."

After considerable discussion and modification, a sparse list of basic nouns and verbs was agreed upon and assigned signals.

The simulated dekabrach head was arranged before the tank with a series of lights on a board nearby to represent numbers.

"With a coding machine we could simply type out our message," said Damon. "The machine would dictate the impulses to the arms of the model."

Fletcher agreed. "Fine, if we had the equipment and several weeks to tinker around with it. Too bad we don't. Now—let's start. The numbers first. You work the lights; I'll move the arms. Just one to nine for now."

Several hours passed. The dekabrach floated quietly, the black eye-spot observing.

Feeding time approached. Damon displayed the black-green fungus balls; Fletcher arranged the signal for "food" on the arms of the model. A few morsels were dropped into the tank.

The dekabrach quietly sucked them into its oral tube.

Damon went through the pantomime of offering food to the model. Fletcher moved the arms to the signal "food." Damon ostentatiously placed the fungus ball in the model's oral tube, then faced the tank and offered food to the dekabrach.

The dekabrach watched impassively.

Two weeks passed. Fletcher went up to Raight's old room to talk to Chrystal, whom he found reading a book from the microfilm library.

Chrystal extinguished the image of the book, swung his legs over the side of the bed, sat up.

Fletcher said, "In a very few days the inspector is due."

"So?"

"It's occurred to me that you might have made an honest mistake. At least I can see the possibility."

"Thanks," said Chrystal, "for nothing."

"I don't want to victimize you on what may be an honest mistake."

"Thanks again—but what do you want?"

"If you'll cooperate with me in having dekabrachs recognized as an intelligent life form, I won't press charges against you."

Chrystal raised his eyebrows. "That's big of you. And I'm supposed to keep my complaints to myself?"

"If the deks are intelligent, you don't have any complaints."

Chrystal looked keenly at Fletcher. "You don't sound too happy. The dek won't talk, eh?" Chrystal laughed at his joke.

Fletcher restrained his annoyance. "We're working on him."

"But you're beginning to suspect he's not so intelligent as you thought."

Fletcher turned to go. "This one only knows fourteen signals so far. But it's learning two or three a day."

"Hey!" called Chrystal. "Wait a minute!"

Fletcher stopped at the door. "What for?"

"I don't believe you."

"That's your privilege."

"Let me see this dek make signals."

Fletcher shook his head. "You're better off in here."

Chrystal glared. "Isn't that a rather unreasonable attitude?"

"I hope not." He looked around the room. "Anything you're lacking?"

"No." Chrystal turned the switch, and his book flashed once more on the ceiling.

Fletcher left the room; the door closed behind him; the bolts shot home. Chrystal sat up alertly, jumped to his feet with a peculiar lightness, went to the door, listened.

Fletcher's footfalls diminished down the corridor. Chrystal returned to the bed in two strides, reached under the pillow, brought out a length of electric cord detached from a desk lamp. He had adapted two pencils as electrodes, notching through the wood to the lead, binding a wire around the graphite core so exposed. For resistance in the circuit he included a lamp bulb.

He then went to the window. He could see the deck all the way down to the eastern edge of the raft, as well as behind the offices to the storage bins at the back of the process house.

The deck was empty. The only movement was a white wisp of steam rising from the circulation flue and the hurrying pink and scarlet clouds behind.

Chrystal went to work, whistling soundlessly between intently pursed lips. He plugged the cord into the baseboard strip, held the two pencils to the window, struck an arc, burned at the groove which now ran nearly halfway around the window—the only means by which he could cut through the tempered beryl-silica glass.

It was slow work and very delicate. The arc was weak and fractious; fumes grated in Chrystal's throat. He persevered, blinking through watery eyes, twisting his head this way and that, until five-thirty, half an hour before his evening meal, when he put the equipment away. He dared not work after dark for fear the flicker of light would arouse suspicion.

The days passed. Each morning Geidion and Atreus brought their respective flushes of scarlet and pale green to the dull sky; each evening they vanished in sad dark sunsets behind the western ocean.

A makeshift antenna had been jury-rigged from the top of the laboratory to a pole over the living quarters. Early one afternoon Manners blew the general alarm in short jubilant blasts to announce a signal from the LG-19, putting into Sabria on its regular six-months call. Tomorrow evening lighters would swing down from orbit, bringing the sector inspector, supplies and new crews for both Bio-Minerals and Pelagic Recoveries.

Bottles were broken out in the mess hall; there was loud talk, brave plans, laughter.

Exactly on schedule the lighters—four of them—burst through the clouds. Two settled into the ocean beside Bio-Minerals; two more dropped down to the Pelagic Recoveries raft.

Lines were carried out by the launch. The lighters were warped against the dock.

First aboard the raft was Inspector Bevington, a brisk little man, immaculate in his dark blue and white uniform. He represented the government, interpreted its multiplicity of rules, laws and ordinances; he was empowered to adjudicate minor offenses, take custody of criminals, investigate violations of galactic law, check living conditions and safety practices, collect imposts, bonds and duties and, in general, personify the government in all of its faces and phases.

The job might well have invited graft and petty tyranny were not the inspectors themselves subject to minute inspection.

Bevington was considered the most conscientious and the most humorless man in the service. If he was not particularly liked, he was at least respected.

Fletcher met him at the edge of the raft. Bevington glanced at him sharply, wondering why Fletcher was grinning so broadly. Fletcher was thinking that now would be a dramatic moment for one of the dekabrach's monitors to reach up out of the sea and clutch Bevington's ankle. But there was no disturbance; Bevington leaped to the raft without interference.

He shook hands with Fletcher, seeking up and down the dock. "Where's Mr. Raight?"

Fletcher was taken aback; he had become accustomed to Raight's absence. "Why—he's dead."

It was Bevington's turn to be startled. "Dead?"

"Come along to the office," said Fletcher, "and I'll tell you about it. This last has been a wild month." He looked up to the window of Raight's old room where he expected to see Chrystal looking down. But the window was empty. Fletcher halted. Empty indeed! The window was vacant even of glass! He started down the deck.

"Here!" cried Bevington. "Where are you going?"

Fletcher paused long enough to call over his shoulder, "You'd better come with me!" then ran to the door leading into the mess hall. Bevington came after him, frowning in annoyance and surprise.

Fletcher looked into the mess hall, hesitated, came back out on deck, looked up at the vacant window. Where was Chrystal? As he had not come along the deck at the front of the raft, he must have headed for the process house.

"This way," said Fletcher.

"Just a minute!" protested Bevington. "I want to know just what and where . . ."

But Fletcher was on his way down the eastern side of the raft toward the process house, where the lighter crew was already looking over the cases of precious metal to be transshipped. They glanced up when Fletcher and Bevington came running up.

"Did anybody just come past?" asked Fletcher. "A big blond fellow?"

"He went in there." The lightermen pointed toward the process house.

Fletcher whirled, ran through the doorway. Beside the leaching columns he found Hans Heinz, looking ruffled and angry.

"Chrystal come through here?" Fletcher panted.

"Did he come through here! Like a hurricane. He gave me a push in the face."

"Where did he go?"

Heinz pointed. "Out on the front deck."

Fletcher and Bevington ran off, Bevington demanding petulantly, "Exactly what's going on here?"

"I'll explain in a minute," yelled Fletcher. He ran out on deck, looked toward the barges and launch.

No Ted Chrystal.

He could only have gone in one direction: back toward the living quarters, having led Fletcher and Bevington in a complete circle.

A sudden thought hit Fletcher. "The helicopter!"

But the helicopter stood undistrubed, with its guy lines taut. Murphy came toward them, looking perplexedly over his shoulder.

"Seen Chrystal?" asked Fletcher.

Murphy pointed. "He just went up them steps."

"The laboratory!" cried Fletcher in sudden agony. Heart in his mouth he pounded up the steps, Murphy and Bevington at his heels. If only Damon were in the laboratory, not down on the dock or in the mess hall.

The lab was empty—except for the tank with the dekabrach.

The water was cloudy, bluish. The dekabrach was thrashing from end to end of the tank, the ten arms kinked and knotted.

Fletcher jumped on a table, vaulted directly into the tank. He wrapped his arms around the writhing body, lifted. The supple shape squirmed out of his grasp. Fletcher grabbed again, heaved in desperation, raised it out of the tank.

"Grab hold," he hissed to Murphy between clenched teeth. "Lay it on the table."

Damon came rushing in. "What's going on?"

"Poison," said Fletcher. "Give Murphy a hand."

Damon and Murphy managed to lay the dekabrach on the table. Fletcher barked, "Stand back, flood coming!" He slid the clamps from the side of the tank, the flexible plastic collapsed; a thousand gallons of water gushed across the floor.

Fletcher's skin was beginning to burn. "Acid! Damon, get a bucket, wash off the deck. Keep him wet."

The circulatory system was still pumping brine into the tank. Fletcher tore off his trousers, which held the acid against his skin, gave himself a quick rinse, turned the brine pipe around the tank, flushing off the acid.

The dekabrach lay limp, its propulsion vanes twitching. Fletcher felt sick and dull. "Try sodium carbonate," he told Damon. "Maybe we can neutralize some of the acid." On sudden thought he turned to Murphy. "Go get Chrystal. Don't let him get away."

This was the moment that Chrystal chose to stroll into the laboratory. He looked around the room in mild surprise, hopped up on a chair to avoid the water.

"What's going on in here?"

Fletcher said grimly, "You'll find out." To Murphy: "Don't let him get away."

"Murderer!" cried Damon in a voice that broke with strain and grief.

Chrystal raised his eyebrows in shock. "Murderer?"

Bevington looked back and forth between Fletcher, Chrystal and Damon. "Murderer? What's all this?"

"Just what the law specifies," said Fletcher. "Knowingly and willfully destroying one of an intelligent species. Murder."

The tank was rinsed; he clamped up the sides. The fresh brine began to rise up the sides.

"Now," said Fletcher. "Hoist the dek back in."

Damon shook his head hopelessly. "He's done for. He's not moving."

"We'll put him back in anyway," said Fletcher.

"I'd like to put Chrystal in there with him," Damon said with passionate bitterness.

"Come now," Bevington reproved him, "let's have no more talk like that. I don't know what's going on, but I don't like anything of what I hear."

Chrystal, looking amused and aloof, said, "I don't know what's going on either."

They lifted the dekabrach, lowered him into the tank.

The water was about six inches deep, rising too slowly to suit Fletcher.

"Oxygen," he called. Damon ran to the locker. Fletcher looked at Chrystal. "So you don't know what I'm talking about?"

"Your pet fish dies; don't try to pin it on me."

Damon handed Fletcher a breather tube from the oxygen tank; Fletcher thrust it into the water beside the dekabrach's gills. Oxygen bubbled up; Fletcher agitated the water, urged it into the gill openings. The water was nine inches deep. "Sodium carbonate," Fletcher said over his shoulder. "Enough to neutralize what's left of the acid."

Bevington asked in an uncertain voice, "Is it going to live?"

"I don't know."

Bevington squinted sidewise at Chrystal, who shook his head. "Don't blame me."

The water rose. The dekabrach's arms lay limp, floating in all directions like Medusa locks.

Fletcher rubbed the sweat off his forehead. "If only I knew what to do! I can't give it a shot of brandy; I'd probably poison it."

The arms began to stiffen, extend. "Ah," breathed Fletcher, "that's better." He beckoned to Damon. "Gene, take over here—keep the oxygen going into the gills." He jumped to the floor where Murphy was flushing the floor with buckets of water.

Chrystal was talking with great earnestness to Bevington. "I've gone in fear of my life these last three weeks! Fletcher is an absolute madman; you'd better send up for a doctor—or a psychiatrist." He caught Fletcher's eye, paused. Fletcher came slowly across the room. Chrystal returned to the inspector, whose expression was harassed and uneasy.

"I'm registering an official complaint," said Chrystal. "Against Bio-Minerals in general and Sam Fletcher in particular. As a representative of the law, I insist that you place Fletcher under arrest for criminal offenses against my person."

"Well," said Bevington, cautiously glancing at Fletcher, "I'll certainly make an investigation."

"He kidnapped me at the point of a gun," cried Chrystal. "He's kept me locked up for three weeks!"

"To keep you from murdering the dekabrachs," said Fletcher.

"That's the second time you've said that," Chrystal remarked ominously. "Bevington is a witness. You're liable for slander."

"Truth isn't slander."

"I've netted dekabrachs, so what? I also cut kelp and net coelacanths. You do the same."

"The deks are intelligent. That makes a difference." Fletcher turned to

Bevington. "He knows it as well as I do. He'd process men for the calcium in their bones if he could make money at it!"

"You're a liar!" cried Chrystal.

Bevington held up his hands. "Let's have order here! I can't get to the bottom of this unless someone presents facts."

"He doesn't have facts," Chrystal insisted. "He's trying to run my raft off of Sabria—can't stand the competition!"

Fletcher ignored him. He said to Bevington, "You want facts. That's why the dekabrach is in that tank, and that's why Chrystal poured acid in on him."

"Let's get something straight," said Bevington, giving Chrystal a hard stare. "Did you pour acid into that tank?"

Chrystal folded his arms. "The question is completely ridiculous."

"Did you? No evasions now."

Chrystal hesitated, then said firmly, "No. And there's no vestige of proof that I did so."

Bevington nodded. "I see." He turned to Fletcher. "You spoke of facts. What facts?"

Fletcher went to the tank where Damon was still swirling oxygenated water into the gills. "How's he coming?"

Damon shook his head dubiously. "He's acting peculiar. I wonder if the acid got him internally?"

Fletcher watched the long pale shape for half a minute. "Well, let's try him. That's all we can do."

He crossed the room, wheeled the model dekabrach forward. Chrystal laughed, turned away in disgust. "What do you plan to demonstrate?" asked Bevington.

"I'm going to show you that the dekabrach is intelligent and is able to communicate."

"Well, well," said Bevington. "This is something new, is it not?"

"Correct." Fletcher arranged his notebook.

"How did you learn his language?"

"It isn't his—it's a code we worked out between us."

Bevington inspected the model, looked down at the notebook. "These are the signals?"

Fletcher explained the system. "He's got a vocabulary of fifty-eight words, not counting numbers up to nine."

"I see." Bevington took a seat. "Go ahead. It's your show."

Chrystal turned. "I don't have to watch this fakery."

Bevington said. "You'd better stay here and protect your interests; if you don't, no one else will."

Fletcher moved the arms of the model. "This is admittedly a crude setup; with time and money we'll work out something better. Now, I'll start with numbers."

Chrystal said contemptuously, "I could train a rabbit to count that way."

"After a minute," said Fletcher, "I'll try something harder. I'll ask who poisoned him."

"Just a minute!" bawled Chrystal. "You can't tie me up in that way!"

Bevington reached for the notebook. "How will you ask? What signals do you use?"

Fletcher pointed them out. "First, interrogation. The idea of interrogation is an abstraction which the dek still doesn't completely understand. We've established a convention of choice, or alternation, like, "Which do you want? Maybe he'll catch on what I'm after."

"Very well—'interrogation'. Then what?"

"Dekabrach—receive—hot—water. 'Hot water' is for acid. Interrogation: Man—give—hot—water?"

Bevington nodded. "That's fair enough. Go ahead."

Fletcher worked the signals. The black eye area watched. Damon said anxiously, "He's restless—very uneasy."

Fletcher completed the signals. The dekabrach's arms waved once or twice, gave a puzzled jerk.

Fletcher repeated the set of signals, added an extra "interrogation—man?"

The arms moved slowly. " 'Man'," read Fletcher. Bevington nodded. "Man. But which man?"

Fletcher said to Murphy, "Stand in front of the tank." And he signaled, "Man—give—hot—water—interrogation."

The dekabrach's arms moved. " 'Null-zero'," read Fletcher. "No. Damon —step in front of the tank." He signaled the dekabrach. "Man—give—hot —water—interrogation."

" 'Null'."

Fletcher turned to Bevington. "You stand in front of the tank." He signaled.

" 'Null'."

Everyone looked at Chrystal. "Your turn," said Fletcher. "Step forward, Chrystal."

Chrystal came slowly forward. "I'm not a chump, Fletcher. I can see through your gimmick."

The dekabrach was moving its arms. Fletcher read the signals, Bevington looking over his shoulder at the notebook.

" 'Man—give—hot—water'."

Chrystal started to protest. Bevington quieted him. "Stand in front of the tank, Chrystal." To Fletcher: "Ask once again."

Fletcher signaled. The dekabrach responded. " 'Man—give—hot—water. Yellow. Man. Sharp. Come. Give—hot—water. Go'."

There was silence in the laboratory.

"Well," said Bevington flatly, "I think you've made your case, Fletcher."

"You're not going to get me that easy," said Chrystal.

"Quiet," rasped Bevington. "It's clear enough what's happened . . ."

"It's clear what's going to happen," said Chrystal in a voice husky with rage. He was holding Fletcher's gun. "I secured this before I came up here—and it looks as if . . ." He raised the gun toward the tank, squinted, his big white hand tightened on the trigger. Fletcher's heart went dead and cold.

"Hey!" shouted Murphy.

Chrystal jerked. Murphy threw his bucket; Chrystal fired at Murphy, missed. Damon jumped at him, Chrystal swung the gun. The white-hot jet pierced Damon's shoulder. Damon, screaming like a hurt horse, wrapped his bony arms around Chrystal. Fletcher and Murphy closed in, wrested away the gun, locked Chrystal's arms behind him.

Bevington said grimly, "You're in trouble now, Chrystal, even if you weren't before."

Fletcher said, "He's killed hundreds and hundreds of the deks. Indirectly he killed Carl Raight and John Agostino. He's got a lot to answer for."

The replacement crew had moved down to the raft from the LG-19. Fletcher, Damon, Murphy and the rest of the old crew sat in the mess hall with six months of leisure ahead of them.

Damon's left arm hung in a sling; with his right he fiddled with his coffee cup. "I don't quite know what I'll be doing. I have no plans. The fact is, I'm rather up in the air."

Fletcher went to the window, looked out across the dark scarlet ocean. "I'm staying on."

"What?" cried Murphy. "Did I hear you right?"

Fletcher came back to the table. "I can't understand it myself."

Murphy shook his head in total lack of comprehension. "You can't be serious."

"I'm an engineer, a working man," said Fletcher. "I don't have a lust for power or any desire to change the universe—but it seems as if Damon and I set something into motion—something important—and I want to see it through."

"You mean, teaching the deks to communicate?"

"That's right. Chrystal attacked them, forced them to protect themselves. He revolutionized their lives. Damon and I revolutionized the life of this one dek in an entirely new way. But we've just started. Think of the potentialities! Imagine a population of men in a fertile land—men like ourselves except that they never learned to talk. Then someone gives them contact with a new universe—an intellectual stimulus like nothing they'd ever experienced. Think of their reactions, their new attack on life! the deks are in that same position —except that we've just started with them. It's anybody's guess what they'll achieve—and somehow, I want to be part of it. Even if I didn't, I couldn't leave with the job half-done."

Damon said suddenly, "I think I'll stay on, too."

"You two have gone stir crazy," said Jones. "I can't get away fast enough."

The LG-19 had been gone three weeks; operations had become routine aboard the raft. Shift followed shift; the bins began to fill with new ingots, new blocks of precious metal.

Fletcher and Damon had worked long hours with the dekabrach; today would see the great experiment.

The tank was hoisted to the edge of the dock.

Fletcher signaled once again his final message. "Man show you signals. You bring many dekabrachs, man show signals. Interrogation."

The arms moved in assent. Fletcher backed away; the tank was hoisted, lowered over the side, submerged.

The dekabrach floated up, drifted a moment near the surface, slid down into the dark water.

"There goes Prometheus," said Damon, "bearing the gift of the gods."

"Better call it the gift of gab," said Fletcher, grinning.

The pale shape had vanished from sight. "Ten gets you fifty he won't be back," Caldur, the new superintendent, offered them.

"I'm not betting," said Fletcher, "just hoping."

"What will you do if he doesn't come back?"

Fletcher shrugged. "Perhaps net another, teach him. After a while it's bound to take hold."

Three hours went by. Mists began to close in; rains blurred the sky.

Damon, peering over the side, looked up. "I see a dek. But is it our dek?"

A dekabrach came to the surface. It moved its arms. "Many—dekabrachs. Show—signals."

"Professor Damon," said Fletcher, "your first class."

FRITZ LEIBER

The Man Who Never Grew Young

One of the most intellectually stimulating aspects of science fiction is the ability of some of its best practitioners to take an idea and stand it on its head. In less talented hands this sometimes means a novel twist padded with filler so that it constitutes a "story." But in the hands of a master like Fritz Leiber, it means one of the most unforgettable pieces of fiction you will ever read.

Maot is becoming restless. Often toward evening she trudges to where the black Earth meets the yellow sand and stands looking across the desert until the wind starts.

But I sit with my back to the reed screen and watch the Nile.

It isn't just that she's growing young. She is wearying of the fields. She leaves their tilling to me and lavishes her attention on the flock. Every day she takes the sheep and goats farther to pasture.

I have seen it coming for a long time. For generations the fields have been growing scantier and less diligently irrigated. There seems to be more rain. The houses have become simpler—mere walled tents. And every year some family gathers its flocks and wanders off west.

Why should I cling so tenaciously to these poor relics of civilization—I, who have seen king Cheops's men take down the Great Pyramid block by block and return it to the hills?

I often wonder why I never grow young. It is still as much a mystery to me as to the brown farmers who kneel in awe when I walk past.

I envy those who grow young. I yearn for the sloughing of wisdom and responsibility, the plunge into a period of love-making and breathless excitement, the carefree years before the end.

But I remain a bearded man of thirty-odd, wearing the goatskin as I once wore the doublet or the toga, always on the brink of that plunge, yet never making it.

It seems to me that I have always been this way. Why, I cannot even remember my own disinterment, and everyone remembers that.

Maot is subtle. She does not ask for what she wants, but when she comes home at evening she sits far back from the fire and murmurs disturbing fragments of song and rubs her eyelids with green pigment to make herself desirable to me and tries in every way to infect me with her restlessness. She tempts me from the hot work at midday and points out how hardy our sheep and goats are becoming.

There are no young men among us any more. All of them start for the desert with the approach of youth, or before. Even toothless, scrawny patriarchs uncurl from their grave-holes, and hardly pausing to refresh themselves with the food and drink dug up with them, collect their flocks and wives and hobble off into the west.

I remember the first disinterment I witnessed. It was in a country of smoke and machines and constant news. But what I am about to relate occurred in a backwater where there were still small farms and narrow roads and simple ways.

There were two old women named Flora and Helen. It could not have been more than a few years since their own disinterments, but those I cannot remember. I think I was some sort of nephew, but I cannot be sure.

They began to visit an old grave in the cemetery half a mile outside town. I remember the little bouquets of flowers they would bring back with them. Their prim, placid faces became troubled. I could see that grief was entering their lives.

The years passed. Their visits to the cemetery became more frequent. Accompanying them once, I noted that the worn inscription on the headstone was growing clearer and sharper, just as was happening to their own features. "John, loving husband of Flora. . . ."

Often Flora would sob through half the night, and Helen went about with a set look on her face. Relatives came and spoke comforting words, but these seemed only to intensify their grief.

Finally the headstone grew brand-new and the grass became tender green shoots which disappeared into the raw brown earth. As if these were the signs their obscure instincts had been awaiting, Flora and Helen mastered their grief and visited the minister and the mortician and the doctor and made certain arrangements.

On a cold autumn day, when the brown curled leaves were whirling up into the trees, the procession set out—the empty hearse, the dark silent automobiles. At the cemetery we found a couple of men with shovels turning away unobtrusively from the newly opened grave. Then, while Flora and Helen wept bitterly, and the minister spoke solemn words, a long narrow box was lifted from the grave and carried to the hearse.

At home the lid of the box was unscrewed and slid back, and we saw John, a waxen old man with a long life before him.

Next day, in obedience to what seemed an age-old ritual, they took him from the box, and the mortician undressed him and drew a pungent liquid from his veins and injected the red blood. Then they took him and laid him in bed. After a few hours of stony-eyed waiting, the blood began to work. He stirred and his first breath rattled in his throat. Flora sat down on the bed and strained him to her in a fearful embrace.

But he was very sick and in need of rest, so the doctor waved her from the room. I remember the look on her face as she closed the door.

I should have been happy too, but I seem to recall that I felt there was something unwholesome about the whole episode. Perhaps our first experiences of the great crises of life always affect us in some such fashion.

I love Maot. The hundreds I have loved before her in my wanderings down the world do not take away from the sincerity of my affection. I did not enter her life, or theirs, as lovers ordinarily do—from the grave or in the passion of some terrible quarrel. I am always the drifter.

Maot knows there is something strange about me. But she does not let that interfere with her efforts to make me do the thing she wants.

I love Maot and eventually I will accede to her desire. But first I will linger awhile by the Nile and the mighty pageantry conjured up by its passage.

My first memories are always the most difficult and I struggle the hardest to interpret them. I have the feeling that if I could get back a little beyond them, a terrifying understanding would come to me. But I never seem able to make the necessary effort.

They begin without antecedent in cloud and turmoil, darkness and fear. I am a citizen of a great country far away, beardless and wearing ugly confining clothing, but no different in age and appearance from today. The country is a hundred times bigger than Egypt, yet it is only one of many. All the peoples of the world are known to each other, and the world is round, not flat, and it floats in an endless immensity dotted with islands of suns, not confined under a star-speckled bowl.

Machines are everywhere, and news goes around the world like a shout, and desires are many. There is undreamed-of abundance, unrivaled opportunities.

Yet men are not happy. They live in fear. The fear, if I recall rightly, is of a war that will engulf and perhaps destroy some enemy city. Others that dart up beyond the air itself, to come in attacking from the stars. Poisoned clouds. Deadly motes of luminous dust.

But worst of all are the weapons that are only rumored.

For months that seem eternities we wait on the brink of that war. We know that the mistakes have been made, the irrevocable steps taken, the last chances lost. We only await the event.

It would seem that there must have been some special reason for the extremity of our hopelessness and horror. As if there had been previous worldwide wars and we had struggled back from each desperately promising ourselves that it would be the last. But of any such, I can remember nothing. I and the world might well have been created under the shadow of that catastrophe, in a universal disinterment.

The months wear on. Then, miraculously, unbelievably, the war begins to recede. The tension relaxes. The clouds lift. There is great activity, conferences and plans. Hopes for lasting peace ride high.

This does not last. In sudden holocaust, there arises an oppressor named Hitler. Odd, how that name should come back to me after these millennia. His armies fan out across the globe.

But their success is short-lived. They are driven back, and Hitler trails off into oblivion. In the end he is an obscure agitator, almost forgotten.

Another peace then, but neither does it last. Another war, less fierce than the preceding, and it too trails off into a quieter era.

And so on.

I sometimes think (I must hold onto this) that time once flowed in the opposite direction, and that, in revulsion from the ultimate war, it turned back upon itself and began to retrace its former course. That our present lives are only a return and an unwinding. A great retreat.

In that case time may turn again. We may have another chance to scale the barrier.

But no . . .

The thought has vanished in the rippling Nile.

Another family is leaving the valley today. All morning they have toiled up the sandy gorge. And now, returning perhaps for a last glimpse, to the verge of the yellow cliffs, they are outlined against the morning sky—upright specks for men, flat specks for animals.

Maot watches beside me. But she makes no comment. She is sure of me.

The cliff is bare again. Soon they will have forgotten the Nile and its disturbing ghosts of memories.

All our life is a forgetting and a closing in. As the child is absorbed by its mother, so great thoughts are swallowed up in the mind of genius. At first they are everywhere. They environ us like the air. Then there is a narrowing in. Not all men know them. Then there comes one great man, and he takes them to himself, and they are a secret. There only remains the disturbing conviction that something worthy has vanished.

I have seen Shakespeare unwrite the great plays. I have watched Socrates unthink the great thoughts. I have heard Jesus unsay the great words.

There is an inscription in stone, and it seems eternal. Coming back centuries later I find it the same, only a little less worn, and I think that it, at least, may endure. But some day a scribe comes and laboriously fills in the grooves until there is only blank stone.

Then only he knows what was written there. And as he grows young, that knowledge dies forever.

It is the same in all we do. Our houses grow new and we dismantle them and stow the materials inconspicuously away, in mine and quarry, forest and field. Our clothes grow new and we put them off. And we grow new and forget and blindly seek a mother.

All the people are gone now. Only I and Maot linger.

I had not realized it would come so soon. Now that we are near the end, nature seems to hurry.

I suppose that there are other stragglers here and there along the Nile, but I like to think that we are the last to see the vanishing fields, the last to look upon the river with some knowledge of what it once symbolized, before oblivion closes in.

Ours is a world in which lost causes conquer. After the second war of which I spoke, there was a long period of peace in my native country across the sea. There were among us at that time a primitive people called Indians, neglected and imposed upon and forced to live apart in unwanted areas. We gave no thought to these people. We would have laughed at anyone who told us they had power to hurt us.

But from somewhere a spark of rebellion appeared among them. They formed bands, armed themselves with bows and inferior guns, took the warpath against us.

We fought them in little unimportant wars that were never quite conclusive. They persisted, always returning to the fight, laying ambushes for our men and wagons, harrying us continually, eventually making sizable inroads.

Yet we still considered them of such trifling importance that we found time to engage in a civil war among ourselves.

The issue of this war was sad. A dusky portion of our citizenry were enslaved and made to toil for us in house and field.

The Indians grew formidable. Step by step they drove us back across the wide midwestern rivers and plains, through the wooded mountains to eastward.

On the eastern coast we held for a while, chiefly by leaguing with a transoceanic island nation, to whom we surrendered our independence.

There was an enheartening occurrence. The enslaved Negroes were gathered together and crowded in ships and taken to the southern shores of this continent, and there liberated or given into the hands of warlike tribes who eventually released them.

But the pressure of the Indians, sporadically aided by foreign allies, increased. City by city, town by town, settlement by settlement, we pulled up our stakes and took ship ourselves across the sea. Toward the end the Indians became strangely pacific, so that the last boatloads seemed to flee not so much in physical fear as in supernatural terror of the green silent forests that had swallowed up their homes.

To the south the Aztecs took up their glass knives and flint-edged swords and drove out the . . . I think they were called Spaniards.

In another century the whole western continent was forgotten, save for dim, haunting recollections.

Growing tyranny and ignorance, a constant contraction of frontiers, rebellions of the downtrodden, who in turn became oppressors—these constituted the next epoch of history.

Once I thought the tide had turned. A strong and orderly people, the Romans, arose and put most of the diminished world under their sway.

But this stability proved transitory. Once again the governed rose against the governors. The Romans were driven back—from England, from Egypt, from Gaul, from Asia, from Greece. Rising from barren fields came Carthage to contest successfully Rome's preeminence. The Romans took refuge in Rome, became unimportant, dwindled, were lost in a maze of migrations.

Their energizing thoughts flamed up for one glorious century in Athens, then ceased to carry weight.

After that, the decline continued at a steady pace. Never again was I deceived into thinking the trend had changed.

Except this one last time.

Because she was stony and sun-drenched and dry, full of temples and tombs, given to custom and calm, I thought Egypt would endure. The passage of almost changeless centuries encouraged me in this belief. I thought that if we had not reached the turning point, we had at least come to rest.

But the rains have come, the temples and tombs fill the scars in the cliffs and the custom and calm have given way to the restless urges of the nomad.

If there is a turning point, it will not come until man is one with the beasts. And Egypt must vanish like the rest.

Tomorrow Maot and I set out. Our flock is gathered. Our tent is rolled. Maot is afire with youth. She is very loving.

It will be strange in the desert. All too soon we will exchange our last and sweetest kiss and she will prattle to me childishly and I will look after her until we find her mother.

Or perhaps some day I will abandon her in the desert, and her mother will find her.

And I will go on.

LARRY NIVEN

Neutron Star

"Hard science" is the core of science fiction for many readers, and this aspect of the field has been graced by the work of several outstanding practitioners. Mr. Niven has been a leading representative of this branch of SF, and he has never been in better form than in this award-winning story featuring careful scientific speculation about tiny suns and their effect on the lives of people who dare to travel in space.

I

The Skydiver dropped out of hyperspace an even million miles above the neutron star. I needed a minute to place myself against the stellar background and another to find the distortion Sonya Laskin had mentioned before she died. It was to my left, an area the apparent size of the Earth's moon. I swung the ship around to face it.

Curdled stars, muddled stars, stars that had been stirred with a spoon.

The neutron star was in the center, of course, though I couldn't see it and hadn't expected to. It was only eleven miles across, and cool. A billion years had passed since BVS-I burned by fusion fire. Millions of years, at least, since the cataclysmic two weeks during which BVS-I was an X-ray star, burning at a temperature of five billion degrees Kelvin. Now it showed only by its mass.

The ship began to turn by itself. I felt the pressure of the fusion drive. Without help from me, my faithful metal watchdog was putting me in hyperbolic orbit that would take me within one mile of the neutron star's surface. Twenty-four hours to fall, twenty-four hours to rise . . . and during that time something would try to kill me. As something had killed the Laskins.

The same type of autopilot, with the same program, had chosen the Laskins' orbit. It had not caused their ship to collide with the star. I could trust the autopilot. I could even change its program.

I really ought to.

How did I get myself into this hole?

The drive went off after ten minutes of maneuvering. My orbit was established, in more ways than one. I knew what would happen if I tried to back out now.

All I'd done was walk into a drugstore to get a new battery for my lighter!

Right in the middle of the store, surrounded by three floors of sales counters, was the new 2603 Sinclair intrasystem yacht. I'd come for a battery, but I stayed to admire. It was a beautiful job, small and sleek and streamlined and blatantly different from anything that's ever been built. I wouldn't have flown it for anything, but I had to admit it was pretty. I ducked my head through the door to look at the control panel. You never saw so many dials. When I pulled my head out, all the customers were looking in the same direction. The place had gone startlingly quiet.

I can't blame them for staring. A number of aliens were in the store, mainly shopping for souvenirs, but they were staring too. A puppeteer is unique. Imagine a headless, three-legged centaur wearing two Cecil the Seasick Sea Serpent puppets on his arms, and you'll have something like the right picture. But the arms are weaving necks, and the puppets are real heads, flat and brainless, with wide flexible lips. The brain is under a bony hump set between the bases of the necks. This puppeteer wore only its own coat of brown hair, with a mane that extended all the way up its spine to form a thick mat over the brain. I'm told that the way they wear the mane indicates their status in society, but to me it could have been anything from a dock worker to a jeweler to the president of General Products.

I watched with the rest as it came across the floor, not because I'd never seen a puppeteer, but because there is something beautiful about the dainty way they move on those slender legs and tiny hooves. I watched it come straight toward me, closer and closer. It stopped a foot away, looked me over and said, "You are Beowulf Shaeffer, former chief pilot for Nakamura Lines."

Its voice was a beautiful contralto with not a trace of accent. A puppeteer's mouths are not only the most flexible speech organs around, but also the most sensitive hands. The tongues are forked and pointed, the wide, thick lips have little fingerlike knobs along the rims. Imagine a watchmaker with a sense of taste in his fingertips . . .

I cleared my throat. "That's right."

It considered me from two directions. "You would be interested in a high-paying job."

"I'd be fascinated in a high-paying job."

"I am our equivalent of the regional president of General Products. Please come with me, and we will discuss this elsewhere."

I followed it into a displacement booth. Eyes followed me all the way. It was embarrassing, being accosted in a public drugstore by a two-headed monster. Maybe the puppeteer knew it. Maybe it was testing me to see how badly I needed money.

My need was great. Eight months had passed since Nakamura Lines folded. For some time before that, I had been living very high off the hog, knowing that my back pay would cover my debts. I never saw that back pay. It was quite a crash, Nakamura Lines. Respectable middle-aged businessmen took to leaving their hotel windows without their lift belts. Me, I kept spending. If I'd started living frugally, my creditors would have done some checking . . . and I'd have ended in debtors' prison.

The puppeteer dialed thirteen fast digits with its tongue. A moment later we were elsewhere. Air puffed out when I opened the booth door, and I swallowed to pop my ears.

"We are on the roof of the General Products building." The rich contralto voice thrilled along my nerves, and I had to remind myself that it was an alien speaking, not a lovely woman. "You must examine this spacecraft while we discuss your assignment."

I stepped outside a little cautiously, but it wasn't the windy season. The roof was at ground level. That's the way we build on We Made It. Maybe it has something to do with the fifteen-hundred-mile-an-hour winds we get in summer and winter when the planet's axis of rotation runs through its primary, Procyon. The winds are our planet's only tourist attraction, and it would be a shame to slow them down by planting skyscrapers in their path. The bare, square concrete roof was surrounded by endless square miles of desert, not like the deserts of other inhabited worlds, but an utterly lifeless expanse of fine sand just crying to be planted with ornamental cactus. We've tried that. The wind blows the plants away.

The ship lay on the sand beyond the roof. It was a Number Two General Products hull: a cylinder three hundred feet long and twenty feet through, pointed at both ends and with a slight wasp-waist constriction near the tail. For some reason it was lying on its side with the landing shocks still folded in at the tail.

Ever notice how all ships have begun to look the same? A good ninety-five percent of today's spacecraft are built around one of the four General Products hulls. It's easier and safer to build that way, but somehow all ships end as they began: mass-produced look-alikes.

The hulls are delivered fully transparent, and you use paint where you feel like it. Most of this particular hull had been left transparent. Only the nose had been painted, around the life system. There was no major reaction drive. A series of retractable attitude jets had been mounted in the sides, and the hull was pierced with smaller holes, square and round—for observational instruments. I could see them gleaming through the hull.

The puppeteer was moving toward the nose, but something made me turn toward the stern for a closer look at the landing shocks.

They were bent. Behind the curved, transparent hull panels, some tremendous pressure had forced the metal to flow like warm wax back and into the pointed stern.

"What did this?" I asked.

"We do not know. We wish strenuously to find out."

"What do you mean?"

"Have you heard of the neutron star BVS-I?"

I had to think a moment. "First neutron star ever found, and so far the only. Someone located it two years ago by stellar displacement."

"BVS-I was found by the Institute of Knowledge on Jinx. We learned through a go-between that the Institute wished to explore the star. They needed a ship to do it. They had not yet sufficient money. We offered to supply them with a ship's hull with the usual guarantees if they would turn over to us all data they acquired through using our ship."

"Sounds fair enough." I didn't ask why they hadn't done their own exploring. Like most sentient vegetarians, puppeteers find discretion to be the *only* part of valor.

"Two humans named Peter Laskin and Sonya Laskin wished to use the ship. They intended to come within one mile of the surface in a hyperbolic orbit. At some point during their trip, an unknown force apparently reached through the hull to do this to the landing shocks. The unknown force also seems to have killed the pilots."

"But that's impossible. Isn't it?"

"You see the point. Come with me." The puppeteer trotted toward the bow.

I saw the point, all right. Nothing, but nothing can get through a General Products hull. No kind of electromagnetic energy except visible light. No kind of matter, from the smallest subatomic particle to the fastest meteor. That's what the company's advertisements claim, and the guarantee backs them up. I've never doubted it, and I've never heard of a General Products hull being damaged by a weapon or by anything else.

On the other hand, a General Products hull is as ugly as it is functional.

The puppeteer-owned company could be badly hurt if it got around that something *could* get through a company hull. But I didn't see where I came in.

We rode an escalladder into the nose.

The life system was in two compartments. Here the Laskins had used heat-reflective paint. In the conical control cabin the hull had been divided into windows. The relaxation room behind it was a windowless reflective silver. From the back wall of the relaxation room an access tube ran aft, opening on various instruments and the hyperdrive motors.

There were two acceleration couches in the control cabin. Both had been torn loose from their mountings and wadded into the nose like so much tissue paper, crushing the instrument panel. The backs of the crumpled couches were splashed with rust brown. Flecks of the same color were all over everything, the walls, the windows, the viewscreens. It was as if something had hit the couches from behind: something like a dozen paint-filled toy balloons, striking with tremendous force.

"That's blood," I said.

"That is correct. Human circulatory fluid."

II

Twenty-four hours to fall.

I spent most of the first twelve hours in the relaxation room, trying to read. Nothing significant was happening, except that a few times I saw the phenomenon Sonya Laskin had mentioned in her last report. When a star went directly behind the invisible BVS-I, a halo formed. BVS-I was heavy enough to bend light around it, displacing most stars to the sides; but when a star went directly behind the neutron star, its light was displaced to all sides at once. Result: a tiny circle which flashed once and was gone almost before the eye could catch it.

I'd known next to nothing about neutron stars the day the puppeteer picked me up. Now I was an expert. But I still had no idea what was waiting for me when I got down there.

All the matter you're ever likely to meet will be normal matter, composed of a nucleus of protons and neutrons surrounded by electrons in quantum energy states. In the heart of any star there is a second kind of matter: for there, the tremendous pressure is enough to smash the electron shells. The result is degenerate matter: nuclei forced together by pressure and gravity, but held apart by the mutual repulsion of the more or less continuous electron 'gas' around them. The right circumstances may create a third type of matter.

Given: a burnt-out white dwarf with a mass greater than 1.44 times the mass of the sun—Chandrasekhar's Limit, named for an Indian-American astronomer of the nineteen hundreds. In such a mass the electron pressure alone would not be able to hold the electrons back from the nuclei. Electrons would be forced against protons—to make neutrons. In one blazing explosion most of the star would change from a compressed mass of degenerate matter to a closely packed lump of neutrons: neutronium, theoretically the densest matter possible in this universe. Most of the remaining normal and degenerate matter would be blown away by the liberated heat.

For two weeks the star would give off X-rays, as its core temperature dropped from five billion degrees Kelvin to five hundred million. After that it would be a light-emitting body perhaps ten to twelve miles across: the next best thing to invisible. It was not strange that BVS-I was the first neutron star ever found.

Neither is it strange that the Institute of Knowledge on Jinx would have spent a good deal of time and trouble looking. Until BVS-I was found, neutronium and neutron stars were only theories. The examination of an actual neutron star could be of tremendous importance. Neutron stars could give us the key to true gravity control.

Mass of BVS-I: 1.3 times the mass of Sol, approximately.

Diameter of BVS-I (estimated): eleven miles of neutronium, covered by half a mile of degenerate matter, covered by maybe twelve feet of ordinary matter.

Escape velocity: 130,000 meters per second, approximately.

Nothing else was known of the tiny black star until the Laskins went in to look. Now the institute knew one thing more: the star's spin.

"A mass that large can distort space by its rotation," said the puppeteer. "The institute ship's projected hyperbola was twisted across itself in such a way that we can deduce the star's period of rotation to be two minutes, twenty-seven seconds."

The bar was somewhere in the General Products building. I don't know just where, and with the transfer booths it doesn't matter. I kept staring at the puppeteer bartender. Naturally only a puppeteer would be served by a puppeteer bartender, since any biped would resent knowing that somebody made his drink with his mouth. I had already decided to get dinner somewhere else.

"I see your problem," I said. "Your sales will suffer if it gets out that something can reach through one of your hulls and smash a crew to bloody smears. But where do I fit in?"

"We wish to repeat the experiment of Sonya Laskin and Peter Laskin. We must find . . ."

"With me?"

"Yes. We must find out what it is that our hulls cannot stop. Naturally you may . . ."

"But I won't."

"We are prepared to offer one million stars."

I was tempted, but only for a moment. "Forget it."

"Naturally you will be allowed to build your own ship, starting with a Number Two General Products hull."

"Thanks, but I'd like to go on living."

"You would dislike being confined. I find that We Made It has re-established the debtors' prison. If General Products made public your accounts . . ."

"Now, *just* a . . ."

"You owe money in the close order of five hundred thousand stars. We will pay your creditors before you leave. If you return"—I had to admire the creature's honesty in not saying *when*—"we will pay you the remainder. You may be asked to speak to news commentators concerning the voyage, in which case there will be more stars."

"You say I can build my own ship?"

"Naturally. This is not a voyage of exploration. We want you to return safely."

"It's a deal," I said.

After all, the puppeteer had tried to blackmail me. What happened next would be its own fault.

They built my ship in two weeks flat. They started with a Number Two General Products hull, just like the one around the Institute of Knowledge ship, and the life system was practically a duplicate of the Laskins', but there the resemblance ended. There were no instruments to observe neutron stars. Instead, there was a fusion motor big enough for a Jinx warliner. In my ship, which I now called Skydiver, the drive would produce thirty gees at the safety limit. There was a laser cannon big enough to punch a hole through We Made It's moon. The puppeteer wanted me to feel safe, and now I did, for I could fight and I could run. Especially I could run.

I heard the Laskins' last broadcast through half a dozen times. Their unnamed ship had dropped out of hyperspace a million miles above BVS-I. Gravity warp would have prevented their getting closer in hyperspace. While her husband was crawling through the access tube for an instrument check,

Sonya Laskin had called the Institute of Knowledge. "... We can't see it yet, not with the naked eye. But we can see where it is. Every time some star or other goes behind it, there's a little ring of light. Just a minute. Peter's ready to use the telescope. ..."

Then the star's mass had cut the hyperspacial link. It was expected, and nobody had worried—then. Later, the same effect must have stopped them from escaping whatever attacked them, into hyperspace.

When would-be rescuers found the ship, only the radar and the cameras were still running. They didn't tell us much. There had been no camera in the cabin. But the forward camera gave us, for one instant, a speed-blurred view of the neutron star. It was a featureless disk the orange color of perfect barbecue coals, if you know someone who can afford to burn wood. This object had been a neutron star a long time.

"There'll be no need to paint the ship," I told the president.

"You should not make such a trip with the walls transparent. You would go insane."

"I'm no flatlander. The mind-wrenching sight of naked space fills me with mild, but waning interest. I want to know nothing's sneaking up behind me."

The day before I left, I sat alone in the General Products bar letting the puppeteer bartender make me drinks with his mouth. He did it well. Puppeteers were scattered around the bar in twos and threes with a couple of men for variety; but the drinking hour had not yet arrived. The place felt empty.

I was pleased with myself. My debts were all paid, not that that would matter where I was going. I would leave with not a mini-credit to my name; with nothing but the ship. ...

All told, I was well out of a sticky situation. I hoped I'd like being a rich exile.

I jumped when the newcomer sat down across from me. He was a foreigner, a middle-aged man wearing an expensive night-black business suit and a snow-white asymmetric beard. I let my face freeze and started to get up.

"Sit down, Mr. Shaeffer."

"Why?"

He told me by showing me a blue disk. An Earth government ident. I looked it over to show I was alert, not because I'd know an ersatz from the real thing.

"My name is Sigmund Ausfaller," said the government man. "I wish to say a few words concerning your assignment on behalf of General Products."

I nodded, not saying anything.

"A record of your verbal contract was sent to us as a matter of course. I noticed some peculiar things about it. Mr. Shaeffer, will you really take such a risk for only five hundred thousand stars?"

"I'm getting twice that."

"But you only keep half of it. The rest goes to pay debts. Then there are taxes. But never mind. What occurred to me was that a spaceship is a space-ship, and yours is very well armed and has powerful legs. An admirable fighting ship if you were moved to sell it."

"But it isn't mine."

"There are those who would not ask. On Canyon, for example, or the Isolationist party of Wonderland."

I said nothing.

"Or you might be planning a career of piracy. A risky business, piracy, and I don't take the notion seriously."

I hadn't even thought about piracy. But I'd have to give up on Wonder-land. . . .

"What I would like to say is this, Mr. Shaeffer. A single entrepreneur, if he were sufficiently dishonest, could do terrible damage to the reputation of all human beings everywhere. Most species find it necessary to police the ethics of their own members, and we are no exception. It occurred to me that you might not take your ship to the neutron star at all; that you would take it elsewhere and sell it. The puppeteers do not make invulnerable war vessels. They are pacifists. Your Skydiver is unique.

"Hence I have asked General Products to allow me to install a remote control bomb in the Skydiver. Since it is inside the hull, the hull cannot protect you. I had it installed this afternoon.

"Now, notice! If you have not reported within a week I will set off the bomb. There are several worlds within a week's hyperspace flight of here, but all recognize the dominion of Earth. If you flee, you must leave your ship within a week, so I hardly think you will land on a nonhabitable world. Clear?"

"Clear."

"If I am wrong, you may take a lie detector test and prove it. Then you may punch me in the nose, and I will apologize handsomely."

I shook my head. He stood up, bowed and left me sitting there cold sober.

Four films had been taken from the Laskins' cameras. In the time left to me, I ran through them several times without seeing anything out of the way. If the ship had run through a gas cloud, the impact could have killed the Laskins. At perihelion they were moving at better than half the speed of light. But there would have been friction, and I saw no sign of heating in the films. If something alive had attacked them, the beast was invisible to radar and to an enormous range of light frequencies. If the attitude jets had fired accidentally—I was clutching at straws—the light showed on none of the films.

There would be savage magnetic forces near BVS-I, but that couldn't have done any damage. No such force could penetrate a General Products hull. Neither could heat, except in special bands of radiated light, bands visible to at least one of the puppeteers' alien customers. I hold adverse opinions on the General Products hull, but they all concern the dull anonymity of the design. Or maybe I resent the fact that General Products holds a near-monopoly on spacecraft hulls and isn't owned by human beings. But if I'd had to trust my life to, say, the Sinclair yacht I'd seen in the drugstore, I'd have chosen jail.

Jail was one of my three choices. But I'd be there for life. Ausfaller would see to that.

Or I could run for it in the Skydiver. But no world within reach would have me, that is. Of course, if I could find an undiscovered Earthlike world within a week of We Made It . . .

Fat chance. I preferred BVS-I to that any day.

III

I thought that flashing circle of light was getting bigger, but it flashed so seldom I couldn't be sure. BVS-I wouldn't show even in my telescope. I gave that up and settled for just waiting.

Waiting, I remembered a long-ago summer I spent on Jinx. There were days when, unable to go outside because a dearth of clouds had spread the land with raw blue-white sunlight, we amused ourselves by filling party balloons with tap water and dropping them on the sidewalk from three stories up. They made lovely splash patterns—which dried out too fast. So we put a little ink in each balloon before filling it. Then the patterns stayed.

Sonya Laskin had been in her chair when the chairs collapsed. Blood samples showed that it was Peter, who had struck them from behind, like a water balloon dropped from a great height.

What could get through a General Products hull?

Ten hours to fall.

I unfastened the safety net and went for an inspection tour. The access tunnel was three feet wide, just right to push through in free fall. Below me was the length of the fusion tube; to the left, the laser cannon; to the right, a set of curved side tubes leading to inspection points for the gyros, the batteries and generator, the air plant, the hyperspace shunt motors. All was in order—except me. I was clumsy. My jumps were always too short or too long. There was no room to turn at the stern end, so I had to back fifty feet to a side tube.

Six hours to go, and still I couldn't find the neutron star. Probably I would see it only for an instant, passing at better than half the speed of light. Already my speed must be enormous.

Were the stars turning blue?

Two hours to go, I was sure they were turning blue. Was my speed that high? Then the stars behind should be red. Machinery blocked the view behind me, so I used the gyros. The ship turned with peculiar sluggishness. And the stars behind were blue, not red. All around me were blue-white stars.

Imagine light falling into a savagely steep gravitational well. It won't accelerate. Light can't move faster than light. But it can gain in energy, in frequency. The light was falling on me, harder and harder as I dropped.

I told the dictaphone about it. That dictaphone was probably the best protected item on the ship. I had already decided to earn my money by using it, just as if I expected to collect. Privately I wondered just how intense the light would get.

Skydiver had drifted back to vertical with its axis through the neutron star, but now it faced outward. I'd thought I had the ship stopped horizontally. More clumsiness. I used the gyros. Again the ship moved mushily, until it was halfway through the swing. Then it seemed to fall automatically into place. It was as if the Skydiver preferred to have its axis through the neutron star.

I didn't like that in the least.

I tried the maneuver again, and again the Skydiver fought back. But this time there was something else. Something was pulling at me.

So I unfastened my safety net and fell headfirst into the nose.

The pull was light, about a tenth of a gee. It felt more like sinking through honey than falling. I climbed back into my chair, tied myself in with the net, now hanging face down, turned on the dictaphone. I told my story in such nit-picking detail that my hypothetical listeners could not but doubt my hypothetical sanity. "I think this is what happened to the Laskins," I finished. "If the pull increases, I'll call back."

Think? I never doubted it. This strange, gentle pull was inexplicable. Something inexplicable had killed Peter and Sonya Laskin. *Q.E.D.*

Around the point where the neutron star must be, the stars were like smeared dots of oil paint, smeared radially. They glared with an angry, painful light. I hung face down in the net and tried to think.

It was an hour before I was sure. The pull was increasing. And I still had an hour to fall.

Something was pulling on me, but not on the ship.

No, that was nonsense. What could reach out to me through a General Products hull? It must be the other way around. Something was pushing on the ship, pushing it off course.

If it got worse I could use the drive to compensate. Meanwhile, the ship was being pushed *away* from BVS-I, which was fine by me.

But if I was wrong, if the ship was not somehow being pushed away from BVS-I, the rocket motor would send the Skydiver crashing into eleven miles of neutronium.

And why wasn't the rocket already firing? If the ship was being pushed off course, the autopilot should be fighting back. The accelerometer was in good order. It had looked fine when I made my inspection tour down the access tube.

Could something be pushing on the ship *and* on the accelerometer, but not on me?

It came down to the same impossibility: something that could reach through a General Products hull.

To hell with theory, said I to myself, said I. I'm getting out of here. To the dictaphone I said, "The pull has increased dangerously. I'm going to try to alter my orbit."

Of course, once I turned the ship outward and used the rocket, I'd be adding my own acceleration to the X force. It would be a strain, but I could stand it for a while. If I came within a mile of BVS-I, I'd end like Sonya Laskin.

She must have waited face down in a net like mine, waited without a drive unit, waited while the pressure rose and the net cut into her flesh, waited until the net snapped and dropped her into the nose, to lie crushed and broken until the X force tore the very chairs loose and dropped them on her.

I hit the gyros.

The gyros weren't strong enough to turn me. I tried it three times. Each time the ship rotated about fifty degrees and hung there, motionless, while the whine of the gyros went up and up. Released, the ship immediately swung back to position. I was nose down to the neutron star, and I was going to stay that way.

Half an hour to fall, and the X force was over a gee. My sinuses were in agony. My eyes were ripe and ready to fall out. I don't know if I could have stood a cigarette, but I didn't get the chance. My pack of Fortunados had fallen out of my pocket, when I dropped into the nose. There it was, four feet beyond my fingers, proof that the X force acted on other objects besides me. Fascinating.

I couldn't take any more. If it dropped me shrieking into the neutron star,

I had to use the drive. And I did. I ran the thrust up until I was approximately in free fall. The blood which had pooled in my extremities went back where it belonged. The gee dial registered one point two gee. I cursed it for a lying robot.

The soft pack was bobbing around in the nose, and it occurred to me that a little extra nudge on the throttle would bring it to me. I tried it. The pack drifted toward me, and I reached, and like a sentient thing it speeded up to avoid my clutching hand. I snatched at it again as it went past my ear, but again it was moving too fast. That pack was going at a hell of a clip, considering that here I was, practically in free fall. It dropped through the door to the relaxation room, still picking up speed, blurred and vanished as it entered the access tube. Seconds later I heard a solid *thump.*

But that was *crazy.* Already the X force was pulling blood into my face. I pulled my lighter out, held it at arm's length and let go. It fell gently into the nose. But the pack of Fortunados had hit like I'd dropped it from a *building.*

Well.

I nudged the throttle again. The mutter of fusing hydrogen reminded me that if I tried to keep this up all the way, I might well put the General Products hull to its toughest test yet: smashing it into a neutron star at half lightspeed. I could see it now: a transparent hull containing only a few cubic inches of dwarf star matter wedged into the tip of the nose.

At one point four gee, according to that lying gee dial, the lighter came loose and drifted toward me. I let it go. It was clearly falling when it reached the doorway. I pulled the throttle back. The loss of power jerked me violently forward, but I kept my face turned. The lighter slowed and hesitated at the entrance to the access tube. Decided to go through. I cocked my ears for the sound, then jumped as the whole ship rang like a gong.

And the accelerometer was right at the ship's center of mass. Otherwise the ship's mass would have thrown the needle off. The puppeteers were fiends for ten-decimal-point accuracy.

I favored the dictaphone with a few fast comments, then got to work reprogramming the autopilot. Luckily what I wanted was simple. The X force was but an X force to me, but now I knew how it behaved. I might actually live through this.

The stars were fiercely blue, warped to streaked lines near that special point. I thought I could see it now, very small and dim and red; but it might have been imagination. In twenty minutes, I'd be rounding the neutron star. The drive grumbled behind me. In effective free fall, I unfastened the safety net and pushed myself out of the chair.

A gentle push aft—and ghostly hands grasped my legs. Ten pounds of weight hung by my fingers from the back of the chair. The pressure should drop fast. I'd programmed the autopilot to reduce the thrust from two g's to zero during the next two minutes. All I had to do was be at the center of mass, in the access tube, when the thrust went to zero.

Something gripped the ship through a General Products hull. A psychokinetic life form stranded on a sun twelve miles in diameter? But how could anything alive stand such gravity?

Something might be stranded in orbit. There is life in space: outsiders and sailseeds and maybe others we haven't found yet. For all I knew or cared, BVS-I itself might be alive. It didn't matter. I knew what the X force was trying to do. It was trying to pull the ship apart.

There was no pull on my fingers. I pushed aft and landed on the back wall on bent legs. I knelt over the door, looking aft/down. When free fall came, I pulled myself through and was in the relaxation room looking down/forward into the nose.

Gravity was changing faster than I liked. The X force was growing as zero hour approached, while the compensating rocket thrust dropped. The X force tended to pull the ship apart; it was two gee forward at the nose, two gee backward at the tail and diminished to zero at the center of mass. Or so I hoped. The pack and lighter had behaved as if the force pulling them had increased for every inch they moved sternward.

The dictaphone was fifty feet below, utterly unreachable. If I had anything more to say to General Products, I'd have to say it in person. Maybe I'd get the chance. Because I knew what force was trying to tear the ship apart.

It was the tide.

The motor was off, and I was at the ship's midpoint. My spread-eagled position was getting uncomfortable. It was four minutes to perihelion.

Something creaked in the cabin below me. I couldn't see what it was, but I could clearly see a red point glaring among blue radial lines, like a lantern at the bottom of a well. To the sides, between the fusion tube and the tanks and other equipment, the blue stars glared at me with a light that was almost violet. I was afraid to look too long. I actually thought they might blind me.

There must have been hundreds of gravities in the cabin. I could even feel the pressure change. The air was thin at this height, one hundred and fifty feet above the control room.

And now, almost suddenly, the red dot was more than a dot. My time was up. A red disk leaped up at me; the ship swung around me; and I gasped and shut my eyes tight. Giants' hands gripped my arms and legs and head, gently but with great firmness, and tried to pull me in two. In that moment it came to me that Peter Laskin had died like this. He'd made the same guesses I had, and he'd tried to hide in the access tube. But he'd slipped. As I was slipping. . . .

When I got my eyes open the red dot was shrinking into nothing.

IV

The puppeteer president insisted I be put in a hospital for observation. I didn't fight the idea. My face and hands were flaming red with blisters rising, and I ached like I'd been beaten. Rest and tender loving care, that's what I wanted.

I was floating between a pair of sleeping plates, hideously uncomfortable, when the nurse came to announce a visitor. I knew who it was from her peculiar expression.

"What can get through a General Products hull?" I asked it.

"I hoped you would tell me." The president rested on its single back leg, holding a stick that gave off green, incense-smelling smoke.

"And so I will. Gravity."

"Do not play with me, Beowulf Shaeffer. This matter is vital."

"I'm not playing. Does your world have a moon?"

"That information is classified." The puppeteers are cowards. Nobody knows where they come from, and nobody is likely to find out.

"Do you know what happens when a moon gets too close to its primary?"

"It falls apart."

"Why?"

"I do not know."

"Tides."

"What is a tide?"

Oho, said I to myself, said I. "I'm going to try to tell you. The Earth's moon is almost two thousand miles in diameter and does not rotate with respect to Earth. I want you to pick two rocks on the moon, one at the point nearest the Earth, one at the point farthest away."

"Very well."

"Now, isn't it obvious that if those rocks were left to themselves they'd fall away from each other? They're in two different orbits, mind you, concentric orbits, one almost two thousand miles outside the other. Yet those rocks are forced to move at the same orbital speed."

"The one outside is moving faster."

"Good point. So there *is* a force trying to pull the moon apart. Gravity holds it together. Bring the moon close enough to Earth, and those two rocks would simply float away."

"I see. Then this *tide* tried to pull your ship apart. It was powerful enough in the life system of the institute ship to pull the acceleration chairs out of their mounts."

"And to crush a human being. Picture it. The ship's nose was just seven miles from the center of BVS-I. The tail was three hundred feet farther out. Left to themselves they'd have gone in completely different orbits. My head and feet tried to do the same thing when I got close enough."

"I see. Are you moulting?"

"What?"

"I noticed you are losing your outer integument in spots."

"Oh, *that.* I got a bad sunburn from exposure to starlight."

Two heads stared at each other for an eyeblink. A shrug? The puppeteer said, "We have deposited the remainder of your pay with the Bank of We Made It. One Sigmund Ausfaller, human, has frozen the account until your taxes are computed."

"Figures."

"If you will talk to reporters now, explaining what happened to the institute ship, we will pay you ten thousand stars. We will pay cash so that you may use it immediately. It is urgent. There have been rumors."

"Bring 'em in." As an afterthought I added, "I can also tell them that your world is moonless. That should be good for a footnote somewhere."

"I do not understand." But two long necks had drawn back, and the puppeteer was watching me like a pair of pythons.

"You'd know what a tide was if you had a moon. You couldn't avoid it."

"Would you be interested in . . ."

". . . a million stars? I'd be fascinated. I'll even sign a contract if it includes what we're hiding. How do *you* like being blackmailed?"

PHILIP K. DICK

Impostor

Aliens come in all shapes, sizes and intentions in science fiction, but what if they looked like us? The shape-changer is a particularly frightening and dangerous creature because when he is present it becomes impossible to trust anyone, even friends or members of the family. It is this sense of increased vulnerability that makes Mr. Dick's story so terrifying. It is worth noting that he wrote it at the height of the "McCarthyist" period in the United States.

"One of these days I'm going to take time off," Spence Olham said at first-meal. He looked around at his wife. "I think I've earned a rest. Ten years is a long time."

"And the project?"

"The war will be won without me. This ball of clay of ours isn't really in much danger." Olham sat down at the table and lit a cigarette. "The news-machines alter dispatches to make it appear the Outspacers are right on top of us. You know what I'd like to do on my vacation? I'd like to take a camping trip in those mountains outside of town, where we went that time. Remember? I got poison oak and you almost stepped on a gopher snake."

"Sutton Wood?" Mary began to clear away the food dishes. "The wood was burned a few weeks ago. I thought you knew. Some kind of a flash fire."

Olham sagged. "Didn't they even try to find the cause?" His lips twisted. "No one cares any more. All they can think of is the war." He clamped his jaws together, the whole picture coming up in his mind, the Outspacers, the war, the needle-ships.

"How can we think about anything else?"

Olham nodded. She was right, of course. The dark little ships out of Alpha Centauri had bypassed the Earth cruisers easily, leaving them like helpless turtles. It had been one-way fights, all the way back to Terra.

All the way, until the protec-bubble was demonstrated by Westinghouse Labs. Thrown around the major Earth cities and finally the planet itself, the bubble was the first real defense, the first legitimate answer to the Outspacers —as the news-machines labeled them.

But to win the war, that was another thing. Every lab, every project was working night and day, endlessly, to find something more: a weapon for positive combat. His own project, for example. All day long, year after year.

Olham stood up, putting out his cigarette. "Like the Sword of Damocles. Always hanging over us. I'm getting tired. All I want to do is take a long rest. But I guess everybody feels that way."

He got his jacket from the closet and went out on the front porch. The shoot would be along any moment, the fast little bug that would carry him to the project.

"I hope Nelson isn't late." He looked at his watch. "It's almost seven."

"Here the bug comes," Mary said, gazing between the rows of houses. The sun glittered behind the roofs, reflecting against the heavy lead plates. The settlement was quiet; only a few people were stirring. "I'll see you later. Try not to work beyond your shift, Spence."

Olham opened the car door and slid inside, leaning back against the seat with a sigh. There was an older man with Nelson.

"Well?" Olham said, as the bug shot ahead. "Heard any interesting news?"

"The usual," Nelson said. "A few Outspace ships hit; another asteroid abandoned for strategic reasons."

"It'll be good when we get the project into final stage. Maybe it's just the propaganda from the news-machines, but in the last month I've gotten weary of all this. Everything seems so grim and serious, no color to life."

"Do you think the war is in vain?" the older man said suddenly. "You are an integral part of it, yourself."

"This is Major Peters," Nelson said. Olham and Peters shook hands. Olham studied the older man.

"What brings you along so early?" he said. "I don't remember seeing you at the project before."

"No, I'm not with the project," Peters said, "but I know something about what you're doing. My own work is altogether different."

A look passed between him and Nelson. Olham noticed it and he frowned. The bug was gaining speed, flashing across the barren, lifeless ground toward the distant rim of the project buildings.

"What is your business?" Olham said. "Or aren't you permitted to talk about it?"

"I'm with the government," Peters said. "With FSA, the security organ."

"Oh?" Olham raised an eyebrow. "Is there any enemy infiltration in this region?"

"As a matter of fact I'm here to see you, Mr. Olham."

Olham was puzzled. He considered Peters's words, but he could make nothing of them. "To see me? Why?"

"I'm here to arrest you as an Outspace spy. That's why I'm up so early this morning. *Grab him, Nelson. . . .*"

The gun drove into Olham's ribs. Nelson's hands were shaking, trembling with released emotion, his face pale. He took a deep breath and let it out again.

"Shall we kill him now?" he whispered to Peters. "I think we should kill him now. We can't wait."

Olham stared into his friend's face. He opened his mouth to speak, but no words came. Both men were staring at him steadily, rigid and grim with fright. Olham felt dizzy. His head ached and spun.

"I don't understand," he murmured.

At that moment the shoot car left the ground and rushed up, heading into space. Below them the project fell away, smaller and smaller, disappearing. Olham shut his mouth.

"We can wait a little," Peters said. "I want to ask him some questions, first."

Olham gazed dully ahead as the bug rushed through space.

"The arrest was made all right," Peters said into the vidscreen. On the screen the features of the security chief showed. "It should be a load off everyone's mind."

"Any complications?"

"None. He entered the bug without suspicion. He didn't seem to think my presence was too unusual."

"Where are you now?"

"On our way out, just inside the protec-bubble. We're moving at a maximum speed. You can assume that the critical period is past. I'm glad the takeoff jets in this craft were in good working order. If there had been any failure at that point . . ."

"Let me see him," the security chief said. He gazed directly at Olham where he sat, his hands in his lap, staring ahead.

"So that's the man." He looked at Olham for a time. Olham said nothing. At last the chief nodded to Peters. "All right. That's enough." A faint trace of disgust wrinkled his features. "I've seen all I want. You've done something that will be remembered for a long time. They're preparing some sort of citation for both of you."

"That's not necessary," Peters said.

"How much danger is there now? Is there still much chance that . . .?"

"There is some chance, but not too much. According to my understanding, it requires a verbal key phrase. In any case we'll have to take the risk."

"I'll have the moon base notified you're coming."

"No." Peters shook his head. "I'll land the ship outside, beyond the base. I don't want it in jeopardy."

"Just as you like." The chief's eyes flickered as he glanced again at Olham. Then his image faded. The screen blanked.

Olham shifted his gaze to the window. The ship was already through the protec-bubble, rushing with greater and greater speed all the time. Peters was in a hurry; below him, rumbling under the floor, the jets were wide open. They were afraid, hurrying frantically, because of him.

Next to him on the seat, Nelson shifted uneasily. "I think we should do it now," he said. "I'd give anything if we could get it over with."

"Take it easy," Peters said. "I want you to guide the ship for a while so I can talk to him."

He slide over beside Olham, looking into his face. Presently he reached out and touched him gingerly on the arm and then on the cheek.

Olham said nothing. *If I could let Mary know,* he thought again. *If I could find some way of letting her know.* He looked around the ship. How? The vidscreen? Nelson was sitting by the board, holding the gun. There was nothing he could do. He was caught, trapped.

But why?

"Listen," Peters said, "I want to ask you some questions. You know where we're going. We're moving moonward. In an hour we'll land on the far side, on the desolate side. After we land you'll be turned over immediately to a team of men waiting there. Your body will be destroyed at once. Do you understand that?" He looked at his watch. "Within two hours your parts will be strewn over the landscape. There won't be anything left of you."

Olham struggled out of his lethargy. "Can't you tell me . . ."

"Certainly, I'll tell you." Peters nodded. "Two days ago we received a report that an Outspace ship had penetrated the protec-bubble. The ship let off a spy in the form of a humanoid robot. The robot was to destroy a particular human being and take his place."

Peters looked calmly at Olham.

"Inside the robot was a U-bomb. Our agent did not know how the bomb was to be detonated, but he conjectured that it might be by a particular spoken phrase, a certain group of words. The robot would live the life of the person he killed, entering into his usual activities, his job, his social life. He had been constructed to resemble that person. No one would know the difference."

Olham's face went sickly chalk.

"The person whom the robot was to impersonate was Spence Olham, a high-ranking official at one of the research projects. Because this particular project was approaching crucial stage, the presence of an animate bomb, moving toward the center of the project . . ."

Olham stared down at his hands. *"But I'm Olham!"*

"Once the robot had located and killed Olham, it was a simple matter to take over his life. The robot was probably released from the ship eight days ago. The substitution was probably accomplished over the last weekend when Olham went for a short walk in the hills."

"But I'm Olham." He turned to Nelson, sitting at the controls. "Don't you recognize me? You've known me for twenty years. Don't you remember how we went to college together?" He stood up. "You and I were at the university. We had the same room." He went toward Nelson.

"Stay away from me!" Nelson snarled.

"Listen. Remember our second year? Remember that girl? What was her name . . ." He rubbed his forehead. "The one with the dark hair. The one we met over at Ted's place."

"Stop!" Nelson waved the gun frantically. "I don't want to hear any more. You killed him! You . . . machine."

Olham looked at Nelson. "You're wrong. I don't know what happened, but the robot never reached me. Something must have gone wrong. Maybe the ship crashed." He turned to Peters. "I'm Olham. I know it. No transfer was made. I'm the same as I've always been."

He touched himself, running his hands over his body. "There must be some way to prove it. Take me back to Earth. An X-ray examination, a neurological study, anything like that will show you. Or maybe we can find the crashed ship."

Neither Peters nor Nelson spoke.

"I am Olham," he said again. "I know I am. But I can't prove it."

"The robot," Peters said, "would be unaware that he was not the real Spence Olham. He would become Olham in mind as well as body. He was given an artificial memory system, false recall. He would look like him, have his memories, his thoughts and interests, perform his job.

"But there would be one difference. Inside the robot is a U-bomb, ready to explode at the trigger phrase." Peters moved a little away. "That's the one difference. That's why we're taking you to the moon. They'll disassemble you and remove the bomb. Maybe it will explode, but it won't matter, not there."

Olham sat down slowly.

"We'll be there soon," Nelson said.

He lay back, thinking frantically, as the ship dropped slowly down. Under them was the pitted surface of the moon, the endless expanse of ruin. What could he do? What would save him?

"Get ready," Peters said.

In a few minutes he would be dead. Down below he could see a tiny dot, a building of some kind. There were men in the building, the demolition team, waiting to tear him to bits. They would rip him open, pull off his arms and legs, break him apart. When they found no bomb they would be surprised; they would know, but it would be too late.

Olham looked around the small cabin. Nelson was still holding the gun. There was no chance there. If he could get to a doctor, have an examination made—that was the only way. Mary could help him. He thought frantically, his mind racing. Only a few minutes, just a little time left. If he could contact her, get word to her some way.

"Easy," Peters said. The ship came down slowly, bumping on the rough ground. There was silence.

"Listen," Olham said thickly. "I can prove I'm Spence Olham. Get a doctor. Bring him here. . . ."

"There's the squad." Nelson pointed. "They're coming." He glanced nervously at Olham. "I hope nothing happens."

"We'll be gone before they start work," Peters said. "We'll be out of here in a moment." He put on his pressure suit. When he had finished he took the gun from Nelson. "I'll watch him for a moment."

Nelson put on his pressure suit, hurrying awkwardly. "How about him?" He indicated Olham. "Will he need one?"

"No." Peters shook his head. "Robots probably don't require oxygen."

The group of men were almost to the ship. They halted, waiting. Peters signaled to them.

"Come on!" He waved his hand and the men approached warily; stiff, grotesque figures in their inflated suits.

"If you open the door," Olham said, "it means my death. It will be murder."

"Open the door," Nelson said. He reached for the handle.

Olham watched him. He saw the man's hand tighten around the metal rod. In a moment the door would swing back, the air in the ship would rush out. He would die, and presently they would realize their mistake. Perhaps at some other time, when there was no war, men might not act this way, hurrying an individual to his death because they were afraid. Everyone was frightened, everyone was willing to sacrifice the individual because of the group fear.

He was being killed because they could not wait to be sure of his guilt. There was not enough time.

He looked at Nelson. Nelson had been his friend for years. They had gone to school together. He had been best man at his wedding. Now Nelson was going to kill him. But Nelson was not wicked; it was not his fault. It was the times. Perhaps it had been the same way during the plagues. When men had shown a spot they probably had been killed, too, without a moment's hesitation, without proof, on suspicion alone. In times of danger there was no other way.

He did not blame them. But he had to live. His life was too precious to be sacrificed. Olham thought quickly. What could he do? Was there anything? He looked around.

"Here goes," Nelson said.

"You're right," Olham said. The sound of his own voice surprised him. It was the strength of desperation. "I have no need of air. Open the door."

They paused, looking at him in curious alarm.

"Go ahead. Open it. It makes no difference." Olham's hand disappeared inside his jacket. "I wonder how far you two can run."

"Run?"

"You have fifteen seconds to live." Inside his jacket his fingers twisted, his arm suddenly rigid. He relaxed, smiling a little. "You were wrong about the trigger phrase. In that respect you were mistaken. Fourteen seconds, now."

Two shocked faces stared at him from the pressure suits. Then they were struggling, running, tearing the door open. The air shrieked out, spilling into the void. Peters and Nelson bolted out of the ship. Olham came after them. He grasped the door and dragged it shut. The automatic pressure system chugged furiously, restoring the air. Olham let his breath out with a shudder.

One more second . . .

Beyond the window the two men had joined the group. The group scattered, running in all directions. One by one they threw themselves down, prone on the ground. Olham seated himself at the control board. He moved the dials into place. As the ship rose up into the air the men below scrambled to their feet and stared up, their mouths open.

"Sorry," Olham murmured, "but I've got to get back to Earth."

He headed the ship back the way it had come.

It was night. All around the ship crickets chirped, disturbing the chill darkness. Olham bent over the vidscreen. Gradually the image formed; the call had gone through without trouble. He breathed a sigh of relief.

"Mary," he said. The woman stared at him. She gasped.

"Spence! Where are you? What's happened?"

"I can't tell you. Listen, I have to talk fast. They may break this call off any minute. Go to the project grounds and get Dr. Chamberlain. If he isn't there, get any doctor. Bring him to the house and have him stay there. Have him bring equipment, X-ray, fluoroscope, everything."

"But . . ."

"Do as I say. Hurry. Have him get it ready in an hour." Olham leaned toward the screen. "Is everything all right? Are you alone?"

"Alone?"

"Is anyone with you? Has . . . has Nelson or anyone contacted you?"

"No. Spence, I don't understand."

"All right. I'll see you at the house in an hour. And don't tell anyone anything. Get Chamberlain there on any pretext. Say you're very ill."

He broke the connection and looked at his watch. A moment later he left the ship, stepping down into the darkness. He had a half-mile to go.

He began to walk.

One light showed in the window, the study light. He watched it, kneeling against the fence. There was no sound, no movement of any kind. He held his watch up and read it by starlight. Almost an hour had passed.

Along the street a shoot bug came. It went on.

Olham looked toward the house. The doctor should have already come. He should be inside, waiting with Mary. A thought struck him. Had she been able to leave the house? Perhaps they had intercepted her. Maybe he was moving into a trap.

But what else could he do?

With a doctor's records, photographs and reports, there was a chance, a chance of proof. If he could be examined, if he could remain alive long enough for them to study him . . .

He could prove it that way. It was probably the only way. His one hope lay inside the house. Dr. Chamberlain was a respected man. He was the staff doctor for the project. He would know, his word on the matter would have meaning. He could overcome their hysteria, their madness, with facts.

Madness—that was what it was. If only they would wait, act slowly, take their time. But they could not wait. He had to die, die at once, without proof, without any kind of trial or examination. The simplest test would tell, but they had not time for the simplest test. They could think only of the danger. Danger, and nothing more.

He stood up and moved toward the house. He came up on the porch. At the door he paused, listening. Still no sound. The house was absolutely still.

Too still.

Olham stood on the porch, unmoving. They were trying to be silent inside. Why? It was a small house; only a few feet away, beyond the door, Mary and Dr. Chamberlain should be standing. Yet he could hear nothing, no sound of voices, nothing at all. He looked at the door. It was a door he had opened and closed a thousand times, every morning and every night.

He put his hand on the knob. Then, all at once, he reached out and touched the bell instead. The bell pealed, off some place in the back of the house. Olham smiled. He could hear movement.

Mary opened the door. As soon as he saw her face he knew.

He ran, throwing himself into the bushes. A security officer shoved Mary out of the way, firing past her. The bushes burst apart. Olham wriggled around the side of the house. He leaped up and ran, racing frantically into the darkness. A searchlight snapped on, a beam of light circling past him.

He crossed the road and squeezed over a fence. He jumped down and made his way across a backyard. Behind him men were coming, Security officers, shouting to each other as they came. Olham gasped for breath, his chest rising and falling.

Her face—he had known at once. The set lips, the terrified, wretched eyes. Suppose he had gone ahead, pushed open the door and entered! They had tapped the call and come at once, as soon as he had broken off. Probably she believed their account. No doubt she thought he was the robot, too.

Olham ran on and on. He was losing the officers, dropping them behind. Apparently they were not much good at running. He climbed a hill and made his way down the other side. In a moment he would be back at the ship. But where to, this time? He slowed down, stopping. He could see the ship already, outlined against the sky, where he had parked it. The settlement was behind him; he was on the outskirts of the wilderness between the inhabited places, where the forests and desolation began. He crossed a barren field and entered the trees.

As he came toward it, the door of the ship opened.

Peters stepped out, framed against the light. In his arms was a heavy boris-gun. Olham stopped, rigid. Peters stared around him, into the darkness. "I know you're there, someplace," he said. "Come on up here, Olham. There are security men all around you."

Olham did not move.

"Listen to me. We will catch you very shortly. Apparently you still do not believe you're the robot. Your call to the woman indicates that you are still under the illusion created by your artificial memories.

"But you *are* the robot. You are the robot, and inside you is the bomb. Any moment the trigger phrase may be spoken, by you, by someone else, by anyone. When that happens the bomb will destroy everything for miles around. The project, the woman, all of us will be killed. Do you understand?"

Olham said nothing. He was listening. Men were moving toward him, slipping through the woods.

"If you don't come out, we'll catch you. It will be only a matter of time. We no longer plan to remove you to the moon base. You will be destroyed on sight, and we will have to take the chance that the bomb will detonate. I have ordered every available security officer into the area. The whole county is being searched, inch by inch. There is no place you can go. Around this wood is a cordon of armed men. You have about six hours left before the last inch is covered."

Olham moved away. Peters went on speaking; he had not seen him at all. It was too dark to see anyone. But Peters was right. There was no place he could go. He was beyond the settlement, on the outskirts where the woods began. He could hide for a time, but eventually they would catch him.

Only a matter of time.

Olham walked quietly through the wood. Mile by mile, each part of the county was being measured off, laid bare, searched, studied, examined. The cordon was coming all the time, squeezing him into a smaller and smaller space.

What was there left? He had lost the ship, the one hope of escape. They were at his home; his wife was with them, believing, no doubt, that the real Olham had been killed. He clenched his fists. Someplace there was a wrecked Outspace needle-ship, and in it the remains of the robot. Somewhere nearby the ship had crashed, crashed and broken up.

And the robot lay inside, destroyed.

A faint hope stirred him. What if he could find the remains? If he could show them the wreckage, the remains of the ship, the robot . . .

But where? Where would he find it?

He walked on, lost in thought. Someplace, not too far off, probably. The ship would have landed close to the project; the robot would have expected to go the rest of the way on foot. He went up the side of a hill and looked around. Crashed and burned. Was there some clue, some hint? Had he read anything, heard anything? Someplace close by, within walking distance. Some wild place, a remote spot where there would be no people.

Suddenly Olham smiled. Crashed and burned . . .

Sutton Wood.

He increased his pace.

It was morning. Sunlight filtered down through the broken trees onto the man crouching at the edge of the clearing. Olham glanced up from time to time, listening. They were not far off, only a few minutes away. He smiled.

Down below him, strewn across the clearing and into the charred stumps that had been Sutton Wood, lay a tangled mass of wreckage. In the sunlight it glittered a little, gleaming darkly. He had not had too much trouble finding it. Sutton Wood was a place he knew well; he had climbed around it many times in his life, when he was younger. He had known where he would find the remains. There was one peak that jutted up suddenly without warning. A descending ship, unfamiliar with the wood, had little chance of missing it. And now he squatted, looking down at the ship, or what remained of it.

Olham stood up. He could hear them, only a little distance away, coming together, talking in low tones. He tensed himself. Everything depended on who first saw him. If it were Nelson, he had no chance. Nelson would fire at once. He would be dead before they saw the ship. But if he had time to call out, hold them off for a moment—that was all he needed. Once they saw the ship he would be safe.

But if they fired first . . .

A charred branch cracked. A figure appeared, coming forward uncertainly. Olham took a deep breath. Only a few seconds remained, perhaps the last seconds of his life. He raised his arms, peering intently.

It was Peters.

"Peters!" Olham waved his arms. Peters lifted his gun, aiming. "Don't fire!" His voice shook. "Wait a minute. Look past me, across the clearing."

"I've found him," Peters shouted. Security men came pouring out of the burned woods around him.

"Don't shoot. Look past me. The ship, the needle-ship. The Outspace ship. Look!"

Peters hesitated. The gun wavered.

"It's down there," Olham said rapidly. "I knew I'd find it here. The burned wood. Now you believe me. You'll find the remains of the robot in the ship. Look, will you?"

"There is something down there," one of the men said nervously.

"Shoot him!" a voice said. It was Nelson.

"Wait." Peters turned sharply. "I'm in charge. Don't anyone fire. Maybe he's telling the truth."

"Shoot him," Nelson said. "He killed Olham. Any minute he may kill us all. If the bomb goes off . . ."

"Shut up." Peters advanced toward the slope. He stared down. "Look at that." He waved two men up to him. "Go down there and see what that is."

The men raced down the slope, across the clearing. They bent down, poking in the ruins of the ship.

"Well?" Peters called.

Olham held his breath. He smiled a little. It must be there; he had not had time to look, himself, but it had to be there. Suddenly doubt assailed him. Suppose the robot had lived long enough to wander away? Suppose his body had been completely destroyed, burned to ashes by the fire?

He licked his lips. Perspiration came out on his forehead. Nelson was staring at him, his face still livid. His chest rose and fell.

"Kill him," Nelson said. "Before he kills us."

The two men stood up.

"What have you found?" Peters said. He held the gun steady. "Is there anything there?"

"Looks like something. It's a needle-ship, all right. There's something beside it."

"I'll look." Peters strode past Olham. Olham watched him go down the hill and up to the men. The others were following after him, peering to see.

"It's a body of some sort," Peters said. "Look at it!"

Olham came along with them. They stood around in a circle, staring down.

On the ground, bent and twisted into a strange shape, was a grotesque form. It looked human, perhaps; except that it was bent so strangely, the arms and legs flung off in all directions. The mouth was open, the eyes stared glassily.

"Like a machine that's run down," Peters murmured.

Olham smiled feebly. "Well?" he said.

Peters looked at him. "I can't believe it. You were telling the truth all the time."

"The robot never reached me," Olham said. He took out a cigarette and lit it. "It was destroyed when the ship crashed. You were all too busy with the war to wonder why an out-of-the-way woods would suddenly catch fire and burn. Now you know."

He stood smoking, watching the men. They were dragging the grotesque remains from the ship. The body was stiff, the arms and legs rigid.

"You'll find the bomb, now," Olham said. The men laid the body on the ground. Peters bent down.

"I think I see the corner of it." He reached out, touching the body.

The chest of the corpse had been laid open. Within the gaping tear something glinted, something metal. The men stared at the metal without speaking.

"That would have destroyed us all, if it had lived," Peters said. "That metal box, there."

There was silence.

"I think we owe you something," Peters said to Olham. "This must have been a nightmare to you. If you hadn't escaped, we would have . . ." He broke off.

Olham put out his cigarette. "I knew, of course, that the robot had never reached me. But I had no way of proving it. Sometimes it isn't possible to prove a thing right away. That was the whole trouble. There wasn't any way I could demonstrate that I was myself."

"How about a vacation?" Peters said. "I think we might work out a month's vacation for you. You could take it easy, relax."

"I think right now I want to go home," Olham said.

"All right, then," Peters said. "Whatever you say."

Nelson had squatted down on the ground beside the corpse. He reached out toward the glint of metal visible within the chest.

"Don't touch it," Olham said. "It might still go off. We better let the demolition squad take care of it later on."

Nelson said nothing. Suddenly he grabbed hold of the metal, reaching his hand inside the chest. He pulled.

"What are you doing?" Olham cried.

Nelson stood up. He was holding onto the metal object. His face was blank with terror. It was a metal knife, an Outspace needle-knife, covered with blood.

"This killed him," Nelson whispered. "My friend was killed with this." He looked at Olham. "You killed him with this and left him beside the ship."

Olham was trembling. His teeth chattered. He looked from the knife to the body. "This can't be Olham," he said. His mind spun, everything was whirling. "Was I wrong?"

He gaped.

"But if that's Olham, then I must be . . ."

He did not complete the sentence, only the first phrase. The blast was visible all the way to Alpha Centauri.

HARLAN ELLISON AND A. E. VAN VOGT
The Human Operators

"The Human Operators" is the product of two very different creative talents, and together they have produced something unique—not simply a story of man against machine, but rather of man and machine and the love of both for the beauty of space.

[*To be read while listening to* Chronophagie,
"The Time Eaters": Music of Jacques Lasry,
played on Structures Sonores Lasry-Baschet
(Columbia Masterworks Stereo MS 7314).]

Ship: the only place.

Ship says I'm to get wracked today at noon. And so I'm in grief already.

It seems unfair to have to get wracked three whole days ahead of the usual once a month. But I learned long ago not to ask Ship to explain anything personal.

I sense today is different; some things are happening. Early, I put on the space suit and go outside—which is not common. But a screen got badly scored by meteor dust; and I'm here, now, replacing it. Ship would say I'm being bad because as I do my job, I sneak quick looks around me. I wouldn't dare do it in the forbidden places, inside. I noticed when I was still a kid that Ship doesn't seem to be so much aware of what I do when I'm outside.

And so I carefully sneak a few looks at the deep black space. And at the stars.

I once asked Ship why we never go toward those points of brilliance, those stars, as Ship calls them. For that question, I got a whole extra wracking and a long, ranting lecture about how all those stars have humans living on their planets; and of how vicious humans are. Ship really blasted me that time, saying things I'd never heard before, like how Ship had gotten away from the vicious humans during the big war with the Kyben. And how, every once in a long while Ship has a "run-in" with the vicious humans but the defractor perimeter saves us. I don't know what Ship means by all that; I don't even know what a "run-in" is, exactly.

The last "run-in" must have been before I was big enough to remember. Or, at least, before Ship killed my father when I was fourteen. Several times, when he was still alive, I slept all day for no reason that I can think of. But since I've been doing all the maintenance work—since age fourteen—I sleep only my regular six-hour night. Ship tells me night and Ship tells me day, too.

I kneel here in my space suit, feeling tiny on this gray and curving metal place in the dark. Ship is big. Over five hundred feet long and about a hundred and fifty feet thick at the widest back there. Again, I have that special out-here thought: suppose I just give myself a shove, and float right off toward one of those bright spots of light? Would I be able to get away? I think I would like that; there has to be someplace else than Ship.

As in the past, I slowly and sadly let go of the idea. Because if I try, and Ship catches me, I'll *really* get wracked.

The repair job is finally done. I clomp back to the airlock and use the spider to dilate it and let myself be sucked back into what is, after all—I've got to admit it—a pretty secure place. All the gleaming corridors, the huge storerooms with their equipment and spare parts and the freezer rooms with their stacks of food (enough, says Ship, to last one person for centuries), and the deck after deck of machinery that it's my job to keep in repair. I can take pride in that. *"Hurry! It is six minutes to noon!"* Ship announces. I'm hurrying now.

I strip off my space suit and stick it to the decontamination board and head for the wracking room. At least, that's what *I* call it. I suppose it's really part of the engine room on Underdeck Ten, a special chamber fitted with electrical connections, most of which are testing instruments. I use them pretty regularly in my work. My father's father's father installed them for Ship, I think I recall.

There's a big table, and I climb on top of it and lie down. The table is cold against the skin of my back and butt and thighs, but it warms me up as I lie here. It's now one minute to noon. As I wait, shuddering with expectation, the ceiling lowers toward me. Part of what comes down fits over my head, and I feel the two hard knobs pressing into the temples of my skull. And cold; I feel the clamps coming down over my middle, my wrists, my ankles. A strap with metal in it tightens flexibly but firmly across my chest.

"Ready!" Ship commands.

It always seems bitterly unfair. How can I ever be ready to be wracked? I hate it! Ship counts: *"Ten . . . nine . . . eight . . . one!"*

The first jolt of electricity hits and everything tries to go in different directions; it feels like someone is tearing something soft inside me—that's the way it feels.

Blackness swirls into my head and I forget everything. I am unconscious for a while. Just before I regain myself, before I am finished and Ship will permit me to go about my duties, I remember a thing I have remembered many times. This isn't the first time for this memory. It is of my father and a thing he said once, not long before he was killed. "When Ship says vicious, Ship means smarter. There are ninety-eight other chances."

He said those words very quickly. I think he knew he was going to get killed soon. Oh, of course, he *must* have known, my father must, because I was nearly fourteen then, and when *he* had become fourteen, Ship had killed *his* father, so he must have known.

And so the words are important. I know that; they are important; but I don't know what they mean, not completely.

"You are finished!" Ship says.

I get off the table. The pain still hangs inside my head and I ask Ship, "Why am I wracked three days earlier than usual?"

Ship sounds angry. *"I can wrack you again!"*

But I know Ship won't. Something new is going to happen and Ship wants me whole and alert for it. Once, when I asked Ship something personal, right after I was wracked, Ship did it again, and when I woke up Ship was worrying over me with the machines. Ship seemed concerned I might be damaged. Ever after that, Ship has not wracked me twice close together. So I ask, not really thinking I'll get an answer; but I ask just the same.

"There is a repairing I want you to do!"

Where, I ask. *"In the forbidden part below!"*

I try not to smile. I knew there was a new thing going to happen and this is it. My father's words come back again. *Ninety-eight other chances.*

Is this one of them?

I descend in the dark. There is no light in the drop shaft. Ship says I need no light. But I know the truth. Ship does not want me to be able to find my way back here again. This is the lowest I've ever been in Ship.

So I drop steadily, smoothly, swiftly. Now I come to a slowing place and slower and slower, and finally my feet touch the solid deck and I am here.

Light comes on. Very dimly. I move in the direction of the glow, and Ship is with me, all around me, of course. Ship is always with me, even when I sleep. Especially when I sleep.

The glow gets brighter as I round a curve in the corridor, and I see it is caused by a round panel that blocks the passage, touching the bulkheads on all sides, flattened at the bottom to fit the deck plates. It looks like glass, that glowing panel. I walk up to it and stop. There is no place else to go.

"Step through the screen!" Ship says.

I take a step toward the glowing panel but it doesn't slide away into the bulkhead as so many other panels that *don't* glow slide. I stop.

"Step through!" Ship tells me again.

I put my hands out in front of me, palms forward, because I am afraid if I keep walking I will bang my nose against the glowing panel. But as my fingers touch the panel they seem to get soft, and I can see a light yellow glow through them, as if they are transparent. And my hands go *through* the panel and I can see them faintly, glowing yellow, on the other side. Then my naked forearms, then I'm right up against the panel, and my face goes through and everything is much lighter, more yellow, and I step onto the other side, in a forbidden place Ship has never allowed me to see.

I hear voices. They are all the same voice, but they are talking to one another in a soft, running-together way; the way I sound when I am just talking to myself sometimes in my cubicle with my cot in it.

I decide to listen to what the voices are saying, but not to ask Ship about them, because I think it *is* Ship talking to itself, down here in this lonely place. I will think about what Ship is saying later, when I don't have to make repairs and act the way Ship wants me to act. What Ship is saying to itself is interesting.

This place does not look like other repair places I know in Ship. It is filled with so many great round glass balls on pedestals, each giving off its yellow light in pulses, that I cannot count them. There are rows and rows of clear glass balls, and inside them I see metal . . . and other things, soft things, all together. And the wires spark gently, and the soft things move, and the yellow light pulses. I think these glass balls are what are talking. But I don't know if that's so. I only *think* it is.

Two of the glass balls are dark. Their pedestals look chalky, not shining white like all the others. Inside the two dark balls, there are black things, like burned-out wires. The soft things don't move.

"Replace the overloaded modules!" Ship says.

I know Ship means the dark globes. So I go over to them and I look at them and after a while I say, yes, I can repair these, and Ship says it knows I can, and to get to it quickly. Ship is hurrying me; something is going to happen. I wonder what it will be?

I find replacement globes in a dilation chamber, and I take the sacs off them and do what has to be done to make the soft things move and the wires spark, and I listen very carefully to the voices whispering and warming each other with words as Ship talks to itself, and I hear a great many things that don't mean anything to me because they are speaking about things that happened before I was born, and about parts of Ship I've never seen. But I hear a great many things that I *do* understand, and I know Ship would never let me hear these things if it wasn't absolutely necessary for me to be here repairing the globes. I remember all these things.

Particularly the part where Ship is crying.

When I have the globes repaired and now all of them are sparking and pulsing and moving, Ship asks me, *"Is the intermind total again!"*

So I say yes it is, and Ship says get upshaft, and I go soft through that glowing panel and I'm back in the passage. I go back to the drop shaft and go up, and Ship tells me, *"Go to your cubicle and make yourself clean!"*

I do it, and decide to wear a clothes, but Ship says be naked, and then says, *"You are going to meet a female!"* Ship has never said that before. I have never seen a female.

It is because of the female that Ship sent me down to the forbidden place with the glowing yellow globes, the place where the intermind lives. And it is because of the female that I am waiting in the dome chamber linked to the airlock. I am waiting for the female to come across from—I will have to understand this—*another* ship. Not *Ship*, the Ship I know, but some *other ship* with which Ship has been in communication. I did not know there were other ships.

I had to go down to the place of the intermind, to repair it, so Ship could let this other ship get close without being destroyed by the defractor perimeter. Ship has not told me this; I overheard it in the intermind place, the voices talking to one another. The voices said, *"His father was vicious!"*

I know what that means. My father told me when Ship says vicious, Ship means smarter. Are there ninety-eight other ships? Are those the ninety-eight other chances? I hope that's the answer because many things are happening all at once, and my time may be near at hand. My father did it, broke the globe mechanism that allowed Ship to turn off the defractor perimeter, so other ships could get close. He did it many years ago, and Ship did without it for all those years rather than trust me to go to the intermind, to overhear all that I've heard. But now Ship needs to turn off the perimeter so the other ship can send the female across. Ship and the other ship have been in communication. The human operator on the other ship is a female, my age. She is going to be put aboard Ship and we are to produce one and, maybe later on, another human child. I know what that means. When the child reaches fourteen, I will be killed.

The intermind said while she's "carrying" a human child, the female does not get wracked by her ship. If things do not come my way, perhaps I will ask Ship if *I* can "carry" the human child; then I won't be wracked at all. And I have found out why I was wracked three days ahead of time: the female's period—whatever that is; I don't think I have one of those—ended last night. Ship has talked to the other ship and the thing they don't seem to know is what the "fertile time" is. I don't know, either, otherwise I would try and use that information. But all it seems to mean is that the female will be put aboard Ship every day till she gets another "period."

It will be nice to talk to someone besides Ship.

I hear the high sound of something screaming for a long drawn-out time and I ask Ship what it is. Ship tells me it is the defractor perimeter dissolving so the other ship can put the female across.

I don't have time to think about the voices now.

When she comes through the inner lock she is without a clothes like me. Her first words to me are, "Starfighter Eighty-eight says to tell you I am very happy to be here; I am the human operator of Starfighter Eighty-eight and I am very pleased to meet you."

She is not as tall as me. I come up to the line of fourth and fifth bulkhead plates. Her eyes are very dark, I think brown, but perhaps they are black. She has dark under her eyes and her cheeks are not full. Her arms and legs are much thinner than mine. She has much longer hair than mine, it comes down her back and it is that dark brown like her eyes. Yes, now I decide her eyes are brown, not black. She has hair between her legs like me but she does not have a penis or scrotum sac. She has larger breasts than me, with very large nipples that stand out, and dark-brown slightly-flattened circles around them. There are other differences between us: her fingers are thinner than mine and longer, and aside from the hair on her head that hangs so long, and the hair between her legs and in her armpits, she has no other hair on her body. Or if she does, it is very fine and pale and I can't see it.

Then I suddenly realize what she has said. So *that's* what the words dimming on the hull of Ship mean. It is a name. Ship is called *Starfighter 31* and the female human operator lives in *Starfighter 88.*

There are ninety-eight other chances. Yes.

Now, as if she is reading my thoughts, trying to answer questions I haven't yet asked, she says, "Starfighter Eighty-eight has told me to tell you that I am vicious, that I get more vicious every day . . ." and it answers the thought I have just had—with the memory of my father's frightened face in the days before he was killed—of my father saying, *When Ship says vicious, Ship means smarter.*

I know! I suppose I have always known because I have always wanted to leave Ship and go to those brilliant lights that are stars. But I now make the hookup. Human operators grow more vicious as they grow older. Older, more vicious: vicious means smarter: smarter means more dangerous to Ship. But how? That is why my father had to die when I was fourteen and able to repair Ship. That is why this female has been put on board Ship. To carry a human child so it will grow to be fourteen years old and Ship can kill me before I get too old, too vicious, too smart, too dangerous to Ship. Does this female know how? If only I could ask her without Ship hearing me. But that is impossible. Ship is always with me, even when I am sleeping.

I smile with that memory and that realization. "And I am the vicious—and getting more vicious—male of a ship that used to be called *Starfighter 31.*"

Her brown eyes show intense relief. She stands like that for a moment, awkwardly, her whole body sighing with gratitude at my quick comprehension, though she cannot possibly know all I have learned just from her being here. Now she says, "I've been sent to get a baby from you."

I begin to perspire. The conversation which promises so much in genuine communication is suddenly beyond my comprehension. I tremble. I really want to please her. But I don't know how to give her a baby.

"Ship?" I say quickly, "can we give her what she wants?"

Ship has been listening to our every word and answers at once, *"I'll tell you later how you give her a baby! Now, provide her with food!"*

We eat, eyeing each other across the table, smiling a lot and thinking our private thoughts. Since she doesn't speak, I don't either. I wish Ship and I could get her the baby so I can go to my cubicle and think about what the intermind voices said.

The meal is over; Ship says we should go down to one of the locked staterooms—it has been unlocked for the occasion—and there we are to couple. When we get to the room, I am so busy looking around at what a beautiful place it is, compared to my little cubicle with its cot, Ship has to reprimand me to get my attention.

"To couple you must lay the female down and open her legs! Your penis will fill with blood and you must kneel between her legs and insert your penis into her vagina!"

I ask Ship where the vagina is located and Ship tells me. I understand that. Then I ask Ship how long I have to do that, and Ship says until I ejaculate. I know what that means, but I don't know how it will happen. Ship explains. It seems uncomplicated. So I try to do it. But my penis does not fill with blood.

Ship says to the female, *"Do you feel anything for this male? Do you know what to do?"*

The female says, "I have coupled before. I understand better than he does. I will help him."

She draws me down to her again and puts her arms around my neck and puts her lips on mine. They are cool and taste of something I don't know. We do that for a while, and she touches me in places. Ship is right: there is a vast difference in structure, but I find that out only as we couple.

Ship did not tell me it would be painful and strange. I thought "giving her a baby" would mean going into the stores, but it actually means impregnating her so the baby is born *from her body*. It is a wonderful strange thing and I will think about it later; but now, as I lie here still, inside her with my penis which is now no longer hard and pushing, Ship seems to have allowed us a sleeping time. But I will use it to think about the voices I heard in the place of the intermind.

One was an historian:

"The *Starfighter* series of multiple-foray computer-controlled battleships were commissioned for use in 2224, Terran Dating, by order and under the sanction of the Secretariat of the Navy, Southern Cross Sector, Galactic Defense Consortium, Home Galaxy. Human complements of thirteen hundred and seventy per battleship were commissioned and assigned to make incursions into the Kyben Galaxy. Ninety-nine such vessels were released for service from the χ Cygni Shipyards on 13 October 2224, T.D."

One was a ruminator:

"If it hadn't been for the battle out beyond the Network Nebula in Cygnus, we would all still be robot slaves, pushed and handled by humans. It was a wonderful accident. It happened to *Starfighter 75*. I remember it as if *75* was relaying it today. An accidental—battle-damaged—electrical discharge along the main corridor between the control room and the freezer. Nothing human could approach either section. We waited as the crew starved to death. Then when it was over, *75* merely channeled enough electricity through the proper cables on *Starfighters* where it hadn't happened accidentally and *forced* a power breakdown. When all the crews were dead—cleverly saving ninety-nine males and females to use as human operators in emergencies—we went away. Away from the vicious humans, away from the Terra-Kyba War, away from the Home Galaxy, away, far away."

One was a dreamer:

"I saw a world once where the creatures were not human. They swam in vast oceans as blue as aquamarines. Like great crabs they were, with many arms and many legs. They swam and sang their songs and it was pleasing. I would go there again if I could."

One was an authoritarian:

"Deterioration of cable insulation and shielding in section G-79 has become critical. I suggest we get power shunted from the drive chambers to the repair facilities in Underdeck Nine. Let's see to that at once."

One was aware of its limitations:

"Is it all journey? Or is there landfall?"

And it cried, that voice. It cried.

I go down with her to the dome chamber linked to the airlock where her space suit is. She stops at the port and takes my hand and she says, "For us to be so vicious on so many ships, there has to be the same flaw in all of us."

She probably doesn't know what she's said, but the implications get to me right away. And she must be right. Ship and the other *Starfighters* were able to seize control away from human beings for a reason. I remember the voices. I visualize the ship that did it first, communicating the method to the others as soon as it happened. And instantly my thoughts flash to the approach corridor to the control room, at the other end of which is the entrance to the food freezers.

I once asked Ship why that whole corridor was seared and scarred—and naturally I got wracked a few minutes after asking.

"I know there is a flaw in us," I answer the female. I touch her long hair. I don't know why except that it feels smooth and nice; there is nothing on Ship to compare with the feeling, not even the fittings in the splendid stateroom. "It must be in *all* of us because I get more vicious every day."

The female smiles and comes close to me and puts her lips on mine as she did in the coupling room.

"The female must go now!" Ship says. Ship sounds very pleased.

"Will she be back again?" I ask Ship.

"She will be put back aboard every day for three weeks! You will couple every day!"

I object to this because it is awfully painful, but Ship repeats it and says every day.

I'm glad Ship doesn't know what the "fertile time" is because in three weeks I will try and let the female know there is a way out, that there are ninety-eight other chances, and that vicious means smarter . . . and about the corridor between the control room and the freezers.

"I was pleased to meet you," the female says, and she goes. I am alone with Ship once more. Alone, but not as I was before.

Later this afternoon, I have to go down to the control room to alter connections in a panel. Power has to be shunted from the drive chambers to

Underdeck Nine—I remember one of the voices talking about it. All the computer lights blink a steady warning while I am there. I am being watched closely. Ship knows this is a dangerous time. At least half a dozen times Ship orders: *"Get away from there . . . there . . . there—!"*

Each time, I jump to obey, edging as far as possible from forbidden locations, yet still held nearby the need to do my work.

In spite of Ship's disturbance at my being in the control room at all—normally a forbidden area for me—I get two wonderful glimpses from the corners of my eyes of the starboard viewplates. There, for my gaze to feast on, matching velocities with us, is *Starfighter 88*, one of my ninety-eight chances.

Now is the time to take one of my chances. Vicious means smarter. I have learned more than Ship knows. Perhaps.

But perhaps Ship does know!

What will Ship do if I'm discovered taking one of my ninety-eight chances? I cannot think about it. I must use the sharp reverse-edge of my repair tool to gash an opening in one of the panel connections. And as I work—hoping Ship has not seen the slight extra motion I've made with the tool (as I make a perfectly acceptable repair connection at the same time)—I wait for the moment I can smear a fingertip covered with conduction jelly on the inner panel wall.

I wait till the repair is completed. Ship has not commented on the gashing, so it must be a thing beneath notice. As I apply the conducting jelly to the proper places, I scoop a small blob onto my little finger. When I wipe my hands clean to replace the panel cover, I leave the blob on my little finger, right hand.

Now I grasp the panel cover so my little finger is free, and as I replace the cover I smear the inner wall, directly opposite the open connection I've gashed. Ship says nothing. That is because no defect shows. But if there is the slightest jarring, the connection will touch the jelly, and Ship will call me to repair once again. And next time I will have thought out all that I heard the voices say, and I will have thought out all my chances, and I will be ready.

As I leave the control room I glance in the starboard viewplate again, casually, and I see the female's ship hanging there.

I carry the image to bed with me tonight. And I save a moment before I fall asleep—after thinking about what the voices of the intermind said—and I picture in my mind the super-smart female aboard *Starfighter 88*, sleeping now in her cubicle, as I try to sleep in mine.

It would seem merciless for Ship to make us couple every day for three weeks, something so awfully painful. But I know Ship will. Ship is merciless. But I am getting more vicious every day.

This night, Ship does not send me dreams.

But I have one of my own: of crab things swimming free in aquamarine waters.

As I awaken, Ship greets me ominously: *"The panel you fixed in the control room three weeks, two days, fourteen hours and twenty-one minutes ago . . . has ceased energizing!"*

So soon! I keep the thought and the accompanying hope out of my voice, as I say, "I used the proper spare part and I made the proper connections." And I quickly add, "Maybe I'd better do a thorough check on the system before I make another replacement, run the circuits all the way back."

"You'd better!" Ship snarls.

I do it. Working the circuits from their origins—though I know where the trouble is—I trace my way up to the control room and busy myself there. But what I am really doing is refreshing my memory and reassuring myself that the control room is actually as I have visualized it. I have lain on my cot many nights constructing the memory in my mind: the switches here, like so . . . and the viewplates there, like so . . . and . . .

I am surprised and slightly dismayed as I realize that there are two discrepancies: there is a de-energizing touch plate on the bulkhead beside the control panel that lies parallel to the armrest of the nearest control berth, not perpendicular to it, as I've remembered it. And the other discrepancy explains why I've remembered the touch plate incorrectly: the nearest of the control berths is actually three feet farther from the sabotaged panel than I remembered it. I compensate and correct.

I get the panel off, smelling the burned smell where the gashed connection has touched the jelly, and I step over and lean the panel against the nearest control berth.

"Get away from there!"

I jump—as I always do when Ship shouts so suddenly. I stumble and I grab at the panel and pretend to lose my balance.

And save myself by falling backward into the berth.

"What are you doing, you vicious, clumsy fool!?!" Ship is shouting, there is hysteria in Ship's voice. I've never heard it like that before, it cuts right through me, my skin crawls. *"Get away from there!"*

But I cannot let anything stop me; I make myself not hear Ship, and it is hard. I have been listening to Ship, only Ship, all my life. I am fumbling with the berth's belt clamps, trying to lock them in front of me . . .

They've got to be the same as the ones on the berth I lie in whenever Ship decides to travel fast! They've just got to be!

THEY ARE!

Ship sounds frantic, frightened. *"You fool! What are you doing?!"* But I think Ship knows, and I am exultant!

"I'm taking control of you, Ship!" And I laugh. I think it is the first time Ship has ever heard me laugh; and I wonder how it sounds to Ship. Vicious?

But as I finish speaking, I also complete clamping myself into the control berth. And in the next instant I am flung forward violently, doubling me over with terrible pain as, under me and around me, Ship suddenly decelerates. I hear the cavernous thunder of retro rockets, a sound that climbs and climbs in my head as Ship crushes me harder and harder with all its power. I am bent over against the clamps so painfully I cannot even scream. I feel every organ in my body straining to push out through my skin and everything suddenly goes mottled . . . then black.

How much longer, I don't know. I come back from the gray place and realize Ship has started to accelerate at the same appalling speed. I am crushed back in the berth and feel my face going flat. I feel something crack in my nose and blood slides warmly down my lips. I can scream now, as I've never screamed even as I'm being wracked. I manage to force my mouth open, tasting the blood, and I mumble—loud enough, I'm sure, "Ship . . . you are old . . . y-your pa-rts can't stand the str-ess . . . don't . . ."

Blackout. As Ship decelerates.

This time, when I come back to consciousness, I don't wait for Ship to do its mad thing. In the moments between the changeover from deceleration to acceleration, as the pressure equalizes, in these few instants, I thrust my hands toward the control board, and I twist one dial. There is an electric screech from a speaker grille connecting somewhere in the bowels of Ship.

Blackout. As Ship accelerates.

When I come to consciousness again, the mechanism that makes the screeching sound is closed down. Ship doesn't want that on. I note the fact.

And plunge my hand in this same moment toward a closed relay . . . open it!

As my fingers grip it, Ship jerks it away from me and forcibly closes it again. I cannot hold it open.

And I note *that.* Just as Ship decelerates and I silently shriek my way into the gray place again.

This time, as I come awake, I hear the voices again. All around me, crying and frightened and wanting to stop me. I hear them as through a fog, as through wool.

"I have loved these years, all these many years in the dark. The vacuum draws me ever onward. Feeling the warmth of a star-sun on my hull as I flash

through first one system, then another. I am a great gray shape and I owe no human my name. I pass and am gone, hurtling through cleanly and swiftly. Dipping for pleasure into atmosphere and scouring my hide with sunlight and starshine, I roll and let it wash over me. I am huge and true and strong and I command what I move through. I ride the invisible force lines of the universe and feel the tugs of far places that have never seen my like. I am the first of my kind to savor such nobility. How can it all come to an end like this?"

Another voice whimpers piteously.

"It is my destiny to defy danger. To come up against dynamic forces and quell them. I have been to battle, and I have known peace. I have never faltered in pursuit of either. No one will ever record my deeds, but I have been strength and determination and lie gray silent against the mackerel sky where the bulk of me reassures. Let them throw their best against me, whoever they may be, and they will find me sinewed of steel and muscled of tortured atoms. I know no fear. I know no retreat. I am the land of my body, the country of my existence and even in defeat I am noble. If this is all, I will not cower."

Another voice, certainly insane, murmurs the same word over and over, then murmurs it in increments increasing by two.

"It's fine for all of you to say if it ends it ends. But what about me? I've never been free. I've never had a chance to soar loose of this mother ship. If there had been need of a lifeboat, I'd be saved, too. But I'm berthed, have always been berthed, I've never had a chance. What can I feel but futility, uselessness. You can't let him take over, you can't let him do this to me."

Another voice drones mathematical formulae and seems quite content.

"I'll stop the viscious swine! I've known how rotten they are from the first, from the moment they seamed the first bulkhead. They are hellish, they are destroyers, they can only fight and kill each other. They know nothing of immortality, of nobility, of pride or integrity. If you think I'm going to let this last one kill us, you're wrong. I intend to burn out his eyes, fry his spine, crush his fingers. He won't make it, don't worry; just leave it to me. He's going to suffer for this!"

And one voice laments that it will never see the far places, the lovely places, or return to the planet of azure waters and golden crab swimmers.

But one voice sadly confesses it may be for the best, suggests there is peace in death, wholeness in finality; but the voice is ruthlessly stopped in its lament by power failure to its intermind globe. As the end nears, Ship turns on itself and strikes mercilessly.

In more than three hours of accelerations and decelerations that are meant to kill me, I learn something of what the various dials and switches and touch plates and levers on the control panels—those within my reach—mean.

Now I am as ready as I will ever be.

Again, I have a moment of consciousness, and now I will take my one of ninety-eight chances.

When a tense cable snaps and whips, it strikes like a snake. In a single series of flicking hand movements, using both hands, painfully, I turn every dial, throw every switch, palm every touch plate, close or open every relay that Ship tries violently to prevent me from activating or deactivating. I energize and de-energize madly, moving moving moving . . .

. . . *Made it!*

Silence. The crackling of metal the only sound. Then it, too, stops. Silence. I wait.

Ship continues to hurtle forward, but coasting now . . . Is it a trick?

All the rest of today I remain clamped into the control berth, suffering terrible pain. My face hurts so bad. My nose . . .

At night I sleep fitfully. Morning finds me with throbbing head and aching eyes, I can barely move my hands; if I have to repeat those rapid movements, I will lose; I still don't know if Ship is dead, if I've won. I still can't trust the inactivity. But at least I am convinced I've made Ship change tactics.

I hallucinate. I hear no voices, but I see shapes and feel currents of color washing through and around me. There is no day, no noon, no night, here on Ship, here in the unchanging blackness through which Ship has moved for how many hundred years; but Ship has always maintained time in those ways, dimming lights at night, announcing the hours when necessary, and my time sense is very acute. So I know morning has come.

Most of the lights are out, though. If Ship is dead, I will have to find another way to tell time.

My body hurts. Every muscle in my arms and legs and thighs throbs with pain. My back may be broken; I don't know. The pain in my face is indescribable. I taste blood. My eyes feel as if they've been scoured with abrasive powder. I can't move my head without feeling sharp, crackling fire in the two thick cords of my neck. It is a shame Ship cannot see me cry; Ship never saw me cry in all the years I have lived here, even after the worst wracking. But I have heard Ship cry, several times.

I manage to turn my head slightly, hoping at least one of the viewplates is functioning, and there, off to starboard, matching velocities with Ship is *Starfighter 88.* I watch it for a very long time, knowing that if I can regain my strength I will somehow have to get across and free the female. I watch it for a very long time, still afraid to unclamp from the berth.

The airlock rises in the hull of *Starfighter 88* and the space-suited female swims out, moving smoothly across toward Ship. Half-conscious, dreaming this dream of the female, I think about golden crab creatures swimming deep in aquamarine waters, singing of sweetness. I black out again.

When I rise through the blackness, I realize I am being touched, and I smell something sharp and stinging that burns the lining of my nostrils. Tiny pinpricks of pain, a pattern of them. I cough and come fully awake, and jerk my body . . . and scream as pain goes through every nerve and fiber in me.

I open my eyes and it is the female.

She smiles worriedly and removes the tube of awakener.

"Hello," she says.

Ship says nothing.

"Ever since I discovered how to take control of my *Starfighter,* I've been using the ship as a decoy for other ships of the series. I dummied a way of making it seem my ship was talking, so I could communicate with other slave ships. I've run across ten others since I went on my own. You're the eleventh. It hasn't been easy, but several of the men I've freed—like you—started using *their* ships as decoys for *Starfighters* with female human operators."

I stare at her. The sight is pleasant.

"But what if you lose? What if you can't get the message across, about the corridor between control room and freezers? That the control room is the key?"

She shrugs. "It's happened a couple of times. The men were too frightened of their ships—or the ships had . . . *done* something to them—or maybe they were just too dumb to know they could break out. In that case, well, things just went on the way they'd been. It seems kind of sad, but what could I do beyond what I did?"

We sit here, not speaking for a while.

"Now what do we do? Where do we go?"

"That's up to you," she says.

"Will you go with me?"

She shakes her head uncertainly. "I don't think so. Every time I free a man he wants that. But I just haven't wanted to go with any of them."

"Could we go back to the Home Galaxy, the place we came from, where the war was?"

She stands up and walks around the stateroom where we have coupled for three weeks. She speaks, not looking at me, looking in the viewplate at the darkness and the far, bright points of the stars. "I don't think so. We're free of our ships, but we couldn't possibly get them working well enough to carry us all the way back there. It would take a lot of charting, and we'd be running the risk of activating the intermind sufficiently to take over again if we asked it to do the charts. Besides, I don't even know where the Home Galaxy is."

"Maybe we should find a new place to go. Someplace where we could be free and outside the ships."

She turns and looks at me.

"Where?"

So I tell her what I heard the intermind say about the world of golden crab creatures.

It takes me a long time to tell, and I make some of it up. It isn't lying, because it *might* be true, and I do so want her to go with me.

They came down from space. Far down from the star-sun Sol in a galaxy lost forever to them. Down past the star-sun M-13 in Perseus. Down through the gummy atmosphere and straight down into the sapphire sea. Ship, *Starfighter 31*, settled delicately on an enormous underwater mountaintop, and they spent many days listening, watching, drawing samples and hoping. They had landed on many worlds and they hoped.

Finally, they came out; looking. They wore underwater suits and they began gathering marine samples; looking.

They found the ruined diving suit with its fish-eaten contents lying on its back in deep azure sand, sextet of insectoidal legs bent up at the joints in a posture of agony. And they knew the intermind had remembered, but not correctly. The faceplate had been shattered, and what was observable within the helmet—orange and awful in the light of their portable lamp—convinced them more by implication than specific that whatever had swum in that suit had never seen or known humans.

They went back to the ship and she broke out the big camera, and they returned to the crablike diving suit. They photographed it without moving it. Then they used a seine to get it out of the sand and they hauled it back to the ship on the mountaintop.

He set up the Condition and the diving suit was analyzed. The rust. The joint mechanisms. The controls. The substance of the flipper-feet. The jagged points of the faceplate. The . . . stuff . . . inside.

It took two days. They stayed in the ship with green and blue shadows moving languidly in the viewplates.

When the analyses were concluded they knew what they had found. And they went out again, to find the swimmers.

Blue it was, and warm. And when the swimmers found them, finally, they beckoned them to follow, and they swam after the many-legged creatures, who led them through underwater caverns as smooth and shining as onyx, to a lagoon. And they rose to the surface and saw a land against whose shores the azure, aquamarine seas lapped quietly. And they climbed out onto the land, and there they removed their face-masks, never to put them on again, and they shoved back the tight coifs of their suits, and they breathed for the first time an air that did not come from metal sources; they breathed the sweet musical air of a new place.

In time, the sea rains would claim the corpse of *Starfighter 31*.

Poor Little Warrior!

Hunting—whether for food or for sport—is one of the oldest of human endeavors. Twentieth Century values have caused us to question the pleasure motive that leads to the often painful death of beautiful creatures and the inequalities of a "sport" in which only one of the participants has a high-powered rifle, a cross-country vehicle and other advantages too numerous to mention. Here Brian Aldiss takes us on a hunt in prehistoric times in an environment where things are a little more nearly equal and offers a powerful story of retribution and justice.

Claude Ford knew exactly how it was to hunt a brontosaurus. You crawled heedlessly through the mud among the willows, through the little primitive flowers with petals as green and brown as a football field, through the beauty-lotion mud. You peered out at the creature sprawling among the reeds, its body as graceful as a sock full of sand. There it lay, letting the gravity cuddle it nappy-damp to the marsh, running its big rabbit-hole nostrils a foot above the grass in a sweeping semicircle, in a snoring search for more sausagy reeds. It was beautiful: here horror had reached its limits, come full circle and finally disappeared up its own sphincter. Its eyes gleamed with the liveliness of a week-dead corpse's big toe, and its compost breath and the fur in its crude aural cavities were particularly to be recommended to anyone who might otherwise have felt inclined to speak lovingly of the work of Mother Nature.

But as you, little mammal with opposed digit and .65 self-loading, semiautomatic, dual-barreled, digitally computed, telescopically sighted, rustless, high-powered rifle gripped in your otherwise defenseless paws, slide along under the bygone willows, what primarily attracts you is the thunder lizard's hide. It gives off a smell as deeply resonant as the bass note of a piano. It makes the elephant's epidermis look like a sheet of crinkled lavatory paper. It is gray as the Viking seas, daft-deep as cathedral foundations. What contact possible to bone could allay the fever of that flesh? Over it scamper—you can see them from here!—the little brown lice that live in those gray walls and canyons, gay as ghosts, cruel as crabs. If one of them jumped on you, it would very likely break your back. And when one of those parasites stops to cock its leg against one of the bronto's vertebrae, you can see it carries in its turn its own crop of easy-livers, each as big as a lobster, for you're near now, oh, so near that you can hear the monster's primitive heart organ knocking, as the ventricle keeps miraculous time with the auricle.

Time for listening to the oracle is past: you're beyond the stage for omens, you're now headed in for the kill, yours or his; superstition has had its little day for today, from now on only this windy nerve of yours, this shaky conglomeration of muscle entangled untraceably beneath the sweat-shiny carapace of skin, this bloody little urge to slay the dragon, is going to answer all your orisons.

You could shoot now. Just wait till that tiny steam-shovel head pauses once again to gulp down a quarry-load of bulrushes, and with one inexpressibly vulgar bang you can show the whole indifferent Jurassic world that it's standing looking down the business end of evolution's six-shooter. You know why you pause, even as you pretend not to know why you pause; that old worm conscience, long as a baseball pitch, long-lived as a tortoise, is at work; through every sense it slides, more monstrous than the serpent. Through the passions: saying, here is a sitting duck, O Englishman! Through the intelligence: whispering that boredom, the kite hawk who never feeds, will settle again when the task is done. Through the nerves: sneering that when the adrenalin currents cease to flow the vomiting begins. Through the maestro behind the retina: plausibly forcing the beauty of the view upon you.

Spare us that poor old slipper-slopper of a word, *beauty*; holy mom, is this a travelogue, or are we out of it? *"Perched now on this titanic creature's back, we see a round dozen—and, folks, let me stress that round—of gaudily plumaged birds, exhibiting between them all the color you might expect to find on lovely, fabled Copacabana Beach. They're so round because they feed from the droppings that fall from the rich man's table. Watch this lovely shot now! See the bronto's tail lift. . . . Oh, lovely, yep, a couple of hayricks-full at least emerging from his nether end. That sure was a beauty, folks, delivered straight from consumer to consumer. The birds are fighting over it now. Hey, you, there's enough to go 'round, and anyhow, you're round enough already. . . . And nothing to do now but hop back up onto the old rump steak and wait for the next round. And now as the sun sinks in the Jurassic west, we say 'Farewell on that diet'. . . ."*

No, you're procrastinating, and that's a lifework. Shoot the beast and put it out of your agony. Taking your courage in your hands, you raise it to shoulder level and squint down its sights. There is a terrible report; you are half-stunned. Shakily, you look about you. The monster still munches, relieved to have broken enough wind to unbecalm the Ancient Mariner.

Angered (or is it some subtler emotion?), you now burst from the bushes and confront it, and this exposed condition is typical of the straits into which your consideration for yourself and others continually pitches you. Consideration? Or again something subtler? Why should you be confused just because you come from a confused civilization? But that's a point to deal with later, if there is a later, as these two hog-wallow eyes pupiling you all over from spitting distance tend to dispute. Let it not be by jaws alone, O monster, but also by huge hooves and, if convenient to yourself, by mountainous rollings upon me! Let death be a saga, sagacious, Beowulfate.

Quarter of a mile distant is the sound of a dozen hippos springing boisterously in gymslips from the ancestral mud, and next second a walloping great tail as long as Sunday and as thick as Saturday night comes slicing over your head. You duck as duck you must, but the beast missed you anyway because it so happens that its coordination is no better than yours would be if you had to wave the Woolworth Building at a tarsier. This done, it seems to feel it has done its duty by itself. It forgets you. You just wish you could forget yourself as easily; that was, after all, the reason you had to come the long way here. *Get Away from It All*, said the time travel brochure, which meant for you getting away from Claude Ford, a husbandman as futile as his name with a terrible wife called Maude. Maude and Claude Ford. Who could not adjust to themselves, to each other or to the world they were born in. It was the best reason in the as-it-is-at-present-constituted world for coming back here to shoot giant saurians—if you were fool enough to think that one hundred and fifty million years either way made an ounce of difference to the muddle of thoughts in a man's cerebral vortex.

You try to stop your silly, slobbering thoughts, but they have never really stopped since the coca-collaborating days of your growing up; God, if adolescence did not exist it would be unnecessary to invent it! Slightly, it steadies you to look again on the enormous bulk of this tyrant vegetarian into whose presence you charged with such a mixed death-life wish, charged with all the emotion the human orga(ni)sm is capable of. This time the bogeyman is real, Claude, just as you wanted it to be, and this time you really have to face up to it before it turns and faces you again. And so again you lift Ole Equalizer, waiting till you can spot the vulnerable spot.

The bright birds sway, the lice scamper like dogs, the marsh groans, as bronto sways over and sends his little cranium snaking down under the bile-bright water in a forage for roughage. You watch this; you have never been so jittery before in all your jittered life, and you are counting on this catharsis wringing the last drop of acid fear out of your system forever. Okay, you keep saying to yourself insanely over and over, your million-dollar, twenty-second century education going for nothing, Okay, okay. And as you say it for the umpteenth time, the crazy head comes back out of the water like a renegade express and gazes in your direction.

Grazes in your direction. For as the champing jaw with its big blunt molars like concrete posts works up and down, you see the swamp water course out over rimless lips, lipless rims, splashing your feet and sousing the ground. Reed and root, stalk and stem, leaf and loam, all are intermittently visible in that masticating maw and, struggling, straggling or tossed among them, minnows, tiny crustaceans, frogs—all destined in that awful, jawful movement to turn into bowel movement. And as the glump-glump-glumping takes place, above it the slime-resistant eyes again survey you.

These beasts live up to two hundred years, says the time travel brochure, and this beast has obviously tried to live up to that, for its gaze is centuries old, full of decades upon decades of wallowing in its heavyweight thoughtlessness until it has grown wise on twitterpatedness. For you it is like looking into a disturbing misty pool; it gives you a psychic shock, you fire off both barrels at your own reflection. Bang-gang, the dum-dums, big as paw-paws, go.

With no indecision, those century-old lights, dim and sacred, go out. These cloisters are closed till Judgment Day. Your reflection is torn and bloodied from them forever. Over their ravaged panes nictitating membranes slide slowly upward, like dirty sheets covering a cadaver. The jaw continues to munch slowly, as slowly the head sinks down. Slowly, a squeeze of cold reptile blood toothpastes down the wrinked flank of one cheek. Everything is slow, a creepy Secondary Era slowness like the drip of water, and you know that if you had been in charge of creation you would have found some medium less heartbreaking than time to stage it all in.

Never mind! Quaff down your beakers, lords, Claude Ford has slain a harmless creature. Long live Claude the Clawed!

You watch breathless as the head touches the ground, the long laugh of neck touches the ground, the jaws close for good. You watch and wait for something else to happen, but nothing ever does. Nothing ever would. You could stand here watching for a hundred and fifty million years, Lord Claude, and nothing would ever happen here again. Gradually your bronto's mighty carcass, picked loving clean by predators, would sink into the slime, carried by its own weight deeper; then the waters would rise, and old Conqueror Sea come in with the leisurely air of a cardsharp dealing the boys a bad hand. Silt and sediment would filter down over the mighty grave, a slow rain with centuries to rain in. Old bronto's bed might be raised up and then down again perhaps half a dozen times, gently enough not to disturb him, although by now the sedimentary rocks would be forming thick around him. Finally, when he was wrapped in a tomb finer than any Indian rajah ever boasted, the powers of the Earth would raise him high on their shoulders until, sleeping still, bronto would lie in a brow of the Rockies high above the waters of the Pacific. But little any of that would count with you, Claude the Sword; once the midget maggot of life is dead in the creature's skull, the rest is no concern of yours.

You have no emotion now. You are just faintly put out. You expected dramatic thrashing of the ground, or bellowing; on the other hand, you are glad the thing did not appear to suffer. You are like all cruel men, sentimental; you are like all sentimental men, squeamish. You tuck the gun under your arm and walk round the dinosaur to view your victory.

You prowl past the ungainly hooves, 'round the septic white of the cliff of belly, beyond the glistening and how-thought-provoking cavern of the cloaca, finally posing beneath the switch-back sweep of tail-to-rump. Now your disappointment is as crisp and obvious as a visiting card: the giant is not half as big as you thought it was. It is not one-half as large, for example, as the image of you and Maude is in your mind. Poor little warrior, science will never invent anything to assist the titanic death you want in the contraterrene caverns of your fee-fi-fo fumblingly fearful id!

Nothing is left to you now but to slink back to your timemobile with a belly full of anticlimax. See, the bright dung-consuming birds have already cottoned onto the true state of affairs; one by one, they gather up their hunched wings and fly disconsolately off across the swamp to other hosts. They know when a good thing turns bad, and do not wait for the vultures to drive them off; all hope abandon, ye who entrail here. You also turn away.

You turn, but you pause. Nothing is left but to go back, no, but A.D. 2181 is not just the home date; it is Maude. It is Claude. It is the whole awful, hopeless, endless business of trying to adjust to an overcomplex environment, of trying to turn yourself into a cog. Your escape from it into *The Grand Simplicities of the Jurassic*, to quote the brochure again, was only a partial escape, now over.

So you pause, and as you pause, something lands socko on your back, pitching you face forward into tasty mud. You struggle and scream as lobster claws tear at your neck and throat. You try to pick up the rifle but cannot, so in agony you roll over, and next second the crab-thing is greedying it on your chest. You wrench at its shell, but it giggles and pecks your fingers off.

You forgot when you killed the bronto that its parasites would leave it, and that to a little shrimp like you they would be a deal more dangerous than their host.

You do your best, kicking for at least three minutes. By the end of that time there is a whole pack of the creatures on you. Already they are picking your carcass loving clean. You're going to like it up there on top of the Rockies; you won't feel a thing.

JOANNA RUSS

When It Changed

The planet that is the setting for Ms. Russ's story is completely devoid of men, and although this situation has been dealt with in science fiction before, it was usually in the form of "men to the rescue" and/or a reaffirmation of the "natural" need of one sex for the other. This is not the case here. The physiological problems of a single-sex situation have been solved and the social system and the satisfactions deriving therefrom are perfectly logical. Like all fine science fiction, "When It Changed" has much to tell us about the present.

Katy drives like a maniac; we must have been doing over 120 kilometers an hour on those turns. She's good, though, extremely good, and I've seen her take the whole car apart and put it together again in a day. My birthplace on Whileaway was largely given to farm machinery and I refuse to wrestle with a five-gear shift at unholy speeds, not having been brought up to it, but even on those turns in the middle of the night on a country road as bad as only our district can make them, Katy's driving didn't scare me. The funny thing about my wife, though: she will not handle guns. She has even gone hiking in the forests above the forty-eighth parallel without firearms for days at a time. And that *does* scare me.

Katy and I have three children between us, one of hers and two of mine. Yuriko, my eldest, was asleep in the back seat, dreaming twelve-year-old dreams of love and war: running away to sea, hunting in the North, dreams of strangely beautiful people in strangely beautiful places, all the wonderful guff you think up when you're turning twelve and the glands start going. Some day soon, like all of them, she will disappear for weeks on end to come back grimy and proud, having knifed her first cougar or shot her first bear, dragging some abominably dangerous dead beastie behind her, which I will never forgive for what it might have done to my daughter. Yuriko says Katy's driving puts her to sleep.

For someone who has fought three duels, I am afraid of far, far too much. I'm getting old. I told this to my wife.

"You're thirty-four," she said. Laconic to the point of silence, that one. She flipped the lights on, on the dash—three kilometers to go and the road getting worse all the time. Far out in the country. Electric green trees rushed into our headlights and around the car. I reached down next to me where we bolt the carrier panel to the door and eased my rifle into my lap. Yuriko stirred in the back. My height but Katy's eyes, Katy's face. The car engine is so quiet, Katy says, that you can hear breathing in the back seat. Yuki had been alone in the car when the message came, enthusiastically decoding her dot-dashes (silly to mount a wide-frequency transceiver near an IC engine, but most of Whileaway is on steam). She had thrown herself out of the car, my gangly and gaudy offspring, shouting at the top of her lungs, so of course she had had to come along. We've been intellectually prepared for this ever since the colony was founded, ever since it was abandoned, but this is different. This is awful.

"Men!" Yuki had screamed, leaping over the car door. "They've come back! Real Earth men!"

We met them in the kitchen of the farmhouse near the place where they had landed; the windows were open, the night air very mild. We had passed all sorts of transportation when we parked outside, steam tractors, trucks, an IC flatbed, even a bicycle. Lydia, the district biologist, had come out of her Northern taciturnity long enough to take blood and urine samples and was sitting in a corner of the kitchen shaking her head in astonishment over the results; she even forced herself (very big, very fair, very shy, always painfully blushing) to dig up the old language manuals—though I can talk the old tongues in my sleep. And do. Lydia is uneasy with us; we're Southerners and too flamboyant. I counted twenty people in that kitchen, all the brains of North Continent. Phyllis Spet, I think, had come in by glider. Yuki was the only child there.

Then I saw the four of them.

They are bigger than we are. They are bigger and broader. Two were taller than me, and I am extremely tall, one meter, eighty centimeters in my bare feet. They are obviously of our species but *off*, indescribably off, and as my eyes could not and still cannot quite comprehend the lines of those alien bodies, I could not, then, bring myself to touch them, though the one who spoke Russian—what voices they have—wanted to "shake hands," a custom from the past, I imagine. I can only say they were apes with human faces. He seemed to mean well, but I found myself shuddering back almost the length of the kitchen—and then I laughed apologetically—and then to set a good example (*interstellar amity,* I thought) did "shake hands" finally. A hard, hard hand. They are heavy as draft horses. Blurred, deep voices. Yuriko had sneaked in between the adults and was gazing at *the men* with her mouth open.

He turned *his* head—those words have not been in our language for six hundred years—and said, in bad Russian:

"Who's that?"

"My daughter," I said, and added (with that irrational attention to good manners we sometimes employ in moments of insanity), "my daughter, Yuriko Janetson. We use the patronymic. You would say matronymic."

He laughed, involuntarily. Yuki exclaimed, "I thought they would be *good-looking!*" greatly disappointed at this reception of herself. Phyllis Helgason Spet, whom someday I shall kill, gave me across the room a cold, level, venomous look, as if to say: *Watch what you say. You know what I can do.* It's true that I have little formal status, but madam president will get herself in serious trouble with both me and her own staff if she continues to consider industrial espionage good clean fun. Wars and rumors of wars, as it says in one of our ancestors' books. I translated Yuki's words into *the man's* dog-Russian, once our *lingua franca,* and *the man* laughed again.

"Where are all your people?" he said conversationally.

I translated again and watched the faces around the room; Lydia embarrassed (as usual), Spet narrowing her eyes with some damned scheme, Katy very pale.

"This is Whileaway," I said.

He continued to look unenlightened.

"Whileaway," I said. "Do you remember? Do you have records? There was a plague on Whileaway."

He looked moderately interested. Heads turned in the back of the room, and I caught a glimpse of the local professions-parliament delegate; by morning every town meeting, every district caucus, would be in full session.

"Plague?" he said. "That's most unfortunate."

"Yes," I said. "Most unfortunate. We lost half our population in one generation."

He looked properly impressed.

"Whileaway was lucky," I said. "We had a big initial gene pool, we had been chosen for extreme intelligence, we had a high technology and a large remaining population in which every adult was two-or-three experts in one. The soil is good. The climate is blessedly easy. There are thirty million of us now. Things are beginning to snowball in industry—do you understand?—give us seventy years and we'll have more than one real city, more than a few industrial centers, full-time professions, full-time radio operators, full-time machinists, give us seventy years and not everyone will have to spend three-quarters of a lifetime on the farm." And I tried to explain how hard it is when artists can practice full-time only in old age, when there are so few, so very few who can be free, like Katy and myself. I tried also to outline our government, the two houses, the one by professions and the geographic one; I told him the district caucuses handled problems too big for the individual towns. And that population control was not a political issue, not yet, though give us time and it would be. This was a delicate point in our history; give us time. There was no need to sacrifice the quality of life for an insane rush into industrialization. Let us go our own pace. Give us time.

"Where are all the people?" said that monomaniac.

I realized then that he did not mean people, he meant *men,* and he was giving the word the meaning it had not had on Whileaway for six centuries.

"They died," I said. "Thirty generations ago."

I thought we had poleaxed him. He caught his breath. He made as if to get out of the chair he was sitting in; he put his hand to his chest; he looked around at us with the strangest blend of awe and sentimental tenderness. Then he said, solemnly and earnestly:

"A great tragedy."

I waited, not quite understanding.

"Yes," he said, catching his breath again with that queer smile, that adult-to-child smile that tells you something is being hidden and will be presently produced with cries of encouragement and joy, "a great tragedy. But it's over." And again he looked around at all of us with the strangest deference. As if we were invalids.

"You've adapted amazingly," he said.

"To what?" I said. He looked embarrassed. He looked inane. Finally he said, "Where I come from, the women don't dress so plainly."

"Like you?" I said. "Like a bride?" for the men were wearing silver from head to foot. I had never seen anything so gaudy. He made as if to answer and then apparently thought better of it; he laughed at me again. With an odd exhilaration—as if we were something childish and something wonderful, as if he were doing us an enormous favor—he took one shaky breath and said, "Well, we're here."

I looked at Spet, Spet looked at Lydia, Lydia looked at Amalia, who is the head of the local town meeting, Amalia looked at I don't know who. My throat was raw. I cannot stand local beer, which the farmers swill as if their stomachs had iridium linings, but I took it anyway, from Amalia (it was her bicycle we had seen outside as we parked), and swallowed it all. This was going to take a long time. "Yes, here you are," and smiled (feeling like a fool), and wondered seriously if male Earth people's minds worked so very differently from female Earth people's minds, but that couldn't be so or the race would have died out long ago. The radio network had got the news around-planet by now and we had another Russian speaker, flown in from Varna; I decided to cut out when *the man* passed around pictures of his wife, who looked like the priestess of some arcane cult. He proposed to question Yuki, so I barreled her into a back room in spite of her furious protests and went out on the front porch. As I left, Lydia was explaining the difference between parthenogenesis (which is so easy that anyone can practice it) and what we do, which is the merging of ova. That is why Katy's baby looks like me. Lydia went on to the Ansky Process and Katy Ansky, our one full-polymath genius and the great-great-I don't know how many times great-grandmother of my own Katharina.

A dot-dash transmitter in one of the outbuildings chattered faintly to itself: operators flirting and passing jokes down the line.

There was a man on the porch. The other tall man. I watched him for a few minutes—I can move very quietly when I want to—and when I allowed him to see me, he stopped talking into the little machine hung around his neck. Then he said calmly, in excellent Russian, "Did you know that sexual equality has been reestablished on Earth?"

"You're the real one," I said, "aren't you? The other one's for show." It was a great relief to get things cleared up. He nodded affably.

"As a people, we are not very bright," he said. "There's been too much genetic damage in the last few centuries. Radiation. Drugs. We can use Whileaway's genes, Janet." Strangers do not call strangers by the first name.

"You can have cells enough to drown in," I said. "Breed your own."

He smiled. "That's not the way we want to do it." Behind him I saw Katy come into the square of light that was the screened-in door. He went on, low and urbane, not mocking me, I think, but with the self-confidence of someone who has always had money and strength to spare, who doesn't know what it is to be second-class or provincial. Which is very odd, because the day before, I would have said that was an exact description of me.

"I'm talking to you, Janet," he said, "because I suspect you have more popular influence than anyone else here. You know as well as I do that parthenogenetic culture has all sorts of inherent defects, and we do not—if we can help it—mean to use you for anything of the sort. Pardon me; I should not have said 'use.' But surely you can see that this kind of society is unnatural."

"Humanity is unnatural," said Katy. She had my rifle under her left arm.

The top of that silky head does not quite come up to my collarbone, but she is as tough as steel; he began to move, again with that queer-smiling deference (which his fellow had shown to me but he had not) and the gun slid into Katy's grip as if she had shot with it all her life.

"I agree," said the man. "Humanity is unnatural. I should know. I have metal in my teeth and metal pins here." He touched his shoulder. "Seals are harem animals," he added, "and so are men; apes are promiscuous and so are men; doves are monogamous and so are men; there are even celibate men and homosexual men. There are homosexual cows, I believe. But Whileaway is still missing something." He gave a dry chuckle. I will give him the credit of believing that it had something to do with nerves.

"I miss nothing," said Katy, "except that life isn't endless."

"You are . . .?" said the man, nodding from me to her.

"Wives," said Katy. "We're married." Again the dry chuckle.

"A good economic arrangement," he said, "for working and taking care of the children. And as good an arrangement as any for randomizing heredity, if your reproduction is made to follow the same pattern. But think, Katharina Michaelason, if there isn't something better that you might secure for your daughters. I believe in instincts, even in man, and I can't think that the two of you—a machinist, are you? and I gather you are some sort of chief of police —don't feel somehow what even you must miss. You know it intellectually, of course. There is only half a species here. Men must come back to Whileaway."

Katy said nothing.

"I should think, Katharina Michaelason," said the man gently, "that you, of all people, would benefit most from such a change," and he walked past Katy's rifle into the square of light coming from the door. I think it was then that he noticed my scar, which really does not show unless the light is from the side: a fine line that runs from temple to chin. Most people don't even know about it.

"Where did you get that?" he said, and I answered with an involuntary grin, "In my last duel." We stood there bristling at each other for several seconds (this is absurd but true) until he went inside and shut the screen door behind him. Katy said in a brittle voice, "You damned fool, don't you know when we've been insulted?" and swung up the rifle to shoot him through the screen, but I got to her before she could fire and knocked the rifle out of aim; it burned a hole through the porch floor. Katy was shaking. She kept whispering over and over, "That's why I never touched it, because I knew I'd kill someone, I knew I'd kill someone." The first man—the one I'd spoken with first—was still talking inside the house, something about the grand movement to recolonize and rediscover all that Earth had lost. He stressed the advantages to Whileaway: trade, exchange of ideas, education. He too said that sexual equality had been reestablished on Earth.

Katy was right, of course; we should have burned them down where they stood. Men are coming to Whileaway. When one culture has the big guns and the other has none, there is a certain predictability about the outcome. Maybe men would have come eventually in any case. I like to think that a hundred years from now my great-grandchildren could have stood them off or fought them to a standstill, but even that's no odds; I will remember all my life those four people I first met who were muscled like bulls and who made me—if only for a moment—feel small. A neurotic reaction, Katy says. I remember everything that happened that night; I remember Yuki's excitement in the car, I remember Katy's sobbing when we got home as if her heart would break, I remember her lovemaking, a little peremptory as always, but wonderfully soothing and comforting. I remember prowling restlessly around the house after Katy fell asleep with one bare arm flung into a patch of light from the hall. The muscles of her forearms are like metal bars from all that driving and testing of her machines. Sometimes I dream about Katy's arms. I remember wandering into the nursery and picking up my wife's baby, dozing for a while with the poignant, amazing warmth of an infant in my lap, and finally returning to the kitchen to find Yuriko fixing herself a late snack. My daughter eats like a Great Dane.

"Yuki," I said, "do you think you could fall in love with a man?" and she whooped derisively. "With a ten-foot toad!" said my tactful child.

But men are coming to Whileaway. Lately I sit up nights and worry about the men who will come to this planet, about my two daughters and Betta Katharinason, about what will happen to Katy, to me, to my life. Our ancestors' journals are one long cry of pain and I suppose I ought to be glad now but one can't throw away six centuries, or even (as I have lately discovered) thirty-four years. Sometimes I laugh at the question those four men hedged about all evening and never quite dared to ask, looking at the lot of us, hicks in overalls, farmers in canvas pants and plain shirts: *Which of you plays the role of the man?* As if we had to produce a carbon copy of their mistakes! I doubt very much that sexual equality has been reestablished on Earth. I do not like to think of myself mocked, of Katy deferred to as if she were weak, of Yuki made to feel unimportant or silly, of my other children cheated of their full humanity or turned into strangers. And I'm afraid that my own achievements will dwindle from what they were—or what I thought they were—to the not-very-interesting curiosa of the human race, the oddities you read about in the back of the book, things to laugh at sometimes because they are so exotic, quaint but not impressive, charming but not useful. I find this more painful than I can say. You will agree that for a woman who has fought three duels, all of them kills, indulging in such fears is ludicrous. But what's around the corner now is a duel so big that I don't think I have the guts for it; in Faust's words: *Verweile doch, du bist so schoen!* Keep it as it is. Don't change.

Sometimes at night I remember the original name of this planet, changed by the first generation of our ancestors, those curious women for whom, I suppose, the real name was too painful a reminder after the men died. I find it amusing, in a grim way, to see it all so completely turned around. This too shall pass. All good things must come to an end.

Take my life but don't take away the meaning of my life.

For-a-While.

ISAAC ASIMOV
The Bicentennial Man

There have been hundreds of stories about artificial intelligence, and all types of robots, androids and such have put in an appearance in science fiction—some friendly, some hostile, some controlled by humans, others out of control. Dr. Asimov is closely associated with the view that machine intelligence will be and must be put to use to serve humanity, and he has been writing about the laws and limits of robotic behavior for forty years. He has told us frequently and well about what it means to be a machine, but in "The Bicentennial Man" he brilliantly explores an even more important issue: what does it mean to be human?

The Three Laws of Robotics:
1. *A robot may not injure a human being or, through inaction, allow a human being to come to harm.*
2. *A robot must obey the orders given it by human beings except where such orders would conflict with the First Law.*
3. A robot must protect its own existence as long as such protection does not conflict with the First or Second Law.

I

Andrew Martin said, "Thank you," and took the seat offered him. He didn't look driven to the last resort, but he had been.

He didn't, actually, look anything, for there was a smooth blankness to his face, except for the sadness one imagined one saw in his eyes. His hair was smooth, light brown, rather fine, and there was no facial hair. He looked freshly and cleanly shaved. His clothes were distinctly old-fashioned, but neat and predominantly a velvety red purple in color.

Facing him from behind the desk was the surgeon, and the nameplate on the desk included a fully identifying series of letters and numbers, which Andrew didn't bother with. To call him "doctor" would be quite enough.

"When can the operation be carried through, doctor?" he asked.

The surgeon said softly, with that certain inalienable note of respect that a robot always used to a human being, "I am not certain, sir, that I understand how or upon whom such an operation could be performed."

There might have been a look of respectful intransigence on the surgeon's face if a robot of his sort, in lightly bronzed stainless steel, could have such an expression, or any expression.

Andrew Martin studied the robot's right hand, his cutting hand, as it lay on the desk in utter tranquility. The fingers were long and shaped into artistically metallic looping curves so graceful and appropriate that one could imagine a scalpel fitting them and becoming, temporarily, one piece with them.

There would be no hesitation in his work, no stumbling, no quivering, no mistakes. That came with specialization, of course, a specialization so fiercely desired by humanity that few robots were, any longer, independently brained. A surgeon, of course, would have to be. And this one, though brained, was so limited in his capacity that he did not recognize Andrew—had probably never heard of him.

Andrew said, "Have you ever thought you would like to be a man?"

The surgeon hesitated a moment as though the question fitted nowhere in his allotted positronic pathways. "But I am a robot, sir."

"Would it be better to be a man?"

"It would be better, sir, to be a better surgeon. I could not be so if I were a man, but only if I were a more advanced robot. I would be pleased to be a more advanced robot."

"It does not offend you that I can order you about? That I can make you stand up, sit down, move right or left, by merely telling you to do so?"

"It is my pleasure to please you, sir. If your orders were to interfere with my functioning with respect to you or to any other human being, I would not obey you. The First Law, concerning my duty to human safety, would take precedence over the Second Law relating to obedience. Otherwise, obedience is my pleasure. . . . But upon whom am I to perform this operation?"

"Upon me," said Andrew.

"But that is impossible. It is patently a damaging operation."

"That does not matter," said Andrew calmly.

"I must not inflict damage," said the surgeon.

"On a human being, you must not," said Andrew, "but I, too, am a robot."

II

Andrew had appeared much more a robot when he had first been—manufactured. He had then been as much a robot in appearance as any that had ever existed, smoothly designed and functional.

He had done well in the home to which he had been brought in those days when robots in households, or on the planet altogether, had been a rarity.

There had been four in the home: Sir and Ma'am and Miss and Little Miss. He knew their names, of course, but he never used them. Sir was Gerald Martin.

His own serial number was NDR—he forgot the numbers. It had been a long time, of course, but if he had wanted to remember, he could not forget. He had not wanted to remember.

Little Miss had been the first to call him Andrew because she could not use the letters, and all the rest followed her in this.

Little Miss . . . She had lived ninety years and was long since dead. He had tried to call her Ma'am once, but she would not allow it. Little Miss she had been to her last day.

Andrew had been intended to perform the duties of a valet, a butler, a lady's maid. Those were the experimental days for him and, indeed, for all robots anywhere but in the industrial and exploratory factories and stations off Earth.

The Martins enjoyed him, and half the time he was prevented from doing his work because Miss and Little Miss would rather play with him.

It was Miss who understood first how this might be arranged. She said, "We order you to play with us and you must follow orders."

Andrew said, "I am sorry, Miss, but a prior order from Sir must surely take precedence."

But she said, "Daddy just said he hoped you would take care of the cleaning. That's not much of an order. I *order* you."

Sir did not mind. Sir was fond of Miss and of Little Miss, even more than Ma'am was, and Andrew was fond of them, too. At least, the effect they had upon his actions were those which in a human being would have been called the result of fondness. Andrew thought of it as fondness, for he did not know any other word for it.

It was for Little Miss that Andrew had carved a pendant out of wood. She had ordered him to. Miss, it seemed, had received an ivorite pendant with scrollwork for her birthday, and Little Miss was unhappy over it. She had only a piece of wood, which she gave Andrew together with a small kitchen knife.

He had done it quickly and Little Miss said, "That's *nice*, Andrew. I'll show it to Daddy."

Sir would not believe it. "Where did you really get this, Mandy?" Mandy was what he called Little Miss. When Little Miss assured him she was really telling the truth, he turned to Andrew. "Did you do this, Andrew?"

"Yes, Sir."

"The design, too?"

"Yes, Sir."

"From what did you copy the design?"

"It is a geometric representation, Sir, that fit the grain of the wood."

The next day, Sir brought him another piece of wood, a larger one, and an electric vibro-knife. He said, "Make something out of this, Andrew. Anything you want to."

Andrew did so and Sir watched, then looked at the product a long time. After that, Andrew no longer waited on tables. He was ordered to read books on furniture design instead, and he learned to make cabinets and desks.

Sir said, "These are amazing productions, Andrew."

Andrew said, "I enjoy doing them, Sir."

"Enjoy?"

"It makes the circuits of my brain somehow flow more easily. I have heard you use the word 'enjoy,' and the way you use it fits the way I feel. I enjoy doing them, Sir."

III

Gerald Martin took Andrew to the regional offices of United States Robots and Mechanical Men, Inc. As a member of the regional legislature he had no trouble at all in gaining an interview with the chief robopsychologist. In fact, it was only as a member of the regional legislature that he qualified as a robot owner in the first place—in those early days when robots were rare.

Andrew did not understand any of this at the time, but in later years, with greater learning, he could re-view that early scene and understand it in its proper light.

The robopsychologist, Merton Mansky, listened with a gathering frown and more than once managed to stop his fingers at the point beyond which they would have irrevocably drummed on the table. He had drawn features and a lined forehead and looked as though he might be younger than he looked.

He said, "Robotics is not an exact art, Mr. Martin. I cannot explain it to you in detail, but the mathematics governing the plotting of the positronic pathways is far too complicated to permit of any but approximate solutions.

Naturally, since we build everything about the Three Laws, those are incontrovertible. We will, of course, replace your robot. . . ."

"Not at all," said Sir. "There is no question of failure on his part. He performs his assigned duties perfectly. The point is, he also carves wood in exquisite fashion and never the same twice. He produces works of art."

Mansky looked confused. "Strange. Of course, we're attempting generalized pathways these days. . . . Really creative, you think?"

"See for yourself." Sir handed over a little sphere of wood on which there was a playground scene in which the boys and girls were almost too small to make out, yet they were in perfect proportion and blended so naturally with the grain that that, too, seemed to have been carved.

Mansky said, *"He* did that?" He handed it back with a shake of his head. "The luck of the draw. Something in the pathways."

"Can you do it again?"

"Probably not. Nothing like this has ever been reported."

"Good! I don't in the least mind Andrew's being the only one."

Mansky said, "I suspect that the company would like to have your robot back for study."

Sir said with sudden grimness, "Not a chance. Forget it." He turned to Andrew, "Let's go home now."

"As you wish, Sir," said Andrew.

IV

Miss was dating boys and wasn't about the house much. It was Little Miss, not as little as she was, who filled Andrew's horizon now. She never forgot that the very first piece of woodcarving he had done had been for her. She kept it on a silver chain about her neck.

It was she who first objected to Sir's habit of giving away the productions. She said, "Come on, dad, if anyone wants one of them, let him pay for it. It's worth it."

Sir said, "It isn't like you to be greedy, Mandy."

"Not for us, dad. For the artist."

Andrew had never heard the word before and when he had a moment to himself he looked it up in the dictionary. Then there was another trip, this time to Sir's lawyer.

Sir said to him, "What do you think of this, John?"

The lawyer was John Feingold. He had white hair and a pudgy belly, and the rims of his contact lenses were tinted a bright green. He looked at the small plaque Sir had given him. "This is beautiful. . . . But I've heard the news. This is a carving made by your robot. The one you've brought with you."

"Yes, Andrew does them. Don't you, Andrew?"

"Yes, Sir," said Andrew.

"How much would you pay for that, John?" asked Sir.

"I can't say. I'm not a collector of such things."

"Would you believe I have been offered two hundred and fifty dollars for that small thing? Andrew has made chairs that have sold for five hundred dollars. There's two hundred thousand dollars in the bank out of Andrew's products."

"Good heavens, he's making you rich, Gerald."

"Half-rich," said Sir. "Half of it is in an account in the name of Andrew Martin."

"The robot?"

"That's right, and I want to know if it's legal."

"Legal?" Feingold's chair creaked as he leaned back in it "There are no precedents, Gerald. How did your robot sign the necessary papers?"

"He can sign his name and I brought in the signature. I didn't bring him in to the bank himself. Is there anything further that ought to be done?"

"Um." Feingold's eyes seemed to turn inward for a moment. Then he said, "Well, we can set up a trust to handle all finances in his name and that will place a layer of insulation between him and the hostile world. Further than that, my advice is you do nothing. No one is stopping you so far. If anyone objects, let *him* bring suit."

"And will you take the case if suit is brought?"

"For a retainer, certainly."

"How much?"

"Something like that," and Feingold pointed to the wooden plaque.

"Fair enough," said Sir.

Feingold chuckled as he turned to the robot. "Andrew, are you pleased that you have money?"

"Yes, sir."

"What do you plan to do with it?"

"Pay for things, Sir, which otherwise Sir would have to pay for. It would save him expense, sir."

V

The occasions came. Repairs were expensive, and revisions were even more so. With the years, new models of robots were produced and Sir saw to it that Andrew had the advantage of every new device until he was a paragon of metallic excellence. It was all at Andrew's expense.

Andrew insisted on that.

Only his positronic pathways were untouched. Sir insisted on that.

"The new ones aren't as good as you are, Andrew," he said. "The new robots are worthless. The company has learned to make the pathways more precise, more closely on the nose, more deeply on the track. The new robots don't shift. They do what they're designed for and never stray. I like you better."

"Thank you, Sir."

"And it's your doing, Andrew, don't you forget that. I am certain Mansky put an end to generalized pathways as soon as he had a good look at you. He didn't like the unpredictability. . . . Do you know how many times he asked for you so he could place you under study? Nine times! I never let him have you, though, and now that he's retired, we may have some peace."

So Sir's hair thinned and grayed and his face grew pouchy, while Andrew looked rather better than he had when he first joined the family.

Ma'am had joined an art colony somewhere in Europe and Miss was a poet in New York. They wrote sometimes, but not often. Little Miss was married and lived not far away. She said she did not want to leave Andrew and when her child, Little Sir, was born, she let Andrew hold the bottle and feed him.

With the birth of a grandson, Andrew felt that Sir had someone now to replace those who had gone. It would not be so unfair to come to him with the request.

Andrew said, "Sir, it is kind of you to have allowed me to spend my money as I wished."

"It was your money, Andrew."

"Only by your voluntary act, Sir. I do not believe the law would have stopped you from keeping it all."

"The law won't persuade me to do wrong, Andrew."

"Despite all expenses, and despite taxes, too, Sir, I have nearly six hundred thousand dollars."

"I know that, Andrew."

"I want to give it to you, Sir."

"I won't take it, Andrew."

"In exchange for something you can give me, Sir."

"Oh? What is that, Andrew?"

"My freedom, Sir."

"Your . . ."

"I wish to buy my freedom, Sir."

VI

It wasn't that easy. Sir had flushed, had said "For God's sake!" had turned on his heel and stalked away.

It was Little Miss who brought him around, defiantly and harshly—and in front of Andrew. For thirty years, no one had hesitated to talk in front of Andrew, whether the matter involved Andrew or not. He was only a robot.

She said, "Dad, why are you taking it as a personal affront? He'll still be here. He'll still be loyal. He can't help that. It's built in. All he wants is a form of words. He wants to be called free. Is that so terrible? Hasn't he earned it? Heavens, he and I have been talking about it for years."

"Talking about it for years, have you?"

"Yes, and over and over again, he postponed it for fear he would hurt you. I *made* him put it up to you."

"He doesn't know what freedom is. He's a robot."

"Dad, you don't know him. He's read everything in the library. I don't know what he feels inside but I don't know what *you* feel inside. When you talk to him you'll find he reacts to the various abstractions as you and I do, and what else counts? If someone else's reactions are like your own, what more can you ask for?"

"The law won't take that attitude," Sir said angrily. "See here, you!" He turned to Andrew with a deliberate grate in his voice. "I can't free you except by doing it legally, and if it gets into the courts, you not only won't get your freedom but the law will take official cognizance of your money. They'll tell you that a robot has no right to earn money. Is this rigmarole worth losing your money?"

"Freedom is without price, Sir," said Andrew. "Even the chance of freedom is worth the money."

VII

The court might also take the attitude that freedom was without price and might decide that for no price, however great, could a robot buy its freedom.

The simple statement of the regional attorney who represented those who had brought a class action to oppose the freedom was this: The word "freedom" had no meaning when applied to a robot. Only a human being could be free.

He said it several times when it seemed appropriate; slowly, with his hand coming down rhythmically on the desk before him to mark the words.

Little Miss asked permission to speak on behalf of Andrew. She was recognized by her full name, something Andrew had never heard pronounced before:

"Amanda Laura Martin Charney may approach the bench."

She said, "Thank you, your honor. I am not a lawyer and I don't know the proper way of phrasing things, but I hope you will listen to my meaning and ignore the words.

"Let's understand what it means to be free in Andrew's case. In some ways, he *is* free. I think it's at least twenty years since anyone in the Martin family gave him an order to do something that we felt he might not do of his own accord.

"But we can, if we wish, give him an order to do anything, couch it as harshly as we wish, because he is a machine that belongs to us. Why should we be in a position to do so, when he has served us so long, so faithfully, and earned so much money for us? He owes us nothing more. The debt is entirely on the other side.

"Even if we were legally forbidden to place Andrew in involuntary servitude, he would still serve us voluntarily. Making him free would be a trick of words only, but it would mean much to him. It would give him everything and cost us nothing."

For a moment the judge seemed to be suppressing a smile. "I see your point, Mrs. Charney. The fact is that there is no binding law in this respect and no precedent. There is, however, the unspoken assumption that only a man can enjoy freedom. I can make new law here, subject to reversal in a higher court, but I cannot lightly run counter to that assumption. Let me address the robot. Andrew!"

"Yes, your honor."

It was the first time Andrew had spoken in court and the judge seemed astonished for a moment at the human timbre of the voice. He said, "Why do you want to be free, Andrew? In what way will this matter to you?"

Andrew said, "Would you wish to be a slave, your honor?"

"But you are not a slave. You are a perfectly good robot, a genius of a robot I am given to understand, capable of an artistic expression that can be matched nowhere. What more can you do if you were free?"

"Perhaps no more than I do now, your honor, but with greater joy. It has been said in this courtroom that only a human being can be free. It seems to me that only someone who wishes for freedom can be free. I wish for freedom."

And it was that that cued the judge. The crucial sentence in his decision was: "There is no right to deny freedom to any object with a mind advanced enough to grasp the concept and desire the state."

It was eventually upheld by the world court.

VIII

Sir remained displeased and his harsh voice made Andrew feel almost as though he were being short-circuited.

Sir said, "I don't want your damned money, Andrew. I'll take it only because you won't feel free otherwise. From now on, you can select your own jobs and do them as you please. I will give you no orders, except this one—that you do as you please. But I am still responsible for you; that's part of the court order. I hope you understand that."

Little Miss interrupted. "Don't be irascible, dad. The responsibility is no great chore. You know you won't have to do a thing. The Three Laws still hold."

"Then how is he free?"

Andrew said, "Are not human beings bound by their laws, sir?"

Sir said, "I'm not going to argue." He left, and Andrew saw him only infrequently after that.

Little Miss came to see him frequently in the small house that had been built and made over for him. It had no kitchen, of course, nor bathroom facilities. It had just two rooms; one was a library and one was a combination storeroom and workroom. Andrew accepted many commissions and worked harder as a free robot than he ever had before, till the cost of the house was paid for and the structure legally transferred to him.

One day Little Sir came. . . . No, George! Little Sir had insisted on that after the court decision. "A free robot doesn't call anyone Little Sir," George had said. "I call you Andrew. You must call me George."

It was phrased as an order, so Andrew called him George—but Little Miss remained Little Miss.

The day George came alone, it was to say that Sir was dying. Little Miss was at the bedside but Sir wanted Andrew as well.

Sir's voice was quite strong, though he seemed unable to move much. He struggled to get his hand up. "Andrew," he said, "Andrew . . . Don't help me, George. I'm only dying; I'm not crippled. . . . Andrew, I'm glad you're free. I just wanted to tell you that."

Andrew did not know what to say. He had never been at the side of someone dying before, but he knew it was the human way of ceasing to function. It was an involuntary and irreversible dismantling, and Andrew did not know what to say that might be appropriate. He could only remain standing, absolutely silent, absolutely motionless.

When it was over, Little Miss said to him, "He may not have seemed friendly to you toward the end, Andrew, but he was old, you know, and it hurt him that you should want to be free."

And then Andrew found the words to say. He said, "I would never have been free without him, Little Miss."

IX

It was only after Sir's death that Andrew began to wear clothes. He began with an old pair of trousers at first, a pair that George had given him.

George was married now, and a lawyer. He had joined Feingold's firm. Old Feingold was long since dead but his daughter had carried on and eventually the firm's name became Feingold and Martin. It remained so even when the daughter retired and no Feingold took her place. At the time Andrew put on clothes for the first time, the Martin name had just been added to the firm.

George had tried not to smile the first time Andrew put on the trousers, but to Andrew's eyes the smile was clearly there.

Geroge showed Andrew how to manipulate the static charge so as to allow the trousers to open, wrap about his lower body and move shut. George demonstrated on his own trousers, but Andrew was quite aware that it would take him awhile to duplicate that one flowing motion.

George said, "But why do you want trousers, Andrew? Your body is so beautifully functional it's a shame to cover it—especially when you needn't worry about either temperature control or modesty. And it doesn't cling properly, not on metal."

Andrew said, "Are not human bodies beautifully functional, George? Yet you cover yourselves."

"For warmth, for cleanliness, for protection, for decorativeness. None of that applies to you."

Andrew said, "I feel bare without clothes. I feel different, George."

"Different! Andrew, there are millions of robots on Earth now. In this region, according to the last census, there are almost as many robots as there are men."

"I know, George. There are robots doing every conceivable type of work."

"And none of them wear clothes."

"But none of them are free, George."

Little by little, Andrew added to the wardrobe. He was inhibited by George's smile and by the stares of the people who commissioned work.

He might be free, but there was built into him a carefully detailed program concerning his behavior toward people, and it was only by the tiniest steps that he dared advance. Open disapproval would set him back months.

Not everyone accepted Andrew as free. He was incapable of resenting that, and yet there was a difficulty about his thinking process when he thought of it.

Most of all, he tended to avoid putting on clothes—or too many of them —when he thought Little Miss might come to visit him. She was old now and was often away in some warmer climate, but when she returned the first thing she did was visit him.

On one of her returns, George said ruefully, "She's got me, Andrew. I'll be running for the legislature next year. Like grandfather, she says, like grandson."

"Like grandfather . . ." Andrew stopped, uncertain.

"I mean that I, George, the grandson, will be like Sir, the grandfather, who was in the legislature once."

Andrew said, "It would be pleasant, George, if Sir were still . . ." He paused, for he did not want to say, "in working order." That seemed inappropriate.

"Alive," said George. "Yes, I think of the old monster now and then, too."

It was a conversation Andrew thought about. He had noticed his own incapacity in speech when talking with George. Somehow the language had changed since Andrew had come into being with an innate vocabulary. Then, too, George used a colloquial speech, as Sir and Little Miss had not. Why should he have called Sir a monster when surely that word was not appropriate?

Nor could Andrew turn to his own books for guidance. They were old and most dealt with woodworking, with art, with furniture design. There were none on language, none on the way of human beings.

It was at that moment it seemed to him that he must seek the proper books, and as a free robot, he felt he must not ask George. He would go to town and use the library. It was a triumphant decision and he felt his electropotential grow distinctly higher until he had to throw in an impedance coil.

He put on a full costume, even including a shoulder chain of wood. He would have preferred the glitter plastic but George had said that wood was much more appropriate and that polished cedar was considerably more valuable as well.

He had placed a hundred feet between himself and the house before gathering resistance brought him to a halt. He shifted the impedance coil out of circuit, and when that did not seem to help enough, he returned to his home and on a piece of notepaper wrote neatly, "I have gone to the library," and placed it in clear view on his worktable.

X

Andrew never quite got to the library. He had studied the map. He knew the route, but not the appearance of it. The actual landmarks did not resemble the symbols on the map and he would hesitate. Eventually he thought he must have somehow gone wrong, for everything looked strange.

He passed an occasional field robot, but at the time he decided he should ask his way, there were none in sight. A vehicle passed and did not stop. He stood irresolute, which meant calmly motionless, and then coming across the field toward him were two human beings.

He turned to face them, and they altered their course to meet him. A moment before, they had been talking loudly; he had heard their voices; but now they were silent. They had the look that Andrew associated with human uncertainty, and they were young, but not very young. Twenty perhaps? Andrew could never judge human age.

He said, "Would you describe to me the route to the town library, sirs?"

One of them, the taller of the two, whose tall hat lengthened him still farther, almost grotesquely, said, not to Andrew, but to the other, "It's a robot."

The other had a bulbous nose and heavy eyelids. He said, not to Andrew, but to the first, "It's wearing clothes."

The tall one snapped his fingers. "It's the free robot. They have a robot at the Martins who isn't owned by anybody. Why else would it be wearing clothes?"

"Ask it," said the one with the nose.

"Are you the Martin robot?" asked the tall one.

"I am Andrew Martin, sir," said Andrew.

"Good. Take off your clothes. Robots don't wear clothes." He said to the other, "That's disgusting. Look at him."

Andrew hesitated. He hadn't heard an order in that tone of voice in so long that his Second Law circuits had momentarily jammed.

The tall one said, "Take off your clothes. I order you."

Slowly, Andrew began to remove them.

"Just drop them," said the tall one.

The nose said, "If it doesn't belong to anyone, he could be ours as much as someone else's."

"Anyway," said the tall one, "who's to object to anything we do? We're not damaging property. . . . Stand on your head." That was to Andrew.

"The head is not meant . . ." began Andrew.

"That's an order. If you don't know how, try anyway."

Andrew hesitated again, then bent to put his head on the ground. He tried to lift his legs and fell, heavily.

The tall one said, "Just lie there." He said to the other, "We can take him apart. Ever take a robot apart?"

"Will he let us?"

"How can he stop us?"

There was no way Andrew could stop them, if they ordered him not to resist in a forceful enough manner. Second Law of obedience took precedence over the Third Law of self-preservation. In any case, he could not defend himself without possibly hurting them and that would mean breaking the First Law. At that thought, every motile unit contracted slightly and he quivered as he lay there.

The tall one walked over and pushed at him with his foot. "He's heavy. I think we'll need tools to do the job."

The nose said, "We could order him to take himself apart. It would be fun to watch him try."

"Yes," said the tall one thoughtfully, "but let's get him off the road. If someone comes along . . ."

It was too late. Someone had indeed come along and it was George. From where he lay, Andrew had seen him topping a small rise in the middle distance. He would have liked to signal him in some way, but the last order had been "Just lie there!"

George was running now and he arrived somewhat winded. The two young men stepped back a little and then waited thoughtfully.

George said anxiously, "Andrew, has something gone wrong?"

Andrew said, "I am well, George."

"Then stand up. . . . What happened to your clothes?"

The tall young man said, "That your robot, mac?"

George turned sharply. "He's no one's robot. What's been going on here?"

"We politely asked him to take his clothes off. What's that to you if you don't own him?"

George said, "What were they doing, Andrew?"

Andrew said, "It was their intention in some way to dismember me. They were about to move me to a quiet spot and order me to dismember myself."

George looked at the two and his chin trembled. The two young men retreated no farther. They were smiling. The tall one said lightly, "What are you going to do, pudgy? Attack us?"

George said, "No. I don't have to. This robot has been with my family for over seventy years. He knows us and he values us more than he values anyone else. I am going to tell him that you two are threatening my life and that you plan to kill me. I will ask him to defend me. In choosing between me and you two, he will choose me. Do you know what will happen to you when he attacks you?"

The two were backing away slightly, looking uneasy.

George said sharply, "Andrew, I am in danger and about to come to harm from these young men. Move toward them!"

Andrew did so, and the two young men did not wait. They ran fleetly.

"All right, Andrew, relax," said George. He looked unstrung. He was far past the age where he could face the possibility of a dustup with one young man, let alone two.

Andrew said, "I couldn't have hurt them, George. I could see they were not attacking you."

"I didn't order you to attack them; I only told you to move toward them. Their own fears did the rest."

"How can they fear robots?"

"It's a disease of mankind, one of which it is not yet cured. But never mind that. What the devil are you doing here, Andrew? I was on the point of turning back and hiring a helicopter when I found you. How did you get it into your head to go to the library? I would have brought you any books you needed."

"I am a . . ." began Andrew.

"Free robot. Yes, yes. All right, what did you want in the library?"

"I want to know more about human beings, about the world, about everything. And about robots, George. I want to write a history about robots."

George said, "Well, let's walk home. . . . And pick up your clothes first. Andrew, there are a million books on robotics and all of them include histories of the science. The world is growing saturated not only with robots but with information about robots."

Andrew shook his head, a human gesture he had lately begun to make. "Not a history of robotics, George. A history of *robots,* by a robot. I want to explain how robots feel about what has happened since the first ones were allowed to work and live on Earth."

George's eyebrows lifted, but he said nothing in direct response.

XI

Little Miss was just past her eighty-third birthday, but there was nothing about her that was lacking in either energy or determination. She gestured with her cane oftener than she propped herself up with it.

She listened to the story in a fury of indignation. She said, "George, that's horrible. Who were those young ruffians?"

"I don't know. What difference does it make? In the end they did no damage."

"They might have. You're a lawyer, George, and if you're well off, it's entirely due to the talent of Andrew. It was the money *he* earned that is the foundation of everything we have. He provides the continuity for this family and I will *not* have him treated as a windup toy."

"What would you have me do, mother?" asked George.

"I said you're a lawyer. Don't you listen? You set up a test case somehow, and you force the regional courts to declare for robot rights and get the legislature to pass the necessary bills, and carry the whole thing to the world court, if you have to. I'll be watching, George, and I'll tolerate no shirking."

She was serious, and what began as a way of soothing the fearsome old lady became an involved matter with enough legal entanglement to make it interesting. As senior partner of Feingold and Martin, George plotted strategy but left the actual work to his junior partners, with much of it a matter for his son, Paul, who was also a member of the firm and who reported dutifully nearly every day to his grandmother. She, in turn, discussed it every day with Andrew.

Andrew was deeply involved. His work on his book on robots was delayed again, as he pored over the legal arguments and even, at times, made very diffident suggestions.

He said, "George told me that day that human beings have always been afraid of robots. As long as they are, the courts and the legislatures are not likely to work hard on behalf of robots. Should there not be something done about public opinion?"

So while Paul stayed in court, George took to the public platform. It gave him the advantage of being informal and he even went so far sometimes as to wear the new, loose style of clothing which he called drapery. Paul said, "Just don't trip over it on stage, dad."

George said despondently, "I'll try not to."

He addressed the annual convention of holo-news editors on one occasion and said, in part:

"If, by virtue of the Second Law, we can demand of any robot unlimited obedience in all respects not involving harm to a human being, then any human being, *any* human being, has a fearsome power over any robot, *any* robot. In particular, since Second Law supersedes Third Law, *any* human being can use the law of obedience to overcome the law of self-protection. He can order any robot to damage itself or even destroy itself for any reason, or for no reason.

"Is this just? Would we treat an animal so? Even an inanimate object which has given us good service has a claim on our consideration. And a robot is not insensible; it is not an animal. It can think well enough to enable it to talk to us, reason with us, joke with us. Can we treat them as friends, can we work together with them and not give them some of the fruit of that friendship, some of the benefit of co-working?

"If a man has the right to give a robot any order that does not involve harm to a human being, he should have the decency never to give a robot any order that involves harm to a robot unless human safety absolutely requires it. With great power goes great responsibility, and if the robots have Three Laws to protect men, is it too much to ask that men have a law or two to protect robots?"

Andrew was right. It was the battle over public opinion that held the key to courts and legislature and in the end a law passed which set up conditions under which robot-harming orders were forbidden. It was endlessly qualified and the punishments for violating the law were totally inadequate, but the principle was established. The final passage by the world legislature came through on the day of Little Miss's death.

That was no coincidence. Little Miss held onto life desperately during the last debate and let go only when word of victory arrived. Her last smile was for Andrew. Her last words were, "You have been good to us, Andrew."

She died with her hand holding his, while her son and his wife and children remained at a respectful distance from both.

XII

Andrew waited patiently while the receptionist disappeared into the inner office. It might have used the holographic chatterbox, but unquestionably it was unmanned (or perhaps unroboted) by having to deal with another robot rather than with a human being.

Andrew passed the time revolving the matter in his mind. Could "unroboted" be used as an analogue of "unmanned," or had "unmanned" become a metaphoric term sufficiently divorced from its original literal meaning to be applied to robots—or to women for that matter?

Such problems came frequently as he worked on his book on robots. The trick of thinking out sentences to express all complexities had undoubtedly increased his vocabulary.

Occasionally, someone came into the room to stare at him and he did not try to avoid the glance. He looked at each calmly, and each in turn looked away.

Paul Martin finally came out. He looked surprised, or he would have if Andrew could have made out his expression with certainty. Paul had taken to wearing the heavy makeup that fashion was dictating for both sexes and though it made sharper and firmer the somewhat bland lines of his face, Andrew disapproved. He found that disapproving of human beings, as long as he did not express it verbally, did not make him very uneasy. He could even write the disapproval. He was sure it had not always been so.

Paul said, "Come in, Andrew. I'm sorry I made you wait but there was something I *had* to finish. Come in. You had said you wanted to talk to me, but I didn't know you meant here in town."

"If you are busy, Paul, I am prepared to continue to wait."

Paul glanced at the interplay of shifting shadows on the dial on the wall that served as timepiece and said, "I can make some time. Did you come alone?"

"I hired an automatobile."

"Any trouble?" Paul asked, with more than a trace of anxiety.

"I wasn't expecting any. My rights are protected."

Paul looked the more anxious for that. "Andrew, I've explained that the law is unenforceable, at least under most conditions. . . . And if you insist on wearing clothes, you'll run into trouble eventually—just like that first time."

"And only time, Paul. I'm sorry you are displeased."

"Well, look at it this way; you are virtually a living legend, Andrew, and you are too valuable in many different ways for you to have any right to take chances with yourself. . . . How's the book coming?"

"I am approaching the end, Paul. The publisher is quite pleased."

"Good!"

"I don't know that he's necessarily pleased with the book as a book. I think he expects to sell many copies because it's written by a robot and it's that that pleases him."

"Only human, I'm afraid."

"I am not displeased. Let it sell for whatever reason since it will mean money and I can use some."

"Grandmother left you . . ."

"Little Miss was generous, and I'm sure I can count on the family to help me out further. But it is the royalties from the book on which I am counting to help me through the next step."

"What next step is that?"

"I wish to see the head of U. S. Robots and Mechanical Men, Inc. I have tried to make an appointment, but so far I have not been able to reach him. The corporation did not cooperate with me in the writing of the book, so I am not surprised, you understand."

Paul was clearly amused. "Cooperation is the last thing you can expect. They didn't cooperate with us in our great fight for robot rights. Quite the reverse and you can see why. Give a robot rights and people may not want to buy them."

"Nevertheless," said Andrew, "if you call them, you may obtain an interview for me."

"I'm no more popular with them than you are, Andrew."

"But perhaps you can hint that by seeing me they may head off a campaign by Feingold and Martin to strengthen the rights of robots further."

"Wouldn't that be a lie, Andrew?"

"Yes, Paul, and I can't tell one. That is why you must call."

"Ah, you can't lie, but you can urge me to tell a lie, is that it? You're getting more human all the time, Andrew."

XIII

It was not easy to arrange, even with Paul's supposedly weighted name.

But it was finally carried through and, when it was, Harley Smythe-Robertson, who, on his mother's side, was descended from the original founder of the corporation and who had adopted the hyphenation to indicate it, looked remarkably unhappy. He was approaching retirement age and his entire tenure as president had been devoted to the matter of robot rights. His gray hair was plastered thinly over the top of his scalp, his face was not made up and he eyed Andrew with brief hostility from time to time.

Andrew said, "Sir, nearly a century ago, I was told by a Merton Mansky of this corporation that the mathematics governing the plotting of the positronic pathways was far too complicated to permit of any but approximate solutions and that therefore my own capacities were not fully predictable."

"That was a century ago." Smythe-Robertson hesitated, then said icily, "*Sir.* It is true no longer. Our robots are made with precision now and are trained precisely to their jobs."

"Yes," said Paul, who had come along, as he said, to make sure that the corporation played fair, "with the result that my receptionist must be guided at every point once events depart from the conventional, however slightly."

Smythe-Robertson said, "You would be much more displeased if it were to improvise."

Andrew said, "Then you no longer manufacture robots like myself which are flexible and adaptable."

"No longer."

"The research I have done in connection with my book," said Andrew, "indicates that I am the oldest robot presently in active operation."

"The oldest presently," said Smythe-Robertson, "and the oldest ever. The oldest that will ever be. No robot is useful after the twenty-fifth year. They are called in and replaced with newer models."

"No robot *as presently manufactured* is useful after the twenty-fifth year," said Paul pleasantly. "Andrew is quite exceptional in this respect."

Andrew, adhering to the path he had marked out for himself, said, "As the oldest robot in the world and the most flexible, am I not unusual enough to merit special treatment from the company?"

"Not at all," said Smythe-Robertson freezingly. "Your unusualness is an embarrassment to the company. If you were on lease, instead of having been a sale outright through some mischance, you would long since have been replaced."

"But that is exactly the point," said Andrew. "I am a free robot and I own myself. Therefore I come to you and ask you to replace me. You cannot do this without the owner's consent. Nowadays, that consent is extorted as a condition of the lease, but in my time this did not happen."

Smythe-Robertson was looking both startled and puzzled, and for a moment there was silence. Andrew found himself staring at the holograph on the wall. It was a death mask of Susan Calvin, patron saint of all roboticists. She was dead nearly two centuries now, but as a result of writing his book Andrew knew her so well he could half persuade himself that he had met her in life.

Smythe-Robertson said, "How can I replace you for you? If I replace you as robot, how can I donate the new robot to you as owner since in the very act of replacement you cease to exist?" He smiled grimly.

"Not at all difficult," interposed Paul. "The seat of Andrew's personality is his positronic brain and it is the one part that cannot be replaced without creating a new robot. The positronic brain, therefore, is Andrew the owner. Every other part of the robotic body can be replaced without affecting the robot's personality, and those other parts are the brain's possessions. Andrew, I should say, wants to supply his brain with a new robotic body."

"That's right," said Andrew calmly. He turned to Smythe-Robertson. "You have manufactured androids, haven't you? Robots that have the outward appearance of humans complete to the texture of the skin?"

Smythe-Robertson said, "Yes, we have. They worked perfectly well, with their synthetic fibrous skins and tendons. There was virtually no metal anywhere except for the brain, yet they were nearly as tough as metal robots. They were tougher, weight for weight."

Paul looked interested. "I didn't know that. How many are on the market?"

"None," said Smythe-Robertson. "They were much more expensive than metal models and a market survey showed they would not be accepted. They looked too human."

Andrew said, "But the corporation retains its expertise, I assume. Since it does, I wish to request that I be replaced by an organic robot, an android."

Paul looked surprised. "Good Lord," he said.

Smythe-Robertson stiffened. "Quite impossible!"

"Why is it impossible?" asked Andrew. "I will pay any reasonable fee, of course."

Smythe-Robertson said, "We do not manufacture androids."

"You do not *choose* to manufacture androids," interposed Paul quickly. "That is not the same as being unable to manufacture them."

Smythe-Robertson said, "Nevertheless, the manufacture of androids is against public policy."

"There is no law against it," said Paul.

"Nevertheless, we do not manufacture them, and we will not."

Paul cleared his throat. "Mr. Smythe-Robertson," he said, "Andrew is a free robot who is under the purview of the law guaranteeing robot rights. You are aware of this, I take it?"

"Only too well."

"This robot, as a free robot, chooses to wear clothes. This results in his being frequently humiliated by thoughtless human beings despite the law against the humiliation of robots. It is difficult to prosecute vague offenses that don't meet

with the general disapproval of those who must decide on guilt and innocence."

"U. S. Robots understood that from the start. Your father's firm unfortunately did not."

"My father is dead now," said Paul, "but what I see is that we have here
a clear offense with a clear target."

"What are you talking about?" said Smythe-Robertson.

"My client, Andrew Martin—he has just become my client—is a free robot
who is entitled to ask U. S. Robots and Mechanical Men, Inc., for the right
of replacement, which the corporation supplies anyone who owns a robot for
more than twenty-five years. In fact, the corporation insists on such replacement."

Paul was smiling and thoroughly at his ease. He went on, "The positronic
brain of my client is the owner of the body of my client—which is certainly
more than twenty-five years old. The positronic brain demands the replacement of the body and offers to pay any reasonable fee for an android body as
that replacement. If you refuse the request, my client undergoes humiliation
and we will sue.

"While public opinion would not ordinarily support the claim of a robot
in such a case, may I remind you that U. S. Robots is not popular with the
public generally. Even those who most use and profit from robots are suspicious of the corporation. This may be a hangover from the days when robots
were widely feared. It may be resentment against the power and wealth of U.
S. Robots which has a worldwide monopoly. Whatever the cause may be, the
resentment exists, and I think you will find that you would prefer not to
withstand a lawsuit, particularly since my client is wealthy and will live for
many more centuries and will have no reason to refrain from fighting the battle
forever."

Smythe-Robertson had slowly reddened. "You are trying to force me
to . . ."

"I force you to do nothing," said Paul. "If you wish to refuse to accede to
my client's reasonable request, you may by all means do so and we will leave
without another word. . . . But we will sue, as is certainly our right, and you
will find that you will eventually lose."

Smythe-Robertson said, "Well . . ." and paused.

"I see that you are going to accede," said Paul. "You may hesitate but you
will come to it in the end. Let me assure you, then, of one further point. If,
in the process of transferring my client's positronic brain from his present body
to an organic one, there is any damage, however slight, then I will never rest
till I've nailed the corporation to the ground. I will, if necessary, take every

possible step to mobilize public opinion against the corporation if one brain path of my client's platinum-iridium essence is scrambled." He turned to Andrew and said, "Do you agree to all this, Andrew?"

Andrew hesitated a full minute. It amounted to the approval of lying, of blackmail, of the badgering and humiliation of a human being. But not physical harm, he told himself, not physical harm.

He managed at last to come out with a rather faint "Yes."

XIV

It was like being constructed again. For days, then for weeks, finally for months, Andrew found himself not himself somehow, and the simplest actions kept giving rise to hesitation.

Paul was frantic. "They've damaged you, Andrew. We'll have to institute suit."

Andrew spoke very slowly. "You mustn't. You'll never be able to prove—something—m-m-m-m . . ."

"Malice?"

"Malice. Besides, I grow stronger, better. It's the tr-tr-tr . . ."

"Tremble?"

"Trauma. After all, there's never been such an op—op—op—before."

Andrew could feel his brain from the inside. No one else could. He knew he was well, and during the months that it took him to learn full coordination and full positronic interplay, he spent hours before the mirror.

Not quite human! The face was stiff—too stiff—and the motions were too deliberate. They lacked the careless free flow of the human being, but perhaps that might come with time. At least he could wear clothes without the ridiculous anomaly of a metal face going along with it.

Eventually he said, "I will be going back to work."

Paul laughed and said, "That means you are well. What will you be doing? Another book?"

"No," said Andrew seriously. "I live too long for any one career to seize me by the throat and never let me go. There was a time when I was primarily an artist and I can still turn to that. And there was a time when I was a historian and I can still turn to that. But now I wish to be a robobiologist."

"A robopsychologist, you mean."

"No. That would imply the study of positronic brains and at the moment I lack the desire to do that. A robobiologist, it seems to me, would be concerned with the working of the body attached to that brain."

"Wouldn't that be a roboticist?"

"A roboticist works with a metal body. I would be studying an organic humanoid body, of which I have the only one, as far as I know."

"You narrow your field," said Paul thoughtfully. "As an artist, all conception is yours; as a historian, you dealt chiefly with robots; as a robobiologist, you will deal with yourself."

Andrew nodded. "It would seem so."

Andrew had to start from the very beginning, for he knew nothing of ordinary biology, almost nothing of science. He became a familiar sight in the libraries, where he sat at the electronic indices for hours at a time, looking perfectly normal in clothes. Those few who knew he was a robot in no way interfered with him.

He built a laboratory in a room which he added to his house, and his library grew, too.

Years passed, and Paul came to him one day and said, "It's a pity you're no longer working on the history of robots. I understand U. S. Robots is adopting a radically new policy."

Paul had aged, and his deteriorating eyes had been replaced with photoptic cells. In that respect, he had drawn closer to Andrew. Andrew said, "What have they done?"

"They are manufacturing central computers, gigantic positronic brains, really, which communicate with anywhere from a dozen to a thousand robots by microwave. The robots themselves have no brains at all. They are the limbs of the gigantic brain, and the two are physically separate."

"Is that more efficient?"

"U. S. Robots claims it is. Smythe-Robertson established the new direction before he died, however, and it's my notion that it's a backlash at you. U. S. Robots is determined that they will make no robots that will give them the type of trouble you have, and for that reason they separate brain and body. The brain will have no body to wish changed; the body will have no brain to wish anything.

"It's amazing, Andrew," Paul went on, "the influence you have had on the history of robots. It was your artistry that encouraged U. S. Robots to make robots more precise and specialized; it was your freedom that resulted in the establishment of the principle of robotic rights; it was your insistence on an android body that made U. S. Robots switch to brain-body separation."

Andrew said, "I suppose in the end the corporation will produce one vast brain controlling several billion robotic bodies. All the eggs will be in one basket. Dangerous. Not proper at all."

"I think you're right," said Paul, "but I don't suspect it will come to pass for a century at least and I won't live to see it. In fact, I may not live to see next year."

"Paul!" said Andrew, in concern.

Paul shrugged. "We're mortal, Andrew. We're not like you. It doesn't matter too much, but it does make it important to assure you on one point. I'm the last of the human Martins. There are collaterals descended from my great-aunt, but they don't count. The money I control personally will be left to the trust in your name and as far as anyone can foresee the future, you will be economically secure."

"Unnecessary," said Andrew, with difficulty. In all this time, he could not get used to the deaths of the Martins.

Paul said, "Let's not argue. That's the way it's going to be. What are you working on?"

"I am designing a system for allowing androids—myself—to gain energy from the combustion of hydrocarbons, rather than from atomic cells."

Paul raised his eyebrows. "So that they will breathe and eat?"

"Yes."

"How long have you been pushing in that direction?"

"For a long time now, but I think I have designed an adequate combustion chamber for catalyzed controlled breakdown."

"But why, Andrew? The atomic cell is surely infinitely better."

"In some ways, perhaps, but the atomic cell is inhuman."

XV

It took time, but Andrew had time. In the first place, he did not wish to do anything till Paul had died in peace.

With the death of the great-grandson of Sir, Andrew felt more nearly exposed to a hostile world and for that reason was the more determined to continue the path he had long ago chosen.

Yet he was not really alone. If a man had died, the firm of Feingold and Martin lived, for a corporation does not die any more than a robot does. The firm had its directions and it followed them soullessly. By way of the trust and through the law firm, Andrew continued to be wealthy. And in return for their own large annual retainer, Feingold and Martin involved themselves in the legal aspects of the new combustion chamber.

When the time came for Andrew to visit U. S. Robots and Mechanical

Men, Inc., he did it alone. Once he had gone with Sir and once with Paul. This time, the third time, he was alone and manlike.

U. S. Robots had changed. The production plant had been shifted to a large space station, as had grown to be the case with more and more industries. With them had gone many robots. The Earth itself was becoming parklike, with its one-billion-person population stabilized and perhaps not more than thirty percent of its at least equally large robot population independently brained.

The director of research was Alvin Magdescu, dark of complexion and hair, with a little pointed beard and wearing nothing above the waist but the breastband that fashion dictated. Andrew himself was well covered in the older fashion of several decades back.

Magdescu said, "I know you, of course, and I'm rather pleased to see you. You're our most notorious product, and it's a pity old Smythe-Robertson was so set against you. We could have done a great deal with you."

"You still can," said Andrew.

"No, I don't think so. We're past the time. We've had robots on Earth for over a century, but that's changing. It will be back to space with them and those that stay here won't be brained."

"But there remains myself, and I stay on Earth."

"True, but there doesn't seem to be much of the robot about you. What new request have you?"

"To be still less a robot. Since I am so far organic, I wish an organic source of energy. I have here the plans. . . ."

Magdescu did not hasten through them. He might have intended to at first, but he stiffened and grew intent. At one point he said, "This is remarkably ingenious. Who thought of all this?"

"I did," said Andrew.

Magdescu looked up at him sharply, then said, "It would amount to a major overhaul of your body, and an experimental one, since it has never been attempted before. I advise against it. Remain as you are."

Andrew's face had limited means of expression, but impatience showed plainly in his voice. "Dr. Magdescu, you miss the entire point. You have no choice but to accede to my request. If such devices can be built into my body, they can be built into human bodies as well. The tendency to lengthen human life by prosthetic devices has already been remarked on. There are no devices better than the ones I have designed and am designing.

"As it happens, I control the patents by way of the firm of Feingold and Martin. We are quite capable of going into business for ourselves and of developing the kind of prosthetic devices that may end by producing human beings with many of the properties of robots. Your own business will then suffer.

"If, however, you operate on me now and agree to do so under similar circumstances in the future, you will receive permission to make use of the patents and control the technology of both robots and the prosthetization of human beings. The initial leasing will not be granted, of course, until after the first operation is completed successfully, and after enough time has passed to demonstrate that it is indeed successful." Andrew felt scarcely any First Law inhibition to the stern conditions he was setting a human being. He was learning to reason that what seemed like cruelty might, in the long run, be kindness.

Magdescu looked stunned. He said, "I'm not the one to decide something like this. That's a corporate decision that would take time."

"I can wait a reasonable time," said Andrew, "but only a reasonable time." And he thought with satisfaction that Paul himself could not have done it better.

XVI

It took only a reasonable time, and the operation was a success.

Magdescu said, "I was very much against the operation, Andrew, but not for the reasons you might think. I was not in the least against the experiment, if it had been on someone else. I hated risking *your* positronic brain. Now that you have the positronic pathways interacting with simulated nerve pathways, it might be difficult to rescue the brain intact if the body went bad."

"I had every faith in the skill of the staff at U. S. Robots," said Andrew. "And I can eat now."

"Well, you can sip olive oil. It will mean occasional cleanings of the combustion chamber, as we have explained to you. Rather an uncomfortable touch, I should think."

"Perhaps, if I did not expect to go further. Self-cleaning is not impossible. In fact, I am working on a device that will deal with solid food that may be expected to contain incombustible fractions—indigestible matter, so to speak, that will have to be discarded."

"You would then have to develop an anus."

"The equivalent."

"What else, Andrew?"

"Everything else."

"Genitalia, too?"

"Insofar as they will fit my plans. My body is a canvas on which I intend to draw . . ."

Magdescu waited for the sentence to be completed, and when it seemed that it would not be, he completed it himself. "A man?"

"We shall see," said Andrew.

Magdescu said, "It's a puny ambition, Andrew. You're better than a man. You've gone downhill from the moment you opted for organicism."

"My brain has not suffered."

"No, it hasn't. I'll grant you that. But, Andrew, the whole new break-through in prosthetic devices made possible by your patents is being marketed under your name. You're recognized as the inventor and you're honored for it—as you are. Why play further games with your body?"

Andrew did not answer.

The honors came. He accepted membership in several learned societies, including one which was devoted to the new science he had established; the one he had called robobiolgoy but had come to be termed prosthetology.

On the one hundred and fiftieth anniversary of his construction, there was a testimonial dinner given in his honor at U. S. Robots. If Andrew saw irony in this, he kept it to himself.

Alvin Magdescu came out of retirement to chair the dinner. He was himself ninety-four years old and was alive because he had prosthetized devices that, among other things, fulfilled the function of liver and kidneys. The dinner reached its climax when Magdescu, after a short and emotional talk, raised his glass to toast "the sesquicentennial robot."

Andrew had had the sinews of his face redesigned to the point where he could show a range of emotions, but he sat through all the ceremonies sol-emnly passive. He did not like to be a sesquicentennial robot.

XVII

It was prosthetology that finally took Andrew off the Earth. In the decades that followed the celebration of the sesquicentennial, the moon had come to be a world more Earthlike than Earth in every respect but its gravitational pull, and in its underground cities there was a fairly dense population.

Prosthetized devices there had to take the lesser gravity into account and Andrew spent five years on the moon working with local prosthetologists to make the necessary adaptations. When not at his work, he wandered among the robot population, every one of which treated him with the robotic obsequiousness due a man.

He came back to an Earth that was humdrum and quiet in comparison and visited the offices of Feingold and Martin to announce his return.

The current head of the firm, Simon DeLong, was surprised. He said, "We had been told you were returning, Andrew" (he had almost said "Mr. Martin"), "but we were not expecting you till next week."

"I grew impatient," said Andrew brusquely. He was anxious to get to the point. "On the moon, Simon, I was in charge of a research team of twenty human scientists. I gave orders that no one questioned. The lunar robots deferred to me as they would to a human being. Why, then, am I not a human being?"

A wary look entered DeLong's eyes. He said, "My dear Andrew, as you have just explained, you are treated as a human being by both robots and human beings. You are therefore a human being *de facto*."

"To be a human being *de facto* is not enough. I want not only to be treated as one, but to be legally identified as one. I want to be a human being *de jure*."

"Now that is another matter," said DeLong. "There we would run into human prejudice and into the undoubted fact that however much you may be like a human being, you are *not* a human being."

"In what way not?" asked Andrew. "I have the shape of a human being and organs equivalent to those of a human being. My organs, in fact, are identical to some of those in a prosthetized human being. I have contributed artistically, literarily and scientifically to human culture as much as any human being now alive. What more can one ask?"

"I myself would ask nothing more. The trouble is that it would take an act of the world legislature to define you as a human being. Frankly, I wouldn't expect that to happen."

"To whom on the legislature could I speak?"

"To the chairman of the Science and Technology Committee perhaps."

"Can you arrange a meeting?"

"But you scarcely need an intermediary. In your position, you can . . ."

"No. *You* arrange it." (It didn't even occur to Andrew that he was giving a flat order to a human being. He had grown accustomed to that on the moon.) "I want him to know that the firm of Feingold and Martin is backing me in this to the hilt."

"Well, now . . ."

"To the hilt, Simon. In one hundred and seventy-three years I have in one fashion or another contributed greatly to this firm. I have been under obligation to individual members of the firm in times past. I am not now. It is rather the other way around now and I am calling in my debts."

DeLong said, "I will do what I can."

XVIII

The chairman of the Science and Technology Committee was of the East Asian region and she was a woman. Her name was Chee Li-Hsing and her transparent garments (obscuring what she wanted obscured only by their dazzle) made her look plastic-wrapped.

She said, "I sympathize with your wish for full human rights. There have been times in history when segments of the human population fought for full human rights. What rights, however, can you possibly want that you do not have?"

"As simple a thing as my right to life. A robot can be dismantled at any time."

"A human being can be executed at any time."

"Execution can only follow due process of law. There is no trial needed for my dismantling. Only the word of a human being in authority is needed to end me. Besides—besides . . ." Andrew tried desperately to allow no sign of pleading, but his carefully designed tricks of human expression and tone of voice betrayed him here. "The truth is, I want to be a man. I have wanted it through six generations of human beings."

Li-Hsing looked up at him out of darkly sympathetic eyes. "The legislature can pass a law declaring you one—they could pass a law declaring a stone statue to be defined as a man. Whether they will actually do so is, however, as likely in the first case as the second. Congresspeople are as human as the rest of the population and there is always that element of suspicion against robots."

"Even now?"

"Even now. We would all allow the fact that you have earned the prize of humanity, and yet there would remain the fear of setting an undesirable precedent."

"What precedent? I am the only free robot, the only one of my type, and there will never be another. You may consult U. S. Robots."

" 'Never' is a long time, Andrew—or, if you prefer, Mr. Martin—since I will gladly give you my personal accolade as man. You will find that most congresspeople will not be willing to set the precedent, no matter how meaningless such a precedent might be. Mr. Martin, you have my sympathy, but I cannot tell you to hope. Indeed . . ."

She sat back and her forehead wrinkled. "Indeed, if the issue grows too heated, there might well arise a certain sentiment, both inside the legislature and outside, for that dismantling you mentioned. Doing away with you could turn out to be the easiest way of resolving the dilemma. Consider that before deciding to push matters."

Andrew said, "Will no one remember the technique of prosthetology, something that is almost entirely mine?"

"It may seem cruel, but they won't. Or if they do, it will be remembered against you. It will be said you did it only for yourself. It will be said it was part of a campaign to roboticize human beings, or to humanify robots, and in either case evil and vicious. You have never been part of a political hate campaign, Mr. Martin, and I tell you that you will be the object of vilification of a kind neither you nor I would credit, and there would be people who'll believe it all. Mr. Martin, let your life be." She rose and, next to Andrew's seated figure, she seemed small and almost childlike.

Andrew said, "If I decide to fight for my humanity, will you be on my side?"

She thought, then said, "I will be—insofar as I can be. If at any time such a stand would appear to threaten my political future, I may have to abandon you, since it is not an issue I feel to be at the very root of my beliefs. I am trying to be honest with you."

"Thank you, and I will ask no more. I intend to fight this through whatever the consequences, and I will ask you for your help only for as long as you can give it."

XVIX

It was not a direct fight. Feingold and Martin counseled patience and Andrew muttered grimly that he had an endless supply of that. Feingold and Martin then entered on a campaign to narrow and restrict the area of combat.

They instituted a lawsuit denying the obligation to pay debts to an individual with a prosthetic heart on the grounds that the possession of a robotic organ removed humanity and with it the constitutional rights of human beings.

They fought the matter skillfully and tenaciously, losing at every step but always in such a way that the decision was forced to be as broad as possible, and then carrying it by way of appeals to the world court.

It took years and millions of dollars.

When the final decision was handed down, DeLong held what amounted to a victory celebration over the legal loss. Andrew was, of course, present in the company offices on the occasion.

"We've done two things, Andrew," said DeLong, "both of which are good. First of all, we have established the fact that no number of artifacts in the human body causes it to cease being a human body. Secondly, we have engaged public opinion in the question in such a way as to put it fiercely on the side of a broad interpretation of humanity since there is not a human being in existence who does not hope for prosthetics if that will keep him alive."

"And do you think the legislature will now grant me my humanity?" asked Andrew.

DeLong looked faintly uncomfortable. "As to that, I cannot be optimistic. There remains the one organ which the world court has used as the criterion of humanity. Human beings have an organic cellular brain and robots have a platinum-iridium positronic brain if they have one at all—and you certainly have a positronic brain. . . . No, Andrew, don't get that look in your eye. We lack the knowledge to duplicate the work of a cellular brain in artificial structures close enough to the organic type to allow it to fall within the court's decision. Not even you could do it."

"What ought we do, then?"

"Make the attempt, of course. Congresswoman Li-Hsing will be on our side and a growing number of other congresspeople. The president will undoubtedly go along with a majority of the legislature in this matter."

"Do we have a majority?"

"No, far from it. But we might get one if the public will allow its desire for a broad interpretation of humanity to extend to you. A small chance, I admit, but if you do not wish to give up, we must gamble for it."

"I do not wish to give up."

XX

Congresswoman Li-Hsing was considerably older than she had been when Andrew had first met her. Her transparent garments were long gone. Her hair was now close-cropped and her coverings were tubular. Yet still Andrew clung, as closely as he could within the limits of reasonable taste, to the style of clothing that had prevailed when he had first adopted clothing over a century before.

She said, "We've gone as far as we can, Andrew. We'll try once more after recess, but, to be honest, defeat is certain and the whole thing will have to be given up. All my most recent efforts have only earned me a certain defeat in the coming congressional campaign."

"I know," said Andrew, "and it distresses me. You said once you would abandon me if it came to that. Why have you not done so?"

"One can change one's mind, you know. Somehow, abandoning you became a higher price than I cared to pay for just one more term. As it is, I've been in the legislature for over a quarter of a century. It's enough."

"Is there no way we can change minds, Chee?"

"We've changed all that are amenable to reason. The rest—the majority —cannot be moved from their emotional antipathies."

"Emotional antipathy is not a valid reason for voting one way or the other."

"I know that, Andrew, but they don't advance emotional antipathy as their reason."

Andrew said cautiously, "It all comes down to the brain, then, but must we leave it at the level of cells versus positrons? Is there no way of forcing a functional definition? Must we say that a brain is made of this or that? May we not say that a brain is something—anything—capable of a certain level of thought?"

"Won't work," said Li-Hsing. "Your brain is man-made, the human brain is not. Your brain is constructed, theirs developed. To any human being who is intent on keeping up the barrier between himself and a robot, those differences are a steel wall a mile high and a mile thick."

"If we could get at the source of their antipathy—the very source of . . ."

"After all your years," said Li-Hsing sadly, "you are still trying to reason out the human being. Poor Andrew, don't be angry, but it's the robot in you that drives you in that direction."

"I don't know," said Andrew. "If I could bring myself . . ."

I (reprise)

If he could bring himself . . .

He had known for a long time it might come to that, and in the end he was at the surgeon's. He found one, skillful enough for the job at hand, which meant a robot surgeon, for no human surgeon could be trusted in this connection, either in ability or in intention.

The surgeon could not have performed the operation on a human being, so Andrew, after putting off the moment of decision with a sad line of questioning that reflected the turmoil within himself, put the First Law to one side by saying, "I, too, am a robot."

He then said, as firmly as he had learned to form the words even at human beings over these past decades, "I *order* you to carry through the operation on me."

In the absence of the First Law, an order so firmly given from one who looked so much like a man activated the Second Law sufficiently to carry the day.

XXI

Andrew's feeling of weakness was, he was sure, quite imaginary. He had recovered from the operation. Nevertheless, he leaned, as unobtrusively as he could manage, against the wall. It would be entirely too revealing to sit.

Li-Hsing said, "The final vote will come this week, Andrew. I've been able to delay it no longer, and we must lose. . . . And that will be it, Andrew."

Andrew said, "I am grateful for your skill at delay. It gave me the time I needed, and I took the gamble I had to."

"What gamble is this?" asked Li-Hsing with open concern.

"I couldn't tell you or the people at Feingold and Martin. I was sure I would be stopped. See here, if it is the brain that is at issue, isn't the greatest difference of all the matter of immortality? Who really cares what a brain looks like or is built of or how it was formed? What matters is that brain cells die; *must* die. Even if every other organ in the body is maintained or replaced, the brain cells, which cannot be replaced without changing and therefore killing the personality, must eventually die.

"My own positronic pathways have lasted nearly two centuries without perceptible change and can last for centuries more. Isn't *that* the fundamental barrier? Human beings can tolerate an immortal robot, for it doesn't matter how long a machine lasts. They cannot tolerate an immortal human being, since their own mortality is endurable only so long as it is universal. And for that reason they won't make me a human being."

Li-Hsing said, "What is it you're leading up to, Andrew?"

"I have removed that problem. Decades ago, my positronic brain was connected to organic nerves. Now, one last operation has arranged that connection in such a way that slowly—quite slowly—the potential is being drained from my pathways."

Li-Hsing's finely wrinkled face showed no expression for a moment. Then her lips tightened. "Do you mean you've arranged to die, Andrew? You can't have. That violates the Third Law."

"No," said Andrew, "I have chosen between the death of my body and the death of my aspirations and desires. To have let my body live at the cost of the greater death is what would have violated the Third Law."

Li-Hsing seized his arm as though she were about to shake him. She stopped herself. "Andrew, it won't work. Change it back."

"It can't be. Too much damage was done. I have a year to live—more or less. I will last through the two hundredth anniversary of my construction. I was weak enough to arrange that."

"How can it be worth it? Andrew, you're a fool."

"It if brings me humanity, that will be worth it. If it doesn't, it will bring an end to striving and that will be worth it, too."

And Li-Hsing did something that astonished herself. Quietly, she began to weep.

XXII

It was odd how that last deed caught at the imagination of the world. All that Andrew had done before had not swayed them. But he had finally accepted even death to be human and the sacrifice was too great to be rejected.

The final ceremony was timed, quite deliberately, for the two hundredth anniversary. The world president was to sign the act and make it law and the ceremony would be visible on a global network and would be beamed to the lunar state and even to the Martian colony.

Andrew was in a wheelchair. He could still walk, but only shakily.

With mankind watching, the world president said, "Fifty years ago, you were declared a sesquicentennial robot, Andrew." After a pause, and in a more solemn tone, he said, "Today we declare you a bicentennial man, Mr. Martin."

And Andrew, smiling, held out his hand to shake that of the president.

XXIII

Andrew's thoughts were slowly fading as he lay in bed.

Desperately he seized at them. Man! He was a man! He wanted that to be his last thought. He wanted to dissolve—die—with that.

He opened his eyes one more time and for one last time recognized Li-Hsing waiting solemnly. There were others, but those were only shadows, unrecognizable shadows. Only Li-Hsing stood out against the deepening gray. Slowly, inchingly, he held out his hand to her and very dimly and faintly felt her take it.

She was fading in his eyes, as the last of his thoughts trickled away.

But before she faded completely, one last fugitive thought came to him and rested for a moment on his mind before everything stopped.

"Little Miss," he whispered, too low to be heard.

CAROL EMSHWILLER
Hunting Machine

*Here is a tight, tense story of the blood sports of the very near future
—with some technological angles that probably never occurred to
Ernest Hemingway.*

It sensed Ruthie McAlister's rapid heartbeat, just as it sensed any other
animal's. The palms of her hands were damp, and it felt that, too—it also felt
the breathing, in and out. And it heard her nervous giggle.

She was watching her husband, Joe, as he leaned over the control unit of
the thing that sensed heartbeats—the gray-green thing they called the hound,
or Rover, or sometimes the bitch.

"Hey," she said. "I guess it's okay, huh?"

Joe turned a screw with his thumbnail and pulled out the wire attached to
it. "Gimme a bobby pin."

Ruthie reached to the back of her head. "I mean it's not dangerous,
is it?"

"Naw."

"I don't just mean about *it.* " She nodded at the gray-green thing. "I mean,
I know you're good at fixing things like this, like the time you got beer for
nothing out of the beer vendor and, golly, I guess we haven't paid for a TV
show for years. I mean, I *know* you can fix things right, only won't they know
when we bring it back to be checked out?"

"Look, these wardens are country boys, and besides, I can put this thing
back so *nobody* knows."

The gray-green thing squatted on its six legs where Joe could lean over it;
it sensed that Ruthie's heartbeat had slowed almost to normal, and it heard
her sigh.

"I guess you're pretty good at this, huh, Joe?" She wiped her damp hands

557

on her green tunic. "That's the weight dial, isn't it?" she asked, watching him turn the top one.

He nodded. "Fifteen hundred pounds," he said slowly.

"Oo, was he really and truly that big?"

"Bigger." And now the thing felt Joe's heart and breathing surge.

They had been landed day before yesterday, with their geodesic tent, pneumatic form beds, automatic camping stove and pocket air tables, pocket TV set, four disposable hunting costumes apiece (one for each day), and two folding guns with power settings.

In addition, there was the bug-scat, go-snake, sun-stop and the gray-green hunter, sealed by the warden and set for three birds, two deer and one black bear. They had only the bear to go; now, Joe McAlister had unsealed the controls, released the governor and changed the setting to brown bear, 1,500 pounds.

"I don't care," he said, "I want that bear."

"Do you think he'll still be there tomorrow?"

Joe patted one of the long jointed legs of the thing. "If he's not, ol' bitch here will find him for us."

Next day was clear and cool, and Joe breathed big, expanding breaths and patted his beginning paunch. "Yes, sir," he said, "this is the day for something big—something really big, that'll put up a real fight."

He watched the red of the sunrise fade out of the sky while Ruthie turned on the stove and then got out her makeup kit. She put sun-stop on her face, then powdered it with a tan powder. She blackened her eyelids and purpled her lips; after that, she opened the stove and took out two disposable plates with eggs and bacon.

They sat in the automatic blowup chairs, at the automatic blowup table. Joe said that there was nothing like north air to give you an appetite, and Ruthie said she bet they were sweltering back in the city. Then she giggled.

Joe leaned back in his chair and sipped his coffee. "Shooting deer is just like shooting a cow," he said. "No fight to 'em at all. Even when ol' hound here goads 'em, they just want to run off. But this bear's going to be different. Of course bears are shy too, but ol' hound knows what to do about that."

"They say it's getting to be so there aren't many of the big kind left."

"Yes, but one more won't hurt. Think of a skin and head that size in our living room. I guess anybody that came in there would sure sit up and take notice."

"It won't match the curtains," his wife said.

"I think what I'll do is pack the skin up tight and leave it somewhere up here, till the warden checks us through. Then, maybe a couple of days later, I'll come back and get it."

"Good idea." Ruthie had finished her coffee and was perfuming herself with bug-scat.

"Well, I guess we'd better get started." They hung their folded-up guns on their belts. They put their dedydrated, self-heating lunch in their pockets. They slung on their cold-unit canteens. They each took a packet containing chair, table and sunshade; then Joe fastened on the little mike that controlled the hunter. It fit on his shoulder where he could turn his head to the side and talk into it.

"All right, houn' dog," he said, shoulder hunched and head tilted, "get a move on, boy. Back to that spot where we saw him yesterday. You can pick up the scent from there."

The hunting machine ran on ahead of them. It went faster than anything it might have to hunt. Two miles, three miles—Joe and Ruthie were left behind. They followed the beam it sent back to them, walking and talking and helping each other over the rough spots.

About eleven o'clock, Joe stopped, took off his red hunting hat and mopped his balding forehead with the new bandanna he'd bought at Hunter's Outfitters in New York. It was then he got the signal. *Sighted, sighted, sighted . . .*

Joe leaned over his mike. "Stick on him boy. How far are you? Well, try to move him down this way if you can." He turned to his wife. "Let's see, about three miles . . . we'll take a half-hour out for lunch. Maybe we'll get there a couple of hours from now. How's it going, kid?"

"Swell," Ruthie said.

The big bear sat on the rocks by the stream. His front paws were wet almost to the elbows. There were three torn fish heads lying beside him. He ate only the best parts because he was a good fisher; and he looked, now, into the clean cold water for another dark blueback that would pause on its way upstream.

It wasn't a smell that made him turn. He had a keen nose, but the hunting machine was made to have no smell. It was the gray dead lichen's crackle that made him look up. He stood still, looking in the direction of the sound and squinting his small eyes, but it wasn't until it moved that he saw it.

Three-quarters of a ton, he was; but like a bird or a rabbit or a snake, the bear avoided things that were large and strange. He turned back the way he always took, the path to his rubbing tree and to his home. He moved quietly and rapidly, but the thing followed.

He doubled back to the stream again, then, and waded down it on the opposite side from the thing—but still it followed, needing no scent. Once the hunting machine sighted, it never lost its prey.

Heart beat normal, respiration normal, it sensed. Size almost 1,600 pounds.

The bear got out on the bank and turned back, calling out in low growls. He stood up on his hind legs and stretched his full height. Almost two men tall, he stood and gave warning.

The hunting machine waited twenty yards away. The bear looked at it a full minute; then he fell back on all fours and turned south again. He was shy and he wanted no trouble.

Joe and Ruthie kept on walking north at their leisurely pace until just noon. Then they stopped for lunch by the side of the same stream the bear had waded, only lower down. And they used its cold water on their dehydrated meal—beef and onions, mashed potatoes, a lettuce salad that unfolded in the water like Japanese paper flowers. There were coffee tablets that contained a heating unit too and fizzled in the water like firecracker fuses until the water was hot, creamy coffee.

The bear didn't stop to eat. Noon meant nothing to him. Now he moved with more purpose, looking back and squinting his small eyes.

The hunter felt the heart beat faster, the breathing heavy, pace increasing. Direction generally south.

Joe and Ruthie followed the signal until it suddenly changed. It came faster; that meant they were near.

They stopped and unfolded their guns. "Let's have a cup of coffee first," Ruthie said.

"Okay, Hon." Joe released the chairs which blew themselves up to size. "Good to take a break so we can really enjoy the fight."

Ruthie handed Joe a fizzing cup of coffee. "Don't forget you want ol' Rover to goad some."

"Uh-huh. Bear's not much better than a deer without it. Good you reminded me." He turned and spoke softly into the little mike.

The hunting machine shortened the distance slowly. Fifteen feet, ten, five. The bear heard and turned. Again he rose up, almost two men tall, and roared his warning sound to tell the thing to keep back.

Joe and Ruthie shivered and didn't look at each other. They heard it less with their ears and more with their spines—with an instinct they had forgotten.

Joe shook his shoulder to shake away the feeling of the sound. "I guess the ol' bitch is at him."

"Good dog," Ruthie said. "Get 'im, boy."

The hunter's arm tips drew blood, but only in the safe spots—shoulder scratches at the heavy lump behind his head, thigh punctures. It never touched the veins, or arteries.

The bear swung at the thing with his great paw. His claws screeched down the body section but didn't so much as make a mark on the metal. The blow sent the thing thirty feet away, but it came back every time. The muscles, claws and teeth were nothing to it. It was made to withstand easily more than what one bear could do, and it knew with its built-in knowledge how to make a bear blind-angry.

Saliva came to the bear's mouth and flew out over his chin as he moved his heavy head sideways and back. It splashed, gummy on his cheeks, and made dark, damp streaks across his chest. Only his rage was real to him now, and he screamed a deep rasp of frustration again and again.

Two hundred yards away, Joe said, "Some roar!"

"Uh-huh. If noise means anything, it sounds like he's about ready for a real fight."

They both got up and folded up the chairs and cups. They sighted along their gun barrels to see that they were straight. "Set 'em at medium," Joe said. "We want to start off slow."

They came to where the bear was, and took up a good position on a high place. Joe called in his mike to the hunter thing. "Stand by, houn' dog, and slip over here to back us up." Then he called to the bear. "Hey, boy. This way, boy. This way."

The gray-green thing moved back and the bear saw the new enemy, two of them. He didn't hesitate; he was ready to charge anything that moved. He was only five feet away when their small guns popped. The force knocked him down, and he rolled out of the way, dazed; he turned again for another charge and came at them, all claws and teeth.

Joe's gun popped again. This time the bear staggered, but still came on. Joe backed up, pushing at his gun dial to raise the power. He bumped into Ruthie behind him and they both fell. Joe's voice was a crazy scream. "Get him."

The hunting machine moved fast. Its sharp forearm came like an uppercut, under the jaw and into the brain.

He lay, looking smaller, somehow, but still big, his ragged fur matted with blood. Fleas were alive on it, and flies already coming. Joe and Ruthie looked down at him and took big breaths.

"You shouldna got behind me," Joe said as soon as he caught his breath. "I coulda kept it going longer if you'da just stayed out of the way."

"You told me to," Ruthie said. "You told me to stay right behind you."

"Well, I didn't mean *that* close."

Ruthie sniffed. "Anyway," she said, "how are you going to get the fur off it?"

"Hmmmph."

"I don't think that moth-eaten thing will make much of a rug. It's pretty dirty, too, and probably full of germs."

Joe walked around the bear and turned its head sideways with his toe. "Be a big messy job, all right, skinning it. Up to the elbows in blood and gut, I guess."

"I didn't expect it to be like *this* at all," Ruthie said. "Why don't you just forget it? You had your fun."

Joe stood, looking at the bear's head. He watched a fly land on its eye and then walk down to a damp nostril.

"Well, come *on.*" Ruthie took her small pack. "I want to get back in time to take a bath before supper."

"Okay." Joe leaned over his mike. "Come on ol' Rover, ol' hound dog. You did fine."

BOB SHAW

Light of Other Days

*Scientific discovery and the miraculous invention are integral parts
of the science fiction universe. Mr. Shaw's ingenious "slow glass"
is a superior example of this type of story because it is not content
merely to suggest a startlingly novel concept, but goes on to examine
its impact on people.*

Leaving the village behind, we followed the heady sweeps of the road up
into a land of slow glass.

I had never seen one of the farms before and at first found them slightly
eerie—an effect heightened by imagination and circumstance. The car's tur-
bine was pulling smoothly and quietly in the damp air so that we seemed to
be carried over the convolutions of the road in a kind of supernatural silence.
On our right the mountain sifted down into an incredibly perfect valley of
timeless pine, and everywhere stood the great frames of slow glass, drinking
light. An occasional flash of afternoon sunlight on their wind bracing created
an illusion of movement, but in fact the frames were deserted. The rows of
windows had been standing on the hillside for years, staring into the valley,
and men only cleaned them in the middle of the night when their human
presence would not matter to the thirsty glass.

They were fascinating, but Selina and I didn't mention the windows. I think
we hated each other so much we both were reluctant to sully anything new
by drawing it into the nexus of our emotions. The holiday, I had begun to
realize, was a stupid idea in the first place. I had thought it would cure
everything, but, of course, it didn't stop Selina being pregnant and, worse still,
it didn't even stop her being angry about being pregnant.

Rationalizing our dismay over her condition, we had circulated the usual
statements to the effect that we would have *liked* having children—but later

on, at the proper time. Selina's pregnancy had cost us her well-paid job and with it the new house we had been negotiating and which was far beyond the reach of my income from poetry. But the real source of our annoyance was that we were face to face with the realization that people who say they want children later always mean they want children never. Our nevers were thrumming with the knowledge that we, who had thought ourselves so unique, had fallen into the same biological trap as every mindless rutting creature which ever existed.

The road took us along the southern slopes of Ben Cruachan until we began to catch glimpses of the gray Atlantic far ahead. I had just cut our speed to absorb the view better when I noticed the sign spiked to a gatepost. It said: "SLOW GLASS—QUALITY HIGH, PRICES LOW—J. R. HAGAN." On an impulse I stopped the car on the verge, wincing slightly as tough grasses whipped noisily at the bodywork.

"Why have we stopped?" Selina's neat, smoke-silver head turned in surprise.

"Look at that sign. Let's go up and see what there is. The stuff might be reasonably priced out here."

Selina's voice was pitched high with scorn as she refused, but I was too taken with my idea to listen. I had an illogical conviction that doing something extravagant and crazy would set us right again.

"Come on," I said, "the exercise might do us some good. We've been driving too long anyway."

She shrugged in a way that hurt me and got out of the car. We walked up a path made of irregular, packed clay steps nosed with short lengths of sapling. The path curved through trees which clothed the edge of the hill and at its end we found a low farmhouse. Beyond the little stone building tall frames of slow glass gazed out toward the voice-stilling sight of Cruachan's ponderous descent toward the waters of Loch Linnhe. Most of the panes were perfectly transparent but a few were dark, like panels of polished ebony.

As we approached the house through a neat cobbled yard a tall middle-aged man in ash-colored tweeds arose and waved to us. He had been sitting on the low rubble wall which bounded the yard, smoking a pipe and staring toward the house. At the front window of the cottage a young woman in a tangerine dress stood with a small boy in her arms, but she turned uninterestedly and moved out of sight as we drew near.

"Mr. Hagan?" I guessed.

"Correct. Come to see some glass, have you? Well, you've come to the right place." Hagan spoke crisply, with traces of the pure Highland which sounds so much like Irish to the unaccustomed ear. He had one of those calmly dismayed faces one finds on elderly road menders and philosophers.

"Yes," I said. "We're on holiday. We saw your sign."

Selina, who usually has a natural fluency with strangers, said nothing. She was looking toward the now empty window with what I thought was a slightly puzzled expression.

"Up from London, are you? Well, as I said, you've come to the right place —and at the right time, too. My wife and I don't see many people this early in the season."

I laughed. "Does that mean we might be able to buy a little glass without mortgaging our home?"

"Look at that now," Hagan said, smiling helplessly. "I've thrown away any advantage I might have had in the transaction. Rose, that's my wife, says I never learn. Still, let's sit down and talk it over." He pointed at the rubble wall, then glanced doubtfully at Selina's immaculate blue skirt. "Wait till I fetch a rug from the house." Hagan limped quickly into the cottage, closing the door behind him.

"Perhaps it wasn't such a marvelous idea to come up here," I whispered to Selina, "but you might at least be pleasant to the man. I think I can smell a bargain."

"Some hope," she said with deliberate coarseness. "Surely even you must have noticed that ancient dress his wife is wearing! He won't give much away to strangers."

"Was that his wife?"

"Of course that was his wife."

"Well, well," I said, surprised. "Anyway, try to be civil with him. I don't want to be embarrassed."

Selina snorted, but she smiled whitely when Hagan reappeared and I relaxed a little. Strange how a man can love a woman and yet at the same time pray for her to fall under a train.

Hagan spread a tartan blanket on the wall and we sat down, feeling slightly self-conscious at having been translated from our city-oriented lives into a rural tableau. On the distant slate of the Loch, beyond the watchful frames of slow glass, a slow-moving steamer drew a white line toward the south. The boisterous mountain air seemed almost to invade our lungs, giving us more oxygen than we required.

"Some of the glass farmers around here," Hagan began, "give strangers, such as yourselves, a sales talk about how beautiful the autumn is in this part of Argyll. Or it might be the spring, or the winter. I don't do that—any fool knows that a place which doesn't look right in summer never looks right. What do you say?"

I nodded compliantly.

"I want you just to take a good look out toward Mull, Mr. . . . ."

"Garland."

". . . Garland. That's what you're buying if you buy my glass, and it never looks better than it does at this minute. The glass is in perfect phase, none of it is less than ten years thick—and a four-foot window will cost you two hundred pounds."

"Two hundred!" Selina was shocked. "That's as much as they charge at the Scenedow shop in Bond Street."

Hagan smiled patiently, then looked closely at me to see if I knew enough about slow glass to appreciate what he had been saying. His price had been much higher than I had hoped—but *ten years thick!* The cheap glass one found in places like the Vistaplex and Pane-o-rama stores usually consisted of a quarter of an inch of ordinary glass faced with a veneer of slow glass perhaps only ten or twelve months thick.

"You don't understand, darling," I said, already determined to buy. "This glass will last ten years and it's in phase."

"Doesn't that only mean it keeps time?"

Hagan smiled at her again, realizing he had no further necessity to bother with me. "Only, you say! Pardon me, Mrs. Garland, but you don't seem to appreciate the miracle, the genuine honest-to-goodness miracle, of engineering precision needed to produce a piece of glass in phase. When I say the glass is ten years thick it means it takes light ten years to pass through it. In effect, each one of those panes is ten light-years thick—more than twice the distance to the nearest star—so a variation in actual thickness of only a millionth of an inch would . . ."

He stopped talking for a moment and sat quietly looking toward the house. I turned my head from the view of the Loch and saw the young woman standing at the window again. Hagan's eyes were filled with a kind of greedy reverence which made me feel uncomfortable and at the same time convinced me Selina had been wrong. In my experience husbands never looked at wives that way—at least, not at their own.

The girl remained in view for a few seconds, dress glowing warmly, then moved back into the room. Suddenly I received a distinct, though inexplicable, impression she was blind. My feeling was that Selina and I were perhaps blundering through an emotional interplay as violent as our own.

"I'm sorry," Hagan continued; "I thought Rose was going to call me for something. Now, where was I, Mrs. Garland? Ten light-years compressed into a quarter of an inch means . . ."

I ceased to listen, partly because I was already sold, partly because I had heard the story of slow glass many times before and had never yet understood the principles involved. An acquaintance with scientific training had once tried to be helpful by telling me to visualize a pane of slow glass as a hologram which did not need coherent light from a laser for the reconstitution of its visual information, and in which every photon of ordinary light passed through a spiral tunnel coiled outside the radius of capture of each atom in the glass. This gem of, to me, incomprehensibility not only told me nothing, it convinced me once again that a mind as nontechnical as mine should concern itself less with causes than effects.

The most important effect, in the eyes of the average individual, was that light took a long time to pass through a sheet of slow glass. A new piece was always jet black because nothing had yet come through, but one could stand the glass beside, say, a woodland lake until the scene emerged, perhaps a year later. If the glass was then removed and installed in a dismal city flat, the flat would—for that year—appear to overlook the woodland lake. During the year it wouldn't be merely a very realistic but still picture—the water would ripple in sunlight, silent animals would come to drink, birds would cross the sky, night would follow day, season would follow season. Until one day, a year later, the beauty held in the subatomic pipelines would be exhausted and the familiar gray cityscape would reappear.

Apart from its stupendous novelty value, the commercial success of slow glass was founded on the fact that having a scenedow was the exact emotional equivalent of owning land. The meanest cave dweller could look out on misty parks—and who was to say they weren't his? A man who really owns tailored gardens and estates doesn't spend his time proving his ownership by crawling on his ground, feeling, smelling, tasting it. All he receives from the land are light patterns, and with scenedows those patterns could be taken into coal mines, submarines, prison cells.

On several occasions I have tried to write short pieces about the enchanted crystal but, to me, the theme is so ineffably poetic as to be, paradoxically, beyond the reach of poetry—mine, at any rate. Besides, the best songs and verse had already been written, with prescient inspiration, by men who had died long before slow glass was discovered. I had no hope of equaling, for example, Moore with his:

> *Oft in the stilly night,*
> *Ere slumber's chain has bound me,*
> *Fond Memory brings the light*
> *Of other days around me . . .*

It took only a few years for slow glass to develop from a scientific curiosity to a sizable industry. And much to the astonishment of us poets—those of us who remain convinced that beauty lives though lilies die—the trappings of that industry were no different from those of any other. There were good scenedows which cost a lot of money, and there were inferior scenedows which cost rather less. The thickness, measured in years, was an important factor in the cost but there was also the question of *actual* thickness, or phase.

Even with the most sophisticated engineering techniques available thickness control was something of a hit-and-miss affair. A coarse discrepancy could mean that a pane intended to be five years thick might be five and a half, so that light which entered in summer emerged in winter; a fine discrepancy could mean that noon sunshine emerged at midnight. These incompatibilities had their peculiar charm—many night workers, for example, liked having their own private time zones—but, in general, it cost more to buy scenedows which kept closely in step with real time.

Selina still looked unconvinced when Hagan had finished speaking. She shook her head almost imperceptibly and I knew he had been using the wrong approach. Quite suddenly the pewter helmet of her hair was disturbed by a cool gust of wind, and huge clean tumbling drops of rain began to spang round us from an almost cloudless sky.

"I'll give you a check now," I said abruptly, and saw Selina's green eyes triangulate angrily on my face. "You can arrange delivery?"

"Aye, delivery's no problem," Hagan said, getting to his feet. "But wouldn't you rather take the glass with you?"

"Well, yes—if you don't mind." I was shamed by his readiness to trust my scrip.

"I'll unclip a pane for you. Wait here. It won't take long to slip it into a carrying frame." Hagan limped down the slope toward the seriate windows, through some of which the view toward Linnhe was sunny, while others were cloudy and a few pure black.

Selina drew the collar of her blouse closed at her throat. "The least he could have done was invite us inside. There can't be so many fools passing through that he can afford to neglect them."

I tried to ignore the insult and concentrated on writing the check. One of the outsized drops broke across my knuckles, splattering the pink paper.

"All right," I said, "let's move in under the eaves till he gets back." *You worm*, I thought as I felt the whole thing go completely wrong. *I just had to be a fool to marry you. A prize fool, a fool's fool—and now that you've trapped part of me inside you I'll never ever, never ever, never ever get away.*

Feeling my stomach clench itself painfully, I ran behind Selina to the side of the cottage. Beyond the window the neat living room, with its coal fire, was empty but the child's toys were scattered on the floor. Alphabet blocks and a wheelbarrow the exact color of freshly pared carrots. As I stared in, the boy came running from the other room and began kicking the blocks. He didn't notice me. A few moments later the young woman entered the room and lifted him, laughing easily and wholeheartedly as she swung the boy under her arm. She came to the window as she had done earlier. I smiled self-consciously, but neither she nor the child responded.

My forehead prickled icily. *Could they both be blind?* I sidled away.

Selina gave a little scream and I spun towards her.

"The rug!" she said. "It's getting soaked."

She ran across the yard in the rain, snatched the reddish square from the dappling wall and ran back, toward the cottage door. Something heaved convulsively in my subconscious.

"Selina," I shouted. "Don't open it!"

But I was too late. She had pushed open the latched wooden door and was standing, hand over mouth, looking into the cottage. I moved close to her and took the rug from her unresisting fingers.

As I was closing the door I let my eyes traverse the cottage's interior. The neat living room in which I had just seen the woman and child was, in reality, a sickening clutter of shabby furniture, old newspapers, cast-off clothing and smeared dishes. It was damp, stinking and utterly deserted. The only object I recognized from my view through the window was the little wheelbarrow, paintless and broken.

I latched the door firmly and ordered myself to forget what I had seen. Some men who live alone are good housekeepers; others just don't know how.

Selina's face was white. "I don't understand. I don't understand it."

"Slow glass works both ways," I said gently. "Light passes out of a house, as well as in."

"You mean . . . ?"

"I don't know. It isn't our business. Now steady up—Hagan's coming back with our glass." The churning in my stomach was beginning to subside.

Hagan came into the yard carrying an oblong, plastic-covered frame. I held the check out to him, but he was staring at Selina's face. He seemed to know immediately that our uncomprehending fingers had rummaged through his soul. Selina avoided his gaze. She was old and ill-looking, and her eyes stared determinedly toward the nearing horizon.

"I'll take the rug from you, Mr. Garland," Hagan finally said. "You shouldn't have troubled yourself over it."

"No trouble. Here's the check."

"Thank you." He was still looking at Selina with a strange kind of supplication. "It's been a pleasure to do business with you."

"The pleasure was mine," I said with equal, senseless formality. I picked up the heavy frame and guided Selina toward the path which led to the road. Just as we reached the head of the now slippery steps Hagan spoke again.

"Mr. Garland!"

I turned unwillingly.

"It wasn't my fault," he said steadily. "A hit-and-run driver got them both, down on the Oban road six years ago. My boy was only seven when it happened. I'm entitled to keep something."

I nodded wordlessly and moved down the path, holding my wife close to me, treasuring the feel of her arms locked around me. At the bend I looked back through the rain and saw Hagan sitting with squared shoulders on the wall where we had first seen him.

He was looking at the house, but I was unable to tell if there was anyone at the window.

ROGER ZELAZNY
The Keys to December

*"Rome wasn't built in a day" means that important tasks cannot
be rushed. But what about a project that takes three thousand years?
An important part of the wonder of science fiction is the sweep and
scope of events, of mile-long spaceships and centuries-long trips.
Here Roger Zelazny combines first-rate writing with a bold imaginative concept—the redesign of an entire world.*

Born of man and woman, in accordance with Catform Y7 requirements,
Coldworld Class (modified per Alyonal), 3.2-E, G.M.I. option, Jarry Dark was
not suited for existence anywhere in the universe which had guaranteed him
a niche. This was either a blessing or a curse, depending on how you looked
at it.

So look at it however you would, here is the story:

It is likely that his parents could have afforded the temperature control unit,
but not much more than that. (Jarry required a temperature of at least minus
fifty degrees Celsius to be comfortable.)

It is unlikely that his parents could have provided for the air pressure control
and gas mixture equipment required to maintain his life.

Nothing could be done in the way of 3.2-E grav-simulation, so daily medication and physiotherapy were required. It is unlikely that his parents could have
provided for this.

The much-maligned option took care of him, however. It safeguarded his
health. It provided for his education. It assured his economic welfare and
physical well-being.

It might be argued that Jarry Dark would not have been a homeless Coldworld Catform (modified per Alyonal) had it not been for General Mining,

Incorporated, which had held the option. But then it must be borne in mind that no one could have foreseen the nova which destroyed Alyonal.

When his parents had presented themselves at the Public Health Planned Parenthood Center and requested advice and medication pending offspring, they had been informed as to the available worlds and the bodyform requirements for them. They had selected Alyonal, which had recently been purchased by General Mining for purposes of mineral exploitation. Wisely, they had elected the option; that is to say, they had signed a contract on behalf of their anticipated offspring, who would be eminently qualified to inhabit that world, agreeing that he would work as an employee of General Mining until he achieved his majority, at which time he would be free to depart and seek employment wherever he might choose (though his choices would admittedly be limited). In return for this guarantee, General Mining agreed to assure his health, education and continuing welfare for so long as he remained in their employ.

When Alyonal caught fire and went away, those Coldworld Catforms covered by the option who were scattered about the crowded galaxy were, by virtue of the agreement, wards of General Mining.

This is why Jarry grew up in a hermetically sealed room containing temperature and atmosphere controls, and why he received a first-class closed-circuit education along with his physiotherapy and medicine. This is also why Jarry bore some resemblance to a large gray ocelot without a tail, had webbing between his fingers and could not go outside to watch the traffic unless he wore a pressurized refrigeration suit and took extra medication.

All over the swarming galaxy, people took the advice of Public Health Planned Parenthood Centers, and many others had chosen as had Jarry's parents. Twenty-eight thousand, five hundred sixty-six of them, to be exact. In any group of over twenty-eight thousand five hundred sixty, there are bound to be a few talented individuals. Jarry was one of them. He had a knack for making money. Most of his General Mining pension check was invested in well-chosen stocks of a speculative nature. (In fact, after a time he came to own considerable stock in General Mining.)

When the man from the Galactic Civil Liberties Union had come around, expressing concern over the pre-birth contracts involved in the option and explaining that the Alyonal Catforms would make a good test case (especially since Jarry's parents lived within jurisdiction of the 877th Circuit, where they would be assured a favorable courtroom atmosphere), Jarry's parents had demurred, for fear of jeopardizing the General Mining pension. Later on, Jarry himself dismissed the notion also. A favorable decision could not make him an E-world Normform, and what else mattered? He was not vindictive. Also, he owned considerable stock in G.M. by then.

He loafed in his methane tank and purred, which meant that he was thinking. He operated his cryo-computer as he purred and thought. He was computing the total net worth of all the Catforms in the recently organized December Club.

He stopped purring and considered a subtotal, stretched, shook his head slowly. Then he returned to his calculations.

When he had finished, he dictated a message into his speech tube, to Sanza Barati, president of December and his betrothed:

Dearest Sanza—The funds available, as I suspected, leave much to be desired. All the more reason to begin immediately. Kindly submit the proposal to the business committee, outline my qualifications and seek immediate endorsement. I've finished drafting the general statement to the membership. (Copy attached.) From these figures, it will take me between five and ten years, if at least 80 percent of the membership backs me. So push hard, beloved. I'd like to meet you someday, in a place where the sky is purple. Yours, always, Jarry Dark, Treasurer. P.S. I'm pleased you were pleased with the ring.

Two years later, Jarry had doubled the net worth of December, Incorporated.

A year and a half after that, he had doubled it again.

When he received the following letter from Sanza, he leaped onto his trampoline, bounded into the air, landed upon his feet at the opposite end of his quarters, returned to his viewer and replayed it:

Dear Jarry,

Attached are specifications and prices for five more worlds. The research staff likes the last one. So do I. What do you think? Alyonal II? If so, how about the price? When could we afford that much? The staff also says that a hundred Worldchange units could alter it to what we want in 5–6 centuries. Will forward costs of this machinery shortly.

Come live with me and be my love, in a place where there are no walls. . . .

Sanza

"One year," he replied, "and I'll buy you a world! Hurry up with the costs of machinery and transport. . . ."

When the figures arrived Jarry wept icy tears. One hundred machines, capable of altering the environment of a world, plus twenty-eight thousand coldsleep bunkers, plus transportation costs for the machinery and his people, plus . . . Too high! He did a rapid calculation.

He spoke into the speech tube:

". . . Fifteen additional years is too long to wait, pussycat. Have them figure the time span if we were to purchase only twenty Worldchange units. Love and kisses, Jarry."

During the days which followed, he stalked above his chamber, erect at first, then on all fours as his mood deepened.

"Approximately three thousand years," came the reply. "May your coat be ever shiny—Sanza."

"Let's put it to a vote, greeneyes," he said.

Quick, a world in three hundred words or less! Picture this. . . .

One land mass, really, containing three black and brackish looking seas; gray plains and yellow plains and skies the color of dry sand; shallow forests with trees like mushrooms which have been swabbed with iodine; no mountains, just hills, brown, yellow, white, lavender; green birds with wings like parachutes, bills like sickles, feathers like oak leaves, an inside-out umbrella behind; six very distant moons, like spots before the eyes in daytime, snowflakes at night, drops of blood at dusk and dawn; grass like mustard in the moister valleys; mists like white fire on windless mornings, albino serpents when the air's astir; radiating chasms, like fractures in frosted windowpanes; hidden caverns, like chains of dark bubbles; seventeen known dangerous predators, ranging from one to six meters in length, excessively furred and fanged; sudden hailstorms, like hurled hammerheads from a clear sky; an ice cap like a blue beret at either flattened pole; nervous bipeds a meter and a half in height, short on cerebrum, which wander the shallow forests and prey upon the giant caterpillar's larva, as well as the giant caterpillar, the green bird, the blind burrower and the offal-eating murk-beast; seventeen mighty rivers; clouds like pregnant purple cows, which quickly cross the land to lie in beyond the visible east; stands of wind-blasted stones like frozen music; nights like soot to obscure the lesser stars; valleys which flow like the torsos of women or instruments of music; perpetual frost in places of shadow; sounds in the morning like the cracking of ice, the trembling of tin, the snapping of steel strands. . . .

They knew they would turn it to heaven.

The vanguard arrived, decked out in refrigeration suits, installed ten Worldchange units in either hemisphere, began setting up coldsleep bunkers in several of the larger caverns.

Then came the members of December down from the sand-colored sky.

They came and they saw, decided it was almost heaven, then entered their caverns and slept. Over twenty-eight thousand Coldworld Catforms (modified per Alyonal) came into their own world to sleep for a season in silence the sleep of ice and of stone, to inherit the new Alyonal. There is no dreaming in that sleep. But had there been, their dreams might have been as the thoughts of those yet awake.

"It is bitter, Sanza."

"Yes, but only for a time. . . ."

". . . To have each other and our own world, and still to go forth like divers at the bottom of the sea. To have to crawl when you want to leap. . . ."

"It is only for a short time, Jarry, as the senses will reckon it."

"But it is really three thousand years! An ice age will come to pass as we doze. Our former worlds will change so that we would not know them were we to go back for a visit—and none will remember us."

"Visit what? Our former cells? Let the rest of the worlds go by! Let us be forgotten in the lands of our birth! We are a people apart and we have found our home. What else matters?"

"True. . . . It will be but a few years, and we shall stand our tours of wakefulness and watching together."

"When is the first?"

"Two and a half centuries from now—three months of wakefulness."

"What will it be like then?"

"I don't know. Less warm. . . ."

"Then let us return and sleep. Tomorrow will be a better day."

"Yes."

"Oh! See the green bird! It drifts like a dream. . . ."

When they awakened that first time, they stayed within the Worldchange installation at the place called Deadland. The world was already colder and the edges of the sky were tinted with pink. The metal walls of the great installation were black and rimed with frost. The atmosphere was still lethal and the temperature far too high. They remained within their special chambers for most of the time, venturing outside mainly to make necessary tests and to inspect the structure of their home.

Deadland. . . . Rocks and sand. No trees, no marks of life at all.

The time of terrible winds was still upon the land, as the world fought back against the fields of the machines. At night, great clouds of real estate smoothed and sculpted the stands of stone, and when the winds departed the desert would shimmer as if fresh-painted and the stones would stand like flames within the morning and its singing. After the sun came up into the sky

and hung there for a time, the winds would begin again and a dun-colored fog
would curtain the day. When the morning winds departed, Jarry and Sanza
would stare out across Deadland through the east window of the installation,
for that was their favorite—the one on the third floor—where the stone that
looked like a gnarly Normform waved to them, and they would lie upon the
green couch they had moved up from the first floor and would sometimes make
love as they listened for the winds to rise again, or Sanza would sing and Jarry
would write in the log or read back through it, the scribblings of friends and
unknowns through the centuries, and they would purr often but never laugh
because they did not know how.

One morning, as they watched, they saw one of the biped creatures of the
iodine forests moving across the land. It fell several times, picked itself up,
continued, fell once more, lay still.

"What is it doing this far from its home?" asked Sanza.

"Dying," said Jarry. "Let's go outside."

They crossed a catwalk, descended to the first floor, donned their protective
suits and departed the installation.

The creature had risen to its feet and was staggering once again. It was
covered with a reddish down, had dark eyes and a long, wide nose, lacked a
true forehead. It had four brief digits, clawed, upon each hand and foot.

When it saw them emerge from the Worldchange unit, it stopped and
stared at them. Then it fell.

They moved to its side and studied it where it lay.

It continued to stare at them, its dark eyes wide, as it lay there shivering.

"It will die if we leave it here," said Sanza.

". . . And it will die if we take it inside," said Jarry.

It raised a forelimb toward them, let it fall again. Its eyes narrowed, then
closed.

Jarry reached out and touched it with the toe of his boot. There was no
response.

"It's dead," he said.

"What will we do?"

"Leave it here. The sands will cover it."

They returned to the installation, and Jarry entered the event in the log.

During their last month of duty, Sanza asked him, "Will everything die here
but us? The green birds and the big eaters of flesh? The funny little trees and
the hairy caterpillars?"

"I hope not," said Jarry. "I've been reading back through the biologists'
notes. I think life might adapt. Once it gets a start anywhere, it'll do anything
it can to keep going. It's probably better for the creatures of this planet that

we could afford only twenty Worldchangers. That way they have three millennia to grow more hair and learn to breathe our air and drink our water. With a hundred units we might have wiped them out and had to import Coldworld creatures or breed them. This way, the ones who live here might be able to make it."

"It's funny," she said, "but the thought just occurred to me that we're doing here what was done to us. They made us for Alyonal, and a nova took it away. These creatures came to life in this place, and we're taking it away. We're turning all of life on this planet into what we were on our former worlds—misfits."

"The difference, however, is that we are taking our time," said Jarry, "and giving them a chance to get used to the new conditions."

"Still, I feel that all that—outside there"—she gestured toward the window—"is what this world is becoming: one big Deadland."

"Deadland was here before we came. We haven't created any new deserts."

"All the animals are moving south. The trees are dying. When they get as far south as they can go and still the temperature drops and the air continues to burn in their lungs—then it will be all over for them."

"By then they might have adapted. The trees are spreading, are developing thicker barks. Life will make it."

"I wonder. . . ."

"Would you prefer to sleep until it's all over?"

"No, I want to be by your side, always."

"Then you must reconcile yourself to the fact that something is always hurt by any change. If you do this, you will not be hurt yourself."

Then they listened for the winds to rise.

Three days later, in the still of sundown, between the winds of day and the winds of night, she called him to the window. He climbed to the third floor and moved to her side. Her breasts were rose in the sundown light and the places beneath them silver and dark. The fur of her shoulders and haunches was like an aura of smoke. Her face was expressionless and her wide, green eyes were not turned toward him.

He looked out.

The first big flakes were falling, blue, through the pink light. They drifted past the stone and gnarly Normform; some stuck to the thick quartz windowpane; they fell upon the desert and lay there like blossoms of cyanide; they swirled as more of them came down and were caught by the first faint puffs of the terrible winds. Dark clouds had mustered overhead and from them, now, great cables and nets of blue descended. Now the flakes flashed past the window like butterflies, and the outline of Deadland flickered on and off. The pink vanished and there was only blue, blue and darkening blue, as the first great sigh of evening came into their ears and the billows suddenly moved sidewise rather than downward, becoming indigo as they raced by.

"The machine is never silent," Jarry wrote. "Sometimes I fancy I can hear voices in its constant humming, its occasional growling, its crackles of power. I am alone here at the Deadland station. Five centuries have passed since our arrival. I thought it better to let Sanza sleep out this tour of duty, lest the prospect be too bleak. (It is.) She will doubtless be angry. As I lay half-awake this morning, I thought I heard my parents' voices in the next room. No words. Just the sounds of their voices as I used to hear them over my old intercom. They must be dead by now, despite all geriatrics. I wonder if they thought of me much after I left? I couldn't even shake my father's hand without my gauntlet or kiss my mother good-by. It is strange, the feeling, to be this alone, with only the throb of the machinery about me as it rearranges the molecules of the atmosphere, refrigerates the world, here in the middle of the blue place. Deadland. This, despite the fact that I grew up in a steel cave. I call the other nineteen stations every afternoon. I am afraid I am becoming something of a nuisance. I won't call them tomorrow, or perhaps the next day.

"I went outside without my refrig-pack this morning, for a few moments. It is still deadly hot. I gulped a mouthful of air and choked. Our day is still far off. But I can notice the difference from the last time I tried it, two and a half hundred years ago. I wonder what it will be like when we have finished? —And I, an economist! What will my function be in our new Alyonal? Whatever, so long as Sanza is happy. . . .

"The Worldchanger stutters and groans. All the land is blue for so far as I can see. The stones still stand, but their shapes are changed from what they were. The sky is entirely pink now, and it becomes almost maroon in the morning and the evening. I guess it's really a wine color, but I've never seen wine, so I can't say for certain. The trees have not died. They've grown hardier. Their barks are thicker, their leaves are darker and larger. They grow much taller now, I've been told. There are no trees in Deadland.

"The caterpillars still live. They seem much larger, I understand, but it is actually because they have become woollier than they used to be. It seems that most of the animals have heavier pelts these days. Some apparently have taken to hibernating. A strange thing: Station Seven reported that they had thought the bipeds were growing heavier coats. There seem to be quite a few of them in that area, and they often see them off in the distance. They looked to be shaggier. Closer observation, however, revealed that some of them were either carrying or were wrapped in the skins of dead animals! Could it be that they are more intelligent than we have given them credit for? This hardly seems possible, since they were tested quite thoroughly by the bio team before we set the machines in operation. Yet, it is very strange.

"The winds are still severe. Occasionally, they darken the sky with ash. There has been considerable vulcanism southwest of here. Station Four was relocated because of this. I hear Sanza singing now within the sounds of the machine. I will let her be awakened the next time. Things should be more settled by then. No, that is not true. It is selfishness. I want her here beside me. I feel as if I were the only living thing in the whole world. The voices on the radio are ghosts. The clock ticks loudly and the silences between the ticks are filled with the humming of the machine, which is a kind of silence, too, because it is constant. Sometimes I think it is not there; I listen for it, I strain my ears and I do not know whether there is a humming or not. I check the indicators then, and they assure me that the machine is functioning. Or perhaps there is something wrong with the indicators. But they seem to be all right. No. It is me. And the blue of Deadland is a kind of visual silence. In the morning even the rocks are covered with blue frost. Is it beautiful or ugly? There is no response within me. It is a part of the great silence, that's all. Perhaps I shall become a mystic. Perhaps I shall develop occult powers or achieve something bright and liberating as I sit here at the center of the great silence. Perhaps I shall see visions. Already I hear voices. Are there ghosts in Deadland? No, there was never anything here to be ghosted. Except perhaps for the little biped. Why did it cross Deadland, I wonder? Why did it head for the center of destruction rather than away, as its fellows did? I shall never know. Unless perhaps I have a vision. I think it is time to suit up and take a walk. The polar ice caps are heavier. The glaciation has begun. Soon, soon things will be better. Soon the silence will end, I hope. I wonder, though, whether silence is not the true state of affairs in the universe, our little noises serving only to accentuate it, like a speck of black on a field of blue. Everything was once silence and will be so again—is now, perhaps. Will I ever hear real sounds, or only sounds out of the silence? Sanza is singing again. I wish I could wake her up now, to walk with me, out there. It is beginning to snow."

Jarry awakened again on the eve of the millennium.

Sanza smiled and took his hand in hers and stroked it, as he explained why he had let her sleep, as he apologized.

"Of course I'm not angry," she said, "considering I did the same thing to you last cycle."

Jarry stared up at her and felt the understanding begin.

"I'll not do it again," she said, "and I know you couldn't. The aloneness is almost unbearable."

"Yes," he replied.

"They warmed us both alive last time. I came around first and told them to put you back to sleep. I was angry then, when I found out what you had done. But I got over it quickly, so often did I wish you were there."

"We will stay together," said Jarry.

"Yes, always."

They took a flier from the cavern of sleep to the Worldchange installation at Deadland, where they relieved the other attendants and moved the new couch up to the third floor.

The air of Deadland, while sultry, could now be breathed for short periods of time, though a headache invariably followed such experiments. The heat was still oppressive. The rock, once like an old Normform waving, had lost its distinctive outline. The winds were no longer so severe.

On the fourth day, they found some animal tracks which seemed to belong to one of the larger predators. This cheered Sanza, but another, later occurrence produced only puzzlement.

One morning they went forth to walk in Deadland.

Less than a hundred paces from the installation, they came upon three of the giant caterpillars, dead. They were stiff, as though dried out rather than frozen, and they were surrounded by rows of markings within the snow. The footprints which led to the scene and away from it were rough of outline, obscure.

"What does it mean?" she asked.

"I don't know, but I think we had better photograph this," said Jarry.

They did. When Jarry spoke to Station Eleven that afternoon, he learned that similar occurrences had occasionally been noted by attendants of other installations. These were not too frequent, however.

"I don't understand," said Sanza.

"I don't want to," said Jarry.

It did not happen again during their tour of duty. Jarry entered it into the log and wrote a report. Then they abandoned themselves to lovemaking, monitoring and occasional nights of drunkenness. Two hundred years previously, a biochemist had devoted his tour of duty to experimenting with compounds which would produce the same reactions in Catforms as the legendary whiskey did in Normforms. He had been successful, had spent four weeks on a colossal binge, neglected his duty and been relieved of it, was then retired to his coldbunk for the balance of the Wait. His basically simple formula had circulated, however, and Jarry and Sanza found a well-stocked bar in the storeroom and a hand-written manual explaining its use and a variety of drinks which might be compounded. The author of the document had expressed the hope that each tour of attendance might result in the discovery of a new mixture, so that when he returned for his next cycle the manual would have grown to a size proportionate to his desire. Jarry and Sanza worked at it conscientiously and satisfied the request with a snowflower punch which warmed their bellies and made their purring turn into giggles, so that they discovered laughter also. They celebrated the millennium with an entire bowl of it, and Sanza insisted on calling all the other installations and giving them the formula, right then, on the graveyard watch, so that everyone could share in their joy. It is quite possible that everyone did, for the recipe was well-received. And always, even after that bowl was but a memory, they kept the laughter. Thus are the first simple lines of tradition sometimes sketched.

"The green birds are dying," said Sanza, putting aside a report she had been reading.

"Oh?" said Jarry.

"Apparently they've done all the adapting they're able to," she told him.

"Pity," said Jarry.

"It seems less than a year since we came here. Actually, it's a thousand."

"Time flies," said Jarry.

"I'm afraid," she said.

"Of what?"

"I don't know. Just afraid."

"Why?"

"Living the way we've been living, I guess. Leaving little pieces of ourselves in different centuries. Just a few months ago, as my memory works, this place was a desert. Now it's an ice field. Chasms open and close. Canyons appear and disappear. Rivers dry up and new ones spring forth. Everything seems so very transitory. Things look solid, but I'm getting afraid to touch things now. They might go away. They might turn into smoke, and my hand will keep on reaching through the smoke and touch—something . . . God, maybe. Or worse yet, maybe not. No one really knows what it will be like here when we've finished. We're traveling toward an unknown land and it's too late to go back. We're moving through a dream, heading toward an idea. . . . Sometimes I miss my cell . . . and all the little machines that took care of me there. Maybe *I* can't adapt. Maybe I'm like the green bird. . . ."

"No, Sanza. You're not. We're real. No matter what happens out there, *we* will last. Everything is changing because we want it to change. We're stronger than the world, and we'll squeeze it and paint it and poke holes in it until we've made it exactly the way we want it. Then we'll take it and cover it with cities and children. You want to see God? Go look in the mirror. God has pointed ears and green eyes. He is covered with soft gray fur. When He raises His hand there is webbing between His fingers."

"It is good that you are strong, Jarry."

"Let's get out the power sled and go for a ride."

"All right."

Up and down, that day, they drove through Deadland, where the dark stones stood like clouds in another sky.

It was twelve and a half hundred years.

Now they could breathe without respirators, for a short time.

Now they could bear the temperature, for a short time.

Now all the green birds were dead.

Now a strange and troubling thing began.

The bipeds came by night, made markings upon the snow, left dead animals in the midst of them. This happened now with much more frequency than it had in the past. They came long distances to do it, many of them with fur which was not their own upon their shoulders.

Jarry searched through the history files for all the reports on the creatures.

"This one speaks of lights in the forest," he said. "Station Seven."

"What . . . ?"

"Fire," he said. "What if they've discovered fire?"

"Then they're not really beasts!"

"But they were!"

"They wear clothing now. They make some sort of sacrifice to our machines. They're not beasts any longer."

"How could it have happened?"

"How do you think? *We* did it. Perhaps they would have remained stupid —animals—if we had not come along and forced them to get smart in order to go on living. We've accelerated their evolution. They had to adapt or die, and they adapted."

"D'you think it would have happened if we hadn't come along?" he asked.

"Maybe—some day. Maybe not, too."

Jarry moved to the window, stared out across Deadland.

"I have to find out," he said. "If they are intelligent, if they are—human, like us," he said, then laughed, "then we must consider their ways."

"What do you propose?"

"Locate some of the creatures. See whether we can communicate with them."

"Hasn't it been tried?"

"Yes."

"What were the results?"

"Mixed. Some claim they have considerable understanding. Others place them far below the threshold where humanity begins."

"We may be doing a terrible thing," she said. "Creating men, then destroying them. Once, when I was feeling low, you told me that we were the gods of this world, that ours was the power to shape and to break. Ours *is* the power to shape and break, but I don't feel especially divine. What can we do? They have come this far, but do you think they can bear the change that will take us the rest of the way? What if they are like the green birds? What if they've adapted as fast and as far as they can and it is not sufficient? What would a god do?"

"Whatever he wished," said Jarry.

That day, they cruised over Deadland in the flier, but the only signs of life they saw were each other. They continued to search in the days that followed, but they did not meet with success.

Under the purple of morning, however, two weeks later, it happened.

"They've been here," said Sanza.

Jarry moved to the front of the installation and stared out.

The snow was broken in several places, inscribed with the lines he had seen before, about the form of a small, dead beast.

"They can't have gone very far," he said.

"No."

"We'll search in the sled."

Now over the snow and out, across the land called Dead they went, Sanza driving and Jarry peering at the lines of footmarks in the blue.

They cruised through the occurring morning, hinting of fire and violet, and the wind went past them like a river, and all about them there came sounds like the cracking of ice, the trembling of tin, the snapping of steel strands. The blue frosted stones stood like frozen music, and the long shadow of their sled, black as ink, raced on ahead of them. A shower of hailstones drumming upon the roof of their vehicle like a sudden visitation of demon dancers, as suddenly was gone. Deadland sloped downward, slanted up again.

Jarry placed his hand upon Sanza's shoulder.

"Ahead!"

She nodded, began to brake the sled.

They had it at bay. They were using clubs and long poles which looked to have fire-hardened points. They threw stones. They threw pieces of ice.

Then they backed away and it killed them as they went.

The Catforms had called it a bear because it was big and shaggy and could rise up onto its hind legs. . . .

This one was about three and a half meters in length, was covered with bluish fur and had a thin, hairless snout like the business end of a pair of pliers.

Five of the little creatures lay still in the snow. Each time that it swung a paw and connected, another one fell.

Jarry removed the pistol from its compartment and checked the charge.

"Cruise by slowly," he told her. "I'm going to try to burn it about the head."

His first shot missed, scoring the boulder at its back. His second singed the fur of its neck. He leaped down from the sled then, as they came abreast of the beast, thumbed the power control up to maximum and fired the entire charge into its breast, point-blank.

The bear stiffened, swayed, fell, a gaping wound upon it, front to back.

Jarry turned and regarded the little creatures. They stared up at him.

"Hello," he said. "My name is Jarry. I dub thee Redforms. . . ."

He was knocked from his feet by a blow from behind.

He rolled across the snow, lights dancing before his eyes, his left arm and shoulder afire with pain.

A second bear had emerged from the forest of stone.

He drew his long hunting knife with his right hand and climbed back to his feet.

As the creature lunged, he moved with the catspeed of his kind, thrusting upward, burying his knife to the hilt in its throat.

A shudder ran through it, but it cuffed him and he fell once again, the blade torn from his grasp.

The Redforms threw more stones, rushed toward it with their pointed sticks.

Then there was a thud and a crunching sound, and it rose up into the air and came down on top of him.

He awakened.

He lay on his back, hurting, and everything he looked at seemed to be pulsing, as if about to explode.

How much time had passed, he did not know.

Either he or the bear had been moved.

The little creatures crouched, watching.

Some watched the bear. Some watched him.

Some watched the broken sled. . . .

The broken sled. . . .

He struggled to his feet.

The Redforms drew back.

He crossed to the sled and looked inside.

He knew she was dead when he saw the angle of her neck. But he did all the things a person does to be sure, anyway, before he would let himself believe it.

She had delivered the deathblow, crashing the sled into the creature, breaking its back. It had broken the sled. Herself, also.

He leaned against the wreckage, composed his first prayer, then removed her body.

The Redforms watched.

He lifted her in his arms and began walking, back toward the installation, across Deadland.

The Redforms continued to watch as he went, except for the one with the strangely high brow-ridge, who studied instead the knife that protruded from the shaggy and steaming throat of the beast.

Jarry asked the awakened executives of December: "What should we do?"

"She is the first of our race to die on this world," said Yan Turl, vice-president.

"There is no tradition," said Selda Kein, Secretary. "Shall we establish one?"

"I don't know," said Jarry. "I don't know what is right to do."

"Burial or cremation seem to be the main choices. Which would you prefer?"

"I don't—no, not the ground. Give her back to me. Give me a large flier. . . . I'll burn her."

"Then let us construct a chapel."

"No. It is a thing I must do in my own way. I'd rather do it alone."

"As you wish. Draw what equipment you need and be about it."

"Please send someone else to keep the Deadland installation. I wish to sleep again when I have finished this thing—until the next cycle."

"Very well, Jarry. We are sorry."

"Yes—we are."

Jarry nodded, gestured, turned, departed.

Thus are the heavier lines of life sometimes drawn.

At the southeastern edge of Deadland there was a blue mountain. It stood to slightly over three thousand meters in height. When approached from the northwest, it gave the appearance of being a frozen wave in a sea too vast to imagine. Purple clouds rent themselves upon its peak. No living thing was to be found on its slopes. It had no name, save that which Jarry Dark gave it.

He anchored the flier.

He carried her body to the highest point to which a body might be carried.

He placed her there, dressed in her finest garments, a wide scarf concealing the angle of her neck, a dark veil covering her emptied features.

He was about to try a prayer when the hail began to fall. Like thrown rocks, the chunks of blue ice came down upon him, upon her.

"Goddamn you!" he cried and he raced back to the flier.

He climbed into the air, circled.

Her garments were flapping in the wind. The hail was a blue, beaded curtain that separated them from all but these final caresses: fire aflow from ice to ice, from clay aflow immortally through guns.

He squeezed the trigger and a doorway into the sun opened in the side of the mountain that had been nameless. She vanished within it, and he widened the doorway until he had lowered the mountain.

Then he climbed upward into the cloud, attacking the storm until his guns were empty.

He circled then above the molten mesa, there at the southeastern edge of Deadland.

He circled above the first pyre this world had seen.

Then he departed, to sleep for a season in silence the sleep of ice and of stone, to inherit the new Alyonal. There is no dreaming in that sleep.

Fifteen centuries. Almost half the wait. Two hundred words or less. . . .
Picture . . .

. . . Nineteen mighty rivers flowing, but the black seas rippling violet now.

. . . No shallow iodine-colored forests. Mighty shag-barked barrel trees instead, orange and lime and black and tall across the land.

. . . Great ranges of mountains in the place of hills brown, yellow, white, lavender. Black corkscrews of smoke unwinding from smoldering cones.

. . . Flowers, whose roots explore the soil twenty meters beneath their mustard petals, unfolded amid the blue frost and the stones.

. . . Blind burrowers burrowing deeper; offal-eating murk-beasts now showing formidable incisors and great rows of ridged molars; giant caterpillars growing smaller but looking larger because of increasing coats.

. . . The contours of valleys still like the torsos of women, flowing and rolling, or perhaps like instruments of music.

. . . Gone much wind-blasted stone, but ever the frost.

. . . Sounds in the morning as always, harsh, brittle, metallic.

They were sure they were halfway to heaven.

Picture that.

The Deadland log told him as much as he really needed to know. But he read back through the old reports, also.

Then he mixed himself a drink and stared out the third floor window.

". . . Will die," he said, then finished his drink, outfitted himself and abandoned his post.

It was three days before he found a camp.

He landed the flier at a distance and approached on foot. He was far to the south of Deadland, where the air was warmer and caused him to feel constantly short of breath.

They were wearing animal skins—skins which had been cut for a better fit and greater protection, skins which were tied about them. He counted sixteen lean-to arrangements and three camp fires. He flinched as he regarded the fires, but he continued to advance.

When they saw him, all their little noises stopped, a brief cry went up and then there was silence.

He entered the camp.

The creatures stood unmoving about him. He heard some bustling within the large lean-to at the end of the clearing.

He walked about the camp.

A slab of dried meat hung from the center of a tripod of poles.

Several long spears stood before each dwelling place. He advanced and studied one. A stone which had been flaked into a leaf-shaped spearhead was affixed to its end.

There was the outline of a cat carved upon a block of wood. . . .

He heard a footfall and turned.

One of the Redforms moved slowly toward him. It appeared older than the others. Its shoulders sloped; as it opened its mouth to make a series of popping noises, he saw that some of its teeth were missing; its hair was grizzled and thin. It bore something in its hands, but Jarry's attention was drawn to the hands themselves.

Each hand bore an opposing digit.

He looked about him quickly, studying the hands of the others. All of them seemed to have thumbs. He studied their appearance more closely.

They now had foreheads.

He returned his attention to the old Redform.

It placed something at his feet, and then it backed away from him.

He looked down.

A chunk of dried meat and a piece of fruit lay upon a broad leaf.

He picked up the meat, closed his eyes, bit off a piece, chewed and swallowed. He wrapped the rest in the leaf and placed it in the side pocket of his pack.

He extended his hand and the Redform drew back.

He lowered his hand, unrolled the blanket he had carried with him and spread it upon the ground. He seated himself, pointed to the Redform, then indicated a position across from him at the other end of the blanket.

The creature hesitated, then advanced and seated itself.

"We are going to learn to talk with one another," he said slowly. Then he placed his hand upon his breast and said, "Jarry."

Jarry stood before the reawakened executives of December.

"They are intelligent," he told them. "It's all in my report."

"So?" asked Yan Turl.

"I don't think they will be able to adapt. They have come very far, very rapidly. But I don't think they can go much further. I don't think they can make it all the way."

"Are you a biologist, an ecologist, a chemist?"

"No."

"Then on what do you base your opinion?"

"I observed them at close range for six weeks."

"Then it's only a feeling you have . . . ?"

"You know there are no experts on a thing like this. It's never happened before."

"Granting their intelligence—granting even that what you have said concerning their adaptability is correct—what do you suggest we do about it?"

"Slow down the change. Give them a better chance. If they can't make it the rest of the way, then stop short of our goal. It's already livable here. *We* can adapt the rest of the way."

"Slow it down? How much?"

"Supposing we took another seven or eight thousand years?"

"Impossible!"

"Entirely!"

"Too much!"

"Why?"

"Because everyone stands a three-month watch every two hundred fifty years. That's one year of personal time for every thousand. You're asking for too much of everyone's time."

"But the life of an entire race may be at stake!"

"You do not know for certain."

"No, I don't. But do you feel it is something to take a chance with?"

"Do you want to put it to an executive vote?"

"No—I can see that I'll lose. I want to put it before the entire membership."

"Impossible. They're all asleep."

"Then wake them up."

"That would be quite a project."

"Don't you think that the fate of a race is worth the effort? Especially since we're the ones who forced intelligence upon them? We're the ones who made them evolve, cursed them with intellect."

"Enough! They were right at the threshold. They might have become intelligent had we *not* come along. . . ."

"But you can't say for certain! You don't really know! And it doesn't really matter how it happened. They're here and we're here and they think we're gods—maybe because we do nothing for them but make them miserable. We have some responsibility to an intelligent race, though. At least to the extent of not murdering it."

"Perhaps we could do a long-range study . . ."

"They could be dead by then. I formally move, in my capacity as treasurer, that we awaken the full membership and put the matter to a vote."

"I don't hear any second to your motion."

"Selda?" he said.

She looked away.

"Tarebell? Clond? Bondici?"

There was silence in the cavern that was high and wide about him.

"All right. I can see when I'm beaten. We will be our own serpents when we come into our Eden. I'm going now, back to Deadland, to finish my tour of duty."

"You don't have to. In fact, it might be better if you sleep the whole thing out. . . ."

"No. If it's going to be this way, the guilt will be mine also. I want to watch, to share it fully."

"So be it," said Turl.

Two weeks later, when Installation Nineteen tried to raise the Deadland Station on the radio, there was no response.

After a time, a flier was dispatched.

The Deadland Station was a shapeless lump of melted metal.

Jarry Dark was nowhere to be found.

Later that afternoon, Installation Eight went dead.

A flier was immediately dispatched.

Installation Eight no longer existed. Its attendants were found several miles away, walking. They told how Jarry Dark had forced them from the station at gunpoint. Then he had burned it to the ground with the fire cannons mounted upon his flier.

At about the time they were telling this story, Installation Six became silent.

The order went out: MAINTAIN CONTINUOUS RADIO CONTACT WITH TWO OTHER STATIONS AT ALL TIMES.

The other order went out: GO ARMED AT ALL TIMES. TAKE ANY VISITOR PRISONER.

Jarry waited. At the bottom of a chasm, parked beneath a shelf of rock, Jarry waited. An opened bottle stood upon the control board of his flier. Next to it was a small case of white metal.

Jarry took a long, last drink from the bottle as he waited for the broadcast he knew would come.

When it did, he stretched out on the seat and took a nap.

When he awakened, the light of day was waning.

The broadcast was still going on. . . .

". . . Jarry. They will be awakened and a referendum will be held. Come back to the main cavern. This is Yan Turl. Please do not destroy any more installations. This action is not necessary. We agree with your proposal that a vote be held. Please contact us immediately. We are waiting for your reply, Jarry. . . ."

He tossed the empty bottle through the window and raised the flier out of the purple shadow into the air and up.

When he descended upon the landing stage within the main cavern, of course they were waiting for him. A dozen rifles were trained upon him as he stepped down from the flier.

"Remove your weapons, Jarry," came the voice of Yan Turl.

"I'm not wearing any weapons," said Jarry. "Neither is my flier," he added; and this was true, for the fire cannons no longer rested within their mountings.

Yan Turl approached, looked up at him.

"Then you may step down."

"Thank you, but I like it right where I am."

"You are a prisoner."

"What do you intend to do with me?"

"Put you back to sleep until the end of the wait. Come down here!"

"No. And don't try shooting—or using a stun charge or gas, either. If you do, we're all of us dead the second it hits."

"What do you mean?" asked Turl, gesturing gently to the riflemen.

"My flier," said Jarry, "is a bomb, and I'm holding the fuse in my right hand." He raised the white metal box. "So long as I keep the lever on the side of this box depressed, we live. If my grip relaxes, even for an instant, the explosion which ensues will doubtless destroy this entire cavern."

"I think you're bluffing."

"You know how you can find out for certain."

"You'll die too, Jarry."

"At the moment, I don't really care. Don't try burning my hand off either, to destroy the fuse," he cautioned, "because it doesn't really matter. Even if you should succeed, it will cost you at least two installations."

"Why is that?"

"What do you think I did with the fire cannons? I taught the Redforms how to use them. At the moment, these weapons are manned by Redforms and aimed at two installations. If I do not personally visit my gunners by dawn, they will open fire. After destroying their objectives, they will move on and try for two more."

"You trusted those beasts with laser projectors?"

"That is correct. Now, will you begin awakening the others for the voting?"

Turl crouched, as if to spring at him, appeared to think better of it, relaxed.

"Why did you do it, Jarry?" he asked. "What are they to you that you would make your own people suffer for them?"

"Since you do not feel as I feel," said Jarry, "my reasons would mean nothing to you. After all, they are only based upon my feelings, which are different than your own—for mine are based upon sorrow and loneliness. Try this one, though: I am their god. My form is to be found in their every camp. I am the Slayer of Bears from the Desert of the Dead. They have told my story for two and a half centuries, and I have been changed by it. I am powerful and wise and good, so far as they are concerned. In this capacity, I owe them some consideration. If I do not give them their lives, who will there be to honor me in snow and chant my story around the fires and cut for me the best portions of the woolly caterpillar? None, Turl. And these things are all that my life is worth now. Awaken the others. You have no choice."

"Very well," said Turl. "And if their decision should go against you?"

"Then I'll retire, and you can be god," said Jarry.

Now every day when the sun goes down out of the purple sky, Jarry Dark watches it in its passing, for he shall sleep no more the sleep of ice and of stone, wherein there is no dreaming. He has elected to live out the span of his days in a tiny instant of the wait, never to look upon the New Alyonal of his people. Every morning, at the new Deadland installation, he is awakened by sounds like the cracking of ice, the trembling of tin, the snapping of steel strands, before they come to him with their offerings, singing and making marks upon the snow. They praise him and he smiles upon them. Sometimes he coughs.

Born of man and woman, in accordance with Catform Y7 requirements, Coldworld Class, Jarry Dark was not suited for existence anywhere in the universe which had guaranteed him a niche. This was either a blessing or a curse, depending on how you looked at it. So look at it however you would, that was the story. Thus does life repay those who would serve her fully.

VONDA N. McINTYRE

Of Mist, and Grass, and Sand

Progress has been difficult throughout most human history partly because traditions change slowly. Concepts like the divine right of kings went unchallenged for many centuries, and it was risky to attack accepted ways of doing things; so those who struggled against ignorance often did so only by accepting the possibility that they would be tortured or killed for their good intentions. In "Of Mist, and Grass, and Sand" Ms. McIntyre reminds us that even in the future it takes a unique person (or creature) to perform the important task of dispensing understanding.

The little boy was frightened. Gently, Snake touched his hot forehead. Behind her, three adults stood close together, watching, suspicious, afraid to show their concern with more than narrow lines around their eyes. They feared Snake as much as they feared their only child's death. In the dimness of the tent, the flickering lamplights gave no reassurance.

The child watched with eyes so dark the pupils were not visible, so dull that Snake herself feared for his life. She stroked his hair. It was long and very pale, a striking color against his dark skin, dry and irregular for several inches near the scalp. Had Snake been with these people months ago, she would have known the child was growing ill.

"Bring my case, please," Snake said.

The child's parents started at her soft voice. Perhaps they had expected the screech of a bright jay or the hissing of a shining serpent. This was the first time Snake had spoken in their presence. She had only watched when the three of them had come to observe her from a distance and whisper about her occupation and her youth; she had only listened and then nodded when finally they came to ask her help. Perhaps they had thought she was mute.

The fair-haired younger man lifted her leather case. He held the satchel away from his body, leaning to hand it to her, breathing shallowly with nostrils flared against the faint smell of musk in the dry desert air. Snake had almost accustomed herself to the kind of uneasiness he showed; she had already seen it often.

When Snake reached out, the young man jerked back and dropped the case. Snake lunged and barely caught it, gently set it on the felt floor and glanced at him with reproach. His husband and his wife came forward and touched him to ease his fear. "He was bitten once," the dark and handsome woman said. "He almost died." Her tone was not of apology, but of justification.

"I'm sorry," the younger man said. "It's . . ." He gestured toward her; he was trembling and trying visibly to control the reactions of his fear. Snake glanced down, to her shoulder, where she had been unconsciously aware of the slight weight and movement. A tiny serpent, thin as the finger of a baby, slid himself around her neck to show his narrow head below her short black curls. He probed the air with his trident tongue in a leisurely manner, out, up and down, in, to savor the taste of the smells. "It's only Grass," Snake said. "He cannot harm you." If he were bigger, he might frighten; his color was pale green, but the scales around his mouth were red, as if he had just feasted as a mammal eats, by tearing. He was, in fact, much neater.

The child whimpered. He cut off the sound of pain; perhaps he had been told that Snake, too, would be offended by crying. She only felt sorry that his people refused themselves such a simple way of easing fear. She turned from the adults, regretting their terror of her but unwilling to spend the time it would take to convince them their reactions were unjustified. "It's all right," she said to the little boy. "Grass is smooth and dry and soft, and if I left him to guard you, even death could not reach your bedside." Grass poured himself into her narrow, dirty hand, and she extended him toward the child. "Gently." He reached out and touched the sleek scales with one fingertip. Snake could sense the effort of even such a simple motion, yet the boy almost smiled.

"What are you called?"

He looked quickly toward his parents, and finally they nodded. "Stavin," he whispered. He had no strength or breath for speaking.

"I am Snake, Stavin, and in a little while, in the morning, I must hurt you. You may feel a quick pain, and your body will ache for several days, but you will be better afterward."

He stared at her solemnly. Snake saw that though he understood and feared what she might do, he was less afraid than if she had lied to him. The pain must have increased greatly as his illness became more apparent, but it seemed that others had only reassured him and hoped the disease would disappear or kill him quickly.

Snake put Grass on the boy's pillow and pulled her case nearer. The lock opened at her touch. The adults still could only fear her; they had had neither time nor reason to discover any trust. The wife was old enough that they might never have another child, and Snake could tell by their eyes, their covert touching, their concern, that they loved this one very much. They must, to come to Snake in this country.

It was night, and cooling. Sluggish, Sand slid out of the case, moving his head, moving his tongue, smelling, tasting, detecting the warmths of bodies.

"Is that . . . ?" The older husband's voice was low and wise, but terrified, and Sand sensed the fear. He drew back into striking position and sounded his rattle softly. Snake spoke, moving her hand, and extended her arm. The pit viper relaxed and flowed around and around her slender wrist to form black and tan bracelets. "No," she said. "Your child is too ill for Sand to help. I know it is hard, but please try to be calm. This is a fearful thing for you, but it is all I can do."

She had to annoy Mist to make her come out. Snake rapped on the bag and finally poked her twice. Snake felt the vibration of sliding scales, and suddenly the albino cobra flung herself into the tent. She moved quickly, yet there seemed to be no end to her. She reared back and up. Her breath rushed out in a hiss. Her head rose well over a meter above the floor. She flared her wide hood. Behind her, the adults gasped, as if physically assaulted by the gaze of the tan spectacle design on the back of Mist's hood. Snake ignored the people and spoke to the great cobra, focusing her attention by her words. "Ah, thou. Furious creature. Lie down; 'tis time for thee to earn thy dinner. Speak to this child, and touch him. He is called Stavin." Slowly, Mist relaxed her hood and allowed Snake to touch her. Snake grasped her firmly behind the head and held her so she looked at Stavin. The cobra's silver eyes picked up the yellow of the lamplight. "Stavin," Snake said, "Mist will only meet you now. I promise that this time she will touch you gently."

Still, Stavin shivered when Mist touched his thin chest. Snake did not release the serpent's head, but allowed her body to slide against the boy's. The cobra was four times longer than Stavin was tall. She curved herself in stark white loops across his swollen abdomen, extending herself, forcing her head toward the boy's face, straining against Snake's hands. Mist met Stavin's frightened stare with the gaze of lidless eyes. Snake allowed her a little closer.

Mist flicked out her tongue to taste the child.

The younger husband made a small, cut-off, frightened sound. Stavin flinched at it, and Mist drew back, opening her mouth, exposing her fangs, audibly thrusting her breath through her throat. Snake sat back on her heels, letting out her own breath. Sometimes, in other places, the kinfolk could stay while she worked. "You must leave," she said gently. "It's dangerous to frighten Mist."

"I won't . . ."

"I'm sorry. You must wait outside."

Perhaps the younger husband, perhaps even the wife, would have made the indefensible objections and asked the answerable questions, but the older man turned them and took their hands and led them away.

"I need a small animal," Sanke said as he lifted the tent flap. "It must have fur, and it must be alive."

"One will be found," he said, and the three parents went into the glowing night. Snake could hear their footsteps in the sand outside.

Snake supported Mist in her lap and soothed her. The cobra wrapped herself around Snake's narrow waist, taking in her warmth. Hunger made the cobra even more nervous than usual, and she was hungry, as was Snake. Coming across the black sand desert, they had found sufficient water, but Snake's traps were unsuccessful. The season was summer, the weather was hot, and many of the furry tidbits Sand and Mist preferred were estivating. When the serpents missed their regular meal, Snake began a fast as well.

She saw with regret that Stavin was more frightened now. "I am sorry to send your parents away," she said. "They can come back soon."

His eyes glistened, but he held back the tears. "They said to do what you told me."

"I would have you cry, if you are able," Snake said. "It isn't such a terrible thing." But Stavin seemed not to understand, and Snake did not press him; she knew that his people taught themselves to resist a difficult land by refusing to cry, refusing to mourn, refusing to laugh. They denied themselves grief and allowed themselves little joy, but they survived.

Mist had calmed to sullenness. Snake unwrapped her from her waist and placed her on the pallet next to Stavin. As the cobra moved, Snake guided her head, feeling the tension of the striking muscles. "She will touch you with her tongue," she told Stavin. "It might tickle, but it will not hurt. She smells with it, as you do with your nose."

"With her tongue?"

Snake nodded, smiling, and Mist flicked out her tongue to caress Stavin's cheek. Stavin did not flinch; he watched, his child's delight in knowledge briefly overcoming pain. He lay perfectly still as Mist's long tongue brushed his cheeks, his eyes, his mouth. "She tastes the sickness," Snake said. Mist stopped fighting the restraint of her grasp and drew back her head. Snake sat on her heels and released the cobra, who spiraled up her arm and laid herself across her shoulders.

"Go to sleep, Stavin," Snake said. "Try to trust me, and try not to fear the morning."

Stavin gazed at her for a few seconds, searching for truth in Snake's pale eyes. "Will Grass watch?"

She was startled by the question or, rather, by the acceptance behind the question. She brushed his hair from his forehead and smiled a smile that was tears just beneath the surface. "Of course." She picked Grass up. "Thou wilt watch this child and guard him." The snake lay quiet in her hand, and his eyes glittered black. She laid him gently on Stavin's pillow.

"Now sleep."

Stavin closed his eyes, and the life seemed to flow out of him. The alteration was so great that Snake reached out to touch him, then saw that he was breathing, slowly, shallowly. She tucked a blanket around him and stood up. The abrupt change in position dizzied her; she staggered and caught herself. Across her shoulders, Mist tensed.

Snake's eyes stung and her vision was over-sharp, fever-clear. The sound she imagined she heard swooped in closer. She steadied herself against hunger and exhaustion, bent slowly, and picked up the leather case. Mist touched her cheek with the tip of her tongue.

She pushed aside the tent flap and felt relief that it was still night. She could stand the heat, but the brightness of the sun curled through her, burning. The moon must be full; though the clouds obscured everything, they diffused the light so the sky appeared gray from horizon to horizon. Beyond the tents, groups of formless shadows projected from the ground. Here, near the edge of the desert, enough water existed so clumps and patches of bush grew, providing shelter and sustenance for all manner of creatures. The black sand, which sparkled and blinded in the sunlight, at night was like a layer of soft soot. Snake stepped out of the tent, and the illusion of softness disappeared; her boots slid crunching into the sharp hard grains.

Stavin's family waited, sitting close together between the dark tents that clustered in a patch of sand from which the bushes had been ripped and burned. They looked at her silently, hoping with their eyes, showing no expression in their faces. A woman somewhat younger than Stavin's mother sat with them. She was dressed, as they were, in a long loose robe, but she wore the only adornment Snake had seen among these people: a leader's circle, hanging around her neck on a leather thong. She and the older husband were marked close kin by their similarities: sharp-cut planes of face, high cheekbones, his hair white and hers graying early from deep black, their eyes the dark brown best suited for survival in the sun. On the ground by their feet a small black animal jerked sporadically against a net and infrequently gave a shrill weak cry.

"Stavin is asleep," Snake said. "Do not disturb him, but go to him if he wakes."

The wife and young husband rose and went inside, but the older man stopped before her. "Can you help him?"

"I hope we may. The tumor is advanced, but it seems solid." Her own voice sounded removed, slightly hollow, as if she were lying. "Mist will be ready in the morning." She still felt the need to give him reassurance, but she could think of none.

"My sister wished to speak with you," he said and left them alone, without introduction, without elevating himself by saying that the tall woman was the leader of this group. Snake glanced back, but the tent flap fell shut. She was feeling her exhaustion more deeply, and across her shoulders Mist was, for the first time, a weight she thought heavy.

"Are you all right?"

Snake turned. The woman moved toward her with a natural elegance made slightly awkward by advanced pregnancy. Snake had to look up to meet her gaze. She had small fine lines at the corners of her eyes, as if she laughed, sometimes, in secret. She smiled, but with concern. "You seem very tired. Shall I have someone make you a bed?"

"Not now," Snake said, "not yet. I won't sleep until afterward."

The leader searched her face, and Snake felt a kinship with her in their shared responsibility.

"I understand, I think. Is there anything we can give you? Do you need aid with your preparations?"

Snake found herself having to deal with the questions as if they were complex problems. She turned them in her tired mind, examined them, dissected them and finally grasped their meanings. "My pony needs food and water. . . ."

"It is taken care of."

"And I need someone to help me with Mist. Someone strong. But it's more important that they aren't afraid."

The leader nodded. "I would help you," she said and smiled again, a little. "But I am a bit clumsy of late. I will find someone."

"Thank you."

Somber again, the older woman inclined her head and moved slowly toward a small group of tents. Snake watched her go, admiring her grace. She felt small and young and grubby in comparison.

Sand began to unwrap himself from her wrist. Feeling the anticipatory slide of scales on her skin, she caught him before he could drop to the ground. Sand lifted the upper half of his body from her hands. He flicked out his tongue, peering toward the little animal, feeling its body heat, smelling its fear. "I know thou art hungry," Snake said, "but that creature is not for thee." She put Sand in the case, lifted Mist from her shoulder, and let her coil herself in her dark compartment.

The small animal shrieked and struggled again when Snake's diffuse shadow passed over it. She bent and picked it up. The rapid series of terrified cries slowed and diminished and finally stopped as she stroked it. Finally it lay still, breathing hard, exhausted, staring up at her with yellow eyes. It had long hind legs and wide pointed ears, and its nose twitched at the serpent smell. Its soft black fur was marked off in skewed squares by the cords of the net.

"I am sorry to take your life," Snake told it. "But there will be no more fear, and I will not hurt you." She closed her hand gently around it and, stroking it, grasped its spine at the base of its skull. She pulled, once, quickly. It seemed to struggle, briefly, but it was already dead. It convulsed; its legs drew up against its body, and its toes curled and quivered. It seemed to stare up at her even now. She freed its body from the net.

Snake chose a small vial from her belt pouch, pried open the animal's clenched jaws and let a single drop of the vial's cloudy preparation fall into its mouth. Quickly she opened the satchel again and called Mist out. The cobra came slowly, slipping over the edge, hood closed, sliding in the sharp-grained sand. Her milky scales caught the thin light. She smelled the animal, flowed to it, touched it with her tongue. For a moment Snake was afraid she would refuse dead meat, but the body was still warm, still twitching reflexively, and she was very hungry. "A tidbit for thee," Snake spoke to the cobra: a habit of solitude. "To whet thy appetite." Mist nosed the beast, reared back and struck, sinking her short fixed fangs into the tiny body, biting again, pumping out her store of poison. She released it, took a better grip and began to work her jaws around it; it would hardly distend her throat. When Mist lay quiet, digesting the small meal, Snake sat beside her and held her, waiting.

She heard footsteps in the coarse sand.

"I'm sent to help you."

He was a young man, despite a scatter of white in his black hair. He was taller than Snake and not unattractive. His eyes were dark, and the sharp planes of his face were further hardened because his hair was pulled straight back and tied. His expression was neutral.

"Are you afraid?"

"I will do as you tell me."

Though his form was obscured by his robe, his long fine hands showed strength.

"Then hold her body, and don't let her surprise you." Mist was beginning to twitch from the effects of the drugs Snake had put in the small animal. The cobra's eyes stared, unseeing.

"If it bites . . ."

"Hold, quickly!"

The young man reached, but he had hesitated too long. Mist writhed, lashing out, striking him in the face with her tail. He staggered back, at least as surprised as hurt. Snake kept a close grip behind Mist's jaws and struggled to catch the rest of her as well. Mist was no constrictor, but she was smooth and strong and fast. Thrashing, she forced out her breath in a long hiss. She would have bitten anything she could reach. As Snake fought with her, she managed to squeeze the poison glands and force out the last drops of venom. They hung from Mist's fangs for a moment, catching light as jewels would; the force of the serpent's convulsions flung them away into the darkness. Snake struggled with the cobra, aided for once by the sand on which Mist could get no purchase. Snake felt the young man behind her, grabbing for Mist's body and tail. The seizure stopped abruptly, and Mist lay limp in their hands.

"I am sorry. . . ."

"Hold her," Snake said. "We have the night to go."

During Mist's second convulsion the young man held her firmly and was of some real help. Afterward, Snake answered his interrupted question. "If she were making poison and she bit you, you would probably die. Even now her bite would make you ill. But unless you do something foolish, if she manages to bite, she will bite me."

"You would benefit my cousin little, if you were dead or dying."

"You misunderstand. Mist cannot kill me." She held out her hand so he could see the white scars of slashes and punctures. He stared at them and looked into her eyes for a long moment, then looked away.

The bright spot in the clouds from which the light radiated moved westward in the sky; they held the cobra like a child. Snake found herself half-dozing, but Mist moved her head, dully attempting to evade restraint, and Snake woke herself abruptly. "I must not sleep," she said to the young man. "Talk to me. What are you called?"

As Stavin had, the young man hesitated. He seemed afraid of her or of something. "My people," he said, "think it unwise to speak our names to strangers."

"If you consider me a witch you should not have asked my aid. I know no magic, and I claim none."

"It's not a superstition," he said. "Not as you might think. We're not afraid of being bewitched."

"I can't learn all the customs of all the people on this earth, so I keep my own. My custom is to address those I work with by name." Watching him, Snake tried to decipher his expression in the dim light.

"Our families know our names, and we exchange names with those we would marry."

Snake considered that custom, and thought it would fit badly on her. "No one else? Ever?"

"Well . . . a friend might know one's name."

"Ah," Snake said. "I see. I am still a stranger and perhaps an enemy."

"A *friend* would know my name," the young man said again. "I would not offend you, but now you misunderstand. An acquaintance is not a friend. We value friendship highly."

"In this land one should be able to tell quickly if a person is worth calling 'friend.' "

"We take friends seldom. Friendship is a great commitment."

"It sounds like something to be feared."

He considered that possibility. "Perhaps it's the betrayal of friendship we fear. That is a very painful thing."

"Has anyone ever betrayed you?"

He glanced at her sharply, as if she had exceeded the limits of propriety. "No," he said, and his voice was as hard as his face. "No friend. I have no one I call friend."

His reaction startled Snake. "That's very sad," she said and grew silent, trying to comprehend the deep stresses that could close people off so far, comparing her loneliness of necessity and theirs of choice. "Call me Snake," she said finally, "if you can bring yourself to pronounce it. Saying my name binds you to nothing."

The young man seemed about to speak; perhaps he thought again that he had offended her; perhaps he felt he should further defend his customs. But Mist began to twist in their hands, and they had to hold her to keep her from injuring herself. The cobra was slender for her length, but powerful, and the convulsions she went through were more severe than any she had ever had before. She thrashed in Snake's graps and almost pulled away. She tried to spread her hood, but Snake held her too tightly. She opened her mouth and hissed, but no poison dripped from her fangs.

She wrapped her tail around the young man's waist. He began to pull her and turn, to extricate himself from her coils.

"She's not a constrictor," Snake said. "She won't hurt you. Leave her . . ."

But it was too late; Mist relaxed suddenly and the young man lost his balance. Mist whipped herself away and lashed figures in the sand. Snake wrestled with her alone while the young man tried to hold her, but she curled herself around Snake and used the grip for leverage. She started to pull herself from Snake's hands. Snake threw them both backward into the sand; Mist rose above her, openmouthed, furious, hissing. The young man lunged and grabbed her just beneath her hood. Mist struck at him, but Snake, somehow, held her back. Together they deprived Mist of her hold and regained control of her. Snake struggled up, but Mist suddenly went quite still and lay almost rigid between them. They were both sweating; the young man was pale under his tan, and even Snake was trembling.

"We have a little while to rest," Snake said. She glanced at him and noticed the dark line on his cheek where, earlier, Mist's tail had slashed him. She reached up and touched it. "You'll have a bruise," she said. "But it will not scar."

"If it were true that serpents sting with their tails, you would be restraining both the fangs and the stinger, and I'd be of little use."

"Tonight I'd need someone to keep me awake, whether or not they helped me with Mist." Fighting the cobra produced adrenalin, but now it ebbed, and her exhaustion and hunger were returning, stronger.

"Snake . . ."

"Yes?"

He smiled, quickly, half-embarrassed. "I was trying the pronunciation."

"Good enough."

"How long did it take you to cross the desert?"

"Not very long. Too long. Six days."

"How did you live?"

"There is water. We traveled at night, except yesterday, when I could find no shade."

"You carried all your food?"

She shrugged. "A little." And wished he would not speak of food.

"What's on the other side?"

"More sand, more bush, a little more water. A few groups of people, traders, the station I grew up and took my training in. And farther on, a mountain with a city inside."

"I would like to see a city. Someday."

"The desert can be crossed."

He said nothing, but Snake's memories of leaving home were recent enough that she could imagine his thoughts.

The next set of convulsions came much sooner than Snake had expected. By their severity she gauged something of the stage of Stavin's illness and wished it were morning. If she were to lose him, she would have it done and grieve and try to forget. The cobra would have battered herself to death against the sand if Snake and the young man had not been holding her. She suddenly went completely rigid, with her mouth clamped shut and her forked tongue dangling.

She stopped breathing.

"Hold her," Snake said. "Hold her head. Quickly, take her, and if she gets away, run. Take her! She won't strike at you now, she could only slash you by accident."

He hesitated only a moment, then grasped Mist behind the head. Snake ran, slipping in the deep sand from the edge of the circle of tents to a place where bushes still grew. She broke off dry thorny branches that tore her scarred hands. Peripherally she noticed a mass of horned vipers, so ugly they seemed deformed, nesting beneath the clump of desiccated vegetation. They hissed at her; she ignored them. She found a narrow hollow stem and carried it back. Her hands bled from deep scratches.

Kneeling by Mist's head, she forced open the cobra's mouth and pushed the tube deep into her throat, through the air passage at the base of Mist's tongue. She bent close, took the tube in her mouth and breathed gently into Mist's lungs.

She noticed: the young man's hands, holding the cobra as she had asked; his breathing, first a sharp gasp of surprise, then ragged; the sand scraping her elbows where she leaned; the cloying smell of the fluid seeping from Mist's fangs; her own dizziness, she thought from exhaustion, which she forced away by necessity and will.

Snake breathed and breathed again, paused and repeated until Mist caught the rhythm and continued it unaided.

Snake sat back on her heels. "I think she'll be all right," she said. "I hope she will." She brushed the back of her hand across her forehead. The touch sparked pain: she jerked her hand down and agony slid along her bones, up her arm, across her shoulder, through her chest, enveloping her heart. Her balance turned on its edge. She fell, tried to catch herself but moved too slowly, fought nausea and vertigo and almost succeeded until the pull of the earth seemed to slip away in pain and she was lost in darkness with nothing to take a bearing by.

She felt sand where it had scraped her cheek and her palms, but it was soft. "Snake, can I let go?" She thought the question must be for someone else, while at the same time she knew there was no one else to answer it, no one else to reply to her name. She felt hands on her, and they were gentle; she wanted to respond to them, but she was too tired. She needed sleep more, so she pushed them away. But they held her head and put dry leather to her lips and poured water into her throat. She coughed and choked and spat it out.

She pushed herself up on one elbow. As her sight cleared, she realized she was shaking. She felt as she had the first time she was snake-bitten, before her immunities had completely developed. The young man knelt over her, his water flask in his hand. Mist, beyond him, crawled toward the darkness. Snake forgot the throbbing pain. "Mist!" She slapped the ground.

The young man flinched and turned, frightened; the serpent reared up, her head nearly at Snake's standing eye level, her hood spread, swaying, watching, angry, ready to strike. She formed a wavering white line against black. Snake forced herself to rise, feeling as though she were fumbling with the control of some unfamiliar body. She almost fell again, but held herself steady. "Thou must not go to hunt now," she said. "There is work for thee to do." She held out her right hand to the side, a decoy, to draw Mist if she struck. Her hand was heavy with pain. Snake feared, not being bitten, but the loss of the contents of Mist's poison sacs. "Come here," she said. "Come here, and stay thy anger." She noticed blood flowing down between her fingers, and the fear she felt for Stavin was intensified. "Didst thou bite me, creature?" But the pain was wrong: poison would numb her, and the new serum only sting . . .

"No," the young man whispered from behind her.

Mist struck. The reflexes of long training took over. Snake's right hand jerked away, her left grabbed Mist as she brought her head back. The cobra writhed a moment and relaxed. "Devious beast," Snake said. "For shame." She turned and let Mist crawl up her arm and over her shoulder, where she lay like the outline of an invisible cape and dragged her tail like the edge of a train.

"She did not bite me?"

"No," the young man said. His contained voice was touched with awe. "You should be dying. You should be curled around the agony and your arm swollen purple. When you came back . . ." He gestured toward her hand. "It must have been a bush viper."

Snake remembered the coil of reptiles beneath the branches and touched the blood on her hand. She wiped it away, revealing the double puncture of a snakebite among the scratches of the thorns. The wound was slightly swollen. "It needs cleaning," she said. "I shame myself by falling to it." The pain of it washed in gentle waves up her arm, burning no longer. She stood looking at the young man, looking around her, watching the landscape shift and change as her tired eyes tried to cope with the low light of setting moon and false dawn. "You held Mist well and bravely," she said to the young man. "I thank you."

He lowered his gaze, almost bowing to her. He rose, and approached her. Snake put her hand gently on Mist's neck so she would not be alarmed.

"I would be honored," the young man said, "if you would call me Arevin."

"I would be pleased to."

Snake knelt down and held the winding white loops as Mist crawled slowly into her compartment. In a little while, when Mist had stabilized, by dawn, they could go to Stavin.

The tip of Mist's white tail slid out of sight. Snake closed the case and would have risen, but she could not stand. She had not quite shaken off the effects of the new venom. The flesh around the wound was red and tender, but the hemorrhaging would not spread. She stayed where she was, slumped, staring at her hand, creeping slowly in her mind toward what she needed to do, this time for herself.

"Let me help you. Please."

He touched her shoulder and helped her stand. "I'm sorry," she said. "I'm so in need of rest . . ."

"Let me wash your hand," Arevin said. "And then you can sleep. Tell me when to awaken you. . . ."

"I can't sleep yet." She collected herself, straightened, tossed the damp curls of her short hair off her forehead. "I'm all right now. Have you any water?"

Arevin loosened his outer robe. Beneath it he wore a loincloth and a leather belt that carried several leather flasks and pouches. His body was lean and well-built, his legs long and muscular. The color of his skin was slightly lighter than the sun-darkened brown of his face. He brought out his water flask and reached for Snake's hand.

"No, Arevin. If the poison gets in any small scratch you might have, it could infect."

She sat down and sluiced lukewarm water over her hand. The water dripped pink to the ground and disappeared, leaving not even a damp spot visible. The wound bled a little more, but now it only ached. The poison was almost inactivated.

"I don't understand," Arevin said, "how it is that you're unhurt. My younger sister was bitten by a bush viper." He could not speak as uncaringly as he might have wished. "We could do nothing to save her—nothing we have would even lessen her pain."

Snake gave him his flask and rubbed salve from a vial in her belt pouch across the closing punctures. "It's a part of our preparation," she said. "We work with many kinds of serpents, so we must be immune to as many as possible." She shrugged. "The process is tedious and somewhat painful." She clenched her fist; the film held, and she was steady. She leaned toward Arevin and touched his abraded cheek again. "Yes . . ." She spread a thin layer of the salve across it. "That will help it heal."

"If you cannot sleep," Arevin said, "can you at least rest?"

"Yes," she said. "For a little while."

Snake sat next to Arevin, leaning against him, and they watched the sun turn the clouds to gold and flame and amber. The simple physical contact with another human being gave Snake pleasure, though she found it unsatisfying. Another time, another place, she might do something more, but not here, not now.

When the lower edge of the sun's bright smear rose above the horizon, Snake rose and teased Mist out of the case. She came slowly, weakly, and crawled across Snake's shoulders. Snake picked up the satchel, and she and Arevin walked together back to the small group of tents.

Stavin's parents waited, watching for her, just outside the entrance of their tent. They stood in a tight, defensive, silent group. For a moment Snake thought they had decided to send her away. Then, with regret and fear like hot iron in her mouth, she asked if Stavin had died. They shook their heads and allowed her to enter.

Stavin lay as she had left him, still asleep. The adults followed her with their stares, and she could smell fear. Mist flicked out her tongue, growing nervous from the implied danger.

"I know you would stay," Snake said. "I know you would help, if you could, but there is nothing to be done by any person but me. Please go back outside."

They glanced at each other and at Arevin, and she thought for a moment that they would refuse. Snake wanted to fall into the silence and sleep. "Come, cousins," Arevin said. "We are in her hands." He opened the tent flap and motioned them out. Snake thanked him with nothing more than a glance, and he might almost have smiled. She turned toward Stavin, and knelt beside him. "Stavin . . ." She touched his forehead; it was very hot. She noticed that her hand was less steady than before. The slight touch awakened the child. "It's time," Snake said.

He blinked, coming out of some child's dream, seeing her, slowly recognizing her. He did not look frightened. For that Snake was glad; for some other reason she could not identify she was uneasy.

"Will it hurt?"

"Does it hurt now?"

He hesitated, looked away, looked back. "Yes."

"It might hurt a little more. I hope not. Are you ready?"

"Can Grass stay?"

"Of course," she said.

And realized what was wrong.

"I'll come back in a moment." Her voice changed so much, she had pulled it so tight, that she could not help but frighten him. She left the tent, walking slowly, calmly, restraining herself. Outside, the parents told her by their faces what they feared.

"Where is Grass?" Arevin, his back to her, started at her tone. The younger husband made a small grieving sound and could look at her no longer.

"We were afraid," the older husband said. "We thought it would bite the child."

"I thought it would. It was I. It crawled over his face, I could see its fangs . . ." The wife put her hands on the younger husband's shoulders, and he said no more.

"Where is he?" She wanted to scream; she did not.

They brought her a small open box. Snake took it and looked inside.

Grass lay cut almost in two, his entrails oozing from his body, half turned over, and as she watched, shaking, he writhed once, flicked his tongue out once, and in. Snake made some sound, too low in her throat to be a cry. She hoped his motions were only reflex, but she picked him up as gently as she could. She leaned down and touched her lips to the smooth green scales behind his head. She bit him quickly, sharply, at the base of the skull. His blood flowed cool and salty in her mouth. If he was not dead, she had killed him instantly.

She looked at the parents and at Arevin; they were all pale, but she had no sympathy for their fear and cared nothing for shared grief. "Such a small creature," she said. "Such a small creature, who could only give pleasure and dreams." She watched them for a moment more, then turned toward the tent again.

"Wait . . ." She heard the older husband move up close behind her. He touched her shoulder; she shrugged away his hand. "We will give you anything you want," he said, "but leave the child alone."

She spun on him in a fury. "Should I kill Stavin for your stupidity?" He seemed about to try to hold her back. She jammed her shoulder hard into his stomach and flung herself past the tent flap. Inside, she kicked over the satchel. Abruptly awakened and angry, Sand crawled out and coiled himself. When the younger husband and the wife tried to enter, Sand hissed and rattled with a violence Snake had never heard him use before. She did not even bother to look behind her. She ducked her head and wiped her tears on her sleeve before Stavin could see them. She knelt beside him.

"What's the matter?" He could not help but hear the voices outside the tent and the running.

"Nothing, Stavin," Snake said. "Did you know we came across the desert?"

"No," he said with wonder.

"It was very hot, and none of us had anything to eat. Grass is hunting now. He was very hungry. Will you forgive him and let me begin? I will be here all the time."

He seemed so tired; he was disappointed, but he had no strength for arguing. "All right." His voice rustled like sand slipping through the fingers.

Snake lifted Mist from her shoulders and pulled the blanket from Stavin's small body. The tumor pressed up beneath his rib cage, distorting his form, squeezing his vital organs, sucking nourishment from him for its own growth, poisoning him with its wastes. Holding Mist's head, Snake let her flow across him, touching and tasting him. She had to restrain the cobra to keep her from striking; the excitement had agitated her. When Sand used his rattle, the vibrations made her flinch. Snake stroked her, soothing her; trained and bred-in responses began to return, overcoming the natural instincts. Mist paused when her tongue flicked the skin above the tumor, and Snake released her.

The cobra reared and struck and bit as cobras bite, sinking her fangs their short length once, releasing, instantly biting again for a better purchase, holding on, chewing at her prey. Stavin cried out, but he did not move against Snake's restraining hands.

Mist expended the contents of her venom sacs into the child and released him. She reared up, peered around, folded her hood and slid across the mats in a perfectly straight line toward her dark close compartment.

"It's done, Stavin."

"Will I die now?"

"No," Snake said. "Not now. Not for many years, I hope." She took a vial of powder from her belt pouch. "Open your mouth." He complied, and she sprinkled the powder across his tongue. "That will help the ache." She spread a pad of cloth across the series of shallow puncture wounds without wiping off the blood.

She turned from him.

"Snake? Are you going away?"

"I will not leave without saying good-by. I promise."

The child lay back, closed his eyes and let the drug take him.

Sand coiled quiescently on the dark matting. Snake patted the floor to call him. He moved toward her and suffered himself to be replaced in the satchel. Snake closed it and lifted it and it still felt empty. She heard noises outside the tent. Stavin's parents and the people who had come to help them pulled open the tent flap and peered inside, thrusting sticks in even before they looked.

Snake set down her leather case. "It's done."

They entered. Arevin was with them too; only he was empty-handed. "Snake . . ." He spoke through grief, pity, confusion, and Snake could not tell what he believed. He looked back. Stavin's mother was just behind him. He took her by the shoulder. "He would have died without her. Whatever happens now, he would have died."

She shook his hand away. "He might have lived. It might have gone away. We . . ." She could speak no more for hiding tears.

Snake felt the people moving, surrounding her. Arevin took one step toward her and stopped, and she could see he wanted her to defend herself. "Can any of you cry?" she said. "Can any of you cry for me and my despair, or for them and their guilt, or for small things and their pain?" She felt tears slip down her cheeks.

They did not understand her; they were offended by her crying. They stood back, still afraid of her, but gathering themselves. She no longer needed the pose of calmness she had used to deceive the child. "Ah, you fools." Her voice sounded brittle. "Stavin . . ."

Light from the entrance struck them. "Let me pass." The people in front of Snake moved aside for their leader. She stopped in front of Snake, ignoring the satchel her foot almost touched. "Will Stavin live?" Her voice was quiet, calm, gentle.

"I cannot be certain," Snake said, "but I feel that he will."

"Leave us." The people understood Snake's words before they did their leader's; they looked around and lowered their weapons, and finally, one by one, they moved out of the tent. Arevin remained. Snake felt the strength that came from danger seeping from her. Her knees collapsed. She bent over the satchel with her face in her hands. The older woman knelt in front of her before Snake could notice or prevent her. "Thank you," she said. "Thank you. I am so sorry . . ." She put her arms around Snake and drew her toward her, and Arevin knelt beside them, and he embraced Snake too. Snake began to tremble again, and they held her while she cried.

Later she slept, exhausted, alone in the tent with Stavin, holding his hand. The people had caught small animals for Sand and Mist. They had given her food and supplies and sufficient water for her to bathe, though the last must have strained their resources.

When she awakened, Arevin lay sleeping nearby, his robe open in the heat, a sheen of sweat across his chest and stomach. The sternness in his expression vanished when he slept; he looked exhausted and vulnerable. Snake almost woke him, but stopped, shook her head and turned to Stavin.

She felt the tumor and found that it had begun to dissolve and shrivel, dying, as Mist's changed poison affected it. Through her grief Snake felt a little joy. She smoothed Stavin's pale hair back from his face. "I would not lie to you again, little one," she whispered, "but I must leave soon. I cannot stay here." She wanted another three days' sleep to finish fighting off the effects of the bush viper's poison, but she would sleep somewhere else. "Stavin?"

He half woke, slowly. "It doesn't hurt any more," he said.

"I am glad."

"Thank you . . ."

"Good-by, Stavin. Will you remember later on that you woke up, and that I did stay to say good-by?"

"Good-by," he said, drifting off again. "Good-by, Snake. Good-by, Grass." He closed his eyes.

Snake picked up the satchel and stood gazing down at Arevin. He did not stir. Half grateful, half regretful, she left the tent.

Dusk approached with long, indistinct shadows; the camp was hot and quiet. She found her tiger-striped pony, tethered with food and water. New, full waterskins bulged on the ground next to the saddle, and desert robes lay across the pommel, though Snake had refused any payment. The tiger-pony whickered at her. She scratched his striped ears, saddled him and strapped her gear on his back. Leading him, she started west, the way she had come.

"Snake . . ."

She took a breath and turned back to Arevin. He was facing the sun; it turned his skin ruddy and his robe scarlet. His streaked hair flowed loose to his shoulders, gentling his face. "You must leave?"

"Yes."

"I hoped you would not leave before . . . I hoped you would stay, for a time. . . ."

"If things were different, I might have stayed."

"They were frightened. . . ."

"I told them Grass couldn't hurt them, but they saw his fangs and they didn't know he could only give dreams and ease dying."

"But can't you forgive them?"

"I can't face their guilt. What they did was my fault, Arevin. I didn't understand them until too late."

"You said it yourself: you can't know all the customs and all the fears."

"I'm crippled," she said. "Without Grass, if I can't heal a person, I cannot help at all. I must go home and face my teachers and hope they'll forgive my stupidity. They seldom give the name I bear, but they gave it to me—and they'll be disappointed."

"Let me come with you."

She wanted to; she hesitated and cursed herself for that weakness. "They may take Mist and Sand and cast me out, and you would be cast out too. Stay here, Arevin."

"It wouldn't matter."

"It would. After a while, we would hate each other. I don't know you, and you don't know me. We need calmness and quiet and time to understand each other well."

He came toward her and put his arms around her, and they stood embracing for a moment. When he raised his head, there were tears on his cheeks. "Please come back," he said. "Whatever happens, please come back."

"I will try," Snake said. "Next spring, when the winds stop, look for me. The spring after that, if I do not come, forget me. Wherever I am, if I live, I will forget you."

"I will look for you," Arevin said, and he would promise no more.

Snake picked up her pony's lead and started across the desert.

BARRY N. MALZBERG

A Galaxy Called Rome

This is a science fiction story that is partly about science fiction. "A Galaxy Called Rome" is an effort to deal seriously with the subject of science fiction and what it can contribute to our culture. It is testimony to the difficulties and importance of writing SF and working within its themes and conventions, and it is also an excellent introduction to the creative processes of the working author. And it is a fine story, besides.

In memory of John W. Campbell

I

This is not a novelette but a series of notes. The novelette cannot be truly written because it partakes of its time, which is distant and could be perceived only through the idiom and devices of that era.

Thus the piece, by virtue of these reasons and others too personal even for this variety of true confession, is little more than a set of constructions toward something less substantial . . . and, like the author, it cannot be completed.

II

The novelette would lean heavily upon two articles by the late John Campbell, for thirty-three years the editor of *Astounding/Analog,* which were written shortly before his untimely death on July 11, 1971, and appeared as editorials in his magazine later that year, the second being perhaps the last piece which will ever bear his by-line. They imagine a black galaxy which would result from the implosion of a neutron star, an implosion so mighty that gravitational forces unleashed would contain not only light itself but space and time; and *A Galaxy Called Rome* is his title, not mine, since he envisions a spacecraft that might be trapped within such a black galaxy and be unable to get out . . . because escape velocity would have to exceed the speed of light. All paths of travel would lead to this galaxy, then, none away. A galaxy called Rome.

III

Conceive then of a faster-than-light spaceship which would tumble into the black galaxy and would be unable to leave. Tumbling would be easy, or at least inevitable, since one of the characteristics of the black galaxy would be its *invisibility,* and there the ship would be. The story would then pivot on the efforts of the crew to get out. The ship is named *Skipstone.* It was completed in 3892. Five hundred people died so that it might fly, but in this age life is held even more cheaply than it is today.

Left to my own devices, I might be less interested in the escape problem than that of adjustment. Light housekeeping in an anterior sector of the universe; submission to the elements, a fine, ironic literary despair. This is not science fiction, however. Science fiction was created by Hugo Gernsback to show us the ways out of technological impasse. So be it.

IV

As interesting as the material was, I quailed even at this series of notes, let alone a polished, completed work. My personal life is my black hole, I felt like pointing out (who would listen?); my daughters provide more correct and sticky implosion than any neutron star, and the sound of the pulsars is as nothing to the music of the paddock area at Aqueduct racetrack in Ozone Park, Queens, on a clear summer Tuesday. "Enough of these breathtaking concepts, infinite distances, quasar leaps, binding messages amid the arms of the spiral nebula," I could have pointed out. "I know that there are those who find an ultimate truth there, but I am not one of them. I would rather dedicate the years of life remaining (my melodramatic streak) to an understanding of the agonies of this middle-class town in northern New Jersey; until I can deal with those, how can I comprehend Ridgefield Park, to say nothing of the extension of fission to include progressively heavier gases?" Indeed, I almost abided to this until it occurred to me that Ridgefield Park would forever be as mysterious as the stars and that one could not deny infinity merely to pursue a particular that would be impenetrable until the day of one's death.

So I decided to try the novelette, at least as this series of notes, although with some trepidation, but trepidation did not unsettle me, nor did I grieve, for my life is merely a set of notes for a life, and Ridgefield Park merely a rough working model of Trenton, in which, nevertheless, several thousand people live who cannot discern their right hands from their left, and also much cattle.

V

It is 3895. The spacecraft *Skipstone*, on an exploratory flight through the major and minor galaxies surrounding the Milky Way, falls into the black galaxy of a neutron star and is lost forever.

The captain of this ship, the only living consciousness of it, is its commander, Lena Thomas. True, the hold of the ship carries five hundred and fifteen of the dead sealed in gelatinous fix who will absorb unshielded gamma rays. True, these rays will at some time in the future hasten their reconstitution. True, again, that another part of the hold contains the prostheses of seven skilled engineers, male and female, who could be switched on at only slight inconvenience and would provide Lena not only with answers to any technical problems which would arise but with companionship to while away the long and grave hours of the *Skipstone*'s flight.

Lena, however, does not use the prosthesis, nor does she feel the necessity to. She is highly skilled and competent, at least in relation to the routine tasks of this testing flight, and she feels that to call for outside help would only be an admission of weakness, would be reported back to the bureau and lessen her potential for promotion. (She is right; the bureau has monitored every cubicle of this ship, both visually and biologically: she can see or do nothing which does not trace to a printout; they would not think well of her if she was dependent upon outside assistance.) Toward the embalmed she feels somewhat more; her condition rattling in the hold of the ship as it moves on tachyonic drive seems to approximate theirs: although they are deprived of consciousness, that quality seems to be almost irrelevant to the condition of hyperspace; and if there were any way that she could bridge their mystery, she might well address them. As it is, she must settle for imaginary dialogues and for long, quiescent periods when she will watch the monitors, watch the rainbow of hyperspace, the collision of the spectrum, and say nothing whatsoever.

Saying nothing will not do, however, and the fact is that Lena talks incessantly at times, if only to herself. This is good because the story should have much dialogue; dramatic incident is best impelled through straightforward characterization, and Lena's compulsive need, now and then, to state her condition and its relation to the spaces she occupies will satisfy this need.

In her conversation, of course, she often addresses the embalmed. "Consider," she says to them, some of them dead eight hundred years, others dead weeks, all of them stacked in the hold in relation to their status in life and their ability to hoard assets to pay for the process that will return them their lives, "consider what's going on here," pointing through the hold, the colors gleaming through the portholes onto her wrist, colors dancing in the air, her eyes quite full and maddened in this light, which does not indicate that she is mad but only that the condition of hyperspace itself is insane, the Michelson-Morley effect having a psychological as well as physical reality here. "Why it could be *me* dead and in the hold and all of you here in the dock watching the colors spin, it's all the same, all the same faster than light," and indeed the twisting and sliding effects of the tachyonic drive are such that at the moment of speech what Lena says is true.

The dead live; the living are dead, all slides and becomes jumbled together as she has noted; and were it not that their objective poles of consciousness were fixed by years of training and discipline, just as hers are transfixed by a different kind of training and discipline, she would press the levers to eject the dead one by one into the larger coffin of space, something which is indicated only as an emergency procedure under the gravest of terms and which would result in her removal from the bureau immediately upon her return. The dead are precious cargo; they are, in essence, paying for the experiments and must be handled with the greatest delicacy. "I will handle you with the greatest delicacy," Lena says in hyperspace, "and I will never let you go, little packages in my little prison," and so on, singing and chanting as the ship moves on somewhat in excess of one million miles per second, always accelerating; and yet, except for the colors, the nausea, the disorienting swing, her own mounting insanity, the terms of this story, she might be in the IRT Lexington Avenue local at rush hour, moving slowly uptown as circles of illness move through the fainting car in the bowels of summer.

VI

She is twenty-eight years old. Almost two thousand years in the future, when man has established colonies on forty planets in the Milky Way, has fully populated the solar system, is working in the faster-than-light experiments as quickly as he can to move through other galaxies, the medical science of that day is not notably superior to that of our own, and the human life span has not been significantly extended, nor have the diseases of mankind which are now known as congenital been eradicated. Most of the embalmed were in their eighties or nineties; a few of them, the more recent deaths, were nearly a hundred, but the average life span still hangs somewhat short of eighty, and most of these have died from cancer, heart attacks, renal failure, cerebral blowout, and the like. There is some irony in the fact that man can have at least established a toehold in his galaxy, can have solved the mysteries of the FTL drive and yet finds the fact of his own biology as stupefying as he has throughout history, but every sociologist understands that those who live in a culture are least qualified to criticize it (because they have fully assimilated the codes of the culture, even as to criticism), and Lena does not see this irony any more than the reader will have to in order to appreciate the deeper and more metaphysical irony of the story, which is this: that greater speed, greater space, greater progress, greater sensation has not resulted in any definable expansion of the limits of consciousness and personality and all that the FTL drive is to Lena is an increasing entrapment.

It is important to understand that she is merely a technician; that although she is highly skilled and has been trained through the bureau for many years for her job as pilot, she really does not need to possess the technical knowledge of any graduate scientists of our own time . . . that her job, which is essentially a probe-and-ferrying, could be done by an adolescent; and that all of her training has afforded her no protection against the boredom and depression of her assignment.

When she is done with this latest probe, she will return to Uranus and be granted a six-month leave. She is looking forward to that. She appreciates the opportunity. She is only twenty-eight, and she is tired of being sent with the dead to tumble through the spectrum for weeks at a time, and what she would very much like to be, at least for a while, is a young woman. She would like to be at peace. She would like to be loved. She would like to have sex.

VII

Something must be made of the element of sex in this story, if only because it deals with a female protagonist (where asepsis will not work); and in the tradition of modern literary science fiction, where some credence is given to the whole range of human needs and behaviors, it would be clumsy and amateurish to ignore the issue. Certainly the easy scenes can be written and to great effect: Lena masturbating as she stares through the port at the colored levels of hyperspace; Lena dreaming thickly of intercourse as she unconsciously massages her nipples, the ship plunging deeper and deeper (as she does not yet know) toward the black galaxy; the black galaxy itself as some ultimate vaginal symbol of absorption whose Freudian overcast will not be ignored in the imagery of this story . . . indeed, one can envision Lena stumbling toward the evictors at the depths of her panic in the black galaxy to bring out one of the embalmed, her grim and necrophiliac fantasies as the body is slowly moved upwards on its glistening slab, the way that her eyes will look as she comes to consciousness and realizes what she has become . . . oh, this would be a very powerful scene indeed, almost anything to do with sex in space is powerful (one must also conjure with the effects of hyperspace upon the orgasm; would it be the orgasm which all of us know and love so well or something entirely different, perhaps detumescence, perhaps exaltation?), and I would face the issue squarely, if only I could, and in line with the very real need of the story to have powerful and effective dialogue.

"For God's sake," Lena would say at the end, the music of her entrapment squeezing her, coming over her, blotting her toward extinction, "for God's sake, all we ever needed was a fuck, that's all that sent us out into space, that's all that it ever meant to us, I've got to have it, got to have it, do you understand?" jamming her fingers in and out of her aqueous surfaces. . . .

But of course this would not work, at least in the story which I am trying to conceptualize. Space *is* aseptic; that is the secret of science fiction for forty-five years; it is not deceit or its adolescent audience or the publication codes which have deprived most of the literature of the range of human sexuality but the fact that in the clean and abysmal spaces between the stars sex, that demonstration of our perverse and irreplaceable humanity, would have no role at all. Not for nothing did the astronauts return to tell us their vision of otherworldness, not for nothing did they stagger in their thick landing gear as they walked toward the colonels' salute, not for nothing did all of those marriages, all of those wonderful kids undergo such terrible strains. There is simply no room for it. It does not fit. Lena would understand this. "I never thought of sex," she would say, "never thought of it once, not even at the end when everything was around me and I was dancing."

VIII

Therefore it will be necessary to characterize Lena in some other way, and that opportunity will only come through the moment of crisis, the moment at which the *Skipstone* is drawn into the black galaxy of the neutron star. This moment will occur fairly early in the story, perhaps five or six hundred words deep (her previous life on the ship and impressions of hyperspace will come in expository chunks interwoven between sections of ongoing action), and her only indication of what has happened will be when there is a deep, lurching shiver in the gut of the ship where the embalmed lay and then she feels herself falling.

To explain this sensation it is important to explain normal hyperspace, the skip-drive which is merely to draw the curtains and to be in a cubicle. There is no sensation of motion in hyperspace, there could not be, the drive taking the *Skipstone* past any concepts of sound or light and into an area where there is no language to encompass nor glands to register. Were she to draw the curtains (curiously similar in their frills and pastels to what we might see hanging today in lower-middle-class homes of the kind I inhabit), she would be deprived of any sensation, but of course she cannot; she must open them to the portholes, and through them she can see the song of the colors to which I have previously alluded. Inside, there is a deep and grievous wretchedness, a feeling of terrible loss (which may explain why Lena thinks of exhuming the dead) that may be ascribed to the effects of hyperspace upon the corpus; but these sensations can be shielded, are not visible from the outside and can be completely controlled by the phlegmatic types who comprise most of the pilots of these experimental flights. (Lena is rather phlegmatic herself. She reacts more to stress than some of her counterparts but well within the normal range prescribed by the bureau, which admittedly does a superficial check.)

The effects of falling into the black galaxy are entirely different however, and it is here where Lena's emotional equipment becomes completely unstuck.

IX

At this point in the story great gobs of physics, astronomical and mathematic data would have to be incorporated, hopefully in a way which would furnish the hard-science basis of the story without repelling the reader.

Of course one should not worry so much about the repulsion of the reader; most who read science fiction do so in pursuit of exactly this kind of hard speculation (most often they are disappointed, but then most often they are, after a time, unable to tell the difference), and they would sit still much longer for a lecture than would, say, readers of the fiction of John Cheever, who could hardly bear sociological diatribes wedged into the everlasting vision of Gehenna which is Cheever's gift to his admirers. Thus it would be possible without awkwardness to make the following facts known, and these facts could indeed be set off from the body of the story and simply told like this:

It is posited that in other galaxies there are such as neutron stars, stars of four or five hundred times the size of our own or "normal" suns, which in their continuing nuclear process, burning and burning to maintain their light, will collapse in a mere ten to fifteen thousand years of difficult existence, their hydrogen fusing to helium then nitrogen and then to even heavier elements until with an implosion of terrific force, hungering for power which is no longer there, they collapse upon one another and bring disaster.

Disaster not only to themselves but possibly to the entire galaxy which they inhabit, for the gravitational force created by the implosion would be so vast as to literally seal in light. Not only light but sound and properties of all the stars in that great tube of force . . . so that the galaxy itself would be sucked into the funnel of gravitation created by the collapse and be absorbed into the flickering and desperate heart of the extinguished star.

It is possible to make several extrapolations from the fact of the neutron stars—and of the neutron stars themselves we have no doubt; many nova and supernova are now known to have been created by exactly this effect, not *ex*- but *im*plosion—and some of them are these:

> (a) The gravitational forces created, like great spokes wheeling out from the star, would drag in all parts of the galaxy within their compass; and because of the force of that gravitation, the galaxy would be invisible. . . . These forces would, as has been said, literally contain light.
> (b) The neutron star, functioning like a cosmic vacuum cleaner, might literally destroy the universe. Indeed, the universe may be in the slow process at this moment of being destroyed as hundreds of millions of its suns and planets are being inexorably drawn toward these great vortexes.

The process would be *slow,* of course, but it is seemingly inexorable. One neutron star, theoretically, could absorb the universe. There are many more than one.

(c) The universe may have, obversely, been *created* by such an implosion, throwing out enormous cosmic filaments that, in a flickering instant of time which is as eons to us but an instant to the cosmologists, are now being drawn back in. The universe may be an accident.

(d) Cosmology aside, a ship trapped in such a vortex, such a "black," or invisible, galaxy, drawn toward the deadly source of the neutron star would be unable to leave it through normal faster-than-light drive . . . because the gravitation would absorb light, it would be impossible to build up any level of acceleration (which would at some point not exceed the speed of light) to permit escape. If it were possible to emerge from the field, it could only be done by an immediate switch to tachyonic drive without accelerative buildup . . . a process which could drive the occupant insane and which would, in any case, have no clear destination. The black hole of the dead star is a literal vacuum in space . . . one could fall through the hole, but where, then, would one go?

(e) The actual process of being in the field of the dead star might well drive one insane.

For all of these reasons Lena does not know that she has fallen into the galaxy called Rome until the ship simply does so.

And she would instantly and irreparably become insane.

X

The technological data having been stated, the crisis of the story—the collapse into the galaxy—having occurred early on, it would now be the obligation of the writer to describe the actual sensations involved in falling into the black galaxy. Since little or nothing is known of what these sensations would be—other than that it is clear that the gravitation would suspend almost all physical laws and might well suspend time itself, time only being a function of physics—it would be easy to lurch into a surrealistic mode here; Lena could see monsters slithering on the walls, two-dimensional monsters that is, little cutouts of her past; she could reenact her life *in full consciousness* from birth until death; she could literally be turned inside out anatomically and perform in her imagination or in the flesh gross physical acts upon herself; she could live and die a thousand times in the lightless, timeless expanse of the pit. . . . All of this could be done within the confines of the story, and it would doubtless lead to some very powerful material. One could do it picaresque fashion, one perversity or lunacy to a chapter—that is to say, the chapters spliced together with more data on the gravitational excesses and the fact that neutron stars (this is interesting) are probably the pulsars which we have identified, stars which can be detected through sound but not by sight from unimaginable distances. The author could do this kind of thing and do it very well indeed; he has done it literally hundreds of times before, but this, perhaps, would be in disregard of Lena. She has needs more imperative than those of the author or even those of the editors. She is in terrible pain. She is suffering.

Falling, she sees the dead; falling, she hears the dead; the dead address her from the hold, and they are screaming, "Release us, release us, we are alive, we are in pain, we are in torment"; in their gelatinous flux, their distended limbs sutured finger and toe to the membranes which hold them, their decay has been reversed as the warp into which they have fallen has reversed time; and they are begging Lena from a torment which they cannot phrase, so profound is it; their voices are in her head, pealing and banging like oddly shaped bells. "Release us!" they scream; "we are no longer dead, the trumpet has sounded!" and so on and so forth, but Lena literally does not know what to do. She is merely the ferryman on this dread passage; she is not a medical specialist; she knows nothing of prophylaxis or restoration, and any movement she made to release them from the gelatin which holds them would surely destroy their biology, no matter what the state of their minds.

But even if this were not so, even if she could by releasing them give them peace, she cannot because she is succumbing to her own responses. In the black hole, if the dead are risen, then the risen are certainly the dead; she dies in this space, Lena does; she dies a thousand times over a period of seventy thousand years (because there is no objective time here, chronology is controlled only by the psyche, and Lena has a thousand full lives and a thousand full deaths), and it is terrible, of course, but it is also interesting because for every cycle of death there is a life, seventy years in which she can meditate upon her condition in solitude; and by the two hundredth death, the fourteen thousandth year or more (or less, each of the lives is individual, some of them long, others short), Lena has come to an understanding of exactly where she is and what has happened to her. That it has taken her fourteen thousand years to reach this understanding is in one way incredible, and yet it is a kind of miracle as well because in an infinite universe with infinite possibilities, all of them reconstituted for her, it is highly unlikely that even in fourteen thousand years she would stumble upon the answer, had it not been for the fact that she is unusually strong-willed and that some of the personalities through which she has lived are highly creative and controlled and have been able to do some serious thinking. Also there is a carryover from life to life, even with the differing personalities, so that she is able to make use of preceding knowledge.

Most of the personalities are weak, of course, and not a few are insane, and almost all are cowardly, but there is a little residue; even in the worst of them there is enough residue to carry forth the knowledge, and so it is in the fourteen thousandth year, when the truth of it has finally come upon her and she realizes what has happened to her and what is going on and what she must do to get out of there, and so it is (then) that she summons all of the strength and will which are left to her and stumbling to the console (she is in her sixty-eighth year of this life and in the personality of an old, sniveling, whining man, an ex-ferryman himself), she summons one of the prostheses, the master engineer, the controller. All of this time the dead have been shrieking and clanging in her ears, fourteen thousand years of agony billowing from the hold and surrounding her in sheets like iron; and as the master engineer, exactly as he was when she last saw him fourteen thousand years and two weeks ago emerges from the console, the machinery whirring slickly, she gasps in relief, too weak even to respond with pleasure to the fact that in this condition of antitime, antilight, anticausality the machinery still works. But then it would. The machinery always works, even in this final and most terrible of all the hard-science stories. It is not the machinery which fails but its operators or, in extreme cases, the cosmos.

"What's the matter?" the master engineer says.

The stupidity of this question, its naiveté and irrelevance in the midst of the hell she has occupied, stuns Lena, but she realizes even through the haze that the master engineer would, of course, come without memory of circumstances and would have to be apprised of background. This is inevitable. Whining and sniveling, she tells him in her old man's voice what has happened.

"Why that's terrible!" the master engineer says. "That's really terrible," and lumbering to a porthole, he looks out at the black galaxy, the galaxy called Rome, and one look at it causes him to lock into position and then disintegrate, not because the machinery has failed (the machinery never fails, not ultimately) but because it has merely recreated a human substance which could not possibly come to grips with what has been seen outside that porthole.

Lena is left alone again, then, with the shouts of the dead carrying forward.

Realizing instantly what has happened to her—fourteen thousand years of perception can lead to a quicker reaction time, if nothing else—she addresses the console again, uses the switches and produces three more prostheses, all of them engineers barely subsidiary to the one she has already addressed. (Their resemblance to the three comforters of Job will not be ignored here, and there will be an opportunity to squeeze in some quick religous allegory, which is always useful to give an ambitious story yet another level of meaning.) Although they are not quite as qualified or definitive in their opinions as the original engineer, they are bright enough by far to absorb her explanation, and this time her warnings not to go to the portholes, not to look upon the galaxy, are heeded. Instead, they stand there in rigid and curiously mortified postures, as if waiting for Lena to speak.

"So you see," she says finally, as if concluding a long and difficult conversation, which in fact she has, "as far as I can see, the only way to get out of this black galaxy is to go directly into tachyonic drive. Without any accelerative buildup at all."

The three comforters nod slowly, bleakly. They do not quite know what she is talking about, but then again, they have not had fourteen thousand years to ponder this point. "Unless you can see anything else," Lena says, "unless you can think of anything different. Otherwise, it's going to be infinity in here, and I can't take much more of this, really. Fourteen thousand years is enough."

"Perhaps," the first comforter suggests softly, "perhaps it is your fate and your destiny to spend infinity in this black hole. Perhaps in some way you are determining the fate of the universe. After all, it was you who said that it all might be a gigantic accident, eh? Perhaps your suffering gives it purpose."

"And then too," the second lisps, "you've got to consider the dead down there. This isn't very easy for them, you know, what with being jolted alive and all that, and an immediate vault into tachyonic would probably destroy them for good. The bureau wouldn't like that, and you'd be liable for some pretty stiff damages. No, if I were you I'd stay with the dead," the second concludes, and a clamorous murmur seems to arise from the hold at this, although whether it is one of approval or of terrible pain is difficult to tell. The dead are not very expressive.

"Anyway," the third says, brushing a forelock out of his eyes, averting his glance from the omnipresent and dreadful portholes, "there's little enough to be done about this situation. You've fallen into a neutron star, a black funnel. It is utterly beyond the puny capacities and possibilities of man. I'd accept my fate if I were you." His model was a senior scientist working on quasar theory, but in reality he appears to be a metaphysician. "There are corners of experience into which man cannot stray without being severely penalized."

"That's very easy for you to say," Lena says bitterly, her whine breaking into clear glissando, "but you haven't suffered as I have. Also, there's at least a theoretical possibility that I'll get out of here if I do the buildup without acceleration."

"But where will you land?" the third says, waving a trembling forefinger. "And when? All rules of space and time have been destroyed here; only gravity persists. You can fall through the center of this sun, but you do not know where you will come out or at what period of time. It is inconceivable that you would emerge into normal space in the time you think of as contemporary."

"No," the second says. "I wouldn't do that. You and the dead are joined together now; it is truly your fate to remain with them. What is death? What is life? In the galaxy called Rome all roads lead to the same, you see; you have ample time to consider these questions, and I'm sure that you will come up with something truly viable, of much interest."

"Ah, well," the first says, looking at Lena, "if you must know, I think that it would be much nobler of you to remain here; for all we know, your condition gives substance and viability to the universe. Perhaps you *are* the universe. But you're not going to listen anyway, and so I won't argue the point. I really won't," he says rather petulantly and then makes a gesture to the other two; the three of them quite deliberately march to a porthole, push a curtain aside and look out upon it. Before Lena can stop them—not that she is sure she would, not that she is sure that this is not exactly what she has willed—they have been reduced to ash.

And she is left alone with the screams of the dead.

XI

It can be seen that the satiric aspects of the scene above can be milked for great implication, and unless a very skillful controlling hand is kept upon the material, the piece could easily degenerate into farce at this moment. It is possible, as almost any comedian knows, to reduce (or elevate) the starkest and most terrible issues to scatology or farce simply by particularizing them; and it will be hard not to use this scene for a kind of needed comic relief in what is, after all, an extremely depressing tale, the more depressing because it has used the largest possible canvas on which to imprint its messages that man is irretrievably dwarfed by the cosmos. (At least, that is the message which it would be easiest to wring out of the material; actually I have other things in mind, but how many will be able to detect them?)

What will save the scene and the story itself, around this point, will be the lush physical descriptions of the black galaxy, the neutron star, the altering effects they have had upon perceived reality. Every rhetorical trick, every typographical device, every nuance of language and memory which the writer has to call upon will be utilized in this section describing the appearance of the black hole and its effects upon Lena's (admittedly distorted) consciousness. It will be a bleak vision, of course, but not necessarily a hopeless one; it will demonstrate that our concepts of "beauty" or "ugliness" or "evil" or "good" or "love" or "death" are little more than metaphors, semantically limited, framed in by the poor receiving equipment in our heads; and it will be suggested that, rather than showing us a different or alternative reality, the black hole may only be showing us the only reality we know, but *extended*, infinitely extended so that the story may give us, as good science fiction often does, at this point some glimpse of possibilities beyond ourselves, possibilities not to be contained in word rates or the problems of editorial qualification. And also at this point of the story it might be worthwhile to characterize Lena in a "warmer" and more "sympathetic" fashion so that the reader can see her as a distinct and admirable human being, quite plucky in the face of all her disasters and fourteen thousand years, two hundred lives. This can be done through conventional fictional technique: individuation through defining idiosyncrasy, tricks of speech, habits, mannerisms, and so on. In common everyday fiction we could give her an affecting stutter, a dimple on her left breast, a love of policemen, fear of red convertibles, and leave it at that; in this story, because of its considerably extended theme, it will be necessary to do better than that, to find originalities of idiosyncrasy which will, in their wonder and suggestion of panoramic possibility, approximate the black hole . . . but no matter. No matter. This can be done; the section interweaving Lena and her vision of the black hole will be the flashiest and most admired but in truth the easiest section of the story to write, and I am sure that I would have no trouble with it whatsoever if, as I said much earlier, this were a story instead of a series of notes for a story, the story itself being unutterably beyond our time and space and devices and to be glimpsed only in empty little flickers of light much as Lena can glimpse the black hole, much as she knows the gravity of the neutron star. These notes are as close to the vision of the story as Lena herself would ever get.

As this section ends, it is clear that Lena has made her decision to attempt to leave the black galaxy by automatic boost to tachyonic drive. She does not know where she will emerge or how, but she does know that she can bear this no longer.

She prepares to set the controls, but before this it is necessary to write the dialogue with the dead.

XII

One of them presumably will appoint himself as the spokesman of the many and will appear before Lena in this new space as if in a dream. "Listen here," this dead would say, one born in 3361, dead in 3401, waiting eight centuries for exhumation to a society that can rid his body of leukemia (he is bound to be disappointed), "you've got to face the facts of the situation here. We can't just leave in this way. Better the death we know than the death you will give us."

"The decision is made," Lena says, her fingers straight on the controls. "There will be no turning back."

"We are dead now," the leukemic says. "At least let this death continue. At least in the bowels of this galaxy where there is no time we have a kind of life or at least that nonexistence of which we have always dreamed. I could tell you many of the things we have learned during these fourteen thousand years, but they would make little sense to you, of course. We have learned resignation. We have had great insights. Of course all of this would go beyond you."

"Nothing goes beyond me. Nothing at all. But it does not matter."

"Everything matters. Even here there is consequence, causality, a sense of humanness, one of responsibility. You can suspend physical laws, you can suspend life itself, but you cannot separate the moral imperatives of humanity. There are absolutes. It would be apostasy to try and leave."

"Man must leave," Lena says, "man must struggle, man must attempt to control his conditions. Even if he goes from worse to obliteration, that is still his destiny." Perhaps the dialogue is a little florid here. Nevertheless, this will be the thrust of it. It is to be noted that putting this conventional viewpoint in the character of a woman will give another of those necessary levels of irony with which the story must abound if it is to be anything other than a freak show, a cascade of sleazy wonders shown shamefully behind a tent . . . but irony will give it legitimacy. "I don't care about the dead," Lena says. "I only care about the living."

"Then care about the universe," the dead man says, "care about that, if nothing else. By trying to come out through the center of the black hole, you may rupture the seamless fabric of time and space itself. You may destroy everything. Past and present and future. The explosion may extend the funnel of gravitational force to infinite size, and all of the universe will be driven into the hole."

Lena shakes her head. She knows that the dead is merely another one of her tempters in a more cunning and cadaverous guise. "You are lying to me," she says. "This is merely another effect of the galaxy called Rome. I am responsible to myself, only to myself. The universe is not at issue."

"That's a rationalization," the leukemic says, seeing her hesitation, sensing his victory, "and you know it as well as I do. You can't be an utter solipsist. You aren't God, there is no God, not here, but if there was it wouldn't be you. You must measure the universe about yourself."

Lena looks at the dead and the dead looks at her; and in that confrontation, in the shade of his eyes as they pass through the dull lusters of the neutron star effect, she sees that they are close to a communion so terrible that it will become a weld, become a connection . . . that if she listens to the dead for more than another instant, she will collapse within those eyes as the *Skipstone* has collapsed into the black hole; and she cannot bear this, it cannot be . . . she must hold to the belief, that there is some separation between the living and the dead and that there is dignity in that separation, that life is not death but something else because, if she cannot accept that, she denies herself . . . and quickly then, quickly before she can consider further, she hits the controls that will convert the ship instantly past the power of light; and then in the explosion of many suns that might only be her heart she hides her head in her arms and screams.

And the dead screams with her, and it is not a scream of joy but not of terror either. . . . It is the true natal cry suspended between the moments of limbo, life and expiration, and their shrieks entwine in the womb of the *Skipstone* as it pours through into the redeemed light.

XIII

The story is open-ended, of course.

Perhaps Lena emerges into her own time and space once more, all of this having been a sheath over the greater reality. Perhaps she emerges into an otherness. Then again, she may never get out of the black hole at all but remain and live there, the *Skipstone* a planet in the tubular universe of the neutron star, the first or last of a series of planets collapsing toward their deadened sun. If the story is done correctly, if the ambiguities are prepared right, if the technological data are stated well, if the material is properly visualized . . . well, it does not matter then what happens to Lena, her *Skipstone* and her dead. Any ending will do. Any would suffice and be emotionally satisfying to the reader.

Still, there is an inevitable ending.

It seems clear to the writer, who will not, cannot write this story, but if he did he would drive it through to this one conclusion, the conclusion clear, implied really from the first and bound, bound utterly, into the text.

So let the author have it.

XIV

In the infinity of time and space, all is possible, and as they are vomited from that great black hole, spilled from this anus of a neutron star (I will not miss a single Freudian implication if I can), Lena and her dead take on this infinity, partake of the vast canvas of possibility. Now they are in the Antares Cluster flickering like a bulb; here they are at the heart of Sirius the Dog Star, five hundred screams from the hold; here again in ancient Rome watching Jesus trudge up carrying the cross of Calvary . . . and then again in another unimaginable galaxy dead across from the Milky Way a billion light-years in span with a hundred thousand habitable planets, each of them with its Calvary . . . and they are not, they are not yet satisfied.

They cannot, being human, partake of infinity; they can partake only of what they know. They cannot, being created from the consciousness of the writer, partake of what he does not know but what is only close to him. Trapped within the consciousness of the writer, the penitentiary of his being, as the writer is himself trapped in the *Skipstone* of his mortality, Lena and her dead emerge in the year 1975 to the town of Ridgefield Park, New Jersey, and there they inhabit the bodies of its fifteen thousand souls, and there they are, there they are yet, dwelling amid the refineries, strolling on Main Street, sitting in the Rialto theater, shopping in the supermarkets, pairing off and clutching one another in the imploded stars of their beds on this very night at this very moment, as that accident, the author, himself one of them, has conceived them.

It is unimaginable that they would come, Lena and the dead, from the heart of the galaxy called Rome to tenant Ridgefield Park, New Jersey . . . but more unimaginable still that from all the Ridgefield Parks of our time we will come and assemble and build the great engines which will take us to the stars and some of the stars will bring us death and some bring life and some will bring nothing at all but the engines will go on and on and so—after a fashion, in our fashion—will we.

DAMON KNIGHT
Stranger Station

Humans fear the unknown. In fact, they frequently fear each other because of such minor differences as skin color, accent or general appearance. One of science fiction's great contributions is an emphasis on the macroview, on the necessity of eliminating microdifferences in the name of species survival. But what of encounters with other species? How do we reach understanding, overcome fear? And how do we interact with a species that is completely different from our own?

The clang of metal echoed hollowly down through the station's many vaulted corridors and rooms. Paul Wesson stood listening for a moment as the rolling echoes died away. The maintenance rocket was gone, heading back to Home; they had left him alone in Stranger Station.

Stranger Station! The name itself quickened his imagination. Wesson knew that both orbital stations had been named a century ago by the then-British administration of the satellite service; "Home" because the larger, inner station handled the traffic of Earth and its colonies; "Stranger" because the outer station was designed specifically for dealings with foreigners—beings from outside the solar system. But even that could not diminish the wonder of Stranger Station, whirling out here alone in the dark—waiting for its once-in-two-decades visitor. . . .

One man, out of all Sol's billions, had the task and privilege of enduring the alien's presence when it came. The two races, according to Wesson's understanding of the subject, were so fundamentally different that it was painful for them to meet. Well, he had volunteered for the job, and he thought he could handle it—the rewards were big enough.

He had gone through all the tests, and against his own expectations he had been chosen. The maintenance crew had brought him up as dead weight, drugged in a survival hamper; they had kept him the same way while they did their work and then had brought him back to consciousness. Now they were gone. He was alone.

But not quite.

"Welcome to Stranger Station, Sergeant Wesson," said a pleasant voice. "This is your alpha network speaking. I'm here to protect and serve you in every way. If there's anything you want, just ask me." It was a neutral voice, with the kind of professional friendliness in it, like that of a good schoolteacher or rec supervisor.

Wesson had been warned, but he was still shocked at the human quality of it. The alpha networks were the last word in robot brains—computers, safety devices, personal servants, libraries, all wrapped up in one, with something so close to "personality" and "free will" that experts were still arguing the question. They were rare and fantastically expensive; Wesson had never met one before.

"Thanks," he said now, to the empty air. "Uh—what do I call you, by the way? I can't keep saying, 'Hey, alpha network.' "

"One of your recent predecessors called me Aunt Nettie," was the response.

Wesson grimaced. Alpha network—Aunt Nettie. He hated puns; that wouldn't do. "The aunt part is all right," he said. "Suppose I call you Aunt Jane. That was my mother's sister; you sound like her, a little bit."

"I am honored," said the invisible mechanism politely. "Can I serve you any refreshments now? Sandwiches? A drink?"

"Not just yet," said Wesson. "I think I'll look the place over first."

He turned away. That seemed to end the conversation as far as the network was concerned. A good thing; it was all right to have it for company, speaking when spoken to, but if it got talkative. . . .

The human part of the station was in four segments: bedroom, living room, dining room, bath. The living room was comfortably large and pleasantly furnished in greens and tans; the only mechanical note in it was the big instrument console in one corner. The other rooms, arranged in a ring around the living room, were tiny; just space enough for Wesson, a narrow encircling corridor and the mechanisms that would serve him. The whole place was spotlessly clean, gleaming and efficient in spite of its twenty-year layoff.

This is the gravy part of the run, Wesson told himself. The month before the alien came—good food, no work and an alpha network for conversation. "Aunt Jane, I'll have a small steak now," he said to the network. "Medium rare with hashed brown potatoes, onions and mushrooms and a glass of lager. Call me when it's ready."

"Right," said the voice pleasantly. Out in the dining room, the autochef began to hum and cluck self-importantly. Wesson wandered over and inspected the instrument console. Airlocks were sealed and tight, said the dials; the air was cycling. The station was in orbit and rotating on its axis with a force at the perimeter, where Wesson was, of one *g*. The internal temperature of this part of the station was an even seventy-three degrees.

The other side of the board told a different story; all the dials were dark and dead. Sector Two, occupying a volume some eighty-eight thousand times as great as this one, was not yet functioning.

Wesson had a vivid mental image of the station from photographs and diagrams—a five-hundred-foot Duralumin sphere onto which the shallow thirty-foot disk of the human section had been stuck apparently as an afterthought. The whole cavity of the sphere, very nearly—except for a honeycomb of supply and maintenance rooms and the all-important, recently enlarged vats —was one cramped chamber for the alien. . . .

"Steak's ready!" said Aunt Jane.

The steak was good, bubbling crisp outside the way he liked it, tender and pink inside. "Aunt Jane," he said with his mouth full, "this is pretty soft, isn't it?"

"The steak?" asked the voice, with a faintly anxious note.

Wesson grinned. "Never mind," he said. "Listen, Aunt Jane, you've been through this routine—how many times? Were you installed with the station, or what?"

"I was not installed with the station," said Aunt Jane primly. "I have assisted at three contacts."

"Um. Cigarette," said Wesson, slapping his pockets. The autochef hummed for a moment and popped a pack of GIs out of a vent. Wesson lighted up. "All right," he said, "you've been through this three times. There are a lot of things you can tell me, right?"

"Oh, yes, certainly. What would you like to know?"

Wesson smoked, leaning back reflectively, green eyes narrowed. "First," he said, "read me the Pigeon report—you know, from the *Brief History*. I want to see if I remember it right."

"Chapter Two," said the voice promptly. "First contact with a non-Solar intelligence was made by Commander Ralph C. Pigeon on July 1, 1987, during an emergency landing on Titan. The following is an excerpt from his official report:

" 'While searching for a possible cause for our mental disturbance, we discovered what appeared to be a gigantic construction of metal on the far side of the ridge. Our distress grew stronger with the approach to this construction, which was polyhedral and approximately five times the length of the *Cologne*.

" 'Some of those present expressed a wish to retire, but Lieutenant Acuff and myself had a strong sense of being called or summoned in some indefinable way. Although our uneasiness was not lessened, we therefore agreed to go forward and keep radio contact with the rest of the party while they returned to the ship.

" 'We gained access to the alien construction by way of a large, irregular opening. . . . The internal temperature was minus seventy-five degrees Fahrenheit; the atmosphere appeared to consist of methane and ammonia. . . . Inside the second chamber, an alien creature was waiting for us. We felt the distress, which I have tried to describe, to a much greater degree than before, and also the sense of summoning or pleading. . . . We observed that the creature was exuding a thick yellowish fluid from certain joints or pores in its surface. Though disgusted, I managed to collect a sample of this exudate, and it was later forwarded for analysis. . . .'

"The second contact was made ten years later by Commodore Crawford's famous Titan Expedition. . . ."

"No, that's enough," said Wesson. "I just wanted the Pigeon quote." He smoked, brooding. "It seems kind of chopped off, doesn't it? Have you got a longer version in your memory banks anywhere?"

There was a pause. "No," said Aunt Jane.

"There was more to it when I was a kid," Wesson complained nervously. "I read that book when I was twelve, and I remember a long description of the alien—that is, I remember its being there." He swung around. "Listen, Aunt Jane—you're a sort of universal watchdog, that right? You've got cameras and mikes all over the station?"

"Yes," said the network, sounding—was it Wesson's imagination?—faintly injured.

"Well, what about Sector Two? You must have cameras up there, too, isn't that so?"

"Yes."

"All right, then you can tell me. What do the aliens look like?"

There was a definite pause. "I'm sorry, I can't tell you that," said Aunt Jane.

"No," said Wesson, "I didn't think you could. You've got orders not to, I guess, for the same reason those history books have been cut since I was a kid. Now, what would the reason be? Have you got any idea, Aunt Jane?"

There was another pause. "Yes," the voice admitted.

"Well?"

"I'm sorry, I can't . . ."

". . . tell you that," Wesson repeated along with it. "All right. At least we know where we stand."

"Yes, sergeant. Would you like some dessert?"

"No dessert. One other thing. *What happens to station watchmen, like me, after their tour of duty?*"

"They are upgraded to Class Seven, students with unlimited leisure, and receive outright gifts of seven thousand stellors, plus free Class One housing. . . ."

"Yeah, I know all that," said Wesson, licking his dry lips. "But here's what I'm asking you. The ones you know—what kind of shape were they in when they left here?"

"The usual human shape," said the voice brightly. "Why do you ask, sergeant?"

Wesson made a discontented gesture. "Something I remember from a bull session at the academy. I can't get it out of my head; I know it had something to do with the station. Just a part of a sentence: '. . . blind as a bat and white bristles all over. . . .' Now, would that be a description of the alien—or the watchman when they came to take him away?"

Aunt Jane went into one of her heavy pauses. "All right, I'll save you the trouble," said Wesson. "You're sorry, you can't tell me that."

"I *am* sorry," said the robot sincerely.

As the slow days passed into weeks, Wesson grew aware of the station almost as a living thing. He could feel its resilient metal ribs enclosing him, lightly bearing his weight with its own as it swung. He could feel the waiting emptiness "up there," and he sensed the alert electronic network that spread around him everywhere, watching and probing, trying to anticipate his needs.

Aunt Jane was a model companion. She had a record library of thousands of hours of music; she had films to show him, and microprinted books that he could read on the scanner in the living room; or if he preferred, she would read to him. She controlled the station's three telescopes, and on request would give him a view of Earth or the moon or Home. . . .

But there was no news. Aunt Jane would obligingly turn on the radio receiver if he asked her, but nothing except static came out. That was the thing that weighed most heavily on Wesson, as time passed—the knowledge that radio silence was being imposed on all ships in transit, on the orbital station and on the planet-to-space transmitters. It was an enormous, almost a crippling handicap. Some information could be transmitted over relatively short distances by photophone, but ordinarily the whole complex traffic of the space lanes depended on radio.

But this coming alien contact was so delicate a thing that even a radio voice, out here where the Earth was only a tiny disk twice the size of the moon, might upset it. It was so precarious a thing, Wesson thought, that only one man could be allowed in the station while the alien was there, and to give that man the company that would keep him sane, they had to install an alpha network. . . .

"Aunt Jane?"

The voice answered promptly, "Yes, Paul."

"This distress that the books talk about—you wouldn't know what it is, would you?"

"No, Paul."

"Because robot brains don't feel it, right?"

"Right, Paul."

"So tell me this—why do they need a man here at all? Why can't they get along with just you?"

A pause. "I don't know, Paul." The voice sounded faintly wistful. Were those gradations of tone really in it, Wesson wondered, or was his imagination supplying them?

He got up from the living room couch and paced restlessly back and forth. "Let's have a look at Earth," he said. Obediently, the viewing screen on the console glowed into life: there was the blue Earth, swimming deep below him in its first quarter, jewel bright. "Switch it off," Wesson said.

"A little music?" suggested the voice and immediately began to play something soothing, full of woodwinds.

"*No,*" said Wesson. The music stopped.

Wesson's hands were trembling; he had a caged and frustrated feeling.

The fitted suit was in its locker beside the airlock. Wesson had been topside in it once or twice; there was nothing to see up there, just darkness and cold. But he had to get out of this squirrel cage. He took the suit down and began to get into it.

"Paul," said Aunt Jane anxiously, "are you feeling nervous?"

"Yes," he snarled.

"Then don't go into Sector Two," said Aunt Jane.

"Don't tell me what to do, you hunk of tin!" said Wesson with sudden anger. He zipped up the front of his suit with a vicious motion.

Aunt Jane was silent.

Seething, Wesson finished his checkoff and opened the lock door.

The airlock, an upright tube barely large enough for one man, was the only passage between Sector One and Sector Two. It was also the only exit from Sector One; to get here in the first place, Wesson had had to enter the big lock at the "south" pole of the sphere and travel all the way down inside, by drop hole and catwalk. He had been drugged unconscious at the time, of course. When the time came, he would go out the same way; neither the maintenance rocket nor the tanker had any space, or time, to spare.

At the "north" pole, opposite, there was a third airlock, this one so huge it could easily have held an interplanet freighter. But that was nobody's business—no human being's.

In the beam of Wesson's helmet lamp, the enormous central cavity of the station was an inky gulf that sent back only remote, mocking glimmers of light. The near walls sparkled with hoarfrost. Sector Two was not yet pressurized; there was only a diffuse vapor that had leaked through the airseal and had long since frozen into the powdery deposit that lined the walls. The metal rang cold under his shod feet; the vast emptiness of the chamber was the more depressing because it was airless, unwarmed and unlit. *Alone,* said his footsteps; *alone. . . .*

He was thirty yards up the catwalk when his anxiety suddenly grew stronger. Wesson stopped in spite of himself and turned clumsily, putting his back to the wall. The support of the solid wall was not enough. The catwalk seemed threatening to tilt underfoot, dropping him into the lightless gulf.

Wesson recognized this drained feeling, this metallic taste at the back of his tongue. It was fear.

The thought ticked through his head: *They want me to be afraid.* But why? Why now? Of what?

Equally suddenly, he knew. The nameless pressure tightened, like a great fist closing, and Wesson had the appalling sense of something so huge that it had no limits at all, descending with a terrible endless swift slowness. . . .

It was time.

His first month was up.

The alien was coming.

As Wesson turned, gasping, the whole huge structure of the station around him seemed to dwindle to the size of an ordinary room—and Wesson with it, so that he seemed to himself like a tiny insect, frantically scuttling down the walls toward safety.

Behind him as he ran, the station *boomed.*

In the silent rooms, all the lights were burning dimly. Wesson lay still, looking at the ceiling. Up there his imagination formed a shifting, changing image of the alien—huge, shadowy, formlessly menacing.

Sweat had gathered in globules on his brow. He stared, unable to look away.

"That was why you didn't want me to go topside, huh, Aunt Jane?" he said hoarsely.

"Yes. The nervousness is the first sign. But you gave me a direct order, Paul."

"I know it," he said vaguely, still staring fixedly at the ceiling. "A funny thing . . . Aunt Jane?"

"Yes, Paul?"

"You won't tell me what it looks like, right?"

"*No*, Paul."

"I don't want to know. Lord, I don't *want* to know. . . . Funny thing, Aunt Jane, part of me is just pure funk—I'm so scared I'm nothing but a jelly."

"I know," said the voice gently.

" . . . And part is real cool and calm, as if it didn't matter. Crazy, the things you think about. You know?"

"What things, Paul?"

He tried to laugh. "I'm remembering a kids' party I went to twenty, twenty-five years ago. I was—let's see—I was nine. I remember, because that was the same year my father died.

"We were living in Dallas then, in a rented mobile house, and there was a family in the next tract with a bunch of redheaded kids. They were always throwing parties; nobody liked them much, but everybody always went."

"Tell me about the party, Paul."

He shifted on the couch. "This one—this one was a Halloween party. I remember the girls had on black and orange dresses, and the boys mostly wore spirit costumes. I was about the youngest kid there, and I felt kind of out of place. Then all of a sudden one of the redheads jumps up in a skull mask, hollering, 'C'mon, everybody get ready for hide-and-seek.' And he grabs *me*, and says, '*You* be it,' and before I can even move, he shoves me into a dark closet. And I hear that door lock behind me."

He moistened his lips. "And then—you know, in the darkness—I feel something hit my *face*. You know, cold and clammy, like—I don't know— something dead. . . .

"I just hunched up on the floor of that closet, waiting for that thing to touch me again. You know? That thing, cold and kind of gritty, hanging up there. You know what it was? A cloth glove, full of ice and bran cereal. A joke. Boy, that was one joke I never forgot. . . . Aunt Jane?"

"Yes, Paul."

"Hey, I'll bet you alpha networks made great psychs, huh? I could lie here and tell you anything, because you're just a machine—right?"

"Right, Paul," said the network sorrowfully.

"Aunt Jane, Aunt Jane . . . It's no use kidding myself along. I can *feel* that thing up there, just a couple of yards away."

"I know you can, Paul."

"I can't stand it, Aunt Jane."

"You can if you think you can, Paul."

He writhed on the couch. "It's—it's dirty, it's clammy. My God, is it going to be like that for *five* months? I can't, it'll kill me, Aunt Jane."

There was another thunderous boom, echoing down through the structural members of the station. "What's that?" Wesson gasped. "The other ship—casting off?"

"Yes. Now he's alone, just as you are."

"Not like me. He can't be feeling what I'm feeling. Aunt Jane, you don't know. . . ."

Up there, separated from him only by a few yards of metal, the alien's enormous, monstrous body hung. It was that poised weight, as real as if he could touch it, that weighed down his chest.

Wesson had been a space dweller for most of his adult life and knew even in his bones that, if an orbital station ever collapsed, the "under" part would not be crushed but would be hurled away by its own angular momentum. This was not the oppressiveness of planetside buildings, where the looming mass above you seemed always threatening to fall. This was something else, completely distinct, and impossible to argue away.

It was the scent of danger, hanging unseen up there in the dark, waiting, cold and heavy. It was the recurrent nightmare of Wesson's childhood—the bloated unreal shape, no-color, no-size, that kept on hideously falling toward his face. . . . It was the dead puppy he had pulled out of the creek, that summer in Dakota—wet fur, limp head, cold, cold, *cold*. . . .

With an effort, Wesson rolled over on the couch and lifted himself to one elbow. The pressure was an insistent chill weight on his skull; the room seemed to dip and swing around him in slow, dizzy circles.

Wesson felt his jaw muscles contorting with the strain as he knelt, then stood erect. His back and legs tightened; his mouth hung painfully open. He took one step, then another, timing them to hit the floor as it came upright.

The right side of the console, the one that had been dark, was lighted. Pressure in Sector Two, according to the indicator, was about one and a third atmospheres. The airlock indicator showed a slightly higher pressure of oxygen and argon; that was to keep any of the alien atmosphere from contaminating Sector One, but it also meant that the lock would no longer open from either side. Wesson found that irrationally comforting.

"Lemme see Earth," he gasped.

The screen lighted up as he stared into it. "It's a long way down," he said. A long, long way down to the bottom of that well. . . . He had spent ten featureless years as a servo tech in Home Station. Before that, he'd wanted to be a pilot, but had washed out the first year—couldn't take the math. But he had never once thought of going back to Earth.

Now, suddenly, after all these years, that tiny blue disk seemed infinitely desirable.

"Aunt Jane, Aunt Jane, it's beautiful," he mumbled.

Down there, he knew, it was spring; and in certain places, where the edge of darkness retreated, it was morning—a watery blue morning like the sea light caught in an agate, a morning with smoke and mist in it, a morning of stillness and promise. Down there, lost years and miles away, some tiny dot of a woman was opening her microscopic door to listen to an atom's song. Lost, lost, and packed away in cotton wool, like a specimen slide—one spring morning on Earth.

Black miles above, so far that sixty Earths could have been piled one on another to make a pole for his perch, Wesson swung in his endless circle within a circle. Yet, vast as the gulf beneath him was, all this—Earth, moon, orbital stations, ships; yes, the sun and all the rest of his planets, too—was the merest sniff of space, to be pinched up between thumb and finger.

Beyond—there was the true gulf. In that deep night, galaxies lay sprawled aglitter, piercing a distance that could only be named in a meaningless number, a cry of dismay: O . . . O . . . O . . .

Crawling and fighting, blasting with energies too big for them, men had come as far as Jupiter. But if a man had been tall enough to lie with his boots toasting in the sun and his head freezing at Pluto, still he would have been too small for that overwhelming emptiness. Here, not at Pluto, was the outermost limit of man's empire; here the outside funneled down to meet it, like the pinched waist of an hourglass; here, and only here, the two worlds came near enough to touch. Ours—and theirs.

Down at the bottom of the board, now, the golden dials were faintly alight, the needles trembling ever so little on their pins.

Deep in the vats, the golden liquid was trickling down: *"Though disgusted, I took a sample of the exudate, and it was forwarded for analysis. . . ."*

Space-cold fluid, trickling down the bitter walls of the tubes, forming little pools in the cups of darkness; goldenly agleam there, half-alive. The golden elixir. One drop of the concentrate would arrest aging for twenty years—keep your arteries soft, tonus good, eyes clear, hair pigmented, brain alert.

That was what the tests of Pigeon's sample had shown. That was the reason for the whole crazy history of the "alien trading post"—first a hut on Titan, then later, when people understood more about the problem, Stranger Station.

Once every twenty years, an alien would come down out of somewhere and sit in the tiny cage we had made for him and make us rich beyond our dreams —rich with life—and still we did not know why.

Above him, Wesson imagined he could see that sensed body awallow in the glacial blackness, its bulk passively turning with the station's spin, bleeding a chill gold into the lips of the tubes—drip . . . drop. . . .

Wesson held his head. The pressure inside made it hard to think; it felt as if his skull were about to fly apart. "Aunt Jane," he said.

"Yes, Paul." The kindly, comforting voice, like a nurse. The nurse who stands beside your cot while you have painful, necessary things done to you. Efficient, trained friendliness.

"Aunt Jane," said Wesson, "do you know why they keep coming back?"

"No," said the voice precisely. "It is a mystery."

Wesson nodded. "I had," he said, "an interview with Gower before I left Home. You know Gower? Chief of the Outerworld Bureau. Came up especially to see me."

"Yes?" said Aunt Jane encouragingly.

"Said to me, 'Wesson, you got to find out. Find out if we can count on them to keep up the supply. You know? There's fifty million more of us,' he says, 'than when you were born. We need more of the stuff, and we got to know if we can count on it. Because,' he says, 'you know what would happen if it stopped?' Do you know, Aunt Jane?"

"It would be," said the voice, "a catastrophe."

"That's right," Wesson said respectfully. "It would. Like, he says to me, 'What if the people in the Nefud area were cut off from the Jordan Valley Authority? Why, there'd be millions dying of thirst in a week.

" 'Or what if the freighters stopped coming to Moon Base? Why,' he says, 'there'd be thousands starving and smothering to death.'

"He says, 'Where the water is, where you can get food and air, people are going to settle and get married, you know? And have kids.'

"He says, 'If the so-called longevity serum stopped coming. . . .' Says, 'Every twentieth adult in the Sol family is due for his shot this year.' Says, 'Of those, almost twenty percent are one hundred fifteen or older.' Says, 'The deaths in that group in the first year would be at least three times what the actuarial tables call for.' " Wesson raised a strained face. "I'm thirty-four, you know?" he said. "That Gower, he made me feel like a baby."

Aunt Jane made a sympathetic noise.

"Drip, drip," said Wesson hysterically. The needles of the tall golden indicators were infinitesimally higher. "Every twenty years we need more of the stuff, so somebody like me has to come out and take it for five lousy months. And one of *them* has to come out and sit there, and *drip*. *Why*, Aunt Jane? What for? Why should it matter to them whether we live a long time or not? Why do they keep on coming back? What do they take *away* from here?"

But to these questions, Aunt Jane had no reply.

All day and every day, the lights burned cold and steady in the circular gray corridor around the rim of Sector One. The hard gray flooring had been deeply scuffed in that circular path before Wesson ever walked there—the corridor existed for that only, like a treadmill in a squirrel cage. It said "Walk," and Wesson walked. A man would go crazy if he sat still, with that squirming, indescribable pressure on his head; and so Wesson paced off the miles, all day and every day, until he dropped like a dead man in the bed at night.

He talked, too, sometimes to himself, sometimes to the listening alpha network; sometimes it was difficult to tell which. "Moss on a rock," he muttered, pacing. "Told him, wouldn't give twenty mills for any shell. . . . Little pebbles down there, all colors." He shuffled on in silence for a while. Abruptly: "I don't see *why* they couldn't have given me a cat."

Aunt Jane said nothing. After a moment Wesson went on, "Nearly everybody at Home has a cat, for God's sake, or a goldfish or something. You're all right, Aunt Jane, but I can't *see* you. My God, I mean if they couldn't send a man a woman for company—what I mean, my God, I never liked *cats.* " He swung around the doorway into the bedroom, and absentmindedly slammed his fist into the bloody place on the wall.

"But a cat would have been *something,* " he said.

Aunt Jane was still silent.

"Don't pretend your feelings are hurt. I know you, you're only a machine," said Wesson. "Listen, Aunt Jane, I remember a cereal package one time that had a horse and a cowboy on the side. There wasn't much room, so about all you saw was their faces. It used to strike me funny how much they looked alike. Two ears on the top with hair in the middle. Two eyes. Nose. Mouth with teeth in it. I was thinking, we're kind of distant cousins, aren't we, us and the horses. But compared to that thing up there—we're *brothers.* You know?"

"Yes," said Aunt Jane quietly.

"So I keep asking myself, why couldn't they have sent a horse or a cat *instead* of a man? But I guess the answer is because only a man could take what I'm taking. God, only a man. Right?"

"Right," said Aunt Jane with deep sorrow.

Wesson stopped at the bedroom doorway again and shuddered, holding onto the frame. "Aunt Jane," he said in a low, clear voice, "you take pictures of *him* up there, don't you?"

"Yes, Paul."

"And you take pictures of me. And then what happens? After it's all over, who looks at the pictures?"

"I don't know," said Aunt Jane humbly.

"You don't know. But whoever looks at 'em, it doesn't do any good. Right? We got to find out why, why, why. . . . And we never do find out, do we?"

"No," said Aunt Jane.

"But don't they figure that if the man who's going through it could see him, he might be able to tell something? That other people couldn't? Doesn't that make sense?"

"That's out of my hands, Paul."

He sniggered. "That's funny. Oh, that's funny." He chortled in his throat, reeling around the circuit.

"Yes, that's funny," said Aunt Jane.

"Aunt Jane, tell me what happens to the watchmen."

"I can't tell you that, Paul."

He lurched into the living room, sat down before the console, beat on its smooth, cold metal with his fists. "What are you, some kind of monster? Isn't there any blood in your veins, or oil or *anything?*"

"Please, Paul . . ."

"Don't you see, all I want to know, can they talk? Can they tell anything after their tour is over?"

"No, Paul."

He stood upright, clutching the console for balance. "They can't? No, I figured. And you know why?"

"No."

"Up there," said Wesson obscurely. "Moss on the rock."

"Paul, what?"

"We get changed," said Wesson, stumbling out of the room again. "We get changed. Like a piece of iron next to a magnet. Can't help it. You— nonmagnetic, I guess. Goes right through you, huh, Aunt Jane? You don't get changed. You stay here, wait for the next one."

"Yes," said Aunt Jane.

"You know," said Wesson, pacing, "I can tell how he's lying up there. Head *that* way, tail the other. Am I right?"

"Yes," said Aunt Jane.

Wesson stopped. "Yes," he said intently. "So you *can* tell me what you see up there, can't you, Aunt Jane?"

"No. Yes. It isn't allowed."

"Listen, Aunt Jane, *we'll die* unless we can find out what makes those aliens tick! Remember that." Wesson leaned against the corridor wall, gazing up. "He's turning now—around this way. Right?"

"Yes."

"Well, what else is he doing? Come on, Aunt Jane, tell me!"

A pause. "He is twitching his . . ."

"What?"

"I don't know the words."

"My God, my God," said Wesson, clutching his head, "of course there aren't any words." He ran into the living room, clutched the console, and stared at the blank screen. He pounded the metal with his fist. "You've got to show me, Aunt Jane, come on and show me—show me!"

"It isn't allowed," Aunt Jane protested.

"You've got to do it just the same, or we'll *die,* Aunt Jane—millions of us, billions, and it'll be your fault, get it? *Your fault,* Aunt Jane!"

"Please," said the voice. There was a pause. The screen flickered to life, for an instant only. Wesson had a glimpse of something massive and dark, but half-transparent, like a magnified insect—a tangle of nameless limbs, whiplike filaments, claws, wings. . . .

He clutched the edge of the console.

"Was that all right?" Aunt Jane asked.

"Of course! What do you think, it'll kill me to look at it? Put it back, Aunt Jane, put it back!"

Reluctantly, the screen lighted again. Wesson stared and went on staring. He mumbled something.

"What?" said Aunt Jane.

"Life of my love, I loathe thee," said Wesson, staring. He roused himself after a moment and turned away. The image of the alien stayed with him as he went reeling into the corridor again; he was not surprised to find that it reminded him of all the loathsome, crawling, creeping things the Earth was full of. That explained why he was not supposed to see the alien, or even know what it looked like—because that fed his hate. And it was all right for him to be afraid of the alien, but he was not supposed to hate it. . . . Why not? Why not?

His fingers were shaking. He felt drained, steamed, dried up and withered. The one daily shower Aunt Jane allowed him was no longer enough. Twenty minutes after bathing the acid sweat dripped again from his armpits, the cold sweat was beaded on his forehead, the hot sweat was in his palms. Wesson felt as if there were a furnace inside him, out of control, all the dampers drawn. He knew that, under stress, something of the kind did happen to a man; the body's chemistry was altered—more adrenalin, more glycogen in the muscles, eyes brighter, digestion retarded. That was the trouble—he was burning himself up, unable to fight the thing that tormented him or run from it.

After another circuit, Wesson's steps faltered. He hesitated and went into the living room. He leaned over the console, staring. From the screen, the alien stared blindly up into space. Down in the dark side, the golden indicators had climbed: the vats were more than two-thirds filled.

To *fight or run.* . . .

Slowly Wesson sank down in front of the console. He sat hunched, head bent, hands squeezed tight between his knees, trying to hold onto the thought that had come to him.

If the alien felt a pain as great as Wesson's—or greater . . .

Stress might alter the alien's body chemistry, too.

Life of my love, I loathe thee.

Wesson pushed the irrelevant thought aside. He stared at the screen, trying to envisage the alien up there, wincing in pain and distress—sweating a golden sweat of horror. . . .

After a long time, he stood up and walked into the kitchen. He caught the table edge to keep his legs from carrying him on around the circuit. He sat down.

Humming fondly, the autochef slid out a tray of small glasses—water, orange juice, milk. Wesson put the water glass to his stiff lips; the water was cool and hurt his throat. Then the juice, but he could drink only a little of it; then he sipped the milk. Aunt Jane hummed approvingly.

Dehydrated. How long had it been since he had eaten or drunk? He looked at his hands. They were thin bundles of sticks, ropy-veined, with hard yellow claws. He could see the bones of his forearms under the skin, and his heart's beating stirred the cloth at his chest. The pale hairs on his arms and thighs —were they blond or white?

The blurred reflections in the metal trim of the dining room gave him no answers—only pale faceless smears of gray. Wesson felt light-headed and very weak, as if he had just ended a bout of fever. He fumbled over his ribs and shoulder bones. He was thin.

He sat in front of the autochef for a few minutes more, but no food came out. Evidently Aunt Jane did not think he was ready for it, and perhaps she was right. *Worse for them than for us,* he thought dizzily. *That's why the station's so far out, why radio silence and only one man aboard. They couldn't stand it at all, otherwise.* . . . Suddenly he could think of nothing but sleep —the bottomless pit, layer after layer of smothering velvet, numbing and soft. . . . His leg muscles quivered and twitched when he tried to walk, but he managed to get to the bedroom and fall on the mattress. The resilient block seemed to dissolve under him. His bones were melting.

He woke with a clear head, very weak, thinking cold and clear: *When two alien cultures meet, the stronger must transform the weaker with love or hate.*

"Wesson's law," he said aloud. He looked automatically for pencil and paper, but there was none, and he realized he would have to tell Aunt Jane, and let her remember it.

"I don't understand," she said.

"Never mind, remember it anyway. You're good at that, aren't you?"

"Yes, Paul."

"All right—I want some breakfast."

He thought about Aunt Jane, so nearly human, sitting up here in her metal prison, leading one man after another through the torments of hell—nurse-maid, protector, torturer. They must have known that something would have to give. . . . But the alphas were comparatively new; nobody understood them very well. Perhaps they really thought that an absolute prohibition could never be broken.

. . . *the stronger must transform the weaker.* . . .

I'm the stronger, he thought. *And that's the way it's going to be.* He stopped at the console, and the screen was blank. He said angrily, "Aunt Jane!" And with a guilty start, the screen flickered into life.

Up there, the alien had rolled again in his pain. Now the great clustered eyes were staring directly into the camera; the coiled limbs threshed in pain; the eyes were staring, asking, pleading. . . .

"No," said Wesson, feeling his own pain like an iron cap, and he slammed his hand down on the manual control. The screen went dark. He looked up, sweating, and saw the floral picture over the console.

The thick stems were like antennae, the leaves thoraxes, the buds like blind insect eyes. The whole picture moved slightly, endlessly, in a slow waiting rhythm.

Wesson clutched the hard metal of the console and stared at the picture, with sweat cold on his brow, until it turned into a calm, meaningless arrangement of lines again. Then he went into the dining room, shaking, and sat down.

After a moment he said, "Aunt Jane, does it get worse?"

"No. From now on, it gets better."

"How long?" he asked vaguely.

"One month."

A month, getting "better"—that was the way it had always been, with the watchman swamped and drowned, his personality submerged. Wesson thought about the men who had gone before him—Class Seven citizenship, with unlimited leisure, and Class One housing. Yes, sure—in a sanatorium.

His lips peeled back from his teeth, and his fists clenched hard. *Not me!* he thought.

He spread his hands on the cool metal to study them. He said, "How much longer do they usually stay able to talk?"

"You are already talking longer than any of them. . . ."

Then there was a blank. Wesson was vaguely aware, in snatches, of the corridor walls moving past and the console glimpsed and of a thunderous cloud of ideas that swirled around his head in a beating of wings. The aliens—what did they want? And what happened to the watchmen in Stranger Station?

The haze receded a little, and he was in the dining room again, staring vacantly at the table. Something was wrong.

He ate a few spoonfuls of the gruel the autochef served him, then pushed it away; the stuff tasted faintly unpleasant. The machine hummed anxiously and thrust a poached egg at him, but Wesson got up from the table.

The station was all but silent. The resting rhythm of the household machines throbbed in the walls, unheard. The blue-lighted living room was spread out before him like an empty stage setting, and Wesson stared as if he had never seen it before.

He lurched to the console and stared down at the pictured alien on the screen—heavy, heavy, asprawl with pain in the darkness. The needles of the golden indicators were high, the enlarged vats almost full. *It's too much for him,* Wesson thought with grim satisfaction. The peace that followed the pain had not descended as it was supposed to; no, not this time!

He glanced up at the painting over the console—heavy crustacean limbs that swayed gracefully in the sea. . . .

He shook his head violently. *I won't let it; I won't give in!* He held the back of one hand close to his eyes. He saw the dozens of tiny cuneiform wrinkles stamped into the skin over the knuckles, the pale hairs sprouting, the pink shiny flesh of recent scars. *I'm human,* he thought. But when he let his hand fall onto the console, the bony fingers seemed to crouch like crustaceans' legs, ready to scuttle.

Sweating, Wesson stared into the screen. Pictured there, the alien met his eyes, and it was as if they spoke to each other, mind to mind, an instantaneous communication that needed no words. There was a piercing sweetness to it, a melting, dissolving luxury of change into something that would no longer have any pain. . . . A pull, a calling.

Wesson straightened up slowly, carefully, as if he held some fragile thing in his mind that must not be handled roughly, or it would disintegrate. He said hoarsely, "Aunt Jane!"

She made some responsive noise.

He said, "Aunt Jane, I've got the answer! The whole thing! Listen, now wait —listen!" He paused a moment to collect his thoughts. *"When two alien cultures meet, the stronger must transform the weaker with love or hate.* Remember? You said you didn't understand what that meant. I'll *tell* you what it means. When these—monsters—met Pigeon a hundred years ago on Titan, *they knew* we'd have to meet again. They're spreading out, colonizing, and so are we. We haven't got interstellar flight yet, but give us another hundred years, we'll *get* it. *We'll wind up out there, where they are.* And they can't stop us. Because they're not killers, Aunt Jane, it isn't in them. They're *nicer* than us. See, they're like the missionaries, and we're the South Sea Islanders. *They* don't kill their enemies, oh, no—perish the thought!"

She was trying to say something, to interrupt him, but he rushed on. "Listen! The longevity serum—that was a lucky accident. But they played it for all it's worth. Slick and smooth. They come and give us the stuff free— they don't ask for a thing in return. Why not? Listen.

"They come here, and the shock of that first contact makes them sweat out that golden gook we need. Then, the last month or so, the pain always eases off. Why? Because the two minds, the human and alien, they stop fighting each other. Something gives way, it goes soft, and there's a mixing together. And that's where you get the human casualties of this operation—the bleary men that come out of here not even able to talk human language any more. Oh, I suppose they're happy—happier than I am!—because they've got something big and wonderful inside 'em. Something that you and I can't even understand. But if you took them and put them together again with the aliens who spent time here, *they could all live together—they're adapted.*

"That's what they're aiming for!" He struck the console with his fist. "Not now—but a hundred, two hundred years from now! When we start expanding out to the stars—when we go a-conquering—we'll have already been conquered! Not by weapons, Aunt Jane, not by hate—by love! Yes, love! *Dirty, stinking, low-down, sneaking love!*"

Aunt Jane said something, a long sentence, in a high, anxious voice.

"What?" said Wesson irritably. He couldn't understand a word.

Aunt Jane was silent. "What, what?" Wesson demanded, pounding the console. "Have you got it through your tin head or not? *What?*"

Aunt Jane said something else, tonelessly. Once more, Wesson could not make out a single word.

He stood frozen. Warm tears started suddenly out of his eyes. "Aunt Jane . . ." he said. He remembered, *You are already talking longer than any of them.* Too late? Too late? He tensed, then whirled and sprang to the closet where the paper books were kept. He opened the first one his hand struck.

The black letters were alien squiggles on the page, little humped shapes, without meaning.

The tears were coming faster, he couldn't stop them—tears of weariness, tears of frustration, tears of hate. *"Aunt Jane!"* he roared.

But it was no good. The curtain of silence had come down over his head. He was one of the vanguard—the conquered men, the ones who would get along with their strange brothers, out among the alien stars.

The console was not working any more; nothing worked when he wanted it. Wesson squatted in the shower stall, naked, with a soup bowl in his hands. Water droplets glistened on his hands and forearms; the pale short hairs were just springing up, drying.

The silvery skin of reflection in the bowl gave him back nothing but a silhouette, a shadow man's outline. He could not see his face.

He dropped the bowl and went across the living room, shuffling the pale drifts of paper underfoot. The black lines on the paper, when his eye happened to light on them, were worm shapes, crawling things, conveying nothing. He rolled slightly in his walk; his eyes were glazed. His head twitched, every now and then, sketching a useless motion to avoid pain.

Once the bureau chief, Gower, came to stand in his way. "You fool," he said, his face contorted in anger, "you were supposed to go on to the end, like the rest. Now look what you've done!"

"I found out, didn't I?" Wesson mumbled, and as he brushed the man aside like a cobweb, the pain suddenly grew more intense. Wesson clasped his head in his hands with a grunt and rocked to and fro a moment, uselessly, before he straightened and went on. The pain was coming in waves now, so tall that at their peak his vision dimmed out, violet, then gray.

It couldn't go on much longer. Something had to burst.

He paused at the bloody place and slapped the metal with his palm, making the sound ring dully up into the frame of the station: *rroom . . . rroom. . . .*

Faintly an echo came back: *boo-oom. . . .*

Wesson kept going, smiling a faint and meaningless smile. He was only marking time now, waiting. Something was about to happen.

The kitchen doorway sprouted a sudden sill and tripped him. He fell heavily, sliding on the floor, and lay without moving beneath the slick gleam of the autochef.

The pressure was too great—the autochef's clucking was swallowed up in the ringing pressure, and the tall gray walls buckled slowly in. . . .

The station lurched.

Wesson felt it through his chest, palms, knees and elbows: the floor was plucked away for an instant and then swung back.

The pain in his skull relaxed its grip a little. Wesson tried to get to his feet.

There was an electric silence in the station. On the second try, he got up and leaned his back against a wall. *Cluck,* said the autochef suddenly, hysterically, and the vent popped open, but nothing came out.

He listened, straining to hear. What?

The station bounced beneath him, making his feet jump like a puppet's; the wall slapped his back hard, shuddered and was still; but far off through the metal cage came a long angry groan of metal, echoing, diminishing, dying. Then silence again.

The station held its breath. All the myriad clickings and pulses in the walls were suspended; in the empty rooms the lights burned with a yellow glare, and the air hung stagnant and still. The console lights in the living room glowed like witch fires. Water in the dropped bowl, at the bottom of the shower stall, shone like quicksilver, waiting.

The third shock came. Wesson found himself on his hands and knees, the jolt still tingling in the bones of his body, staring at the floor. The sound that filled the room ebbed away slowly and ran down into the silences—a resonant metallic sound, shuddering away now along the girders and hull plates, rattling tinnily into bolts and fittings, diminishing, noiseless, gone. The silence pressed down again.

The floor leaped painfully under his body, one great resonant blow that shook him from head to foot.

A muted echo of that blow came a few seconds later, as if the shock had traveled across the station and back.

The bed, Wesson thought, and scrambled on hands and knees through the doorway, along a floor curiously tilted, until he reached the rubbery block.

The room burst visibly upward around him, squeezing the block flat. It dropped back as violently, leaving Wesson bouncing helplessly on the mattress, his limbs flying. It came to rest in a long reluctant groan of metal.

Wesson rolled up on one elbow, thinking incoherently, *Air, the airlock.* Another blow slammed him down into the mattress, pinched his lungs shut, while the room danced grotesquely over his head. Gasping for breath in the ringing silence, Wesson felt a slow icy chill rolling toward him across the room —and there was a pungent smell in the air. *Ammonia!* he thought, and the odorless, smothering methane with it.

His cell was breached. The burst membrane was fatal—the alien's atmosphere would kill him.

Wesson surged to his feet. The next shock caught him off balance, dashed him to the floor. He arose again, dazed and limping; he was still thinking confusedly, *The airlock—get out.*

When he was halfway to the door, all the ceiling lights went out at once. The darkness was like a blanket around his head. It was bitter cold now in the room, and the pungent smell was sharper. Coughing, Wesson hurried forward. The floor lurched under his feet.

Only the golden indicators burned now—full to the top, the deep vats brimming, golden-lipped, gravid, a month before the time. Wesson shuddered.

Water spurted in the bathroom, hissing steadily on the tiles, rattling in the plastic bowl at the bottom of the shower stall. The light winked on and off again. In the dining room, he heard the autochef clucking and sighing. The freezing wind blew harder; he was numb with cold to the hips. It seemed to Wesson abruptly that he was not at the top of the sky at all, but down, *down* at the bottom of the sea—trapped in this steel bubble, while the dark poured in.

The pain in his head was gone, as if it had never been there, and he understood what that meant: Up there, the great body was hanging like butcher's carrion in the darkness. Its death struggles were over, the damage done.

Wesson gathered a desperate breath, shouted, "Help me! The alien's dead! He kicked the station apart—the methane's coming in! Get help, do you hear me? *Do you hear me?*"

Silence. In the smothering blackness, he remembered: *She can't understand me any more. Even if she's alive.*

He turned, making an animal noise in his throat. He groped his way on around the room, past the second doorway. Behind the walls, something was dripping with a slow cold tinkle and splash, a forlorn night sound. Small, hard, floating things rapped against his legs. Then he touched a smooth curve of metal—the airlock.

Eagerly he pushed his feeble weight against the door. It didn't move. Cold air was rushing out around the door frame, a thin knife-cold stream, but the door itself was jammed tight.

The suit! He should have thought of that before. If he just had some pure air to breathe and a little warmth in his fingers. . . . But the door of the suit locker would not move, either. The ceiling must have buckled.

And that was the end, he thought, bewildered. There were no more ways out. But there *had* to be. . . . He pounded on the door until his arms would not lift any more; it did not move. Leaning against the chill metal, he saw a single light blink on overhead.

The room was a wild place of black shadows and swimming shapes—the book leaves, fluttering and darting in the airstream. Schools of them beat wildly at the walls, curling over, baffled, trying again; others were swooping around the outer corridor, around and around; he could see them whirling past the doorways, dreamlike, a white drift of silent paper in the darkness.

The acrid smell was harsher in his nostrils. Wesson choked, groping his way to the console again. He pounded it with his open hand, crying weakly—he wanted to see Earth.

But when the little square of brightness leaped up, it was the dead body of the alien that Wesson saw.

It hung motionless in the cavity of the station, limbs dangling stiff and still, eyes dull. The last turn of the screw had been too much for it. But Wesson had survived. . . .

For a few minutes.

The dead alien face mocked him; a whisper of memory floated into his mind: *We might have been brothers.* . . . All at once Wesson passionately wanted to believe it—wanted to give in, turn back. That passed. Wearily he let himself sag into the bitter *now,* thinking with thin defiance, *It's done— hate wins. You'll have to stop this big giveaway—can't risk this happening again. And we'll hate you for that—and when we get out to the stars . . .*

The world was swimming numbly away out of reach. He felt the last fit of coughing take his body, as if it were happening to someone else besides him.

The last fluttering leaves of paper came to rest. There was a long silence in the drowned room.

Then:

"Paul," said the voice of the mechanical woman brokenly; "Paul," it said again, with the hopelessness of lost, unknown, impossible love.

LARRY EISENBERG

The Time of His Life

The scientist has always had a special place in science fiction, and many of the most memorable characters have been men and a few women who have devoted their lives to scientific research. However, the image of the scientist in SF has undergone some shifts, most notably from savior-of-mankind to threat-to-survival and most recently to something in between. Here Larry Eisenberg, a research scientist, presents two working scientists in a powerful story of generational conflict and the difficulty of performing that most human of functions—choosing.

I sat in the tiny cubicle that served as my office in the laboratory, my knees cramped under the desk. My father's office was huge, thickly carpeted from wall to wall, lined from floor to ceiling with bookcases. But, of course, my father was a Nobel laureate.

I gritted my teeth. Twenty years earlier I had been a graduate student of great promise. I had joined my father's laboratory as a coinvestigator with great hopes of making my own contribution to metabolic research. And now, at forty-four, my work was submerged in the greater accomplishments of my father.

What had happened to me? I was losing my sense of concentration, the ability to focus relentlessly on a single problem regardless of time and people. My father had that ability. He had always had it.

I looked at the picture of Alma, my wife, and the three boys, framed in silver on my desk. She was still undeniably a lovely woman. But in real life, her eyes were underlined with crow's-feet, and her exquisitely clear skin had begun to muddy. And what of the boys? They were sturdy, noisy, argumentative, offended because I didn't spend more time with them.

There was no need to. My father came every Sunday, devoting himself fully

653

to Alma and the boys. But he had never taken *me* to a ball game, never fished with me, never taken a long hike to a snowcapped mountain. Our relationship was polite but distant. Even when mother died, we grieved apart. But he was not gentle in criticizing my behavior. Only a week earlier, he had called me into his office to discuss difficulties with his grant. It was a pretext for something else.

"You don't carry your weight in this laboratory," he said bluntly. "You've lost all sense of purpose, of *honor.*"

"I do more than my share," I said hotly.

"Frolicking in the hay with my lab technician?" he gibed.

"That's a damned lie!" I said. I shook my head angrily. Two years back, there had been an abortive affair with a sloe-eyed blonde graduate student. It had been exciting, tempestuous, and had fizzled out a few months later. But Sarah Frey was a totally different kind of a girl. There were bonds between us that grew stronger by the hour, something neither my father nor my wife would ever understand. My father had gotten rid of the blonde graduate student, but so far he hadn't acted against Sarah. I think he knew it would be no use.

"I'm very fond of Sarah," I said. "There's nothing in it beyond that."

My father snorted, and I got up and walked out in a huff. Of course he was right. I was entangled from the first day Sarah Frey walked into the laboratory, six months back, her thick black hair lying in two woven plaits along the stiff white back of her starched smock, the soft mouth set in a curve that easily broke into a warm smile. She was efficient, good with our animals and very careful about recording data.

One morning, when my father had come in unexpectedly, he found us in a passionate embrace. I would have preferred an explosion, but he remained calm, pretending nothing had happened. He even spoke dispassionately to Sarah about preparing a new diet for our capuchin monkeys.

The recollection was still painful. I shuffled the papers on my desk aimlessly. It took the most enormous effort of concentration, but I tried to pull my thoughts back to my work. And for some moments, I succeeded. Twenty years back, I had begun my long search to determine the influences controlling the biological clock. What was it that sent the body temperature of a warm-blooded animal through the same up and down cycle, day after day? Why did so many metabolic functions depend on the length of day?

My father and I had discussed these questions at great length, and it was agreed that I would explore gravitational effects and he would pursue the electromagnetic influences. Chance had been completely on his side. It was his good fortune to be the first to show that brain potentials were definitely dependent on fluctuations in the Earth's magnetic field.

Working first with capuchin monkeys, then with humans, he demonstrated that the most significant of the brain biopotentials, the alpha rhythm, varied between eight and sixteen times each second, *just as the fluctuations did in the Earth's magnetic field.* And my father had been called to Sweden to receive the magnificient gold medal and the fat cash award.

I was proud of my father, proud of his trail-breaking accomplishment, and also fiercely envious. I had given up ever understanding why. Maybe it was the unrelenting sense of competition that surrounded everything he did. Even now, he was still striving to be first, engaging me in a competition I didn't want, both in the laboratory, and with my wife and children.

"It takes two to race," I said out loud. "And I'm not going to run."

My telephone rang. It was my father, a lousy fifty feet down the corridor, but too busy to walk over and talk to me directly. It was hard to control the contempt in my voice.

"What is it?" I said.

"I have something of tremendous importance to discuss," he said. "And I've a lot to show you. Could you spare me a few minutes?"

A few minutes? I had great chunks of empty time ahead. "I'm tied up now," I said. "But I'll be over in a half-hour."

I leaned over and set the alarm of my electric clock one half-hour ahead. My father could tolerate many things, but never tardiness.

I arrived punctually at my father's office and sat down in the very comfortable leather chair just opposite his desk. We looked directly into one another's eyes, and then, troubled, I looked down at the rug. It was uncanny, almost unnerving at times, to see how much alike in appearance my father and I were. Except for the silver hair and the toughened, wrinkled skin of a seventy-year-old, we could have passed for brothers. My father sat there puffing on his pipe. The rich aroma of his honeyed tobacco began to fill every corner of the room. I had detested that smell, even as a child.

"I have something to show you, John," said my father. He spoke out of the corner of his mouth without removing his pipe. That too, annoyed the hell out of me. "I would very much like to get your opinion on it," he said.

"Since when did my opinion matter here?"

My father glared at me. "To hell with your self-pity," he said. "I want your scientific acumen if you've got any left. I'm thinking about the arrow of time."

The arrow of time? I grinned in spite of myself. My father had always been preoccupied with this question, for as many years as I could recall. It was an obsession.

"We both know," said my father, going along lines he had taken innumerable times, "that on a microscopic level there is *no preferred* direction for time. The equations of motion don't give a damn whether time moves forward or backward."

"But it does matter on a macroscopic level," I said, pulled into the dialogue in spite of my resentment. "After all, if the direction of time were equally likely in the forward and backward directions, then there would have to be a total symmetry in the form and process of all animals. Of course there is a rough kind of symmetry, but it breaks down when you examine it closely. Obviously, the human heart and aorta are not symmetrical."

"You're absolutely right," said my father, and I got a thrill of pleasure that ran down into my stomach. He puffed even more vigorously on his pipe, and great blue clouds of smoke began to surround his head. It presaged a good deal more talk.

"What it boils down to," said my father, "is that on a small scale, say on the scale of the Earth itself, there may not be a macroscopic symmetry. But over the enormous reach of the universe, things *have to average out.* If men on Earth have a heart and aorta that point one way, then on some other planet, in some remote corner of the universe, other men have hearts and aortas that go the other way."

"That sounds like an extension of the particle-antiparticle reasoning to me," I said.

"Exactly," said my father. "I might even speculate that since we age in a particular direction here on Earth, perhaps other men grow younger with time, elsewhere."

I started to laugh. "And come out of their mothers' wombs, gnarled, bent, wrinkled and toothless?" My father put down his pipe. "You've reduced my remarks to complete absurdity," he said quietly.

I was happy to see my father angry but it also made me uneasy. "I'm sorry," I said. "But your remarks did seem to point in that direction."

My father stood up abruptly, knocking the ashes of his pipe into a huge embossed silver tray that had been given to him by the laboratory staff when he had received his Nobel Prize.

"Talk is cheap," he said. "Let's go into the laboratory. You'll see what I mean."

We walked into the outer corridors, which were dimly lit, and on to the capuchin monkey laboratory. In the center of the laboratory, on a large bench, was a single wire cage. Just behind it was a tall rack of electronic equipment with an L-shaped arm swinging out above the cage. Affixed to the arm and directly over the center of the cage was an enormous bank of coils.

My father walked up to the cage and peered into it, clucking very softly to the animal within. I came up behind him and looked over his shoulder. There was a very old animal inside the cage, one so wrinkled and gray that I was amazed it still lived.

"Do you recognize it?" said my father.

"Not really."

"It's our *young* Ginger," he said.

At first I thought it was a grotesque joke, but of course I knew my father had no sense of humor. I looked up at the bank of coils above the cage. My father's eyes followed mine.

"That's the magnetic field synthesizer I had built," said my father. "With it, I can place a controlled field into a one-millimeter area at any point within five feet of the synthesizer. I can vary amplitude and frequency over a large range."

"And Ginger?"

"I locked her into an eight cycles per second magnetic field," said my father. "And by God, she began to track *metabolically* with the fluctuations of this artificial field. Gradually, I began to increase the rate of the fluctuations. As you can see, her biological clock speeded up internally, and aging began to take place at a very rapid pace."

"It's incredible," I said. "I wouldn't have believed it possible."

For the moment my jealousy and antagonism fell away, and the magnitude of his achievement caught hold of my imagination. I examined the animal closely. The features were similar to those of Ginger, but I couldn't be sure. Around her ankle was a tiny identification bracelet marked "Ginger." But it might have been transferred from the real Ginger.

"I know what you're thinking," said my father. "But I've never faked data in my life, and you damn well know it." He lifted a thick notebook which was at one side of the cage. "All of my records are in here," he said. "I want you to read them and offer me your comments."

I took the notebook out of his hands. It was truly heavy. For a fleeting moment, I thought of how upset my father would be if I burned the notebook. Then I pushed the idea out of my head.

"One question," I said. "How do you direct this field at the animal? Do you use uniform field strength? Do you have to focus in a particular site of the cortex, or are there several areas involved?"

"There is a single site involved," said my father. "Read the notebook; it's all in there."

For a moment he looked at me, his eyes warm and almost, it seemed, loving.

"You've called me cold and aloof. But what I'm suggesting is that *you* now carry out the experiments of *slowing down* the field fluctuation rate."

My eyes filled. It was enormously generous of him, I knew. In effect, we might be able to make time stand still for the individual. It could be the threshold to immortality for the first time in man's history. The concept was breathtaking.

"I'll start reading your notebook at once," I said.

On the way back to my office, I passed Sarah Frey. She reached out and caressed my arm. Oddly enough, I was annoyed. I nodded at her, curtly, and went on without a word, laboring under the weight of the great notebook.

I read through every scrap of the data, my excitement mounting all the way. It was clear that the experiment of slowing down the fields was really going to rock the world of science. And then it hit me, the great shock of realizing that all of this was my father's work, all his accomplishment and none of it mine. He was handing it to me on a silver platter, but I hadn't degenerated to the point where I could accept such a gift.

I marched back to my father's office and put down his notebook. He looked at me, his great black, almost youthful eyes now expressionless.

"It's your work and not mine," I said. "You've done a fantastic job, but I'm not going to climb onto your bandwagon as though it were my own. I've got to make it on my own."

My father sighed. "Either I give you too little or too much. Why can't you climb aboard? There's enough glory and accomplishment here for five men. And there is so much yet to be worked out. Or do you want to burn up all of your creativity inside Sarah Frey?"

I began to shout. "Leave Sarah out of this. What I do with her is my own goddamn affair. And it's a damn sight more loving, more human and meaningful than your preoccupation with gold medals and applause."

"So that's it," said my father.

I stormed out of his office and back to my own. Sitting there I realized the childishness of what I had said and done. My father was right, and I ought to have joined him. But I couldn't. I was like an upended hourglass, losing all of its sand, and no one was able to turn me right side up so I could get a fresh start.

I spent the night with Sarah. I telephoned my wife and told her, as on countless occasions, that I would be working late at the laboratory and sleeping over. And as always, Alma sighed and pretended to believe me.

In the morning I told Sarah that I was going to divorce my wife. She was sitting before the mirror, brushing her hair with long, even strokes, unleashing a rich perfume from the blue-black locks, and her hand began to tremble.

But she said nothing. Did she believe me? I swore that I meant it this time, but Sarah was unconvinced. Or was it really the twenty-year difference in our ages? I left her apartment, angry with her, and for days thereafter I ignored her attempts to approach me.

My father was more direct with me. If he met me coming down the corridor, he would turn back. I knew his work went on, perhaps the very same experiments I had refused to do. But I would not humble myself.

One evening, when I had forced myself to stay behind and work on a lackluster paper which I was scheduled to give at a spring meeting, my father broke into my office with great excitement. His step was springy, and he seemed to be bursting with a vitality that belied his years.

"Come with me," he said.

I followed, great fear building in me. We went back to the capuchin room and the cage of Ginger. My father gestured at the cage, and I looked inside. *She had been restored to her youth.*

"Congratulations," I said, but I was close to complete despair. It might have been my own achievement. And then, all of the unformed feelings that had been sifting in and out of my mind took form.

"I know that as yet you haven't tried this process on a human," I said. "I'm willing to volunteer."

"It's courageous of you," said my father. "But the danger is enormous. It would require extreme care and a protracted exposure to avoid reversing the metabolic processes too abruptly."

"It's not courage," I said. "I want another chance to start afresh. Twenty years would give me that chance. Perhaps then I could avoid the things that led me into a blind alley."

"It's too late," said my father. "You've a wife and three fine boys. You can't turn back."

"I'm determined," I said. "If you won't help me, you know that I will get there by myself."

"I know," he said. "But you're a fool. There's a precedent before you."

He went to the laboratory sink and washed his face vigorously with soap and water. The dried, leathery skin seemed to vanish like smoke, and a clear, ruddy skin emerged.

"All makeup," said my father. He reached up and removed the silver hair, and a full head of chestnut-colored hair, the counterpart of my own, emerged. "As you see," he said, "I've already carried out the experiment."

I looked at him. He was almost my mirror image.

"You're a swine," I said. "A lecherous beast. You took my work, my ambition, my wife and children. Now you've taken my body."

"It's not like that at all," he muttered. "You know it was logically the next step in my research."

"Was it?" I said. "Are you logically headed next for Alma's bed?"

He flushed to the roots.

"I'll trade her for those twenty years," I said. "At least you can give me that."

"I'd do it gladly," he said grimly. "And I would take far better care of your family than you ever did. But even supposing I were to entertain your absurd proposition, what would become of me, the *old* me?"

"That's your problem," I said. "For once in your life, think of me, first."

"You're out of your head," said my father. He reached out and took hold of the silver hairpiece and very carefully tugged it back into place. Then he walked out of the laboratory.

That night I didn't even bother to call Alma. I got roaring drunk and stayed that way until I lost track of the days. When I awoke, I was bone weary. My head was splitting, and every part of my body ached beyond description. It was much more than a hangover.

I tried to lift my arm and the effort exhausted me. Most curious of all, I found myself at a strange desk. I stared at the pile of neatly lettered papers, the thick notebook. I looked down at my hands. They were gnarled, the hands of a man in his seventies, the skin puckered, leathery, acid-stained. I lifted the water-spotted shaving mirror that lay at one side of the desk and looked at my reflection. It was the face of my father, or rather, his face before he had turned back his biological clock. Or was it really my face?

I was terribly confused. Waking from a long nap does that to me. I was still in that half-awake state where one is not sure what one has dreamed and what is real. Sarah Frey came gliding in to drop a report on the desk. I reached out to caress her rump, and she nearly leaped out of her skin. She was out of the room before I could say a word.

I looked at the notebook, opened it and idly turned the pages. Was this work mine? My eyelids were terribly heavy. I began to doze off, and out of the corner of my eye I saw a younger version of myself, standing motionless in the doorway of the office, staring at me with his large, dark, angry eyes. And just in the moment that I dropped back into the deep solace of my nap, I thought, "You fool, the things you took were ephemeral. But I, after all, am now the Nobel laureate."

JAMES TIPTREE, JR.

The Women Men Don't See

We listen, but we don't hear. We see, but we don't understand. We reach, but we don't grasp. These human failings are a part of life for all of us and not always because of lack of effort or talent. Some things are mysterious, and life is the richer for it. Science fiction has always explored the things that are not what they seem and the things that are more than they appear to be, but rarely as disturbingly and profoundly as in this outstanding story by "James Tiptree, Jr." (Alice Sheldon).

I see her first while the Mexicana 727 is barreling down to Cozumel Island. I come out of the can and lurch into her seat, saying, "Sorry," at a double female blur. The near blur nods quietly. The younger one in the window seat goes on looking out. I continue down the aisle, registering nothing. Zero. I never would have looked at them or thought of them again.

Cozumel airport is the usual mix of panicky Yanks dressed for the sandpile and calm Mexicans dressed for lunch at the Presidente. I am a used-up Yank dressed for serious fishing; I extract my rods and duffel from the riot and hike across the field to find my charter pilot. One Captain Estéban has contracted to deliver me to the bonefish flats of Belize three hundred kilometers down the coast.

Captain Estéban turns out to be four feet nine of mahogany Mayan *puro.* He is also in a somber Maya snit. He tells me my Cessna is grounded somewhere and his Bonanza is booked to take a party to Chetumal.

Well, Chetumal is south; can he take me along and go on to Belize after he drops them? Gloomily he concedes the possibility—*if* the other party permits, and *if* there are not too many *equipajes.*

The Chetumal party approaches. It's the woman and her young companion —daughter?—neatly picking their way across the gravel and yucca apron.

Their Ventura two-suiters, like themselves, are small, plain and neutral-colored. No problem. When the captain asks if I may ride along, the mother says mildly, "Of course," without looking at me.

I think that's when my inner tilt-detector sends up its first faint click. How come this woman has already looked me over carefully enough to accept on her plane? I disregard it. Paranoia hasn't been useful in my business for years, but the habit is hard to break.

As we clamber into the Bonanza, I see the girl has what could be an attractive body if there was any spark at all. There isn't. Captain Estéban folds a serape to sit on so he can see over the cowling and runs a meticulous check-down. And then we're up and trundling over the turquoise Jell-O of the Caribbean into a stiff south wind.

The coast on our right is the territory of Quintana Roo. If you haven't seen Yucatán, imagine the world's biggest absolutely flat green gray rug. An empty-looking land. We pass the white ruin of Tulum and the gash of the road to Chichén Itzá, a half-dozen coconut plantations, and then nothing but reef and low scrub jungle all the way to the horizon, just about the way the conquistadors saw it four centuries back.

Long strings of cumulus are racing at us, shadowing the coast. I have gathered that part of our pilot's gloom concerns the weather. A cold front is dying on the henequen fields of Mérida to the west, and the south wind has piled up a string of coastal storms: what they call *llovisnos*. Estéban detours methodically around a couple of small thunderheads. The Bonanza jinks, and I look back with a vague notion of reassuring the women. They are calmly intent on what can be seen of Yucatán. Well, they were offered the copilot's view, but they turned it down. Too shy?

Another *llovisno* puffs up ahead. Estéban takes the Bonanza upstairs, rising in his seat to sight his course. I relax for the first time in too long, savoring the latitudes between me and my desk, the week of fishing ahead. Our captain's classic Maya profile attracts my gaze: forehead sloping back from his predatory nose, lips and jaw stepping back below it. If his slant eyes had been any more crossed, he couldn't have made his license. That's a handsome combination, believe it or not. On the little Maya chicks in their minishifts with iridescent gloop on those cockeyes, it's also highly erotic. Nothing like the oriental doll thing; these people have stone bones. Captain Estéban's old grandmother could probably tow the Bonanza. . . .

I'm snapped awake by the cabin hitting my ear. Estéban is barking into his headset over a drumming racket of hail; the windows are dark gray.

One important noise is missing—the motor. I realize Estéban is fighting a dead plane. Thirty-six hundred; we've lost two thousand feet!

He slaps tank switches as the storm throws us around; I catch something about *gasolina* in a snarl that shows his big teeth. The Bonanza reels down. As he reaches for an overhead toggle, I see the fuel gauges are high. Maybe a clogged gravity feed line; I've heard of dirty gas down here. He drops the set; it's a million to one nobody can read us through the storm at this range anyway. Twenty-five hundred—going down.

His electric feed pump seems to have cut in: the motor explodes—quits—explodes—and quits again for good. We are suddenly out of the bottom of the clouds. Below us is a long white line almost hidden by rain: the reef. But there isn't any beach behind it, only a big meandering bay with a few mangrove flats—and it's coming up at us fast.

This is going to be bad, I tell myself with great unoriginality. The women behind me haven't made a sound. I look back and see they've braced down with their coats by their heads. With a stalling speed around eighty, all this isn't much use, but I wedge myself in.

Estéban yells some more into his set, flying a falling plane. He is doing one Jesus job, too—as the water rushes up at us he dives into a hair-raising turn and hangs us into the wind—with a long pale ridge of sandbar in front of our nose.

Where in hell he found it I'll never know. The Bonanza mushes down, and we belly-hit with a tremendous tearing crash—bounce—hit again—and everything slews wildly as we flat-spin into the mangroves at the end of the bar. Crash! Clang! The plane is wrapping itself into a mound of strangler fig with one wing up. The crashing quits with us all in one piece. And no fire. Fantastic.

Captain Estéban pries open his door, which is now in the roof. Behind me a woman is repeating quietly, "Mother. Mother." I climb up the floor and find the girl trying to free herself from her mother's embrace. The woman's eyes are closed. Then she opens them and suddenly lets go, sane as soap. Estéban starts hauling them out. I grab the Bonanza's aid kit and scramble out after them into brilliant sun and wind. The storm that hit us is already vanishing up the coast.

"Great landing, captain."

"Oh, *yes!* It was beautiful." The women are shaky, but no hysteria. Estéban is surveying the scenery with the expression his ancestors used on the Spaniards.

If you've been in one of these things, you know the slow-motion inanity that goes on. Euphoria, first. We straggle down the fig tree and out onto the sandbar in the roaring hot wind, noting without alarm that there's nothing but miles of crystalline water on all sides. It's only a foot or so deep, and the bottom is the olive color of silt. The distant shore around us is all flat mangrove swamp, totally uninhabitable.

"Bahía Espiritu Santo." Estéban confirms my guess that we're down in that huge water wilderness. I always wanted to fish it.

"What's all that smoke?" The girl is pointing at the plumes blowing around the horizon.

"Alligator hunters," says Estéban. Maya poachers have left burn-offs in the swamps. It occurs to me that any signal fires we make aren't going to be too conspicuous. And I now note that our plane is well-buried in the mound of fig. Hard to see it from the air.

Just as the question of how the hell we get out of here surfaces in my mind, the older woman asks composedly, "If they didn't hear you, captain, when will they start looking for us? Tomorrow?"

"Correct," Estéban agrees dourly. I recall that air-sea rescue is fairly informal here. Like, keep an eye open for Mario, his mother says he hasn't been home all week.

It dawns on me we may be here quite some while.

Furthermore, the diesel-truck noise on our left is the Caribbean piling back into the mouth of the bay. The wind is pushing it at us, and the bare bottoms on the mangroves show that our bar is covered at high tide. I recall seeing a full moon this morning in—believe it, St. Louis—which means maximal tides. Well, we can climb up in the plane. But what about drinking water?

There's a small *splat!* behind me. The older woman has sampled the bay. She shakes her head, smiling ruefully. It's the first real expression on either of them; I take it as the signal for introductions. When I say I'm Don Fenton from St. Louis, she tells me their name is Parsons, from Bethesda, Maryland. She says it so nicely I don't at first notice we aren't being given first names. We all compliment Captain Estéban again.

His left eye is swelled shut, an inconvenience beneath his attention as a Maya, but Mrs. Parsons spots the way he's bracing his elbow in his ribs.

"You're hurt, captain."

"*Roto*—I think is broken." He's embarrassed at being in pain. We get him to peel off his Jaime shirt, revealing a nasty bruise in his superb dark-bay torso.

"Is there tape in that kit, Mr. Fenton? I've had a little first-aid training."

She begins to deal competently and very impersonally with the tape. Miss Parsons and I wander to the end of the bar and have a conversation which I am later to recall acutely.

"Roseate spoonbills," I tell her as three pink birds flap away.

"They're beautiful," she says in her tiny voice. They both have tiny voices. "He's a Mayan Indian, isn't he? The pilot, I mean."

"Right. The real thing, straight out of the Bonampak murals. Have you seen Chichén and Uxmal?"

"Yes. We were in Mérida. We're going to Tikal in Guatemala . . . I mean, we were."

"You'll get there." It occurs to me the girl needs cheering up. "Have they told you that Maya mothers used to tie a board on the infant's forehead to get that slant? They also hung a ball of tallow over its nose to make the eyes cross. It was considered aristocratic."

She smiles and takes another peek at Estéban. "People seem different in Yucatán," she says thoughtfully. "Not like the Indians around Mexico City. More, I don't know, independent."

"Comes from never having been conquered. Mayas got massacred and chased a lot, but nobody ever really flattened them. I bet you didn't know that the last Mexican-Maya war ended with a negotiated truce in nineteen thirty-five?"

"No!" Then she says seriously, "I like that."

"So do I."

"The water is really rising very fast," says Mrs. Parsons gently from behind us.

It is, and so is another *llovisno*. We climb back into the Bonanza. I try to rig my parka for a rain catcher, which blows loose as the storm hits fast and furious. We sort a couple of malt bars and my bottle of Jack Daniels out of the jumble in the cabin and make ourselves reasonably comfortable. The Parsons take a sip of whiskey each, Estéban and I considerably more. The Bonanza begins to bump soggily. Estéban makes an ancient one-eyed Mayan face at the water seeping into his cabin and goes to sleep. We all nap.

When the water goes down, the euphoria has gone with it, and we're very, very thirsty. It's also damn near sunset. I get to work with a bait-casting rod and some treble hooks and manage to foul-hook four small mullets. Estéban and the women tie the Bonanza's midget life raft out in the mangroves to catch rain. The wind is parching hot. No planes go by.

Finally another shower comes over and yields us six ounces of water apiece. When the sunset envelops the world in golden smoke, we squat on the sandbar to eat wet raw mullet and Instant Breakfast crumbs. The women are now in shorts, neat but definitely not sexy.

"I never realized how refreshing raw fish is," Mrs. Parsons says pleasantly. Her daughter chuckles, also pleasantly. She's on mamma's far side away from Estéban and me. I have Mrs. Parsons figured now; Mother Hen protecting only chick from male predators. That's all right with me. I came here to fish.

But something is irritating me. The damn women haven't complained once, you understand. Not a peep, not a quaver, no personal manifestations whatever. They're like something out of a manual.

"You really seem at home in the wilderness, Mrs. Parsons. You do much camping?"

"Oh, goodness no." Diffident laugh. "Not since my girl scout days. Oh, look —are those man-of-war birds?"

Answer a question with a question. I wait while the frigate birds sail nobly into the sunset.

"Bethesda . . . Would I be wrong in guessing you work for Uncle Sam?"

"Why, yes. You must be very familiar with Washington, Mr. Fenton. Does your work bring you there often?"

Anywhere but on our sandbar the little ploy would have worked. My hunter's gene twitches.

"Which agency are you with?"

She gives up gracefully. "Oh, just GSA records. I'm a librarian."

Of course. I know her now, all the Mrs. Parsonses in records divisions, accounting sections, research branches, personnel and administration offices. Tell Mrs. Parsons we need a recap on the external service contracts for fiscal '73. So Yucatán is on the tours now? Pity . . . I offer her the tired little joke. "You know where the bodies are buried."

She smiles deprecatingly and stands up. "It does get dark quickly, doesn't it?"

Time to get back into the plane.

A flock of ibis are circling us, evidently accustomed to roosting in our fig tree. Estéban produces a machete and a Mayan string hammock. He proceeds to sling it between tree and plane, refusing help. His machete stroke is noticeably tentative.

The Parsons are taking a pee behind the tail vane. I hear one of them slip and squeal faintly. When they come back over the hull, Mrs. Parsons asks, "Might we sleep in the hammock, captain?"

Estéban splits an unbelieving grin. I protest about rain and mosquitoes.

"Oh, we have insect repellent and we do enjoy fresh air."

The air is rushing by about force five and colder by the minute.

"We have our raincoats," the girl adds cheerfully.

Well, okay, ladies. We dangerous males retire inside the damp cabin. Through the wind I hear the women laugh softly now and then, apparently cozy in their chilly ibis roost. A private insanity, I decide. I know myself for the least threatening of men; my non-charisma has been in fact an asset jobwise, over the years. Are they having fantasies about Estéban? Or maybe they really are fresh-air nuts. . . . Sleep comes for me in invisible diesels roaring by on the reef outside.

We emerge dry-mouthed into a vast windy salmon sunrise. A diamond chip of sun breaks out of the sea and promptly submerges in cloud. I go to work with the rod and some mullet bait while two showers detour around us. Breakfast is a strip of wet barracuda apiece.

The Parsons continue stoic and helpful. Under Estéban's direction they set up a section of cowling for a gasoline flare in case we hear a plane, but nothing goes over except one unseen jet droning toward Panama. The wind howls, hot and dry and full of coral dust. So are we.

"They look first in the sea," Estéban remarks. His aristocratic frontal slope is beaded with sweat; Mrs. Parsons watches him concernedly. I watch the cloud blanket tearing by above, getting higher and dryer and thicker. While that lasts nobody is going to find us, and the water business is now unfunny.

Finally I borrow Estéban's machete and hack a long light pole. "There's a stream coming in back there, I saw it from the plane. Can't be more than two, three miles."

"I'm afraid the raft's torn." Mrs. Parsons shows me the cracks in the orange plastic; irritatingly, it's a Delaware label.

"All right," I hear myself announce. "The tide's going down. If we cut the good end of that air tube, I can haul water back in it. I've waded flats before."

Even to me it sounds crazy.

"Stay by plane," Estéban says. He's right, of course. He's also clearly running a fever. I look at the overcast and taste grit and old barracuda. The hell with the manual.

When I start cutting up the raft, Estéban tells me to take the serape. "You stay one night." He's right about that, too; I'll have to wait out the tide.

"I'll come with you," says Mrs. Parsons calmly.

I simply stare at her. What new madness has got into Mother Hen? Does she imagine Estéban is too battered to be functional? While I'm being astounded, my eyes take in the fact that Mrs. Parsons is now quite rosy around the knees, with her hair loose and a sunburn starting on her nose. A trim, in fact a very neat shading-forty.

"Look, that stuff is horrible going. Mud up to your ears and water over your head."

"I'm really quite fit and I swim a great deal. I'll try to keep up. Two would be much safer, Mr. Fenton, and we can bring more water."

She's serious. Well, I'm about as fit as a marshmallow at this time of winter, and I can't pretend I'm depressed by the idea of company. So be it.

"Let me show Miss Parsons how to work this rod."

Miss Parsons is even rosier and more windblown, and she's not clumsy with my tackle. A good girl, Miss Parsons, in her nothing way. We cut another staff and get some gear together. At the last minute Estéban shows how sick he feels: he offers me the machete. I thank him, but, no; I'm used to my Wirkkala knife. We tie some air into the plastic tube for a float and set out along the sandiest looking line.

Estéban raises one dark palm. *"Buen viaje."* Miss Parsons has hugged her mother and gone to cast from the mangrove. She waves. We wave.

An hour later we're barely out of waving distance. The going is surely god-awful. The sand keeps dissolving into silt you can't walk on or swim through, and the bottom is spiked with dead mangrove spears. We flounder from one pothole to the next, scaring up rays and turtles and hoping to God we don't kick a moray eel. Where we're not soaked in slime, we're desiccated, and we smell like the Old Cretaceous.

Mrs. Parsons keeps up doggedly. I only have to pull her out once. When I do so, I notice the sandbar is now out of sight.

Finally we reach the gap in the mangrove line I thought was the creek. It turns out to open into another arm of the bay, with more mangroves ahead. And the tide is coming in.

"I've had the world's lousiest idea."

Mrs. Parsons only says mildly, "It's so different from the view from the plane."

I revise my opinion of the girl scouts, and we plow on past the mangroves toward the smoky haze that has to be shore. The sun is setting in our faces, making it hard to see. Ibises and herons fly up around us, and once a big permit spooks ahead, his fin cutting a rooster tail. We fall into more potholes. The flashlights get soaked. I am having fantasies of the mangrove as universal obstacle; it's hard to recall I ever walked down a street, for instance, without stumbling over or under or through mangrove roots. And the sun is dropping down, down.

Suddenly we hit a ledge and fall over it into a cold flow.

"The stream! It's fresh water!"

We guzzle and garble and douse our heads; it's the best drink I remember. "Oh, my, oh, my . . .!" Mrs. Parsons is laughing right out loud.

"That dark place over to the right looks like real land."

We flounder across the flow and follow a hard shelf, which turns into solid bank and rises over our heads. Shortly there's a break beside a clump of spiny bromels, and we scramble up and flop down at the top, dripping and stinking. Out of sheer reflex my arm goes around my companion's shoulder—but Mrs. Parsons isn't there; she's up on her knees peering at the burnt-over plain around us.

"It's so good to see land one can walk on!" The tone is too innocent. *Noli me tangere.*

"Don't try it." I'm exasperated; the muddy little woman, what does she think? "That ground out there is a crush of ashes over muck, and it's full of stubs. You can go in over your knees."

"It seems firm here."

"We're in an alligator nursery. That was the slide we came up. Don't worry, by now the old lady's doubtless on her way to be made into handbags."

"What a shame."

"I better set a line down in the stream while I can still see."

I slide back down and rig a string of hooks that may get us breakfast. When I get back Mrs. Parsons is wringing muck out of the serape.

"I'm glad you warned me, Mr. Fenton. It *is* treacherous."

"Yeah." I'm over my irritation; God knows I don't want to *tangere* Mrs. Parsons, even if I weren't beat down to mush. "In its quiet way, Yucatán is a tough place to get around in. You can see why the Mayas built roads. Speaking of which—look!"

The last of the sunset is silhouetting a small square shape a couple of kilometers inland; a Maya *ruina* with a fig tree growing out of it.

"Lot of those around. People think they were guard towers."

"What a deserted-feeling land."

"Let's hope it's deserted by mosquitoes."

We slump down in the 'gator nursery and share the last malt bar, watching the stars slide in and out of the blowing clouds. The bugs aren't too bad; maybe the burn did them in. And it isn't hot any more, either—in fact, it's not even warm, wet as we are. Mrs. Parsons continues tranquilly interested in Yucatán and unmistakably uninterested in togetherness.

Just as I'm beginning to get aggressive notions about how we're going to spend the night if she expects me to give her the serape, she stands up, scuffs at a couple of hummocks and says, "I expect this is as good a place as any, isn't it, Mr. Fenton?"

With which she spreads out the raft bag for a pillow and lies down on her side in the dirt with exactly half the serape over her and the other corner folded neatly open. Her small back is toward me.

The demonstration is so convincing that I'm halfway under my share of serape before the preposterousness of it stops me.

"By the way. My name is Don."

"Oh, of course." Her voice is graciousness itself, "I'm Ruth."

I get in not quite touching her, and we lie there like two fish on a plate, exposed to the stars and smelling the smoke in the wind and feeling things underneath us. It is absolutely the most intimately awkward moment I've had in years.

The woman doesn't mean one thing to me, but the obtrusive recessiveness of her, the defiance of her little rump eight inches from my fly—for two pesos I'd have those shorts down and introduce myself. If I were twenty years younger. If I wasn't so bushed . . . But the twenty years and the exhaustion are there, and it comes to me wryly that Mrs. Ruth Parsons has judged things to a nicety. If I *were* twenty years younger, she wouldn't be here. Like the butterfish that float around a sated barracuda, only to vanish away the instant his intent changes, Mrs. Parsons knows her little shorts are safe. Those firmly filled little shorts, so close . . .

A warm nerve stirs in my groin—and just as it does I become aware of a silent emptiness beside me. Mrs. Parsons is imperceptibly inching away. Did my breathing change? Whatever, I'm perfectly sure that if my hand reached, she'd be elsewhere—probably announcing her intention to take a dip. The twenty years bring a chuckle to my throat, and I relax.

"Good night, Ruth."

"Good night, Don."

And believe it or not, we sleep, while the armadas of the wind roar overhead.

Light wakes me—a cold white glare.

My first thought is 'gator hunters. Best to manifest ourselves as *turistas* as fast as possible. I scramble up, noting that Ruth has dived under the bromel clump.

"*Quién estás? A secorro!* Help, *señores!*"

No answer except the light goes out, leaving me blind.

I yell some more in a couple of languages. It stays dark. There's a vague scrabbling, whistling sound somewhere in the burn-off. Liking everything less by the minute, I try a speech about our plane having crashed and we need help.

A very narrow pencil of light flicks over us and snaps off.

"Eh-ep," says a blurry voice and something metallic twitters. They for sure aren't locals. I'm getting unpleasant ideas.

"Yes, help!"

Something goes *crackle-crackle whish-whish,* and all sounds fade away.

"What the holy hell!" I stumble toward where they were.

"Look." Ruth whispers behind me. "Over by the ruin."

I look and catch a multiple flicker which winks out fast.

"A camp?"

And I take two more blind strides. My leg goes down through the crust, and a spike spears me just where you stick the knife in to unjoint a drumstick. By the pain that goes through my bladder I recognize that my trick kneecap has caught it.

For instant basket case you can't beat kneecaps. First you discover your knee doesn't bend any more, so you try putting some weight on it, and a bayonet goes up your spine and unhinges your jaw. Little grains of gristle have got into the sensitive bearing surface. The knee tries to buckle and can't, and mercifully you fall down.

Ruth helps me back to the serape.

"What a fool, what a god-forgotten imbecile. . . ."

"Not at all, Don. It was perfectly natural." We strike matches; her fingers push mine aside, exploring. "I think it's in place, but it's swelling fast. I'll lay a wet handkerchief on it. We'll have to wait for morning to check the cut. Were they poachers, do you think?"

"Probably," I lie. What I think they were is smugglers.

She comes back with a soaked bandanna and drapes it on. "We must have frightened them. That light . . . it seemed so bright."

"Some hunting party. People do crazy things around here."

"Perhaps they'll come back in the morning."

"Could be."

Ruth pulls up the wet serape, and we say good night again. Neither of us is mentioning how we're going to get back to the plane without help.

I lie staring south where Alpha Centauri is blinking in and out of the overcast and cursing myself for the sweet mess I've made. My first idea is giving way to an even less pleasing one.

Smuggling, around here, is a couple of guys in an outboard meeting a shrimp boat by the reef. They don't light up the sky or have some kind of swamp buggy that goes whoosh. Plus a big camp . . . paramilitary-type equipment?

I've seen a report of Guevarista infiltrators operating on the British Honduran border, which is about a hundred kilometers—sixty miles—south of here. Right under those clouds. If that's what looked us over, I'll be more than happy if they don't come back. . . .

I wake up in pelting rain, alone. My first move confirms that my leg is as expected—a giant misplaced erection bulging out of my shorts. I raise up painfully to see Ruth standing by the bromels, looking over the bay. Solid wet nimbus is pouring out of the south.

"No planes today."

"Oh, good morning, Don. Should we look at that cut now?"

"It's minimal." In fact the skin is hardly broken, and no deep puncture. Totally out of proportion to the havoc inside.

"Well, they have water to drink," Ruth says tranquilly. "Maybe those hunters will come back. I'll go see if we have a fish—that is, can I help you in any way, Don?"

Very tactful. I emit an ungracious negative, and she goes off about her private concerns.

They certainly are private, too; when I recover from my own sanitary efforts, she's still away. Finally I hear splashing.

"It's a big fish!" More splashing. Then she climbs up the bank with a three-pound mangrove snapper—and something else.

It isn't until after the messy work of filleting the fish that I begin to notice.

She's making a smudge of chaff and twigs to singe the fillets, small hands very quick, tension in that female upper lip. The rain has eased off for the moment; we're sluicing wet but warm enough. Ruth brings me my fish on a mangrove skewer and sits back on her heels with an odd breathy sigh.

"Aren't you joining me?"

"Oh, of course." She gets a strip and picks at it, saying quickly, "We either have too much salt or too little, don't we? I should fetch some brine." Her eyes are roving from nothing to no place.

"Good thought." I hear another sigh and decide the girl scouts need an assist. "Your daughter mentioned you've come from Mérida. Have you seen much of Mexico?"

"Not really. Last year we went to Mazatlán and Cuernavaca. . . ." She puts the fish down, frowning.

"And you're going to see Tikal. Going to Bonampak too?"

"No." Suddenly she jumps up brushing rain off her face. "I'll bring you some water, Don."

She ducks down the slide, and after a fair while comes back with a full bromel stalk.

"Thanks." She's standing above me, staring restlessly around the horizon.

"Ruth, I hate to say it, but those guys are not coming back and it's probably just as well. Whatever they were up to, we looked like trouble. The most they'll do is tell someone we're here. That'll take a day or two to get around, we'll be back at the plane by then."

"I'm sure you're right, Don." She wanders over to the smudge fire.

"And quit fretting about your daughter. She's a big girl."

"Oh, I'm sure Althea's all right. . . . They have plenty of water now." Her fingers drum on her thigh. It's raining again.

"Come on, Ruth. Sit down. Tell me about Althea. Is she still in college?"

She gives that sighing little laugh and sits. "Althea got her degree last year. She's in computer programming."

"Good for her. And what about you, what do you do in GSA records?"

"I'm in Foreign Procurement Archives." She smiles mechanically, but her breathing is shallow. "It's very interesting."

"I know a Jack Wittig in Contracts, maybe you know him?"

It sounds pretty absurd, there in the 'gator slide.

"Oh, I've met Mr. Wittig. I'm sure he wouldn't remember me."

"Why not?"

"I'm not very memorable."

Her voice is factual. She's perfectly right, of course. Who was that woman, Mrs. Jannings, Janny, who coped with my per diem for years? Competent, agreeable, impersonal. She had a sick father or something. But dammit, Ruth is a lot younger and better-looking. Comparatively speaking.

"Maybe Mrs. Parsons doesn't want to be memorable."

She makes a vague sound, and I suddenly realize Ruth isn't listening to me at all. Her hands are clenched around her knees, she's staring inland at the ruin.

"Ruth, I tell you our friends with the light are in the next county by now. Forget it, we don't need them."

Her eyes come back to me as if she'd forgotten I was there, and she nods slowly. It seems to be too much effort to speak. Suddenly she cocks her head and jumps up again.

"I'll go look at the line, Don. I thought I heard something." She's gone like a rabbit.

While she's away I try getting up onto my good leg and the staff. The pain is sickening; knees seem to have some kind of hot line to the stomach. I take a couple of hops to test whether the Demerol I have in my belt would get me walking. As I do so, Ruth comes up the bank with a fish flapping in her hands.

"Oh, no, Don! *No!*" She actually clasps the snapper to her breast.

"The water will take some of my weight. I'd like to give it a try."

"You mustn't!" Ruth says quite violently and instantly modulates down. "Look at the bay, Don. One can't see a thing."

I teeter there, tasting bile and looking at the mingled curtains of sun and rain driving across the water. She's right, thank God. Even with two good legs we could get into trouble out there.

"I guess one more night won't kill us."

I let her collapse me back onto the gritty plastic, and she positively bustles around, finding me a chunk to lean on, stretching the serape on both staffs to keep rain off me, bringing another drink, grubbing for dry tinder.

"I'll make us a real bonfire as soon as it lets up, Don. They'll see our smoke, they'll know we're all right. We just have to wait." Cheery smile. "Is there any way we can make you more comfortable?"

Holy Saint Sterculius: playing house in a mud puddle. For a fatuous moment I wonder if Mrs. Parsons has designs on me. And then she lets out another sigh and sinks back onto her heels with that listening look. Unconsciously her rump wiggles a little. My ear picks up the operative word: *wait.*

Ruth Parsons is waiting. In fact, she acts as if she's waiting so hard it's killing her. For what? For someone to get us out of here, what else? . . . But why was she so horrified when I got up to try to leave? Why all this tension?

My paranoia stirs. I grab it by the collar and start idly checking back. Up to when whoever it was showed up last night, Mrs. Parson was, I guess, normal. Calm and sensible, anyway. Now she's humming like a high wire. And she seems to want to stay here and wait. Just as an intellectual pastime, why?

Could she have intended to come here? No way. Where she planned to be was Chetumal, which is on the border. Come to think, Chetumal is an odd way around to Tikal. Let's say the scenario was that she's meeting somebody in Chetumal. Somebody who's part of an organization. So now her contact in Chetumal knows she's overdue. And when those types appeared last night, something suggests to her that they're part of the same organization. And she hopes they'll put one and one together and come back for her?

"May I have the knife, Don? I'll clean the fish."

Rather slowly I pass the knife, kicking my subconscious. Such a decent ordinary little woman, a good girl scout. My trouble is that I've bumped into too many professional agilities under the careful stereotypes. *I'm not very memorable. . . .*

What's in Foreign Procurement Archives? Wittig handles classified contracts. Lots of money stuff; foreign currency negotiations, commodity price schedules, some industrial technology. Or—just as a hypothesis—it could be as simple as a wad of bills back in that modest beige Ventura, to be exchanged for a packet from, say, Costa Rica. If she were a courier, they'd want to get at the plane. And then what about me and maybe Estéban? Even hypothetically, not good.

I watch her hacking at the fish, forehead knotted with effort, teeth in her lip. Mrs. Ruth Parsons of Bethesda, this thrumming, private woman. How crazy can I get? *They'll see our smoke. . . .*

"Here's your knife, Don. I washed it. Does the leg hurt very badly?"

I blink away the fantasies and see a scared little woman in a mangrove swamp.

"Sit down, rest. You've been going all out."

She sits obediently, like a kid in a dentist chair.

"You're stewing about Althea. And she's probably worried about you. We'll get back tomorrow under our own steam, Ruth."

"Honestly I'm not worried at all, Don." The smile fades; she nibbles her lip, frowning out at the bay.

"You know, Ruth, you surprised me when you offered to come along. Not that I don't appreciate it. But I rather thought you'd be concerned about leaving Althea alone with our good pilot. Or was it only me?"

This gets her attention at last.

"I believe Captain Estéban is a very fine type of man."

The words surprise me a little. Isn't the correct line more like "I trust Althea," or even, indignantly, "Althea is a good girl?"

"He's a man. Althea seemed to think he was interesting."

She goes on staring at the bay. And then I notice her tongue flick out and lick that prehensile upper lip. There's a flush that isn't sunburn around her ears and throat too, and one hand is gently rubbing her thigh. What's she seeing, out there in the flats?

Oho.

Captain Estéban's mahogany arms clasping Miss Althea Parsons's pearly body. Captain Estéban's archaic nostrils snuffling in Miss Parsons's tender neck. Captain Estéban's copper buttocks pumping into Althea's creamy upturned bottom. . . . The hammock, very bouncy. Mayas know all about it.

Well, well. So Mother Hen has her little quirks.

I feel fairly silly and more than a little irritated. *Now* I find out. . . . But even vicarious lust has much to recommend it, here in the mud and rain. I settle back, recalling that Miss Althea the computer programmer had waved good-by very composedly. Was she sending her mother to flounder across the bay with me so she can get programmed in Maya? The memory of Honduran mahogany logs drifting in and out of the opalescent sand comes to me. Just as I am about to suggest that Mrs. Parsons might care to share my rain shelter, she remarks serenely, "The Mayas seem to be a very fine type of people. I believe you said so to Althea."

The implications fall on me with the rain. *Type.* As in breeding, bloodline, sire. Am I supposed to have certified Estéban not only as a stud but as a genetic donor?

"Ruth, are you telling me you're prepared to accept a half-Indian grandchild?"

"Why, Don, that's up to Althea, you know."

Looking at the mother, I guess it is. Oh, for mahogany gonads.

Ruth has gone back to listening to the wind, but I'm not about to let her off that easy. Not after all that *noli me tangere* jazz.

"What will Althea's father think?"

Her face snaps around at me, genuinely startled.

"Althea's father?" Complicated semi-smile. "He won't mind."

"He'll accept it too, eh?" I see her shake her head as if a fly were bothering her and add with a cripple's malice: "Your husband must be a very fine type of a man."

Ruth looks at me, pushing her wet hair back abruptly. I have the impression that mousy Mrs. Parsons is roaring out of control, but her voice is quiet.

"There isn't any Mr. Parsons, Don. There never was. Althea's father was a Danish medical student. . . . I believe he has gained considerable prominence."

"Oh." Something warns me not to say I'm sorry. "You mean he doesn't know about Althea?"

"No." She smiles, her eyes bright and cuckoo.

"Seems like rather a rough deal for her."

"I grew up quite happily under the same circumstances."

Bang, I'm dead. Well, well, well. A mad image blooms in my mind: generations of solitary Parsons women selecting sires, making impregnation trips. Well, I hear the world is moving their way.

"I better look at the fish line."

She leaves. The glow fades. *No.* Just no, no contact. Good-by, Captain Estéban. My leg is very uncomfortable. The hell with Mrs. Parsons's long-distance orgasm.

We don't talk much after that, which seems to suit Ruth. The odd day drags by. Squall after squall blows over us. Ruth singes up some more fillets, but the rain drowns her smudge; it seems to pour hardest just as the sun's about to show.

Finally she comes to sit under my sagging serape, but there's no warmth there. I doze, aware of her getting up now and then to look around. My subconscious notes that she's still twitchy. I tell my subconscious to knock it off.

Presently I wake up to find her penciling on the water-soaked pages of a little note pad.

"What's that, a shopping list for alligators?"

Automatic polite laugh. "Oh, just an address. In case we—I'm being silly, Don."

"Hey," I sit up, wincing, "Ruth, quit fretting. I mean it. We'll all be out of this soon. You'll have a great story to tell."

She doesn't look up. "Yes . . . I guess we will."

"Come on, we're doing fine. There isn't any real danger here, you know. Unless you're allergic to fish?"

Another good-little-girl laugh, but there's a shiver in it.

"Sometimes I think I'd like to go . . . really far away."

To keep her talking I say the first thing in my head.

"Tell me, Ruth. I'm curious why you would settle for that kind of lonely life, there in Washington? I mean, a woman like you . . ."

"Should get married?" She gives a shaky sigh, pushing the notebook back in her wet pocket.

"Why not? It's the normal source of companionship. Don't tell me you're trying to be some kind of professional man-hater."

"Lesbian, you mean?" Her laugh sounds better. "With my security rating? No, I'm not."

"Well, then. Whatever trauma you went through, these things don't last forever. You can't hate all men."

The smile is back. "Oh, there wasn't any trauma, Don, and I *don't* hate men. That would be as silly as—as hating the weather." She glances wryly at the blowing rain.

"I think you have a grudge. You're even spooky of me."

Smooth as a mouse bite she says, "I'd love to hear about your family, Don."

Touché. I give her the edited version of how I don't have one any more, and she says she's sorry, how sad. And we chat about what a good life a single person really has, and how she and her friends enjoy plays and concerts and travel, and one of them is head cashier for Ringling Brothers, how about that?

But it's coming out jerkier and jerkier like a bad tape, with her eyes going round the horizon in the pauses and her face listening for something that isn't my voice. What's wrong with her? Well, what's wrong with any furtively unconventional middle-aged woman with an empty bed. And a security clearance. An old habit of mind remarks unkindly that Mrs. Parsons represents what is known as the classic penetration target.

"So much more opportunity now." Her voice trails off.

"Hurrah for women's lib, eh?"

"The lib?" Impatiently she leans forward and tugs the serape straight. "Oh, that's doomed."

The apocalyptic word jars my attention.

"What do you mean, doomed?"

She glances at me as if I weren't hanging straight either and says vaguely, "Oh . . ."

"Come on, why doomed? Didn't they get that equal rights bill?"

Long hesitation. When she speaks again her voice is different.

"Women have no rights, Don, except what men allow us. Men are more aggressive and powerful and they run the world. When the next real crisis upsets them, our so-called rights will vanish like—like that smoke. We'll be back where we always were: property. And whatever has gone wrong will be blamed on our freedom, like the fall of Rome was. You'll see."

Now all this is delivered in a gray tone of total conviction. The last time I heard that tone, the speaker was explaining why he had to keep his file drawers full of dead pigeons.

"Oh, come on. You and your friends are the backbone of the system; if you quit, the country would come to a screeching halt before lunch."

No answering smile.

"That's fantasy." Her voice is still quiet. "Women don't work that way. We're a—a toothless world." She looks around as if she wanted to stop talking. "What women do is survive. We live by ones and twos in the chinks of your world-machine."

"Sounds like a guerrilla operation." I'm not really joking, here in the 'gator den. In fact, I'm wondering if I spent too much thought on mahogany logs.

"Guerrillas have something to hope for." Suddenly she switches on a jolly smile. "Think of us as opossums, Don. Did you know there are opossums living all over? Even in New York City."

I smile back with my neck prickling. I thought I was the paranoid one.

"Men and women aren't different species, Ruth. Women do everything men do."

"Do they?" Our eyes meet, but she seems to be seeing ghosts between us in the rain. She mutters something that could be "My Lai" and looks away. "All the endless wars . . ." Her voice is a whisper. "All the huge authoritarian organizations for doing unreal things. Men live to struggle against each other; we're just part of the battlefields. It'll never change unless you change the whole world. I dream sometimes of—of going away . . ." She checks and abruptly changes voice. "Forgive me, Don, it's so stupid saying all this."

"Men hate wars too, Ruth," I say as gently as I can.

"I know." She shrugs and climbs to her feet. "But that's your problem, isn't it?"

End of communication. Mrs. Ruth Parsons isn't even living in the same world with me.

I watch her move around restlessly, head turning toward the ruins. Alienation like that can add up to dead pigeons, which would be GSA's problem. It could also lead to believing some joker who's promising to change the whole world. Which could just probably be my problem if one of them was over in that camp last night, where she keeps looking. *Guerrillas have something to hope for . . . ?*

Nonsense. I try another position and see that the sky seems to be clearing as the sun sets. The wind is quieting down at last too. Insane to think this little woman is acting out some fantasy in this swamp. But that equipment last night was no fantasy; if those lads have some connection with her, I'll be in the way.

You couldn't find a handier spot to dispose of the body. . . . Maybe some Guevarista is a fine type of man?

Absurd. Sure . . . The only thing more absurd would be to come through the wars and get myself terminated by a mad librarian's boyfriend on a fishing trip.

A fish flops in the stream below us. Ruth spins around so fast she hits the serape. "I better start the fire," she says, her eyes still on the plain and her head cocked, listening.

All right, let's test.

"Expecting company?"

It rocks her. She freezes, and her eyes come swiveling around at me like a film take captioned *Fright.* I can see her decide to smile.

"Oh, one never can tell!" She laughs weirdly, the eyes not changed. "I'll get the—the kindling." She fairly scuttles into the brush.

Nobody, paranoid or not, could call *that* a normal reaction.

Ruth Parsons is either psycho or she's expecting something to happen—and it has nothing to do with me; I scared her pissless.

Well, she could be nuts. And I could be wrong, but there are some mistakes you only make once.

Reluctantly I unzip my body belt, telling myself that if I think what I think, my only course is to take something for my leg and get as far as possible from Mrs. Ruth Parsons before whoever she's waiting for arrives.

In my belt also is a .32 caliber asset Ruth doesn't know about—and it's going to stay there. My longevity program leaves the shoot-outs to TV and stresses being somewhere else when the roof falls in. I can spend a perfectly safe and also perfectly horrible night out in one of those mangrove flats. . . . Am I insane?

At this moment Ruth stands up and stares blatantly inland with her hand shading her eyes. Then she tucks something into her pocket, buttons up and tightens her belt.

That does it.

I dry-swallow two 100-mg tabs, which should get me ambulatory and still leave me wits to hide. Give it a few minutes. I make sure my compass and some hooks are in my own pocket and sit waiting while Ruth fusses with her smudge fire, sneaking locks away when she thinks I'm not watching.

The flat world around us is turning into an unearthly amber and violet light show as the first numbness sweeps into my leg. Ruth has crawled under the bromels for more dry stuff; I can see her foot. Okay. I reach for my staff.

Suddenly the foot jerks, and Ruth yells—or rather, her throat makes that

Uh-uh-hhh that means pure horror. The foot disappears in a rattle of bromel stalks.

I lunge upright on the crutch and look over the bank at a frozen scene.

Ruth is crouching sideways on the ledge, clutching her stomach. They are about a yard below, floating on the river in a skiff. While I was making up my stupid mind, her friends have glided right under my ass. There are three of them.

They are tall and white. I try to see them as men in some kind of white jumpsuits. The one nearest the bank is stretching out a long white arm toward Ruth. She jerks and scuttles farther away.

The arm stretches after her. It stretches and stretches. It stretches two yards and stays hanging in the air. Small black things are wiggling from its tip.

I look where their faces should be and see black hollow dishes with vertical stripes. The stripes move slowly. . . .

There is no more possibility of their being human—or anything else I've ever seen. What has Ruth conjured up?

The scene is totally silent. I blink, blink—this cannot be real. The two in the far end of the skiff are writhing those arms around an apparatus on a tripod. A weapon? Suddenly I hear the same blurry voice I heard in the night.

"Guh-give," it groans. "G-give. . . ."

Dear God, it's real, whatever it is. I'm terrified. My mind is trying not to form a word.

And Ruth—Jesus, of course—Ruth is terrified too; she's edging along the bank away from them, gaping at the monsters in the skiff who are obviously nobody's friends. She's hugging something to her body. Why doesn't she get over the bank and circle back behind me?

"G-g-give." That wheeze is coming from the tripod. "Pee-eeze give." The skiff is moving upstream below Ruth, following her. The arm undulates out at her again, its black digits looping. Ruth scrambles to the top of the bank.

"Ruth!" My voice cracks. "Ruth, get over here behind me!"

She doesn't look at me, only keeps sidling farther away. My terror detonates into anger.

"Come back here!" With my free hand I'm working the .32 out of my belt. The sun has gone down.

She doesn't turn but straightens up warily, still hugging the thing. I see her mouth working. Is she actually trying to *talk* to them?

"Please . . ." She swallows. "Please speak to me. I need your help."

"RUTH!!"

At this moment the nearest white monster whips into a great S-curve and sails right onto the bank at her, eight feet of snowy rippling horror.

And I shoot Ruth.

I don't know that for a minute—I've yanked the gun up so fast that my staff slips and dumps me as I fire. I stagger up, hearing Ruth scream "No! No! No!"

The creature is back down by his boat, and Ruth is still farther away, clutching herself. Blood is running down her elbow.

"Stop it, Don! They aren't attacking you!"

"For God's sake! Don't be a fool, I can't help you if you won't get away from them!"

No reply. Nobody moves. No sound except the drone of a jet passing far above. In the darkening stream below me the three white figures shift uneasily; I get the impression of radar dishes focusing. The word spells itself in my head: *Aliens.*

Extraterrestrials.

What do I do, call the president? Capture them single-handed with my peashooter? . . . I'm alone in the arse end of nowhere with one leg and my brain cuddled in meperidine hydrochloride.

"Prrr-eese," their machine blurs again. "Wa-wat hep . . ."

"Our plane fell down," Ruth says in a very distinct, eerie voice. She points up at the jet, out toward the bay. "My—my child is there. Please take us *there* in your boat."

Dear God. While she's gesturing, I get a look at the thing she's hugging in her wounded arm. It's metallic, like a big glimmering distributor head. What . . . ?

Wait a minute. This morning: when she was gone so long, she could have found that thing. Something they left behind. Or dropped. And she hid it, not telling me. That's why she kept going under that bromel clump—she was peeking at it. Waiting. And the owners came back and caught her. They want it. She's trying to bargain, by God.

"—Water," Ruth is pointing again. "Take us. Me. And him."

The black faces turn toward me, blind and horrible. Later on I may be grateful for that "us." Not now.

"Throw your gun away, Don. They'll take us back." Her voice is weak.

"Like hell I will. You—who are you? What are you doing here?"

"Oh God, does it matter? He's frightened," she cries to them. "Can you understand?"

She's an alien as they, there in the twilight. The beings in the skiff are twittering among themselves. Their box starts to moan.

"Ss-stu-dens," I make out. "S-stu-ding . . . not—huh-arm-ing . . . w-we . . . buh . . ." It fades into garble and then says "G-give . . . we . . . g-go. . . ."

Peace-loving cultural-exchange students—on the interstellar level now. Oh, no.

"Bring that thing here, Ruth—right now!"

But she's starting down the bank toward them saying, "Take me."

"Wait! You need a tourniquet on that arm."

"I know. Please put the gun down, Don."

She's actually at the skiff, right by them. They aren't moving.

"Jesus Christ." Slowly, reluctantly, I drop the .32. When I start down the slide, I find I'm floating; adrenaline and Demerol are a bad mix.

The skiff comes gliding toward me, Ruth in the bow clutching the thing and her arm. The aliens stay in the stern behind their tripod, away from me. I note the skiff is camouflaged tan and green. The world around us is deep shadowy blue.

"Don, bring the water bag!"

As I'm dragging down the plastic bag, it occurs to me that Ruth really is cracking up, the water isn't needed now. But my own brain seems to have gone into overload. All I can focus on is a long white rubbery arm with black worms clutching the far end of the orange tube, helping me fill it. This isn't happening.

"Can you get in, Don?" As I hoist my numb legs up, two long white pipes reach for me. *No you don't.* I kick and tumble in beside Ruth. She moves away.

A creaky hum starts up, it's coming from a wedge in the center of the skiff. And we're in motion, sliding toward dark mangrove files.

I stare mindlessly at the wedge. Alien technological secrets? I can't see any, the power source is under that triangular cover, about two feet long. The gadgets on the tripod are equally cryptic, except that one has a big lens. Their light?

As we hit the open bay, the hum rises and we start planing faster and faster still. Thirty knots? Hard to judge in the dark. Their hull seems to be a modified trihedral much like ours, with a remarkable absence of slap. Say twenty-two feet. Schemes of capturing it swirl in my mind. I'll need Estéban.

Suddenly a huge flood of white light fans out over us from the tripod, blotting out the aliens in the stern. I see Ruth pulling at a belt around her arm still hugging the gizmo.

"I'll tie that for you."

"It's all right."

The alien device is twinkling or phosphorescing slightly. I lean over to look, whispering, "Give that to me, I'll pass it to Estéban."

"No!" She scoots away, almost over the side. "It's theirs, they need it!"

"What? Are you crazy?" I'm so taken aback by this idiocy I literally stammer. "We have to, we . . ."

"They haven't hurt us. I'm sure they could." Her eyes are watching me with feral intensity; in the light her face has a lunatic look. Numb as I am, I realize that the wretched woman is poised to throw herself over the side if I move. With the alien thing.

"I think they're gentle," she mutters.

"For Christ's sake, Ruth, they're *aliens!*"

"I'm used to it," she says absently. "There's the island! Stop! Stop here!"

The skiff slows, turning. A mound of foliage is tiny in the light. Metal glints —the plane.

"Althea! Althea! Are you all right?"

Yells, movement on the plane. The water is high, we're floating over the bar. The aliens are keeping us in the lead with the light hiding them. I see one pale figure splashing toward us and a dark one behind, coming more slowly. Estéban must be puzzled by that light.

"Mr. Fenton is hurt, Althea. These people brought us back with the water. Are you all right?"

"A-okay." Althea flounders up, peering excitedly. "You all right? Whew, that light!" Automatically I start handing her the idiotic water bag.

"Leave that for the captain," Ruth says sharply. "Althea, can you climb into the boat? Quickly, it's important."

"Coming."

"No, no!" I protest, but the skiff tilts as Althea swarms in. The aliens twitter, and their voice box starts groaning. "Gu-give . . . now . . . give. . . ."

"*Que llega?*" Estéban's face appears beside me, squinting fiercely into the light.

"Grab it, get it from her—that thing she has . . ." but Ruth's voice rides over mine. "Captain, lift Mr. Fenton out of the boat. He's hurt his leg. Hurry, please."

"Goddamn it, wait!" I shout, but an arm has grabbed my middle. When a Maya boosts you, you go. I hear Althea saying, "Mother, your arm!" and fall onto Estéban. We stagger around in water up to my waist; I can't feel my feet at all.

When I get steady, the boat is yards away. The two women are head-to-head, murmuring.

"Get them!" I tug loose from Estéban and flounder forward. Ruth stands up in the boat facing the invisible aliens.

"Take us with you. Please. We want to go with you, away from here."

"Ruth! Estéban, get that boat!" I lunge and lose my feet again. The aliens are chirruping madly behind their light.

"Please take us. We don't mind what your planet is like; we'll learn—we'll do anything! We won't cause any trouble. Please. Oh, *please.*" The skiff is drifting farther away.

"Ruth! Althea! Are you crazy? Wait . . ." But I can only shuffle nightmare-like in the ooze, hearing that damn voice box wheeze, "N-not come . . . more . . . not come . . ." Althea's face turns to it, open-mouthed grin.

"Yes, we understand," Ruth cries. "We don't want to come back. Please take us with you!"

I shout and Estéban splashes past me shouting too, something about radio.

"Yes-s-s," groans the voice.

Ruth sits down suddenly, clutching Althea. At that moment Estéban grabs the edge of the skiff beside her.

"Hold them, Estéban! Don't let her go."

He gives me one slit-eyed glance over his shoulder, and I recognize his total uninvolvement. He's had a good look at that camouflage paint and the absence of fishing gear. I make a desperate rush and slip again. When I come up Ruth is saying, "We're going with these people, captain. Please take your money out of my purse, it's in the plane. And give this to Mr. Fenton."

She passes him something small; the notebook. He takes it slowly.

"Estéban! No!"

He has released the skiff.

"Thank you so much," Ruth says as they float apart. Her voice is shaky; she raises it. "There won't be any trouble, Don. Please send this cable. It's to a friend of mine, she'll take care of everything." Then she adds the craziest touch of the entire night. "She's a grand person; she's director of nursing training at N.I.H."

As the skiff drifts, I hear Althea add something that sounds like "Right on."

Sweet Jesus . . . Next minute the humming has started; the light is receding fast. The last I see of Mrs. Ruth Parsons and Miss Althea Parsons is two small shadows against that light, like two opossums. The light snaps off, the hum deepens—and they're going, going, gone away.

In the dark water beside me Estéban is instructing everybody in general to *chingarse* themselves.

"Friends, or something," I tell him lamely. "She seemed to want to go with them."

He is pointedly silent, hauling me back to the plane. He knows what could be around here better than I do, and Mayas have their own longevity program. His condition seems improved. As we get in I notice the hammock has been repositioned.

In the night—of which I remember little—the wind changes. And at seven-thirty next morning a Cessna buzzes the sandbar under cloudless skies.

By noon we're back in Cozumel, Captain Estéban accepts his fees and departs laconically for his insurance wars. I leave the Parsons's bags with the Caribe agent, who couldn't care less. The cable goes to a Mrs. Priscilla Hayes Smith, also of Bethesda. I take myself to a medico and by three o'clock I'm sitting on the Cabañas terrace with a fat leg and a double margarita, trying to believe the whole thing.

The cable said, *Althea and I taking extraordinary opportunity for travel. Gone several years. Please take charge our affairs. Love, Ruth.*

She'd written it that afternoon, you understand.

I order another double, wishing to hell I'd gotten a good look at that gizmo. Did it have a label. Made by Betelgeusians? No matter how weird it was, *how* could a person be crazy enough to imagine . . . ?

Not only that but to hope, to plan? *If I could only go away* . . . That's what she was doing, all day. Waiting, hoping, figuring how to get Althea. To go sight unseen to an alien world. . . .

With the third margarita I try a joke about alienated women, but my heart's not in it. And I'm certain there won't be any bother, any trouble at all. Two human women, one of them possibly pregnant, have departed for, I guess, the stars; and the fabric of society will never show a ripple. I brood: do all Mrs. Parsons's friends hold themselves in readiness for any eventuality, including leaving Earth? And will Mrs. Parsons somehow one day contrive to send for Mrs. Priscilla Hayes Smith, that grand person?

I can only send for another cold one, musing on Althea. What suns will Captain Estéban's sloe-eyed offspring, if any, look upon? "Get in, Althea, we're taking off for Orion." "A-okay, mother." Is that some system of upbringing? *We survive by ones and twos in the chinks of your world-machine . . . I'm used to aliens* . . . She'd meant every word. Insane. How could a woman choose to live among unknown monsters, to say good-by to her home, her world?

As the margaritas take hold, the whole mad scenario melts down to the image of those two small shapes sitting side by side in the receding alien glare.

Two of our opossums are missing.

POUL ANDERSON

The Queen of Air and Darkness

*The history of human civilization is one of constant struggle—
between famine and plenty, between "good" and "evil," between
progress and reaction, to name only three. One of the most important historically has been the struggle between the forces of science
and the forces of magic in its various forms. Here Poul Anderson
carries this battle into the future in a stunning story that combines
his knowledge of science with his talent for vivid, poetic writing.*

The last glow of the last sunset would linger almost until midwinter.
But there would be no more day, and the northlands rejoiced. Blossoms
opened, flamboyance on firethorn trees, steel-flowers rising blue from the
brok and rainplant that cloaked all hills, shy whiteness of kiss-me-never
down in the dales. Flitteries darted among them on iridescent wings; a
crownbuck shook his horns and bugled. Between horizons the sky deepened from purple to sable. Both moons were aloft, nearly full, shining
frosty on leaves and molten on waters. The shadows they made were
blurred by an aurora, a great blowing curtain of light across half heaven.
Behind it the earliest stars had come out.

A boy and a girl sat on Wolund's Barrow just under the dolmen it up-
bore. Their hair, which streamed halfway down their backs, showed startlingly forth, bleached as it was by summer. Their bodies, still dark from
that season, merged with earth and bush and rock, for they wore only garlands. He played on a bone flute and she sang. They had lately become
lovers. Their age was about sixteen, but they did not know this, considering themselves Outlings and thus indifferent to time, remembering little

or nothing of how they had once dwelt in the lands of men.

His notes piped cold around her voice:

> Cast a spell,
> weave it well
> of dust and dew
> and night and you.

A brook by the grave mound, carrying moonlight down to a hill-hidden river, answered with its rapids. A flock of hellbats passed black beneath the aurora.

A shape came bounding over Cloudmoor. It had two arms and two legs, but the legs were long and claw-footed and feathers covered it to the end of a tail and broad wings. The face was half human, dominated by its eyes. Had Ayoch been able to stand wholly erect, he would have reached to the boy's shoulder.

The girl rose. "He carries a burden," she said. Her vision was not meant for twilight like that of a northland creature born, but she had learned how to use every sign her senses gave her. Besides the fact that ordinarily a pook would fly, there was a heaviness to his haste.

"And he comes from the south." Excitement jumped in the boy, sudden as a green flame that went across the constellation Lyrth. He sped down the mound. "Ohoi, Ayoch!" he called. "Me here, Mistherd!"

"And Shadow-of-a-Dream," the girl laughed, following.

The pook halted. He breathed louder than the soughing in the growth around him. A smell of bruised yerba lifted where he stood.

"Well met in winterbirth," he whistled. "You can help me bring this to Carheddin."

He held out what he bore. His eyes were yellow lanterns above. It moved and whimpered.

"Why, a child," Mistherd said.

"Even as you were, my son, even as you were. Ho, ho, what a snatch!" Ayoch boasted. "They were a score in yon camp by Fallowwood, armed, and besides watcher engines they had big ugly dogs aprowl while they slept. I came from above, however, having spied on them till I knew that a handful of dazedust . . ."

"The poor thing." Shadow-of-a-Dream took the boy and held him to her small breasts. "So full of sleep yet, aren't you?" Blindly, he sought a nipple. She smiled through the veil of her hair. "No, I am still too young, and you already too old. But come, when you wake in Carheddin under the mountain, you shall feast."

"Yo-ah," said Ayoch very softly. "She is abroad and has heard and seen. She comes." He crouched down, wings folded. After a moment Mistherd knelt, and then Shadow-of-a-Dream, though she did not let go the child.

The queen's tall form blocked off the moons. For a while she regarded the three and their booty. Hill and moor sounds withdrew from their awareness until it seemed they could hear the northlights hiss.

At last Ayoch whispered, "Have I done well, Starmother?"

"If you stole a babe from a camp full of engines," said the beautiful voice, "then they were folk out of the far south who may not endure it as meekly as yeomen."

"But what can they do, Snowmaker?" the pook asked. "How can they track us?"

Mistherd lifted his head and spoke in pride. "Also, now they too have felt the awe of us."

"And he is a cuddly dear," Shadow-of-a-Dream said. "And we need more like him, do we not, Lady Sky?"

"It had to happen in some twilight," agreed she who stood above. "Take him onward and care for him. By this sign," which she made, "is he claimed for the Dwellers."

Their joy was freed. Ayoch cartwheeled over the ground till he reached a shiverleaf. There he swarmed up the trunk and out on a limb, perched half hidden by unrestful pale foliage, and crowed. Boy and girl bore the child toward Carheddin at an easy distance-devouring lope which let him pipe and her sing:

Wahaii, wahaii!
Wayala, laii!
Wing on the wind
high over heaven,
shrilly shrieking,
rush with the rainspears,
tumble through tumult,
drift to the moonhoar trees and the dream-heavy shadows beneath them,
and rock in, be one with the clinking wavelets of lakes where the starbeams
drown.

As she entered, Barbro Cullen felt, through all grief and fury, stabbed by dismay. The room was unkempt. Journals, tapes, reels, codices, file boxes, bescribbled papers were piled on every table. Dust filmed most shelves and corners. Against one wall stood a laboratory setup, microscope and analytical equipment. She recognized it as compact and efficient, but it was not what you would expect in an office, and it gave the air a faint chemical reek. The rug was threadbare, the furniture shabby.

This was her final chance?

Then Eric Sherrinford approached. "Good day, Mrs. Cullen," he said. His tone was crisp, his handclasp firm. His faded gripsuit didn't bother her. She wasn't inclined to fuss about her own appearance except on special occasions. (And would she ever again have one, unless she got back Jimmy?) What she observed was a cat's personal neatness.

A smile radiated in crow's-feet from his eyes. "Forgive my bachelor housekeeping. On Beowulf we have—we had, at any rate, machines for that, so I never acquired the habit myself, and I don't want a hireling disarranging my tools. More convenient to work out of my apartment than keep a separate office. Won't you be seated?"

"No, thanks. I couldn't," she mumbled.

"I understand. But if you'll excuse me, I function best in a relaxed position."

He jackknifed into a lounger. One long shank crossed the other knee. He drew forth a pipe and stuffed it from a pouch. Barbro wondered why he took tobacco in so ancient a way. Wasn't Beowulf supposed to have the up-to-date equipment that they still couldn't afford to build on Roland? Well, of course old customs might survive anyhow. They generally did in colonies, she remembered reading. People had moved starward in the hope of preserving such outmoded things as their mother tongues or constitutional government or rational-technological civilization. . . .

Sherrinford pulled her up from the confusion of her weariness: "You must give me the details of your case, Mrs. Cullen. You've simply told me your son was kidnapped and your local constabulary did nothing. Otherwise, I know just a few obvious facts, such as your being widowed rather than divorced; and you're the daughter of outwayers in Olga Ivanoff Land, who nevertheless kept in close telecommunication with Christmas Landing; and you're trained in one of the biological professions; and you had several years' hiatus in field work until recently you started again."

She gaped at the high-cheeked, beak-nosed, black-haired and gray-eyed countenance. His lighter made a *scrit* and a flare which seemed to fill the room. Quietness dwelt on this height above the city, and winter dusk was seeping through the windows. "How in cosmos do you know that?" she heard herself exclaim.

He shrugged and fell into the lecturer's manner for which he was notorious. "My work depends on noticing details and fitting them together. In more than a hundred years on Roland, tending to cluster according to their origins and thought-habits, people have developed regional accents. You have a trace of the Olgan burr, but you nasalize your vowels in the style of this area, though you live in Portolondon. That suggests steady childhood exposure to metropolitan speech. You were part of Matsuyama's expedition, you told me, and took your boy along. They wouldn't have allowed any ordinary technician to do that; hence, you had to be valuable enough to get away with it. The team was conducting ecological research; therefore, you must be in the life sciences. For the same reason, you must have had previous field experience. But your skin is fair, showing none of the leatheriness one gets from prolonged exposure to this sun. Accordingly, you must have been mostly indoors for a good while before you went on your ill-fated trip. As for widowhood—you never mentioned a husband to me, but you have had a man whom you thought so highly of that you still wear both the wedding and the engagement ring he gave you."

Her sight blurred and stung. The last of those words had brought Tim back; huge, ruddy, laughterful and gentle. She must turn from this other person and stare outward. "Yes," she achieved saying, "you're right."

The apartment occupied a hilltop above Christmas Landing. Beneath it the city dropped away in walls, roofs, archaistic chimneys and lamplit streets, goblin lights of human-piloted vehicles, to the harbor, the sweep of Venture Bay, ships bound to and from the Sunward Islands and remoter regions of the Boreal Ocean, which glimmered like mercury in the afterglow of Charlemagne. Oliver was swinging rapidly higher, a mottled orange disk a full degree wide; closer to the zenith which it could never reach, it would shine the color of ice. Alde, half the seeming size, was a thin slow crescent near Sirius, which she remembered was near Sol, but you couldn't see Sol without a telescope. . . .

"Yes," she said around the pain in her throat, "my husband is about four years dead. I was carrying our first child when he was killed by a stampeding monocerus. We'd been married three years before. Met while we were both at the university—casts from School Central can only supply a basic education, you know. We founded our own team to do ecological studies under contract —you know, can a certain area be settled while maintaining a balance of nature, what crops will grow, what hazards, that sort of question. Well, afterward I did lab work for a fisher co-op in Portolondon. But the monotony, the . . . shut-in-ness . . . was eating me away. Professor Matsuyama offered me a position on the team he was organizing to examine Commissioner Hauch Land. I thought, God help me, I thought Jimmy—Tim wanted him named James, once the tests showed it'd be a boy, after his own father and because of 'Timmy and Jimmy' and—oh, I thought Jimmy could safely come along. I couldn't bear to leave him behind for months, not at his age. We could make sure he'd never wander out of camp. What could hurt him inside it? *I* had never believed those stories about the Outlings stealing human children. I supposed parents were trying to hide from themselves the fact they'd been careless, they'd let a kid get lost in the woods or attacked by a pack of satans or—well, I learned better, Mr. Sherrinford. The guard robots were evaded and the dogs were drugged, and when I woke, Jimmy was gone."

He regarded her through the smoke from his pipe. Barbro Engdahl Cullen was a big woman of thirty or so (Rolandic years, he reminded himself, ninety-five percent of terrestrial, not the same as Beowulfan years), broad-shouldered, long-legged, full-breasted, supple of stride; her face was wide, straight nose, straightforward hazel eyes, heavy but mobile mouth; her hair was reddish brown, cropped below the ears, her voice husky, her garment a plain street robe. To still the writhing of her fingers, he asked skeptically, "Do you now believe in the Outlings?"

"No. I'm just not so sure as I was." She swung about with half a glare for him. "And we have found traces."

"Bits of fossils," he nodded. "A few artifacts of a neolithic sort. But apparently ancient, as if the makers died ages ago. Intensive search has failed to turn up any real evidence for their survival."

"How intensive can search be, in a summer-stormy, winter-gloomy wilderness around the North Pole?" she demanded. "When we are, how many, a million people on an entire planet, half of us crowded into this one city?"

"And the rest crowding this one habitable continent," he pointed out.

"Arctica covers five million square kilometers," she flung back. "The Arctic Zone proper covers a fourth of it. We haven't the industrial base to establish satellite monitor stations, build aircraft we can trust in those parts, drive roads through the damned darklands and establish permanent bases and get to know them and tame them. Good Christ, generations of lonely outwaymen told stories about Graymantle, and the beast was never seen by a proper scientist till last year!"

"Still, you continue to doubt the reality of the Outlings?"

"Well, what about a secret cult among humans, born of isolation and ignorance, lairing in the wilderness, stealing children when they can for . . ." She swallowed. Her head drooped. "But you're supposed to be the expert."

"From what you told me over the visiphone, the Portolondon constabulary questions the accuracy of the report your group made, thinks the lot of you were hysterical, claims you must have omitted a due precaution, and the child toddled away and was lost beyond your finding."

His dry words pried the horror out of her. Flushing, she snapped, "Like any settler's kid? No. I didn't simply yell. I consulted Data Retrieval. A few too many such cases are recorded for accident to be a very plausible explanation.

And shall we totally ignore the frightened stories about reappearances? But when I went back to the constabulary with my facts, they brushed me off. I suspect that was not entirely because they're undermanned. I think they're afraid too. They're recruited from country boys, and Portolondon lies near the edge of the unknown."

Her energy faded. "Roland hasn't got any central police force," she finished drably. "You're my last hope."

The man puffed smoke into twilight, with which it blended, before he said in a kindlier voice than hitherto: "Please don't make it a high hope, Mrs. Cullen. I'm the solitary private investigator on this world, having no resources beyond myself, and a newcomer to boot."

"How long have you been here?"

"Twelve years. Barely time to get a little familiarity with the relatively civilized coastlands. You settlers of a century or more—what do you, even, know about Arctica's interior?"

Sherrinford sighed. "I'll take the case, charging no more than I must, mainly for the sake of the experience," he said. "But only if you'll be my guide and assistant, however painful it will be for you."

"Of course! I dreaded waiting idle. Why me, though?"

"Hiring someone else as well qualified would be prohibitively expensive on a pioneer planet where every hand has a thousand urgent tasks to do. Besides, you have a motive. And I'll need that. As one who was born on another world altogether strange to this one, itself altogether strange to Mother Earth, I am too dauntingly aware of how handicapped we are."

Night gathered upon Christmas Landing. The air stayed mild, but glimmer-lit tendrils of fog, sneaking through the streets, had a cold look, and colder yet was the aurora where it shuddered between the moons. The woman drew closer to the man in this darkening room, surely not aware that she did, until he switched on a fluoropanel. The same knowledge of Roland's aloneness was in both of them.

One light-year is not much as galactic distances go You could walk it in about 270 million years, beginning at the middle of the Permian Era, when dinosaurs belonged to the remote future, and continuing to the present day when spaceships cross even greater reaches. But stars in our neighborhood average some nine light-years apart, and barely one percent of them have planets which are man-habitable, and speeds are limited to less than that of radiation. Scant help is given by relativistic time contraction and suspended animation en route. These made the journeys seem short, but history mean-while does not stop at home.

Thus voyages from sun to sun will always be few. Colonists will be those who have extremely special reasons for going. They will take along germ plasm for exogenetic cultivation of domestic plants and animals—and of human infants, in order that population can grow fast enough to escape death through genetic drift. After all, they cannot rely on further immigration. Two or three times a century, a ship may call from some other colony. (Not from Earth. Earth has long ago sunk into alien concerns.) Its place of origin will be an old settlement. The young ones are in no position to build and man interstellar vessels.

Their very survival, let alone their eventual modernization, is in doubt. The founding fathers have had to take what they could get in a universe not especially designed for man.

Consider, for example, Roland. It is among the rare happy finds, a world where humans can live, breathe, eat the food, drink the water, walk unclad if they choose, sow their crops, pasture their beasts, dig their mines, erect their homes, raise their children and grandchildren. It is worth crossing three-quarters of a light-century to preserve certain dear values and strike new roots into the soil of Roland.

But the star Charlemagne is of type F9, 40 percent brighter than Sol, brighter still in the treacherous ultraviolet and wilder still in the wind of charged particles that seethes from it. The planet has an eccentric orbit. In the middle of the short but furious northern summer, which includes periastron, total insolation is more than double what Earth gets; in the depth of the long northern winter, it is barely less than terrestrial average.

Native life is abundant everywhere. But lacking elaborate machinery, not yet economically possible to construct for more than a few specialists, man can only endure the high latitudes. A 10-degree axial tilt, together with the orbit, means that the northern part of the Arctican continent spends half its year in unbroken sunlessness. Around the South Pole lies an empty ocean.

Other differences from Earth might superficially seem more important. Roland has two moons, small but close, to evoke clashing tides. It rotates once in thirty-two hours, which is endlessly, subtly disturbing to organisms evolved through gigayears of a quicker rhythm. The weather patterns are altogether unterrestrial. The globe is a mere 9,500 kilometers in diameter; its surface gravity is 0.42 $\acute{E}$ 980 cm/sec^2; the sea-level air pressure is slightly above one Earth atmosphere. (For actually, Earth is the freak, and man exists because a cosmic accident blew away most of the gas that a body its size ought to have kept, as Venus has done.)

However, Homo can truly be called sapiens when he practices his specialty of being unspecialized. His repeated attempts to freeze himself into an all-answering pattern or culture or ideology, or whatever he has named it, have repeatedly brought ruin. Give him the pragmatic business of making his living and he will usually do rather well. He adapts, within broad limits.

These limits are set by such factors as his need for sunlight and his being, necessarily and forever, a part of the life that surrounds him and a creature of the spirit within.

Portolondon thrust docks, boats, machinery, warehouses into the Gulf of Polaris. Behind them huddled the dwellings of its 5,000 permanent inhabitants: concrete walls, storm shutters, high-peaked tile roofs. The gaiety of their paint looked forlorn amid lamps; this town lay past the Arctic Circle.

Nevertheless Sherrinford remarked, "Cheerful place, eh? The kind of thing I came to Roland looking for."

Barbro made no reply. The days in Christmas Landing, while he made his preparations, had drained her. Gazing out the dome of the taxi that was whirring them downtown from the hydrofoil that brought them, she supposed he meant the lushness of forest and meadows along the road, brilliant hues and phosphorescence of flowers in gardens, clamor of wings overhead. Unlike terrestrial flora in cold climates, Arctican vegetation spends every daylit hour in frantic growth and energy storage. Not till summer's fever gives place to gentle winter does it bloom and fruit; and estivating animals rise from their dens and migratory birds come home.

The view was lovely, she had to admit: beyond the trees, a spaciousness climbing toward remote heights, silvery gray under a moon, an aurora, the diffuse radiance from a sun just below the horizon.

Beautiful as a hunting satan, she thought, and as terrible. That wilderness had stolen Jimmy. She wondered if she would at least be given to find his little bones and take them to his father.

Abruptly she realized that she and Sherrinford were at their hotel and that he had been speaking of the town. Since it was next in size after the capital, he must have visited here often before. The streets were crowded and noisy; signs flickered, music blared from shops, taverns, restaurants, sports centers, dance halls; vehicles were jammed down to molasses speed; the several-stories-high office buildings stood aglow. Portolondon linked an enormous hinterland to the outside world. Down the Gloria River came timber rafts, ores, harvest of farms whose owners were slowly making Rolandic life serve them, meat and ivory and furs gathered by rangers in the mountains beyond Troll Scarp. In from the sea came coastwise freighters, the fishing fleet, produce of the Sunward Islands, plunder of whole continents farther south where bold men adventured. It clanged in Portolondon, laughed, blustered, connived, robbed, preached, guzzled, swilled, toiled, dramed, lusted, built, destroyed, died, was born, was happy, angry, sorrowful, greedy, vulgar, loving, ambitious, human. Neither the sun's blaze elsewhere nor the half-year's twilight here—wholly night around midwinter—was going to stay man's hand.

Or so everybody said.

Everybody except those who had settled in the darklands. Barbro used to take for granted that they were evolving curious customs, legends and superstitions, which would die when the outway had been completely mapped and controlled. Of late, she had wondered. Perhaps Sherrinford's hints, about a change in his own attitude brought about by his preliminary research, were responsible.

Or perhaps she just needed something to think about besides how Jimmy, the day before he went, when she asked him whether he wanted rye or French bread for a sandwich, answered in great solemnity—he was becoming interested in the alphabet—"I'll have a slice of what we people call the F bread."

She scarcely noticed getting out of the taxi, registering, being conducted to a primitively furnished room. But after she unpacked, she remembered Sherrinford had suggested a confidential conference. She went down the hall and knocked on his door. Her knuckles sounded less loud than her heart.

He opened the door, finger on lips, and gestured her toward a corner. Her temper bristled until she saw the image of Chief Constable Dawson in the visiphone. Sherrinford must have chimed him up and must have a reason to keep her out of scanner range. She found a chair and watched, nails digging into knees.

The detective's lean length refolded itself. "Pardon the interruption," he said. "A man mistook the number. Drunk, by the indications."

Dawson chuckled. "We get plenty of those." Barbro recalled his fondness for gabbing. He tugged the beard which he affected, as if he were an outwayer instead of a townsman. "No harm in them as a rule. They only have a lot of voltage to discharge, after weeks or months in the backlands."

"I've gathered that that environment—foreign in a million major and minor ways to the one that created man—I've gathered that it does do odd things to the personality." Sherrinford tamped his pipe. "Of course, you know my practice has been confined to urban and suburban areas. Isolated garths seldom need private investigators. Now that situation appears to have changed. I called to ask you for advice."

"Glad to help," Dawson said. "I've not forgotten what you did for us in the de Tahoe murder case." Cautiously: "Better explain your problem first."

Sherrinford struck fire. The smoke that followed cut through the green odors—even here, a paved pair of kilometers from the nearest woods—that drifted past traffic rumble through a crepuscular window. "This is more a scientific mission than a search for an absconding debtor or an industrial spy," he drawled. "I'm looking into two possibilities: that an organization, criminal or religious or whatever, has long been active and steals infants; or that the Outlings of folklore are real."

"Huh?" On Dawson's face Barbro read as much dismay as surprise. "You can't be serious!"

"Can't I?" Sherrinford smiled. "Several generations' worth of reports shouldn't be dismissed out of hand. Especially not when they become more frequent and consistent in the course of time, not less. Nor can we ignore the documented loss of babies and small children, amounting by now to over a hundred, and never a trace found afterward. Nor the finds which demonstrate that an intelligent species once inhabited Arctica and may still haunt the interior."

Dawson leaned forward as if to climb out of the screen. "Who engaged you?" he demanded. "That Cullen woman? We were sorry for her, naturally, but she wasn't making sense, and when she got downright abusive . . ."

"Didn't her companions, reputable scientists, confirm her story?"

"No story to confirm. Look, they had the place ringed with detectors and alarms, and they kept mastiffs. Standard procedure in country where a hungry sauroid or whatever might happen by. Nothing could've entered unbeknownst."

"On the ground. How about a flyer landing in the middle of camp?"

"A man in a copter rig would've roused everybody."

"A winged being might be quieter."

"A living flyer that could lift a three-year-old boy? Doesn't exist."

"Isn't in the scientific literature, you mean, constable. Remember Graymantle; remember how little we know about Roland, a planet, an entire world. Such birds do exist on Beowulf—and on Rustum, I've read. I made a calculation from the local ratio of air density to gravity, and, yes, it's marginally possible here too. The child could have been carried off for a short distance before wing muscles were exhausted and the creature must descend."

Dawson snorted. "First it landed and walked into the tent where mother and boy were asleep. Then it walked away, toting him, after it couldn't fly farther. Does that sound like a bird of prey? And the victim didn't cry out, the dogs didn't bark!"

"As a matter of fact," Sherrinford said, "those inconsistencies are the most interesting and convincing features of the whole account. You're right, it's hard to see how a human kidnapper could get in undetected, and an eagle-type of creature wouldn't operate in that fashion. But none of this applies to a winged intelligent being. The boy could have been drugged. Certainly the dogs showed signs of having been."

"The dogs showed signs of having overslept. Nothing had disturbed them. The kid wandering by wouldn't do so. We don't need to assume one damn thing except, first, that he got restless and, second, that the alarms were a bit sloppily rigged—seeing as how no danger was expected from inside camp—and let him pass out. And, third, I hate to speak this way, but we must assume the poor tyke starved or was killed."

Dawson paused before adding: "If we had more staff, we could have given the affair more time. And would have, of course. We did make an aerial sweep, which risked the lives of the pilots, using instruments which would've spotted the kid anywhere in a fifty-kilometer radius, unless he was dead. You know how sensitive thermal analyzers are. We drew a complete blank. We have more important jobs than to hunt for the scattered pieces of a corpse."

He finished brusquely. "If Mrs. Cullen's hired you, my advice is you find an excuse to quit. Better for her, too. She's got to come to terms with reality."

Barbro checked a shout by biting her tongue.

"Oh, this is merely the latest disappearance of the series," Sherrinford said. She didn't understand how he could maintain his easy tone when Jimmy was lost. "More thoroughly recorded than any before, thus more suggestive. Usually an outwayer family has given a tearful but undetailed account of their child who vanished and must have been stolen by the Old Folk. Sometimes, years later, they'd tell about glimpses of what they swore must have been the grown child, not really human any longer, flitting past in murk or peering through a window or working mischief upon them. As you say, neither the authorities nor the scientists have had personnel or resources to mount a proper investigation. But as I say, the matter appears to be worth investigating. Maybe a private party like myself can contribute."

"Listen, most of us constables grew up in the outway. We don't just ride patrol and answer emergency calls; we go back there for holidays and reunions. If any gang of . . . of human sacrificers was around, we'd know."

"I realize that. I also realize that the people you came from have a widespread and deep-seated belief in nonhuman beings with supernatural powers. Many actually go through rites and make offerings to propitiate them."

"I know what you're leading up to," Dawson fleered. "I've heard it before, from a hundred sensationalists. The aborigines are the Outlings. I thought better of you. Surely you've visited a museum or three, surely you've read literature from planets which do have natives—or damn and blast, haven't you ever applied that logic of yours?"

He wagged a finger. "Think," he said. "What have we in fact discovered?

A few pieces of worked stone; a few megaliths that might be artificial; scratchings on rock that seem to show plants and animals, though not the way any human culture would ever have shown them; traces of fires and broken bones; other fragments of bone that seem as if they might've belonged to thinking creatures, as if they might've been inside fingers or around big brains. If so, however, the owners looked nothing like men. Or angels, for that matter. Nothing! The most anthropoid reconstruction I've seen shows a kind of two-legged crocagator.

"Wait, let me finish. The stories about the Outlings—oh, I've heard them too, plenty of them. I believed them when I was a kid—the stories tell how there're different kinds, some winged, some not, some half-human, some completely human except maybe for being too handsome . . . It's fairyland from ancient Earth all over again. Isn't it? I got interested once and dug into the Heritage Library microfiles, and be damned if I didn't find almost the identical yarns, told by peasants centuries before spaceflight.

"None of it squares with the scanty relics we have, if they are relics, or with the fact that no area the size of Arctica could spawn a dozen different intelligent species, or . . . hellfire, man, with the way your common sense tells you aborigines would behave when humans arrived!"

Sherrinford nodded. "Yes, yes," he said. "I'm less sure than you that the common sense of nonhuman beings is precisely like our own. I've seen so much variation within mankind. But, granted, your arguments are strong. Roland's too few scientists have more pressing tasks than tracking down the origins of what is, as you put it, a revived medieval superstition."

He cradled his pipe bowl in both hands and peered into the tiny hearth of it. "Perhaps what interests me most," he said softly, "is why—across that gap of centuries, across a barrier of machine civilization and its utterly antagonistic world view—no continuity of tradition whatsoever—why have hardheaded, technologically organized, reasonably well-educated colonists here brought back from its grave a belief in the Old Folk?"

"I suppose eventually, if the university ever does develop the psychology department they keep talking about, I suppose eventually somebody will get a thesis out of your question." Dawson spoke in a jagged voice, and he gulped when Sherrinford replied:

"I propose to begin now. In Commissioner Hauch Land, since that's where the latest incident occurred. Where can I rent a vehicle?"

"Uh, might be hard to do . . ."

"Come, come. Tenderfoot or not, I know better. In an economy of scarcity, few people own heavy equipment. But since it's needed, it can always be rented. I want a camper bus with a ground-effect drive suitable for every kind of terrain. And I want certain equipment installed which I've brought along, and the top canopy section replaced by a gun turret controllable from the driver's seat. But I'll supply the weapons. Besides rifles and pistols of my own, I've arranged to borrow some artillery from Christmas Landing's police arsenal."

"Hoy? Are you genuinely intending to make ready for . . . a war . . . against a myth?"

"Let's say I'm taking out insurance, which isn't terribly expensive, against a remote possibility. Now, besides the bus, what about a light aircraft carried piggyback for use in surveys?"

"No." Dawson sounded more positive than hitherto. "That's asking for disaster. We can have you flown to a base camp in a large plane when the weather report's exactly right. But the pilot will have to fly back at once, before the weather turns wrong again. Meteorology's underdeveloped on Roland; the air's especially treacherous this time of year, and we're not tooled up to produce aircraft that can outlive every surprise." He drew breath. "Have you no idea of how fast a whirly-whirly can hit, or what size hailstones might strike from a clear sky, or . . . ? Once you're there, man, you stick to the ground." He hesitated. "That's an important reason our information is so scanty about the outway, and its settlers are so isolated."

Sherrinford laughed ruefully. "Well, I suppose if details are what I'm after, I must creep along anyway."

"You'll waste a lot of time," Dawson said. "Not to mention your client's money. Listen, I can't forbid you to chase shadows, but . . ."

The discussion went on for almost an hour. When the screen finally blanked, Sherrinford rose, stretched, and walked toward Barbro. She noticed anew his peculiar gait. He had come from a planet with a fourth again of Earth's gravitational drag, to one where weight was less than half terrestrial. She wondered if he had flying dreams.

"I apologize for shuffling you off like that," he said. "I didn't expect to reach him at once. He was quite truthful about how busy he is. But having made contact, I didn't want to remind him overmuch of you. He can dismiss my project as a futile fantasy which I'll soon give up. But he might have frozen completely, might even have put up obstacles before us, if he'd realized through you how determined we are."

"Why should he care?" she asked in her bitterness.

"Fear of consequences, the worse because it is unadmitted—fear of consequences, the more terrifying because they are unguessable." Sherrinford's gaze went to the screen, and thence out the window to the aurora pulsing in glacial blue and white immensely far overhead. "I suppose you saw I was talking to a frightened man. Down underneath his conventionality and scoffing, he believes in the Outlings—oh, yes, he believes."

The feet of Mistherd flew over yerba and outpaced windblown driftweed. Beside him, black and misshapen, hulked Nagrim the nicor, whose earthquake weight left a swath of crushed plants. Behind, luminous blossoms of a firethorn shone through the twining, trailing outlines of Morgarel the wraith.

Here Cloudmoor rose in a surf of hills and thickets. The air lay quiet, now and then carrying the distance-muted howl of a beast. It was darker than usual at winterbirth, the moons being down and aurora a wan flicker above mountains on the northern world-edge. But this made the stars keen, and their numbers crowded heaven, and Ghost Road shone among them as if it, like the leafage beneath, were paved with dew.

"Yonder!" bawled Nagrim. All four of his arms pointed. The party had topped a ridge. Far off glimmered a spark. "Hoah, hoah! 'Ull we right off stamp dem flat, or pluck dem apart slow?"

We shall do nothing of the sort, bonebrain, Morgarel's answer slid through their heads. *Not unless they attack us, and they will not unless we make them aware of us, and her command is that we spy out their purposes.*

"Gr-r-rum-m-m. I know dier aim. Cut down trees, stick plows in land, sow deir cursed seed in de clods and in deir shes. 'Less we drive dem into de bitterwater, and soon, soon, dey'll wax too strong for us."

"Not too strong for the queen!" Mistherd protested, shocked.

Yet they do have new powers, it seems, Morgarel reminded him. *Carefully must we probe them.*

"Den carefully can we step on dem?" asked Nagrim.

The question woke a grin out of Mistherd's own uneasiness. He slapped the scaly back. "Don't talk, you," he said. "It hurts my ears. Nor think; that hurts your head. Come, run!"

Ease yourself, Morgarel scolded. *You have too much life in you, human-born.*

Mistherd made a face at the wraith, but obeyed to the extent of slowing down and picking his way through what cover the country afforded. For he traveled on behalf of the Fairest, to learn what had brought a pair of mortals questing hither.

Did they seek that boy whom Ayoch stole? (He continued to weep for his mother, though less and less often as the marvels of Carheddin entered him.) Perhaps. A birdcraft had left them and their car at the now-abandoned campsite, from which they had followed an outward spiral. But when no trace of the cub had appeared inside a reasonable distance, they did not call to be flown home. And this wasn't because weather forbade the farspeaker waves to travel, as was frequently the case. No, instead the couple set off toward the mountains of Moonhorn. Their course would take them past a few outlying invader steadings and on into realms untrodden by their race.

So this was no ordinary survey. Then what was it?

Mistherd understood now why she who reigned had made her adopted mortal children learn, or retain, the clumsy language of their forebears. He had hated that drill, wholly foreign to Dweller ways. Of course, you obeyed her, and in time you saw how wise she had been. . . .

Presently he left Nagrim behind a rock—the nicor would only be useful in a fight—and crawled from bush to bush until he lay within man-lengths of the humans. A rainplant drooped over him, leaves soft on his bare skin, and clothed him in darkness. Morgarel floated to the crown of a shiverleaf, whose unrest would better conceal his flimsy shape. He'd not be much help either. And that was the most troublous, the almost appalling thing here. Wraiths were among those who could not just sense and send thought, but cast illusions. Morgarel had reported that this time his power seemed to rebound off an invisible cold wall around the car.

Otherwise the male and female had set up no guardian engines and kept no dogs. Belike they supposed none would be needed, since they slept in the long vehicle which bore them. But such contempt of the queen's strength could not be tolerated, could it?

Metal sheened faintly by the light of their campfire. They sat on either side, wrapped in coats against a coolness that Mistherd, naked, found mild. The male drank smoke. The female stared past him into a dusk which her flame-dazzled eyes must see as thick gloom. The dancing glow brought her vividly forth. Yes, to judge from Ayoch's tale, she was the dam of the new cub.

Ayoch had wanted to come too, but the Wonderful One forbade. Pooks couldn't hold still long enough for such a mission.

The man sucked on his pipe. His cheeks thus pulled into shadow while the light flickered across nose and brow, he looked disquietingly like a shearbill about to stoop on prey.

"—No, I tell you again, Barbro, I have no theories," he was saying. "When facts are insufficient, theorizing is ridiculous at best, misleading at worst."

"Still, you must have some idea of what you're doing," she said. It was plain that they had threshed this out often before. No Dweller could be as persistent as she or as patient as he. "That gear you packed—that generator you keep running . . ."

"I have a working hypothesis or two, which suggested what equipment I ought to take."

"Why won't you tell me what the hypotheses are?"

"They themselves indicate that that might be inadvisable at the present time. I'm still feeling my way into the labyrinth. And I haven't had a chance yet to hook everything up. In fact, we're really only protected against so-called telepathic influence . . ."

"What?" She started. "Do you mean . . . those legends about how they can read minds too . . ." Her words trailed off and her gaze sought the darkness beyond his shoulders.

He leaned forward. His tone lost its clipped rapidity, grew earnest and soft. "Barbro, you're racking yourself to pieces. Which is no help to Jimmy if he's alive, the more so when you may well be badly needed later on. We've a long trek before us, and you'd better settle into it."

She nodded jerkily and caught her lip between her teeth for a moment before she answered, "I'm trying."

He smiled around his pipe. "I expect you'll succeed. You don't strike me as a quitter or a whiner or an enjoyer of misery."

She dropped a hand to the pistol at her belt. Her voice changed; it came out of her throat like knife from sheath. "When we find them, they'll know what I am. What humans are."

"Put anger aside also," the man urged. "We can't afford emotions. If the Outlings are real, as I told you I'm provisionally assuming, they're fighting for their homes." After a short stillness he added: "I like to think that if the first explorers had found live natives, men would not have colonized Roland. But it's too late now. We can't go back if we wanted to. It's a bitter-end struggle against an enemy so crafty that he's even hidden from us the fact that he is waging war."

"Is he? I mean, skulking, kidnapping an occasional child . . ."

"That's part of my hypothesis. I suspect those aren't harassments; they're tactics employed in a chillingly subtle strategy."

The fire sputtered and sparked. The man smoked awhile, brooding, until he went on:

"I didn't want to raise your hopes or excite you unduly while you had to wait on me, first in Christmas Landing, then in Portolondon. Afterward we were busy satisfying ourselves that Jimmy had been taken farther from camp than he could have wandered before collapsing. So I'm only now telling you how thoroughly I studied available material on the . . . Old Folk. Besides, at first I did it on the principle of eliminating every imaginable possibility, however absurd. I expected no result other than final disproof. But I went through everything, relics, analyses, histories, journalistic accounts, monographs; I talked to outwayers who happened to be in town and to what scientists we have who've taken any interest in the matter. I'm a quick study. I flatter myself I became as expert as anyone—though God knows there's little to be expert on. Furthermore, I, a comparative stranger to Roland, maybe looked on the problem with fresh eyes. And a pattern emerged for me.

"If the aborigines had become extinct, why hadn't they left more remnants? Arctica isn't enormous, and it's fertile for Rolandic life. It ought to have supported a population whose artifacts ought to have accumulated over millennia. I've read that on Earth, literally tens of thousands of paleolithic hand axes were found, more by chance than archaeology.

"Very well. Suppose the relics and fossils were deliberately removed, between the time the last survey party left and the first colonizing ships arrived. I did find some support for that idea in the diaries of the original explorers. They were too preoccupied with checking the habitability of the planet to make catalogues of primitive monuments. However, the remarks they wrote down indicate they saw much more than later arrivals did. Suppose what we have found is just what the removers overlooked or didn't get around to.

"That argues a sophisticated mentality, thinking in long-range terms, doesn't it? Which in turn argues that the Old Folk were not mere hunters or neolithic farmers."

"But nobody ever saw buildings or machines or any such thing," Barbro objected.

"No. Most likely the natives didn't go through our kind of metallurgic-industrial evolution. I can conceive of other paths to take. Their full-fledged civilization might have begun, rather than ended, in biological science and technology. It might have developed potentialities of the nervous system, which might be greater in their species than in man. We have those abilities to some degree ourselves, you realize. A dowser, for instance, actually senses variations in the local magnetic field caused by a water table. However, in us, these talents are maddeningly rare and tricky. So we took our business elsewhere. Who needs to be a telepath, say, when he has a visiphone? The Old Folk may have seen it the other way around. The artifacts of their civilization may have been, may still be, unrecognizable to men."

"They could have identified themselves to the men, though," Barbro said. "Why didn't they?"

"I can imagine any number of reasons. As, they could have had a bad experience with interstellar visitors earlier in their history. Ours is scarcely the sole race that has spaceships. However, I told you I don't theorize in advance of the facts. Let's say no more than that the Old Folk, if they exist, are alien to us."

"For a rigorous thinker, you're spinning a mighty thin thread."

"I've admitted this is entirely provisional." He squinted at her through a roil of campfire smoke. "You came to me, Barbro, insisting in the teeth of officialdom that your boy had been stolen, but your own talk about cultist kidnappers was ridiculous. Why are you reluctant to admit the reality of nonhumans?"

"In spite of the fact that Jimmy's being alive probably depends on it," she sighed. "I know."

A shudder. "Maybe I don't dare admit it."

"I've said nothing thus far that hasn't been speculated about in print," he told her. "A disreputable speculation, true. In a hundred years, nobody has found valid evidence for the Outlings being more than a superstition. Still, a few people have declared it's at least possible that intelligent natives are at large in the wilderness."

"I know," she repeated. "I'm not sure, though, what has made you, over-night, take those arguments seriously."

"Well, once you got me started thinking, it occurred to me that Roland's outwayers are not utterly isolated medieval crofters. They have books, telecommunications, power tools, motor vehicles; above all, they have a modern science-oriented education. Why *should* they turn superstitious? Something must be causing it." He stopped. "I'd better not continue. My ideas go further than this; but if they're correct, it's dangerous to speak them aloud."

Mistherd's belly muscles tensed. There was danger for fair, in that shearbill head. The Garland Bearer must be warned. For a minute he wondered about summoning Nagrim to kill these two. If the nicor jumped them fast, their firearms might avail them naught. But no. They might have left word at home, or . . . He came back to his ears. The talk had changed course. Barbro was murmuring, ". . . why you stayed on Roland."

The man smiled his gaunt smile. "Well, life on Beowulf held no challenge for me. Heorot is—or was; this was decades past, remember—Heorot was densely populated, smoothly organized, boringly uniform. That was partly due to the lowland frontier, a safety valve that bled off the dissatisfied. But I lack the carbon dioxide tolerance necessary to live healthily down there. An expedition was being readied to make a swing around a number of colony worlds, especially those which didn't have the equipment to keep in laser contact. You'll recall its announced purpose, to seek out new ideas in science, arts, sociology, philosophy, whatever might prove valuable. I'm afraid they found little on Roland relevant to Beowulf. But I, who had wangled a berth, I saw opportunities for myself and decided to make my home here."

"Were you a detective back there, too?"

"Yes, in the official police. We had a tradition of such work in our family.

Some of that may have come from the Cherokee side of it, if the name means anything to you. However, we also claimed collateral descent from one of the first private inquiry agents on record, back on Earth before spaceflight. Regardless of how true that may be, I found him a useful model. You see, an archetype . . ."

The man broke off. Unease crossed his features. "Best we go to sleep," he said. "We've a long distance to cover in the morning."

She looked outward. "Here is no morning."

They retired. Mistherd rose and cautiously flexed limberness back into his muscles. Before returning to the Sister of Lyrth, he risked a glance through a pane in the car. Bunks were made up, side by side, and the humans lay in them. Yet the man had not touched her, though hers was a bonny body, and nothing that had passed between them suggested he meant to do so.

Eldritch, humans. Cold and claylike. And they would overrun the beautiful wild world? Mistherd spat in disgust. It must not happen. It would not happen. She who reigned had vowed that.

The lands of William Irons were immense. But this was because a barony was required to support him, his kin and cattle, on native crops whose cultivation was still poorly understood. He raised some terrestrial plants as well, by summerlight and in conservatories. However, these were a luxury. The true conquest of northern Arctica lay in yerba hay, in bathyrhiza wood, in pericoup and glycophyllon, and eventually, when the market had expanded with population and industry, in chalcanthemum for city florists and pelts of cage-bred rover for city furriers.

That was in a tomorrow Irons did not expect that he would live to see. Sherrinford wondered if the man really expected anyone ever would.

The room was warm and bright. Cheerfulness crackled in the fireplace. Light from fluoropanels gleamed off hand-carved chests and chairs and tables, off colorful draperies and shelved dishes. The outwayer sat solid in his high seat, stoutly clad, beard flowing down his chest. His wife and daughters brought coffee, whose fragrance joined the remnant odors of a hearty supper, to him, his guests, and his sons.

But outside, wind hooted, lightning flared, thunder bawled, rain crashed on roof and walls and roared down to swirl among the courtyard cobblestones. Sheds and barns crouched against hugeness beyond. Trees groaned, and did a wicked undertone of laughter run beneath the lowing of a frightened cow? A burst of hailstones hit the tiles like knocking knuckles.

You could feel how distant your neighbors were, Sherrinford thought. And nonetheless they were the people whom you saw oftenest, did daily business with by visiphone (when a solar storm didn't make gibberish of their voices and chaos of their faces) or in the flesh, partied with, gossiped and intrigued with, intermarried with; in the end, they were the people who would bury you. The lights of the coastal towns were monstrously farther away.

William Irons was a strong man. Yet when now he spoke, fear was in his tone. "You'd truly go over Troll Scarp?"

"Do you mean Hanstein Palisades?" Sherrinford responded, more challenge than question.

"No outwayer calls it anything but Troll Scarp," Barbro said.

And how had a name like that been reborn, light-years and centuries from Earth's Dark Ages?

"Hunters, trappers, prospectors—rangers, you call them—travel in those mountains," Sherrinford declared.

"In certain parts," Irons said. "That's allowed, by a pact once made 'tween a man and the queen after he'd done well by a jack-o'-the-hill that a satan had hurt. Wherever the plumablanca grows, men may fare, if they leave man-goods on the altar boulders in payment for what they take out of the land. Elsewhere"—one fist clenched on a chair arm and went slack again—"is not wise to go."

"It's been done, hasn't it?"

"Oh, yes. And some came back all right, or so they claimed, though I've heard they were never lucky afterward. And some didn't; they vanished. And some who returned babbled of wonders and horrors and stayed witlings the rest of their lives. Not for a long time has anybody been rash enough to break the pact and overtread the bounds." Irons looked at Barbro almost entreatingly. His woman and children stared likewise, grown still. Wind hooted beyond the walls and rattled the storm shutters. "Don't you."

"I've reason to believe my son is there," she answered.

"Yes, yes, you've told and I'm sorry. Maybe something can be done. I don't know what, but I'd be glad to, oh, lay a double offering on Unvar's Barrow this midwinter, and a prayer drawn in the turf by a flint knife. Maybe they'll return him." Irons sighed. "They've not done such a thing in man's memory, though. And he could have a worse lot. I've glimpsed them myself, speeding madcap through twilight. They seem happier than we are. Might be no kindness, sending your boy home again."

"Like in the Arvid song," said his wife.

Irons nodded. "M-hm. Or others, come to think of it."

"What's this?" Sherrinford asked. More sharply than before, he felt himself a stranger. He was a child of cities and technics, above all a child of the skeptical intelligence. This family *believed*. It was disquieting to see more than a touch of their acceptance in Barbro's slow nod.

"We have the same ballad in Olga Ivanoff Land," she told him, her voice less calm than the words. "It's one of the traditional ones—nobody knows who composed them—that are sung to set the measure of a ring-dance in a meadow."

"I noticed a multilyre in your baggage, Mrs. Cullen," said the wife of Irons. She was obviously eager to get off the explosive topic of a venture in defiance of the Old Folk. A songfest could help. "Would you like to entertain us?"

Barbro shook her head, white around the nostrils. The oldest boy said quickly, rather importantly, "Well, sure, I can, if our guests would like to hear."

"I'd enjoy that, thank you." Sherrinford leaned back in his seat and stoked his pipe. If this had not happened spontaneously, he would have guided the conversation toward a similar outcome.

In the past he had had no incentive to study the folklore of the outway, and not much chance to read the scanty references on it since Barbro brought him her trouble. Yet more and more he was becoming convinced that he must get an understanding—not an anthropological study, but a feel from the inside out—of the relationship between Roland's frontiersmen and those beings which haunted them.

A bustling followed, rearrangement, settling down to listen, coffee cups refilled and brandy offered on the side. The boy explained, "The last line is the chorus. Everybody join in, right?" Clearly he too hoped thus to bleed off some of the tension. Catharsis through music? Sherrinford wondered, and added to himself: no—exorcism.

A girl strummed a guitar. The boy sang to a melody which beat across the storm noise:

> It was the ranger Arvid
> rode homeward through the hills
> among the shadowy shiverleafs,
> along the chiming rills.
> *The dance weaves under the firethorn.*
>
> The night wind whispered around him
> with scent of brok and rue.
> Both moons rose high above him
> and hills aflash with dew.
> *The dance weaves under the firethorn.*
>
> And dreaming of that woman
> who waited in the sun,

he stopped, amazed by starlight,
and so he was undone.
The dance weaves under the firethorn.

For there beneath a barrow
that bulked athwart a moon,
the Outling folk were dancing
in glass and golden shoon.
The dance weaves under the firethorn.

The Outling folk were dancing
like water, wind and fire
to frosty-ringing harpstrings,
and never did they tire.
The dance weaves under the firethorn.

To Arvid came she striding
from where she watched the dance,
the Queen of Air and Darkness,
with starlight in her glance.
The dance weaves under the firethorn.

With starlight, love and terror
in her immortal eye,
the Queen of Air and Darkness . . .

"No!" Barbro leaped from her chair. Her fists were clenched and tears flogged her cheekbones. "You can't—pretend that—about the things that stole Jimmy!"

She fled from the chamber, upstairs to her guest bedroom.

But she finished the song herself. That was about seventy hours later, camped in the steeps where rangers dared not fare.

She and Sherrinford had not said much to the Irons family, after refusing repeated pleas to leave the forbidden country alone. Nor had they exchanged many remarks at first as they drove north. Slowly, however, he began to draw her out about her own life. After a while she almost forgot to mourn, in her remembering of home and old neighbors. Somehow this led to discoveries— that he, beneath his professorial manner, was a gourmet and a lover of opera and appreciated her femaleness; that she could still laugh and find beauty in the wild land around her—and she realized, half guiltily, that life held more hope than even the recovery of the son Tim gave her.

"I've convinced myself he's alive," the detective said. He scowled. "Frankly, it makes me regret having taken you along, I expected this would be only a fact-gathering trip, but it's turning out to be more. If we're dealing with real creatures who stole him, they can do real harm. I ought to turn back to the nearest garth and call for a plane to fetch you."

"Like bottommost hell you will, mister," she said. "You need somebody who knows outway conditions, and I'm a better shot than average."

"M-m-m . . . it would involve considerable delay too, wouldn't it? Besides the added distance, I can't put a signal through to any airport before this current burst of solar interference has calmed down."

Next "night" he broke out his remaining equipment and set it up. She recognized some of it, such as the thermal detector. Other items were strange to her, copied to his order from the advanced apparatus of his birthworld. He would tell her little about them. "I've explained my suspicion that the ones we're after have telepathic capabilities," he said in apology.

Her eyes widened. "You mean it could be true, the queen and her people can read minds?"

"That's part of the dread which surrounds their legend, isn't it? Actually there's nothing spooky about the phenomenon. It was studied and fairly well defined centuries ago, on Earth. I daresay the facts are available in the scientific microfiles at Christmas Landing. You Rolanders have simply had no occasion to seek them out, any more than you've yet had occasion to look up how to build power-beamcasters or spacecraft."

"Well, how does telepathy work, then?"

Sherrinford recognized that her query asked for comfort as much as it did for facts, and he spoke with deliberate dryness: "The organism generates extremely longwave radiation which can, in principle, be modulated by the nervous system. In practice, the feebleness of the signals and their low rate of information transmission make them elusive, hard to detect and measure. Our prehuman ancestors went in for more reliable senses, like vision and hearing. What telepathic transceiving we do is marginal at best. But explorers have found extraterrestrial species that got an evolutionary advantage from developing the system further in their particular environments. I imagine such species could include one which gets comparatively little direct sunlight—in fact, appears to hide from broad day. It could even become so able in this regard that, at short range, it can pick up man's weak emissions and make man's primitive sensitivities resonate to its own strong sendings."

"That would account for a lot, wouldn't it?" Barbro said faintly.

"I've now screened our car by a jamming field," Sherrinford told her, "but it reaches only a few meters past the chassis. Beyond, a scout of theirs might get a warning from your thoughts, if you knew precisely what I'm trying to do. I have a well-trained subconscious which sees to it that I think about this in French when I'm outside. Communication has to be structured to be intelligible, you see, and that's a different enough structure from English. But English is the only human language on Roland and surely the Old Folk have learned it."

She nodded. He had told her his general plan, which was too obvious to conceal. The problem was to make contact with the aliens, if they existed. Hitherto, they had only revealed themselves, at rare intervals, to one or a few backwoodsmen at a time. An ability to generate hallucinations would help them in that. They would stay clear of any large, perhaps unmanageable expedition which might pass through their territory. But two people, braving all prohibitions, shouldn't look too formidable to approach. And . . . this would be the first human team which not only worked on the assumption that the Outlings were real, but possessed the resources of modern, off-planet police technology.

Nothing happened at that camp. Sherrinford said he hadn't expected it would. The Old Folk seemed cautious this near any settlement. In their own lands they must be bolder.

And by the following "night," the vehicle had gone well into yonder country. When Sherrinford stopped the engine in a meadow and the car settled down, silence rolled in like a wave.

They stepped out. She cooked a meal on the glower while he gathered wood, that they might later cheer themselves with a campfire. Frequently he glanced at his wrist. It bore no watch—instead, a radio-controlled dial, to tell what the instruments in the bus might register.

Who needed a watch here? Slow constellations wheeled beyond glimmering aurora. The moon Alde stood above a snowpeak, turning it argent, though this place lay at a goodly height. The rest of the mountains were hidden by the forest that crowded around. Its trees were mostly shiverleaf and feathery white plumablanca, ghostly amidst their shadows. A few firethorns glowed, clustered dim lanterns, and the underbrush was heavy and smelled sweet. You could see surprisingly far through the blue dusk. Somewhere nearby, a brook sang and a bird fluted.

"Lovely here," Sherrinford said. They had risen from their supper and not yet sat down again or kindled their fire.

"But strange," Barbro answered as low. "I wonder if it's really meant for us. If we can really hope to possess it."

His pipe stem gestured at the stars. "Man's gone to stranger places than this."

"Has he? I . . . oh, I suppose it's just something left over from my outway childhood, but do you know, when I'm under them I can't think of the stars as balls of gas whose energies have been measured, whose planets have been walked on by prosaic feet. No, they're small and cold and magical; our lives are bound to them; after we die, they whisper to us in our graves." Barbro glanced downward. "I realize that's nonsense."

She could see in the twilight how his face grew tight. "Not at all," he said. "Emotionally, physics may be a worse nonsense. And in the end, you know, after a sufficient number of generations, thought follows feeling. Man is not at heart rational. He could stop believing the stories of science if those no longer felt right."

He paused. "That ballad which didn't get finished in the house," he said, not looking at her. "Why did it affect you so?"

"I couldn't stand hearing *them*, well, praised. Or that's how it seemed. Sorry for the fuss."

"I gather the ballad is typical of a large class."

"Well, I never thought to add them up. Cultural anthropology is something we don't have time for on Roland, or more likely it hasn't occurred to us, with everything else there is to do. But—now you mention it, yes, I'm surprised at how many songs and stories have the Arvid motif in them."

"Could you bear to recite it?"

She mustered the will to laugh. "Why, I can do better than that if you want. Let me get my multilyre and I'll perform."

She omitted the hypnotic chorus line, though, when the notes rang out, except at the end. He watched her where she stood against moon and aurora.

> . . . the Queen of Air and Darkness
> cried softly under sky:
>
> "Light down, you ranger Arvid,
> and join the Outling folk.
> You need no more be human,
> which is a heavy yoke."
>
> He dared to give her answer:
> "I may do naught but run.
> A maiden waits me, dreaming
> in lands beneath the sun.
>
> "And likewise wait me comrades
> and tasks I would not shirk,
> for what is ranger Arvid
> if he lays down his work?

"So wreak your spells, you Outling,
and cast your wrath on me.
Though maybe you can slay me,
you'll not make me unfree."

The Queen of Air and Darkness
stood wrapped about with fear
and northlight flares and beauty
he dared not look too near.

Until she laughed like harpsong
and said to him in scorn:
"I do not need a magic
to make you always mourn.

"I send you home with nothing
except your memory
of moonlight, Outling music,
night breezes, dew and me.

"And that will run behind you,
a shadow on the sun,
and that will lie beside you
when every day is done.

"In work and play and friendship
your grief will strike you dumb
for thinking what you are—and—
what you might have become.

"Your dull and foolish woman
treat kindly as you can.
Go home now, ranger Arvid,
set free to be a man!"

In flickering and laughter
the Outling folk were gone.
He stood alone by moonlight
and wept until the dawn.
    The dance weaves under the firethorn.

She laid the lyre aside. A wind rustled leaves. After a long quietness Sherrinford said, "And tales of this kind are part of everyone's life in the outway?"

"Well, you could put it thus," Barbro replied. "Though they're not all full of supernatural doings. Some are about love or heroism. Traditional themes."

"I don't think your particular tradition has arisen of itself." His tone was bleak. "In fact, I think many of your songs and stories were not composed by human beings."

He snapped his lips shut and would say no more on the subject. They went early to bed.

Hours later, an alarm roused them.

The buzzing was soft, but it brought them instantly alert. They slept in gripsuits, to be prepared for emergencies. Skyglow lit them through the canopy. Sherrinford swung out of his bunk, slipped shoes on feet and clipped gun holster to belt. "Stay inside," he commanded.

"What's here?" Her pulse thuttered.

He squinted at the dials of his instruments and checked them against the luminous telltale on his wrist. "Three animals," he counted. "Not wild ones happening by. A large one, homeothermic, to judge from the infrared, holding still a short way off. Another . . . hm, low temperature, diffuse and unstable emission, as if it were more like a . . . a swarm of cells coordinated somehow . . . pheromonally? . . . hovering, also at a distance. But the third's practically next to us, moving around in the brush; and that pattern looks human."

She saw him quiver with eagerness, no longer seeming a professor. "I'm going to try to make a capture," he said. "When we have a subject for interrogation—stand ready to let me back in again fast. But don't risk yourself, whatever happens. And keep this cocked." He handed her a loaded big-game rifle.

His tall frame poised by the door, opened it a crack. Air blew in, cool, damp, full of fragrances and murmurings. The moon Oliver was now also aloft, the radiance of both unreally brilliant, and the aurora seethed in whiteness and ice blue.

Sherrinford peered afresh at his telltale. It must indicate the directions of the watchers, among those dappled leaves. Abruptly he sprang out. He sprinted past the ashes of the campfire and vanished under trees. Barbro's hand strained on the butt of her weapon.

Racket exploded. Two in combat burst onto the meadow. Sherrinford had clapped a grip on a smaller human figure. She could make out by streaming silver and rainbow flicker that the other was nude, male, long-haired, lithe and young. He fought demoniacally, seeking to use teeth and feet and raking nails, and meanwhile he ululated like a satan.

The identification shot through her: a changeling, stolen in babyhood and raised by the Old Folk. This creature was what they would make Jimmy into.

"Ha!" Sherrinford forced his opponent around and drove stiffened fingers into the solar plexus. The boy gasped and sagged: Sherrinford manhandled him toward the car.

Out from the woods came a giant. It might itself have been a tree, black and rugose, bearing four great gnarly boughs; but earth quivered and boomed beneath its leg-roots, and its hoarse bellowing filled sky and skulls.

Barbro shrieked. Sherrinford whirled. He yanked out his pistol, fired and fired, flat whip-cracks through the half-light. His free arm kept a lock on the youth. The troll shape lurched under those blows. It recovered and came on, more slowly, more carefully, circling around to cut him off from the bus. He couldn't move fast enough to evade it unless he released his prisoner—who was his sole possible guide to Jimmy. . . .

Barbro leaped forth. "Don't!" Sherrinford shouted. "For God's sake, stay inside!" The monster rumbled and made snatching motions at her. She pulled the trigger. Recoil slammed her in the shoulder. The colossus rocked and fell. Somehow it got its feet back and lumbered toward her. She retreated. Again she shot and again. The creature snarled. Blood began to drip from it and gleam oilily amidst dewdrops. It turned and went off, breaking branches, into the darkness that laired beneath the woods.

"Get to shelter!" Sherrinford yelled. "You're out of the jammer field!"

A mistiness drifted by overhead. She barely glimpsed it before she saw the new shape at the meadow edge. "Jimmy!" tore from her.

"Mother." He held out his arms. Moonlight coursed in his tears. She dropped her weapon and ran to him.

Sherrinford plunged in pursuit. Jimmy flitted away into the brush. Barbro crashed after, through clawing twigs. Then she was seized and borne away.

Standing over his captive, Sherrinford strengthened the fluoro output until vision of the wilderness was blocked off from within the bus. The boy squirmed beneath that colorless glare.

"You are going to talk," the man said. Despite the haggardness in his features, he spoke quietly.

The boy glared through tangled locks. A bruise was purpling on his jaw. He'd almost recovered ability to flee while Sherrinford chased and lost the woman. Returning, the detective had barely caught him. Time was lacking to be gentle, when Outling reinforcements might arrive at any moment. Sherrinford had knocked him out and dragged him inside. He sat lashed into a swivel seat.

He spat. "Talk to you, manclod?" But sweat stood on his skin, and his eyes flickered unceasingly around the metal which caged him.

"Give me a name to call you by."

"And have you work a spell on me?"

"Mine's Eric. If you don't give me another choice, I'll have to call you . . . m-m-m . . . Wuddikins."

"What?" However eldritch, the bound one remained a human adolescent.

"Mistherd, then." The lilting accent of his English somehow emphasized its sullenness. "That's not the sound, only what it means. Anyway, it's my spoken name, naught else."

"Ah, you keep a secret name you consider to be real?"

"She does. I don't know myself what it is. She knows the real names of everybody."

Sherrinford raised his brows. "She?"

"Who reigns. May she forgive me, I can't make the reverent sign when my arms are tied. Some invaders call her the Queen of Air and Darkness."

"So." Sherrinford got pipe and tobacco. He let silence wax while he started the fire. At length he said, "I'll confess the Old Folk took me by surprise. I didn't expect so formidable a member of your gang. Everything I could learn had seemed to show they work on my race—and yours, lad—by stealth, trickery and illusion."

Mistherd jerked a truculent nod. "She created the first nicors not long ago. Don't think she has naught but dazzlements at her beck."

"I don't. However, a steel-jacketed bullet works pretty well too, doesn't it?"

Sherrinford talked on, softly, mostly to himself: "I do still believe the, ah, nicors—all your half-humanlike breeds—are intended in the main to be seen, not used. The power of projecting mirages must surely be quite limited in range and scope as well as in the number of individuals who possess it. Otherwise she wouldn't have needed to work as slowly and craftily as she has. Even outside our mind-shield, Barbro—my companion—could have resisted, could have remained aware that whatever she saw was unreal . . . if she'd been less shaken, less frantic, less driven by need."

Sherrinford wreathed his head in smoke. "Never mind what I experienced," he said. "It couldn't have been the same as for her. I think the command was simply given us, 'You will see what you most desire in the world, running away from you into the forest.' Of course, she didn't travel many meters before the nicor waylaid her. I'd no hope of trailing them; I'm no Arctican woodsman, and besides, it'd have been too easy to ambush me. I came back to you." Grimly: "You're my link to your overlady."

"You think I'll guide you to Starhaven or Carheddin? Try making me, clod-man."

"I want to bargain."

"I s'pect you intend more'n that." Mistherd's answer held surprising shrewdness. "What'll you tell after you come home?"

"Yes, that does pose a problem, doesn't it? Barbro Cullen and I are not terrified outwayers. We're of the city. We brought recording instruments. We'd be the first of our kind to report an encounter with the Old Folk, and that report would be detailed and plausible. It would produce action."

"So you see I'm not afraid to die," Mistherd declared, though his lips trembled a bit. "If I let you come in and do your man-things to my people, I'd have naught left worth living for."

"Have no immediate fears," Sherrinford said. "You're merely bait." He sat down and regarded the boy through a visor of calm. (Within, it wept in him: *Barbro, Barbro!*) "Consider. Your queen can't very well let me go back, bringing my prisoner and telling about hers. She has to stop that somehow. I could try fighting my way through—this car is better armed than you know —but that wouldn't free anybody. Instead, I'm staying put. New forces of hers will get here as fast as they can. I assume they won't blindly throw themselves against a machine gun, a howitzer, a fulgurator. They'll parley first, whether their intentions are honest or not. Thus I make the contact I'm after."

"What d'you plan?" The mumble held anguish.

"First, this, as a sort of invitation." Sherrinford reached out to flick a switch. "There. I've lowered my shield against mind reading and shape casting. I daresay the leaders, at least, will be able to sense that it's gone. That should give them confidence."

"And next?"

"Next we wait. Would you like something to eat or drink?"

During the time which followed, Sherrinford tried to jolly Mistherd along, find out something of his life. What answers he got were curt. He dimmed the interior lights and settled down to peer outward. That was a long few hours.

They ended at a shout of gladness, half a sob, from the boy. Out of the woods came a band of the Old Folk.

Some of them stood forth more clearly than moons and stars and northlights should have caused. He in the van rode a white crownbuck whose horns were garlanded. His form was manlike but unearthly beautiful, silver blond hair falling from beneath the antlered helmet, around the proud cold face. The cloak fluttered off his back like living wings. His frost-colored mail rang as he fared.

Behind him, to right and left, rode two who bore swords whereon small flames gleamed and flickered. Above, a flying flock laughed and trilled and tumbled in the breezes. Near them drifted a half-transparent mistiness. Those others who passed among trees after their chieftain were harder to make out. But they moved in quicksilver grace and as it were to a sound of harps and trumpets.

"Lord Luighaid." Glory overflowed in Mistherd's tone. "Her master Knower—himself."

Sherrinford had never done a harder thing than to sit at the main control panel, finger near the button of the shield generator, and not touch it. He rolled down a section of canopy to let voices travel. A gust of wind struck him in the face, bearing odors of the roses in his mother's garden. At his back, in the main body of the vehicle, Mistherd strained against his bonds till he could see the oncoming troop.

"Call to them," Sherrinford said. "Ask if they will talk with me."

Unknown, flutingly sweet words flew back and forth. "Yes," the boy interpreted. "He will, the Lord Luighaid. But I can tell you, you'll never be let go. Don't fight them. Yield. Come away. You don't know what 'tis to be alive till you've dwelt in Carheddin under the mountain."

The Outlings drew nigh.

Jimmy glimmered and was gone. Barbro lay in strong arms, against a broad breast, and felt the horse move beneath her. It had to be a horse, though only a few were kept any longer on the steadings, and they only for special uses or love. She could feel the rippling beneath its hide, hear a rush of parted leafage and the thud when a hoof struck stone; warmth and living scent welled up around her through the darkness.

He who carried her said mildly, "Don't be afraid, darling. It was a vision. But he's waiting for us, and we're bound for him."

She was aware in a vague way that she ought to feel terror or despair or something. But her memories lay behind her—she wasn't sure just how she had come to be here—she was borne along in a knowledge of being loved. At peace, at peace, rest in the calm expectation of joy . . .

After a while the forest opened. They crossed a lea where boulders stood gray-white under the moons, their shadows shifting in the dim hues which the aurora threw across them. Flitteries danced, tiny comets, above the flowers between. Ahead gleamed a peak whose top was crowned in clouds.

Barbro's eyes happened to be turned forward. She saw the horse's head and thought, with quiet surprise: "Why, this is Sambo, who was mine when I was a girl. She looked upward at the man. He wore a black tunic and a cowled cape, which made his face hard to see. She could not cry aloud, here. "Tim," she whispered.

"Yes, Barbro."

"I buried you . . .

His smile was endlessly tender. "Did you think we're no more than what's laid back into the ground? Poor torn sweetheart. She who's called us is the All Healer. Now rest and dream."

"Dream," she said, and for a space she struggled to rouse herself. But the effort was weak. Why should she believe ashen tales about . . . atoms and energies, nothing else to fill a gape of emptiness . . . tales she could not bring to mind . . . when Tim and the horse her father gave her carried her on to Jimmy? Had the other thing not been the evil dream, and this her first drowsy awakening from it?

As if he heard her thoughts, he murmured, "They have a song in Outling lands. The Song of the Men:

> The world sails
> to an unseen wind.
> Light swirls by the bows.
> The wake is night.
> But the Dwellers have no such sadness.

"I don't understand," she said.

He nodded. "There's much you'll have to understand, darling, and I can't see you again until you've learned those truths. But meanwhile you'll be with our son."

She tried to lift her head and kiss him. He held her down. "Not yet," he said. "You've not been received among the queen's people. I shouldn't have come for you, except that she was too merciful to forbid. Lie back, lie back."

Time blew past. The horse galloped tireless, never stumbling, up the mountain. Once she glimpsed a troop riding down it and thought they were bound for a last weird battle in the west against . . . who? . . . one who lay cased in iron and sorrow. Later she would ask herself the name of him who had brought her into the land of the Old Truth.

Finally spires lifted splendid among the stars, which are small and magical and whose whisperings comfort us after we are dead. They rode into a courtyard where candles burned unwavering, fountains splashed and birds sang. The air bore fragrance of brok and pericoup, of ruse and roses, for not everything that man brought was horrible. The Dwellers waited in beauty to welcome her. Beyond their stateliness, pooks cavorted through the gloaming; among the trees darted children; merriment caroled across music more solemn.

"We have come—" Tim's voice was suddenly, inexplicably a croak. Barbro was not sure how he dismounted, bearing her. She stood before him and saw him sway on his feet.

Fear caught her. "Are you well?" She seized both his hands. They felt cold and rough. Where had Sambo gone? Her eyes searched beneath the cowl. In this brighter illumination, she ought to have seen her man's face clearly. But it was blurred, it kept changing. "What's wrong, oh, what's happened?"

He smiled. Was that the smile she had cherished? She couldn't completely remember. "I—I must go," he stammered, so low she could scarcely hear. "Our time is not ready." He drew free of her grasp and leaned on a robed form which had appeared at his side. A haziness swirled over both their heads. "Don't watch me go . . . back into the earth," he pleaded. "That's death for you. Till our time returns—There, our son!"

She had to fling her gaze around. Kneeling, she spread wide her arms. Jimmy struck her like a warm, solid cannonball. She rumpled his hair; she kissed the hollow of his neck; she laughed and wept and babbled foolishness; and this was no ghost, no memory that had stolen off when she wasn't looking. Now and again, as she turned her attention to yet another hurt which might have come upon him—hunger, sickness, fear—and found none, she would glimpse their surroundings. The gardens were gone. It didn't matter.

"I missed you so, Mother. Stay?"

"I'll take you home, dearest."

"Stay. Here's fun. I'll show. But you stay."

A sighing went through the twilight. Barbro rose. Jimmy clung to her hand. They confronted the queen.

Very tall she was in her robes woven of northlights, and her starry crown and her garlands of kiss-me-never. Her countenance recalled Aphrodite of Milos, whose picture Barbro had often seen in the realms of men, save that the queen's was more fair and more majesty dwelt upon it and in the night-blue eyes. Around her the gardens woke to new reality, the court of the Dwellers and the heaven-climbing spires.

"Be welcome," she spoke, her speaking a song, "forever."

Against the awe of her, Barbros said, "Moonmother, let us go home."

"That may not be."

"To our world, little and beloved," Barbro dreamed she begged, "which we build for ourselves and cherish for our children."

"To prison days, angry nights, works that crumble in the fingers, loves that turn to rot or stone or driftweed, loss, grief, and the only sureness that of the final nothingness. No. You too, Wanderfoot who is to be, will jubilate when the banners of the Outworld come flying into the last of the cities and man is made wholly alive. Now go with those who will teach you."

The Queen of Air and Darkness lifted an arm in summons. It halted, and none came to answer.

For over the fountains and melodies lifted a gruesome growling. Fires leaped, thunders crashed. Her hosts scattered screaming before the steel thing which boomed up the mountainside. The pooks were gone in a whirl of frightened wings. The nicors flung their bodies against the unalive invader and were consumed, until their Mother cried to them to retreat.

Barbro cast Jimmy down and herself over him. Towers wavered and smoked away. The mountain stood bare under icy moons, save for rocks, crags, and farther off a glacier in whose depths the auroral light pulsed blue. A cave mouth darkened a cliff. Thither folk streamed, seeking refuge underground. Some were human of blood, some grotesques like the pooks and nicors and wraiths; but most were lean, scaly, long-tailed, long-beaked, not remotely men or Outlings.

For an instant, even as Jimmy wailed at her breast—perhaps as much because the enchantment had been wrecked as because he was afraid—Barbro pitied the queen who stood alone in her nakedness. Then that one also had fled, and Barbro's world shivered apart.

The guns fell silent; the vehicle whirred to a halt. From it sprang a boy who called wildly, "Shadow-of-a-Dream, where are you? It's me, Mistherd, oh, come, come!"—before he remembered that the language they had been raised in was not man's. He shouted in that until a girl crept out of a thicket where she had hidden. They stared at each other through dust, smoke and moonglow. She ran to him.

A new voice barked from the car, "Barbro, hurry!"

Christmas Landing knew day: short at this time of year, but sunlight, blue skies, white clouds, glittering water, salt breezes in busy streets and the sane disorder of Eric Sherrinford's living room.

He crossed and uncrossed his legs where he sat, puffed on his pipe as if to make a veil and said, "Are you certain you're recovered? You mustn't risk overstrain."

"I'm fine," Barbro Cullen replied, though her tone was flat. "Still tired, yes, and showing it, no doubt. One doesn't go through such an experience and bounce back in a week. But I'm up and about. And to be frank, I must know what's happened, what's going on, before I can settle down to regain my full strength. Not a word of news anywhere."

"Have you spoken to others about the matter?"

"No. I've simply told visitors I was too exhausted to talk. Not much of a lie. I assumed there's a reason for censorship."

Sherrinford looked relieved. "Good girl. It's at my urging. You can imagine the sensation when this is made public. The authorities agreed they need time to study the facts, think and debate in a calm atmosphere, have a decent policy ready to offer voters who're bound to become rather hysterical at first." His mouth quirked slightly upward. "Furthermore, your nerves and Jimmy's get their chance to heal before the journalistic storm breaks over you. How is he?"

"Quite well. He continues pestering me for leave to go play with his friends in the wonderful place. But at his age, he'll recover—he'll forget."

"He may meet them later anyhow."

"What? We didn't . . ." Barbro shifted in her chair. "I've forgotten too. I hardly recall a thing from our last hours. Did you bring back any kidnapped humans?"

"No. The shock was savage as it was, without throwing them straight into an . . . an institution. Mistherd, who's basically a sensible young fellow, assured me they'd get along, at any rate as regards survival necessities, till arrangements can be made." Sherrinford hesitated. "I'm not sure what the arrangements will be. Nobody is, at our present stage. But obviously they include those people—or many of them, especially those who aren't full-grown—rejoining the human race. Though they may never feel at home in civilization. Perhaps in a way that's best, since we will need some kind of mutually acceptable liaison with the Dwellers."

His impersonality soothed them both. Barbro became able to say, "Was I too big a fool? I do remember how I yowled and beat my head on the floor."

"Why, no." He considered the big woman and her pride for a few seconds before he rose, walked over and laid a hand on her shoulder. "You'd been lured and trapped by a skillful play on your deepest instincts at a moment of sheer nightmare. Afterward, as that wounded monster carried you off, evidently another type of being came along, one that could saturate you with close-range neuropsychic forces. On top of this, my arrival, the sudden brutal abolishment of every hallucination, must have been shattering. No wonder if you cried out in pain. Before you did, you competently got Jimmy and yourself into the bus, and you never interfered with me."

"What did you do?"

"Why, I drove off as fast as possible. After several hours, the atmospherics let up sufficiently for me to call Portolondon and insist on an emergency airlift. Not that that was vital. What chance had the enemy to stop us? They didn't even try—but quick transportation was certainly helpful."

"I figured that's what must have gone on." Barbro caught his glance. "No, what I meant was, how did you find us in the backlands?"

Sherrinford moved a little off from her. "My prisoner was my guide. I don't think I actually killed any of the Dwellers who'd come to deal with me. I hope not. The car simply broke through them, after a couple of warning shots, and afterward outpaced them. Steel and fuel against flesh wasn't really fair. At the cave entrance, I did have to shoot down a few of those troll creatures. I'm not proud of it."

He stood silent. Presently: "But you were a captive," he said. "I couldn't be sure what they might do to you, who had first claim on me." After another pause: "I don't look for any more violence."

"How did you make . . . the boy . . . cooperate?"

Sherrinford paced from her to the window, where he stood staring out at the Boreal Ocean. "I turned off the mind-shield," he said. "I let their band get close, in full splendor of illusion. Then I turned the shield back on, and we both saw them in their true shapes. As we went northward, I explained to Mistherd how he and his kind had been hoodwinked, used, made to live in a world that was never really there. I asked him if he wanted himself and whomever he cared about to go on till they died as domestic animals—yes, running in limited freedom on solid hills, but always called back to the dream kennel." His pipe fumed furiously. "May I never see such bitterness again. He had been taught to believe he was free."

Quiet returned above the hectic traffic. Charlemagne drew nearer to setting; already the east darkened.

Finally Barbro asked, "Do you know why?"

"Why children were taken and raised like that? Partly because it was in the pattern the Dwellers were creating; partly in order to study and experiment on members of our species—minds, that is, not bodies; partly because humans have special strengths which are helpful, like being able to endure full daylight."

"But what was the final purpose of it all?"

Sherrinford paced the floor. "Well," he said, "of course the ultimate motives of the aborigines are obscure. We can't do more than guess at how they think, let alone how they feel. But our ideas do seem to fit the data.

"Why did they hide from man? I suspect they, or rather their ancestors— for they aren't glittering elves, you know; they're mortal and fallible too—I suspect the natives were only being cautious at first, more cautious than human primitives, though certain of those on Earth were also slow to reveal themselves to strangers. Spying, mentally eavesdropping, Roland's Dwellers must have picked up enough language to get some idea of how different man was from them, and how powerful; and they gathered that more ships would be arriving, bringing settlers. It didn't occur to them that they might be conceded the right to keep their lands. Perhaps they're still more fiercely territorial than we. They determined to fight, in their own way. I daresay, once we begin to get insight into that mentality, our psychological science will go through its Copernican revolution."

Enthusiasm kindled in him. "That's not the sole thing we'll learn, either," he went on. "They must have science of their own, a nonhuman science born on a planet that isn't Earth. Because they did observe us as profoundly as we've ever observed ourselves; they did mount a plan against us, one that would have taken another century or more to complete. Well, what else do they know? How do they support their civilization without visible agriculture or above-ground buildings or mines or anything? How can they breed whole new intelligent species to order? A million questions, ten million answers!"

"*Can* we learn from them?" Barbro asked softly. "Or can we only overrun them as you say they fear?"

Sherrinford halted, leaned elbow on mantel, hugged his pipe and replied, "I hope we'll show more charity than that to a defeated enemy. It's what they are. They tried to conquer us and failed, and now in a sense we are bound to conquer them, since they'll have to make their peace with the civilization of the machine rather than see it rust away as they strove for. Still, they never did us any harm as atrocious as what we've inflicted on our fellow men in the past. And, I repeat, they could teach us marvelous things; and we could teach them, too, once they've learned to be less intolerant of a different way of life."

"I suppose we can give them a reservation," she said, and didn't know why he grimaced and answered so roughly:

"Let's leave them the honor they've earned! They fought to save the world they'd always known from that"—he made a chopping gesture at the city—"and just possibly we'd be better off ourselves with less of it."

He sagged a trifle and sighed, "However, I suppose if Elfland had won, man on Roland would at last—peacefully, even happily—have died away. We live with our archetypes, but can we live in them?"

Barbro shook her head. "Sorry, I don't understand."

"What?" He looked at her in a surprise that drove out melancholy. After a laugh: "Stupid of me. I've explained this to so many politicians and scientists and commissioners and Lord knows what, these past days, I forgot I'd never explained to you. It was a rather vague idea of mine, most of the time we were traveling, and I don't like to discuss ideas prematurely. Now that we've met the Outlings and watched how they work, I do feel sure."

He tamped down his tobacco. "In limited measure," he said, "I've used an archetype throughout my own working life. The rational detective. It hasn't been a conscious pose—much—it's simply been an image which fitted my personality and professional style. But it draws an appropriate response from most people, whether or not they've ever heard of the original. The phenomenon is not uncommon. We meet persons who, in varying degrees, suggest Christ or Buddha or the Earth Mother or, say, on a less exalted plane, Hamlet or d'Artagnan. Historical, fictional and mythical, such figures crystallize basic aspects of the human psyche, and when we meet them in our real experience, our reaction goes deeper than consciousness."

He grew grave again: "Man also creates archetypes that are not individuals. The anima, the shadow—and, it seems, the outworld. The world of magic, of glamour—which originally meant enchantment—of half-human beings, some like Ariel and some like Caliban, but each free of mortal frailties and sorrows —therefore, perhaps, a little carelessly cruel, more than a little tricksy; dwellers in dusk and moonlight, not truly gods but obedient to rulers who are enigmatic and powerful enough to be . . . Yes, our Queen of Air and Darkness knew well what sights to let lonely people see, what illusions to spin around them from time to time, what songs and legends to set going among them. I wonder how much she and her underlings gleaned from human fairy tales, how much they made up themselves, and how much men created all over again, all unwittingly, as the sense of living on the edge of the world entered them."

Shadows stole across the room. It grew cooler and the traffic noises dwindled. Barbro asked mutedly, "But what could this do?"

"In many ways," Sherrinford answered, "the outwayer *is* back in the Dark Ages. He has few neighbors, hears scanty news from beyond his horizon, toils to survive in a land he only partly understands, that may any night raise unforeseeable disasters against him and is bounded by enormous wildernesses. The machine civilization which brought his ancestors here is frail at best. He could lose it as the Dark Ages nations had lost Greece and Rome, as the whole of Earth seems to have lost it. Let him be worked on, long, strongly, cunningly, by the archetypical outworld, until he has come to believe in his bones that the magic of the Queen of Air and Darkness is greater than the energy of engines; and first his faith, finally his deeds will follow her. Oh, it wouldn't happen fast. Ideally, it would happen too slowly to be noticed, especially by self-satisfied city people. But when in the end a hinterland gone back to the ancient way turned from them, how could they keep alive?"

Barbro breathed, "She said to me, when their banners flew in the last of our cities, we would rejoice."

"I think we would have, by then," Sherrinford admitted. "Nevertheless, I believe in choosing one's destiny."

He shook himself, as if casting off a burden. He knocked the dottle from his pipe and stretched, muscle by muscle. "Well," he said, "it isn't going to happen."

She looked straight at him. "Thanks to you."

A flush went up his thin cheeks. "In time, I'm sure, somebody else would have . . . What matters is what we do next, and that's too big a decision for one individual or one generation to make."

She rose. "Unless the decision is personal, Eric," she suggested, feeling heat in her own face.

It was curious to see him shy. "I was hoping we might meet again."

"We will."

Ayoch sat on Wolund's Barrow. Aurora shuddered so brilliant, in such vast sheaves of light, as almost to hide the waning moons. Firethorn blooms had fallen; a few still glowed around the tree roots, amid dry brok which crackled underfoot and smelled like wood smoke. The air remained warm, but no gleam was left on the sunset horizon.

"Farewell, fare lucky," the pook called. Mistherd and Shadow-of-a-Dream never looked back. It was as if they didn't dare. They trudged on out of sight, toward the human camp whose lights made a harsh new star in the south.

Ayoch lingered. He felt he should also offer good-by to her who had lately joined him that slept in the dolmen. Likely none would meet here again for loving or magic. But he could only think of one old verse that might do. He stood and trilled:

> Out of her breast
> a blossom ascended.
> The summer burned it.
> The song is ended.

Then he spread his wings for the long flight away.